MODERN HUMANITIES RESEARCH ASSOCIATION
CRITICAL TEXTS
VOLUME 71

EDITOR
STEFANO EVANGELISTA
(ENGLISH)

JEWELLED TORTOISE
VOLUME 7

EDITORS
STEFANO EVANGELISTA
CATHERINE MAXWELL

HUBERT CRACKANTHORPE: SELECTED WRITINGS

EDITED WITH AN INTRODUCTION AND NOTES BY
WILLIAM GREENSLADE AND EMANUELA ETTORRE

Hubert Crackanthorpe: Selected Writings

Edited with an introduction and notes by
William Greenslade and Emanuela Ettorre

Modern Humanities Research Association
2020

Published by

The Modern Humanities Research Association
Salisbury House
Station Road
Cambridge CB1 2LA
United Kingdom

© *Modern Humanities Research Association 2020*

First published 2020

ISBN 978-1-78188-965-7 (paperback)
ISBN 978-1-78188-966-4 (hardback)

Copies may be ordered from www.tortoise.mhra.org.uk

CONTENTS

ACKNOWLEDGEMENTS

About ten years ago, during one of many stimulating conversations, we discovered a mutual interest in Hubert Crackanthorpe. We both thought that to work on his writing would be challenging, possibly foolhardy: his short stories had never been properly edited after their first publication, and very few scholars had published on him, and then at no great length. But despite this, our enthusiasm for Crackanthorpe's writing grew and this volume is the result.

We owe a particular debt of gratitude to Hubert's grand-nephew, David Crackanthorpe, for his readiness to assist us with our various queries, including translation questions, and for generously sharing with us both his unsurpassed knowledge of Hubert's life and work and his personal recollections of the Crackanthorpe family.

We would like to extend our sincere thanks to Gerard Lowe at the MHRA and to the Jewelled Tortoise series editors, Stefano Evangelista and Catherine Maxwell, for supporting our initial proposal so positively, for their careful editing of our drafts and for their cheerful, constructive approach in conversations both at the early stages and throughout the process.

Special thanks are due to John Stokes, who read parts of the manuscript and shared, virtually on demand, his deep knowledge of the literature and the arts of the 1890s, unerringly pointing to the best route through, in the best phrase. We would also like to thank Nick Freeman and Regenia Gagnier, each of whom brought their extensive knowledge of the British *fin de siècle* to bear on their acute writing on Crackanthorpe that informed our own work at an early stage.

In addition we would like to acknowledge the assistance given to us, in a variety of ways, by Lorenzo Buonvivere, Roger Clarke, Marion Doyen, Jason Hall, Philip Horne, Keith McClelland, Sati McKenzie, Lorella Martinelli, Greg W. Matthias, Chantal Morel, Alex Murray, and Marco Olivieri.

We would also like to thank Ms Bay James, the holder of copyright for Henry James's letters, and the staff of: the British Library; the Senate House Library; the London Library; the Library of Scotland, Edinburgh; the library of the University of West of England; and the library of the University of Bristol.

William Greenslade would like to thank his colleagues at the University of the West of England for sharing their scholarship, as well as dispensing friendly criticism, over many years. He would like to acknowledge the support of his family, particularly Hannah, Emily, Danny, and Alex, and that of his enquiring, often surprisingly well-informed, friends. Nina Behrman has been an outstanding source of personal encouragement and ready editorial advice.

Emanuela Ettorre extends her gratitude to Adrian Tait for his invaluable ideas and strong encouragement while she was working on this edition. She also acknowledges the support of the two Heads of the Department of Languages, Literatures and Modern Cultures at 'Gabriele d'Annunzio' University of Chieti-Pescara for enabling her to attend conferences and spend time in the British Library and the Senate House Library, over the last two years. For various reasons, she should like to thank her graduate students who might have found her enthusiasm for Crackanthorpe baffling, but were always willing to listen. Above all, she wishes to give special thanks to Pierfrancesco, who never complained when Hubert kept her far from home, or when she regularly monopolized all the tables in the house with the bibliographical material, and finally to Martina, for her constant presence.

INTRODUCTION

Life, Contexts, and Criticism

by William Greenslade

I

'Does the side-wind of the poor dismal little Hubert Crackanthorpe tragedy reach you over there?', Henry James enquired of his friend Grace Norton, on 28 December 1896. James had just recently learnt of the news, announced by *The Times* and other London papers on 26 December, that a body had been discovered in the River Seine in Paris two days earlier. On Christmas Day the body, unrecognizable due to advanced decomposition, was identified as that of Hubert Crackanthorpe by his two brothers, Dayrell and Oliver, from a signet ring, cuff links, and medals found in his pocket. The corpse was swiftly reclaimed, enclosed in a sealed coffin, and returned to London on 26 December.

Hubert's body had probably been in the river for seven weeks. It had been discovered near the Pont d'Alma, downstream from the Quai Voltaire where he had last been seen following his departure from his mother's hotel in the company of John Hills at 11.30 pm on 5 November 1896. They had walked together along the Quai, next to the river on the left bank, before Hubert left Hills, at 11.50 pm, to walk alone. Hills was the solicitor for Hubert's wife, Leila, whom she had summoned from London the previous day to instigate divorce proceedings against Hubert, proceedings which included the scandalous charge of 'legal cruelty' — that Hubert had infected her with a venereal disease.[1]

This crisis marked the culmination of what James called a 'somewhat small sordid drama of crude, incompatible youthful matrimony'.[2] Hubert had been married to the poet and writer Leila Macdonald (1871–1944) for just under

[1] David Crackanthorpe, *Hubert Crackanthorpe and English Realism in the 1890s* (Columbia and London: University of Missouri Press, 1977), p. 59 (hereafter abbreviated to DC); John Waller Hills (1867–1938), Eton and Oxford, solicitor, later Liberal Unionist politician and author, in April 1897 married Stella Duckworth (1869–1897), who died of peritonitis that July. Stella was the daughter of Herbert Duckworth, barrister, and Julia Prinsep Jackson, who married the man of letters Leslie Stephen in 1878 and so was half-sister to Vanessa and Virginia Stephen. Henry James observed to Grace Norton that 'She [Leila] foolish girl, the wife, is a cousin of the silent solicitor young Hills, to whom the still more silent Stella Duckworth is engaged and was Mrs. Hubert's legal advisor' (James to Grace Norton, 28 December 1896 (ALS Houghton bMS Am 1094 (1008))).

[2] Henry James to Grace Norton, 28 December 1896.

three years. Leila's parents died young, and she was brought up by her nurse who became housekeeper to her maternal grandfather, Sir William Grove, a judge and scientist. Through her father she was indirectly related to the Scottish Jacobite Flora Macdonald. Her writing career mostly coincided with the period of her marriage to Crackanthorpe, with four contributions to the *Yellow Book*: a story (October 1894), two poems (January and October 1895), and some lyrical 'Refrains' (April 1895). Her poem in dramatic form, 'The Love of the Poor', appeared in the second number of *The Savoy*, and her *A Wanderer and Other Poems* was published by T. Fisher Unwin in 1904.[3]

Their shared literary interests and enjoyment of travel in Europe initially promised well, but by Spring 1896, with Leila recovering from a miscarriage, their marriage broke down. The reasons for their incompatibility, in the absence of firm evidence, remain a matter of speculation. Both Hubert and Leila took lovers: Elizabeth 'Sissie' Welch (1868–1907), wife of the actor James Welch and a sister of poet and journalist Richard Le Gallienne, and the Comte d'Artaux, an artist. Hubert and Sissie left London for Paris sometime in August 1896, while Leila and d'Artaux were alone in Italy before they, too, arrived in Paris, in early September 1896.

The two couples established an improbable *ménage à quatre* in an apartment off the Champs-Elysées, an 'experiment in luxurious bohemianism', inevitably doomed by the deteriorating relations between Hubert and Leila.[4] On 4 November, prompted by Hills, Leila, aided by the clinching testimony of a *femme de chambre*, found the necessary evidence in Sissie's bedroom with which to compromise Hubert in her pursuit of divorce proceedings. She then immediately left the apartment to stay in a hotel with d'Artaux. Late that evening Hubert attempted to find her, failed to do so and returned to Sissie at the apartment. The following morning, on the 5th, after sending Sissie back to London, Hubert traced Leila to her hotel: there was a row, and, threatened by Leila with the police, he telegraphed for parental help. With her husband unavailable, his mother, Blanche, immediately took the boat train, arriving, very likely, at the Hôtel du Quai Voltaire later that day. We can only speculate about how candid Hubert felt he could be with her during their conversations at Blanche's hotel. But what is known is that mother and son planned to return to London together 'by the night train' and that, in the event, Blanche was 'left to travel alone'.[5]

---

[3]   DC, p. 59; Jad Adams, 'The Drowning of Hubert Crackanthorpe and the Persecution of Leila Macdonald', *English Literature in Transition 1880–1920*, 52.1 (2009), 6–34 (p. 29).

[4]   DC, p. 131.

[5]   DC, p. 137. This account of the tragedy, together with other biographical material in this Introduction, is reliant on David Crackanthorpe's indispensable study, *Hubert Crackanthorpe and English Realism in the 1890s*, ch. 5. All papers relating to Hubert Crackanthorpe came into the possession of David Crackanthorpe, on the death in 1950 of

'In the days following', writes David Crackanthorpe, 'the anxiety at Rutland Gate [...] must have been intense as all efforts to trace Hubert failed'.[6] For James, 'the whole ugliness has brushed a little and darkened that immaculate and lovable house'. 'Siss is of course very upset', wrote Le Gallienne on hearing the news.[7] Under his protection, Sissie Welch had returned to her husband in London. The 'responsibility for protecting her from the scandal' fell to Hubert's brother Dayrell, who 'assum[ed] a tenderness for his brother's mistress that perhaps augmented his dislike of the widow'. That dislike showed itself in an angry, accusatory letter to Leila, written on 25 November 1896, three weeks after Hubert's disappearance, and is a key source for David Crackanthorpe's masterly account of the tragedy on which we have relied.

Dayrell Crackanthorpe (1872–1950) was a man who, in his grandson's words, 'held discretion to be almost the first of virtues', and had evolved, 'to a high degree, manipulative skills in dealing with those around him'.[8] Dayrell's mission, at this point, was to protect the Crackanthorpe family from any taint of scandal. Despite widespread press speculation that Hubert might have been murdered, he was happy to accept the view of the chief investigating detective that suicide was the most likely cause of death and that no inquest was necessary, thus facilitating, under his direction, the speedy return of Hubert's coffin to England. And in his desire to silence public speculation, Dayrell sought to throw 'the whole responsibility for what had happened onto Leila and her desertion'.[9] A young, aspiring Foreign Office diplomat, he was adept at presenting Hubert as an innocent party, subject to the unaccountable and irrational behaviour of an uncaring wife; Leila's accusation of 'legal cruelty' was, in his words, a 'foul & beastly charge [...] a dastardly outrage on the sanctity of married life'.[10]

Archival research by Jad Adams reveals that Leila, who on leaving Paris for London in the immediate aftermath sought the protection of *Yellow Book* editor Henry Harland and his wife and the assistance of its publisher, John Lane, was effectively marginalized by the Crackanthorpe family, persuaded, later, through an intermediary, to 'abandon any claims she might have against Crackanthorpe's estate'.[11] And, whatever the influence of the Crackanthorpes,

---

his grandfather, Dayrell Crackanthorpe. They are now deposited at the Kendal Archive Centre.

[6] DC, p. 137. Rutland Gate was the London home of Montague and Blanche Crackanthorpe.

[7] James to Grace Norton, 28 December 1896; Richard Whittington–Egan and Geoffrey Smerdon, *The Quest of the Golden Boy: The Life and Letters of Richard Le Gallienne* (London: Unicorn Press, 1960), p. 306.

[8] DC, p. 21.

[9] DC, p. 140.

[10] DC, p. 136.

[11] Adams, 'The Drowning of Hubert Crackanthorpe', p. 27.

and the friends of Hubert who mourned his death, the episode appeared to mark the end of her hoped-for literary career.

II

The critical challenge of how to evaluate the brief life of a writer and a necessarily modest body of writing was treated head-on by James in his subtle memorial essay 'Hubert Crackanthorpe', written at the request of his friend Blanche Crackanthorpe for inclusion in the posthumous *Last Studies* (1897):

> There remained the sense of a relation formed and from which there was much more to come; but before scarce anything could come, arrived, with violence, the young man's sudden death, anticipating opportunities and bringing with it specific regrets. So it became a question of reading into what he had done and intended other things still than symptoms of an influence and softly-reflected lights [...] Hubert Crackanthorpe's death, for those who knew him, could only give him more meaning and, as I may say, more life — something that, for the subject, in especial, of the demonstration I have mentioned, could constitute more of a tie. Such a memory seemed offered, in its vivid contraction, instead of the longer chance.[12]

The key phrase, 'a question of reading', is brought into focus since the very 'event of his death gives him "more meaning." '[13] The brief life might be thought to discourage interpretation through the sheer paucity of recorded evidence, but the awareness of a life 'in its vivid contraction', in James's phrase, serves to increase the temptation to interpret and formulate a narrative of what *is* known. For James the brief life in effect constitutes 'more of a tie' and so lends itself to, or even compels, a 'reading'. Elsewhere, in two brief epistolary accounts, James reads or frames Crackanthorpe's life as fit for formal representation when he speaks of 'a somewhat small sordid drama', or a 'very complete little history'.[14]

In the generations which followed the *fin de siècle*, the tragic 'drama', the 'history' of Hubert Crackanthorpe's life became assimilated into a larger narrative prompted largely by feelings of nostalgia and regret, in which a generation of Decadent writers were marked out by their doomed youth or a special proclivity to self-destructive excess. Publication of Crackanthorpe's work was notably sparse; his stories appearing, only intermittently, in journals and anthologies of limited reach. Only in the late 1960s was there the beginning of a

---

[12] Henry James, 'Hubert Crackanthorpe', *Last Studies* (London: William Heinemann, 1897), pp. xi–xxiii (pp. xii–xiii).
[13] Shafquat Towheed, 'Reading the Life and Art of Hubert Crackanthorpe', *English Literature in Transition 1880–1920*, 43.1 (2000), 51–65.
[14] Henry James to Grace Norton, 28 December 1896 (ALS Houghton bMS Am 1094 (1008)); Henry James to Edwin Lawrence Godkin, 2 February 1897 (Unpub. 34DVG TS Houghton bMS Am 1083 (418)).

more concerted effort to anthologize his work (see Appendix: 'Crackanthorpe's Writings Selected for this Edition: A Bibliographical Survey'). And such typecasting also meant that critical appraisal of Crackanthorpe's achievement as a writer and critic, as with that of his literary and artistic contemporaries, was noticeably checked. Holbrook Jackson, in his still indispensable *The Eighteen Nineties* (1913), had already placed Crackanthorpe, along with Oscar Wilde, Aubrey Beardsley, Ernest Dowson, Charles Conder, Lionel Johnson, Henry Harland, James Thompson, and John Davidson, as one of the 'restless and tragic figures' of the 1890s, most of whom 'died young, several [...] scarcely youths'.[15] W. B. Yeats later contributed to the mythologizing of the period, writing, notoriously, that after 1900 'nobody drank absinthe with his black coffee; nobody went mad; nobody committed suicide; nobody joined the catholic church', a calculated overstatement which did little to dislodge the perception that the 'literatures of decadence' could be 'safely quarantined in the 1890s', a period bathed in images 'of absinthe and hansom cabs, perfumed with patchouli and cigar smoke'.[16]

The impressionist-symbolist Crackanthorpe of *Vignettes* appealed to bohemian Greenwich Village in the person of the avant-garde small press editor Guido Bruno (1884–1942), who published, somewhat erratically (from his 'Garret on Washington Square'), six of Crackanthorpe's vignettes as '*Vignettes: Pastels in Prose*, taken from the *Saturday Review*'.[17] The critic Vincent Starrett was likewise keen to praise Crackanthorpe's late, experimental work, noting in 1921 the 'vivid impressionism toward which he was tending': Crackanthorpe, he said, had 'amazing promise', 'one of the group of brilliant young men who made the eighteen-nineties an outstanding renascent period in English letters'.[18] The post-war period also saw Osbert Burdett, in a wide-ranging assessment, picking out Crackanthorpe's 'scrupulous loyalty to his material' and 'splendid' talent for

[15]   Holbrook Jackson, *The Eighteen Nineties* (1913; Harmondsworth: Pelican, 1950), p. 16.
[16]   Introduction to *The Oxford Book of Modern Verse, 1892–1935* (Oxford: Clarendon Press, 1936), p. xi. Quoted by John Stokes, *In the Nineties* (London: Harvester Wheatsheaf, 1989), p. xix; Kate Hext and Alex Murray, 'Introduction', in *Decadence in the Age of Modernism*, ed. by Kate Hext and Alex Murray (Baltimore: John Hopkins University Press, 2019), p. 5; Nick Freeman, 'Decadent Paths and Percolations after 1895', in *Decadence in the Age of Modernism*, pp. 84–85.
[17]   *Bruno Chap Books*, ed. by Guido Bruno, 1.8 (1915), 98–106. Bruno claimed these 'Pastels in Prose' were 'hitherto uncollected', which was not strictly true since all six had appeared in Crackanthorpe's 1896 volume. The link of course was the erstwhile *Saturday Review* editor Frank Harris, a friend of Bruno's who employed him on *Pearson's Magazine*, of which Harris was editor.
[18]   Vincent Starrett, 'Two Suicides', in *Buried Caesars: Essays in Literary Appreciation* (Chicago: Covici–McGee, 1923), pp. 133–45 (p. 140); Headnote to 'Three Prose Pieces', *The Double-Dealer: A National Magazine From the South Published at New Orleans*, 2 (December 1921), pp. 252–55 (p. 252).

dialogue; 'if he had not died so young, he should have written plays'.[19] 'Behind all this impenetrably impersonal bitter play of human passions in these short stories', wrote Bernard Muddiman in 1920, 'one feels [...] the distant beats of the author's compassionate heart'.[20] Frank Harris recorded an affectionate reminiscence, as did Richard Le Gallienne in his *The Romantic '90s* (1925), speaking of the 'scrupulous, almost fanatical "objectivity" of his "artistic aim"'.[21] And reminding readers of his innovatory contribution to the short story form, Edward J. H. O'Brien suggested in 1919 that 'a new edition of Hubert Crackanthorpe would be a fine public service'.[22] Arthur Symons, though, was less keen to rehabilitate him. In 1923, as part of his essay 'Impressionist Writing', he republished, in shortened form, his December 1896 review of Crackanthorpe's *Vignettes*; in the course of the transmission from 1890s journal article to post-war essay Crackanthorpe and *Vignettes* became anonymized to 'the writer' of 'a certain book'.[23]

While the inter-war period saw further reminiscences of the 1890s by Arthur Waugh (1931), Grant Richards (1932; 1934), and J. Lewis May (1936), in which Crackanthorpe briefly featured, there are few examples of any sustained critical attention being paid to the writer.[24] With the exception of William Frierson's perceptive commentaries of 1928 and (more fully) of 1942, and Holbrook Jackson's sympathetic reminiscence of 1946, there was little Crackanthorpe criticism of note (apart from one re-examination of his debt to Maupassant by George J. Worth (1957)) until the 1960s.[25] From that decade American scholars Wendell Harris (1962; 1963; 1963) and William Peden (1970) took him up, as a pioneering author from the underwritten period of 'transition' (1880–1920),

[19]   Osbert Burdett, *The Beardsley Period: An Essay in Perspective* (London: John Lane/The Bodley Head, 1925), pp. 230–31.
[20]   Bernard Muddiman, *The Men of the Nineties* (London: Danielson, 1920), pp. 77–78.
[21]   Frank Harris, 'Lionel Johnson and Hubert Crackanthorpe', in *Contemporary Portraits: Second Series* (New York: Frank Harris, 1919), pp. 179–91; Richard Le Gallienne, *The Romantic '90s* (1925; London: Robin Clark, 1993), p. 140.
[22]   Edward J. H. O'Brien, Introduction to *The Great Modern English Stories* (New York: Boni and Liveright, 1919), p. ix.
[23]   Arthur Symons, 'Mr. Crackanthorpe's Vignettes in Prose', *Saturday Review*, 82 (26 December 1896), 678; Symons, 'Impressionistic Writing', in *Dramatis Personae* (Indianapolis: Bobbs-Merrill Co., 1923), pp. 343–50 (p. 344).
[24]   Arthur Waugh, *One Man's Road: Being a Picture of Life in a Passing Generation* (London: Chapman and Hall, 1931); Grant Richards, *Memories of a Misspent Youth 1872–1896* (London: William Heinemann, 1932); Richards, *Author Hunting* (London: Hamish Hamilton, 1934); J. Lewis May, *John Lane and the Nineties* (London: John Lane, 1936).
[25]   William C. Frierson, 'Hubert Crackanthorpe: Analyst of the Affections', *Sewanee Review*, 36.4 (1928), 462–74; William Frierson, *The English Novel in Transition 1885–1940* (Norman: University of Oklahoma Press, 1942); Holbrook Jackson, 'Hubert Crackanthorpe: Impressionist of Fiction', *Windmill*, 2.2 (1946), 8–16; George G. Worth, 'The English "Maupassant School" of the 1890's: Some Reservations', *Modern Language Notes*, 72 (1957), 337–40.

with Harris producing the first reliable bibliographical account in 1963, and Peden producing the first facsimile edition of Crackanthorpe's stories in 1969.[26] The 1970s saw the publication of David Crackanthorpe's *Hubert Crackanthorpe and English Realism in the 1890s* (1977) which, for the first time, made available evidence of family papers and the extent of Crackanthorpe's reading, in a much-needed authoritative, full-length study of the writer. David Crackanthorpe also contributed compact essays on Crackanthorpe and two of his short story collections, *Wreckage* and *Sentimental Studies & A Set of Village Tales*, to *The 1890s: An Encyclopedia of British Literature, Art, and Culture*, published in 1993.[27]

In more recent years Crackanthorpe has received overdue bibliographical attention, with a *DNB* entry eventually arriving in 2004,[28] in new surveys of British *fin-de-siècle* writing and the evolution of the short story in the 1890s.[29]

Criticism solely devoted to Crackanthorpe has come in a handful of essays.

---

[26] Wendell V. Harris, 'Identifying the Decadent Fiction of the Eighteen-Nineties', *English Fiction in Transition*, 5.5 (1962), 1–13; Wendell Harris, 'Hubert Crackanthorpe as Realist', *English Literature in Transition 1880–1920*, 6.2 (1963), 76–84; Wendell Harris, 'A Bibliography of Writings about Hubert Crackanthorpe', *English Literature in Transition 1880–1920*, 6.2 (1963), 85–91; William Peden: 'Hubert Crackanthorpe: Forgotten Pioneer', *Studies in Short Fiction*, 7.4 (1970), 539–48; *Collected Stories (1893–1897) of Hubert Crackanthorpe*, ed. by William Peden (Gainesville: Scholar's Facsimiles and Reprints, 1969).

[27] *Hubert Crackanthorpe and English Realism in the 1890s* (Columbia: University of Missouri Press, 1977); 'Hubert Crackanthorpe'; 'Wreckage'; 'Sentimental Studies & A Set of Village Tales', in *The 1890s: An Encyclopedia of British Literature, Art, and Culture*, ed. by G. A. Cevasco (New York and London: Garland, 1993), pp. 128–30, 684–85, 540–41.

[28] Kenneth Womack, 'Hubert Crackanthorpe', *Dictionary of National Biography, Vol. 13* (Oxford: Oxford University Press, 2004), pp. 911–12; *New Cambridge Bibliography of English Literature*, ed. by George Watson, 5 vols (Cambridge: Cambridge University Press, 1969–1977), III, p. 1044; *The Longman Companion to Victorian Fiction*, ed. by John Sutherland (London: Longman, 1988), p. 155; Benjamin Franklin Fisher IV, 'Hubert Crackanthorpe', *Dictionary of Literary Biography Vol. 135 (British Short-Fiction Writers, 1880–1914: The Realist Tradition)*, ed. by William B. Thesing (Detroit: Gale Research, 1994), pp. 60–74.

[29] Winnie Cran, 'The Yellow Book Circle and the Culture of the Literary Magazine', in *The Cambridge History of the English Short Story*, ed. by Dominic Head (Cambridge: Cambridge University Press, 2016), pp. 118–34; *The Decadent Short Story: An Annotated Anthology*, ed. by Kostas Boyiopoulos and others (Edinburgh: Edinburgh University Press, 2015); David Malcolm, *The British and Irish Short Story Handbook* (New Jersey: John Wiley, 2012); *A Companion to the British and Irish Short Story*, ed. by Cheryl Alexander Malcolm and David Malcolm (Oxford: Wiley-Blackwell, 2008); Adrian Hunter, *The Cambridge Introduction to the Short Story in English* (Cambridge: Cambridge University Press, 2007); Elke D'hoker, 'Artist Stories of the 1890s: Life, Art and Sacrifice', in *Reconnecting Aestheticism and Modernism: Continuities, Revisions, Speculations*, ed. by Bénédicte Coste and others (London: Routledge, 2016), pp. 281–331; *Decadent Verse: An Anthology of Late-Victorian Poetry, 1872–1900*, ed. by Caroline Blyth (London: Anthem Press, 2009); Nicholas Freeman, *Conceiving the City: London, Literature, and Art 1870–1914* (Oxford: Oxford University Press, 2007); Regenia Gagnier, *The Insatiability of Human Wants: Economics and Aesthetics in Market Society* (Chicago: University of Chicago Press, 2000).

For Shafquat Towheed (2000) Crackanthorpe both experienced and was haunted by the prospect of literary failure, and 'his choice of subject [...] almost calculated in its unpopularity' is painfully symptomatic of the dilemmas facing the serious 'literary artist' at the *fin de siècle*. Jad Adams (2009) drew on unpublished correspondence in a number of archives to examine how contradictory and misleading information enveloped the debacle of the final months of Crackanthorpe's life leading to his tragic death and its aftermath, and in 'Hubert Crackanthorpe 1870–1896' (2010) he offered a succinct, well-informed account of his life and literary career. William Greenslade (2011) viewed Crackanthorpe as a shrewd observer of the literary scene in the early 1890s who sought to navigate an innovative course between a realist-naturalist literature of 'disagreeable details' and a Jamesian aesthetics of detachment, and Emanuela Ettorre, in her translation into Italian of five of Crackanthorpe's stories from *Wreckage: Seven Studies*, stressed the importance of his avant-garde style, which included fragmented phraseology and broken syntax, and produced an effect of disorientation in the face of the inscrutability of the human dramas performed in the stories.[30]

A welcome edition of the complete *Wreckage* was published in 2019, edited by David Malcolm for Edinburgh University Press.[31] His critical introduction included attention to *Wreckage* itself, and to Crackanthorpe's 'career and reception', 'the fin de siècle', and 'remaining fiction'. A set of appendices carried Crackanthorpe's 'Realism in France and England', 'Reticence in Literature', 'The Haseltons', 'The White Maize', and three *Vignettes*, together with stories by Maupassant ('The Rendezvous') and Leila Macdonald ('Jeanne-Marie').

III

Of unusual emotional intelligence, generosity of spirit, and unostentatiously held convictions, Hubert Crackanthorpe — 'Bertie' or 'Crackie', as he was affectionately called by his friends — seemed to have made a universally favourable impression. 'Everyone loved him', said the writer Ella D'Arcy; he was

---

[30] Towheed, 'Reading the Life and Art of Hubert Crackanthorpe', pp. 51–65; Adams, 'The Drowning of Hubert Crackanthorpe', pp. 6–34; Jad Adams, 'Hubert Crackanthorpe', *The Yellow Nineties Online*, ed. by Denis Denisoff and Lorraine Janzen Kooistra (Ryerson University, 2010) <http://www.1890s.ca/HTML.aspx?s=crackanthorpe_bio.html> [accessed 9 June 2020]. William Greenslade, 'Naturalism and Decadence: The Case of Hubert Crackanthorpe', in *Decadent Poetics: Literature and Form at the British Fin de Siècle*, ed. by Jason David Hall and Alex Murray (Basingstoke: Palgrave, 2013), pp. 163–80; Emanuela Ettorre, '"Those little documents of Hell": Hubert Crackanthorpe e l'ossessione del reale', Introduction to *Hubert Crackanthorpe: Racconti*, ed. by Emanuela Ettorre (Napoli: Edizioni Scientifiche Italiane, 2015), pp. 9–32.

[31] Hubert Crackanthorpe, *Wreckage: Seven Studies*, ed. by David Malcolm (Edinburgh: Edinburgh University Press, 2019).

'so gentle, and chivalric, and romantic [with] a lovable boyish presence', wrote his friend Richard Le Gallienne. James spoke of the 'generosity of his youth', while Lionel Johnson invoked his 'fair and cordial friend' in his moving elegy 'In Memory of Hubert Crackanthorpe'.[32]

Naturally reserved, Crackanthorpe was also capable of moments and episodes of dashing extroversion, such as his spontaneous decision, when holidaying in Dieppe in summer 1895, to join Sanger's Circus as an interpreter; he was last seen departing 'on the back of an enormous elephant' by his friends, who had got up at five in the morning to see him off.[33] According to Johnson, he 'took his literary life, as he took to travel, movement, the open air, with an eager animation and delighted energy'[34] and he was, by all accounts, an engaging companion, not to mention proficient horseman and card player. He was indeed 'the happiest of fortunate youth', in Le Gallienne's phrase,[35] the beneficiary of material comfort, social privilege, and the intellectual encouragement that a creative family life might offer — all of this sustained by the financial support, given to him, within limits, by his father.

But Crackanthorpe's extrovert side was accompanied by darker moods. Frank Harris recalled that his 'shy ingenious manners and outbursts of enthusiasm' were 'soon followed by fits of unaccountably black depression'.[36] Indeed, it is likely that he suffered from a form of manic depression, possibly a tendency within the family, and that he was in the grip of such an episode at the end.[37]

Montague Crackanthorpe (1832–1911) was a Queen's Council and Doctor of Civil Law, a talented and professionally accomplished figure who successfully straddled the worlds of law and of academia. A liberal in politics, he was a reformer on legal questions: 'the very last thing we should do in legal reform', he wrote in 1892, 'is to increase the advantages which the rich unavoidably possess

---

[32] Katherine Lyon Mix, *A Study in Yellow: The Yellow Book and its Contributors* (London: Constable, 1960), p. 58; quoted by DC, p. 42; *The Romantic '90s* (London: G. P. Putnam's Sons, 1925), p. 140; James, 'Hubert Crackanthorpe', *Last Studies*, p. xiii; *The Complete Poems of Lionel Johnson*, ed. by Ian Fletcher (London: The Unicorn Pres, 1953), p. 252.

[33] DC, pp. 24, 104; J. Lewis May, *John Lane and the Nineties* (London: John Lane, 1936), pp. 82–83; Nicholas Freeman, *1895: Drama, Disaster and Disgrace in Late Victorian Britain* (Edinburgh: Edinburgh University Press, 2011), p. 166. His friends included the publisher and editor of *The Yellow Book*, John Lane and Henry Harland, and the painter Walter Sickert. This four-day episode is re-lived in his attractive account 'Bread and the Circus', *Yellow Book*, 7 (October 1895), pp. 235–57. It was a pity that Blanche left it out of the posthumous *Last Studies* (1897) — the taint of decadent association lingering on; see Adams, 'The Drowning of Hubert Crackanthorpe', p. 27.

[34] Lionel Johnson, 'Hubert Crackanthorpe', *The Academy*, 52 (20 November 1897), 428–29.

[35] Le Gallienne, *The Romantic '90s*, p. 140.

[36] Harris, 'Lionel Johnson and Hubert Crackanthorpe', in *Contemporary Portraits*, pp. 179–91 (p. 180).

[37] David Crackanthorpe, personal communication, 17 October 2019.

over the poor.'[38] Montague later became President of the Eugenics Society (1909–1911), which he had established with Francis Galton, the founder of eugenics in Britain. But unlike Galton, he urged 'positive' rather than 'negative' eugenic policies, as in his advocacy of the 'voluntary principle', a code for birth control which he first advocated in 1872 and then explored, at fuller length, in his *Population and Progress* (1907): the voluntary principle would ensure that 'those children only are born who are desired before, and are warmly welcomed after birth'.[39]

Hubert's mother, Blanche Alethea Crackanthorpe (1847–1928), was a progressively minded, feminist author of three well-regarded articles on aspects of the Woman Question in the mid-1890s, a number of plays, including her banned *The Turn of the Wheel* (1901), and a novel.[40] A well-read literary and theatrical enthusiast, she was also a considerable hostess and 'networker'. Leading writers of the day, including Thomas Hardy and George Meredith, circulated at the soirees and parties held at the Crackanthorpes' Knightsbridge home.[41] Of her closer literary acquaintances, Henry James appeared to be in a category of his own, privy, it seems, to the details of the family tragedy, and the painful emotions it generated. At Blanche's invitation, he stepped up to write an extended meditation on Hubert's life and work for her compilation of some hitherto uncollected stories: *Last Studies* was published in late 1897 by William Heinemann (with whom Blanche was also on good terms).

Crackanthorpe was certainly fortunate in being the son of a free-thinking, financially secure, cultured mother and the beneficiary of her social skills, drive, and ambition — energies which were partly directed at nurturing her son's writing career, and, indeed, at curating his posthumous reputation. Blanche, in turn, was happy with her able, self-propelling son, whose own youthful drive matched her own, even if his creative talent surpassed hers. In any case there seemed little evidence of parental coercion on the one hand, or callow resentment of parental interference on the other. Here, it seemed, was

---

[38] Montague Crackanthorpe, 'The Revision of Criminal Sentences', *The Albermarle: A Monthly Review*, 1.4 (1892), 144–48 (p. 148).

[39] Montague Crackanthorpe, *Population and Progress* (London: Chapman and Hall, 1907), pp. 9–10, quoted in DC, pp. 9–10.

[40] 'The Revolt of the Daughters', *Nineteenth Century*, 35 (1894), 23–31; 'A Last Word on "The Revolt"', *Nineteenth Century*, 35 (1894), 424–29; 'Sex in Modern Literature', *Nineteenth Century*, 37 (1895), 607–16. For a description of *The Turn of the Wheel* see Kerry Powell, *Women and Victorian Theatre* (Cambridge: Cambridge University Press, 1997), pp. 137–38. See also 'Crackanthorpe, Blanche, Alethea', in *Dictionary of Nineteenth-Century Journalism in Great Britain and Ireland*, ed. by Laurel Brake and Marysa Demoor (London: Academia Press and The British Library, 2009), p. 150.

[41] See DC, p. 12. Other literary friends and acquaintances of Blanche's included Stopford Brooke, Elizabeth Robins, Lillah McCarthy, 'Laurence Hope', Robert Hitchens, and Marie Belloc Lowndes.

a sympathetic, familial relationship enhanced by forms of cultural affiliation — to literature, theatre, and the arts — and the London circles, albeit of contrasting kinds, in which the leading writers and critics of the period moved.

An example is a shared enthusiasm for the plays of Ibsen. Crackanthorpe and his parents were each members of the Independent Theatre Society founded in 1891 by J. T. Grein, the engine room of advanced drama in the early 1890s. Crackanthorpe himself would later put up a one-act play to Grein for his 1894–95 season, but it was never staged because of Grein's growing financial worries for the company.[42]

Through his encouraging parents Hubert enjoyed unusual opportunities as a young man. While his younger brothers would proceed, conventionally, from public school to university, Crackanthorpe left Eton in March 1888, after only five years at the school, to pursue a novel path. In her essay 'The Revolt of the Daughters' (1894) Blanche Crackanthorpe took it for granted that a mother's 'best-loved son must have his *wanderjahre*', which approximated in Crackanthorpe's case to 'the period between leaving Eton [...] and his next emergence from obscurity in the spring of 1889'.[43] Details of this phase in his life are scarce, but it was about this time that he was mentored by Selwyn Image (1849–1930), an artist, designer, and poet much influenced by Walter Pater and prominent in the Century Guild, established in 1882 'to render all branches of art the sphere no longer of the tradesman but the artist'.[44] In 1889, together with other Guild members Arthur Mackmurdo (another friend of Blanche's) and Lionel Johnson, Image set up a fashionably bohemian 'settlement' in London's Fitzroy Street.[45]

---

[42] DC, pp. 40–41; 'Dramatic Gossip', *The Athenaeum*, 3 November 1894, pp. 613–14; Michael Orme, *J. T. Grein: The Story of a Pioneer 1862–1935* (London: John Murray, 1936), pp. 142–43.

[43] 'The Revolt of the Daughters', *Nineteenth Century*, 35 (January 1894), 23–31 (p. 27); DC, p. 33.

[44] Quoted by Lisa Tickner, 'Selwyn Image', in *The 1890s*, pp. 300–01 (p. 300).

[45] DC, p. 38; *Complete Poems of Lionel Johnson*, ed. by Ian Fletcher (London: The Unicorn Press, 1953), p. xxxix. Crackanthorpe may also have been taught at this time by the novelist George Gissing, who had become known to the Crackanthorpes through a mutual friend, the positivist thinker Frederick Harrison. Pierre Coustillas notes from internal evidence from *George Gissing's Commonplace Book* (ed. by Jacob Korg (New York Public Library, 1962), p. 57) that Gissing listed the 'young aristocrats' he had tutored between September 1887 and December 1888, including the 'sons of Montague Cookson, QC', leaving it open as to whether he tutored Hubert or Dayrell (Oliver being too young) or both. In that *Commonplace Book* entry, Gissing's phrase 'in days gone by' leads Coustillas to conclude that the most likely period was 'in the mid-eighties' ('Gissing and Crackanthorpe: A Note on Their Relationship', *Notes and Queries*, 28.5 (1981), 421–22 (p. 422)), but given that Hubert and Dayrell were still at their respective senior schools at that point, this seems improbable. Since Hubert left Eton in 1888, David Crackanthorpe's estimate of March 1888 to Spring 1889 (DC, p. 33) would seem more likely: the *Commonplace Book* entry cited by Coustillas would still allow for the possibility that Gissing could have tutored one or more of the

Through such contacts Crackanthorpe experienced a unique form of cultural induction at a crucial stage in his own creative development. What was open to him was the opportunity to become immersed in the language, literature, and culture of France as a dedicated Francophile, in keeping with the continental sympathies of the Decadent writers and artists he had begun to meet through Image in London's Fitzrovia, and who associated with members of the Rhymers Club, including Johnson, Symons, Dowson, and Yeats. Crackanthorpe's knowledge of nineteenth-century French literature, particularly fiction — together with his association with talented tutors and up and coming writers — made for a thorough-going alternative cultural induction, which combined the privilege of an eighteenth-century gentleman's cultural peregrination with a Victorian dedication to the hard pounding of literary acculturation — of making himself *au courant*.[46] His 'aptitude for French and [...] interest in French literature', notes David Crackanthorpe, had been nurtured by an experienced French master at Eton, Francis Tarver. The literary critic Percy Lubbock (nine years Crackanthorpe's junior) fondly remembered the experience of Tarver's attractively cultured French classes: 'What I acquired in those hours', he wrote, 'had no vulgar usefulness [...] after all these years an imagination is working on a grain of material that was given it by old Tarver'.[47]

Crackanthorpe certainly possessed the facility to work on 'a grain of material' that fell to him; a capacity for making text out of experience came easily and early. Aged twelve, in August 1882, he compiled the 'Mayes Gazette', one of a number of handwritten magazines arising from family holidays in Sussex, and for a further four years, from 1883 to 1887, the 'Howtownian' in Westmorland, orchestrated along with Dayrell.[48] An unusual process of early writerly self-making could be glimpsed from those precocious family productions. Much later, a journalistic awareness and enterprise, supported by ample parental encouragement — material and intellectual — would lead to his establishing, at the age of 21, a major, if short-lived, new journal, *The Albermarle: A Monthly Review*.[49]

Crackanthorpe boys (more likely Hubert) between March and December 1888.

[46] David Crackanthorpe records his reading in Zola, Gustave Flaubert, Maupassant, Bourget, Barrès, the Goncourts, and Pierre Loti in the original, drawing attention to some of the many marked passages from his reading (DC, pp. 43, 180–83).

[47] DC, p. 26; Percy Lubbock, *Shades of Eton* (London: Jonathan Cape, 1929), pp. 133–35.

[48] DC, pp. 22–24.

[49] It was originally conceived in the summer of 1891 as a 'London weekly journal' with the title 'The Torpedo' (*Penrith Observer*, 14 July 1891, p. 6, col. 2).

IV

Announcing its 'individual independence of thought' in its opening number (January 1892), *The Albermarle* carried 'spirited discussions of remedies for the economic ills of the time and fictionalized indictments of society's cruelty to its outcasts'.[50] It sought to chime with liberal opinion on contemporary social questions, employing, possibly through the Crackanthorpes' many contacts, a number of eminent political figures from across the political spectrum, including Charles Dilke, David Lloyd George, and Ben Tillett.[51]

It is likely that Crackanthorpe's co-editor, W. H. Wilkins (1860–1905), had a hand in soliciting the articles by the more politically conservative of these figures. Wilkins, a future novelist and royal biographer, was, by today's standards, a questionable choice for co-editor, since his association with the Association for the Preventing of Destitute Aliens (of which he was Secretary) would have been known about and even better-known on the publication of his study *The Alien Invasion* (1892). But Wilkins may have been installed on the advice of Montague, who was financing the periodical, and may have warmed to the fact of his well-connected administrative experience. It is true that Montague himself was on record at this time as lamenting the influence of 'ruinous competition' from Jewish aliens on 'our working class'.[52] But Wilkins travelled further, into social-Darwinian territory on the issue, by claiming that 'just as the lower organisms in animal life can continue to exist under circumstances which are intolerable to higher organisms, so can these aliens live, and even to a certain extent thrive, under conditions which to the more highly developed Englishman involve disease and death'.[53] However, there is no evidence to suggest that such fashionable degenerationism offered any currency for Montague, let alone for Hubert.

The Albermarle aimed to be visually distinctive, carrying an original

---

[50]   Harris, 'Hubert Crackanthorpe as Realist', p. 78.
[51]   The Trades Union leader Ben Tillett is likely to have contributed at Hubert's invitation, rather than at Montague's. The following year Hubert was writing in support of miners on strike in autumn 1893: 'The coal-strike has been interesting us keenly; we have been longing for some spare pounds to send to the miners' (Letter to Mrs Heywood, 28 September 1893, quoted by Jad Adams, pp. 12–13, 32 n. 14). Further, albeit slim, evidence of Crackanthorpe's reforming instincts comes from Conal O'Riordan, who had been present at Crackanthorpe's lecture on 'The Art of Fiction' (February 1894) and recalled that '[i]n 1895 he and I sat on a committee to further popular education' ('Bloomsbury and Beyond In the Eighteen-Nineties'. The Tredegar Memorial Lecture (11 September 1946), [Paper Read to the Royal Society of Literature of the United Kingdom] in *Essays By Divers Hands. The Transactions of the Royal Society of Literature of the United Kingdom* (London: Geoffrey Cumberlege/ Oxford University Press, 1948), pp. 63–86 (p. 78)). No corroboration of this claim has been traced, to date.
[52]   William J. Fishman, *East End Jewish Radicals 1875–1914* (London: Duckworth, 1975), p. 74.
[53]   'The Alien Question', *The Albermarle: A Monthly Review*, 2.1 (1892), 25–29 (pp. 28–29).

lithograph by James Whistler, 'A Song on Stone', in the opening number, and subsequent contributions by Walter Sickert, Wilson Steer, Henri Fantin-Latour, and others. The result was to offer its readers, in Linda Dowling's words, 'an extraordinary artistic bonus [...] for the irresistible (and heavily subsidized) price of sixpence', and so proof of Crackanthorpe's 'striking commitment to fine graphic art'.[54] And the journal gave Crackanthorpe an outlet for his early literary journalism and creative work. His first essay, 'Henry James as a Playwright', a precociously critical piece, appeared in its opening number, followed by his 'Interview with M. Emile Zola' in the next. His first published story, 'He Wins Who Loses', came out in the March number and his next, 'Dissolving View', in August. Among other notable contributions to the journal were poems by leading Decadent writers — Dowson, Johnson, Image, Le Gallienne, and Herbert Horne — and literary essays by Herbert Beerbohm Tree, John Gray, Maurice Barrès, and G. B. Shaw. *The Albermarle* also carried art criticism with a distinct emphasis on impressionism through contributions from the artist Charles Furse and the critic D. S. MacColl, both associated with the New English Art School.[55]

Contributions from both Bourget and Maupassant had been secured but could not be published before the periodical suddenly folded in September 1892. 'Alas! The "Albermarle" is dead. Peace to its ashes', Dowson exclaimed on news of its closure.[56] But alongside feelings of regret for its passing there was praise: 'a high-class review', wrote the *Guardian*, 'very popular with a wide circle of readers'; for *The Speaker* it had been 'the most promising of the new magazines'.[57] A later commentator on the magazines of the 1890s concluded that *The Albermarle* was 'in all points a strictly high class periodical, but it was too modern, too clever, to be a financial success'.[58]

Crackanthorpe had proved himself to be a skilful editor, showing flair in locating questions and issues of contemporary interest to his intended readers, impressively au fait with trends of opinion in literature and the arts and in contemporary social and political debate, and prescient in his commissioning of significant criticism and creative work. While the termination of his father's funding was a disappointment, it probably came as little surprise.

---

[54] Linda Dowling, 'Letterpress and Picture in the Literary Periodicals of the 1890s', *Yearbook of English Studies*, 16 (1986), 117–31 (p. 120).

[55] The New English Art Club, started in 1886, comprised 'a little body of young artists, who had got their training in Paris, were enthusiastic over French ideas and methods, and a good deal opposed to the narrowness of The Academy, and the sort of taste it patronized and encouraged' (Selwyn Image to John Image, 17 November 1893, *Selwyn Image Letters*, ed. by A. H. Mackmurdo (London: Grant Richards, 1932), pp. 82–83 (p. 82)).

[56] Dowson to Charles Sayle, late November 1889 [wrongly dated], *New Letters From Ernest Dowson*, ed. by Desmond Flower (Andoversford: Whittington Press, 1984), p. 16.

[57] Quoted by DC, p. 57.

[58] E. Leonore Casford, 'The Magazines of the 1890s', *Language and Literature Series* (University of Oregon), 1.1 (1929), 1–39 (p. 11).

And he could now look forward, rather than back, to developing his writing career, with criticism and two stories published, others in the pipeline, the prospect of a first short story collection from Heinemann on the horizon, and, in his personal life, a romance with Leila Macdonald, initiated, perhaps, at 'literary gatherings associated with the *Albermarle*', which would shortly lead to their marriage in February 1893.[59] Yet the desire to edit never left him. Four years later, in late October 1896, with his relationship with Leila in crisis, an opportunity which he thought might fall to him, via Grant Richards, to take over the editorship of Symons and Beardsley's *The Savoy*, suddenly evaporated: coming at that vulnerable moment, disappointment tipped, very possibly, into depression.[60]

Crackanthorpe's talent as a literary editor was not unconnected with his ability to engage sympathetically with other writers, to proffer open-minded, practical encouragement — all qualities which spoke of the optimistic side of his temperament and his maturity of judgement.[61] Testimony to his capacity to offer creative support to other writers could be found in his dealings with the French nature poet Francis Jammes (1868–1938), whom Crackanthorpe first met in Orthez, in the Béarn region of south-west France, in 1889 as part of his youthful project of self-education. Crackanthorpe stayed there for at least three months, striking up a strong creative rapport with Jammes, for whom Crackanthorpe had been 'le truchement de ces premières sympathies'.[62] He paid a second visit to the Béarn in Spring 1893, this time with Leila, the couple renting a nearby house found for them by Jammes. It was Crackanthorpe who encouraged the poet to gather his poems into a first collection, *Vers*. And according to Jacqueline Ansaloni, Crackanthorpe's involvement with Jammes's plans for publication was decisive: 'C'est lui qui fit le choix des vingt et un poèmes que Jammes devait publier sous le titre de *Vers*.'[63] When Jammes's volume was published in May 1893, there was a dedication to two men, the artist

---

[59] Adams, 'The Drowning of Hubert Crackanthorpe', p. 10.

[60] See Richards, *Memories of a Misspent Youth 1872–1896*, pp. 342–45; DC, pp. 30–32.

[61] Evidence of Crackanthorpe's solicitude towards an aspiring author comes in a report in the *Bookman Gallery* for November 1907 of a meeting between Crackanthorpe and Betinna Riddle von Hutten (1874–1957), an American heiress and prolific novelist. 'It was in the "City of Flowers"', gushed the journalist, Beatrice Marshall, 'that the gifted and vivacious girl formed a friendship with the late Hubert Crackanthorpe, who although he forbade her to read his own gloomy and neurotic works, inspired her with the desire to write. He discovered a distinctly original talent in her sketches, alike piquant and tender of the Italian peasant life, many of which will be remembered by readers of the Westminster Gazette, in which paper they appeared' (p. 74).

[62] 'the channel for these first sympathies'. G. Jean-Aubry, 'Hubert Crackanthorpe et Stéphane Mallarmé', *Hommage à Hubert Crackanthorpe*, Association Francis Jammes, Bulletin No. 14 (1990), 2–3 (p. 3).

[63] 'La Morte (Nouvelle)', *Nouvelle Revue Des Deux Mondes* (Fevrier 1973), 338–55 (p. 338). 'It was he who selected the twenty-one poems which Jammes would publish with the title of *Vers*.'

Charles Lacoste, and Crackanthorpe: 'A Toi, Crackanthorpe, déjà célèbre en ton pays et qui a senti passer en toi le souffle de l'amour et de la pitié humaine'.[64] Crackanthorpe returned the compliment by taking Jammes's collection to Paris to bring it to the attention of the poet Stéphane Mallarmé, and the writers André Gide and Henri de Régnier.[65]

It is possible that in the course of that visit Crackanthorpe attended one of Mallarmé's famous 'Mardis', the weekly gatherings the poet hosted at his apartment in Paris for other notable writers, which by now included Arthur Symons. Later that year Crackanthorpe was one of several writers present at one of a number of meetings organized by Symons in London for the poet Paul Verlaine, on an invited three-week visit to England.[66] By late 1893 it was clear that Crackanthorpe was being recognized, on both sides of the Channel, not least by Symons, as a writer — even an advanced Decadent — whose time had come.

V

'Oh! what dreary affectation it all is! what stupidity! what is the use of any of us trying to contend against these damned, dull, posing idiots of fellowcountrymen': this was the response of Crackanthorpe's mentor, Selwyn Image, on 1 November 1888 to the news that the publisher Henry Vizetelly had been fined £100 at the Central Criminal Court in London on a charge of 'obscene libel' for publishing translations, albeit in lightly expurgated versions, of three novels by Emile Zola: *La Terre*, *Nana*, and *Pot-Bouille*.[67] An additional fifteen translations had appeared from 1884, each of which Vizetelly was now forced to withdraw. Doubtless encouraged by Image, Crackanthorpe could look to affiliate with a liberal cultural politics which demanded that the French writer be defended against those 'idiots of fellowcountrymen' who sat in judgement on Vizetelly and were effectively responsible for placing him in the dock. And it was fortunate for Crackanthorpe that, when the Vizetelly storm broke, he found himself well positioned to negotiate these cross-currents as an aspiring young writer and critic.

Back in May, with the support of the increasingly strident National Vigilance Association and fired up by the polemical stance of W. T. Stead, the campaigning

---

[64] '[to] You, Crackanthorpe, who are already celebrated in your own country, and through whom the breath of love and human compassion has already passed.'
[65] 'Hubert Crackanthorpe vu par Francis Jammes', *Hommage à Hubert Crackanthorpe*, Association Francis Jammes, Bulletin, No. 14 (1990), 31–33 (p. 33).
[66] Karl Beckson, *Arthur Symons: A Life* (Oxford: Clarendon Press, 1987), pp. 93–95; Jad Adams, *Madder Music, Stronger Wine: The Life of Ernest Dowson, Poet and Decadent* (London and New York: I. B. Taurus, 2000), p. 74.
[67] Selwyn Image to Herbert P. Horne, 1 November 1888, *Selwyn Image Letters*, p. 60.

editor of the *Pall Mall Gazette*, the MP Samuel Smith named Vizetelly the 'chief culprit' in a debate in Parliament about 'Pernicious Literature', declaring of Zola that 'nothing more diabolical has ever been written by the pen of man'.[68] A few months later, in March 1889, the elderly and infirm Vizetelly found himself again on trial for his publication of a further eight Zola novels, having conspicuously failed 'to keep the peace for a year', as the court had directed. Committed to Holloway Prison for three months, he died five years later, 'a broken and ruined man'.[69]

The Vizetelly case brought to a head contentious issues debated through the 1880s and into the 1890s about freedom of artistic expression and where and how the boundaries of acceptable material in literature should be drawn — the matter, in fact, of 'reticence' in literature, the subject of a debate staged in the opening numbers of the *Yellow Book* in 1894 which would feature Crackanthorpe's most important critical intervention.[70] While *The Times* could congratulate itself after the first trial that '[i]n future [...] any one who publishes translations of Zola's novels and works of a similar character will do so at his peril',[71] many writers were appalled. A petition to the Home Secretary appealing for Vizetelly's early release, organized by the novelist George Moore and Henry's son Ernest, secured the support of leading writers of the day, including Hardy, Edmund Gosse, Symons, and Havelock Ellis.[72]

Moore, never backward in self-promotion, had been prominent in defending freedom of expression for writers ever since his own novel, *A Modern Lover* (1883), had been condemned as an 'immoral publication' by Mudie's Circulating Library. The stranglehold exerted by the circulating libraries, most prominently Mudie's and W. H. Smith, over their writers throughout the 1880s was a longstanding source of annoyance for serious novelists, including Hardy, and found early expression in Moore's brash polemic *Literature at Nurse, or Circulating Morals*, which Vizetelly published in 1885. In part a protest against Mudie's for refusing to stock his novel *A Mummer's Wife* (1885), Moore asserted that it was 'the librarian' who 'rules the roost; he crows, and every chanticleer pitches his note in the same key. He [...] is the author of modern fiction'.[73] For

---

[68] Susan Bassnett and Peter France, 'Translation, Politics and the Law', in *The Oxford History of Literary Translation in English: Volume 4 1790–1900*, ed. by Peter France and Kenneth Haynes (Oxford: Oxford University Press, 2006), pp. 48–58 (p. 54).

[69] Bassnett and France, 'Translation, Politics and the Law', p. 54.

[70] Arthur Waugh, 'Reticence in Literature', *The Yellow Book: An Illustrated Quarterly*, 1 (April 1894), 201–19; Hubert Crackanthorpe, 'Reticence in Literature: Some Roundabout Remarks', *The Yellow Book: An Illustrated Quarterly*, 2 (July 1894), 259–69.

[71] *The Times*, 1 November 1888, p. 9, col. 5. Quoted by Bassnett and France, 'Translation, Politics and the Law', p. 54.

[72] Bassnet and France, 'Translation, Politics and the Law', p. 54; Eileen Horne, *Zola and the Victorians* (London: MacLehose Press, 2015), p. 216.

[73] *Literature at Nurse or Circulating Morals* (London: Vizetelly & Co., 1885), pp. 16, 20.

Hardy, the libraries, 'acting under the censorship of prudery', had led novelists into practices of bad faith, such as 'arranging a *dénouement* which he knows to be indescribably unreal and meretricious'.[74]

The scandalous nature of Zola's subject matter, together with its frank treatment in novels such as *L'Assomoir* and *Nana*, had been a target for conservative critics, such as Robert Buchanan and Andrew Lang, from the early 1880s. Discussion of Zola's naturalism prompted by his 'Le Roman Expérimental' (1880) had inevitably generated questions which Henry James's debate with the novelist Walter Besant in 1884 had begun to formulate. How might fiction aim to be more than a straightforward transcription of life? What aesthetic choices might be involved in the attempt? What balance should be struck in fiction between content and treatment — between 'the school of facts and the school of effects', as Oscar Wilde put it?[75] By the end of the decade Zola was still at the centre of arguments over realism and its future, over where and how the boundaries of taste in literature should be drawn — indeed, over the very status of fiction, current and future.

These issues lay behind some of the questions directed at Zola by Crackanthorpe himself in an interview with him, conducted probably in late 1891, which he proceeded to publish in *The Albermarle* the following February.[76] In comparison with Moore's self-aggrandizing version of his own interview with Zola conducted a couple of years later, Crackanthorpe attempts, as far as possible, to render an objective account: as respectful interlocutor he allows Zola's opinions a plentiful airing.[77] The interview is interesting, not only for Zola's reported views — on contemporary realism, English fiction, the essential Protestant character of English writers and their status in France — but for the choice of questions with which Crackanthorpe prompts him. Sensitive to a discussion in England about 'the supposed death of realism in France', Zola elicits from Crackanthorpe a confirming '[y]es, and is it not so? Are there not on all sides signs of a reaction?'. To Zola's own suggestion that 'our conception

[74] 'Candour in English Fiction' (1890); repr. in *Thomas Hardy's Personal Writings*, ed. by Harold Orel (London: Macmillan, 1967), pp. 125–33 (pp. 129, 130).

[75] 'London Models', *English Illustrated Magazine*, 6.64 (January 1889), 313–19 (p. 313), repr. in *The Complete Works of Oscar Wilde: Vol VII: Journalism Part II*, ed. by John Stokes and Mark W. Turner (Oxford: Oxford University Press, 2013), pp. 133–38 (p. 134). The editors note that '"effects not facts" was a slogan commonly adopted by advanced art critics' (note to p. 134 (p. 450)). Wilde's own famous attack on Zola's work, 'entirely wrong from beginning to end [...] on the ground of art', came in his 'The Decay of Lying', published the same month in *Nineteenth Century*.

[76] 'Realism in France and England. An Interview with M. Emile Zola', *The Albermarle: A Monthly Review*, 1.2 (February 1892), 39–43; see pp. 388–94.

[77] George Moore, 'My Impressions of Zola', *English Illustrated Magazine* (February 1894), 477–89; David Trotter, *The English Novel in History 1895–1920* (London: Routledge, 1993), p. 115.

of realistic fiction is probably destined to be developed, transformed' and that 'there will be an expansion of our formula', Crackanthorpe follows up with: 'And what shape do you think that this expansion will take?', and shortly after, 'Do you think then that this reaction is near at hand?'. This question produces from Zola a familiar, full-flowing defence of '[o]ur realistic movement' as 'the outcome of the temper of our age' (p. 390) which Crackanthorpe reports without comment. With no 'immediate reaction' in the novel imminent, in Zola's view, Crackanthorpe then shifts attention to poetry — prompting Zola to denigrate contemporary symbolism: 'vague scribbling, in obscure, stuttering verses'. Acknowledging that the British stage 'is getting emancipated' and that the founding of the Independent Theatre 'is an excellent sign', he is unenthused by Crackanthorpe's observation that 'we have had several of Ibsen's plays produced in London this year'; his work, says Zola, is '*bien obscur*' (p. 392). The 'furious entry of a little black spaniel, who flew barking and snapping round my chair' brings us neatly back to the occasion of the interview: Crackanthorpe takes this as his cue to leave, accompanied by Zola's good wishes for *The Albermarle*. A concluding pronouncement from the 'great man', '*Il vous faut de la patience en Angleterre .. de la patience. Tout vient à qui sait attendre*', rounds off his report.[78]

By the early 1890s more complicated interpretations of Zola could be detected in discussions by critics for whom defence of the writer had necessarily become synonymous with the upholding of freedom of artistic expression. In a generally sympathetic treatment of Zola's procedures, Havelock Ellis nevertheless questioned Zola's pursuit of 'disagreeable details', accumulated through painstaking note-taking and observation, and asked 'do they make-up reality?'.[79] In another piece Ellis looked forward to 'a synthesis of naturalism and romanticism'; 'we need to reconstitute the complete man, instead of studying him in separate pieces; to put a living soul in the clothed body'.[80] Gosse, while conceding that Zola offered a 'large, competent, and profound view of the movement of life [...] the results of a most laudable attempt to cultivate the estate outside the kitchen-garden', suggested that Zola's 'earnest disciples' had reached 'the limits of realism' with their 'sombre, grimy, and dreary studies of pathology, clinical bulletins of a soul dying in atrophy'.[81]

---

[78] 'You must have patience in England, patience. Everything comes to those that can wait.' Crackanthorpe, 'Realism in France and England', p. 394.
[79] 'Tolstoi', in *The New Spirit*, 4th edn (London: Constable, 1926), pp. 174–227 (p. 213); see William Greenslade, 'Naturalism and Decadence', p. 169.
[80] Havelock Ellis, 'A Note on Paul Bourget', *Pioneer* (October 1889), repr. in *Views and Reviews: A Selection of Uncollected Articles 1884–1932. First Series: 1884–1919* (London: Desmond Harmsworth, 1932), pp. 48–60 (p. 60).
[81] 'The Tyranny of the Novel', in *Questions At Issue* (London: William Heinemann, 1893), pp. 3–31 (pp. 26–27); 'The Limits of Realism in Fiction', in *Questions At Issue*, pp. 137–54 (p. 151).

Other critics made more concerted efforts to defend Zola on aesthetic grounds. For John Addington Symonds, with *La Bête Humaine* in mind, Zola is a consummate realist, but an idealist, too, in his formal achievement: his weaving together of the 'separate parcels of plot', the 'dominating conception [...] which gives unity to the whole work', so that 'we are not in the real region of reality, but in the region of the constructive imagination'.[82] 'Brutal as his [Zola's] facts often are', wrote Hubert's mother Blanche a little later in the same vein, 'they are always grouped round a great central principle, a great governing idea, and so far may M. Zola be counted as an Idealist'. The Real and Ideal must 'have allotted to them equal rights and equal powers'.[83]

The 'hyperbolic, metaphorical quality' of Zola's writing was flagged up by Vernon Lee in her 1893 essay 'The Moral Teaching of Zola'. Lee suggested that 'in estimating the moral bearings of Zola's novels we must not separate the mere facts from their oratorical setting; but on the contrary, submit to be acted upon by both'. The unarranged nature of reality, where 'good and evil are [...] scattered about with no sense of pattern', 'or in Whistlerian language, *symphonies*', is actually given shape by Zola's 'elaborate arrangements', by which we come to understand 'the various sorts and systems of the world's tolerated evil'. The 'gigantic spider's web of lust, greed, vanity, and sloth' which Zola spins implicates us all: 'into [this web] is fatally caught every inferior one of us, *every inferior portion of ourselves*' (my italics).[84] This important insight gestures towards both Lee's proto-psychoanalytic understanding of the self and the act of reading. We don't know whether Crackanthorpe read her essay, the most sophisticated treatment of Zola of the 1890s, but it is hard to imagine him not endorsing her conclusions: 'it is well to be forced to think on cause and effect while being made to feel other folk's woes; and still more to feel them as really living, while one is wondering on their cause and effect'.[85] Lee validates not simply Zola's sociological skill and affective achievement, but, crucially, as the reader experiences it, their sustaining interdependence. It is an insight which could apply to Crackanthorpe's own negotiation with the mode of the short story, as he filters his gift for realist observation through the gauze of aestheticism.

There are good reasons, then, for Jesse Matz's view that Lee 'essentially claims Zola's naturalism for aestheticism'.[86] And at this moment, in the early

[82] 'La Bête Humaine: A Study in Zola's Idealism', *Fortnightly Review*, 50 (October 1891), 453–62 (p. 462).
[83] 'Sex in Modern Literature', p. 616.
[84] Vernon Lee, 'The Moral Teaching of Zola', *Contemporary Review*, 63 (February 1893), 196–212 (pp. 199, 211).
[85] Lee, 'The Moral Teaching of Zola', p. 211.
[86] 'Impressionism, Naturalism and Aestheticism: Novel Theory 1880–1914', in *The Oxford History of the Novel in English Volume 4: The Reinvention of the British and Irish Novel*

1890s, this means literary impressionism. There were other straws in the wind, of course, not least the impact of Ibsen's *Hedda Gabler* (first performed in London in 1891), judged 'a bit of sheer "impressionism"' by the theatre critic A. B. Walkley,[87] or the conversation Hardy staged between naturalism and impressionism in his 1892 introduction to *Tess of the d'Urbervilles*. Matz rightly sees impressionism at this period as 'naturalism's subjective counterpart, a safer private way to pursue the analysis that naturalism pursued for public reasons, and to public opprobrium'.[88] And, again, with Crackanthorpe in mind, literary impressionism is best seen as a movement, not so much in opposition to realism-naturalism as in a fluid, dynamic, relationship with it — the boundaries, however they were being drawn, intriguingly unclear.

Crackanthorpe would undoubtedly have absorbed the felicitous argument of Charles Furse's essay 'Impressionism: What It Means', which invited readers of *The Albermarle* to consider that pictures were 'never interesting as a journalist's catalogue of facts, but as an appeal to the imagination from the mind of the painter'. While the appeal of a 'lauded' painting, Luke Fildes's 'Doctor', was essentially 'histrionic', depending 'for its interest in tickling the lachrymose sensibilities of the spectator', Whistler's 'sneered at' 'portrait of Miss Corder' was characterized by 'grace and movement of the figure, the dignity of the simple profile, the reserve in every inch of the canvas'. 'It is not the painter's business to record what he sees', Furse wrote, 'but to suggest what he feels, for the poetry of nature lies in its suggestiveness'.[89]

VI

The death of Henry Vizetelly on New Year's Day 1894 prompted a raft of correspondence in the *Daily Chronicle* throughout early January. Crackanthorpe took the opportunity to announce himself publicly in support of Zola, and argued for the right of authors to freedom of expression without fear of censorship. But while reservations about Zola's naturalism made by critics that Crackanthorpe respected were one thing, public support for Zola, in a fractious literary climate, was quite another. Crackanthorpe's unwavering support for Zola, dating back, as we have seen, to at least 1888, was, in the broadest sense, political: to defend Zola, and to continue to defend him, was now an absolute requirement — tantamount to defending the principle of artistic freedom itself.

The debate was kicked off by the critic, poet and dramatist Robert Buchanan,

---

1880–1940, ed. by Patrick Parrinder and Andrzej Gąsiorek (Oxford: Oxford University Press, 2010), pp. 539–54 (p. 548).

[87] See John Stokes, *Resistible Theatres* (London: Paul Elek, 1972), p. 157.

[88] Matz, 'Impressionism, Naturalism and Aestheticism: Novel Theory 1880–1914', p. 547.

[89] Charles W. Furse, 'Impressionism: What It Means', *The Albermarle: A Monthly Review*, 2.2 (August 1892), 47–51 (pp. 48–49).

a controversialist heavily invested in advertising lost causes, including himself. Buchanan criticized the timidity of journalists at the time of Vizetelly's imprisonment, asking '[w]hy was it left for a discredited person like myself to champion the cause of the imprisoned publisher?'.[90] Given that Buchanan was apt to use any opportunity to point up the sordidness of Zolaism (along with other *bêtes noire* such as the 'parochialism' of 'New Womanhood'), this was not a little disingenuous. Frank Harris, now editor (and part-owner) of the *Saturday Review*, replied two days later that Buchanan was 'too sweeping in his condemnation of journalists', reminding readers that he, himself, had offered to fund Vizetelly's defence case (a point actually contested by Vizetelly's son Ernest in a letter to the *Daily Chronicle* the following day). But the thrust of Harris's letter was to draw attention 'to the public importance of the facts incidentally exposed by this case'. Whereas '[i]n France, the artist and man of letters is supported by the organized opinion of his fellows', in England with 'grocerdom [...] organised in conventicle and church, and rancorously articulate', 'men of letters [...] are unorganised and powerless', with 'English novel-writers [...] debarred from holding "the mirror up to nature" by the antipathies, moral and commercial, of the tallow-chandlers'. Harris ended by asking '[w]hen shall the man of letters win the freedom accorded to the thinker and artist? He could win it at once with organisation. Is organisation impossible?'[91]

Crackanthorpe's intervention came in the *Daily Chronicle* the following day. He sidestepped Harris's by now familiar Arnoldian lamentation of the philistine tastes of the middle classes but picked up Harris's interrogatives. 'What we lack in this matter of literary freedom', he wrote, 'is an organised opinion of artists and men of letters' to combat any further instance of writer prosecution, while acknowledging that 'there has been a very considerable advance in public opinion since the prosecution of Mr. Vizetelly'. The 'cause of literary freedom' would be furthered by 'influential men of letters' combining together, rather than allowing single publishers, like Vizetelly, to be picked off individually and so forced to fight 'single-handed'. Glancing back to the attempted suppression of Zola's work five years before, he suggested a 'test case' for the future: 'publication of an English translation of, say, "Nana" or "Au bonheur des Dames"' undertaken by 'men of letters', and that the 'brunt of the prosecution', should one arise, be 'borne, not by a single unfortunate publisher, but by an organisation which includes every writer of eminence who has the cause of literary freedom at heart'.[92]

Crackanthorpe's proposal appeared to be answered almost immediately, but only in part, by an initiative of the Lutetian Society, which went on to publish

[90] Buchanan, Letter to the *Daily Chronicle*, 6 January 1894, p. 3, col. 7.
[91] Harris, Letter to the *Daily Chronicle*, 8 January 1894, p. 3, col. 5.
[92] Crackanthorpe, Letter to the *Daily Chronicle*, 9 January 1894, p. 3, col. 7.

a limited number of Zola translations as well as works by Maupassant and Bourget, entirely unexpurgated, in the light of the editorial compromises forced onto the Vizetellys. Its members were among the leading Decadent writers of the day — Symons, Dowson, and other Rhymers' Club members, Victor Plarr and Ellis. The certain threat of prosecution was circumvented by the secrecy of the project and the restricted intended readership for the editions. The six volumes (which included Symons's translation of *L'Assomoir* (1894), Plarr's *Nana* (1894), Dowson's *La Terre* (1895), and Ellis's *Germinal* (1895)) ran only to 300 copies on hand-made paper, with 10 on 'Japanese vellum'.[93] As Plarr recalled: 'We had the fearful example of Mr Vizetelly before our eyes [...] but we were writing for scholars, and were protected by our manifest sincerity and by prohibitive prices.'[94] The project, if nothing else, advertised the determinedly Francophile nature of Decadent allegiance and practice and something of the extent to which '[t]he cosmopolitanism of the 1890s was hospitable to translation'.[95] Symons, Dowson, and Gray had each published collections blending translations from poets such as Verlaine and their own work. At least half the poems in Gray's *Silverpoints* (1893), for example, were translations from Baudelaire, Mallarmé, Verlaine, and Rimbaud, and several of Symons's volumes carried translations of Baudelaire.[96] Such facility for poetic translation and incorporation was in itself evidence of the determination of these writers to extend the reach of French literary culture to British readers in a spirit of combative Decadence. Precisely by not answering in full Crackanthorpe's rather noble proposal, the Lutetian project performed an appropriately Decadent work of exposure, by demonstrating the still impossible task of allowing challenging works of fiction to become available to a wider readership.

What Crackanthorpe had spotted about Buchanan, meanwhile, was that while he professed to defend artistic freedom, hard-won by Vizetelly and his supporters, his stated position on advanced literature, such as that of Zola, was simplistic and backward-looking. Crackanthorpe was keen to advance on this front by tangling not so much with the perceived philistine readership, sceptical as they might be of the frankness of contemporary realism, as with the unwillingness and ill-preparedness of a powerful strand of critical opposition (Buchanan being an example), as he saw it, to give such literature a fair critical hearing.

---

[93]   These translators would have endorsed Le Gallienne's aperçu: 'all nature is on the side of limited editions' (*Limited Editions: A Prose Fancy: Together With Confessio Amantis. A Sonnet* (London: Elkin Mathews/John Lane, 1893), p. 7).

[94]   *Ernest Dowson 1888–1897: Reminiscences, Unpublished Letters and Marginalia* (London: Elkin Mathews, 1914), pp. 96–97; Chantal Morel, '"Did you say ... the Lutetian Society?"', *Bulletin of the Émile Zola Society*, 16 (September 1997), 6–15.

[95]   Haynes, 'Translation and British Literary Culture', p. 13.

[96]   Haynes, 'Translation and British Literary Culture', p. 13.

Buchanan's next intervention may have helped Crackanthorpe to burnish his own line of attack in his 'Reticence in Literature' essay for the *Yellow Book* later that year. Buchanan clarified that his objection was not to Harris's philistine readers but to 'The "Critic up to Date, the Militant Editor, the Flamboyant Journalist"': in other words, the critical elite which persisted, he thought, in betraying standards of taste in their championing of realism-naturalism and, in particular, Zola. While Buchanan conceded 'the genius of M. Zola' and 'approved its full and free manifestation', it did not stop him from 'believing and saying that Zolaism is an ugly, a corrupt, and an evil influence on literature, generally, and that the whole series of the Rougon-Macquart is a monument of great genius misapplied'. He went on to condemn, in what were by now rather conventional epithets, Zola's 'colour-blind[ness] to character', his deafness to the 'still small voice of humanity', his ears 'stopped with ordure', his search 'chiefly for the Execrable'.[97]

For Crackanthorpe, these assaults were less the point than the limitations of the critical position which they exposed, particularly as the tide of criticism had turned towards a greater acceptance of Zola (and so a reduced necessity to defend him). Crackanthorpe had almost certainly been present when the French author arrived in London in September 1893 at the invitation of the Institute of Journalists, so formalizing, rather dubiously, the rehabilitation of Zola's reputation — at least for those who had doubted it. 'His reception [...] has been very remarkable', wrote George Gissing, adding that 'the change of opinion is strange enough. All the papers now speak of him with high respect — even the most conservative.'[98] And Crackanthorpe himself later recalled that '[i]t is not so long since a publisher was sent to prison for issuing English translations of celebrated specimens of French realism; yet, only the other day we vied with each other in doing honour to the chief figure-head of that tendency across the Channel' (p. 398). His wider point, though, was that the easing, though not cessation, of hostilities towards Zola since the Vizetelly trials was part of a changing climate in which 'the opposition to the renascence of fiction as a conscientious interpretation of life is not what it was [...] Books are published, stories are printed, in old-established reviews, which would never have been tolerated a few years ago' (pp. 397–98).

Buchanan's position on Zola was of course tired, not to say trite. Crackanthorpe was happy to affiliate himself to a body of open-minded critical opinion open to Decadent experiment (and the type of figure represented by Buchanan's 'The Critic up to Date, the Militant Editor, the Flamboyant Journalist'). However,

[97]   Buchanan, Letter to the *Daily Chronicle*, 11 January 1894, p. 3, col. 6.

[98]   Gissing to Eduard Bertz, 29 September 1893, repr. in *The Collected Letters of George Gissing Volume Five: 1892–1895*, ed. by Paul Matthiesen and others (Athens: Ohio University Press, 1994), p. 149.

Crackanthorpe's current priority was to establish an aesthetic position as a critic which would not be defined by Zola's naturalism but would neither involve wholesale dismissal of this methods.

VII

The up-and-coming reviewer and critic Arthur Waugh (1866–1943), future father of Evelyn, was alert to these developments. Waugh could not fail to have spotted the saliency of Arthur Symons's essay, published in November 1893, 'The Decadent Movement in Literature'.[99] Now 'Decadence' threatened to become not only a fashionable but a significant literary force and focus for controversy — all of which helped set the terms for a debate on 'Reticence in Literature' between Waugh and Crackanthorpe, staged by *Yellow Book* co-editor Henry Harland, for the first and second volumes of the new periodical, which appeared in April and July 1894.

Crackanthorpe had first trailed aspects of the argument of his own essay in an invited lecture, 'The Art of Fiction', the title probably a conscious allusion to Henry James's influential essay of 1884. Delivered on 11 February 1894 in a series of 'Sunday Popular Debates' hosted by J. T. Grein, the director of the Independent Theatre, it was well received, though poorly reported.[100] Gosse, who had accepted Crackanthorpe's invitation to chair his 'little paper', would shortly have the pleasure of hearing his own recently republished essay on 'The Limits of Realism in Fiction' quoted by Crackanthorpe in his 'Reticence' essay for the *Yellow Book*.[101]

Rather like Buchanan, but with more urbanity, Waugh argued that contemporary literature had dispensed with 'the restraining, the saving influence of reticence'. This was founded on his judgement that

> [t]he standard of taste in literature [...] should be regulated by the normal state of the hale and cultured man of its age: it should steer a middle course between the prudery of the manse, which is for hiding everything vital, and the effrontery of the pot-house, which makes for ribaldry and bawdry.[102]

[99] Arthur Symons, 'The Decadent Movement in Literature', *Harper's New Monthly Magazine*, 87 (1893), pp. 858–67.
[100] Hubert Crackanthorpe, 'The Art of Fiction'. ("Sunday Popular Debates"), Royalty Theatre, London. Reported in the *Daily Chronicle*, 13 February 1894, p. 3, col. 6; see Edward Baugh, 'Hubert Crackanthorpe and the Cause of "Literary Freedom"', *Notes & Queries*, n.s., 18.3 (March 1971), 105–07; Foreword [by Conal O'Riordan] to Orme, *J. T. Grein*, p. 12. Grein's choice of the Royalty Theatre was apposite given that it had become, for the time, 'the home on and off of the New Drama', offering productions of Shaw's *Widowers' Houses* (1892) and Ibsen's *Ghosts* (1891), *A Doll's House* (1893), and *The Wild Duck* (1894). See Mander and Mitchenson, *The Lost Theatres of London*, p. 420.
[101] DC, p. 82.
[102] Waugh, 'Reticence in Literature', p. 218.

Relief was needed from 'small poets and smaller novelists [who] bring out their sick into the thoroughfare, and stop the traffic while they give us a clinical lecture upon their sufferings'.[103] There had been a falling-away from that 'universal standard of good taste that has from the days of Milo distinguished between the naked and the nude. We are losing the distinction now; the cry for realism, naked and unashamed, is borne in upon us from every side.' '[L]iterature has never survived', he said, '[w]ithout dignity, without self-restraint, without the morality of art'.[104]

While Waugh was evidently gratified by his essay's positive reception, as a piece of criticism it compares unfavourably to Crackanthorpe's 'reply'.[105] Crackanthorpe's essay is an arresting, acute performance, informed by his practice as a creative writer and showing a shrewd understanding of the potential of contemporary literary production. Where Waugh is bound by moralized considerations of the effect of literature on his implied reader — the dominant question of taste, the naked versus the nude — Crackanthorpe sees in the history of literature a continuing and necessary alternation. The 'pendulum of production' swings between the claims of 'the jealous worship of beauty — which we term idealism — and the jealous worship of truth — which we term realism', so that 'no hard and fast line can be drawn between the one spirit and the other' (p. 396). He deals with Waugh's alarm at the virus of contemporary 'realism, naked and unashamed', not by justifying his own credentials as a realist writer, still less conceding any commitment to slavish dependency on empirical fact, but by positioning literature as a 'creative rather than purely mimetic art'.[106] 'Art is not invested with the futile function of perpetually striving after imitation or reproduction of Nature', he suggests; rather 'she endeavours to produce, through the adaptation of a restricted number of natural facts, an harmonious and satisfactory whole' (p. 397). The relationship between 'idealism' and 'realism' is altogether dynamic, progressive, irresistible — the Darwinian inflections clearly sounded:

> in this very process of adaptation and blending together, lies the main and greater task of the artist. And the novel, the short story, even the impression of a mere incident, convey each of them, the imprint of the temper in which their creator has achieved this process of adaptation and blending together of his material. (p. 397)

Not wishing to disavow a commitment to realism, he nonetheless registers the Jamesian perception that a novel 'is in its broadest definition a personal,

[103] Waugh, 'Reticence in Literature', p. 218.
[104] Waugh, 'Reticence in Literature', pp. 218–19, 219.
[105] Waugh later drew attention to *The Academy*'s notice of it: '"a sane and manly, an instructed and well-written essay."' See *One Man's Road: Being a Picture of Life in a Passing Generation* (London: Chapman and Hall, 1931), p. 257.
[106] Freeman, *Conceiving the City*, p. 41.

a direct impression of life'.[107] 'A work of art', he contends, 'can never be more than a corner of Nature, seen through the temperament of a single man. Thus, all literature is, must be, essentially subjective; for style is but the power of individual expression' (p. 397).[108] It follows that a firm distinction is required between literature and fact-dependent journalists chasing copy: 'The disparity which separates literature from the reporter's transcript is ineradicable' (p. 397). That declarative feels like a concession he still needs to make to face down critics like Buchanan and Waugh who were still heavily invested in pointing up the scandal of realism-naturalism; but it is a measure of Crackanthorpe's determination to advance to a more Jamesian position of 'ultimate suggestiveness' that he noticeably plays down the importance of an 'attitude of objectivity, or of impersonality towards his subject [...] assumed by the artist'. This is a significant concession because such an 'attitude' had been admired by the reviewers of *Wreckage* — a point that Crackanthorpe seems to acknowledge when he notes that the 'attitude of objectivity, or of impersonality [...] nowadays provokes so considerable an admiration'. Nonetheless, such an attitude 'can be attained only in a limited degree' (p. 397).

And Crackanthorpe's adopted aesthetic position now aligns him more closely with his Decadent contemporaries in that he seeks to try out new angles of vision which require him to go beyond an 'objectivity, or impersonality' in representation (for which he has adeptly drawn on Zola, the Goncourts, Maupassant, and Flaubert), to the more psychologically complex, if unwieldy, realism of his *Sentimental Studies* (1895) and the posthumous *Last Studies* (1897), and to a more explicitly impressionist form of writing, in the prose poems of his *Vignettes* (1896).

At this point in 1894 Crackanthorpe is notably hopeful for the future of literature, remarking that 'during the past year things have been moving very rapidly' (p. 398) — an observation which equally could be applied to his own fast-developing career. Now '[t]he position of the literary artist towards Nature, his great inspirer, has become more definite, more secure' (p. 398), even though to write about Nature now means taking into account Wilde's post-Romantic characterization of it: its 'lack of design, her curious crudities, her extraordinary monotony, her absolutely unfinished condition'.[109] Here Crackanthorpe allows

---

[107] 'The Art of Fiction', in *Henry James: Selected Literary Criticism*, ed. by Morris Shapira (1963; London: Peregrine Books, 1968), pp. 78–97 (p. 83).
[108] This is a near-quotation of Zola's definition of a work of art as 'un coin de la création vu à travers un tempérament' ('a corner of life seen through a temperament'), briefly alluded to in Wilde's 1889 essay 'London Models' (Stokes and Turner (ed.), *Journalism Part II* in *Complete Works of Oscar Wilde*, pp. 137, 452 n.).
[109] Oscar Wilde, 'The Decay of Lying' (1889) repr. in *The Complete Works of Oscar Wilde: Vol IV: Criticism*, ed. by Josephine Guy (Oxford: Oxford University Press, 2009), pp. 72–103 (p. 73).

himself a moment of self-congratulation when he identifies a 'tendency of the time' with which he can affiliate, spurred on by a 'sound, organised opinion of men of letters' (p. 398) — the precise formation to which he had appealed in his *Daily Chronicle* letter of January 1894.

What helped to give him such confidence was knowing that his own perception of the 'tendency of the time' was shared by one of those 'men of letters', Arthur Symons. January 1894 was the month in which Symons, looking back over 'English Literature in 1893', had detected telling evidence:

> Foreign influences [...] have begun to have more and more effect upon the making of such literature as is produced in England nowadays; we have seen '[a] certain acceptance of Ibsen, a popular personal welcome of Zola, and literary homage paid to Verlaine'.[110]

All this chimed, even journalistically, with Crackanthorpe's own sense of living through a dynamic, exciting period of literary and cultural change. It helped, of course, that, in addition to favourable appraisals of work produced by Dowson, John Davidson, and Yeats, Symons had placed Crackanthorpe and his *Wreckage* 'at the head of the short stories of the year'.[111] Symons's overall prognosis was decidedly and attractively upbeat: 'literature is coming to be appreciated as literature [...] a poet is once more a person of importance'.[112]

'All this is exceedingly comforting', says Crackanthorpe, 'and yet, perhaps, it is not a matter for absolute congratulation' (p. 398). With regard to fiction, any new growth in literary production will best flourish in a Hegelian and Darwinian state of creative conflict with readers who may have little invested in the importance of poets. For in order that 'this new evolution in the art of fiction' can 'achieve any definite, ultimate fineness of expression', it needs 'a healthy, vigorous, if not wholly intelligent, body of opponents' who can, with salutary effect, 'knock a lot of nonsense out of us' and 'spur us on to bring out the best' (p. 398). And in a prelude to launching his own bespoke assault, Crackanthorpe goes out of his way in a Beerbohm-esque satiric flourish to applaud the mediocrity of 'grocerdom' embodied in the figure of the 'moral objector'. All that fighting talk from Frank Harris is simply striking at the wrong enemy. Critics like Harris mistakenly persist in characterizing the 'moral objector' as an alarming 'ogre in the fairy tale':

> the gentleman who objects to realistic fiction on moral grounds [...] has been labelled a Philistine [...] It is confidently asserted that he comes from Putney, or from Sheffield, and that, when he is not busy abolishing the art of English literature, he is employed in safeguarding the interests of the grocery or tallow-chandler's trade. Strange and cruel tales of him have been

[110] Arthur Symons, 'English Literature in 1893', *The Athenaeum*, 6 January 1894, p. 18.
[111] Symons, 'English Literature in 1893', p. 18.
[112] Symons, 'English Literature in 1893', p. 18.

printed in the monthly reviews [...] but why start to shatter brutally their dainty charm by a soulless process of investigation? [...] Let us remember that he has never professed to understand Art, and the deep debt of gratitude that every artist in the land should consequently owe to him; let us remember that he is above us, for he belongs to the great middle classes [...] he is delightful, because he is intelligible. (pp. 398–99)

Rather than submit him to the 'soulless process of investigation', the 'moral ogre', who has 'no subtly exacting demand', requiring only 'a plain moral lesson', should not be denigrated but actually cherished for his 'delightful [...] intelligible' incomprehension (pp. 399–400). And since the 'business of art is to create for us fine interests, to make of our human nature a more complete thing', it follows, says Crackanthorpe, that all 'great art is moral in the wider and the truer sense of the word' (p. 400). On this point there can simply be no agreement with the denizen of Putney or Sheffield, since '[t]o him, morality is concerned only with the established relations between the sexes and with fair dealing between man and man: to him the subtle, indirect morality of Art is incomprehensible' (p. 400).[113] And yet, for Crackanthorpe, this 'moral objector', 'healthy, vigorous, if not wholly intelligent', is a necessary, desirable adversary.

Crackanthorpe's principal target, though, is the much less desirable 'artistic objector' to realist fiction, 'the aesthetic philistine who opposes the innovatory in terms of the art of the past', as John Goode has put it.[114] And in its final section the essay addresses this topic by circling back to the question of 'reticence' and Arthur Waugh. For Goode, the distinction Waugh draws between 'nakedness' and 'nudity' — a distinction grounded in an aesthetics requiring the maintenance of a 'universal standard of good taste' — reflects a very partial version of literary and cultural tradition, one which allows art to be incorporated 'within a totalized mode of seeing [...] that Crackanthorpe attacks in the name of productive excellence'.[115] Waugh is simply the latest recruit to that band of prominent critics who have commanded, in some cases for over a decade, a disproportionate cultural authority in their flaunting of opposition to innovative literature, particularly realism — familiar, influential figures like Andrew Lang, William Barry, Clement Scott, and J. A. Spender ('The Philistine'), as well as (less securely) Buchanan.

Crackanthorpe's impressive grasp of the terms of this longstanding literary and cultural conflict animates the rest of his essay. The 'artistic objector to

---

[113] It is a definition anticipated by Crackanthorpe's aesthete, Eustace, in his dialogue 'After The Play — A Conversation': '"Morality", as we commonly understand it, is concerned only with sexual relations, and with fair dealing between man and man [...] "morals" and art have no point of contact' (*The Albermarle: A Monthly Review*, 1.6 (June 1892), 216–18 (p. 217)).

[114] John Goode, 'The Decadent Writer as Producer', in *Collected Essays of John Goode*, ed. by Charles Swann (Keele: Keele University Press, 1995), pp. 336–54 (p. 339).

[115] Goode, 'The Decadent Writer as Producer', p. 339.

realist fiction', he says, has quitted the 'camp of the lovers of Art' in order to solicit, even imitate, attitudes taken to art by the 'moral objector'. Not short of adroitness, '[h]e can patter to us glibly of the "gospel of ugliness"; of the "cheerlessness of modern literature"; he can even juggle with that honourable property-piece, the maxim of Art for Art's sake' (p. 400). But

> when even this feat has proved ineffective, and someone has started scoffing at his pretended 'delight in pure rhythm or music of the phrase,' and flippantly assured him that he is talking nonsense, and that style is a mere matter of psychological suggestion [he] passes dexterously to his curtain effect — a fervid denunciation of express trains, evening newspapers, Parisian novels, or the first number of THE YELLOW BOOK. (pp. 400–01)

Treading a fine line between playful mockery and contempt, Crackanthorpe anatomizes how the traditionalist 'artistic' critic mirrors the moral objector's promiscuous way with categories in his worried search for decadence, as he flits from literature to modernity and then back, via Paris, to the dubious *avant-garde*. It is neatly done and playfully mimics the circular procedures of both philistine and traditionalist critics who embrace the very condition which gives rise to the symptoms they decry. And it is a critically telling point because it is eloquent about both the state of criticism itself and the authority exerted on it by a conservative critical elite.

'The whole business' can be explained by the invention of the 'weird word' of 'Decadence'. Crackanthorpe exposes here the 'absurdity' and instability of the term 'Decadent', that 'favourite, meaningless word of that time' as Yeats put it.[116] He does so by ventriloquizing the voice of anxiety and bafflement in the most frequently quoted passage from the essay:

> Decadence, decadence: you are all decadent nowadays. Ibsen, Degas, and the New English Art Club; Zola, Oscar Wilde, and the Second Mrs. Tanqueray. Mr. Richard Le Gallienne is hoist with his own petard; even the British playwright has not escaped the taint. Ah, what a hideous spectacle. All whirling along towards one common end. And the elegant voice of the artistic objector floating behind: '*Après vous le deluge.*' (pp. 401–02)

'Lumping things together' in the manner of the critics of Decadent art, Crackanthorpe anticipates, not least in his choice of writers, the remorseless positivist symptomology of 'the Jeremiah of the period', Max Nordau, who sought to lay bare what he saw as the inadequacies of the age in his *Degeneration* (1895), first published as *Entartung* (1892).[117] Nowhere does Crackanthorpe make direct reference to *Degeneration*, but Blanche Crackanthorpe did — neatly skewering Nordau's procedures as the 'prince of graphomaniacs' in her essay

---

[116] See Goode, 'The Decadent Writer', p. 338; W. B. Yeats, *Memoirs*, ed. by Denis Donoghue (London: Macmillan, 1988), p. 97.
[117] Stokes, *In the Nineties*, p. 11; Jackson, *The Eighteen Nineties*, p. 16.

'Sex in Modern Literature'.[118] Voicing the anxieties of both philistine, 'moral objector', and cultured, 'artistic objector', *Degeneration* ran to seven editions in six months, a period coinciding with the Wilde trials and the dethroning of the so-called 'Decadent' movement.[119] Crackanthorpe may dispense with 'the umbrella word', writes Goode, but 'he is nevertheless affirming a movement', certain in the knowledge that quite unlike the counter-Decadent readership to which Nordau appeals, '[a] new public has been created — appreciative, eager and determined'.[120] Now Crackanthorpe cites what has become a familiar passage from Gosse's essay on 'The Limits of Realism in Fiction' to underscore the combative role that realism still has to play in answering the needs of this readership:

> we cannot return, in serious novels, to the inanities and impossibilities of the old well-made plot, to the children changed at nurse, to the madonna-heroine and the god-like hero, to the impossible virtues and melodramatic vices. In future, even those who sneer at realism and misrepresent it most wilfully, will be obliged to put their productions more in accordance with veritable experience.

The critically demanding public, tired of these contrivances, has, in Gosse's metaphor, 'eaten of the apple of knowledge' (p. 403).[121] It is a familiar defence of realism, of course, but the terms that Gosse chose might well have given impetus to Crackanthorpe's interest in foregrounding, in a spirit of critical Decadence, the performance of 'sentiment', melodrama, and the 'old well-made plot' in his stories.

But then there is something of a critical lapse:

> Fiction has taken her place amongst the arts. The theory that writing resembles the blacking of boots, the more boots you black, the better you do it, is busy evaporating. The excessive admiration for the mere idea of a book or a story is dwindling; so is the comparative indifference to slovenly treatment. True is it that the society lady, dazzled by the brilliancy of her own conversation, and the serious-minded spinster, bitten by some sociological theory, still decide in the old jaunty spirit, that fiction is the obvious medium through which to astonish or improve the world. Let us beware of the despotism of the intelligent amateur [...] deadliest of Art's enemies, [who] is creeping up in our midst. (p. 404)

Crackanthorpe's elision of the 'serious-minded spinster' with the 'intelligent

---

[118] B. A. Crackanthorpe, 'Sex in Modern Literature', p. 611, and note.
[119] See William Greenslade, *Degeneration, Culture and the Novel 1880–1940* (Cambridge: Cambridge University Press, 1994), p. 120 and, generally, pp. 120–29.
[120] Goode, 'The Decadent Writer', p. 339; Crackanthorpe, 'Reticence in Literature', pp. 396–405.
[121] This passage is taken, verbatim, from Gosse's essay 'The Limits of Realism in Fiction' (1890), repr. in *Questions At Issue*, pp. 152–53.

amateur' as the 'deadliest of Art's enemies' (a point he made earlier in his
February 1894 'Art of Fiction' lecture and repeated in the essay, virtually
verbatim) marks a failure of judgement in its denigration of contemporary
'romans à thèse', the New Woman novels, just then appearing in the 1890s,
lending weight to Jane Eldridge Miller's verdict that Crackanthorpe 'had no
objection to the subject matter or candor of realism in the hands of men, but
saw a great danger in the female usurpers who had the temerity to think that
they too could be realists'.[122] And the point threatens to unbalance the burden
of the earlier, innovative argument. In urging that Art should be a matter
of 'treatment', of 'life' in fiction, 'without rearrangement', as James had it,
Crackanthorpe now undervalues the work of the 'intelligent amateur' — the
female writer — whose innovative use of fiction with which 'to astonish or
improve the world' cannot be seriously entertained. Crackanthorpe sounds
here too much like the 'artistic objector' he has decried. On the other hand,
his error could be chargeable to his need to validate the efforts of innovative
writers as serious professionals who have to contend with the prejudice of the
'popular mind' — that 'the one thing needed [...] to produce good fiction' is 'an
ingenious idea, or "plot" [...] The rest is a mere matter of handwriting' (p. 404).

Crackanthorpe's final move is to return to the 'artistic objector', Arthur
Waugh, and to sidestep his phobia about 'realism, naked and unashamed'.
Crackanthorpe contends that there is 'scanty merit' in 'the mere selection',
by a writer, 'of any particular subject, however ingenious or daring it may
appear at first sight'. An 'ingenious or daring' choice of subject was, of course,
a cornerstone of Zola's naturalist project; after all, his scientific method
had licensed the idea that, as with scientific enquiry, there was logically no
subject matter that literature could or should not be capable of treating. But
Crackanthorpe leaves it clear that

> a man is not an artist, simply because he writes about heredity or the demi-
> monde, that to call a spade a spade requires no extraordinary literary gift,
> and that the essential is contained in the frank, fearless acceptance by every
> man of his entire artistic temperament, with its qualities and its flaws.
> (pp. 404–05)

The 'Reticence' essay is an important 'Decadent' document in that it exemplified
a spirit of critical combativeness that Goode, and most recently Alex Murray,
have identified as central to the cultural politics of the Decadent avant-garde:
its 'protest' against 'popular journalism; sexual conservatism; "high Victorian"
literary forms (the triple-decker novel and the epic poem); middle-class thrift;
nationalism; new media forms; provincialism'. Indeed it was a 'response to a
whole range of Victorian values' involving 'primarily, a rejection of the all too

[122] Jane Eldridge Miller, Rebel Women: Feminism, Modernism and the Edwardian Novel
(London: Virago, 1994), p. 17.

easy forms of moral judgement that the very term "decadent" conveyed'.[123] Such a spirit of deconstructive, critical iconoclasm animates, in a variety of ways, Crackanthorpe's experiments with the form of the short story.

[123] Alex Murray, *Landscapes of Decadence: Literature and Place at the Fin de Siècle* (Cambridge: Cambridge University Press, 2016), p. 8.

The Stories and the Prose Poems

by Emanuela Ettorre

VIII

By the 1890s the short story, 'with its emphasis on artistic delicacy and style at the expense of traditional moral cliché', had become 'the most suitable platform' for the expression of the aesthetic and moral challenge of literary Decadence.[124] Whether gathered in *avant-garde* publications such as the *Yellow Book* or *The Savoy*, or in outlets which sought a broader appeal, like *The Strand*, '[n]o short story of the slightest distinction', as H. G. Wells famously observed, 'went for long unrecognised'.[125] The short story had come to prominence during the previous decade alongside a striking increase in new periodicals catering for the tastes of a growing urban readership.[126] New publications, such as *Black and White* and *The Sketch*, featured a story each week, and newspapers like *The Star* found room for them on a regular basis, commissioning their first from Hubert Crackanthorpe himself; it appeared in February 1896.[127]

With the demise of the three-volume novel in 1894, the rise of the short story as a genre was perhaps inevitable. Shorter fictional pieces were changing substantially from the productions of the mid-century when they had been generally read as 'stray chapters from longer works'.[128] By the end of the century the short story had modulated into an autonomous form, an appropriate narrative instrument with which 'to do the complicated thing with a strong brevity and lucidity'.[129]

Crackanthorpe's volumes were important staging-posts in the evolution of the short story in Britain. During his brief literary career, he interpreted this form flexibly: from the relatively compact stories in *Wreckage*, which

---

[124] Kostas Boyiopoulos and others, Introduction to *The Decadent Short Story: An Annotated Anthology*, p. 1.

[125] H. G. Wells, Introduction to *The Country of the Blind and Other Stories* (London: Thomas Nelson and Sons, 1913), p. v.

[126] Peter Keating provides the evidence for the growth in numbers of 'weekly, monthly and quarterly magazines': from 643 in 1875 to 1298 in 1885 and 2081 in 1895 (*The Haunted Study: A Social History of the English Novel 1875–1914* (London: Secker and Warburg, 1989), p. 34).

[127] 'A Latter-Day Highwayman (An Adventure in Miniature)', *The Star*, 1 February 1896, p. 2, cols 1–2.

[128] Phillip Mallett, 'Thomas Hardy and the Story-teller's Art', Postfazione in *Thomas Hardy: L'immaginazione di una donna e altri racconti*, ed. by Emanuela Ettorre (Massa: Transeuropa, 2012), p. 117.

[129] Henry James, Preface to 'The Lesson of the Master', in *The Art of the Novel: Critical Prefaces* (London: Charles Scribner's Sons, 1935), pp. 217–31 (p. 231).

shared a thematic focus and 'unity of impression',[130] to the more elaborate, psychologically complex productions of *Sentimental Studies* and *Last Studies*, and from the fable-like *A Set of Village Tales* to the impressionistic fragments of *Vignettes*.

For early reviewers still disturbed by the disquieting challenge of literary naturalism, Crackanthorpe's narratives were 'nothing if not Zola-esque' in their shocking representation of 'deliberate crudities [...] by which to catch the public ear'.[131] Critics called out the 'ferocious Crackanthorpe',[132] considering his stories 'morbid' and 'loathsome', preoccupied by 'the more sordid aspects of life',[133] or tracing them, in an assessment fashionably derived from Nordau and *Degeneration*, to the convolutions of 'a diseased mind who finds pleasure in writing of diseased mortals'.[134]

Crackanthorpe's subject matter *was* unquestionably challenging. The world of his *Wreckage*, for example, is peopled by characters who build their lives upon the illusions of a love that is doomed to die, or which degenerates into abject forms of manipulation, seduction, deceit, and abandonment, not to mention prostitution. From the naturalist toolbox of Zola and the Goncourts, he 'made full use of the decline-plot',[135] the naturalist downward trajectory which described all sorts and conditions of disabling states — physical, psychological, moral. Crackanthorpe's figures are quite capable of expressing their malaise pathologically, in sudden fits of rage, states of psycho-physical prostration, in a cultivation of isolation that verges on misanthropy, or in self-destructive life-choices and suicidal impulses. For readers, these characteristics can still be less than captivating: it is difficult to approach some of Crackanthorpe's characters with feelings of unalloyed compassion, since the perverse choices they are drawn into making, not to say their occasional vulgarity, ineptitude, or manifest refusal to live, make for decidedly 'uncomfortable reading',[136] prompting reactions of irritation, exasperation — even of disgust.

Together with other practitioners of the short story in the 1890s, amongst them George Egerton, Marion Hepworth Dixon, Ella D'Arcy, and Netta Syrett, Hubert Crackanthorpe was spoken of as one of the exponents of 'new realism'. New realism 'pushed forward into new realms of subject matter', wrote Wendell Harris; 'it insisted upon the right to present a pessimistic view of life,

---

[130] Edgar Allan Poe, 'The Philosophy of Composition', in *Edgar Allan Poe: Essays and Reviews*, ed. by G. R. Thompson (New York, The Library of America, 1984), p. 15.

[131] H. D. Traill, 'Literature', *New Review*, 8 (May 1893), 602–09 (p. 607).

[132] Anon., 'A Yellow Melancholy', *The Speaker*, 28 April 1894, p. 469.

[133] 'Our Library Table', *The Athenaeum*, 29 April 1893, p. 535.

[134] Jeanette Gilder, 'The Lounger', *Critic*, 27, 2 January 1897, p. 9.

[135] Trotter, *The English Novel in History*, p. 115.

[136] Harris, 'Hubert Crackanthorpe as Realist', p. 77.

and it denied the necessity of an elaborate or ingeniously fascinating plot'.[137] But the new realism of Crackanthorpe's 'little documents of hell'[138] coalesces with a conscious aestheticizing of his subject matter, one facet of which was his deliberately dispassionate handling of the human predicaments in the stories. For Terry Eagleton, '[a]estheticizing the unacceptable' had become 'a common *fin-de-siècle* pastime'.[139] And indeed, Crackanthorpe's desolate land of human relationships, unfulfilled desires, and negated love was infused with an innovative, aesthetic colouring. In so doing he was expressing both his realist-naturalist commitment, and giving rein to his compulsions as a critical writer of Decadence.

For many reviewers, the publication of *Wreckage: Seven Studies* established Crackanthorpe as a disciple of the French realist school, an author whose 'directness in his manner of telling a story and [...] sharpness in his brief delineations of character [are] rarely found in English novel-writers'.[140] Crackanthorpe was frequently compared to France's leading short story writer, Guy de Maupassant, 'both in approval and in contempt',[141] and there was little doubt that Maupassant was influential: Crackanthorpe's new realism chimed with Maupassant's aim, as a realist, not to 'show us a banal photograph of life, but to provide us with a vision that is at once more complete, more startling, and more convincing than reality itself'.[142] His indebtedness to Maupassant was evident, too, in the way that the French author dealt with human misery and the more brutal aspects of reality. For Elizabeth Bowen, Maupassant 'transcribed passions in the only terms possible — dispassionate understatement';[143] similarly, Crackanthorpe's 'abstemiousness', and the 'refinement of his reticence', as Lionel Johnson put it,[144] are central to his narrative approach. But

---

[137] Wendell V. Harris, 'Identifying the Decadent Fiction of the Eighteen-Nineties', p. 4.

[138] Richard Le Gallienne, 'The Real Book', in *The Junk Man and Other Poems* (New York and Toronto: Doubleday, Page & C., 1921), p. 227.

[139] Terry Eagleton, 'The Flight to the Real', in *Cultural Politics at the Fin de Siècle*, ed. by Sally Ledger and Scott McCracken (Cambridge: Cambridge University Press, 1995), pp. 11–21 (p. 16).

[140] *The Athenaeum*, 29 April 1893, p. 535. The volume appeared in Dutch translation, four years later, as *Wrakhout: zeven schesten*, trans. by Titia van der Tuuk (Almelo: W. Hilarius, 1897).

[141] Malcolm, Introduction to Hubert Crackanthorpe, *Wreckage: Seven Studies*, p. xxi. His debt to Maupassant was acknowledged by many critics: William C. Frierson later traced his beneficial influence on Crackanthorpe in his scorning of 'tricks of plot, elements of adventure, and dénouements', but thought, too, that Crackanthorpe lacked Maupassant's 'broad scope of subject-matter' (William C. Frierson, p. 471).

[142] Guy de Maupassant, 'The Novel', in *Pierre et Jean*, trans. by Julie Mead (Oxford: Oxford University Press, 2001), pp. 3–14 (p. 7).

[143] Elizabeth Bowen, Introduction to *The Faber Book of Modern Stories* (London: Faber and Faber, 1937), p. 9.

[144] Johnson, 'Hubert Crackanthorpe', p. 428.

there were divergences, too. Arthur Symons had observed that the two authors shared a 'cynical acceptance of the animal passions as being really at the root of things',[145] yet the abiding note of cynicism in Maupassant's work is attenuated in Crackanthorpe's more compassionate treatment of relationships. Furthermore, Crackanthorpe's representation of suffering is more sympathetically, and, arguably, more profoundly, engaged: his 'telling of the misery', in Johnson's words, 'becomes a thing of dreadful beauty, and in its intensity goes near[er] to the heart of the whole dark matter than many a moving sermon'.[146]

Other sympathetic critics detected in his writing the realization of an aesthetic project in which his subject matter, however troubling, was treated with an 'art of restraint, of reticence, of abstinence', producing 'the visual effect of lines from the etching needle'.[147] Looking back over Crackanthorpe's brief writing career, Henry James felt able to praise his 'imaginative reaction against the smug and superficial', his 'excellent felicity of dreariness', and 'his troubled individual note — a note so rare in England', all of which determined the force of his experiments in fiction.[148] James recognized the significance of Crackanthorpe's 'consciousness of the cruelty of life, the expression, from volume to volume, of the deep insecurity of things', but he was also taken by his attention to language and style, and in particular, by his effort to 'summarize and compress for purposes of presentation'.[149] Appreciative reviewers, like William Archer, had already noticed that '[t]he real excellence of Mr Crackanthorpe's work [...] lies in the conciseness and concreteness of his style'.[150] That 'style' tends to foreground economical presentation: it is characterized by short sentences, unadorned diction, a paratactic phraseology that often relies on the juxtaposition and accumulation of images, and by phrases that either lack coordination, or are connected only by a full stop or semicolon. Sequences of short paragraphs and simple sentences lend his prose a powerful, impressionistic expressiveness, further reinforced by ellipsis, graphical markers (asterisks and suspension points), blunt dialogue, free indirect speech, and a succession of brief chapters interspersed in the narration. These unconventional narratological features testify to the challenge Crackanthorpe faced, and invariably surmounted, in translating the complexity of lived experience into his work of fiction.

Notwithstanding the controversial subject matter of his stories, his 'impersonality in narration'[151] prevents him from depicting the world through

[145] Symons, 'English Literature in 1893', p. 18.
[146] Johnson, 'Hubert Crackanthorpe', p. 428.
[147] Anon., 'A Decadent Proseman', *Daily Chronicle*, 23 March 1893, p. 3.
[148] Henry James, 'Hubert Crackanthorpe', in *Last Studies*, pp. xix, xx, xiv, xxii.
[149] James, 'Hubert Crackanthorpe', p. xxii.
[150] William Archer, 'Wreckage', *Westminster Gazette*, 25 March 1893, p. 3.
[151] Malcolm, Introduction to Hubert Crackanthorpe, *Wreckage: Seven Studies*, p. xxii.

the lens of a pervasive moralism, or a Manichean conception of society. Crackanthorpe's understanding of reality rarely assumes preconceptions or judgement, since he sees 'another kind of world', as Symons ventriloquized, 'in which no one is quite good or quite bad, in which nothing extraordinary happens, but which is full of mean troubles, and sordid cares, [...] and in which love, and death, and pity, and wrong-doing come and go under dim masks and soiling disguises'.[152]

Crackanthorpe's singularly dispassionate treatment of disturbing subjects is bound up in interesting ways with his awareness of the inadequacy of any categorical interpretation of human behaviour. Accordingly, at a formal level, his stories greeted readers with an indeterminate sense of closure and resolution, with any denouement left inconclusive and open-ended. These formal strategies anticipate modernist techniques of narrative, and they would inevitably have challenged the expectations of any complacent late Victorian reader.

IX

In 'Profiles', the arresting opening story in *Wreckage*, 'the material for a Victorian three-decker is condensed into fifty-three pages'.[153] In seventeen short chapters, it skilfully dramatizes the destructive complexities of romantic and sexual relations. Maurice Radford and Lilly are engaged and about to get married: he is a young officer; she is an orphan who has never known her mother, and has only a vague recollection of her father. Forced to live with an aunt whom she detests 'with an instinctive, imperious loathing' (p. 81), she decides to leave her home and follow Maurice to London, having first struggled with her homicidal instincts towards her aunt. The two lovers spend some days together in a hotel — a choice that Lilly makes spontaneously — but it is after this sexual experience, conducted outside marriage, that we witness her inexorable descent towards self-destruction. Lilly becomes attracted to an acquaintance of Maurice, Adrian Safford, who comes to represent a disruptive force in the narrative; he allures Lilly with his 'bushy eyebrows, heavy, black moustache and vermilion lips' (p. 87), his 'lustrous black eyes' and 'strong muscles on each side of the bull-like throat' (p. 88). Lilly falls in love with Adrian, whose close resemblance to a 'traditional sexual villain'[154] anticipates the unfortunate epilogue of this infatuation. Lilly abandons Maurice for Adrian, but on her awakening in his sombre chambers, Adrian is clearly annoyed by her very presence — 'his feeling was one of pure disgust' (pp. 91–92). The conclusion of the story is predictable:

[152] Arthur Symons, 'Hubert Crackanthorpe', *Saturday Review*, 85 (8 January 1898), 52–53 (p. 52).
[153] Cheryl Alexander Malcolm and David Malcolm, p. 12.
[154] DC, p. 66.

Adrian disappears, while Maurice unsuccessfully tries to regain Lilly's affection despite her infidelity and her inevitable turn to prostitution.

'Profiles' textualizes the loss of illusions and a descent into amoral decadence through the fall of a woman of 'strong passions' and 'desperate sensuality' (p. 86); her sexual desires cannot be accommodated in society without her experiencing a loss of self, and a concomitant loss of self-respect. Lilly rejects the stability of a suitable marriage, only to find herself condemned by the perversity of her choices:

> the seething turmoil of the great city, ruthless in its never-flagging lust, caught up the frailty of her helpless beauty, and playing with it, marred it, mutilated it. Like a flower, frost-bitten in the hour of its budding, she drooped and withered. [...] She grew careless of her dress and of her person, and at last callous to all around her. She sunk into the irretrievable morass of *impersonal* prostitution. She ceased to live; mechanically she trudged on across the swamp-level of existence. (p. 96, my italics)

Unable to preserve her purity in the corrupting city, Lilly is brought to a state of self-annihilation; she is a restless, unstable figure who drifts inexorably downwards into prostitution, invisibility, and ultimately silence.

In the next story, 'A Conflict of Egoisms', Crackanthorpe dramatizes the growing discomfort and afflictions of 'two ambitious but monadic individuals who marry as if to escape their respective solitudes'.[155] It is a story which skilfully navigates the dichotomic relationship between life and artistic production, 'shown to be at odds', as Elke D'hoker observes, since 'the artist's absorption in his art and, consequently, in himself allows for no other affections'.[156] Oswald Nowell is a frustrated and solitary writer, unable to complete what he considers to be a remarkable work of art; Letty Moore, an editor of a weekly magazine, is an exponent of female emancipation who ironically surrenders to the idea of marriage. At the beginning of the story they live in the same building, but they are oblivious to each other, sheltered as they are in their solitude. When they finally meet, Letty is fascinated by the image of Oswald as a writer; she reads all his books and immediately accepts his lukewarm marriage proposal in the hope of a passionate life together. But the two characters very soon realize the impossibility of experiencing a loving relationship. Oswald's alienation from Letty is chilling:

> It had been a strange thing this marriage of his — a thing so sudden, so impulsive, that, as he thought, he marvelled at it. This woman by his side, her full-lipped mouth quivering with an expression that he disliked — all at once, she seemed no longer near him; but, from a distance, as it were, he

---

[155] Gagnier, *The Insatiability of Human Wants*, p. 170.
[156] D'hoker, 'Artist Stories of the 1890s', p. 291.

> was looking at her as one looks upon a stranger — a stranger who had come
> into his life and who was changing it all for him. (pp. 113–14)

As the marriage gradually withers and the dread of being with Letty increasingly torments him, Oswald paradoxically recovers 'the fever of creation' (p. 117). Yet his obsession with writing is now so overwhelming that his nervous system is overstrained, rendering him even more distant from his wife, who has now become a disturbing, not to say nauseating, presence to him. On her side, Letty feels a growing despair at the lack of the kind of love for which she had hoped.

Something of the depressing absence of marital harmony between them is conveyed by the narrator's linguistic choices: the phraseological units are mainly attributive-nominal, dialogues are brusque and characterized by simple language, and collide with passages in which phrasing becomes artificial, loaded down with adjectives and adverbs which appear redundant, disproportionate, even oxymoronic: 'grim serenity', 'chilly apathy', 'fierce delight', 'pitiless obstinacy', 'weary docility', 'frenzied fierceness', 'blind recklessness'.

The ending of the story enacts a massive failure. Unable to endure a married life of apathy and uneasiness, Letty destroys her husband's manuscript, tearing it into fragments. Oswald does not even succeed in committing suicide by throwing himself into the river Thames, but dies on the bridge, victim of a probable stroke. His failed suicide strikes a note, rather shockingly, of dark comedy:

> He stood in the middle of the suspension bridge, peering down through the
> iron-work at the river [...] and gripping the stanchions, prepared to swing
> himself on to the top of them. As he did so, a blackness filled his eyes; a
> dull thud; his body dropped back on to the roadway — dead. (pp. 120–21)

Several other of Crackanthorpe's protagonists are driven to contemplate suicidal extremes. The wretched wife in 'A Struggle for Life' appears to be on the verge of suicide as she leans over the parapet of a bridge; only the commodification of her body can save her from drowning. In 'Battledore and Shuttlecock', Helen 'attempted to take poison' (p. 205), while in 'A Commonplace Chapter', Hillier Haselton, occasionally tormented by the insignificance of life and 'the horrid squalor of death', 'muse[s] vaguely on suicide as the only fitting termination' (p. 184, p. 196). The presence of a suicidal tendency in Crackanthorpe's narratives finds an explanation in Émile Durkheim's *On Suicide* (1897):

> It is the moral constitution of society that determines at any moment the
> number of voluntary deaths. [...] The movements that the victim carries
> out — which, at first sight, seem to express only his personal temperament
> — are in reality the outcome and extension of a social state to which they
> give external form.[157]

---

[157] Émile Durkheim, *On Suicide* (1897; London: Penguin, 2006), p. 331.

In Durkheim's terms the expressions of egotism, lassitude, or anomie that distinguish these self-destructive characters testify to a pervasive social malaise. Yet Crackanthorpe refuses any clear-cut interpretation of suicide: the suicidal impulse or act may signal surrender or escape, but it may also constitute a form of heroic defence against the slough of despond.

In 'A Conflict of Egoisms' Crackanthorpe's ruthless depiction of humanity reaches a notable pitch of macabre sarcasm, given his stark recognition here of the impossibility of establishing harmonious relationships in an urban society characterized by the coexistence of solitary lives. In this, and other stories, Crackanthorpe perfectly captures the sad predicament of figures who wander the streets, victims of paralyzing routine or humiliating failure, for whom loneliness and disappointment lead all too often to catatonic behaviour and forms of psychosis. These anti-heroes experience the fragmentation of a world in which there appears little room for the display of courage, decisiveness, and the exercise of the creative impulse.

In their investigation of this world, Crackanthorpe's stories also confront the problematic issue of gender relations in original ways. His narratives explore the complexities of femininity by representing a variety of women who range from the perverse to the agreeable prostitute, from the greedy and frivolous opportunist to the fragile victim of a merciless environment, or the betrayed wife. By contrast, he exposes male characters, such as Oswald, who are paralyzed by their own fears, and by a masochistic passivity when confronted with the vital but destabilizing forms of female desire. These inadequate men, 'emasculated, domesticated' male figures, as Adrian Hunter puts it, wrestle 'with their own conflicted mentalities'. Hunter's further, valuable point is that the psychological realism of the type that Crackanthorpe practises is itself 'associated with the perceived "feminization" of social and political life', and the 'diminishment of male cultural authority'.[158] The decline of patriarchal assumptions of superiority is exemplified by Oswald, but also by the character of Frank Gorridge in the later story 'Embers'. Trapped in the fixed roles society has devised for them, both these figures suppress their sexual desire and suffer emotional breakdown. Alongside the more typical male seducer — a Vivian Marston, untroubled by the consequences of adultery and promiscuity in 'Dissolving View' — sit these more intriguing, complex figures, in whom conventionally masculine qualities of virility, vigour, and ambitiousness seem entirely lacking.

The degraded face of the city, and the human penalties it exacts, is the focus of 'The Struggle for Life', the shortest story in *Wreckage*, peopled by 'dregs of a population' (p. 122): 'bargemen with grimy furrows across their bronzed faces', 'typical river casuals sucking stumpy clay-pipes', 'pasty-faced youths

---

[158] *The Cambridge Introduction to the Short Story in English*, pp. 36, 35.

quarrelling over their greasy cards', and 'riverside prostitutes, their cheap finery all bedraggled with mud' (p. 122). These unsympathetically drawn figures have little means of improving their condition of life or escaping the paralysis of their existence. And the stark Darwinian echo in the title carries an antiphrastic undertone: if in nature 'the struggle for life' is essential for the fittest to survive and proliferate, the 'struggle' here revolves around a permanent condition of immobility, or death.

The detached narrator of the story invites us on a 'chilly October night' to enter 'a notorious "den"' (p. 122), a public house in which a mason indulges his passion for drinking in the company of a prostitute. He refuses to go home even when his wife arrives and implores him to leave with her, or to give her money to feed their children. After his peremptory, cruel refusal, she quits the pub and walks to the parapet of a bridge where she is driven to sell herself to a passer-by for half a crown, so ironically saving herself from a probable suicide attempt. The homodiegetic narrator has observed the whole scene with detachment: when the young wife 'dropping her head [...] ran out of the room like a hunted animal' (p. 123), he follows her movements and, without expressing compassion, directs his gaze beyond the building to observe her desperate reaction: 'When the girl passed out, I followed her, curious to see the end of it' (p. 123).

The ending of the story provides a good example of how Crackanthorpe seeks to aestheticize 'the unacceptable'. The unmistakably naturalist trajectory of the victimized woman's struggle for survival, and the sensationalist associations of the story's degraded spaces, play against, but also receive validation from, the knowing, but detached, narrator. Yet these narrative features are themselves displaced by a further imaginative stroke. At the riverside, moments before her capitulation, we receive an 'impressionistic evocation' of her abject condition, now lit by moonlight: this 'poised pictorial' 'made her pinched face seem whiter than ever' (p. 123).[159] This memorable story draws on naturalist 'facts' and Decadent 'effects' to create a sense of the real on Crackanthorpe's own creative terms: his sordid pictures do indeed 'becom[e] a thing of dreadful beauty'.[160]

In 'Dissolving View' any possibility of fulfilment in human relationships is foreclosed by the presentation of a male figure so dominated by his vanity that he is incapable of ennobling his own existence, or that of others. Vivian Marston is the embodiment of bourgeois entitlement, a man who finds delight in his own well-being and prosperity, in the cosiness of his 'luxuriously furnished room' (p. 125), while the cold wind rages against 'the wretches who, cut by its blast, [are left] shivering outside' (p. 125). Marston has no compassion for the

[159] Nick Freeman, 'Curious Intricacies: Some Versions of City Writing at the Fin de Siècle', in *The Edinburgh Companion to Fin-de-Siècle Literature, Culture and the Arts*, ed. by Josephine M. Guy (Edinburgh: Edinburgh University Press, 2018), pp. 239–307 (p. 270); Greenslade, 'Naturalism and Decadence', p. 171.
[160] Johnson, 'Hubert Crackanthorpe', p. 428.

destitute; he ignores them. Wrapped up in a golden solitude, his only concern is to make an advantageous marriage with the beautiful Gwynnie, 'the biggest triumph of all' (p. 125). Marston is portrayed as a *homo faber*, the maker of his own destiny, whose narcissistic behaviour leads him to conceive of women only as convenient sexual objects.

As he traces the past through his own memories, he lingers on one of his ex-lovers, Kit, an unknown, illiterate dancer who won him over, but then abandoned him for a young musician. He discovers an overlooked letter in which she reveals that she has been seriously ill, having just given birth to a child who, Marston now realizes, is his own son. Annoyed and distressed to the point of feeling 'a dizzy faintness and a sickening feeling in his stomach' (p. 127) for putting at risk his reputation and his future marriage, he reaches Kit's lodgings only to discover that she has just died, together with her child. The news of her death prompts in him relief and even a sense of joy, now that his marriage to Gwynnie can be celebrated without any compromise to his reputation. The story ends with renewed cynicism, as Marston sits 'before his breakfast-table, eating voraciously; for the morning excursion had given him a splendid appetite' (p. 129).

In 'Dissolving View' the bourgeois space is contrasted with the unwholesome and dangerous slums that Marston visits to reach Kit's dwelling. This is a collision between two separate worlds that cannot be reconciled: within his 'luxuriously furnished room', Marston basks in his own egotism, while the world outside is cast as 'indecent' and 'repulsive' (p. 128). The story gives us close access to the convolutions of Marston's rationalizing mind, and to the sequence of emotions he feels — from self-satisfaction and pride to anxiety and exasperation — which thread through the interplaying sequences of his recollections, delusions, and anticipations. Crackanthorpe's narrator vividly renders his state of mind as he takes a cab, bound for the proletarian district of his past lover:

> As the hansom rolled along, Vivian's thoughts rushed back over the past. Incident after incident crowded up in his memory, and this hideous sequel to his love for Kit gave to each a new, ugly significance. [...] He was going to see Kit. [...] And he understood how he hated going, how he shrunk from bringing her back into his life. But for the irresistible force inside him, urging him forward, he would have turned homeward again. Gwynnie, how could he marry her after this? [...] But perhaps she was dead — oh! To know for certain that it was so; and the sense of relief, which he knew to be a delusion, was so keen that it hurt him. But the child? — the child — that would live on. They always did. Gloomily, incoherently, he brooded over what was to be done with it. (pp. 127–28)

Here, free indirect speech blurs the boundaries between the thoughts of the characters and those of the narrator. In the fusion of the diegetic and the mimetic, the narrator's presence is partially eclipsed, his judgements eluded 'in the analysis of the psychological mechanisms of the mind, and in particular in the sinuous sophistries by which it deceives itself'.[161] As in the other stories, these inner conflicts are reported without ever being brought to a definitive resolution.

'A Dead Woman' is another story that dwells on the complexities of married life and their unforeseen consequences. It focuses on the gradual realization by Richard Rushout, a public house landlord, of his dead wife's infidelity with a neighbouring farmer, Jonathan Hays. The more Richard's suspicions grow, the more his devotion towards his wife 'reasserted itself in all the earnestness of its profundity' (p. 139). Then his recollections of his life with her begin to transform the 'anguish of his doubt' and the intensity of his pain into an unforeseen acceptance of his circumstances: 'day and night he longed for her; could she have returned he would have shared her with Jonathan willingly' (p. 139). Richard and Jane had a childless marriage, but the creature to which she was devoted was a white mare, whose possession, now that the lady is dead, becomes the symbolic centre of the story. Despite Jonathan's desire to own her, Richard sells the mare to someone else, only to see the horse poorly treated and reduced to lameness. Within the economy of the text, the white mare symbolizes the dead woman, who is evidently replaced by the animal, whose shapes, movement, and posture parallel those of a human being: 'her legs, straight, slender, sinewy; her lithe and gracefully rounded body; her undersized head erect' (p. 135). As a character, Jane exists only in terms of a vivid remembrance. She resides in the memory of both her husband and her lover as an elusive but powerful presence: 'And each remembered that she had belonged to the other, and, at that moment, they felt instinctively drawn together: each was conscious of a craving to talk about her, to hear the other mention her name' (p. 144). The reconciliation of the two rivals is possible now that the object of desire is dead, and that love is no more synonymous with promises, illusions, or expectations. Crackanthorpe frequently addresses 'the fearful emotional discrepancies in the sex relation that arise from illusion, from prior fantasy or from egoistic hope',[162] but in this story it becomes possible to overcome emotional pain, to accept adultery, and acquiesce in death.

Strikingly, 'A Dead Woman' displays a marked absence of any predictable expressions of sentiment or of conventional definitions of gender roles: clichés of masculine behaviour are re-positioned through a counter-narrative which supports an unromantic articulation of feelings, and a decidedly non-heroic resolution of problems. Richard Rushout's gradual accommodation of his wife's lover revises performances of manliness conventionally based on ideas

---

[161] Harris, 'Hubert Crackanthorpe as Realist', p. 78.
[162] DC, p. 89.

of virility and honour. If in 'A Conflict of Egoisms' and 'Dissolving View' the obsessive characters remain unchanged throughout the whole story, the protagonist of 'A Dead Woman' is able to evolve, so as to achieve some kind of psychological balance, quite against the odds. The presiding influence here is less Zola or Hardy than George Eliot.

In 'Embers' Frank Gorridge is an apathetic and methodical scribe living a monotonous life in his dull apartment. He constantly thinks about Maggie, his wife, who abandoned him, apparently without reason, a few years before. Unlike Vivian Marston — who is distressed by the recollection of his ex-lover, after the shocking truth has surfaced — Gorridge's memories attenuate in a process of gradual acceptance and a sense of resignation, since 'five years of unconscious retrospective crystallisation had vaguely beautified them for him' (p. 147). When Mag suddenly reappears in his life, her only concern is to get money from him with reiterated and blunt requests, whose intimidating effect is to reduce him to a state of immoveable depression and financial ruin:

> Back his life dropped into the old groove, till it all seemed like a bad dream [...] he was unable to pay his weekly bill [...] And he began to age strangely, thinner and thinner his hair became, till he was almost quite bald. (p. 151)

Whereas Vivian Marston was obstinate in his search for the truth about the dancer's fate, Gorridge is extremely passive when confronted with the insolence of his wife: when she first haughtily re-emerges in his life, he is consumed by an inexplicable impulse of prodigality that ultimately leads him to a state of irreversible prostration. While victimizing her husband, Mag demonstrates her frivolousness and opportunism; devoted to alcohol and driven by the logic of money and consumerism, she wanders from one public house to another. The remarkable aspect of Frank and Mag's relationship is that she treats her husband with the same inhumanity that Marston shows towards his women. It is notable that in Crackanthorpe's stories both male and female characters show a capacity for malevolence and emotional exploitation that condemns them to solitude and failure. The reader of 'Embers' might well wonder why Mag got married to Frank only to leave him, even though she could have taken advantage of her husband's magnanimity, but the text offers few clues; their emotional turmoil remains relatively unexplained, along with the choices they make, presented as matters of fact. Mag had suddenly 'gone with not a word of explanation' (p. 147), and Frank only remembers the date, 18 February, marking the beginning of a monotonous, lonely phase of his life.

X

Crackanthorpe's second collection of stories, *Sentimental Studies & A Set of Village Tales*, published in July 1895, showed a development in his writing that inevitably divided the critics. Henry Harland praised the 'clearness of his psychological insights' and 'the intensity of his realization';[163] the *Saturday Review* found that he had 'toppled over into a flood of psychoanalysis [in wishing] to exercise all his cleverness upon analysis'.[164] For Johnson, 'Sentimental Studies [...] are more spacious and elaborate, richlier worded and of ampler rhythm'; however the 'longeurs' of this volume 'are disproportionate to the interest of the situation'.[165] In *Sentimental Studies* Crackanthorpe reassesses, only to deconstruct, the paradigm of Victorian sentimentality, characterized by Michael Bell as 'mawkish self-indulgent and actively pernicious modes of feeling'.[166] In these stories the appeal to sentiment rarely leads to states of 'lachrymose excess',[167] since the method Crackanthorpe employs is, in a sense, scientific. In their dispassionate approach, *Sentimental Studies* become, in effect, case studies in sentiment.

The volume opens with 'A Commonplace Chapter', a narrative that testifies to Crackanthorpe's development of the short story form. Not only is he experimenting with a longer narrative, here composed of two linked sections of thirty-one chapters, he is also moving away from the rather dramatic and impressionistic mode of *Wreckage*. This story assumes a more elaborate and analytic form that relies on a detailed investigation of the characters, of their emotional drives, and of the tortuous personal dilemmas faced by a couple whose initially happy relationship will result in disillusionment. At first, the marriage between Hillier and his wife, Ella, symbolizes an ideal, the possibility of 'regeneration', a moment of 'great, unknown happiness' (p. 157, p. 155) for both of them. But as the story unfolds, their experience of married life becomes marked by fluctuating but unmistakably discomforting feelings — jealousy, listlessness, resentment, even disgust. Hillier is an ambitious and successful writer,[168] while Ella is an unpretentious and naïve girl whose heart's desire has always been to marry. Initially, she sees her husband as 'kind and unselfish', even though he very quickly reveals his own nature: he is arrogant and conceited, scornful of those around him, and gripped by a 'moody restlessness', resorting to performances of self-loathing and self-abnegation when faced with the challenge of reciprocating Ella's love for him:

> Ella [...] trusted in him as a man above all other men; and his very self-

---

[163] [Henry Harland], 'A Letter to the Editor and an offer of a Prize from "The Yellow Dwarf"', *The Yellow Book*, 7 (October 1895), 125–43 (p. 141).

[164] 'Mr. Crackanthorpe's New Volume', *Saturday Review*, 80 (27 July 1895), 117–18 (pp. 117–18).

[165] Johnson, 'Hubert Crackanthorpe', p. 428.

[166] Michael Bell, *Sentimentalism, Ethics and the Culture of Feeling* (London, Palgrave Macmillan, 2000), p. 2.

[167] Bell, *Sentimentalism*, p. 118.

[168] In the first, periodical version of the story, 'Ray' Haselton is an up-and-coming lawyer.

absorption made each fresh sign of this trust of hers an acute suffering to him, till, racked by remorse, he longed weakly to besmirch himself altogether in her eyes. (p. 157)

What begins as a relatively uneventful narrative generates dramatic momentum when Hillier is unfaithful to his wife, and ratchets up his psychological control over her: Ella is treated as a subjugated animal — 'If she had been a dog he could not have spoken more brutally' (p. 174) — and their only child, Claude, receives 'perfunctory attention' from his father (p. 186). And throughout, Hillier oscillates between feelings of 'remorse' and displays of 'haughtiness' (p. 172).

In this story, Crackanthorpe investigates the way in which sentimental relationships deteriorate and degenerate into forms of possession or deception; the protagonists are trapped and isolated by their state of emotional turmoil, a condition which offers no resolution to their dilemmas. The appropriately open, indeterminate ending leaves the reader with just one certainty: any relief can only be achieved through the relinquishing of emotional drives:

> By-and-bye, the recent revelation of his unfaithfulness seemed to recede slowly into the misty past, and, fading, losing its sharpness of outline, its distinctness of detail, to resemble an irreparable fact to which familiarity had inured her.
>
> And all the uneasiness of her mistrustfulness, the pain of her fluctuating doubtings ceased; her comprehension of him was all at once clarified, rendered vivid and indisputable; and she was conscious of a certain sense of relief. She was eased of those feverish, spasmodic gaspings of her half-starved love; at first the dullness of sentimental atrophy seemed the more endurable. (p. 200)

Since the spasms of love and the experience of desire prove to be detrimental because deceptive or unattainable, Ella's 'sentimental atrophy' seems to be the only way to endure her husband's betrayal and their 'slow tale of decorous lovelessness' (p. 200).

In 'Battledore and Shuttlecock', Ronald Thornycroft is the naïve protagonist of the story; his progressive disenchantment with the world of sentiment stems from his impossible relationship with Midge, a prostitute who unexpectedly lifts him out of the monotony of a life whose only point appears to be cramming for the army examination. His unexpected encounter with Midge in a London theatre is a revelation. Awakened from his torpor and exhilarated by the possibilities of his new experience with the girl, he accepts Midge unconditionally: in his innocent eyes she remains quite untainted. Midge is kind-hearted and amiable: she can even, in a fit of 'sentimental melancholy' (p. 216), cry at the thought of her past. But Midge is looking only for a chaste friendship with Ronald, one that might offer her a redemptive rite of passage, allowing her to settle eventually into the role of an obliging wife and mother.

Crackanthorpe's depiction of the prostitute here challenges the typical idea of the fallen woman displayed in much Victorian literature, for Midge directs her own life in a way that requires no display of remorse from her, nor compassion from us: there is 'no rankling remembrance of male cruelty; no savagely revolting realization of the part she played. She had found men pleasant, affectionate, generous' (p. 216). And, as if welcoming the inevitability of her choices, she confesses to Ronald: 'But I'm like that. I always do things just as they come. It's my way — I can't help it' (p. 213). Surprisingly, it is the young protagonist who feels 'clumsy and clownish' (p. 208) before her; it is his inexperience, his blind expectations, and his 'libidinal damming-up' that condemn their relationship to failure.[169] This is another story which deconstructs the idealistic conception of love. Whilst the prostitute insists on the chastity of their relationship, Ronald's hope for a sentimental and sexual union with Midge can only lead to frustration. The story removes the possibility of any further encounter, let alone reconciliation, for by the end Midge will be living a completely new life far from London, where nobody knows about her past, and where she can finally be considered respectable. Ronald's experience embodies the bitter impact of these altogether dissonant expectations, and is marked by feelings of 'regret, starved hope, or heart-burnings', as Hardy phrases it.[170] Conversely, Midge emerges almost unscathed from the torments of love and emotional distress, turning Ronald's innocent love for her into a liberating, therapeutic resource that will help in her rescue. At the same time, her abandonment of prostitution coincides with an acceptance of convention which enables her to be rehabilitated into the social sphere. Such lightness of being, such capacity to resist the dangers of sentiment, allows Midge to survive, making her one of the few characters in Crackanthorpe's turbulent fictional world who is not, altogether, denied hope.

By contrast, the relatively brief 'Modern Melodrama' revolves around the paradigm of death, a subject the story addresses dispassionately and with notable directness. A young woman, Daisy, dying of consumption, implores her servant to listen in to the conversation between her partner and the doctor who is visiting her. The story successfully creates a mood of dejection, to which it adds layers of hypocrisy, meanness, and deceit. The servant does as she is asked, but only in exchange for money; the partner falsely reassures Daisy by saying she will soon be well again; the doctor continues to recommend useless therapies, knowing that she will not live beyond 'the end of February' (p. 259). In depicting the inexorability of Daisy's demise, Crackanthorpe makes particularly effective use of free indirect discourse, by which the voice of the narrator merges with that of Daisy to convey her torment as she reckons on the horror of her impending death:

[169] DC, p. 102.
[170] Thomas Hardy, 'Before Life and After' (line 6), in *Thomas Hardy: The Complete Poems*, ed. by James Gibson (Basingstoke: Macmillan, 1978), p. 277.

> It would be just nothing — like a sleep. Not even painful: she'd be just shut down in a coffin, and she wouldn't know that they were doing it. Ah! but they might do it before she was quite dead! It had happened sometimes. And she wouldn't be able to get out. The lid would be nailed, and there would be earth on the top. And if she called no one would hear. (p. 260)

The mental processes of the young woman are relayed with compelling exactness; Daisy's obsessive whirl of thoughts, such as her anxiety about being buried alive, gives the story a horrific edge. With its blunt dialogue and dispassionate descriptions, the story effectively brings to life Daisy's experience of fear, and her physical and mental affliction, whilst denying her (and the reader) any form of consolation. As in other of Crackanthorpe's stories, an attitude of resignation seems to be the only way for his characters to bear their sufferings.

But Crackanthorpe approaches this tragic and sensational subject matter in a distinctive way. Fully aware, it seems, of its potential for both melodramatic (as well as sentimental) treatment, he upends these inherited Victorian categories in the spirit of critical Decadence we have referred to earlier. While the narrator is focused on the depiction of Daisy's torments and heightened emotions resulting in 'spasms of weeping, harsh and gasping', and in her desperate supplication — ' "Let me live — let me live — I'll be straight — I'll go to church — I'll do anything! Take it away — it hurts — I can't bear it!" ' (p. 259) — the predominating melodramatic mood is suddenly punctured by the contrapuntal effect of a music-hall song that, coming from the street outside, undercuts the pathos of the scene. Crackanthorpe's 'modern' melodrama involves a deconstruction of its basic components, 'the indulgence of strong emotionalism; moral polarization and schematisation; extreme states of being'.[171] He invokes the idea of melodrama only to dismantle, in front of us, its implicit moralism, its 'clarity of recognition of what is being fought for and against'.[172] Melodrama has become a matter of empty gesture, even for the dispassionate narrator of the fraught marriage in the later 'The Turn of the Wheel', a 'melodrama grown grotesque' (p. 322).[173]

'In Cumberland' is a further case study of what Hardy in *The Return of the Native* described as 'the night-side of sentiment'.[174] The emasculated protagonist of this story suffers from an immoderate outbreak of sentiment that dooms him to a kind of hysteria, a form of emotional excess that will pathologically detach

---

[171] Peter Brooks, *The Melodramatic Imagination: Balzac, Henry James, Melodrama and the Mode of Excess* (New Haven and London: Yale University Press, 1995), p. 11.
[172] Brooks, *The Melodramatic Imagination*, p. 206.
[173] When describing the sour reaction of a female character in 'A Dead Woman' the narrator focuses on her features, that become 'grotesque with passion' (p. 141).
[174] Thomas Hardy, *The Return of the Native*, ed. by Amanda Hodgson (London: J. M. Dent, 1995), p. 73.

him from reality. Alec Burkett, the modest vicar of Scarsdale,[175] an isolated
Lake District parish, falls severely ill as a result of overwork and, unable to
continue with his parish duties, is forced to take to his bed. Alec looks back
over his past life to 'his single chapter of romance' with Ethel Winn: 'she and
he had promised their lives to one another' (p. 237), but Ethel deserted him
for a wealthy solicitor. As Alec's health further deteriorates, he considers the
possibility of death with a serenity grounded in his religious faith. The story
reaches its melodramatic climax when he is visited by Ethel: she stands by his
bedside, and out of pity for his condition (he repeatedly tells her he is about
to die), she kisses him, an empathic act which he wrongly interprets as an
expression of love. Alec gradually recovers, but now his thoughts are morbidly
focused on the epiphany of Ethel's visit that creates in his mind the certainty
of an 'indissoluble bond' (p. 248) between them. He now invents an impossible
future life with her, but it is a sentimental self-deception, which inevitably
results in a final disdainful rejection by Ethel of his impossible overture to her.

If Crackanthorpe's characters are rarely able to adapt themselves to life's
challenges (if, in fact, they are misguided by sentiment), it usually follows
that the price they pay in order to survive will be some kind of renunciation,
in turn resulting in a life half-lived. But in this story the alternative is worse,
for Alec will lose his mind chasing an impossible fantasy. With the exception
of the story 'He Wins who Loses', in which the artist renounces his love but
finds resources of artistic inspiration, Crackanthorpe's narratives textualize
a world in which renunciation is unaccompanied by any compensation. In
'In Cumberland' the frequent reiteration of disquieting adverbial expressions
— 'listless brooding', 'accumulating disquietude' (p. 251), 'throbbing with
triumphant exhilaration' (p. 251) — testifies to the heightened emotional pitch
of a story in which an excess of misdirected passion brings with it inevitable
pain and disenchantment. Its melancholic and nihilistic colouring is reflected
even in its descriptions of the natural environment, from the war-like metaphor
of 'A phantom regiment of giant mist-pillars swept silently across the valley', to
similes that link it to the semantic field of disease, such as 'the peat-hags gaped
like black, dripping flesh-wounds in the earth's side' (p. 233).

'A Set of Village Tales', the six brief stories that make up a separate section
of the Sentimental Studies volume, are set in the villages of Béarn in south-
west France, which Crackanthorpe had visited on several occasions. In these
fable-like narratives Crackanthorpe's presentation of rural life is shaped by the
imperatives of traditional oral storytelling that, as Andrew Harrison puts it,
'instil specific moral/religious values, and [...] record cultural practices, passing
on the wisdom of the ages while reinforcing a collective sense of identity among

---

[175]　Scarsdale: invented.

members of a given community, nation or religious group'.[176] His storyteller is a perceptive narrator, a visitor to the villages who sympathetically observes and registers stories, memories, and anecdotes of the rural community — a community of people of relatively limited ambitions and opportunities that seems to echo Alphonse Daudet's Provence, or Hardy's Wessex. Both Daudet's *Lettres de mon Moulin* (*Letters from my Windmill*, 1866) and Hardy's 'A Few Crusted Characters' (in *Life's Little Ironies*, 1894) sport a cast of local inhabitants who weave in and out of their separate stories, and *A Set of Village Tales* follows this generic pattern. The most visible of the recurring characters is the semi-paralyzed 'old Cauhapé', who embodies the traditions of the villages, and whose recollections inform the stories he recounts to the homodiegetic narrator.

In 'Lisa-la-Folle', the title itself signals a paradox. The name Lisa, with its phonic resemblance to the French 'lys' (lily), embodies purity and chastity in Christian iconography, but in the story Lisa subverts any such association: 'she lived alone', she is 'black-haired', and 'devilish proud' (p. 262). Before returning to her native village, she has spent years in Paris, and it is presumably the 'glamorous, sinful life' (p. 262) she led there which accounts for the attribution of madness by the community, with the narrator's ironic collusion. But it is rather the obscure nature of femininity that this brief tale evokes — an obscurity often represented by the image of the witch, not unlike Rhoda Brooke, the 'thin, fading woman' with deep dark eyes and 'abundant dark hair', of Hardy's story 'The Withered Arm' (1888).[177] Like Rhoda, Lisa is an isolated figure, avoided with superstitious apprehension by her community.

Crackanthorpe's presentation of Lisa, with 'raven hair [...] and an unfortunate destiny',[178] might appear to conform to the paradigmatic opposition black/evil and light/good that, some decades before, Wilkie Collins had identified as one of the clichés exploited by Victorian writers. But in fact Crackanthorpe dignifies the figure of Lisa, making her not just the diligent worker, who has for years tended 'four kilometres of road, in rain, sunshine, and storm' (p. 263) near the village, but the bearer, too, of a cosmic message of 'sexual betrayal and of [...] eternal penance',[179] when she reveals to the narrator the most ancient story of the celestial spaces, the amorous but ill-fated union between the sun and moon — a story that he will be able to pass on to the people of his land. Yet even here, the figure of the moon serves as a reminder of Lisa's own alienated condition.[180]

---

[176] Andrew Harrison, 'Fable, Myth and Folk Tale: The Writing of Oral and Traditional Forms', in *The Cambridge History of the English Short Story*, p. 86.

[177] Thomas Hardy, 'The Withered Arm', in *Wessex Tales*, ed. by Kathryn R. King (Oxford: Oxford University Press, 2009), pp. 57, 85.

[178] Wilkie Collins, 'A Petition to the Novel Writers', in *My Miscellanies* (London: Chatto and Windus, 1875), p. 113.

[179] DC, p. 113.

[180] The cosmic metaphor also has animistic connotations, recalling a passage from *Tess of*

'Etienne Mattou' is also set in the rural community of Amou. If 'Lisa-la-Folle' introduces the themes of exclusion and estrangement from society on the basis of madness, here it is the simulation of a 'convenient' suicide which is the cause of the separation from the community. Etienne, like Lisa, is a rebellious figure, but he is also prone to malevolent actions: 'A fierce haggler, a man of many wiles, a man of stubborn greed, a man without a pity, a bully, an evil-natured cheat' (p. 266); with him, even his wife Jeanne 'had grown evil-hearted too' (p. 267). This is a tale of multiple deceptions: Etienne cheats his clients as a speculator and merchant, kills a beggar, and plays the part of a dead man; his wife, Jeanne, cheats him out of his fortune and of the money obtained from the insurance after his presumed death. As the story unfolds, and the narrator seeks clues about Etienne's true story, old Cauhapé's interventions divert the solution of the mystery by his propounding 'half-a-dozen theories concerning it' (p. 268). The history of Etienne Mattou resembles a proto-detective story, with sensational implications that are generated through a non-linear plot structure: eventually the narrator-protagonist discovers the truth about Etienne's death only by chance, and not through a careful investigation.

These stories, thematically and structurally inspired by folkloric tales, offer melancholic accounts of the rural community in which the unifying element is the malicious gossip that circulates around ambiguous characters like Lisa, who destabilizes the tranquillity of her village with her choices and behaviour, like Jeanne who chooses to spend her life in a convent after having swindled her husband, or like Etienne, who pretends to commit suicide in order to gain a new life.

It is in these 'half-dozen vivid little chapters', Henry James wrote, that Crackanthorpe expresses his 'brief, hard, controlled intensity', in representing 'the sweetness and the sadness [...] of strong country aspects, of the sharp, local folk and out-of-the-way places'.[181] Here, as he would do in *Vignettes*, he succeeds in blending 'sweetness' and 'sadness', balancing his love for rural life and its traditions with an unblinkered depiction of human coarseness and malevolent intent.

XI

Crackanthorpe's final collection of stories was issued posthumously as *Last Studies* in late 1897, a volume which also included a poem by Stopford Brooke and an 'Appreciation' by Henry James. The three stories in the collection, 'Anthony

---

the d'Urbervilles in which the eponymous heroine recites lines from the *Benedicite*, evoking the sun and the moon. Thomas Hardy, *Tess of the d'Urbervilles*, ed. by Tim Dolin (London: Penguin, 2003), p. 104.

[181] James, 'Hubert Crackanthorpe', p. xx.

Garstin's Courtship', 'Trevor Perkins', and 'The Turn of the Wheel', represent a movement back to 'psychological investigation',[182] and were generally well received. For *The Academy*, *Last Studies* 'makes clear the loss which modern literature suffered by the death of Mr. Crackanthorpe',[183] and *The Spectator* wrote that the stories testify to 'his very considerable power of style. He had, indeed, a really marvellous capacity for describing the essential characteristics of scenery.'[184] When 'Anthony Garstin's Courtship' fell onto the editor's desk for consideration in *The Savoy*, Arthur Symons recognized that it constituted 'something almost like a reaching out in more or less a new direction'.[185]

In this story, Crackanthorpe's introspective method is applied to another of his anti-heroes, this time characterized by a stolid pride that prevents him from experiencing a fulfilling relationship with women or, more generally, with others. In 'Anthony Garstin's Courtship' the homonymous protagonist is frequently depicted in terms of his pride: 'And soon, he came to take a sturdy, secret pride' (p. 282); 'In the exaltation of his pride' (p. 290); 'He felt with a swelling pride that God had entrusted to him this great charge — to tend her' (p. 292). Such 'stubborn confidence in himself' (p. 292) can only result in a distorted perception of reality, and, consequently, in unreliable, even reckless, choices. Anthony Garstin is a hill farmer in his mid-forties who lives a dull life and works with his mother in the valleys of Cumberland. He is determined to share his future with Rosa Blencarn, a young woman whose only pleasure lies in rejoicing at her 'tribe of rustic admirers' (p. 284); certain that she 'had not been brought up to be a farmer's wife' (p. 292), she 'found life in the valley intolerably dull', and 'longed for [...] the exciting bustle of the streets' (p. 284). Obstinate in his unrequited love for her, Anthony idealistically accepts the illegitimate child she is carrying as his own, and asks her to marry him. The development of the plot leads to a bitterly ironic denouement: Rosa agrees to marry him even though she does not love him; Mrs Garstin accommodates Rosa into her house only after Anthony has perjured himself by swearing on the Bible, but she soon announces that she is going to disinherit her son because of his choice.

Unlike the other two stories in *Last Studies*, 'Anthony Garstin's Courtship' is set in a rural environment and offers a compelling portrait of a closed, if not claustrophobic, community in which faith, morality, and gossip are tied together. At its centre is Anthony's mother, whose intolerance and rigid adherence to conventional morality are explicable mainly by the nature of the environment she lives in, one that relies on the steady pull of the seasons, on the cycles of hard work, and the distant but ever-present prospect of economic

---

[182] Crackanthorpe, 'Hubert Crackanthorpe', in *The 1890s*, ed. by Cevasco, pp. 128–30 (p. 129).
[183] 'Book Reviews Reviewed', *The Academy*, 52 (4 December 1897), 503–04 (p. 503).
[184] *The Spectator*, 18 December 1897, p. 24.
[185] 'Hubert Crackanthorpe', p. 52.

hardship. This rural environment is harsh, cramped, always there to be fought against, offering little room for the expression of finer feelings; a constant reminder to those who live there of their marginal, impoverished existence.

Crackanthorpe's realism allows for the recognition of the pull of tradition (the Garstin's farming way of life goes back three hundred years), with the narrator emphasizing how the environment in which they have striven has shaped their characters:

> They had been a race of few words, "keeping themselves to themselves," as
> the phrase goes; beholden to no man, filled with a dogged, churlish pride
> — an upright, old-fashioned race, stubborn, long-lived, rude in speech, slow
> of resolve. (p. 280)

People and place are convincingly interfused, so that Anthony's quality of stubborn persistence is at one with his tough life in the valleys, along with modest expectations of life. But the young Rosa Blencarn, who will later disrupt the relationship between mother and son, shows little empathy with country life and its mores. The depiction of Anthony's life as a hill farmer is achieved through convincing realism: life and work in the countryside are hard and grim, the rural setting, with its 'brown, lumpy grass', often 'wrapped in darkness' (p. 272, p. 273), or covered by a 'sombre, drifting sky' (p. 277), is remorselessly bleak. But layered onto a conventionally realist specificity — here the influence of the agricultural way of life on character — is a condition of emotional paralysis, pervasively felt in Crackanthorpe's writing: whether they live in rural or urban environments, his protagonists suffer the predicament of 'emotional mutilation, or of resistance against it',[186] regardless of their origins or situated experience.

Once again the pattern of romantic closure is checked, since the marriage between Anthony and Rosa is simply a bargain, a convenient choice in the face of the censorious attitudes and narrow horizons of a rural community: the child will have a father, the father a bride, and the wife will eventually inherit from the parson. The alternatives would be a life of solitude for Anthony, and the stigma of sinfulness for the young woman.

In 'Trevor Perkins. A Platonic Episode' the city of London, with its crowded streets and parks, is the backdrop to the alienated existence of the protagonist. Trevor is a young autodidact whose narcissistic impulses estrange him from the company of relatives and friends, bringing him to a form of emotional apathy. Victim of his own misanthropic feelings, 'he [shrinks] from the coarse contact of men [and] from their blatant glorification of their animal instincts' (p. 299). A previous and unsuccessful relationship with a woman has only reinforced the sense of bitter disillusionment that now inhibits him from having other

---

[186] DC, p. 149.

love affairs. He suffers from 'an indefinable disquietude [...] and morbid dissatisfaction' (p. 299), a characteristic *fin-de-siècle* condition that leads him to a tormented acquiescence in his own lot, and a pervasive solipsism that makes him conceive of the world as an extension of himself. The only chance of escape and apparent relief is offered by his absorption in books and literature. Trevor is a self-made intellectual who 'had studied Shakespeare diligently [...] to elevate his conception of life' (p. 297), however his idea of culture mostly relies on received commonplaces that remind us of the neurasthenic and alienated figures in Gissing's short stories, such as Philip Dolamore, the idle protagonist of 'The Pessimist of Plato Road' (1894), who finds self-satisfaction in his own melancholic disposition, and who conceals his own frustrations behind his literary and pseudo-philosophic knowledge.[187] Uncritically, Trevor absorbs the texts he reads, and he does so almost mechanically. Thus, his habit of quoting from those texts simply underlines his solipsism, pointing up the irreconcilable gap between the protagonist's self and the outer world. Despite his efforts to achieve intellectual emancipation, he remains an outsider, a 'frightened non-hero', as William Peden put it, 'left in an emotional vacuum, lonely prototype of a thousand literary descendants'.[188]

In this story Crackanthorpe invokes romantic clichés, only to deconstruct them. It is with bitter irony that on the night of his encounter with Emily Hammond, a young, naïve waitress, Trevor gazes up at the stars, trying 'to lose himself in the wondrous immensity of the firmament, to comprehend the infinite insignificance of human life' (p. 302). The couple meet in 'the Park' when 'a dark, romantic sky quivered with a myriad glittering stars — an infinity of distant worlds, dimly winking through measureless miles of space' (p. 302). But Trevor is a tormented and cynical soul, who cannot enjoy the beauties of nature, and he is similarly unable to find relief in a potential relationship with Emily. His feelings towards her are lukewarm, and even on the only occasion in which his whole being starts to 'throb with a mad, passionate yearning', and he kisses her 'with a fierce and feverish desperation' (p. 304), the force of disenchantment is overwhelming, and his 'tranquil self-detachment' prevents him from being emotional. Johnson saw 'a curious tender cruelty'[189] in this story of a Decadent character who, in a spirit of bitter irony, embraces his own hollowness, all too aware of his inability to love.

In 'The Turn of the Wheel' Crackanthorpe explores the destructive and morbid tendencies at work in human relationships. Between husband and wife, lovers engaged in extramarital affairs, daughter and parents, or engaged

---

[187] George Gissing, 'The Pessimist of Plato Road', *English Illustrated Magazine*, 12 (November 1894), 51–59, repr. in *Collected Short Stories by George Gissing, Vol. 2*, ed. by Pierre Coustillas (Grayswood: Grayswood Press, 2012), pp. 132–43.

[188] William Peden, Introduction to *Collected Stories of Hubert Crackanthorpe*, p. xxi.

[189] Johnson, 'Hubert Crackanthorpe', p. 429.

couples, trust is replaced by suspicion; frankness by hypocrisy and deceit. If relationships ultimately prove to be a failure, it is because the characters are either trapped by their narcissistic impulses and cynicism, or paralyzed by disenchantment, leading to feelings of inadequacy, hatred and contempt, all of which prevent the expression of affection and fellow-feeling.

Hilda Lingard is a young woman who blindly worships her father, Eardley, a proud and ambitious man devoted to his 'double career, commercial and political' (p. 307) and, despite his long marriage to his wife Bessie, to his mistresses. Bessie Lingard is a fragile woman who, after twenty-five years of marriage, has been almost completely excluded from her husband's world, spending most of her time in their country residence with an old and invalid aunt in 'apathetic content' (p. 315), leaving Eardley to enjoy his professional career and the pleasures of society in London. Bessie is characterized by a state of Decadent listlessness; she is 'inertly immobile with fatigue', 'absorbed by a hebetude of over-ripe middle-age, a lax and puffy lethargy' (p. 308), a woman who is 'sluggishly living from day to day' (p. 309). After an initial expression of feeble resentment towards Eardley, she has learnt to accommodate her feelings of exclusion from family life and from her daughter's affections; moreover, she is aware that 'Hilda had altogether supplanted her, driven her into the background, transformed her into a person of no consequence' (p. 309).

On her side, Hilda is unaware of her father's love affairs, but she accepts his indifference towards his wife since, like him, she has assumed a 'cynical attitude of worldliness' (p. 312). Arrogant, insensitive, and 'insurgent' (p. 311), she conceives of life as a continuous struggle to assert herself. Sentimentally, Hilda is not easily roused: her idea of marriage as a makeshift bargain renders her 'apathetic' towards her two suitors, the ambitious Greaves Chamney and the modest but dull Stephen Walsh. The revelation by her aunt of the extent of Eardley's unscrupulousness marks the story's climactic phase. A disbelieving Hilda reaches her father's home only to discover that he has fallen seriously ill; during the febrile delirium which precedes his death, Eardley unwittingly confesses his betrayals, leaving Hilda in a state of anguish, 'embittered against the humiliation of the smirched memory he had left behind him' (p. 344). When the truth about her father's life is revealed, her feelings of resentment at being deceived by him displace those of conventional grief. In her efforts to reconcile her belated recognition of her father's ignoble life with her own blind faith in him, she turns against a world that is 'tainted'; she breaks her engagement with Greaves Chamney and nurtures 'a weary yearning after goodness; a burning remorse for the empty, useless egoism of her former self' (p. 345).

That her 'yearning' is 'weary' is indicative of her continuing confusion: her 'aching longing' for her dead father allows her to blame 'her mother's inadequacy' for his serial infidelities, with her mother the object of her rancour.

In this distressed emotional state, Hilda accepts a loveless marriage to Walsh, a man of simple virtues who, earlier, had provoked in her feelings of 'shallow, thoughtless contempt' (p. 347). Now, as a form of belated gratitude, if not of expiation, Hilda tries to appreciate his noble qualities, hoping that 'she would be able, without difficulty, to conceal from him that she did not care for him, as he cared for her' (pp. 350–51). But the story's ending is once more, indeterminate. Hilda's final refusal to kiss her husband points forward to a marriage of starved and impoverished emotions, leaving us to wonder if, and when, the wheel will turn again.

The challenging nature of 'male–female relationships, whether by way of marriage or unauthorised liaison',[190] is a characteristic feature of Crackanthorpe's work, not least in the early story, not included in his published collections, 'He Wins Who Loses'. Here the writer captures the psychological isolation of his protagonists, doomed, it seems, to experience and accept the impossible relation between the desires of the self and the world they inhabit. Kate is a lonely, unsatisfied woman, despite her marriage to the wealthy but taciturn John Hayward. Through marriage Hayward has allowed her to escape poverty and dependency, but '[h]e did not seem to have many ideas, he did not look at things as she did, and he was thirteen years older than herself' (p. 355). Kate is frequently absorbed by thoughts of her past days in London, but these recollections only reinforce her sense that her relationship with John has resulted in 'bitter disappointment' (p. 355): for both of them marriage is a constraint that accentuates their sense of solitude and apathy. But what is remarkable in the story is that Kate renounces the opportunity of an epistolary friendship with Lord Flamborough, a well-known artist towards whom she feels a deep empathy, an empathy which is immediately reciprocated. Despite the extraordinary 'elective affinity' between the two, and the fraction of happiness they bring to each other's life, Kate's final words to him only emphasize the sad but inexorable acceptance of her own lot:

> I will not take what you offer me — your friendship. It is the very thing I would soonest have on earth — but I will not. Life is very difficult — I mean it is very difficult to do what we know to be right, to keep ideals steadily in front of us. It would be harder than ever to me, so I would rather not see you or write to you again. I won't ask you to forget me — I don't want you to forget me — I want to be remembered, as I shall remember, one chamber in my heart is yours, where no other has the right to enter. (p. 362)

This is a blunt, disenchanted confession, but it contributes to the narrative's plausibility: given the social and moral constraints, what else could she and Lord Flamborough do? Necessarily, they have to accommodate themselves to their circumstances, and continue to lead decent lives. Nonetheless, in 'He

---

[190] Malcolm, Introduction to Hubert Crackanthorpe, *Wreckage: Seven Studies*, p. xxiii.

Wins who Loses' Crackanthorpe describes the human condition as a state of internal exile — a state that every human being is doomed to endure through a loss of affections, love, and prospects.

This story is a delicate portrait of the characters' emotional sphere, partly disclosed through the formal device of the letters exchanged between Mrs Hayward and Lord Flamborough, a device which substitutes a dialogic perspective for that of the heterodiegetic narrator. Yet the letters both reveal and conceal the feelings of the protagonists: their strongest emotions remain unstated, and their dreams are never completely expressed. If 'He Wins who Loses' can be read as a story of renunciation, it also suggests that artistic enthusiasm and inspiration can survive, if not bloom, through the painful experiences of denied hope. At the end of the story, Hayward reads, over breakfast, a review in *The Times* of a painting by Lord Flamborough, portraying a landscape and a figure at dawn. According to the reviewer, 'the picture possesses a grandeur and depth of feeling such as can only emanate from a great artist' (p. 363). The painting is the imaginative outcome of his decision to renounce his love for Mrs Hayward, proof that artistic creativity, in subsuming the experience of pain, can neutralize its most destructive effects.

The second uncollected story included in this edition is 'A Latter-Day Highwayman (An Adventure in Miniature)'. It is set in the area of the Lake District above the Eden Valley, and it is unusually told by a homodiegetic narrator whose presence in the action lends the events considerable dramatic immediacy. This brief narrative centres on an encounter between the anonymous narrator-protagonist and an unidentified tramp, a 'highwayman', on a winter evening in snowy, inhospitable moorland. Despite the simple structure of the diegesis, and the almost uneventful plot, the story is cleverly constructed from a series of dichotomies that turn on the level of characterization (the ordinary man vs the outcast), the axiological dimension (good vs evil), and the topographical one (outside = the moorland vs inside = a disused cattle shed), all of which serve to destabilize conventionally codified notions of identity, morality, and social class.

The story is interesting, too, in that it very obviously offers itself as a critically Decadent production which consciously plays with images of the contemporary indigent — the degenerate 'other' who traps and threatens the apparently normative narrator. Indeed, such a perspective purposely contradicts the confident heroism of the old-fashioned highwayman, more specifically the 'Dick Turpin' figure mentioned at the very end of the story. Instead, this Decadent, 'latter day' character, with his air of 'sorry burlesque' (p. 369), his 'luxurious sigh' (p. 368), his resemblance to 'a decadent Father Christmas' (p. 366), and actions which fluctuate between the 'solem[n]' and the 'ingloriou[s]', testifies to Crackanthorpe's deconstruction of the clichés of contemporary representations of degeneracy. Moreover, there is fascinating tension manifested in the narrator's focalization of the events, between his self-deprecation and his obtuseness, between his moments of insight and his thoroughly conventionalized way of seeing. At times, he displays a pronounced snobbery, at others he cannot conceal his social sympathy with the outcast figure, a sympathy that cuts against the scandal of the narrator's remarkably close physical proximity to the 'highwayman'. Significantly, the emphasis of the story lies in Crackanthorpe's rejection of the simplistic typologizing of the outcast, and in his creation of an open ending (as in 'A Fellside Tragedy', discussed below) characterized by a series of interrogative sentences that vocalize the reader's response. Such a dialogic configuration is a further instance of a proto-modernist tendency in Crackanthorpe's narrative approach — one that avoids definitive closure and invites the reader to participate in the construction and understanding of the text.

The action of the last uncollected story, 'A Fellside Tragedy', is also set in the broad Lake District region, here a 'lonely Westmorland valley' (p. 370). The very simple plot revolves around the tragic existence of Jenny King, a farm girl from the fells. In order to help her quick-tempered boyfriend, who has killed a man with a pitchfork, she steals money from her mistress which she then gives to him. Most of the story centres on Jenny's reactions to this appalling incident — reactions that involve fear, a sense of guilt, terror, nightmares, and her night wanderings throughout the valley, which culminate in her unexpectedly gruesome death.

Onto this simple diegetic structure the narrator superimposes the interior experience of the protagonist: she is troubled by the consequences of her action, which haunt her mind and produce the most anxious thoughts. Eventually she falls asleep, and the experience of her disturbing dreams is related by the narrator in all its vividness. The reader can follow the mental processes of Jenny's dreams in a way that makes it difficult to distinguish the real experience she is undergoing from that of her nightmares. Within these blurred boundaries even the temporal order is fragmented: the diegetic sequence is interrupted by the description of her awful dream, characterized by onomatopoeic words ('buzzing', 'thud, thud, thud', (p. 372)), a hyperbolic verbal register, and a rhetorical density felt in her insistent self-questioning, and in the anaphoric sequence of 'On, on, she climbed', at the beginning of two consecutive paragraphs (p. 372), thus emphasizing the oneiric experience of the protagonist. The dream anticipates what is really going to happen to her: Jenny is trying to escape, and finds herself shivering with fear and 'mortal anxiety' (p. 373). This oscillation between wakefulness and dream suggests a sort of *mise en abîme* into which Jenny's mind seems to have fallen. In this story the chosen form of narration used to express Jenny's inner world is free indirect speech: the narrator has unrestricted access to her thoughts and becomes the interpreter of her memories, fears, and wishes, to the point where her words are presented directly, without quotation marks or introductory reporting clauses.

The increasing intensity of the story leads to a climax and a macabre denouement:

> As the days went by a strange, horrible odour came from the rick-yard. They pulled down the rick and found poor Jenny's body. The forks of the men had pierced her through and through. Was it these wounds that had killed her, or had she passed away before the rising of the sun?
> Who shall tell? (p. 374)

The shocking discovery of Jenny's decomposing body is narrated in Crackanthorpe's characteristically dispassionate manner, which serves to intensify the tragic effect of a story notable for its author's 'unvoiced but constantly present sympathy for his luckless heroine'.[191]

XII

'Who among us has not dreamed, in his ambitious days', wrote Baudelaire in his Preface to *Petits Poèmes en Prose*, 'of the miracle of a poetic prose, musical without rhythm or rhyme, supple enough and jarring enough to be adapted to the soul's lyrical movements, to the undulations of reverie, to the twists and turns that consciousness takes?'[192] Crackanthorpe's impressionistic collection of 'prose poems', *Vignettes: A Miniature Journal of Whim and Sentiment*,[193]

---

[191] William Peden, '"A Fellside Tragedy": An Uncollected Crackanthorpe Story', *Studies in Short Fiction*, 9.4 (1972), 401–02 (p. 402).

[192] Charles Baudelaire, *Paris Spleen and La Fanfarlo*, trans. by Raymond N. MacKenzie (Indianapolis: Hackett Publishing Company, 2008), p. 3.

[193] For Le Gallienne, reviewing *Sentimental Studies & a Set of Village Tales* in July 1895, Crackanthorpe's 'sincerity towards his impressions' issued in 'descriptions [which] make one hope that he will some day publish a volume of those "Vignettes" of which he has already published a few examples in various periodicals'. Le Gallienne, *Retrospective Reviews: A Literary Log Vol. II (1893–1895)* (London: John Lane/The Bodley Head, 1896), p. 278. There were at least thirty-nine such 'examples', published separately, in groups, in *The Westminster Gazette*, *The Speaker*, and the *Saturday Review* between 1894 and 1896. Le Gallienne's hope came to fruition when in October 1896 John Lane brought out *Vignettes: A Miniature Journal of Whim and Sentiment* which, together with two newly-published items ('At Villeneuve-les-Avignon' and 'In St. James's Park'), included all but seven of the hitherto published newspaper and periodical 'vignettes'. The excluded items were: 'At Chenies, Buckinghamshire', *Westminster Gazette*, 23 June 1894, p. 3, col. 1; 'On the Road to Arthez', *Westminster Gazette*, 23 June 1894, p. 3, col. 1; 'Kensington Gdns.', *Westminster Gazette*, 12 July 1894, p. 3, col. 1; 'Melodramatic Storm', *The Speaker*, 8 December 1894, pp. 635–36 [transposed into 'A Commonplace Chapter — II', *Sentimental Studies*, p. 86]; 'Femme incomprise', *The Speaker*, 8 December 1894, p. 636 [transposed into 'A Commonplace Chapter — II', *Sentimental Studies*, pp. 91–93]; 'Ullswater', *The Speaker*, 8 December 1894, p. 636; 'The old Garden', *The Speaker*, 8 December 1894, p. 636 [transposed into 'Yew-Trees and Peacocks', *Sentimental Studies*, p. 227].

draws on the musical and artistic correspondences for states of being which Baudelaire's model displayed, a model mediated through other French and British exponents of the form, including Joris-Karl Huysmans's *Croquis Parisiens* (1880), Wilde's *Poems in Prose* (1894), and Le Gallienne's *Prose Fancies* (1894; second series, 1896). By the 1890s the prose poem had become a cherished form for Decadent writers, with close affinities to the evanescent, fragmentary poetics cultivated by the Rhymers.

Crackanthorpe's work was partly associated with his encounters with people and places during his journeys in Europe, but he also linked his impressionism to London — appropriately, perhaps, since Baudelaire himself had applied the prose poem in *Le Spleen de Paris*, the original title of his work, to the subject of the city. *Vignettes* consists of a series of sketches, stories of impressions, pictures of crystallized moments, observations of places, whose aim was less to provide a series of memoirs than to register a striking variety of moods and feelings, revealing, in places, a spiritual yearning for some totalising state of reality. Through a modality that oscillates between the photographic and the phantasmagorical, Crackanthorpe engages in a hermeneutic process in which writing becomes a means of self-discovery, as the observation of place is transformed into a projection of his soul. '*Tout paysage est un état d'âme*', he writes in 'Lausanne' (p. 380), and in this sense the brief descriptions in *Vignettes* transcend the realistic plane, expressing what Vincent Starrett had identified as his 'vivid impressionism'.[194] James, too, was taken with *Vignettes*, praising Crackanthorpe's 'tiny collection' for 'working the impression down to a few square inches of water-colour'.[195] Not all critics, though, were enthusiastic: Symons highlighted Crackanthorpe's limitations as an impressionist writer: he has, he wrote, 'a sharp, hard, brutal, efficacious grasp on fact, on the fact of events, character, temperament, outward detail. He sees colour strongly, but without distinction between its subtler shades'.[196]

Yet Crackanthorpe's sketches in *Vignettes* do succeed in catching the elusiveness of feeling and the evanescent 'subtler shades' of the real. The painterliness of Crackanthorpe's fragments, together with their sudden shifts in subject, tone and location, all call attention to their qualities of composition. The powerful sensuousness of the descriptions permit the reader to imagine the world with a luridly colourful palette that transforms reality into a kaleidoscope: we see a sunset 'of liquid gold', the hills 'all indigo' ('In the Basque Country'); 'the old gold and scarlet of hanging meat; the metallic green of mature cabbages; the wavering russet of piled potatoes' ('Our Lady of the Lane'); Paris 'white and a-glitter', or the 'ruddy earth' in 'La Côte D'Or from the Train'.

---

[194] Vincent Starrett, 'Two Suicides', p. 140.
[195] James, 'Hubert Crackanthorpe', p. xxi.
[196] Symons, 'Mr. Crackanthorpe's Vignettes in Prose', p. 678.

Crackanthorpe's prose is marked, too, by what Caroline Blyth terms the 'phantasmagoric', produced by, but also in tension with, a heightened realism: it is an effect characteristic of *fin-de-siècle* poetics, prompted by 'a growing unease with Nature, a sense of its phantasmagoric weirdness, its "unnaturalness" as an agency rather than its consoling spiritual power'.[197] Nature, it seems, revels in its 'vital materiality',[198] as in 'In the Basque Country', where the viewer is given a vivid impression of 'lusty sunlight, of quivering golden-green' (p. 377), of 'blue brawling rivers' (p. 377), of 'soft shadows stealing beneath the still, silent oaks' (p. 377), of 'the great snow-mountains, vague, phantasmagoric, like a mirage in the sky' (p. 377).

The recurrent personifications and the metaphorical use of language make the natural environment more vibrant and exuberant than the peopled world, a world that appears either as 'a thick, drifting tide of men and women' ('Ascension Day at Arles', p. 377), as 'a figure' out of the darkness ('In the Landes', p. 378), or as 'a retreating figure [...] alone in the quiet' ('On Chelsea Embankment', p. 378). In 'In the Strand', the spirit of a decadent city is conveyed by a noisy and turbulent humanity that is almost on the verge of insanity:

> The city disgorges.
> All along the Strand, down the great, ebbing tide, the omnibuses, a congested press of gaudy craft, drift westwards, jostling and jamming their tall, loaded decks, with a clanking of chains, a rumble of lumbering wheels, a thudding of quick-loosed brakes, a humming of hammering hoofs....
> The empty hansoms slink silently past; the street hawkers — a long row of dingy figures — line the pavement-edge; troops of frenzied newsboys dart yelling through the traffic; and here and there a sullen-faced woman struggles to stem the tide of men. (pp. 382–83)

An anonymous crowd pours out into the streets of London; the strident noises produced by the means of transport that traverse it intensify the sense of a dehumanized environment, and give it an apocalyptic mood. Metaphors that connote plurality ('tide of men', 'troops of frenzied newsboys'), together with onomatopoeic forms ('thudding', 'humming', 'clanking'), and the alliterative effect given by various sequences of words ('clanking of chains', 'jostling and jamming', 'humming of hammering hoofs'), express excess and disorder: the deafening noises and the continuous and rapid movements create an urbanscape in which characters wither and languish.

The selection of fragments from *Vignettes* included in this edition are exemplary in that they encompass both Crackanthorpe's snapshots of London — assimilated, mostly verbatim, into his posthumously published story *The Turn*

---

[197] Caroline Blyth (ed.), *Decadent Verse*, p. 33.
[198] Jane Bennett, *Vibrant Matter: A Political Ecology of Things* (Durham and London: Duke University Press, 2010), p. vii.

of the Wheel — and observations from his travels around Italy, France, Spain, and Switzerland. The titles of the fragments furnish interesting topographical data about the extent of his travels in Europe with Leila, drawing together Arles, the Basque Country, Chelsea, Paris, La Côte d'Or, Lausanne, and Perugia, but these landscapes are, in truth, physical projections of inner worlds, mental constructions that often become eidetic images of the female body: at dusk, Lausanne 'lies white, tranquil, statuesque, like a beautiful, sleeping woman' (p. 380), while 'the pale green plain' of the Côte d'Or is 'hesitating and soft as the lines of a woman's body' (p. 379).

Crackanthorpe's symbolic topography in *Vignettes* is further emphasized by the two fragments 'Enfantillage' and 'In the Campo Santo at Perugia', in which different spaces evoke two different stages of human experience. If the idea of childhood is conveyed by a sky full of 'milk-white summer clouds [...] slow and sleek and swelling' (p. 385), the arrival of death in the churchyard coincides with an 'empty and darkening' land, where 'every alley is black with the press of people' (p. 380, p. 381). *Vignettes* moves between a series of antitheses, each subsumed under the dichotomy of life versus death: the sun reawakens nature in 'Sunrise'; the new year begins in 'New Year's Eve', and the most sparkling colours of the landscapes (crimson, gold, green, yellow, and white) are connected to the reviving dimension of life. Conversely, autumnal, chromatic elements suggest the impending presence of death, such as the 'dead branches, still rustling their brown, winter leaves' in 'Rêverie April 15' (p. 384), or the 'frail, russet leaves' that fall down in 'Paris in October' (p. 379), with the vivid colours of twilight that mark the end of the day, and the silent night that invades the places with obscurity.

But it is striking, too, that the texts contain elements that conjoin life and death: the 'bank of inky cloud' (p. 384) that obscures the sun in 'Rêverie April 15' is the same element that allows the narrator to escape from reality and surrender to imagination in 'Enfantillage'; fog is both a haze that dims and hides reality in 'Lausanne', and the brilliant shade ('the russet fog') that pervades 'On Chelsea Embankment' (p. 378). In *Vignettes* the tension between life and death, light and darkness, happiness and melancholy is dissolved with paradox: 'Death [...] becomes [...] almost gay' ('In the Campo Santo at Perugia', p. 381), or in the oxymoronic 'sullen glow' in 'In St. James's Park' (p. 382), which annuls any attempt to separate antithetic emotions. Crackanthorpe's non-disjunctive habit of mind is expressed in his ambiguous attraction both to the exuberance of life and to the mysterious condition of death. And it is in these narrative fragments that he unveils, most completely, a fascination with and a fear of mortality. If in 'Rêverie April 15' the narrator cannot conceal the enchantment of the 'violet night [...] wrapping all earth and sky in her mysterious, impenetrable blackness' (p. 385), the appearance of a train 'charging [...] into the dark country beyond'

('On Chelsea Embankment', p. 378) reveals, in equal measure, his anxiety at something threatening and definitive.

In these symbolic fragments Crackanthorpe unravels fixed polarities and overcomes the torpor of despair in the cathartic logic of oxymoron and paradox that he adopts, as well as in the extraordinary arrangement of 'passages of grim, quick irony', interleaved with 'passages of a quiet lyrical melancholy and compassion'.[199] Those phrases were Lionel Johnson's, and we leave it to Johnson, Crackanthorpe's finest critic, to put it with his customary delicate precision. The pages of *Vignettes*, he wrote, 'are full of joyousness and buoyancy. But there steals in the note of distrust in the stability of happiness; the sense, as he goes through the world, that this delight and that pleasure are fatally precarious'.[200]

[199] Johnson, 'Hubert Crackanthorpe', p. 429.
[200] Johnson, 'Hubert Crackanthorpe', p. 428.

SELECT BIBLIOGRAPHY

Primary Works

Collections

Wreckage: Seven Studies (London: William Heinemann, 1893)
Sentimental Studies & A Set of Village Tales (London: William Heinemann, 1895)
Vignettes: A Miniature Journal of Whim and Sentiment (London: John Lane, The
   Bodley Head, 1896)
Last Studies (London: William Heinemann, 1897)

Fiction

'He Wins Who Loses', *The Albermarle: A Monthly Review*, 1.3 (March 1892), 104–11
'At Chenies, Buckinghamshire', *The Westminster Gazette*, 23 June 1894, p. 3, col. 1
'On the Road to Arthez', *The Westminster Gazette*, 23 June 1894, p. 3, col. 1
'Melodramatic Storm', *The Speaker*, 8 December 1894, pp. 635–36
'Femme incomprise', *The Speaker*, 8 December 1894, p. 636
'Ullswater', *The Speaker*, 8 December 1894, p. 636
'The Old Garden', *The Speaker*, 8 December 1894, p. 636
'A Latter-Day Highwayman (An Adventure in Miniature)', *The Star*, 1 February
   1896, p. 2, cols 1–2
'A Fellside Tragedy', *The Northern Counties Magazine*, 1, February 1901, pp. 287–91

Other Writings

Letter to the *Pall Mall Gazette* (on the financial consequences for staff of the closing
   of music-halls and theatres), *Pall Mall Gazette*, 19 January 1892, p. 2, cols 2–3
'Mr. Henry James as a Playwright', *The Albermarle: A Monthly Review*, 1.1 (January
   1892), 34–35
'Realism in France and England: An Interview with M. Emile Zola', *The Albermarle:
   A Monthly Review*, 1.2 (February 1892), 39–43
'After The Play: A Conversation', *The Albermarle: A Monthly Review*, 1.6 (June
   1892), 216–18
'Mr. Vizetelly and Literary Freedom', Letter to Editor of *The Daily Chronicle*, 9
   January 1894, p. 3, col. 7
'Reticence in Literature: Some Roundabout Remarks', *Yellow Book: An Illustrated
   Quarterly*, 2 (July 1894), 259–69
'Bread and the Circus', *Yellow Book: An Illustrated Quarterly*, 7 (October 1895),
   235–57
'Notes for a Paper on Barrès and Bourget', *To-Morrow: A Monthly Review
   Conducted by J. T. Grein*, 3 (January–June 1897), 83–92

The Light Sovereign: A Farcical Comedy in Three Acts [with Henry Harland], [n.d.] (London: Lady Henry Harland, 1917)

'The Art of Fiction' ('Sunday Popular Debates'), Lecture [Royalty Theatre, London], Reported in *The Daily Chronicle*, 13 February 1894, p. 3, col. 6

Secondary Works

Editions

ETTORRE, EMANUELA, *Hubert Crackanthorpe: Racconti* (Napoli: Edizioni Scientifiche Italiane, 2015)

MALCOLM, DAVID, *Hubert Crackanthorpe. Wreckage: Seven Studies* (Edinburgh: Edinburgh University Press, 2019)

PEDEN, WILLIAM, *Collected Stories (1893–1897) of Hubert Crackanthorpe* (Gainesville, Florida: Scholar's Facsimiles and Reprints, 1969)

Biographical Studies and General Surveys

ADAMS, JAD, 'Hubert Crackanthorpe 1870–1896', in *The Yellow Nineties Online*, ed. by Dennis Denisoff and Lorraine Janzen Kooistra (Ryerson University, 2010) <https://beta.1890s.ca/crackanthorpe_bio> [accessed 9 June 2020]

BURNS, JIM, 'The Pity of It: Hubert Crackanthorpe', *London Magazine*, 37.9 & 10 (1997/ 1998), 52–57

CRACKANTHORPE, DAVID, *Hubert Crackanthorpe and English Realism in the 1890s* (Columbia: University of Missouri Press, 1977)

—— 'Hubert Crackanthorpe', in *The 1890s: An Encyclopedia of British Literature, Art, and Culture*, ed. by G. A. Cevasco (New York and London: Garland, 1993), pp. 128–30

JACKSON, HOLBROOK, 'Hubert Crackanthorpe: Impressionist of Fiction', *Windmill*, 2.2 (1946), 8–16

SUTHERLAND, JOHN, 'Hubert Crackanthorpe', in *The Longman Companion to Victorian Fiction* (London: Longman, 1988), p. 155

Bibliographical Entries

FISHER, BENJAMIN F., 'Hubert Crackanthorpe', in *British Short-Fiction Writers, 1880–1914: The Realist Tradition*, ed. by William B. Thesing, *Dictionary of Literary Biography*, vol. 135 (Detroit: Gale, 1994), pp. 60–74

HARRIS, WENDELL, 'A Bibliography of Writings about Hubert Crackanthorpe', *English Literature in Transition*, 6.2 (1963), 85–91

WATSON, GEORGE (ed.), 'Hubert Crackanthorpe', in *The New Cambridge Bibliography of English Literature*, ed. by George Watson, 5 vols (Cambridge: Cambridge University Press, 1969–1977), III, p. 1044

WOMACK, KENNETH, 'Hubert Crackanthorpe', in *Dictionary of National Biography, Vol. 13* (Oxford: Oxford University Press, 2004), pp. 911–12

Secondary Material

ADAMS, JAD, 'The 1890s Woman', *The Edinburgh Companion to Fin-de-Siècle Literature, Culture and the Arts*, ed. by Josephine M. Guy (Edinburgh: Edinburgh University Press, 2018), pp. 968–1020

—— 'The Drowning of Hubert Crackanthorpe and the persecution of Leila Macdonald', *English Literature in Transition 1880-1920*, 52.1 (2009), 6–34

ASSOCIATION FRANCIS JAMMES, *Homage à Hubert Crackanthorpe*, Bulletin No. 14 (1990)

BAEDEKER, K., *London and its Environs: Handbook for Travellers* (London: Dulau and Co., 1889)

BASSNETT, SUSAN, and PETER FRANCE, 'Translation, Politics and the Law', in *The Oxford History of Literary Translation in English: Volume 4 1790-1900*, ed. by Peter France and Kenneth Haynes (Oxford: Oxford University Press, 2006), pp. 48–58

BAUGH, EDWARD, 'Hubert Crackanthorpe and the Cause of "Literary Freedom"', *Notes & Queries*, n.s., 18.3 (1971), 105–07

BEAUMONT, MATTHEW (ed.), *Walter Pater: Studies in the History of the Renaissance* (Oxford: Oxford University Press, 2010)

BECKSON, KARL, *Arthur Symons: A Life* (Oxford: Clarendon Press, 1987)

—— *London in the 1890s: A Cultural History* (New York: W. W. Norton, 1992)

BORG, MONICA, 'Resistance From the Margins: Studies of Subversion in British Short Fiction in the Fin de Siècle' (unpublished doctoral thesis, University of Birmingham, 1999)

BOYIOPOULOS, KOSTAS, YOONJOUNG CHOI, and MATTHEW BRINTON (eds), *The Decadent Short Story: An Annotated Anthology* (Edinburgh: Edinburgh University Press, 2015)

BROOKS, PETER, *The Melodramatic Imagination: Balzac, Henry James, Melodrama and the Mode of Excess* (New Haven and London: Yale University Press, 1995)

BURDETT, OSBERT, *The Beardsley Period: An Essay in Perspective* (London: John Lane/The Bodley Head, 1925)

COUSTILLAS, PIERRE, 'Gissing and Crackanthorpe: A Note on Their Relationship', *Notes and Queries*, 28.5 (1981), 421–22

CRACKANTHORPE, DAVID, 'Sentimental Studies and a Set of Village Tales', in *The 1890s: An Encyclopedia of British Literature, Art, and Culture*, ed. by G. A. Cevasco (New York: Garland, 1993), pp. 540–41

—— 'Wreckage', in *The 1890s: An Encyclopedia of British Literature, Art, and Culture*, ed. by G. A. Cevasco (New York: Garland, 1993), pp. 684–85

CRAN, WINNIE, 'The Yellow Book Circle and the Culture of the Literary Magazine', in *The Cambridge History of the English Short Story* (Cambridge: Cambridge University Press, 2016), pp. 118–34

DENISOFF, DENNIS, and LORRAINE KOOISTRA (eds), *The Yellow Nineties Online* <https://beta.1890s.ca>

D'HOKER, ELKE, 'Artist Stories of the 1890s: Life, Art and Sacrifice', in *Reconnecting Aestheticism and Modernism: Continuities, Revisions, Speculations*, ed. by Bénédicte Coste, Catherine Delyfer, and Christine Reynier (London: Routledge, 2016), pp. 281–331

DOWLING, LINDA, 'Letterpress and Picture in the Literary Periodicals of the 1890s', *Yearbook of English Studies*, 16 (1986), 117–31

ETTORRE, EMANUELA, '"Those little documents of Hell": Hubert Crackanthorpe e l'ossessione del reale', Introduction to *Hubert Crackanthorpe: Racconti*, ed. by Emanuela Ettorre (Napoli: Edizioni Scientifiche Italiane, 2015), pp. 9–32

FLETCHER, IAN (ed.), *British Poetry and Prose 1870–1905* (Oxford: Oxford University Press, 1987)

—— (ed.), *The Complete Poems of Lionel Johnson* (London: The Unicorn Press, 1953)

—— *W. B. Yeats and his Contemporaries* (Brighton: Harvester Press, 1987)

FREEMAN, NICHOLAS (ed.), *Arthur Symons: Spiritual Adventures* (Cambridge: MHRA, 2017)

—— *1895: Drama, Disaster and Disgrace in Late Victorian Britain* (Edinburgh: Edinburgh University Press, 2011)

—— *Conceiving the City: London, Literature, and Art 1870–1914* (Oxford: Oxford University Press, 2007)

—— 'Curious Intricacies: Some Versions of City Writing at the Fin de Siècle', in *The Edinburgh Companion to Fin-de-Siècle Literature, Culture and the Arts*, ed. by Josephine M. Guy (Edinburgh: Edinburgh University Press, 2018), pp. 239–307

GAGNIER, REGENIA, *The Insatiability of Human Wants: Economic and Aesthetics in Market Society* (Chicago: University of Chicago Press, 2000)

GERBER, HELMUT E. (ed.), *The English Short Story in Transition 1880–1920* (New York: Pegasus, 1967)

GOODE, JOHN, 'The Decadent Writer as Producer', in *Collected Essays of John Goode*, ed. by Charles Swann (Keele: Keele University Press, 1995), pp. 336–54

GREENSLADE, WILLIAM, *Degeneration, Culture and the Novel 1880–1940* (Cambridge: Cambridge University Press, 1994; 2010)

—— 'Naturalism and Decadence: The Case of Hubert Crackanthorpe', in *Decadent Poetics: Literature and Form at the British Fin de Siècle*, ed. by Jason David Hall and Alex Murray (Basingstoke: Palgrave Macmillan, 2013), pp. 163–80

HALL, JASON DAVID, and ALEX MURRAY (eds), *Decadent Poetics: Literature and Form at the British Fin de Siècle* (Basingstoke: Palgrave Macmillan, 2013)

HANSON, CLARE, *Short Stories, and Short Fictions 1880–1980* (London: Macmillan, 1985)

HARRIS, WENDELL V., 'Hubert Crackanthorpe as Realist', *English Literature in Transition 1880–1920*, 6.2 (1963), 6–84

—— 'Identifying the Decadent Fiction of the Eighteen-Nineties', *English Fiction in Transition*, 5.5 (1962), 1–13

HORNE, EILEEN, *Zola and the Victorians* (London: MacLehose Press, 2015)

HUNTER, ADRIAN, *The Cambridge Introduction to the Short Story in English* (Cambridge: Cambridge University Press, 2007)

JACKSON, HOLBROOK, *The Eighteen Nineties: A Review of Art and Ideas at the Close of the Nineteenth Century* (London: Grant Richards, 1913; Harmondsworth: Penguin, 1950)

JAMES, HENRY, 'The Art of Fiction' (1884), in *Henry James: Selected Literary Criticism*, ed. by Morris Shapira (1963; London: Peregrine Books, 1968), pp. 78–97

JAMMES, FRANCIS, *Mémoires* (Paris: Mercure de France, 1971)

Khalil, Nelly Aziz, 'Hubert Crackanthorpe: his Life and Work' (unpublished doctoral thesis, University of Manchester, 1973)

Le Gallienne, Richard, *The Romantic '90s* (1926; London: Robin Clark, 1993)

Malcolm, Cheryl Alexander, and David Malcolm, 'The British and Irish Short Story to 1945', in *A Companion to the British and Irish Short Story*, ed. by Cheryl Alexander Malcolm and David Malcolm (Oxford: Wiley-Blackwell, 2008), pp. 5–16

Malcolm, David, *The British and Irish Short Story Handbook* (Chichester: Wiley-Blackwell, 2012)

—— 'Introduction', in *Hubert Crackanthorpe. Wreckage: Seven Studies* (Edinburgh: Edinburgh University Press, 2019), pp. vii–xxxix

Matz, Jesse, 'Impressionism, Naturalism, and Aestheticism: Novel Theory, 1880–1914', in *The Reinvention of the British and Irish Novel 1880–1940* [*The Oxford History of the Novel in English Volume 4*], ed. by Patrick Parrinder and Andrzej Gasiorek (Oxford: Oxford University Press, 2001), pp. 539–54

May, J. Lewis, *John Lane and the Nineties* (London: John Lane, 1936)

Miller, Jane Eldridge, *Rebel Women: Feminism, Modernism and the Edwardian Novel* (London: Virago, 1994)

Mix, Katherine Lyon, *A Study in Yellow: The Yellow Book and its Contributors* (London: Constable, 1960)

Murray, Alex, *Landscapes of Decadence: Literature and Place at the Fin de Siècle* (Cambridge, Cambridge University Press, 2016)

Peden, William, '"A Fellside Tragedy": An Uncollected Crackanthorpe Story', *Studies in Short Fiction*, 9.4 (1972), 401–02

—— 'Hubert Crackanthorpe: Forgotten Pioneer', *Studies in Short Fiction*, 7.4 (1970), 539–48

—— 'Introduction', in *Hubert Crackanthorpe: Collected Short Stories* (Gainesville, FL: Scholars' Facsimiles and Reprints, 1969), p. vii–xxv

Stanford, Derek (ed.), *Stories of the '90s* (London: John Baker, 1968)

—— (ed.), *Writing of the 'Nineties: From Wilde to Beerbohm* (London: J. M. Dent, 1971)

Stokes, John, *In the Nineties* (London: Harvester Wheatsheaf, 1989)

—— *Resistible Theatres: Enterprise and Experiment in the Late Nineteenth Century* (London: Paul Elek, 1972)

Thornton, R. K. R., *The Decadent Dilemma* (London: Arnold, 1983)

Towheed, Shafquat, 'Reading the Life and Art of Hubert Crackanthorpe', *English Literature in Transition 1880–1920*, 43.1 (2000), 51–65

Weintraub, Stanley, *The Savoy: Nineties Experiment* (Pennsylvania State University Press, 1965)

Whittington-Egan, Richard, and Geoffrey Smerdon (eds), *The Quest of the Golden Boy: The Life and Letters of Richard Le Gallienne* (London: The Unicorn Press, 1960)

Worth, George G., 'The English "Maupassant School" of the 1890's: Some Reservations', *Modern Language Notes*, 72 (1957), 337–40

A NOTE ON THE TEXT
AND EDITORIAL DECISIONS

Hubert Crackanthorpe's writing achievement, although of brief duration, deserves to be much better known. We hope that this edition, in offering a powerful selection of his work, will help introduce this exciting writer to new or interested readers. In wishing to emphasize both the variety and reach of his writing we include all but two of the stories published in his volumes *Wreckage* and *Sentimental Studies*, and all three of the stories in the posthumous *Last Studies*. We have also included two of Crackanthorpe's 'A Set of Village Tales' and a representative selection from his *Vignettes*. This has left us the space to present two lesser-known stories, 'He Wins Who Loses' and 'A Fellside Tragedy' (published only in later short story anthologies), and one further story, 'A Latter-Day Highwayman (An Adventure in Miniature)', which is published here for the first time. We have also chosen three of Crackanthorpe's seven published examples of non-fiction, which we believe throw light on the extent of his critical engagement with pressing issues for writers of the 1890s.

Given the relative scarcity of critical and scholarly attention devoted to Crackanthorpe's work, we have provided a 'Bibliographical Survey' of each item selected for this edition.

The copy-text for those stories brought together for publication in *Wreckage* (1893), *Sentimental Studies & A Set of Village Tales* (1895), and *Last Studies* (1897), is the first editions of those volumes. We reprint our selection of pieces in *Vignettes* (1896), the majority of which were first published in periodical form, as they appear in that volume. In the case of the two uncollected stories, 'He Wins Who Loses' and 'A Fellside Tragedy', which were anthologized many years after Crackanthorpe's death, we use the versions which first appeared in periodical form. In the case of 'A Latter-Day Highwayman (An Adventure in Miniature)', the copy-text is the sole newspaper version. Our selection of Crackanthorpe's critical writings reprints the original journal, newspaper, and periodical versions, respectively.

All references to Crackanthorpe's writings are to this edition and are given parenthetically in the text.

We have modernized Crackanthorpe's hyphenation of words, such as 'afternoon', 'any-more', 'good-bye', 'note-paper', 'note-book', 'now-a-days', 'some-one' 'up-stairs', 'to-morrow', 'to-day', throughout. The original spelling of words such as 'any more' or 'some one' has been retained, as has Crackanthorpe's original punctuation, grammar, and use of italicization. Any printers' errors have been silently corrected.

All translations are our own, unless indicated. In our annotations we have abbreviated David Crackanthorpe's seminal study *Hubert Crackanthorpe and English Realism in the 1890s* (Columbia, MO: University of Missouri Press, 1977) to 'DC'.

A CRACKANTHORPE CHRONOLOGY

1870 Hubert Montague Cookson is born in London on 12 May, to Montague Cookson (later Crackanthorpe) (b. 1832) and Blanche Alethea Cookson (neé Holt) (b. 1846). He is the elder brother of Dayrell (b. 1872) and Oliver (b. 1874).

1882 Produces the *Mayes Gazette* (22 August), the first of several handwritten holiday magazines associated with family holidays in Sussex and from 1883–1887, in Westmorland, the *Howtownian*, written with his younger brother, Dayrell.

1883 Attends Eton College until March 1888, leaving before entering the sixth form.

1888 Following death of his cousin, William Crackanthorpe, Hubert's father, Montague, inherits Newbiggin, Westmorland, a 7000-acre estate, and takes his name.

March–December possibly tutored by George Gissing.

Stays in Orthez in the Béarn, south-west France. Meets the poet Francis Jammes (spring).

Meets Emile Zola, Stéphane Mallarmé, André Gide, and Henri de Régnier, and possibly Maurice Barrès, Paul Bourget, and Guy de Maupassant (1889–1891).

Later in 1889 returns to England and studies in London under Selwyn Image, the art historian and co-editor of the *Hobby Horse*. Through Image makes contact with the Fitzroy Group. Also makes contact with the Rhymers' Club.

1891 Becomes a member, along with his parents, of J. T. Grein's Independent Theatre Society.

September–October: is attending social events in Carlisle and Kendal.

Is writing his first stories (1891–1892).

Probably in late 1891 interviews Zola in Paris.

1892 Establishes and co-edits with W. H. Wilkins *The Albermarle: A Monthly Review*, financed by his father (January–September).

His first published critical essay, 'Mr. Henry James as a Playwright', appears in its opening number; his next is his 'Interview with M. Emile Zola' in February.

His first published story, 'He Wins Who Loses', appears in the March number, and 'Dissolving View' comes out in August.

His engagement to Leila Macdonald is announced in July.

Montague Crackanthorpe withdraws his funding and the *Albermarle* promptly closes (September).

1893 Marries Leila Macdonald at St Paul's Church, Knightsbridge (14 February).
Hubert and Leila honeymoon in the Béarn, near Sallespisse, in a house
found for them by Jammes.
Wreckage: Seven Studies is published by William Heinemann (March).
Encourages Jammes to publish his poems. Jammes's collection *Vers* is
dedicated to him. Hubert delivers copies of *Vers* to Mallarmé, Gide, and
Régnier in Paris.
Is with Leila in Pamplona, Spain; they return to Sallespisse (early April).
While picnicking with Hubert and Jammes, Leila suffers damage to her
eyes in a spirit stove accident, necessitating treatment from specialists over
the next two years.
Attends dinner in honour of Zola hosted by the Authors' Club (28
September).
In November meets Paul Verlaine who is in England for three weeks,
at the invitation of Arthur Symons and York Powell, at Symons's home,
Fountain Court, in the company of, among others, Symons, Edward
Dowson, John Lane, and Herbert Horne.
By end of 1893 Hubert and Leila have taken a flat at 36 Chelsea Gardens
overlooking Chelsea Hospital.

1894 On 12 January his letter ('Literary Freedom') is published in the *Daily
Chronicle*.
Delivers a two-hour lecture, 'The Art of Fiction', to J. T. Grein's 'Sunday
Popular Debates' (11 February); Edmund Gosse is in the Chair; George
Moore, Dowson, and Conal O'Riordan attend.
His 'A Commonplace Chapter' appears in the *New Review* in February
and March. (The second part of the story, 'The Hasletons', appears in the
Yellow Book: An Illustrated Quarterly in April 1895.)
April: Arthur Waugh's essay 'Reticence in Literature' appears in the
opening number of the *Yellow Book*.
June and July: publication (in the *Westminster Gazette*) of a selection of his
Vignettes.
July: his rejoinder essay, 'Reticence in Literature: Some Roundabout
Remarks', appears in the second number of the *Yellow Book*.
Is writing one or more one-act plays for the Independent Society
programme (September) which are never performed.
Hubert and Leila are abroad from April through to October in Avignon,
Tuscany, Florence, the Apennines, Lausanne, and Paris (visiting Maurice
Maeterlinck, Edmond de Goncourt, and Jammes).
October: his story 'A Study in Sentimentality' appears in the *Yellow Book*.
The first of Leila's four contributions to the *Yellow Book*, a story, 'Jeanne-
Marie', is published (October).
Late Autumn–January 1895: he and Leila are in London (socializing with
Selwyn Image and Richard Le Gallienne).

December sees first publication (in the *Speaker*) of a selection of his *Vignettes*. Further batches of *Vignettes* will appear in the *Speaker* in January, April, and November 1895.

1895   He and Leila spend the Spring in the Béarn.

June sees publication (in the *Saturday Review*) of a selection of his *Vignettes*. Further batches of *Vignettes* will appear in the *Saturday Review* in August 1895 and October 1896.

In July *Sentimental Studies & A Set of Village Tales* is published by William Heinemann.

Spends the summer in Normandy, Dieppe, then Villerville; has contact with the English artistic colony in Dieppe, comprising Dowson, Symons, Lane, Henry Harland, and Walter Sickert.

While in Dieppe briefly joins Lord George Sanger's Travelling Circus, which is on its way to Le Havre, as an interpreter. The piece 'Bread and the Circus' for the *Yellow Book* (October) is his published account of this four-day escapade.

He and Leila are back at Villerville, then at Wiesbaden (with Leila consulting an oculist).

August–September: he and Leila are in London.

Later that Autumn they visit France, Switzerland, Italy, and Spain.

Their flat at 36 Chelsea Gardens is taken over by Julie Norregard, Danish journalist and writer, later Richard Le Gallienne's mistress and second wife (December).

Hubert and Leila move to their new home, 96 Cheyne Walk, Chelsea (James Whistler's home until 1878), decorated by Roger Fry.

At the end of 1895 Leila is pregnant.

1896   Leila miscarries sometime between New Year and her departure for Italy in the spring of 1896 (she does not return to London).

In April the *Savoy Magazine* publishes Leila's 'The Love of the Poor', a poem in dramatic form.

Hubert lives on alone in Cheyne Walk until August. He has now become involved with Mary, Elizabeth ('Sissie') Welch, a sister of Le Gallienne.

Leila is at Viareggio, Tuscany, having begun an affair with an artist, the Comte d'Artaux.

In July his 'Anthony Garstin's Courtship' is published in the *Savoy Magazine*.

He is 'summoned for furiously riding a bicycle in Piccadilly' on 29 July. Fined 5s., with 4s. costs.

In August, Hubert and his lover, Sissie Welch, are travelling openly to Paris, where he lives until his death in November.

In September his 'Trevor Perkins: A Platonic Episode' is published in the *Illustrated English Magazine*.

Beginning of September: Leila arrives in Paris from Italy accompanied by her lover, d'Artaux.

Hubert takes apartment with Leila and d'Artaux and, shortly after, with Sissie at 18 avenue Kléber.

Discussions between Hubert and the publisher Grant Richards through October concerning the possibility of taking over the *Savoy*, which is ailing under Arthur Symons and Leonard Smithers.

He and Richards agree to meet again in a few weeks, but no further meeting comes about.

His *Vignettes* is published by John Lane (end of October).

End of October–beginning of November, severe rainfall results in the river Seine at highest level for thirty years, but level subsides (4–5 November).

Beginning of November: Leila sends for her solicitor, John Hills.

4 November: Hills arrives in Paris. Leila sees Hubert and Sissie together in the apartment, providing evidence for case for separation. Leila abruptly leaves apartment with d'Artaux. On return from opera late evening Hubert finds note from Leila — tries unsuccessfully to find her.

5 November: Hubert sends Sissie back to London. Traces Leila to Hôtel Mirabeau, Rue de la Paix: the interview results in a threat by Leila to call police. His mother, Blanche, arrives from London probably at the Hôtel Quai de Voltaire, where Hubert joins her. Hubert summons Hills, who informs him that the case brought against him by Leila is 'legal cruelty', in addition to the charge of adultery. After an evening conference with Hills and Blanche, leaves his mother at her hotel at about 11.30 pm and walks with Hills along the Quai Voltaire. The men part there at about 11.50 pm. Hubert is never seen alive again. Blanche takes the night train back to London.

25 November: the Crackanthorpe family is convinced that Hubert is dead. Dayrell writes his 'all-embracing indictment' letter to Leila.

24 December: his body is discovered by workmen near Pont d'Alma, a few hundred yards downstream from the Quai de Voltaire.

25 December: identification of Hubert's body by his brothers Dayrell and Oliver.

26 December: his body is returned to London and incinerated at Woking.

1897 1 January: funeral service at All Saints, Knightsbridge, conducted by Edward Lyttleton, Hubert's classical tutor at Eton.

His ashes are taken to the chapel at the family seat, Newbiggin, Westmorland.

Last Studies is published by William Heinemann in November.

31 December: a midnight service is held in Newbiggin church, Westmorland, in his memory.

PART I: FICTION

From
Wreckage: Seven Studies (1893)[1]

[1]   Crackanthorpe's epigraph to the volume is: 'Que le roman ait cette religion que le siècle passé appelait de ce large et vaste nom: "Humanité": — il lui suffit de cette conscience: son droit est là': 'If the Novel has that religion which the last century called by the wide, vast name of *Humanity*, the consciousness of this is sufficient for it, and implies its right' (Edmond and Jules De Goncourt, 'Preface', *Germinie Lacerteux: A Realistic Novel* (London: Vizetelly & Co., 1887), pp. v–vii (p. vii)).

Profiles

It was one of the first warm afternoons of the year; the vigorous rays of the sun lent the young leaves, whose delicate green suffused the wood, an exquisite transparency.

All was still; the rushes clustered immobile on the banks of the little stream; no breath of wind ruffled its surface.

Alone a water-rat splashed, and gently rippling the water, swam across.

On the bank a girl was sitting, her white cotton dress rucked about her knees, displaying a small pair of muddy boots, which dangled close to the water's surface. Her body was thrust forward in a cramped position, as with both hands she held a long, clumsy-looking fishing-rod. She was watching intently the movements of a fat, red float, which bobbed excitedly up and down.

She was bareheaded, and her crisp, auburn hair was riotously tumbling about her ears and neck.

Quite pale was her skin, but pale, transparent, soft; exquisite was the modelling of her fresh, firm lips.

There were great possibilities of beauty in the face; but now an all-absorbing look filled it, the forehead puckered over the eyebrows, the lips set tight together.

A little way off, on the grass, a young man, in a grey flannel suit, was lying on his back, his face shaded by her big-brimmed straw hat, inside the ribbon of which were tucked some bunches of primroses; one hand thrust in the armhole of his waistcoat, the other thrown back over his head — the limp abandon of his pose betrayed that he was asleep.

Down darted the fat, red float. Awkwardly the girl tugged at the rod; the line tightened, swaying about from side to side.

"Maurice!" she called; then louder, as he did not wake.

Maurice started, pushed the hat from off his eyes, murmuring sleepily —

"Hullo! what's up?"

"Make haste, do! I can't hold the rod any more."

He jumped up, took it, and in a minute or two the fish was floundering on the grass, its sleek, silver sides gleaming in the sunlight.

"Why, Lilly, it's quite a big one," he exclaimed.

Tall, with fine, broad shoulders, and a small, well-shaped head, evidently not a quite young man; but a trick of raising his eyebrows with an air of boyish surprise, made him appear some years younger.

"He pulled like anything. I should have had to let go the rod in another minute. My arms ache all over," she added, ruefully.

"That rod's too heavy for you. I'll have to get another, if we're coming fishing again."

"Oh, yes! Of course we are. I love it."

She looked altogether beautiful, her face lit up in a delicate flush of excitement.

"Put on another worm, quick. There's sure to be some more, aren't there?"

Maurice pulled out his watch.

"Nearly four o'clock," he said, shaking his head.

"I've got a guard at half-past five. We must pack up."

At once her face clouded, the eyes half-closed, the mouth drooped, the chin pouted.

A pettish exclamation was on her lips, but, catching sight of an amused twinkle in Maurice's eyes, she checked herself, and her face cleared.

Together they unscrewed the rod, and when they had put the joints into their canvas case, they started off through the wood, along the narrow path that led to the village.

Maurice, with the rod under his arm, and a long cigar in the corner of his mouth, Lilly bareheaded, her hair more unruly than ever, carrying her hat and her parasol in her hand.

II

They were engaged to be married, Lilly and Maurice. It had been so for nearly three months.

Lilly lived with her Aunt Lisbet in a semi-detached villa on the outskirts of Guildford,[1] where Maurice's regiment was quartered.

She had never known her mother; when she ransacked the dim memories of her childhood, there was nobody further back than Aunt Lisbet. Her father she scarcely remembered at all, for he had died when she was quite a little girl. He had been a bookmaker, and a coloured photograph of him — a burly, red-faced man, in a white top-hat, and a long, grey dust-coat with a scarlet flower in the button-hole — hung over the fire-place in Aunt Lisbet's bedroom. Underneath the photograph was written, James Maguire — "Big Jock."

During his lifetime "Big Jock's" good luck had been almost proverbial, so that he was reputed to be worth a "tidy pile." But at his death, when all his debts had been paid, scarcely a hundred pounds remained.[2] What had become of it all no one knew, and Aunt Lisbet had never forgiven her brother for this mystery. The disappearance of the money itself exasperated her; but the thought that for years he had been secretly making away with large sums without a word to her,

---

[1]   Guildford is a town in Surrey, twenty-seven miles south-west of London.
[2]   The current equivalent value is about £8000.

his sister, who had kept house for him since his wife's death, and who had been a second mother to his child, made her especially furious.

This bitter feeling against her brother, instead of subsiding as time went on, only rankled the more in her mind, and now, except in terms of abuse she never mentioned his name.

She was a thin, sharp-boned, little woman, with red lids to her greenish-coloured eyes, a long, aquiline nose and a pointed chin. When she spoke to Lilly of her father, there came into her voice a curious, rasping intonation.

Aunt Lisbet drank; chiefly brandy, and her drunkenness took the form of fits of ungovernable passion.

These outbursts were almost always directed against Lilly; not that Aunt Lisbet had any particular personal animosity towards her niece, but because Lilly was the handiest object on which to vent her feelings.

She would begin by recalling some evil trait in Jock's character. Lilly had no really tender affection for her father's memory, the little she knew of him was far from creditable. But this disparagement of him by Aunt Lisbet somehow made her blood boil, and at times the scenes between them were very violent.

And though, except for these occasions, they seldom quarrelled, Lilly loathed Aunt Lisbet with an instinctive, imperious loathing.

And this afternoon, as she drove home in the dog-cart[3] by Maurice's side, her hatred for her aunt seemed fiercer than it had ever been before.

III

The horse's hoofs rang clear on the hard, white road, as they sped swiftly along, Lilly leaning against Maurice's shoulder, plunged in a brown study.[4]

Presently she said, meditatively: "What is the earliest date on which your father can arrive?"

"Well, he won't leave Bombay for another fortnight, then he'll not hurry himself on the journey, so it will be at least a month before he reaches England. It's a beastly long time, isn't it?"

"Oh, Maurice! What's the good of waiting? He will never consent, let's get married at once."

Recklessly he dropped the reins and taking her face in his gloved hands, held it up to his. Their lips met, and putting both his arms round her, he strained her to him. The kiss was a long one; at last she gave a little moan; he let her go.

"You don't know the old gentleman, you see," he continued. "My infernal busybodies of relations have been writing all sorts of tales about you — at least, not about you, but about your aunt and your father, and about — well, a lot of

---

[3] A dog-cart is a light horse-drawn vehicle.
[4] A brown study is a state of serious absorption or abstraction.

damned rot." But directly he's seen you, I shall be able to make it all right with him. Of course, if you really wish it, we could get married next week, but I think it would be more prudent to wait. The very fact that I had not waited till his return might put his back up, and he might cut off my allowance on the spot."

"Of course, Maurice, we'll wait. It was selfish of me to think of it. But — but — "

"Well?"

"I do hate Aunt Lisbet so."

"I know; but it's not so very long now."

They were entering the town.

"Shall I drive you to the door?"

"No, drop me at St. Luke's. I'll walk home from there."

He pulled up and she got down.

"Be at Mrs. Newton's in good time tomorrow afternoon," he called out, as, smartly flicking the horse, he rattled away down the street.

IV

The solitary candle flickering on the dressing-table made the shadows of the coming night creep back into the corners of the room, as Lilly, with swollen eyelids, and red patches on her cheeks, looked out through the window-pane.

All was still. The earth slept.

The moon poured her white light on the meadows opposite; a few fleecy clouds lazily chased one another across the sky. In the distance a dog barked, then all was again still.

Lilly threw herself on the bed, burying her face in the pillow.

And presently the cool linen began to soothe her burning forehead.

It had passed, the wild impulse to throw herself out of the window that people might know to what Aunt Lisbet had driven her. Now the resolve never to see her again ousted all else from her mind. Absolute, irrevocable was this resolve: any departure from it was as a physical impossibility. Only she must wait till morning, and she turned to a cooler spot on the pillow.

And as she did so, a vivid vision of the scene in the kitchen below started before her eyes. Aunt Lisbet leaning against the dresser, her hair slipping down on one side, and in her voice a hissing sound.

It was the first time that she had said things about Maurice; that was what had made it worse than it had ever been before.

A blind desire to silence her, to stamp the life out of her, swept over Lilly. Seizing the parasol which lay on the kitchen-table, with all her strength she hit Aunt Lisbet across the side of the head.

And over the thought of that blow she lingered, recalling it again and again, repeating it in her mind with a strange, exquisite pleasure. For into it she had put the hatred of years.

Aunt Lisbet uttered a low, plaintive moan — the curious moan of sudden pain — and fell, dragging with her onto the floor a pile of plates.

The crash sent every nerve in Lilly's body tingling, piercing her through and through; in a fit of hysterical sobbing she sank into an armchair.

Slowly Aunt Lisbet rose to her feet, and muttering incoherently under her breath, staggered out of the room.

Round and round all these incidents Lilly's thoughts revolved, dwelling on them, brooding over them, unable to escape from them.

And each time that she thought of the hissing sound in Aunt Lisbet's voice, the blind, murderous feeling swept over her, and each time that the thud of Aunt Lisbet's head on the floor sounded in her ears, the tears welled up in her eyes.

V

The Charing Cross platform was alive with people, some hurrying hither and thither, others standing together in groups or sauntering up and down.[5]

The fierce panting of an engine echoed through the building, and a cloud of dense smoke rose to melt away under the curved roof.

It was nearly a quarter to one, for when Lilly had awoken in her little bedroom at Aunt Lisbet's, weary and unrefreshed through having slept in her clothes, the morning was already half gone. Downstairs and out of the house she had crept, meeting only the servant-girl, who told her with a smirk that her aunt was still sleeping.

Her first impulse had been to go straight to the "Barracks" to ask Maurice to take her away and marry her at once. It seemed the only alternative, for never again would she set foot in Aunt Lisbet's house.

But, as she hurried through the town, there came upon her, like a spasm of physical pain, a feeling of irresolution. She remembered what Maurice had said yesterday — "It's not for so very long." She foresaw that he would advise her to go back and put up with it for a few weeks more, and that she would have to argue with him about it. The courage to face such a prospect was wanting.

No, there was only one thing, take the train for London, telegraph to Maurice to meet her there. Then he *must* understand how impossible it was for her to go back.

And this she had done.

---

[5] Charing Cross Station, off the Strand (see note, below) and close to Trafalgar Square in central London: it served passengers travelling to and from south London and the southeast of England.

Three hours and three quarters to wait till the next train from Guildford, even if Maurice got the telegram in time. He might not be at the barracks when it arrived. At four, of course, he would go to Mrs. Newton's, as they had arranged yesterday. But would he go back home beforehand? And if not, would his servant send on the telegram, or keep it till his return? These and many other possibilities whirled through Lilly's brain as anxiously she paced the platform.

*   *   *   *   *

Four hours had passed. The porters lined the platform edge as rapidly the train drew up. The doors flung open; out swarmed the crowd.

But Maurice was nowhere to be seen. Eagerly Lilly looked for him, up and down; once she fancied that she saw him talking to a porter at the other end of the train.

Desperately she pushed through the crowd, only to find herself face to face with a stranger.

There was not another train till five, and then not another till half-past seven.

With a numb feeling of hopelessness she wandered out into the Strand.[6]

It had just stopped raining. Noisily the omnibuses splashed past, while the hansoms,[7] one after another, crawled along the edge of the pavement.

Some hungry-looking boys were yelling the contents of an evening paper, two flower-girls and an old man selling bootlaces, stood in the gutter. Along the pavement, brown, and a-glimmer with the wet, poured a continual stream of men and women.

No one took any notice of Lilly, they only jostled roughly past her. And somehow the sight of all these strange faces and the movement of this seething turmoil made her feel sick and faint.

For the first time she realised her absolute loneliness.

*   *   *   *   *

The five-o'clock train and the seven-o'clock train had both come in, but still no signs of Maurice.

The last train was due at twenty minutes past nine.

Lilly sat staring lifelessly before her. She had scarcely eaten anything all day; exhausted, she was suffering much, but so great was her nervous tension, that she did not know that it was hunger.

What she would do if Maurice did not come she never considered. All her

---

[6]   The Strand 'so named from its skirting the bank of the river [it] is the great artery of traffic between the City and the West End' (K. Baedeker, *London and its Environs: Handbook for Travellers* (London: Dulau and Co., 1889), p. 141).

[7]   Hansoms are two-wheeled horse-drawn cabs.

energy was occupied in counting the minutes till the train was due.

At last! That must be it! She had not the strength to move, but intently watched the passengers as they poured out through the barrier.

Yes! Maurice! — hastening towards her, yet somehow not looking as she had expected him to look.

VI

Maurice, rising abruptly from the breakfast-table, and throwing open the window, looked down onto the crowded street, for their rooms in the hotel faced the Strand.

Delicate, grey-blue streaks of smoke curled restlessly upwards; in streamed the morning sunlight, bathing Lilly in its full flood.

A newspaper lay before her on the sofa; but she was observing Maurice with stealthy glances from under her dark eyelashes.

Solemnly the clock ticked, while, with obvious constraint, he hummed discontentedly to himself.

An instant ago their voices were raised in angry dispute — not the first, though they had been but three days together. And Maurice, as he gazed out onto the sea of roof-tops, recalled the trivial incident from which their quarrel had sprung. The thought formed a central spot of pain amid the monotony of his gloom.

For the twentieth time he was aimlessly brooding on the change that had come over her.

Never for a moment had he treated her dislike for Aunt Lisbet seriously, though he had sympathised with it, vaguely, distantly. Lilly was to blame for this he thought: beyond occasional references, she had told him nothing, and, in his blind contentedness, he had never troubled to question her. Besides, instinctively, even in thought, he had shrunk from that side of her life. It jarred upon him.

They had spent the night after his arrival together; it had seemed the more natural thing. Maurice only had hesitated for an instant with an indefinable shrinking. And when in the morning Lilly suddenly sat up in bed, and began the explanation of her flight, he listened impatiently to what seemed a series of clumsy and unnecessary exaggerations. He had imagined, with a subtle tickling of vanity, that somehow she had been driven to it out of love for him, and he felt an annoyance, vague but real, at learning that it was not so.

But in a minute or two this had passed; in bewilderment he lay watching her.

Tremulously, with a look of passionate fierceness, her face was working as if some strange light were playing on it.[8]

---

[8]   Tremulously: along with the adjective, 'tremulous', it fuses the uncertainty of feeling

She had done. He knew that every word was true.

And afterwards, if, at odd moments, the improbability of it all flashed upon him, the recollection of that look would at once drive all doubt from his mind.

No longer could he love her lazily as before. The half-girl, half-child, simple and heedless, with occasional moods of confiding dreamy gravity, and fits of charming pettishness, the easy dispelling of which he had enjoyed, was gone.

The events of the past few days had broken down the barrier, behind which the strong passions of her nature had laid dormant, and now, let loose for the first time, they mastered her; she was their slave.

Capricious and irritable, with outbursts of nervous exasperation, followed by hot tears of remorse and a desperate sensuality that disturbed and almost frightened him.

And strangest of all, when he had proposed yesterday that they should be married at the end of the week, with an evasive reply she had at once started another topic.

As he turned to throw away his cigarette, he saw that she was by his side. How silently she had crossed the room! Putting both hands on his shoulders, she murmured:

"Maurice, dear Maurice, kiss me; don't be angry with me."

VII

"We must go back to Guildford, tomorrow," he said, after a pause. "I can't get any more leave, and there are all kinds of arrangements to be made down there — fresh quarters, servants, and heaps of things. You can stay at Mrs. Newton's till everything is ready," he went on hurriedly, "it will only take a few days and then we will come back here and get married. I will keep on the room, so that there will be no difficulty about a licence."

"I don't want to go back. I hate the place," she muttered sullenly.

"But, Lilly dear, do be reasonable. There's nothing else to be done."

"You can go alone, I shall stay here till you come back."

Angrily he was on the point of replying, but the words died away on his lips. Expostulation, he saw, would be worse than useless.

He went on to tell her about a red-tiled house just outside the town, on which he had had his eye for months, but catching sight of her face, he stopped short, and burst out despairingly:

and its transmission, central to the poetics of Decadence of the 1890s, prompted by Walter Pater's sense of the 'perpetual flight' of our impressions. 'To such a tremulous wisp constantly reforming itself on the stream, to a single sharp impression, with a sense in it, a relic more or less fleeting, of such moments gone by, what is real in our life fines itself down' (Pater, 'Conclusion', *Studies in the History of the Renaissance*, ed. by Matthew Beaumont (Oxford: Oxford University Press, 2010), p. 119).

"Why, Lilly, doesn't it interest you?"

"I don't think I could ever go back," she answered slowly.

"But we can't live anywhere else, unless I exchange, and that would take time."[9]

A pause, during which she was nervously tearing strips off the edge of the newspaper.

"How long will you be away?" she asked at length.

"Let's see, today's Wednesday. If I go tomorrow morning, I ought to be back by Friday night or Saturday morning. But what on earth will you do with yourself?"

"I don't know, but I can't go back there. You don't know how impossible it is."

"But after we are married?"

"Perhaps it will be different then," she answered musingly.

He drew her to the sofa, and putting both arms round her, began with infinite tenderness:

"Lilly, darling, what is it? Tell me. Is it that you don't care for me as you did? What is it? Tell me, little woman. Oh! I can't bear the thought of leaving you here all alone by yourself."

"Maurice, I don't know what it is. Only I feel very miserable. Everything seems in such a tangle. I feel as if something strange were going to happen to me. I want to think about lots of things. That's why I want to be alone, quite alone."

VIII

Eight o'clock had just struck; a continuous hum resounded through the restaurant, a Babel[10] of voices and a clatter of knives and forks.

"I do love the crowd, the bustle, and all that," exclaimed Lilly, excitedly.

Then,

"Oh! Maurice, who's that? I'm sure he knows you; look!"

Against the pillar in the centre of the room a powerfully built, dark-faced man was leaning. His face, in contrast to the whiteness of his shirt-front, seemed copper-coloured, and there was a singular massiveness about it; bushy eyebrows, heavy, black moustache and vermilion lips.

Dominating the whole room, he stood leisurely casting his eyes over the crowd of diners.

"That man by the pillar?" answered Maurice. "Yes, I know him a little. His name is Adrian Safford. Some more soup?" And he went on with his dinner.

---

9   Exchange, in this context, means to be transferred.
10   Babel here refers to the fact that there are people talking various different languages, therefore, presumably, foreigners.

Safford's eyes were on them now, travelling from one to the other with a deliberateness that was almost insolent.

Lilly's eyelids dropped; she hurriedly crumbled a piece of bread.

But the temptation was irresistible; nervously she glanced up. Quite close now, his back towards her, both hands in his pockets, and a crush hat tucked under one arm.

"Maurice, he can't find a seat."

"Can't find a seat — who can't?"

"That big man — Mr. Safford. Tell him that there's room next you."

In the glass opposite she could see the reflection of his face. As she spoke he made a sudden, half-arrested movement of his head. He had overheard.

Maurice touched him on the shoulder. And, as shaking hands they exchanged greetings, Lilly noticed the prickliness of his eyebrows, and the strong muscles on each side of the bull-like throat.

And Maurice introduced him to her; under the stare from his lustrous black eyes she flushed hotly.

He was speaking, his voice sounded slow, drawling almost.

But she scarcely heard what he was saying, she was watching his hands, as they smoothed the cloth in front of him — white and fat, tipped with pink finger-nails, carefully trimmed to a point.

IX

All the morning and during luncheon Maurice had been gloomily taciturn; this had induced in Lilly a strained, nervous gaiety.

The moment of parting drew near and the tension became more and more painful.

Yet it did not snap till they were slowly pacing the platform before the departure of the train. Then, of a sudden, he turned his face, contorted as in acute physical pain, and with a dryness in his voice, passionately implored her to return.

But he did not touch her. Strange that she was observing him, curiously, for the first time conscious of distinct antipathy towards him. He looked — yes, ridiculous, as if ashamed of having betrayed his emotion. The sight of this emotion sent a spasm of irritation through her. Next she felt an almost uncontrollable inclination to laugh.

But he did not press her any longer, for he dimly saw how it was. The porters began to slam the doors; in silence he entered the train.

After it had gone she sauntered about the streets, staring at the people, reading the posters on the hoardings, gazing into the shop windows, now and then buying with the money he had given her little objects that took her fancy.

At last, hot and dusty, she found herself back at the hotel. Tired out, she stretched herself on the sofa, and, closing her eyes, let thoughts float aimlessly across her brain.

There passed visions of a woman with yellow hair indolently[11] reclining against the cushions of a Victoria;[12] of the red-bearded policeman who had told her the way to the hotel; of the stare of a thin man in frock coat pinched at the waist; of the gold-spotted veil, and of the brooch set in imitation pearls, which she had carried home with her.

Then the bronzed countenance of Safford, his bright, red lips, and fat, white hands appeared as he leant against the central pillar of the restaurant.

And now Maurice was there too. Side by side they disputed for her. Maurice troubled, with tears in his eyes; Safford still, massive as a statue.

"Which loves her best?" cried the crowd.

"I do," answered his slow tones. He encircled her cheeks with his hands, which were soft and warm, and his bright, red lips kissed her softly on the eyes.

X

Abruptly, without effort, her eyes opened. And immediately their gaze fell upon Safford. For an instant, the impression of her dream remained vivid; to see him there seemed natural. But before the returning sense of reality, it faded quickly; bewilderment sweeping in, arrested all thought.

Astride of a chair, the broad expanse of his back blocking the light, he sat, looking out of the window, apparently absorbed in the street below. This unconcernedness alarmed her.

How did he come there?

A minute or two slipped by, then he shifted his chair, as if to rise. Her eyes shut hastily, involuntarily; she pretended to be asleep. He came to her, so close that his breath played on her cheek, but in spite of the loud throbbing of her heart, she never stirred. He moved away: his heavy tread sounded about the room. Then silence.

Had he gone? No, she would have heard the click of the door-handle. The darkness, the suspense became intolerable, yet it was a full minute before she could summon courage to reopen her eyes.

Her gaze met his.

"I say, if I couldn't sham better than that, I wouldn't try at all," and his broad teeth gleamed.

---

[11] Indolently: a favourite word of the Decadent poets; see Arthur Symons, 'Arques: I: Noon. Amoris Exsul: XI': 'Idly, I watch them indolently play' (line 9) (*Poems by Arthur Symons Volume I* (London: Martin Secker, 1923), p. 292).
[12] A Victoria is a light four-wheeled horse-drawn carriage with a folding hood.

Somehow his voice calmed her. His self-possession communicated itself to her, giving her confidence.

"I wasn't shamming."

"I could see it."

"How?"

"Your eyes were trembling."

She smiled, almost frankly.

"Weren't you surprised to see me?"

"Yes, no — I mean yes."

"Where's Radford?"

"Maurice? He's gone."

"Gone? Where?"

"To Guildford."

"And you're here all alone?"

She nodded.

A moment's pause — he thoughtfully jingling some money in his trouser-pocket; she, wondering that he looked so much darker than he had done in evening dress.

"When is he coming back?"

"I'm not sure, either tomorrow night or Saturday morning."

Another pause.

"What did you do last night — after I went away?"

"We went to the theatre."

"Did you like it?"

"Yes, awfully."

"You're fond of the theatre?"

"I've only been twice — in London at least."

"Would you like to go again tonight?"

"I couldn't."

"Why not?"

"Maurice — I promised him."

"What a pity! You'd have liked it."

"Yes, I should."

"Look here, it will be all right; he won't mind, he knows me well enough." And again the broad teeth gleamed.

"I don't know — perhaps ——"

But as she spoke, his soft, warm hands encircled her face, his bright, red lips kissed her on the eyes, just as in her dream.

The blood rushed to her face, in hot gasps her breath came and went, everything but Safford swam in a mist and was gone; impulsively she lifted her burning face to his and murmured:

"Tell me that you love me. Then I'll come."

XI

Adrian Safford's chambers were sombre; even on this summer morning shadows lurked in the corners of the lofty spacious room. There was no window; the light struggled in as best it could, through a ground glass skylight. On the walls, maroon-coloured hangings; from the fireplace to the ceiling reached a huge overmantel of black, carved oak. The rich scent of a burning pastille[13] struck a note of sensuous mystery. It was all curiously characteristic of the man.

Amid the dark tints, a single patch of colour — the white table-cloth on which an exquisitely fresh breakfast was laid. Safford had just seated himself before it, a scowl deepening the bronze of his face. Yet he ate in a vigorous, business like way. His appetite was always splendidly regular.

The girl asleep in the next room was the cause of his scowl.

Something about the crispness of her hair; something about the modelling of her chin; something in the questioning look that darted out from the liquidness of her big eyes; something — he knew not what — had haunted him, ever since their first meeting. A spark of caprice fanned into fitful flame by the offensiveness of Radford's ill-concealed pride of possession.

And so the day before yesterday he had gone to the hotel. To find her alone was more than he had hoped for, but directly he saw her lying asleep on the sofa, he knew instinctively that she was his. Women were so easy.

The rest had been the old story, only this time more commonplace than ever — a dinner at the Café Royal,[14] a box at the Empire,[15] and back to his chambers afterwards. And yet she was different from the others; she remained; he kept her for her mutinous freshness.

He had asked nothing about her relations with Radford. He had made a rule never to question them about themselves; the tedious monotony of their stories bored him immensely.

It was she who, in her wilfulness, had blurted it all out. He saw it coming and did his best to stop her. But it was not to be. And when he heard that she and Radford were to have been married in a day or two, his feeling was one of

[13]   A burning pastille produces incense by burning pellets.
[14]   The Café Royal was a fashionable cafe-restaurant in Regent Street, London, patronised by artists and writers, including Walter Sickert, Aubrey Beardsley, James Whistler, and Oscar Wilde.
[15]   The Empire: Leicester Square, London. First built in 1881 as the Royal London Panorama, it re-opened in 1887 as a music-hall, notable for its dance spectacles. The autumn of 1894 saw a highly publicised spat prompted by the 'Prudes', led by Mrs Ormiston Chant of the British Women's Temperance Association, and the National Vigilance Association, who campaigned against the Empire and the Alhambra (also in Leicester Square) because of 'impropriety on the stage and disorderliness in the auditorium', due in particular to the activities of prostitutes who routinely touted for business in the Promenade areas of the theatres. See John Stokes, *In the Nineties* (Hemel Hempstead: Harvester Wheatsheaf, 1989), p. 56. See note on the Alhambra on p. 208.

pure disgust — not disgust at her treachery, but disgust at the blunder he had committed — blunder ahead of which he foresaw a whole series of unpleasant complications.

And in that instant he tired of her — her passion, from being a thing to be toyed with complacently, suddenly filled him with active dislike. The very searching gaze which had amused him before now seemed merely stupid. With the exasperation of a trapped animal, he realised that she was one of the clinging sort, whose dismissal was generally difficult, always disagreeable.

"Damn," he muttered, savagely biting the end of a cigar.

XII

Safford, his huge frame stretched on two chairs, from time to time carefully inserted the cigar between his teeth. He smoked thoughtfully, deliberately, yet the cigar had nearly burnt to an end before Lilly ran in, with the fresh morning bloom upon her.

"Why, how late! Ten o'clock," she cried. "And you've eaten nearly all the breakfast. For shame! I believe that's why you got up without waking me."

"There's some left under the cover. Ring for more if it's cold," he answered, without removing the cigar from his mouth.

But she, in her radiant unconsciousness, did not notice his gloom.

"Do come and cut this bread for me," she called out presently, "it hurts my fingers, it's so awfully hard." He did as she asked; then flicking the ash from his cigar, stood looking down at her as she ate.

"Sugar, please. I say, what shall we do today? It's so splendid out. I can't stop inside. Besides, it's so stuffy in here." Safford shifted his feet uneasily. "I tell you what — I know. We'll go down to Kingston and go on the river.[16] It's awfully jolly down there. I went once last summer."

"With Radford, I suppose?"

"Why, I believe you're jealous of him — yes, you are, else you wouldn't look so solemn. Come, aren't you?"

No answer.

She rose, and both hands toying with the lapels of his coat, said hurriedly:

"But I don't care for him — not a bit. He seems like a stranger now. It seems months since I saw him. I love you — oh! I can never tell you how I love you. I want to be with you always — you know I do. Come kiss, kiss me again like the first time." Her voice, though rapid, had great earnestness in it.

With an impatient movement he repulsed her.

"You must go back this morning," he said, more brutally than he had

---

[16]   Kingston: the town of Kingston was established on the east bank of the river Thames. Once in Surrey, it is now in Greater London.

intended, but his exasperation had got the better of him. "When I sent for your things yesterday, they said he would return this morning."

She stepped back, as if he had struck her; the light went out of her face; her eyes blinked quickly as she tried to grasp his meaning, her under-lip began to twitch.

"You're joking! Oh! don't! Say it's a joke! You don't know how it hurts!"

"No, I'm quite serious. Now be sensible and listen. I should never have brought you here if I'd known about you and him. You must go back — at once."

"You really mean it?"

"Yes, I mean it."

"Then you don't love me any more," she burst out. "I don't believe you ever did. It was only just to amuse yourself that you brought me here. You made me love you, and now that you've had enough of me you want to send me back to him. You ——"

Unheeding, he went on slowly:

"Besides, I'm going away."

"It's a lie! You only want to get rid of me."

"Do as I tell you, and don't make a fuss." There was an imperiousness in his voice that cowed her. The passionate fierceness left her. "And if you are careful," he went on, "it will be all right; not a soul knows where you've been. Very likely he won't find out that you've been away. And even if he does, he's quite fool enough" — and with a grim smile at the words that were rising to his lips, he checked himself.

But she did not hear what he was saying. Like some nightmare procession, the incidents in her life since her departure from Guildford were passing before her.

"I sha'n't tell any lies. I shall tell him straight out," she said half to herself.

Impatiently he shrugged his shoulders.

"And then, when I've told him, I may come back, mayn't I?"

"Come back? Here?"

"Yes, when it's all over with him. I mean when he's gone away again."

"It's quite impossible. Just understand that."

"But what am I to do, then?" It was the cry of concentrated despair.

"You've got to do what I've told you. It will be all right. I know what I'm talking about. If you don't choose to — well, then, it's your lookout. You can't come back here, that's certain. I'm going away."

She was not looking at him; her big eyes, wide-open, were staring vacantly at something beyond.

"Where are you going?" she said faintly, after a pause.

"Never mind. Nowhere where you can come."

"Oh! for God's sake, don't send me away." The vacant expression had given way to the feverish[17] pleading of her childish passion. "You will kill me if you do. Can't you see how I love you. There seems to be nothing else in the world for me but you. Perhaps you think that I shall be in the way. But I promise you that I will do whatever you tell me; I will be no trouble; I will not speak to you if you do not want me to — I will do anything." And down streamed the tears.

"Poor little devil," he muttered under his breath. He drew her towards him and her frail body shook convulsively on his chest.

"Lilly, dear, you must go, you really must. It's for your own good. There are lots of reasons why you must, that you don't understand — you will soon forget all about this. Now come, kiss me, and say you will go quietly."

Her sobbing had ceased. His slow tones had mastered her.

She looked up through her tears and nodded. "I will go," she said through her teeth, "because I can't help doing what you tell me. But I shall come back."

So absorbing was his sense of relief that he did not hear her last words.

"Make haste and get your hat. I'll see you into a hansom. I'll get your things packed and sent after you at once. And remember all that I told you. You've only got to play your cards well, and it will be all right."

So fearful was he lest she should repent her submission, that the unnatural calm which had come over her passed unnoticed.

XIII

"Lieutenant Radford has just come back; he was asking for you just now ma'am," said a waiter as she mounted the staircase.

Pushing past him, she laid her hand on the door of the room. As she did so, it opened suddenly from within, and a man, whom she recognised as the manager of the hotel, held it open for her to pass.

Maurice was seated at the table, writing.

"Lilly," he cried as she entered. "Thank God!"

Wildly he poured kisses on her hair and face. She submitted passively, quite white, her teeth set, in her eyes a stony stare.

The first rush of emotion passed, he let her go.

"But where have you been?"

She made no answer, only a dangerous light — a light that boded mischief — suddenly animated her face. He was so different from him whom she had just left. And, as she recalled Safford's massive frame and bronzed countenance, she found herself looking at Maurice, critically, as at some stranger, each detail of

---

[17]   Feverish: an adjective favoured by Decadent writers in conveying states of confusion, or even, as here, abjection; see Symons's poem 'White Heliotrope': 'The feverish room and that white bed, | The tumbled skirts upon a chair' (lines 1–2 in *Arthur Symons: Selected Early Poems*, ed. by Jane Desmarais and Chris Baldick (Cambridge: MHRA, 2017), p. 115).

whose person was acutely repulsive. But for him Safford would never have sent her away. She hated him for it.

"Lilly, they tell me that you've been away since Thursday. What have you been doing?"

She had expected anger; but there was none in his voice, only a tone of tender entreaty that made her wince. An irresistible, evil desire to wound him came to her.

"I've been with Adrian."

"Adrian? Who? Safford?"

"Good God!" and as the truth dawned on him, with a gradual, ugly contraction, his face turned a greyish colour.

Sinking into a chair, he buried his head in his hands.

Some minutes passed, but he did not stir. The silence soon became intolerable to Lilly; fiercely she fidgeted with her glove, pulling at a button, trying to wrench it off.

At last she could bear it no longer. She spoke, and as she did so, the sound of her own voice startled her.

"Have you anything more to say to me?"

He looked up, tears were in his eyes.

"What do you mean?"

"I'm going if you haven't anything more to say."

"Going? Where?"

"Back. I only came to tell you."

In supreme unconsciousness of his suffering, she spoke quite naturally, as if the matter was of no consequence.

His lips moved, but he uttered no words, only a choking, gurgling sound.

Again dropping his head in his hands, he sobbed audibly.

The sobs rose, and fell regularly, harshly. It was the first time that she had seen a man cry. And an element of contempt entered into her bitterness.

Then for one short moment she pitied him. Vaguely, as one pities an animal in pain.

She stepped forward, as if to say something, but almost immediately the impulse died away. She went quickly out through the door, closing it softly behind her.

And Maurice, blinded by his grief, did not know that she was gone.

XIV

Lilly was now alone. Maurice and she had parted — probably for ever. And Safford had disappeared. They had told her at his chambers that he was gone. At first she believed that they were lying, and obstinately waited for him during long hours. But it was in vain. Then she searched for him in the streets, wandering hither and thither in the hope of meeting him. But amid the crowd there were no signs of his massive frame.

So for several days. And then the seething turmoil of the great city, ruthless in its never-flagging lust, caught up the frailty of her helpless beauty, and playing with it, marred it, mutilated it. Like a flower, frost-bitten in the hour of its budding, she drooped and withered.

Against the inevitable she made no continuous resistance. How could she? Only for a while; with the feeble struggles of a drowning creature she clung to the memory of her great love for Safford, and to every little thing that reminded her of it.

First, it was a dark-faced foreigner about Safford's build and height. He was kind to her — at least he treated her with no selfish brutality — and listened indulgently when she opened her heart to him. As he listened she would feverishly strive to delude herself into believing that he was the lover she had lost. But even this consolation of self-deception was denied her.

After a while, she somehow lost sight of him, and then it was anyone who by some detail of his person recalled Safford to her — a drawling voice heard one night in a restaurant; two prickly eyebrows caught sight of one night under a lamp-post in Piccadilly; a red and black necktie like the one he wore the afternoon that he had come to the hotel.[18]

Fierce, fitful loves, prompted by curious twistings of caprice, born to die within an hour or two.

She grew careless of her dress and of her person, and at last callous to all around her. She sunk into the irretrievable morass of impersonal prostitution. She ceased to live; mechanically she trudged on across the swamp-level of existence.

One evening, before starting out, as she dragged through the ceremony of her toilet, wearily staring in her glass, there flashed across her murky brain a resemblance between her own wasted, discoloured face, and the hard angularity of Aunt Lisbet's features.

After that the recollections of her girlhood — Aunt Lisbet, Maurice and even Safford faded into the twilight of the past. With no common speed, the end was drawing near.

---

[18] Lilly falls into prostitution in the streets around Piccadilly, a magnet for London prostitutes and their clients in the Victorian period. 'When the Shaftesbury Memorial Fountain, otherwise known as Eros, was unveiled in 1893 at Piccadilly Circus, it was only a few yards from the infamous Haymarket where mothers brought their young daughters for sale' (Peter Ackroyd, *London: The Biography* (London: Vintage, 2001), p. 379).

XV

Pain beyond a certain degree of intensity ceases to be pain. Thus it was with Maurice. In a state of mental numbness he went back to Guildford. His mind, stunned as it was, could only feebly revolve about these words of Lilly's: "I'm going back to him. I only came to tell you." All else was blurred; this alone, and the vision of her white, set face, and stony stare stood out distinct and sharp.

It was many days before consciousness began to return, before his thoughts, emerging from their torpor, started to explore the extent of his pain.

But when the awakening came, with a morbid craving for self-inflicted torture, he lingered over every detail; starting from the very beginning, he lived once again through the events of the last three months.

Now and then, the memory of some happy day they had spent together would come back so vividly as to drive away the dull pain, but it was only for an instant. With a quiver like that caused by the turning of a knife in an old wound, he heard the words ringing once more in his ears: "I'm going back to him. I only came to tell you."

And yet, realising the grim hideousness of it, he felt no resentment against her.

Of a sudden, an infinite pity for her filled him. From that moment all was changed. His love for her, which had lived on in spite of it all, and the new-born pity, each nourishing the other, lessened the sense of his pain, lifting him above it.

For the first time the mechanism of her nature was laid bare before him. He saw many things that he had never heeded before, passing them over as of no significance, things that now, with curious intuition, he understood.

And the exaltation of his love and of his pity rose.

The tragedy was no longer his, but hers. It was not his life that was spoilt, but hers. Pitilessly he upbraided himself — to have left her in the hands of a brute like Safford (the very thought of the man's swarthy skin made his blood boil) — Lilly — his Lilly — who was to have been his wife. How had he ever done it? How contemptible, what a weak creature he was! Poor little child!

And the exaltation of his love and his pity rose still higher.

Yes, he must save her. It was not too late. All the fine elements in his nature forced their way to the front in support of this resolve.

This resolve was the outcome of no blind impulse; he knew to the full the extent of the sacrifice he was about to make. His eyes were opened; he had counted the cost, but he never wavered.

On the contrary, the very sense of her unfitness to be his wife only strengthened his determination to do what was right.

XVI

A small servant-girl, slatternly in her dress, led the way up some narrow stairs, and Maurice stumbled once or twice, catching his feet in the torn stair-carpet, which was colourless with dirt.

"This is the room," she said, and he followed her in.

The first thing that struck him was its shameless disorder — on the table, in the centre, a great litter of old newspapers; some tattered, yellow-backed novels; a half-finished cup of tea, stale and greasy; the remains of a cake, with crumbs scattered on the floor; a packet of cigarettes,[19] two almost empty glasses. There were only three chairs, and on each some article of clothing had been thrown, a bonnet, a petticoat, or a pair of stockings. On the mantelpiece lay a bunch of withered roses, and opposite the mantelpiece stretched a curtain which evidently divided off the bedroom.

Presently a voice — her voice, just the same as in the old days — called out from behind the curtain.

"Who's there?"

"It's someone to see you," answered the servant-girl.

"All right. I'll be out in a minute."

A sound of splashing water, and the strained humming of a music-hall song.

"I say, who are you?" she called out.

He did not answer.

"Speak up, don't be shy. You're Dick? Ned Chalmers, then? Eh? Well, I give it up. Just wait till I've brushed my hair a bit, and I'll come and see for myself."

At each fresh word revealing the extent of her downfall, he winced.

But his resolve was as strong as ever.

The curtain moved. In a gaudy, pink dressing-gown, stained and torn, she stood before him. Lilly, and yet not Lilly — like, but different with a difference that chilled him.

At the sight of him, her whole body stiffened in astonishment.

"Maurice!" she gasped.

Face to face they stood, looking into each other's eyes, "Lilly," he heard himself saying at last, "come away." He could find no other words, so imperious was the desire to remove her immediately out of these loathsome surroundings.

"Come away," he repeated, "away from all this."

"Yes, it is rather messy," she assented, looking round the room with a forced smile. "But I'll get the girl to tidy up a bit. Sit down, chuck those things onto

---

[19]   In the 1890s cigarette-smoking was associated with the unwomanly pursuit of 'pleasure and independence' by New Women; see Angelique Richardson, Introduction to *Women Who Did: Stories By Men and Women, 1890–1914* (London: Penguin, 2002), p. xxxiii. Here, though, the presence of cigarettes in Lilly's disorderly room is one symptom of her state of abjection.

the floor. How it took me aback seeing you all of a sudden like that! Fancy your finding me out. I never expected to see you again. I thought you had forgotten all about me." (She spoke hurriedly to conceal her agitation.) "Just look at this table, did you ever see such a beastly mess? The people here never think of cleaning out the room."

"Lilly," he heard himself saying again, "you must come away with me at once. You shall make a fresh start with me. I will marry you, and together we will forget all this awful time."

"You're quite serious?" she asked slowly. "You want to marry me now — after all that has happened?"

"Yes," he answered steadily, yet with the absolute futility of it quite clear before him.

"Well, you're more curious than I thought you were," was all her reply.

"What have you been doing all this time?" she added presently.

"I've been back at Guildford. But you must come away from here first. I can't talk things over with you in this horrible place."

"All right, I'll come if you like. But it's no good."

"What do you mean?"

"I mean about your marrying me. I could never marry a man I didn't care for."

He took a full minute to grasp her meaning. The possibility of this had never crossed his mind.

"But you can't go on like this." He was so staggered that words failed him. "Do you know what the life you're leading means? Don't you see how it must all end?"

"Oh! I know all that as well as you do. You don't suppose I find it so extra pleasant, do you?" she burst out bitterly. "But they say it won't last long; that's one comfort. I'm done for, and the sooner it's over the better."

Her voice was hard and reckless.

"For Heaven's sake don't talk like that."

"Look here," she interrupted almost fiercely. "It's no good your going on about it. I could never marry a man I didn't love. And I don't love you. I thought I did once. But it was all different then."

"Is there anyone else then?"

"Anyone else," and there was a savageness in her voice as she caught up his words. "They're just a lot of beasts, the whole lot of them. And if you go on talking about it you'll make me just mad — yes, they're all beasts — I hate them — every one of them, and the sooner it's all over the better. Have a cigarette, there's some on the table. For God's sake do something, say something; don't stand staring at me like that — you've seen me often enough. I'm a precious fright, I know. But how's a girl to keep her looks in this hell of a life?"

"But it's not too late to mend it all."

"Oh! don't go on saying that over and over again. Just get the idea out of your head, once and for all. That's my last word."

And he saw that she meant it. Somehow an immense relief that it was not to be came to him and struggled with his pity for her.

"At least give up this life. Here's some money. Go away somewhere, where you can make a fresh start."

She took the sovereigns from his hand, quickly, with an angry movement as if to fling them on the floor. But, instead, she poured them into a china box on the mantelpiece.

"I'll see about it," she answered.

But he saw the deceit written on her face, and he could bear the strain no longer. An irresistible longing to escape from the stifling atmosphere of the room, to be once more in the street, swept over him.

And as he groped his way down the dirty staircase he felt physically sick.

XVII

The next day Maurice went back to her lodgings.

She was gone, leaving no address behind. He set to work to trace her, and found her at last, late one rainy night, in the Charing Cross Road,[20] but she passed by without recognising him.

And when he entreated her, she was sullenly obdurate.

In despair he went back to his regiment.

For some time more she was seen at intervals in a little public-house at the back of Regent Street. Then she disappeared. What had become of her, no one knew and no one cared.

Maurice alone remembered her, but he never saw her again.

---

[20]   The Charing Cross Road, central London: a road that skirts London's entertainment district of Soho, making it clear that these are not safe, respectable surroundings.

A Conflict of Egoisms

I

The sun must have gone down some time ago, for the room was darkening rapidly. Still Oswald Nowell went on writing, covering page after page with a bold, irregular scrawl. Since breakfast he had been there, and large sheets of paper littered the table and the floor around it. In front of him, by the inkstand, was a plate filled with half-burnt cigarettes.

Of a sudden he became aware that the light was very bad; so he laid down his pen, rose and paced up and down impatiently, his canvas shirt unbuttoned at the throat, his coat discoloured, and worn quite threadbare at the elbows, his thin, grey hair dishevelled as after a sleepless night; his eyes with the dull look of brain exhaustion in them.

For some moments he stood blinking thoughtfully down at the sheets on the floor, and passed his fingers roughly across his forehead, and once more sat down at the writing-table; with the reckless pluck of a blood-horse,[1] struggling on for a few minutes longer. But in vain. He was dead beat.

This was how he always worked — a brief spell of magnificent effort following weeks of listless idleness.

For twelve years he had been writing. In all, he had published five novels and a volume of short stories. The work was singularly unequal, now so dreamy and vague as to be almost unintelligible, now grand with largeness of handling and a power of vision that lifted it at once into the front rank. He had learnt nothing from modern methods, neither French nor English; he belonged to no clique, he had no followers, he stood quite alone. He knew nothing of the disputes that were raging in the world of letters around him: when they told him that a popular critic had set him up as a chief of the idealist school, to do battle with an aggressive and prosperous band of young realists, he puckered his eyebrows and smiled a faint, expressionless smile. For in reality, he had grown accustomed to his own ignorance of what was going on around him, and, when people talked to him of such things, he never expected to understand. And so, day by day, his indifference grew more and more impregnable. His books achieved a *succès d'éstime* readily enough,[2] but the figures of their sale were quite mediocre: the last one, however, probably owing to his having been labelled chief of a school, had run through several editions.

All by himself, in a quiet corner of Chelsea,[3] he lived, at the top of a pile

---

[1]   Blood-horse: a thoroughbred, purebred horse, bred especially for racing.
[2]   'This should be "succès d'estime". The French phrase means critical as opposed to popular or commercial success.' Hubert Crackanthorpe, *Wreckage*, ed. by Malcolm, p. 25.
[3]   A district of West London, skirting the River Thames.

of flats overlooking the river. And each year the love of solitude had grown stronger within him, so that now he regularly spent the greater part of the day alone. Not that he had not a considerable circle of acquaintances; but very few of them had he admitted into his life ungrudgingly. This was not from misanthropy, sound or morbid, but rather the accumulated result of years of voluntary isolation. People sometimes surmised that he must have had some great love trouble in his youth from which he had never recovered. But it was not so. In the interminable day-dreams, which had filled so many hours of his life, no woman's image had ever long occupied a place. It was the sex, abstract and generalised, that appealed to him; for he lived as it were too far off to distinguish particular members. In like manner, his whole view of human nature was a generalised, abstract view: he saw no detail, only the broad lights and shades. And, since he started with no preconceived ideas or prejudices concerning the people with whom he came in contact, he accepted them as he found them, absolutely; and this, coupled with the effects of his solitary habits, gave him a supreme tolerance — the tolerance of indifference. This indifference lent a background of strength to his artistic personality. It was for this reason perhaps, and also because no one knew much about him, that everyone spoke of him with respect.

Just now his power of work was exhausted: stretching himself on a sofa and shutting his eyes, he loosened the tension which was causing his brain to ache. His thoughts, as if astonished at their sudden liberation, for a minute or two flitted about aimlessly; then sank to rest as he fell into a dull slumber.

II

Below, in a tiny sitting-room, daintily, but inexpensively furnished, a woman, broad-shouldered and large-limbed, was stirring a cup of tea, with the unconstraint of habitual solitude. She sat facing the light, which exposed the faint wrinkle-marks about the eyes and mouth and made her seem several years older than she probably was; and these, coupled with the absence of colour in her cheeks, gave to the whole face a worn look, as if the effort of living had for her been no slight one.

And so indeed it was.

Eight of the best years of her life had slipped away in a hard-fought, all-absorbing struggle for independence. At last, a year and a half ago, it had come, and ever since, the emotional side of her nature, hitherto cramped and undeveloped, had been expanding with a passionateness that was almost painful.

Her childhood and her girlhood till she was nineteen, had been spent with her father, who was sub-editor of a halfpenny evening daily — a joyless, homeless existence, moving from boarding-house to boarding-house. Then one dirty November evening brought the first turning-point in her life. An omnibus knocked down her father as he was crossing the Strand,[4] and the wheels passed over his chest. Death was quite instantaneous. Letty gave way to no explosion of grief, only she uttered a little gasp of horror at the sight of the distorted, dead face.

She had never cared for her father, the outbreaks of whose almost uncontrollable temper were the only dark incidents that relieved the dreariness of her colourless memories; and she had never learnt to pretend what she did not feel.

Old Stephen Moore, thriftless and dissolute all his life, left behind him nothing but a month's unpaid salary.

A couple of days after the funeral, she appeared at the office, and doggedly demanded to be given something to do. The manager peered suspiciously through his glasses at this gawky, overgrown girl and put one or two questions to her. Her apparent friendlessness and her determined spirit touched him; he promised to see what could be done.

The next day, and every day for the following six years, she spent in and out of the narrow, grimy building in Fleet Street, doing all manner of odd jobs, carrying messages, copying and answering letters, after awhile working up paragraphs and even writing leaderettes.[5] Into whatever she was set to do, she threw her whole soul, always bright-faced and quick of intelligence, always eager to learn. And three or four times her salary was raised.

Then the sub-editorship of a ladies' weekly was offered her. She accepted it eagerly, for, though it meant but a little more money, there seemed good prospect of promotion. Here, as before, she was indefatigable. Two years later the editor died; the post was at once given to her.

The new sense of authority and of responsibility was a source of great pleasure to her; she liked to recall the old Fleet Street days, when she was at everyone's beck and call, to remind herself that no one had helped her, that her exertions alone had done it all. This thought repeated itself constantly, never failing to send through her a warm thrill of self-satisfaction. Hitherto she had had no desire, no interest outside her work; in complete unconsciousness of self, in complete ignorance of her own emotional possibilities, she had lived on, day after day.

Little by little, she began to realise herself in her relation to the corner of the world in which she mixed; insensibly to compare herself with others; dimly

---

4   See note 6 on p. 84.
5   Fleet Street was where national newspapers had their offices until the mid-1980s, and so a metonym for London journalism. Leaderettes are short editorials, printed in the same type as a newspaper's leaders.

to perceive that life had perhaps many things in store for her, that were not included in the daily routine of work. And this process of awakening, once begun, proceeded with a curious rapidity.

Formerly she had always spent the couple of hours between her dinner and bed-time typewriting or doing other light work, making or mending her own clothes.

Now the necessity for this was gone, and at first she found the filling of the daily gap by no means easy, for she had never learnt how to be idle. She could, of course, have found plenty of work for herself in connection with the paper, but when she thought of it, she became aware that somehow the idea was distasteful. In reality an undefinable but growing longing for something — what she knew not — was unsettling her.

One evening the dinginess of her lodgings struck her, and from that moment she took a violent dislike to them. A week later she moved into the rooms she now occupied, half-way up the pile of flats overlooking the river.

The choosing of the furniture gave her a fortnight of excitement, for she set about it, as she set about everything, with an intense seriousness.

Next followed a period of restless arranging and rearranging; directly the dinner was cleared away, hammering in nails and wrenching them out again, pushing chairs and tables from one corner of the room to another, the whole accompanied by protracted consultations with the newly engaged servant-girl.

Sometimes on her way back from the office, it would occur to her that the looking-glass ought to be hung higher or lower, or that the table-cloth on the square table would look better on the round one; hastening home, and without waiting to take off her hat and gloves, she would at once try the effect of the alteration.

And, when everything was done, the clean, new chintzes, the stiff, white muslin curtains, the Japanese fans, and the hundred and one other bright-coloured knick-knacks on the walls, all, instead of delighting her, as she had expected, made her feel awkward and ill at ease.[6] Her well-worn work-a-day-clothes seemed out of place in this new interior, which made their deficiencies appear all the more glaring. In her daily work she had of necessity acquired a considerable knowledge of the fashions, but to use that knowledge for the adornment of herself had never occurred to her before.

The new elegancies in her dress led her to self-admiration, and to the delicious discovery of her own beauty. It came one afternoon, through a glimpse caught

[6] Chintzes: patterned cotton fabrics with a glazed finish. Japanese fans, appropriated in the West as a decorative fashion item, were associated with the rise in popularity of Japanese culture in the second half of the nineteenth century. *The Mikado; or, The Town of Titipu*, the immensely popular operetta by W. S. Gilbert and Sir Arthur Sullivan, which premiered in 1885, both fed off and contributed to the craze. Japanese art and design were much admired by Decadent artists, including Aubrey Beardsley.

of the reflection of her own profile in a shop window. She stopped, turned and passed before it five or six times, examining herself anxiously. Then, as she walked on homewards, she found herself eagerly comparing her own appearance, which remained clearly visualised, with that of the passers-by.

About this time, too, she became infected with a passion for reading — chiefly inferior, sentimental novels. A considerable number of these were sent each week to the office for review. One afternoon, when things were slack, she happened to open one of these volumes that was lying on her table. Before long her attention was absorbed, and, in the evening, she carried the book home with her. All through her dinner, and on till nearly twelve o'clock, she pored over it, till the three volumes were finished.

The habit, once set going, rapidly ate its way into her life, so that, soon, she never sat down to a meal without a novel before her. And directly one book was finished, she would start on another; hence she remembered scarcely anything of what they contained, but their incidents, piled up and jumbled together in her mind, inflamed her imagination and brought on inexplicable fits of dissatisfaction and depression. Her thoughts took to dwelling on man's love; vaguely she marvelled that it had always been divorced from her life, that no one had ever whispered softly to her, "Letty, darling, I love you."

But surely one day, now that she was well dressed and smart — yes, it seemed that it must be, when she thought of the others, dull and ugly, who were married. And the care with which she dressed herself each morning was for the sake of this unknown new-comer, for whom she was waiting with vague expectation.

This evening however, as she sat over her half-finished cup of tea, her expression — sensitive reflection of all that was passing in her mind — started to fluctuate from radiancy to perplexity, from perplexity to despair.

III

"I beg your pardon," he said, "but may I offer you half of my umbrella? It's not quite so bad now."

The shower had been a fierce one covering the roadway with a thick crop of rain spikes, filling the gutters with rushing rivulets of muddy water; now, through a rift in the ink-coloured clouds, the sunlight was filtering feebly, and the swirl of the downpour had subsided to a gentle patter.

Under a doorway they stood, side by side. Having no umbrella, she had fled there for shelter, when the shower had overtaken her on her way home from the office. And as soon as she had recovered her breath, she saw that he was there too, leaning against the wall, staring absently before him, puffing at a short pipe, his hat pulled over his eyes, his clothes hanging loosely about his large frame. She knew him well by sight from having passed him often on the stairs of the flat; but they had never exchanged a word.

When she had first learnt who he was, she had bought his books, and had set about reading them, not as she usually read, but attentively, almost religiously, because the fact that she was constantly meeting him, and that he lived overhead, gave her an almost personal interest in them. And hence, though there was much in them that she did not understand, they remained distinct in her memory.

She encouraged her servant to repeat to her all sort of gossip about the inmates of the flats, and in this way she learnt much concerning him. And all that she so learnt, coupled with his picturesque appearance, only set her imagination working the more. So that, insensibly, she slipped into the habit of thinking a great deal about him.

As he spoke, she flushed under her veil, and endeavoured by an anxious scrutiny of the sky to disguise her nervousness.

"Thank you," she answered. "Thank you very much; but I think it would be better to wait a few minutes longer. It looks, over there, as if it were going to quite stop."

Two or three minutes passed. She was waiting for him to speak; but he said nothing. She was growing angry with herself for not having gone with him at once: the silence oppressed her. A dozen different ways of breaking it passed through her mind, but she rejected them all as soon as they occurred to her. Why did he not say something?

She glanced at him — back in the listless attitude, gazing vacantly across the street; the sight of this unconsciousness considerably relieved her embarrassment.

Presently he seemed to become aware that she was looking at him; rousing himself, he took the pipe from his mouth and said:

"I think you should be getting home; you ought not to stand here in your wet clothes." He spoke easily, with a quiet familiarity, as if he had known her for a long time.

They started out together: quite slowly, for in order to keep herself out of the rain, she was obliged to accommodate herself to his pace. And as they strolled along through the drizzle, he clumsily pecked at her hat from time to time with the points of his umbrella. She longed to ask him to walk quicker, or to let her hold the umbrella; but she dared not, on account of his self-possession. He was talking leisurely, questioning her about herself, about her life, with a directness that would have been presumptuous but for the half-disguised indifference of his tone. Then gradually the uncomfortable edge of the strangeness wore off and his calm communicated itself to her.

She was not listening attentively to what he was saying; she was thinking about him as the author of his books, vaguely wondering that he did not talk as she had expected him to talk.

There was a pause; he had done speaking and she had nothing to answer.

Suddenly, almost with surprise, she found herself saying:

"I've read your books." And immediately she felt a sense of relief flowing through her, as if the weight of some heavy thing had been all at once removed.

He started and answered with a change of tone:

"Which ones?"

"All of them."

For the first time he seemed embarrassed, uncertain what to say. Surprised at his silence, she looked, and saw that his lips were moving hesitatingly; but he said nothing. Then a crash, just behind her — a heavy dray-horse fell, and lay helplessly floundering on the slimy pavement.[7] They turned and stood watching its vain efforts to rise.

"What a shame not to put down some sand!" she exclaimed.

But he answered:

"Did you like the last — 'Kismet'?"[8]

Smiling a little at the irrelevancy of his question, she answered him at first with trite, meaningless phrases; but as she tried to explain how it had affected her, she found herself talking as she had never talked before, as it were inventing ideas that sounded astonishingly clever and well expressed. And, one after another, they rose to her lips.

She was unconsciously charmed by this new pleasure of listening to her own talk; oblivious of all else, she walked on by his side, till the sight of the familiar, red-brick doorway abruptly brought back the sense of reality.

"Goodbye," she said hurriedly. "Thank you so much. I hope," — she wanted to apologise for her outburst of garrulity — she wanted to express a hope that he would come to see her — to tea some afternoon; but somehow she did neither, and without finishing her sentence, mounted the stairs. He waited till she was gone; then filling his pipe again, lit it, and went out slowly, his large figure growing more and more indistinct as it receded down the brown pavement.

The rain was over: the countless little streams that trickled down the roadway gleamed yellow in the sunlight.

IV

On the morrow, as Letty, hastening homewards, approached the spot in the Strand where she had met him yesterday, she became aware of a thrill of expectation; for she was half counting on seeing him leaning against the doorway, his hat pulled over his eyes, his short pipe in the corner of his mouth.

---

[7] A dray-horse is a powerful horse used for pulling heavy loads.
[8] Kismet, from the Persian *qismat*, meaning fate or destiny.

She even stopped and looked about her. But the crowd flowed thick on the pavement; there was no sign of him. And, since he was not there, just as she had imagined he would be, her expectation died away, her thoughts drifting to other things.

And so till she was home; then, by the entrance to the flats, she caught sight of him — how she liked the loose way his coat hung from his shoulders!

"Won't you come up and have some tea?" she said nervously.

"Thank you," he answered, and they mounted the stairs together.

She had been scheming the evening before, as she lay awake in bed, how she should get him to come to tea with her; she had imagined him sitting in her armchair, consulting her about his books, or admiring her yellow silk curtains and the plush hangings behind the door. But with their entry into the room, a constraint seemed to come over both of them. Without even glancing around him, he sat down and drank his tea, awkwardly, obviously not accustomed to holding his cup in his hand. And when he spoke — and he said but little — it was with a slight stammer that she had not noticed before. She, too, was ill at ease: it had been easy enough to talk to him in the street, now she could think of nothing to say. And more and more keenly she resented her disappointment, growing quite indignant with him because it was all so different from what she had expected. So that, when at last he rose to go it was almost a relief, and her petulance was scarcely concealed. And he, noticing her change of manner, gave her a look half-puzzled, half-pained.

* * * * *

During the week that followed, she met him almost every day on her way home: each time it was in the same, absent, almost casual manner that he accosted her. But she knew that he came out expressly to meet her. All day, as she went about her work in her little room at the office, she would look forward to the walk home by his side; in the evening she would sit, as it were, living every incident of it over again. Beyond his books they had found no common interest, so they talked of little else; but this alone seemed to her full of possibilities, indefinable but endless.

One evening she was sorting a bundle of letters she had brought home from the office, when her servant opened the door and he walked in.

"I can't get on with that chapter; I want to talk to you," he said abruptly.

She saw the yellow look on his face; she noticed, too, that his shirt was unbuttoned at the throat, and that there were inkstains on his fingers; it was as if he had risen from his writing-table and had come straight down to her.

"I can't get on with it at all," he repeated, half to himself.

There was something in this appeal which, outside her own personal feeling for him, went straight to her heart, and put her quite at her ease.

He began to talk, walking up and down the room, and, in a minute or two, she perceived that he had forgotten all about her. For he was not talking to her, but to himself, thinking aloud; now blurting out headless, tailless phrases, now breaking into long, rhythmical sentences which he recapitulated and corrected as he went along. She was listening, a little impatiently, waiting till he should stop, anxious to turn the conversation. But when at last there was a pause, it seemed impossible for her to break the silence with any other topic, so impregnated did the very air of the room seem with his words.

"And after that, what happens?" she asked, not really wanting to know, but only to hear him speak again.

He gave her a sudden glance, as if surprised that she should have overheard him; then, picking up the thread of his thought, continued as before.

Presently he stopped abruptly, just in front of her.

"Goodnight."

She held out her hand: he took it in both of his.

"Goodnight," he repeated absently, "things are much clearer now."

"Then I have really helped you?" Her eyes fell on her hand which he still held, and she flushed a little, drawing it away. But he never noticed her movement: he was staring straight in front of him.

"Yes, things are much clearer. I think I'll go up and put them on paper. I'm afraid I've disturbed you," he added, glancing at the papers on the table. "It was good of you to listen to me for so long." And with his hand on the door he continued: "It is all well marked out in my mind now."

She stood listening to his footsteps, as they died away up the staircase. Then glancing down at her right hand, as it hung by her side, she flushed again, more deeply this time, and moved almost impatiently to the chair by the table. She took up the paper again, but it was only for a minute or two. The loneliness of the little room struck her: the knick-knacks that brightened it irritated her, and this for the first time. Her head sunk on her hands.

"I have really helped you?"

"Yes, things are much clearer now."

The question, the answer, and the faint smile which had accompanied it were repeating themselves in her mind over and over again.

*　*　*　*　*

How long she had been there she did not know, for she was thinking of him, sitting at his writing-table upstairs, putting it all on paper as he had said he would do. What was his room like, she wondered, for she had never seen it. Of a sudden — a step — his step — coming down the stairs. Instinctively she felt that he was coming back to her; so she rose and opened the door. Without a word he walked in, she following him. So continuously had she been thinking of him that the strangeness of his proceeding never struck her: it seemed quite natural that he should return.

"Well?" she said inquiringly, as he did not speak.

"I've done it, it's all come splendidly. Thank you, thank you."

A pause.

"But I came down again because I want to ask you something, Miss Moore." He spoke with the slight stammer that she had noticed once already, and he called her by her name, which sounded strange, as if he had never done so before.

"Well? what is it?"

"Would you care to be my wife?" He said it quite easily.

"Yes," she answered, quite easily also, not realising the situation, but knowing by instinct that there was no other answer possible.

"I haven't much, only a few hundreds a year, about four or five I think.[9] I don't suppose I spend half of it myself. There will be enough for both of us."

At the sound of this bald statement of the practical side of the matter, she winced; but almost immediately, with a woman's quick intuition, she saw that the words had not come naturally, that he had only said them in a blundering endeavour to rise to the situation.

"I don't see many people," he went on in the same, clumsy way, "but I think it would help me having you — with the work, I mean. Would you really care to live with me?"

"Yes." The word came back through her set teeth with a little hissing sound. Her joy struggled with the disappointment she could not help feeling at the way he had said it, and the struggle hurt her considerably.

He crossed the room and stood quite close to her.

"May I kiss you?"

In answer she held up her face; the light of the lamp fell on it, and there was no colour in it. As he bent down, with a sudden movement she clasped both arms round his neck and dragging his face down to hers, said:

"You will love me, won't you?"

"Yes, of course."

There was a silence painful to each of them. At last with an evident effort he broke it.

"Goodnight once more."

But she had caught his hand and was holding it tightly, looking anxiously into his face.

"Please," she whispered.

"I — I don't understand."

The blood rushed to her face.

---

9   The current equivalent value is approximately £32,000–£40,000.

"Please," she repeated under her breath.

He understood; and when he had kissed her, he went slowly out. On the landing he stumbled heavily over the mat, for the gas on the stairs had been turned off.

V

Mechanically, in a state of unnatural passivity, drifting on as if impelled by some invisible outside force, she lived through the next few days. Some great thing was about to happen to her, but somehow she shrank from questioning herself concerning it. Outwardly there was little change in her daily life. She went down to the office as usual, for to throw up her situation at a moment's notice was impossible; besides, she clung to the old life instinctively; partly because at the thought that soon it would all be gone, a feeling of dismay, almost of terror, would creep over her; partly because its daily routine enabled her to ignore her own suppressed excitement.

She saw him a good deal oftener now, for every evening he would come down and sit with her. He no longer talked to her about his work since that strange night, now far receded into the past, when he had asked her to marry him; all his fever for it seemed to have passed away. And so, for the first time, their conversation drifted to other things, to the insignificant incidents of their daily existence. Then came the first half-realisation of her ignorance of him, which bewildered her.

For he was quite different now — so different that at times on looking back over the old days she could scarcely believe that he was the same man. The abrupt self-absorption had given way to a simple kindliness, with a trustful look in his eyes, which sent all her love for him leaping up within her. He had no variation of mood, his easy familiarity, at once gentle and respectful, was always the same.

And, as for Letty, her feeling for him, sprung at first out of her own overwrought sentimental imagination, soon began to grow each day in strength and richness. Into this newborn love for him her whole being fused itself in impetuous rebellion again the life of solitude which had cramped it for so long. With a rapidity, that at first sight seemed startling, she absorbed every detail concerning him, till the whole perspective of her life veered round, everything being subordinated to its relation to him. And all these new things accumulated themselves within her, till their accumulation was painful to endure. For through his easy kindliness of manner she soon divined his supreme unconsciousness of all that the marriage meant to her, and thus her yearning to bring herself at once quite close to him became anguish; looming in front of her, as it were, she began to dimly perceive the barrier of his own personality, a barrier which was the outcome of years of accumulated habit, and which had grown so natural to him that he ignored its very existence. Yet, following a common paradox of human nature, the further she felt herself from him, the more she loved him.

As the days went by her listlessness concerning practical details became almost wilful, so that he was driven to making most of the arrangements for the marriage, foreign though it all was to his nature. Of course there was to be no ceremony; everything was to be as simple as possible. One morning they were to walk together to the Registrar's office in the King's Road[10] — that was all; and there was no need to hunt for fresh lodgings, for Oswald's flat contained two empty rooms. When he suggested this as he sat with her one evening, she assented without a word of comment. Next, the matter of the moving up of her furniture arose.

"I should think it could all be done in a day," he murmured, looking vaguely round the room.

"Yes, while we're away."

He looked up, puzzled.

"Away?" he repeated after her.

"Yes, we're going away, aren't we — for — for — the honeymoon," and her voice quavered a little.

"Of course — of course," he answered hurriedly, "but where?" There was a despairing accent in his voice, so dismayed was he at this new, unforeseen difficulty.

The comic side to it never struck her, only she continued, staring vacantly before her:

"I should like to go where we could walk together under tall pine trees, where the bracken grows high and thick, where there are mossy banks to rest oneself upon, and a little inn by the roadside with a gabled roof."

"But I don't know where it is," he said blankly.

"Nor do I," she answered. "I must have read about it in some book."

So they never left London; but on the marriage day, he took her down to Greenwich by steamer instead.[11]

VI

The crowd, black and restless, swarmed aimlessly round the flaring kiosque, from whence rose and fell the sensuous cadence of a Strauss waltz;[12] behind,

---

[10]　The King's Road runs through Chelsea, and so near to where the couple lives.
[11]　Greenwich is a district of south-east London, just over five miles east-south-east of Charing Cross, situated on the Thames. It was then, as now, a popular destination for boat excursions on the river.
[12]　Kiosques (i.e. kiosks) are movable booths dispensing light refreshments, cigarettes,

amid the tress, winked yellow and sea-green lights, lending an air at once weird and fascinating; while beyond, the buildings of the Exhibition lifted their fire-rimmed roofs.[13]

Oswald and Letty were sitting a little apart from the rest. Since they had come there, the band had played, and ceased, and played and ceased again several times; but, as yet, neither of them had spoken. At last, however, Letty began, realising as she spoke, the length of their silence.

"Look at the people. How silent and sad, all of them! Why is it? Why is everyone so sad tonight?"

But not a muscle of his face stirred; he had not heard her.

"Tell me, why is it? Why is everyone so sad tonight?" she continued, a shrill note of exasperation in her voice.

Still his lips did not move, and she began moodily to dig up the gravel with the point of her umbrella.

After a pause, with perverse determination to make him speak, she broke out again:

"I wonder if any of them are as unhappy as I am."

This time at her words he started; he did not know to what she was referring, but the tone of her voice made the anger rise within him. He resented this unhappiness of hers which he saw she was trying to force under his notice. And now he remembered how soon after their marriage it had begun — reproachful generalities, fits of inexplicable irritability, of exacting affection, or of studied coldness. They had been married several weeks; how many he scarcely knew, only the old life seemed to have receded far, far into the past.

Since the night when he had asked her to marry him he had done no work. There was nothing strange in this, for in between the outbreaks of work-fever, he had always been accustomed to spend weeks without once putting pen to paper — unbroken weeks of eventless peace, as it seemed to him tonight. But now she was always there, with her air of suppressed discontent, from which he shrank, never meeting it openly, pretending to ignore it. To arrive at an explanation of it he never attempted. The necessary effort, and a vague dread of consequences were more than sufficient to deter him.

It had been a strange thing this marriage of his — a thing so sudden, so impulsive, that, as he thought, he marvelled at it. This woman by his side, her full-lipped mouth quivering with an expression that he disliked — all at once,

newspapers, etc. The waltz, 'the most popular ballroom dance of the nineteenth century', was energetically promoted by the enterprising Strauss family, Johann (1804–1849) and his sons, Johann, Joseph, and Eduard, who elevated the Viennese Waltz in particular to a 'consummate form' (*New Grove Dictionary of Music and Musicians*, ed. by Stanley Sadie, 29 vols (London: Macmillan, 2001), XXVII, p. 72).

[13]   This refers to the Crystal Palace: designed for the Great Exhibition of 1851, it was rebuilt in 1852–1854 at Sydenham Hill, south London, and destroyed by fire in 1936.

she seemed no longer near him; but, from a distance, as it were, he was looking at her as one looks upon a stranger — a stranger who had come into his life and who was changing it all for him.

Back his thoughts drifted to his unfinished book, and the craving for work returned, coming as a great relief. Tomorrow morning he would start again. There were passages, especially in the last chapter, that sadly needed revision. Yes, tonight he would begin. And, all at once, a whole multitude of ideas, leaping up, chased one another across his brain. Expressionless his eyes stared out across the crowd, while a wonderful intuition seemed for a moment to lay bare the whole secret of his life. But it was for a moment only, gloriously it all flitted past and was gone.

He rose.

"Shall we go home?" Letty asked. There was a note of penitent tenderness in her voice.

"Yes, I want to look over a manuscript. I'm going to begin work again tomorrow morning. Come, this is the shortest way. We can get a cab at the entrance."

"Oh! my Oswald," she exclaimed, "I *am* glad. You will talk it all over with me, just as you used to do before, in the old days, won't you? That will be splendid. And I will help you — ever so much. Listen, I've thought of something. Do you remember how once you said to me that ideas came to you in talking, but that when you tried to write them down, they all slipped away? Well, you shall talk to me, I will write it all down. I can write quite quickly enough, I'm sure. I used to take down articles like that years ago at the office, when they were in a hurry. That will help you, won't it?"

They had left the gardens and were walking rapidly down the main hall, she, her face lit up to excited radiancy, he, preoccupied, frowning a little.

VII

The next morning, when she awoke, he was already dressed and gone. Should she slip on a dressing-gown and go to him? Not just yet — presently; for she shrank from the reality that awaited her. So she lay on in bed, and closing her eyes, half asleep and half awake, dreamed that they were together on a desert island and that he was loving her in a new, wonderful way. After awhile she awoke more completely, and she grew restlessly curious to find out what he was doing.

Breakfast was ready in the little dining-room, but only a single place was laid.

"Mr. Nowell's writing in his room, ma'am, and he said he shouldn't want no breakfast, and that he mustn't be disturbed," explained the servant.

She sat down; but beyond a cup of tea and half a slice of dry toast, she could eat nothing.

A mental pain, dull at first, growing in intensity as she brooded over it, was settling down upon her. This was the first time that she had breakfasted alone since their marriage: so he did not want her — yet last night, when she had proposed that she should help him — no, it struck her now that he had made no movement of assent. And she had somehow taken for granted that he would like it. How happy the thought of it had made her. For a long while as he slept heavily by her side, she had lain awake thinking of it in a state of excited happiness. "He mustn't be disturbed" — that was his message. All at once, tumultuously, her wounded pride rose within her. He did not want her — she, who had loved him — ah! how she had loved him. There was nothing she would not have done for him; and he scorned it all — who was he to treat her in this way? She had thrown herself away on him — he did not care for her, not a bit; a dozen small signs of his indifference occurred to her. Why had he married her, then? Oh! why had he made her love him, since he did not care for her? And in bitter, reckless desire for self-inflicted pain, she strove to conjure up all the silly day-dreams she had had about him.

Then, of a sudden, her mood changed. Her love for him, pent up and unsatisfied, cried out in anguish, "Oswald, Oswald," and big teardrops rolled down her cheeks. "Come to me, my Oswald, you are the whole world to me." Yes, she would go to him and tell him all; she would break down this barrier that lay between them. But not now. He was at work. She must not disturb him. He would not like it. Perhaps he would answer her crossly. And, with a rush, her pride broke forth again, fiercer this time. Thus, while the hands of the clock slipped round, they wrangled together, her wounded pride and her wounded love.

*   *   *   *   *

"Mr. Nowell says you needn't wait lunch for him, ma'am; I've just taken him some coffee and bread-and-butter, and he says he won't want anything more till tea-time."

*   *   *   *   *

Tea-time — so he meant to stop work at tea-time — nearly four hours to wait. A quarter of an hour of it she killed, trying to eat some luncheon. After this she fetched her bonnet and went out, wandering disconsolately down the Embankment.[14] Unconsciously she took the way along which she had walked so often with him. And her thoughts were very bitter.

[14]   The Embankment was constructed between 1868 and 1874 to run alongside the north side of the river Thames in west London. By the 1890s it had become something of a magnet for the city's homeless and destitute. It is sadly appropriate that Letty finds herself 'wandering disconsolately' along it.

*   *   *   *   *

With Oswald hour after hour was slipping by — only the scratching of the pen, and the tick-tick of the clock. How good he felt, as two or three times he leant back, stretching his arms, back to the regular grind after the nerve-exasperating idleness of the past weeks! Then he would turn to again.

As for Letty, her image never once crossed his mind. Outside the work in which, with the exhilaration of new-found freedom, he was revelling, he had forgotten everything; all things were alike.

When he had finished, he strolled downstairs and out into the street, never looking to see what she was doing. The summer evening was clear and cool, the roadway glowed like a track of beaten gold, and his brain, lazily drinking it all in, sank into a delicious torpor.

*   *   *   *   *

About five o'clock he came in. Letty was already drinking her tea; she had not waited for him. She gave him no word of greeting; only a look expressive, as a woman alone can give.

But he noticed nothing; he did not even remember that he had not spoken to her before that day.

"It's been splendid," he broke out. "Splendid. I feel a different man."

"Your tea is getting cold," she answered in icy exasperation.

"I've written that last chapter from beginning to end, and nearly finished another one," he went on, taking up the cup, "there's a real rhythm about the last three pages."

"The muffin is down by the fire."

"Look here," putting down his tea untasted, "I'll just fetch them and read them."

In a minute he was back again, the manuscript in his hand.

He walked up and down, trying the sound of the sentences sometimes over and over again before passing on to the next, or appealing to her as to the justness of a word or continuing without waiting for her verdict.

The scene in her own old little room underneath, the evening that he had asked her to marry him, came back to Letty. She felt that she could bear it no longer, but, with a last effort, clenching her teeth, she restrained herself.

When he had finished he turned to her:

"Well?"

But there was no answer from the white, set face.

"Come, say something," he went on almost roughly.

Slowly her head began to droop, the lips pressed tighter and tighter together, till they were quite bloodless. Suddenly, burying her face in her hands, she burst into a passionate fit of sobbing.

"What on earth's the matter with you?" he exclaimed, making no attempt to conceal his annoyance.

"Can't you see?" she burst out. "Are you as heartless as that?"

"Heartless! What do you mean? Whatever do you want?"

"Oh! nothing," she answered in a hard voice, and there the conversation ended; a few minutes afterwards he went back to his study.

VIII

After this, in grim serenity, a whole month passed, while the breach between them steadily widened. On Letty's part all signs of the smouldering fire within her disappeared beneath a permanent attitude of chilly apathy. By a mutual, tacit understanding neither spoke to the other, beyond attempting now and then some forced commonplace remark, when the tension of silence became especially intolerable. But even this pretence of intercourse was rare, for, except during the evening meal, they were never together. And, as often as not, Letty would sit with an open book before her plate, taking refuge in the old habit of reading, which she had dropped since her marriage.

All this while, the fever of creation was consuming Oswald more rapidly than it had ever done before. In a sort of blind recklessness, fostered, at first, to a considerable extent by an instinctive striving to forget the strain of the daily life with Letty, he would shut himself up in his study every morning, and struggle on till evening, with scarcely any food, till his eyes throbbed and it seemed that endless regiments of heavy soldiers were tramping across his brain. When he had done, he would lie in his armchair, a helpless prey to fits of depression, inexplicable as it seemed to him, but which were in reality the reaction that inevitably followed the long hours of cerebral excitement. The effort required to seat himself each morning at his writing-table grew greater and greater, and the progress achieved was each day less and less. His brain under the continual, accumulated strain, became impotent with exhaustion, and he would sit for hours, feebly grappling with a single sentence.

Letty never appeared to observe that anything was the matter with him; she made no comment when his appetite grew smaller and smaller. Only once, as he furtively glanced across the table at her, he perceived that she was scrutinising him with a strange, searching look that he did not understand.

And, with the acute sensitiveness of an over-strained nervous system, he grew to hate this half-hour face to face with her over the evening meal; in her presence he felt painfully uneasy, as if there were hanging over his head a storm, which, at any moment, might break and overwhelm him. So that every time she began to speak to him, he was conscious of a spasm of alarm; and all through the day, the dread of meeting her was present in his mind.

One evening — he had been working later than usual — when the servant came in to tell him that dinner was ready, and that Letty had already begun, he felt that he could bear it no longer. He waited till the girl was gone back to the kitchen; then crept stealthily along the passage, took down his hat from the peg behind the door, and hurried out down the stairs, into the street.

From the river came a fresh breeze. Before he had walked a dozen yards, his brain began to reel, and a black mist floated before his eyes. He clutched at a railing to steady himself, and crawled onto an eating-house round the corner.

The place was sordid-looking and far from cleanly, and a hot smell of cooking pervaded it. Oswald found his way to one of the narrow tables covered with greasy and yellow oilcloth and sat down. Presently a young man, in his shirt-sleeves, fetched him from the counter at the far end a steaming plateful of hot food. Oswald began to eat feebly, glancing up at the door between each mouthful. Letty! if she should come and find him out here; and he fancied she was standing before him, beckoning to him to follow her. His fork slipped from his hand. He was asleep over his food.

He awoke with a start; someone was shaking him roughly by the shoulders. It was the young man in his shirt-sleeves who had waited upon him. The room was empty, and all the lights but one had been extinguished. With a shiver, Oswald rose and went home, slinking up the stairs of the flats. All was dark; Letty had gone to bed. For the first time since their marriage, he unlocked the door of the room where he had always slept in the old days. And, fetching some blankets from a cupboard, he arranged them, as best he could, on the narrow bedstead.

So that now they were separated day and night.

The next day Letty expressed no surprise at his behaviour, and that evening and each following evening, he went out to the eating-house round the corner, sitting there stupidly over his food, till the young man in his shirt-sleeves turned out the lights.

And as time went on the thought of death began to haunt him till it became a constant obsession. In the daytime, fascinated by it, he would lay down his pen and sit brooding on it; at night, he would lie tossing feverishly from side to side, with the blackness that was awaiting ever before him. And with the sickly light of the early morning, there met him the early relief of having dragged on one day nearer the end.

IX

"Don't go out this evening. I ask you to stay in to dinner. I have a particular reason."

She was standing in the doorway of his study, on her face a look of infinite pleading, strangely out of harmony with the stiffness of her phrases.

All day he had been writing, squandering in a sort of fierce delight the last desperate rally of his brain, and now that he felt his strength to be running low, goading himself on with pitiless obstinacy.

After she had spoken, there was silence, for he could not immediately transfer his thoughts to what she had said. When at last he did so, it was in savage irritation that he answered:

"I can't — I don't know — I'm busy."

* * * * *

An hour and a half later the servant came in to tell him that his wife was waiting dinner for him. The phase of irritability was gone. With weary docility he collected the scattered sheets of paper and followed her into the dining-room, the manuscript in his hand.

He was unaware whether the expression with which she greeted him was angry or pained, for he never looked at her. Without a word he walked straight to his place and sat down. Putting the manuscript on his plate, he began mechanically to turn over the pages. In a few minutes he ceased, and leant back wearily in his chair.

* * * * *

A long while, a short while, he knew not which, and consciousness began to return. A white table before him — a half finished pudding. He was alone; she had gone. The manuscript! — surely he had had it in front of him. Where is it? — gone! He looked up, and the first thing that met his glance was Letty, her face half turned away from him, evidently unaware that he was awake, on her lap the manuscript. Presently the crackling sound of crumbling paper, next, the harsh noise of tearing; she was tearing it, slowly, deliberately. Then, again and again; it was with a sort of frenzied fierceness that she was tearing now, and the fragments were fluttering onto the floor. She stood upright, and quickly, without heeding him, went past.

It was dead; she had killed it — this was the end. He picked up some of the fragments, handling them gently, tenderly almost. A wild look came into his face: he followed her out of the room.

* * * * *

Softly he pushed the door open, and stood, in hesitation, on the threshold. From below, through the open window, came the rattle of wheels and an instant after the distant wail of a steam-tug.[15] The room was almost dark, only the dim night-light from outside. Yet he was quite familiar with its arrangement, and this somehow astonished him a little. Almost simultaneously two thoughts occurred to him. That it was a long time since he had been inside the room, and that he had slept there with her many nights. Where was she? Suddenly, quite close to him, so close that he shuddered, the sound of heavy breathing. It was she. He could see her huddled form, shapeless in the dark, crouching by the bedside. The rumble of wheels died away, the noise of her breathing grew in intensity till it filled the whole room.

Holding his breath in dread lest she should discover him, he peered through the obscurity at her. By degrees he perceived that she was kneeling with her head buried between her two arms, which were stretched out straight on the bed in front of her. Then, a queer muffled sound, breaking in upon the stillness — she was speaking, and his fingers closed on the door handle.

"Oh God! Merciful God! Listen to me; hear me. Almighty God! They say that Thou helpest people who are in trouble. Surely it cannot be much to Thee just to help me. Dear God! (here she began to sob) I cannot bear it any longer, indeed I cannot. Bring him back to me, God, just for a moment. I wanted him. Oh, how I wanted him! And I will give up my whole life to You. I swear it, my whole life shall be Yours. I have been wicked, very wicked in the past. Give me this one thing, and I will do whatever Thou wishest. Almighty, merciful God, say that You will help me!"

For a while her sobs choked her utterance. Oswald's fingers pressed tighter and tighter on the door-handle. She broke out again:

"Oswald, my Oswald, come back to me. Oswald, Oswald, my husband, speak to me — oh! speak to me, just one little word. What have I done that you will not speak to me? What is it that has taken you from me? Oh! I want you, I want your love. Oswald, my Oswald, I cannot live without it. Come back to me, come back to me. I cannot bear it any longer. It is killing me. Oh! it is killing me. If only it could be."

X

He stood in the middle of the suspension bridge, peering down through the iron-work at the river.

A long fall through the air — the water black, cold and slimy, the rush down his throat, the fight for breath, to sink down, down at once, and the yearning for the peace of death swept through him.

Could he crawl through the iron-work? No, it was too small. And someone might see him. He must clamber over, quickly. As he looked round him to see if

[15]   A steam-tug is a small, powerful steamboat used to tow other vessels.

he were observed, his eyes fell on a heap of flints a few yards off, where the road was under repair. He went up to it, and stooping down, began, with the feeble slowness of an old man, to fill his pockets with the stones. Then he went back to the bridge edge, and gripping the stanchions,[16] prepared to swing himself onto the top of them. As he did so, a blackness filled his eyes; a dull thud; his body dropped back on to the roadway — dead.

[16]   Stanchions are fixed vertical bars or poles used as supports.

The Struggle for Life

It was a chilly October night in a notorious "den" beyond the water — since closed by the police.[1]

Half a dozen gross gas-jets lit up the long, low room, making a procession of queer-shaped shadows dance restlessly about the walls: here and there, dotted about, crudely coloured chromos of the Queen, the Prince of Wales, and one or two half-naked prize-fighters.[2]

It was a Saturday night, so the place was quite full — bargemen with grimy furrows across their bronzed faces; plenty of typical river casuals sucking stumpy clay-pipes; in a corner a group of pasty-faced youths quarrelling over their greasy cards; and scattered about the room some riverside prostitutes, their cheap finery all bedraggled with mud. A veritable Babel rose from these dregs of a population — hoarse laughter, snatches of songs and oaths.[3]

It was hot: a foul, unhealthy heat; the very walls were sweating, and a bluish haze was filling the room up to the blackened ceiling.

I was vainly looking about me for a seat, when a mason, whose corduroys were still white with lime, pulled my arm and motioned me to a place next him, at the same time lifting the woman who was occupying it onto his knees.

Then he began again to beat the table, with an empty pewter-pot, to the refrain of a popular song.[4] At intervals he would stop, grin across at me, and hug his companion.

She, too, was young: perhaps she had been striking-looking once; at least her eyes were still fine, but the lips were shapeless, the voice was hoarse and overpitched, and the complexion was muddy-coloured. I was watching this typical couple, when suddenly I heard a plaintive voice behind me.

A girl stood there, death-white, with dark rings round her eyes. The corners of her bloodless lips were quivering, as though she were in great pain.

"Jack," murmured the plaintive voice, "ain't yer comin' back?"

The mason looked across at her with drunken solemnity, shrugged his shoulders, and put his arms round the woman on his knees.

In one flash the eyes of the two women met; of a sudden the whole expression of the young girl's face changed. Like wild beasts, they glared at each other: the one, with all the exasperated fury of interrupted appetite; the other, with the instinctive desperate hatred of a mother defending her young.

---

[1] Den: a hollow or cavern used as a hideout, or a resort of criminals and, here, opium den — a setting of abjection and illegality.

[2] Chromos: short for chromolithographs, coloured prints produced by lithography, a method of printing from a metal or stone surface.

[3] See note 10 on p. 87.

[4] A pewter-pot or pewter: a drinking vessel made of a grey alloy of tin and lead.

She clutched at a pewter-pot as if to fling it in her rival's face, but the impulse passed away, and letting it fall listlessly, she turned again to the mason and said in the same, plaintive voice:

"Jack, come along, do."

"'Ee knows when 'ee's well off, my dear," said the prostitute, pursing up her heavy lips and offering them to her companion.

"At least give us some money," went on the other, "the kids ain't touched a bit since morning, and I've nothing."

The mason, by this time exasperated, burst out, bringing his fist down on the table:

"Go to hell!"

"But baby'll die, if she don't get something," persisted the girl.

A hoarse laugh from the prostitute was all the reply.

This little scene was beginning to attract the attention of the occupants of the surrounding tables — the gambling group in the corner threw down their cards at the prospect of a fight; two women opposite began to jeer.

Whiter than ever, the girl stood there, braving them all; then dropping her head, she ran out of the room like a hunted animal. I had already left my seat and was watching the scene from the doorway. When the girl passed out, I followed her, curious to see the end of it.

She hurried along, through the ill-lit streets till she came to the river.

It was a starless night, but the full moon had just risen from behind the thin, headless necks of a cluster of chimneys which stood out black against the lurid glow reflected by the lights of the city; across the river lay a ragged pathway of quivering, silver light.

There was an uncanny stillness about the spot. The water flowed sluggishly, stealthily by; not a sign of life on board the black hulks[5] moored to the banks, only from the distance came the feverish rumble of the great city.

A cab was crawling up, its yellow lamps gleaming like the round eyes of some great night beetle; nearer, at the street corner, a policeman and a woman stood talking. The girl, crossing the road, made straight for the river; and the policeman turned to follow her. She stopped when she came to the edge, for she saw the policeman was close behind her; leaning against the parapet she stared down at the water, her head between her hands.

I passed close by her. The moonlight made her pinched face seem whiter than ever.

I sat down on a bench a few yards off and waited.

Presently, the small, black figure of a man came slinking along under the wall. When he saw the girl leaning over the parapet, he stopped and went slowly up to her.

[5]   Hulks are cargo ships.

He passed behind her, turned, and passed again. She had not stirred. He was now standing by her side, examining her from head to foot, cynically, as a horse-dealer examines a horse. Presently he put his hand on her arm and spoke to her.

I could not hear what they were saying; but I saw the girl shake her head several times, while the other seemed to be speaking very fast.

After a while, they moved away together, and as they passed in front of the bench where I was sitting, I heard her saying in a broken voice:

"Half a crown then,[6] and I can go home in an hour."

---

[6]   A half-crown was worth two shillings and sixpence, a fourteenth of what the average male worker earned in the 1890s, which was 35s (i.e. 1.75 pounds) per week.

Dissolving View[1]

In a low, roomy armchair, puffing gently at a long-stemmed pipe, Vivian Marston was listening to the wail of the wind as it swept fitfully down the street, complacently pitying the wretches who, cut by its blast, were shivering outside, this bleak November evening. Slowly his eyes travelled round the luxuriously furnished room, every detail of which reminded him of his own cosiness, and he became conscious of a vague glow of internal satisfaction. Resting his feet on the fender-bar, he began to think of himself.

Leisurely he recapitulated all that conduced to his self-satisfaction. His silky hair, which one woman had liked to stroke; his large, grey eyes, "expressive," another had called them; his money it pleased him to remember that he was rich, richer even than most rich people; next, how his new hunter,[2] thanks to the excellent line he had taken, had shown the whole field the way on Saturday, and how, last week, he had crumpled up pheasant after pheasant in a tearing wind, when the others couldn't touch them; last, of Gwynnie, the biggest triumph of all, Gwynnie, his Gwynnie, whom he was going to marry in the spring. And before him defiled, in a grotesque procession, all the men who wanted to marry her; each one, as he passed, looking up in jealous admiration.

From Gwynnie, his thoughts wandered to the others to whom he had made love before her. And a gentle, sentimental melancholy, which was delicious, stole over him. The images of most of them were blurred, half-effaced by time; one alone remained clear-cut. Many weeks it was since he had thought of her, for there was nothing in his life now to remind him of her. She was only a little chorus-girl, yellow-eyed and freckled, with a cracked voice that grated on the ear. He wondered, looking back over it all, what had been the link between them. Perhaps her splendid masses of hair, dark chestnut shot with gold; perhaps her quaint, clinging winsomeness. Towards the end she had grown capricious and fretful, and he had tired considerably of her; but that he did not remember. Only he heard once again the small imperfect voice raised in anger, as they stood together the last evening in the narrow, theatre corridor, with the single gas jet flaring behind. The next day she was gone, with a Frenchman who played third fiddle in the orchestra, so they said. And Vivian, the first moment of pique over, forgot her. With curious ease she dropped out of his life. At the

---

[1] 'Dissolving Views' (the forerunner of the cinematic 'dissolve') were a popular type of nineteenth-century magic lantern show exhibiting a gradual transition from one projected image to another: projectionists, or 'lanternists', used specially designed lantern slides to create the illusion of movement, as in day into night, or a winter scene into a summer one. The image applies to Marston's facile capacity for burying or dissolving his encounter with, and attraction to, the abject real, in the person of his working-class mistress.
[2] A hunter is a horse used for hunting.

end of a week the gap she had left was scarce perceptible. All that happened ten months ago.

He unlocked a drawer in the writing-table, and took from it a packet of letters — ten or perhaps a dozen in all, and three of them much longer than the rest. These last she had written in the autumn when he was away in the Mediterranean yachting. One after the other he read them, and, as he did so, a curious uncomfortable feeling crept over him. The vision of the thick, rich hair, encircling the yellow eyes, and little freckled face, seemed to change, charged with new meaning. Between the lines he began to read all that the misspelt scrawlings on these cheap, shiny half-sheets of notepaper had meant for her. He remembered how their illegibility had used to amuse him, and he was puzzled that he had not understood them then as he did now. There was one, worse written than the others, full of reproaches, that she had not seen him for three days. After that he read no more, but impatiently threw the packet into the blazing grate.

He lit another pipe, and for some little time more sat on exasperated, trying to force his thoughts into another channel.

*   *   *   *   *

96 Paxton Street, W.C.
Sunday.

"DEAR VIV,

"i am very ill the Dr says i shall get better but it is not true. i have got a little boy he was born last tusday you are his farther so you will see to him when i am ded will you not dear Viv. Louis is gone to Parris he was mad because of the child. Viv dear for the sake of old times com and see me gest once it is not a grand place were i am but i do long to see your dear face again. Plese Viv forgiv me for going of with Louis but i thought you did not care for me anny more and it made me mad i am sending this to the old adress i hope you will get it alright.

"Your loving

"KIT."

Motionless, he was staring at the sheet of paper in his hand. He could not think; stunned, his brain refused to function. Thus a whole minute passed. At last, mechanically, he picked up the envelope which was lying on the breakfast-table. He turned it over, absently at first, but, with returning consciousness, he noticed that there were two addresses on it; it must have been forwarded from his old lodgings, and, looking closer, he saw that one of the postmarks was nearly a month old. Once more he read the letter through, then again, and then a third time. Gradually a dizzy faintness and a sickening feeling in his stomach came over him. The air seemed close and stifling, but he had not the strength to cross the room to open the window. He sat down feebly by the fire, and, as he did so, he became aware that his hands were clammy with perspiration.

A moment or two and it passed. His thoughts were liberated; he was able to think again.

Kit was dying; by this time perhaps dead. Kit dead — stiff and cold between white sheets, lying flat all but her feet, which, upright, projected at the foot of the bed, her face expressionless, the freckles yellower than ever against the death-pale skin. And the child? He felt a thrill of exasperation against the useless, unwanted child. But it was his child — then it was he who —

Suddenly the door opened. He started, every nerve in his body tingling. It was the servant bringing in his breakfast. The man set down the shining covers and steaming coffee-urn, while Vivian, half-dazed, watched him curiously, for there seemed something strangely unreal about his unconcernedness.

At last he moved towards the door.

"Get me a cab," said Vivian, huskily. Then perceiving the astonished look on the man's face, he added hurriedly:

"I have to go out — at once — important business."

* * * * *

As the hansom[3] rolled along, Vivian's thoughts rushed back over the past. Incident after incident crowded up in his memory, and this hideous sequel to his love for Kit gave to each a new, ugly significance. It was the culmination towards which all the rest pointed. The cab shot past an omnibus lumbering city-ward, and he found himself marvelling at the difference between the people seated inside it and him. Surely they had never had things like this in their lives. And his thoughts writhed under the increasing pain — then, a quick twinge of hunger, reminding him that he had had no breakfast. Back came the object of his journey. He was going to see Kit. It was as if he and she had never had anything in common, as if he only knew of her by hearsay — but somehow, she and her child had spoilt everything for him. And he understood how he hated going, how he shrunk from bringing her back into his life. But for the irresistible force inside him, urging him forward, he would have turned homeward again. Gwynnie, how could he marry her after this? Strange that he felt no anger against Kit, for having come between them, only he wondered vaguely if it would be easy to get rid of her. But perhaps she was dead — oh! to

---

[3]   See note 7 on p. 84.

know for certain that it was so; and the sense of relief, which he knew to be a delusion, was so keen that it hurt him. But the child? — the child — that would live on. They always did. Gloomily, incoherently, he brooded over what was to be done with it.

The cab turned into a side street, scattering some squalid children from off the narrow, asphalted road. There was an untidiness about the neighbourhood, an untidiness that was almost indecent, the untidiness of a bed that has been slept in. Here and there, in the doorways, lounged slatternly women in dirty, colourless petticoats. As the cab passed they looked up, and under their gaze, Vivian winced. All the repulsive features of the neighbourhood stared him brutally in the face. Surely it must be close now? Here? The hansom pulled up before a dingy Italian restaurant: the driver was asking the way of some men smoking cigarettes before the door. They were foreigners, and answered him, all speaking at once, with gestures. A spasm of impotent rage passed over Vivian: he could almost have struck them. The cab moved slowly along: then stopped again at the end of the street. Vivian got out.

He knocked, and, before the narrow seedy-looking door, stood waiting. His excitement made his teeth chatter as with cold. This annoyed him, and, in the struggle to divert his thoughts, he forced himself to take stock of the house. There was nothing peculiar about it; its sordidness was neither greater nor less than that of those next to it or opposite to it. Only across the ground-floor window there stretched a card bearing the words "Apartments."

Kit was inside this house: perhaps in the very room into which he could almost see from the doorstep. He imagined himself arguing with her, persuading her, reminding her of the old days, giving her money — a large sum of money, the loss of which he would not feel — enough to make her and the child comfortable for life — doing anything and everything to get her to go away at once, to some spot where he would never even hear of her again. Surely she would agree to that. It would be for her own benefit, quite as much as for his. Yes, after all, he would be doing the handsome thing by her, and for an instant, he deluded himself into a glimmer of self-satisfaction.

The sound of a voice, breaking the train of his thoughts — in the area below a grimy woman, her sleeves rolled back over her red arms.

"Well, what d'yer want?" she asked, defiantly.

"I want to see Miss Gilston."

"Thur ain't no Miss Gilston livin' 'ere," she called back fiercely, evidently angry at having been disturbed for nothing. She prepared to re-enter the house.

"But," Vivian went on, "didn't she — about a month ago."

"No, I tell yer, I ain't 'ad no Miss Gilston 'ere. Thur was a Mrs. Marston" — at the sound of his own name shouted up through the area railings, Vivian's hands clenched and instinctively he glanced up the street to see if anyone was within ear-shot — "a few weeks back, but she was took ill with a baby, and she died, poor soul."

Mrs. Marston — his name — she had taken it then, — and his head began to swim a little — but she was dead — dead — gone — dead!

"What's become of the child?" he heard himself asking. The sound of his own voice startled him, for he did not recognise it.

"The baby died along with 'er," shouted the woman. "She didn't leave a blessed sixpence behind 'er. Two week and a arf rent she owed me, besides 'er food, all sorts of delictasses[4] I used to git for 'er." Then with a change of tone, perhaps desirous of a gossip, perhaps struck by Vivian's prosperous appearance, "Jest wait a minute. I'll come up and tell yer all about it."

He was leaning against the area railings, scarcely hearing what she was saying, conscious only of the immense relief that was creeping over him. The child dead too. Both of them gone for ever. He became aware that the high-pitched voice had ceased; the woman had left the area. And he looked feebly around for her, the monotonous squalor of the close-packed, brown-brick houses hurt him more than before — oh! to get out of it, away from it, quickly, at once. Kit — it was as if she had never existed. It was like an episode in another man's life.

With a sudden, imperious impulse, he left the doorstep and walked rapidly away down the street.

Twenty minutes later he was seated before his breakfast-table, eating voraciously; for the morning excursion had given him a splendid appetite.

*　*　*　*　*

A month afterwards, Gwynnie and he were married. It was a smart wedding. There was a fashionable crowd, and the couple started to spend their honeymoon in Italy.

---

[4]　Delictasses are delicacies.

A Dead Woman

I

"Mary, two bitters and a small Scotch to the Commercial Room, and a large Irish[1] for Mr. Hays here."

"Yes, Mr. Rushout," answered the girl, measuring out the spirit and swinging down the silver-knobbed handles.

Then she whisked herself out of the room, and the two men were alone. Neither spoke, but their silence evidently resulted from no constraint; it was quite natural that each should be all content with his own thoughts.

There was no mistaking the dejection of Rushout, the landlord. His corpulent and unwieldy frame lay inert; the features of his smooth, congested face hung limp in gloomy abstraction.

Opposite him, stiffly upright on the edge of his chair, sat Jonathan Hays, bony and gaunt in his rough frieze coat, corduroy leggings and iron-bound boots, while his bushy, red hair and untrimmed beard added not a little to the uncouthness of his appearance.

One end of the room gave on to the entrance of the inn, through a window, across which stretched the broad, brown shelf that did duty for the bar. On either side of this opening were ranged row upon row of glasses, of all shapes and sizes, and all along the edges of the shelves were suspended glistening pewter mugs. Sporting prints, a rack-full of walking sticks and hunting crops, a large coloured almanack,[2] some pictures of fattened sheep and cattle, illustrating the results of using certain artificial foods, adorned the rest of the room. In the grate glowed a lavish fire, before which a cat lay curled.

"Are ye takin' nothin' yeself?" asked Jonathan, as he filled up his glass from the water-bottle. "Have a drop o' port: it'll cheer ye, maybe."

Rushout made a faint sign of dissent.

"Ye're for a smoke then," persisted the other, producing a battered tin box, half full of tobacco.

"Nay, I've lost all inclination for't."

The farmer pulled out a blackened pipe and filled it with slow precision. He had all but finished when there burst down the passage a strident guffaw of laughter.

"That'll be Mike, I'll swear." "Ay," Rushout replied listlessly.

"How's t' house doing, Richard?" asked Jonathan.

"Middlin'."

---

[1]   Scotch is whisky distilled in Scotland; Irish is whiskey distilled in Ireland.

[2]   An almanack (almanac) is a yearly calendar giving statistical information on events and phenomena.

The other drank and sucked his moustache appreciatively.

"Jonathan," Rushout began.

"Well?"

"It'll be a twelvemonth today."

"Ay, sure, that it be," and he started all at once to puff vigorously at his pipe. "Ay, jest a twelvemonth. Lord, how time flies! It don't seem as it was last back end, do it? Ye'll best be soon looking about ye, Richard. T' house can never prosper while there be no missus, and jest to look at that broomstick woman ye've got now is sufficient to drive even Mike over the way. I tell ye man, ye'll have to bestir yeself," he continued, raising his voice as he saw that his words had produced no effect on the other's apathy, "the custom'll go to pieces, right off, mark my words."

And, with an air of profound conviction, he repeated, "Mark my words, Richard."

"Jonathan," said Rushout presently, "I'm partin' with the white mare."

"What? — not ——"

"Ay, *her* mare. She be jest spoilin' herself in stable and I can't abide drivin' her myself."

"Who's for buy in' her?"

"Dr. Wilkinson. He was in this mornin' about her."

"What're ye askin'?"

"Forty-five."

Once more they both relapsed into silence. It was again Rushout who spoke first.

"Jonathan, it's a twelvemonth today. I'm goin' to drink to her soul." He drained the wineglass to the dregs and set it down again with almost reverent precaution. The other stared at him in stolid astonishment; then mutely raised his glass to his lips and did likewise. The glances of the two men met, and parted again hastily. It was as if the one had detected the other in some secret deed. The publican obstinately examined the fire; the farmer toyed with his glass, rinsing the spirit round and round.

"Did ye part with them ewes?" asked Rushout. He was obviously struggling to appear unconcerned; but the huskiness of his utterances belied the effort.

"Every one of them. 'Twas a good job too; they were always a troublesome lot."

"Jonathan, do ye believe in ghosts?" A shout of laughter from down the passage followed immediately on the question which was delivered in impressive solemnity.

The farmer took time before answering: the matter was too serious to be settled off-hand.

"I don't know but what I should, if I se'ed one," he said at last.

"It'll be near eleven likely?"

"It wants half an hour."

"I believe she'll come tonight."

Jonathan started violently; his clay pipe fell to the floor, smashing into a dozen pieces.

"Ye're a fool, Richard," he exclaimed, stooping forward and ruefully picking up the fragments.

"Ye never knew her when that likeness was taken," Rushout continued, pointing to a photograph surrounded by a deep black border, which hung on the wall. "I had it done jest after we were married. It's simply magnificent. That was when we kept the 'King's Head' at Dewston. She *was* a beauty in them days. Why the whole place was jest wild about her. And we'd ha' been married thirteen years come Martinmas.[3] God! it do take the life out of a man!" he concluded. His speech had grown thick, and the gurgle of a stifled sob sounded through the room.

Jonathan was engaged in fitting together the fragments of his broken pipe. Gradually his fingers stiffened, his eyebrows contracted, a sullen look swept over his face. He never raised his eyes but kept them fixed on his fingers. Next he blurted out, pushing back his chair roughly:

"I'll ha' to be gettin' home."

"Goodnight, old man," answered the other feebly, without moving.

Jonathan went out. In the passage he stumbled over his dog who lay across the doorway; with a vicious kick he sent him yelping into the street. The night was clear and frosty, and his footfall over the cobbles, as he strode away, broke with strange brutality the silence of the sleeping village.

II

The village shops were drowsily divesting themselves of their shutters, and the two or three loafers hanging about the parapet of the bridge over the river, their hands thrust deep in their trouser pockets, were stolidly watching the rickety one-horsed omnibus as it rattled past on its way to meet the early train, when Jonathan, his collie at his heels, swung round the corner.

One of the men on the bridge jerked a "marnin'" at him as he strode by; then he had passed, and through the swing door of the "Bear," disappeared.

Inside, the discordant note of a woman's angry voice met his ear. "It was that 'broomstick woman' giving it to the girl," he guessed. And so it was.

The flow of her wrath ceased when she caught sight of him; screwing up her

---

[3]   Martinmas is traditionally celebrated on 11 November, honouring the story of St Martin, patron saint of beggars and outcasts, who was known for bringing warmth and light to those in need.

ill-conditioned countenance into a caricature of a smile:

"Good morning, Mr. Hays; grand mornin' this," and turning to the girl cried: "Now what're ye standin' gapin' there for? Get along and see after that breakfast for the coffee-room."

"Ye do let her have it," remarked Jonathan dryly.

"Let her have it," she retorted, "let her have it. I should like to know who wouldn't let her have it, lazy, good-for-nothin' hussy. Her goin's on 'ud try the patience of a saint, and as for her impudence, why ——"

"Is t' master in?" interrupted Jonathan.

"In! In! Gracious! In! where d'ye think he'd be? In, indeed! Why it 'ud be a wonder if he's out o' bed yet. And for all the trouble he gives himself he might jest as well stay there. Jest settin' and mopin', the whole blessed day. Senseless, downright senseless. I call it. Ye'd think his wife had been a sort of female paragon, to see the way he behaves himself. *She* wasn't such a lot to mourn over, by all accounts. No better than she should be, and there he sets, moonin' and soakin'[4] like a great baby."

"Stop that jabberin'," shouted Jonathan, banging his stick down flat on the bar. "Ye know nought agin' her."

"Oh! I know nothin', don't I? Oh! very well, I know nothin'. No, of course I don't. How should I? Only let folks as pretends to have nothin' on their conscience and can't keep a civil tongue in their heads — let 'em look out, I say. I'll teach 'em to march in here with their airs and graces."

But of a sudden the rest died away on her lips, and snatching up a tray, she bounced down the passage into the kitchen. Jonathan faced about seeking the reason for her precipitate departure: behind him stood Rushout.

The landlord's vitality had perceptibly bettered since last night, for he sent an angry glance in the direction of the kitchen-door.

"Mornin'. I thought ye were off to the auction mart."[5]

"Nay, I thought better on't. There's scarce bit doin' jest now."

"Ye'll take a drop to warm ye. It's raw."

"Nay. I've come for a bit o' business."

"Ye're welcome, business or no business. Step inside."

He led the way into the room where they had sat the night before.

"Well," said Rushout, when he had settled down in his chair.

"I've come to buy t' mare."

"Not the white one?"

"Ay, that's her."

Rushout reflected: "What, in the name of goodness, d'ye want with her?"

"I want her," answered the farmer doggedly.

---

4 Soakin': drinking heavily.
5 Marts are markets.

"But what for?" testily retorted the other.

"Maybe I've taken a fancy to her."

Rushout's face broadened to a smile.

"Are ye lookin' for a bit of blood to spank ye to church?"[6]

"Never ye mind, Richard. It's none o' your business why I'm wantin' her," replied Jonathan, nettled.

"Well, it don't make much odds, anyway,[7] because ye can't have her."

"She's not gone yet?"

"Nay, she's not gone, but she's promised. I told Dr. Wilkinson he should have her. Ye know that."

"He's givin' ye forty-five."

Rushout nodded.

"I'll give ye fifty."

"I tell ye man, it's no good. The affair's concluded. Dr. Wilkinson's to have her. Why if I'd advertised her, I'd have got half that price again, and many a time over, easy. She's jest about the bonniest mare, for her size, I ever saw. And I'm determined Dr. Wilkinson shall have her, and cheap too; for (lowering his voice) there's not another doctor in the neighbourhood as would have done what he did for Jane."

"Settle yer own figure then, I'll give it ye. I'll make it a hundred," persisted Jonathan.

"Are ye crazy?"

"I tell ye I want her."

"And I tell ye, ye can't have her."

"When's she goin'?"

"Tomorrow mornin'."

"I'll come back this afternoon. Maybe ye'll have changed yer mind."

And, with that, he marched out into the street.

III

But neither that afternoon nor that evening did Jonathan return to the "Bear." For about sundown, while he was re-penning some sheep in a bare field all strewn with half-gnawed turnips, he heard the stride of the white mare pounding down the road towards him. Ay, t'was she: many a time had he waited before, listening for her action along the road. Behind, in his mustard-coloured ulster,[8] sat Dr. Wilkinson. On perceiving Jonathan, he reined up and called out over the hedge:

---

[6] Spank: that is, at a spanking (fast) pace.

[7] It don't make much odds: it doesn't matter.

[8] An ulster is a long overcoat.

"How are the sheep doing, Hays?"

"But the question fell unheeded on Jonathan's ears. He was surveying the mare — her legs, straight, slender, sinewy; her lithe and gracefully rounded body; her undersized head erect, neck arched, and ears cocked, while at regular intervals she shot out bars of breath from her quivering nostrils.

"Isn't she a beauty?" said the doctor, following Jonathan's gaze. "By Jove, she does take some driving, too. She hasn't been between the shafts these ten days. By the way she rushes at her work, you'd think she hadn't stretched her legs since poor Jane Rushout's death."

Jonathan did not answer, so the doctor continued:

"Ah! there wasn't a prettier whip this side of the county than poor Jane Rushout. It was a sad thing! And Richard's getting in a very bad way. I wish something could be done for him. He's got no spirit left — just as cut up as if it all happened yesterday. When I sent my man just now to fetch the mare, he was as overcome as if he were parting with an only child. It *was* a pity they never had any children."

The mare, who had been fidgeting with her bit, now began to paw the ground. The doctor, poking the rug under his legs with the whip-stock, lifted the reins preparatory to starting again.

"Hold hard, doctor," broke in Jonathan. He pushed fiercely through the hedge and laid one hand on the mare's neck, pressing his cheek against her nose and speaking softly and soothingly to her. This for a few seconds, till she tossed up her head, and he was forced to let her go.

"Good day, doctor."

"Good day to you, Hays."

Jonathan watched the retreating gig till it was gone round the corner; then, roughly brushing the back of his hand across his eyes, climbed back into the field. The sheep lifted their heads a moment and fell to nibbling the turnips again. Folding his arms across the top of a hurdle, he rested his chin on them, gazing straight out before him. His ruddy beard glowed as the light from the setting sun caught it, and the look of suppressed suffering on his face lent a curious refinement to its ruggedness. And the fantastic tracery of a couple of gnarled oaks stood out against the glare as of some burning city on the horizon.

IV

After this an obstinate combination of calamities made a busy time for Jonathan — an outbreak of sickness among his sheep, coupled with the unexpected departure of his shepherd, and the destruction of fence after fence by a sudden rising of the river; and as his energy, dogged, desperate almost at times, overcame one difficulty, a fresh one would discover itself.

Two miles away, in the village, the procession of eventless days defiled in sluggish regularity. Rushout rose from his bed in the morning only to lie torpid for hours before the fire in the little room behind the bar, now staring into the glowing coals, now sunk in stupid slumber.

At all hours the shrill voice of the "broomstick woman," as Jonathan had nicknamed her, grated on his ears, till he agreed with himself that she must go. Yet he took no step, procrastinating, first for one reason, then for another. Every hour saw his indifference to the mechanism of the little world around him take deeper root.

One morning, however, he was conscious that the wrangling voices in the kitchen waxed higher than usual, and presently Mary, the maid, stood before him, her cheeks aflame, and her voice tremulous with emotion. "She couldn't stop to be treated like dirt. She desired to give warning[9] — she had put up with it long enough." And when Rushout, remonstrating, endeavoured to soothe her, the girl, bursting into sobs, poured an elaborate, though spasmodic, category of the abuse, tyranny and insults to which she had been subjected. "It'd never ha' been so if the poor missus were here." And, at these words, Rushout felt all his apathy lift, like a curtain of fog, and the momentary recovery of his old self, stirred him strangely.

"There, there, lass; ye needna' fash yerself so," he said.[10] "I'll not part with ye. Faith! I'd sooner give her the sack this forenoon[11] right off, than lose ye."

And at the end of three or four such speeches the girl, pacified, returned to the kitchen.

She had not been gone a moment before the wrangle of voices recommenced, as fierce, nay fiercer, than before. Then the door burst open violently, and the other woman, her soured face, grotesque with passion, stalked into the room.

"I jest want to ask ye, Mr. Rushout, if ye told that girl just now that ye intended me to go sooner than her?"

"Ye're quite correct." He spoke with quiet determination that was not without dignity.

For nearly a minute she was unable to articulate a word.

"Then ye mean to signify that I'm to clear out to suit that chit of a gal."

"If ye can't give over frettin' agin her from mornin' till night," he answered. "She's a downright good girl, that she is; she's been with me these three years and a half, and I've had scarce a fault to find with her, and my wife had never a word agin her."

"Oh! that's it, is it? It's for that that ye're wanting to turn me off — me that's

---

[9]   To give warning, here, is to give notice to leave her employment.
[10]   Fash yerself is to get angry: from the French, *se fâcher*, it often appears in Scots dialect as 'dinna fash yersel the noo'.
[11]   Forenoon: the part of the day before noon, i.e. the morning.

slaved my soul out to keep the custom in the house, while ye lie soakin' over the fire. Yer wife never had a word to say agin' her — nothin' to say agin' her (mimicking Rushout's intonation). Where's the wonder? I'm not surprised. Of course she hadn't — she was too busy gallivanting about the country."

Rushout struggled to his feet, and advanced threateningly towards her.

"By God! ye dare to say another word agin' her. Ye jade, why ye aren't fit to scrape the dirt off her gig-wheels."[12]

"Ay, ye great, louting coward ye — ye'd be for strikin' me, wouldn't ye? But jest lay so much as yer little finger on me, and I'll have the law agin' ye. Who be ye to call me names? Jade, indeed! D'ye mean to insinuate that I'm not what I should be?"

"Nay, it 'd be powerful curious if ye'd ever had the chance." The adroitness of his retort pleased Rushout, restoring his self-possession.

The woman craned her neck, as if to break into a torrent of abuse; but her impulse changed. With deliberate and concentrated venom she began:

"Ye poor deluded fool, Richard Rushout! Ye little think how that doll-faced minx hocussed ye the minute yer back was turned. Ye little reckon the proper laughin'-stock she made of ye."

"Shut that sewer of a mouth," thundered Rushout. His wrath had trebled in intensity with its return flow, and the hue of his face darkened to an apoplectic purple.

But the woman was not to be silenced.

"I'll teach ye to throw mud at honest respectable women," she cried back, "a giddy, wanton thing she was, I tell ye. Did ye fancy she'd be satisfied with the boozing good-for-nothing that ye are."

"It's a blasted lie!"

"A lie, is it? Ye can spare me your filthy language, Richard Rushout. Ask Jonathan Hays if it's a lie. Ask Jonathan Hays if he never had his arms round her. Ask Jonathan Hays if he never ——"

A spasm of atrocious suffering convulsed Rushout's face — the poison was doing its work. Snatching at both her wrists, he wrenched her onto her knees.

"Ye'll not stop me — nay, not if ye beat my head in," she hissed. "I'll teach ye to throw mud at me. Ask Jonathan Hays, I tell ye. Ask him where she used to drive that high stepping horse of hers, when ye sat soakin' yeself with a roomful of sots.[13] Ask Jonathan Hays, I ——"

"Ye she-devil," shouted Richard, with a guttural cry of anguish, as he flung her into the passage.

Then dizzy and dazed, he dropped into a chair.

---

[12]   A jade is literally a 'worn-out horse', so applied to a woman it may also signify 'worn-out whore', hence the woman's umbrage below.
[13]   Sots are habitual drunkards.

V

Rushout never saw the woman again, though her voice resounded outside several times. He sent her out her wages and her railway fare back to Newcastle, whence she came, by Mary with a message that the omnibus would call to convey her luggage to the station. After which he ate his lunch, cold beef, beer and cheese, which was all quite tasteless. And early in the afternoon he heard her depart. The rumble of the omnibus died away in the distance bringing him real relief, for as long as her presence in the house continued to irritate the activity of his rage against her, he felt himself unable to settle down and grapple, face to face, with the new anguish of his doubt. And this he longed to do.

But now that all was still again, he unhooked the photograph from the wall and stood looking into the eyes, long and earnestly. They told him nothing. The guileless candour of their gaze seemed to exhale first tenderness, then mockery. Which was the truth? He set the photograph down on the table, and, going back to his chair, started to ransack the incidents of the past. "Where did she go when she went out driving?" the woman had said. "The white mare." And the first time that they had sat together behind her, the day after he had bought her, came back to him — a crisp, frosty morning, with the sunlight sparkling coldly on the whitened hedges. Next, another time, the week of the Agricultural Show; after lunch they had set off along the North Road to a farm where he had some business, she holding the reins, he smoking by her side. When they arrived, she had declined to come in, declaring that the mare was too hot to stand, and he, with a glow of pride at her work-manlike solicitude for the animal, why, he himself had asked her to take a message up to Jonathan's about some heifers he was entering for the President's prize. Perhaps — God! — and in his mind's eye he saw the two, locked in each other's arms. He watched the whole scene as it was played before him; she, giving herself with all the gestures and caresses with which he was familiar, till its vividness became almost unbearable. He lifted up the photograph once more. But underneath the faint smile lurked a wealth of smothered corruption; on the half-parted lips he detected the imprint of Jonathan's kisses. Hemmed in, as it were, on every side, he appealed as a last resource to the memories of all their common life; but these, obstinately blurred and confused, came not to the rescue, and his belief in her, losing foothold irrevocably, tumbled headlong into the abyss. Then by sheer intensity his desire to establish the certitude of her faithlessness was fulfilled. Fragments of conversations, chance meetings and exclamations, all were pregnant with damnatory clues. Even meaningless remarks he interpreted as fresh proofs of her guilt.

And if Jonathan, why not with others? With Mike, who was in and out of the house all day — with this and that acquaintance. On, on, the Satanic extravagance of his imagination whirled, till at the zenith of his agony, he was conscious that he loathed her virulently. This discovery made him uneasy, and by some quick, unaccountable process his mind wandered off to the advisability of giving a trial to a new blend of whisky, a prospectus of which had reached him that morning. For the moment, all else, receding into the background, was forgotten; outside this fresh track of thought his mind was a blank. The spirit was cheaper, certainly; but that would be balanced by heavier carriage, unless indeed, he ordered a large quantity. But he was not certain concerning the flavour. As he debated the matter with himself, the idea occurred to consult Jonathan. Immediately the full strength of his pain was upon him once more. And once more the whole round of self-torturing doubt recommenced, each time with a fresh crop of detail, new pretexts for suffering. That night in his longing for forgetfulness he went to bed drunk. And he had been sober for years.

VI

He made no effort to acquire fresh proofs. The seed of suspicion sprouted in his mind with the luxuriant growth of a noxious weed; and at the same time his devotion to his dead wife reasserted itself in all the earnestness of its profundity, so that he would turn without transition from the contemplation of her faithlessness to tender recollections of her personality. There was no lifting of the gloom of existence without her; day and night he longed for her; could she have returned he would have shared her with Jonathan willingly. In the sluggish meanderings of his mind he often faced such a contingency, and the consideration of it was in nowise painful. Jonathan — he had never settled with himself what attitude he should adopt when next they met; indeed, whether he felt any vindictiveness against him or not, he did not know. It was that he simply never considered him in the present, apart from his connection in the past with her who still was everything to him, connection of which now his certitude was quite absolute.

After a while it began to seem many days since he had seen him, and he fell to expecting that he would be in, day after day. That it was because Dr. Wilkinson had got the white mare, he guessed, and he resented no longer the other's anxiety to possess her, though the reason for it was now quite clear. And the thought that the doctor had got her, ceased to give him satisfaction; for he understood how carefully Jonathan would have treated her. He was sorry he had spoken so sharply to him about it.

In the mornings when he woke, then the depression lay heaviest, the fatigue at the joyless prospect of the day in front of him. He cared not a jot that the custom of the house was dwindling daily, that every corner revealed some sign of dirt and slovenliness. Everything outside his own bodily wants was growing indifferent to him. And the expectation of seeing Jonathan was the solitary daily event that remained.

One Sunday evening, about six o'clock, there began to fall, slowly, silently, big flakes of snow, so that by the time the congregation trooped out of the square-towered church the white carpet lay soft and thick on the ground. Rushout elbowed his way through the group, loitering in the porch, and buttoning up his coat, hurried down the street, as briskly as his ungainly gait permitted. As he pushed through the swing door of the "Bear" the first sound that struck his ear was Jonathan's voice:

"Ye can cart the load Tuesday forenoon," he was saying.

"Right, Mr. Hays, that'll suit," answered another voice.

Rushout walked straight into the commercial room, whence the sound came. As he entered the third man greeted him with the cordiality due to the landlord, but Jonathan remained silent. Rushout stood irresolute: the sight of his beard and pale face caused him an unexpected agitation. It brought back the past with, as it were, a change of perspective, that filled him with excitement. He discovered that there was something about Jonathan's physiognomy offensive, violently, imperiously. Yet it was not all at once that he realised this impression, so overwhelming was its unexpectedness.

Presently the third man bid them goodnight, and the door banged behind him.

Almost immediately Jonathan, awkward-looking in his ill-fitting Sunday suit and stiff, black hat, prepared to depart also.

"A wintry evening," he mumbled.

"Nay, ye cannot go," said Richard in a voice at once low and full of determination. And he blocked the doorway. "Sit ye down again."

The farmer obeyed. He turned his hat round and round on his lap: a twinge shot across his face and was gone. It was evident that he had guessed what was coming.

Then he waited, stolidly resigned. Rushout was still too agitated to determine where to begin. At last, when for a moment his astonishment got the better of his anger, he broke the silence with:

"How did she come to be fond of ye?"

Jonathan shifted his feet in noisy uneasiness.

"It commenced with the Foresters' picnic, three years ago."

"Where did ye used to see her?"

"At Coney Standish's old cottage, along the North Road."

The blow was a heavy one; but Rushout never winced. All outward signs of his agitation had vanished.

"Ye might have let me have the mare," Jonathan went on, powerless to keep back the bitter thought that lay uppermost in his mind.

"How often did ye use to meet her?" asked Rushout, entirely ignoring the other's remark.

Jonathan paused to consider.

"On Mondays and Fridays, mostly."

A sudden thought struck Rushout.

"Did she go there that time I was away at my father's funeral?"

Jonathan nodded.

For a long time they remained silent, as if oblivious of each other's presence. Of a sudden Rushout looked up; from around his eyes all the blood had retreated, leaving broad, white rings, and making a deep-toned patch of red on either cheek. He seemed to have come to some great resolution, for the whole expression of his face was different.

"Jonathan Hays," he said solemnly, "there'll not be room for both of us."

The farmer did not answer. And there was nothing in his face to reveal whether he had heard.

This time the silence was longer than ever, then Rushout continued:

"I'll be at Helton cross-roads at ten."

Jonathan slowly uncrossed his legs, and walked to the door. And, as he crossed the threshold, he blurted out:

"Ye'll find me there."

VII

After the darkness of night had descended, savage gusts of wind started to sweep across the country, mysterious-looking, clad in tatters of ghostly white. And the myriad snowflakes, which had ceased awhile previously, appeared again, fleeing before the wind; the big trees moved their limbs as if racked with pain; the little trees writhed, taking queer, fantastic shapes.

Inside the "Bear," each time that the wind passed in its frenzied passage down the village street the windows rattled, and the smoke burst into the room from under the mantelpiece in dense puffs, as if it shrank from facing the storm outside. Rushout raised the tumbler to his lips, unsteadily, knocking the edge of the glass against his chin.

The hands of the slow-ticking clock pointed to close upon ten. Presently he must set off to meet Jonathan at the cross-roads. He was quite hazy as to what would happen there; but he had a vague notion that something was to be settled between them — and, indeed, he cared but little. Jonathan had wronged him, and the consciousness of injury begat a spirit of quarrelsomeness within him amounting to pugnacity, fitfully violent.

The rush of the wind gave way to a crooning wail of distress: the window shook furiously in its casement. Too stupefied to heed the storm, he added some more spirit to his glass.

It was half-past ten before he had put on his great-coat and crammed his hat all awry onto his head. He stepped into the street and immediately the blinding force of the wind and driven snow struck him: he tottered, and only kept on his legs by clutching at the wall. Catching at his breath he paused. His senses were sufficiently dulled to render him indifferent to the cutting cold of the blast and the icy wet of the snow: besides, the strain of maintaining a foothold demanded all his attention.

By the parapet of the bridge he halted, hopelessly struggling to rally his faculties. The strangeness of the storm completed his bewilderment. Behind him, out of the blackness, trooped the multitude of snowflakes: in front of him, back into the blackness, they disappeared. Where was he? Had he crossed the bridge? Then he knew that the night air had made him drunk. It was a vague sense of unfulfilled purpose that roused him again — he must avenge the memory of Jane. And he started forward once more. He crossed the bridge and even mounted the ascent on the other side, though the journey took him a long time.

Now the cold was beginning to penetrate him. The cross-roads were scarcely a hundred yards distant; but he was completely ignorant of his whereabouts. Then his foot tripped against something, and he floundered headlong in the snow.

*   *   *   *   *

"I jest catchéd seet o' him, leein' all o' a heap by t' road-side: ef I had'na stoppéd he'd ha bin leein' there yet," said the carter.

"Lift him onto the sofa — here," called the ostler.[14]

"Get your arms under him — now then."

"He be na featherweight," the carter remarked, as they deposited the body.

"However did he come there?" asked the maid.

The three figures stood grouped together. The carter's lantern was on the table: there was no other light.

"Light one of them candles; let's have a look at him," said the ostler.

The maid did so.

But the draught blew the flame to a tiny spark.

"Shut the door — the outside door. Hark to the wind!"

"There's a nasty place on his forehead," said the carter.

"Ye'd best run for the doctor," suggested the maid.

The ostler went out.

"He be jest stupified-like," remarked the carter.

[14]   An ostler is a stableman, especially at a coaching inn.

"I reckon I'll loose him at t' throat."

Five minutes later Dr. Wilkinson was in the room, directing the two men how to carry him upstairs to bed. And when that was done, the carter went on his way.

VIII

All traces of the snow were gone; the sun glinted warm on the house-tops opposite; inside, a red hot fire was piled up in the little room behind the bar, and before it, extended in his accustomed armchair, lay Rushout. His half-grown beard transformed his whole physiognomy, veiling the coarseness of it here, adding vitality to it there. Since his illness the ruddiness of his face had paled considerably. After the fever-tossed delirium had come the gentle lassitude of convalescence.

Mary was bustling about the room, retailing divers scraps of village gossip which had accumulated during the past fortnight.

"And Mr. Hays, too," she was saying, "he's been in most every day to ask how ye was doin'. I bid him come upstairs many a time; but he was frightened to disturb ye. He'll be around this afternoon sure; I told him ye were for coming downstairs."

Unreal, shadowy as a dream, the past — the storm, the white snow, the slippery road, the story about Jonathan and Jane — came back to Rushout. Jonathan and Jane — his thoughts lingered over them — not angrily, not bitterly, not sadly. His bodily weakness rendered his emotions indolent, and this indolence precluded any feeling but that of passive goodwill. Only he wondered lazily concerning it all.

Then he heard the triple slam of the swing door outside, and Jonathan was before him.

"There, Mr. Hays," cried the girl, "ye see he's come downstairs after all."

"Jonathan, I'm downright glad to see ye," Rushout found himself saying, and just for an instant it seemed a little odd that he should speak so.

The farmer gripped him by the hand with unfeigned cordiality; as their eyes met his red beard and pale face looked at once strange and familiar.

"I scarce should ha' known ye, Richard, the beard makes ye look different." And he seated himself opposite, adding:

"Mary, jest a drop of Scotch — the same that I had yesterday."

"What's your opinion of the spirit?" asked Rushout.

"It's just to my taste. Ye'll be feelin' feeble-like?"

"Ay, I do a bit."

"It was a close touch of it ye had."

"I reckon it was."

"By God! it was a wild night."

Richard shot across an inquisitive glance, but he did not speak. And simultaneously there appeared to both of them a vision of the dead woman — to Jonathan clear-cut and living, to Richard half-effaced by time. And each remembered that she had belonged to the other, and, at that moment, they felt instinctively drawn together: each was conscious of a craving to talk about her, to hear the other mention her name. All this was keener with Jonathan, hence it was he who began:

"Richard, she *was* a grand woman."

"That she was — sich splendid hair."

"Nay, but t'was her eyes that were the finest."

"Black — jet-black."

"Did you ever take notice of the lashes?"

"And a dresser — more style than any lady. And the cleverest understander of horseflesh!"

Here they paused.

"Richard," Jonathan began again at last in an altered tone, "the white mare's gone lame."

"Lame!" Rushout sat of a sudden upright as he repeated the word after him. "Lame!"

"It's a nasty strain on t' hind fetlock. The doctor says she's been kickin' in the stable."

"Stuff and nonsense," Rushout retorted angrily.

"Kickin' in the stable — she's as quiet as a sheep. He's been drivin' of her too hard, that's what it is. A hammerin' of her over the stones. He isn't fit to sit behind her."

"I'm goin' to put her out to grass."

"Ye goin' to! But the doctor? Isn't he for usin' of her?"

"He's parted with her. He reckoned she would na stand his work."

"And it's ye that have bought her?"

Jonathan assented.

Rushout reflected, then:

"Jonathan, I'm powerful glad. I've always regretted ye didn't have her first. I reckon Jane would ha' sooner that ye had her, if she was to go."

"And to mind that on her death-bed she bade ye be tender with the animal. I'd ha' given most anything for her to ha' kept sound," returned Jonathan reproachfully.

"Ay, I know ye would," answered Rushout repentantly.

Yet a moment later he began again:

"D'ye mind how wild she was the day I was for lettin' young Will Dykes drive the mare?"

"That I do."

"Were ye sweet on her then?" he put the question in hesitating timidity.

"'Twas the first occasion I had a kiss from her," answered Jonathan, defiantly.

"When was that?"

"Whilst ye were fetchin' the new skin rug."

*   *   *   *   *

"What made ye fix on that old house of Coney Standish's?"

"I canna rightly say. There was a great amount o' reasons — it's a long tale. Yet I don't know but what I've any objection to relating it to ye. I reckon it'd be best out."

"Ay, ye're right. Ye know I bear ye no malice. Hold on though till the girl fetches me a drop more of this barley-drink. It's grand coolin' stuff when ye're feverish."

Embers

The room was small, but the twilight shadows made it appear larger. An iron bedstead; two tables, one covered with papers, the other with a white cloth; a chair by the door, and on it a mud-splashed pair of trousers and a dirty shirt, with a pair of old slippers, trodden down at the heels, underneath; a black, shiny armchair, its horsehair stuffing protruding in places; a deal chest of drawers — this was all the furniture. No kind of ornament, bare walls, not a spot of colour to relieve the cheerlessness.

Yet presently, as one looked, two or three details betrayed something of the individuality of the occupant.

The papers on the writing-table were arranged in neat stacks; the shirt on the chair had been carefully folded; the slippers lay side by side; but it was the mechanical precision of habit, and not a love of tidiness; for the room was far from clean, and looked almost squalid.

But when he came in, he noticed none of these things.

A lean young man, with a hesitating gait and tired stoop; lank hair streaked with grey; a yellow, parchment-like skin that puckered in wrinkles round the eyes, and gave a shrivelled look to the whole face; and in the eyes a startling dulness.

He lit the little lamp with the green cardboard shade, hung up his hat and his overcoat behind the door, took off his boots and laid them together, just as he had done every evening for the last five years.

He lifted up the dirty shirt, and, after looking closely at the cuffs, folded it again, and replaced it on the chair. Then he fetched a brush from off the chest of drawers, and began carefully to clean the mud-splashed trousers.

When he had nearly finished, the servant-girl brought in his dinner.

"Good evening," he said, without looking up.

"Good evening, Mr. Gorridge," she answered.

And he began to eat the cold mutton and the boiled potatoes methodically.

As a rule, when his dinner was finished, he seated himself at the writing-table, to copy manuscripts at a half-penny a folio or to address envelopes at fourpence a hundred. It was not so much for the sake of the money, for he had but few wants, and his salary was more than enough to supply them. He had taken to it long ago, when the mechanical work had kept him from brooding over his trouble; and gradually the habit had grown upon him, till it was an inseparable part of his existence. Narrower and narrower had become the groove in which his life ran, and now each day was a counterpart of the preceding one.

But tonight, when the servant girl had taken away the half-finished leg of mutton, he turned round his chair and stared into the empty grate.

February 18th, said the almanack[1] on the wall opposite. February 18th, the day on which she had gone. With a yearning, dull and immense, like the yearning for home of the solitary traveller, he was thinking of his married life — quite hazily; for five years of unconscious retrospective crystallisation had vaguely beautified them for him.

And then he lived over again the moment when he had come back from the City[2] to find her gone, gone with not a word of explanation.

Most of that night and all the next day he had spent in wild search for her. The next three days he was in bed, unable to get up. On the morning of the fourth day, fearing to lose his place, he had dragged himself down to the City as usual. And afterwards, for weeks, every evening as he mounted the stairs, his heart thumped excitedly with the hope that he would find her back again. But she never came.

He changed his lodgings, for the hundred and one little things that brought her back to him made the rooms unbearable.

* * * * *

Outside, a drizzling rain. The gas lamps shone a dim, filthy yellow, streaking the slimy pavement with their reflections. There was no sky, only a murky atmosphere overhead. And save for a woman creeping along, the street was deserted. Her slatternly clothes hung loosely about her; her skirt trailed in the mud. She was quite wet, for she had no umbrella.

Underneath his window she stopped, and for a moment she stood in the doorway out of the rain.

During that moment, the thoughts of the man in the little bedroom above, sitting staring into the empty grate, and the thoughts of the bedraggled figure in the doorway below, went out towards each other.

She could only think in a foggy sort of way, for she had already had a drink or two. There were many things which were blurred; many things about which she was not sure. Her recollection of their separation was dim; she scarcely understood how it had come about. She wondered feebly where he was, what he was doing. Yet her cunning instinct told her he would take her back, in spite of it all, and that once more she could do with him what she would. It seemed that they were together. He was so simple, so confiding,[3] that during the day when he was down at the City, she did what she liked. She was careful, of course, so that he never found out anything.

Then she moved out again into the wet, and stumbled along towards the lights of the public house at the corner.

1   See note 2 on p. 130.
2   The City is the financial and business district of London.
3   Confiding: here in the sense of 'trusting'.

*   *   *   *   *

It was inevitable that it would come, sooner or later, for she slept over the public-house at the end of the street, and he passed it every day on his way to the City. Yet it was several days before she saw him. When he went by in the morning, she was seldom out of bed, and when he came back in the evening, she was generally drunk.

But once she woke early, and looked out through the grimy window-pane.

There he was! She could see his back, as he hurried away down the street. But there was no mistaking the narrow, sloping shoulders, the jerky, nervous gait, with the head thrust forward. She even remembered the black overcoat; he had bought it just after their marriage. It used to be a shiny one, several sizes too large for him, and to hang in baggy wrinkles about the armpits. And she fell to dreaming, recalling vague, half-blurred little incidents.

He was found now. A quarter to nine. He was on his way to the City; well she knew that, when evening came, he would return by the same way. All she had to do was to wait for him, and to keep her head clear. So back she went to her dirty bed and fell into a fitful sleep.

About three o'clock, with a low, sickly feeling, she awoke. But as she slipped into her tawdry garments, her spirits rose. This was the last day; tomorrow she would be a respectable married woman in comfortable lodgings, with a man to earn money for her. She went down to the bar, and ordered a large pewter of beer. She always lunched off a large pewter, never having any appetite till evening.

Presently two women, one of whom she knew, came in. She felt in her pocket. Half a crown. Her last. But what odds?[4] Tomorrow he would give her plenty more. So she recklessly stood drinks to the new-comers.

And thus through the afternoon, and with the idea that she must catch him on his return increasing in force as she grew more and more drunk.

She talked loudly and volubly, explaining to the two others all about him, and dilating on all the things she would do when he had taken her back. They listened stupidly, nodding gravely at intervals.

About six o'clock they found themselves with no more money and with nothing more to drink, so, holding each other by the arm, they sallied forth into the street to wait for him.

*   *   *   *   *

He was hastening home, thinking of the bundle of manuscript which bulged his pocket, whether he would be able to copy it all before eleven, the hour when he always went to bed.

---

[4]   But what odds: but what did it matter?

Of a sudden something clutching at his arm — a woman! — looking up into his face, with the glare of the gas-lamp lighting up her senseless leer. She did not speak, only leered the more, and hung heavier and heavier on his arm.

He made a half frightened, half indignant movement to shake her off. Next he recognised her. She did not know that he had done so, for he did not start, nor make any sound. Only first his features, then his whole body stiffened, till he stood as if petrified.

"Don't you know me Frank?" she stuttered.

There was no reply, and it dawned upon her that he did.

"What are you looking so scared at? One would think you'd never seen me before," she continued with a sickly smile. "I'm not as I was, I know that. I've had a hard time of it, a cruel hard time of it," she whined; "but I've come back to be your dutiful wife once more," and she leered the same, senseless leer. "Where are your digs? Somewhere along this way, eh?" And pulling him by the arm, she dragged him down the street. His feeble resistance only lasted an instant.

When they reached the door, his hand shook so violently, that it was nearly a minute before he could fit the key into the keyhole. Automatically he lit the little lamp with the green cardboard shade, hung up his hat and overcoat behind the door, and was about to take off his boots, when his eyes fell on her. With a start he stopped short.

She was lying in an armchair, looking round the room.

"No great shakes, this drawing-room of yours. Just you wait till I've been here a day or two, and see how I'll smarten it up. It's beastly cold and no fire."

At this moment the servant-girl came in to lay the cloth. On seeing the stranger, she stepped back, looking in astonishment from one to the other.

"Well, stupid, what are you staring at? Look sharp. I'm hungry. Let's see. Soup — soup to begin with. Fish, no, no fish — beastly smelly stuff, I can't stomach it. Tripe and baked potatoes to follow, and here, fetch a bottle of beer, look alive; don't stand there like a blasted lamp-post."

The servant-girl fled, slamming the door behind her. And the two relapsed into silence, he, standing staring at her, in terror-stricken rigidity.

Exasperated, she turned to him.

"What the devil's the matter with you? A nice way to receive back your loving wife, after all these years. Good God! man, you look like a blooming mummy!"

The door opened violently. In burst a heavy, stout woman, her face flushed with passion.

"Now, Mr. Gorridge," she cried. "What's the meaning of this? I'm not going to stand it, d'ye hear? What are you looking so dazed at? Why, God bless my soul, I believe the man's off his head!" And raising her voice still louder: "Now then, hussy, clear out quick. What do you take me for, I should like to know? I've always kept a respectable house, and I ain't goin' to begin to have the likes of you about now!"

"Dry up your damned impudence," stuttered the other, staggering to her feet. "Why, I'm his lawful wife. We were married in church. I've been away on business, these last three years. And it's a hard time of it that I've had," and she wound up with a whine.

"Get out, you drunken beast," shouted the elder woman, "or if you don't I'll soon make you."

And, seizing her by the shoulders, she began to push her towards the door. The other kicked and struggled, but it was of no use. There was a scuffle on the staircase, an oath from the drunken woman, a crash as of something falling, and the front door banged.

"If you ever dare to set foot inside my house again," called the landlady through the door, "I'll send the police after you."

And, as she re-entered the room: "Mr. Gorridge, just you understand this, I'll have none of these goings on in my house. You ought to be ashamed of yourself, at your age."

But he lay in a heap in the armchair, staring fixedly into the empty grate.

Seeing that he paid no heed, she bounced out of the room with a snort of contempt.

Quite still he lay, his limbs huddled together while the servant-girl, openly casting indignant glances at him, prepared his dinner.

Half an hour passed. The food was untouched. He had not moved.

"Ain't you going to have no dinner, Mr. Gorridge?" asked the girl, with a touch of compassion in her voice.

He made no sound, so she took away the things.

How long he had been there he did not know. He was cold; the cramped position had stiffened his legs; the lamp had gone out; it was quite dark.

He struck a match, and clumsily lit it again. Then, undressing, crept into bed.

* * * * *

When he awoke his mind was blank. Mechanically he looked at the chair on which his clothes always lay folded. It was empty. In a heap, there they were on the floor.

A quick spasm, contracting his features, and he remembered, and, with a gesture of indescribable weariness, began to dress.

That day he did his work at the office as usual, only he looked more yellow and more wizened than ever. But no one noticed it.

In the evening, he no longer hurried along the street towards home, absently with his head thrust forward. Slowly he crept, with cautious, cat-like movements.

From a doorway, out burst a boy with a basket. He started aside like a frightened animal.

It was only when he had passed the spot where she had met him yesterday, that he seemed reassured. Quickening his pace, he fell again into his accustomed, jerky gait.

But presently, he caught sight of something coming in the distance. By instinct he knew that it was she. On he hastened, his eyes on the pavement, till they came face to face.

"Frank," she began in a voice broken by maudlin sobs, "don't you think that I'm going to bother you any more. I'm a miserable, lost creature. I know I am. I'll never trouble you again, Frank; only give me something to keep body and soul together. I haven't a blessed sixpence," here she stopped, watching him intently.

He had pulled out his purse, and was emptying its contents into his hand. Three half-crowns, a shilling and four coppers[5] — he handed them all to her, and, without a word, turned to go in.

"Goodnight, Frank my darling," she called after him. "You're a trump,[6] you are."

* * * * *

The next three days passed, and she never appeared.

Back his life dropped into the old groove, till it all seemed like a bad dream, and sometimes he wondered whether it had really happened.

Then she met him again, with the same maudlin tears. He gave her a sovereign, for that morning he had received his salary.

After this she took to waylaying him almost every evening. Sometimes, he could only give her a copper or two, sometimes half a crown, sometimes — on Saturdays — gold.[7] He scarcely ever spoke to her, and seemed relieved when she left him on the doorstep. Once she spoke of coming up.

"Tomorrow is Saturday," he said in a hurried voice. She understood, and went away.

At the end of a fortnight, he was unable to pay his weekly bill. This was the first time since he had lodged there, and the thought gnawed him night and day.

His landlady said nothing, but when at the end of the second week no money was forthcoming, she grumbled sullenly.

And he began to age strangely, thinner and thinner his hair became, till he was almost quite bald.

---

[5] Coppers are pennies. Before decimalisation (pre-1971) there were 240 pence to the pound (twelve pence to the shilling and twenty shillings to the pound). A half-crown was worth two shillings and sixpence. Frank hands over a total of eight shillings and ten pence, about a quarter of what the average male worker earned in the 1890s, which was 35s (i.e. 1.75 pounds) per week.
[6] Trump is slang for a dependable person.
[7] A gold sovereign was worth one pound.

*   *   *   *   *

… About three weeks later — night-time — the little street was black and still — on the doorstep, two figures.

"I am going on Saturday," said he.

"Going? Why? Where?" she answered.

"I can't pay the rent," he said simply.

Face to face they stood. In his eyes the vacant stare of complete weariness; in hers a look of silent suffering. Quicker and quicker her face quivered. Big tears rolled down her cheeks.

And as he watched her, his vacant stare passed away; in its place came the soft light of compassion.

"Don't cry, Mag," he said gently.

At the sound of this little pet name, coming again for the first time at the end of all these years, she broke down.

It was the hysterical sobbing of a ruined nervous system; it was very painful to hear.

"Don't cry, Mag," he repeated.

But she sobbed on, her frame rocking with convulsive throbs.

Bewildered he looked about him. Then timidly, he put his arm round her saying once more:

"Don't cry, little Mag."

By degrees the fit spent itself. She stood quite still at last, her head resting on his shoulder. After a moment, she stepped back and looked again into his eyes.

The features were quite composed, but the lips were bloodless.

"Frank," she said with an intenseness that revealed the tumult within. "Frank, will you forgive me?"

The old spasm of pain, contracting the features, came back.

She saw it.

"I don't mean that," she said hurriedly. "I'm too bad for that. Only say that you forgive me."

He pondered a moment perplexed, his eyes blinking rapidly. Then looking at her, and seeing that she was waiting for his answer:

"I forgive you," he murmured.

Holding out her hand — "goodbye," she said.

"Goodbye," he answered mechanically.

And she stepped onto the pavement, and moved slowly away down the street.

From
Sentimental Studies
and
A Set of Village Tales (1895)

A Commonplace Chapter — I

I

The two women stood by the door, face to face. Impulsively the elder one lifted her arms, caught the younger one to her, and kissed her.

"God bless you, my darling …. God bless you!"

The struggle to stifle the rising sobs made the words come irregularly, in gasps.

"There, there, mother dear," murmured the girl, soothingly, while she smoothed the elder woman's hair. "There, there. You mustn't cry."

"No, no; it's over now," the other answered hastily, lifting her face.

The girl brushed the tears from the wrinkled cheeks, and held them an instant between her hands, smiling encouragingly.

And the mother smiled back bravely. Once more she drew the girl to her and kissed her greedily.

"Goodnight, Nell darling."

"Goodnight, mother."

They looked into each other's eyes; the girl still smiling encouragingly; the mother still gulping with her grief.

Then the door shut gently.

Mechanically Ella knelt down by the bedside. The words of her habitual evening prayer rose to her lips:

"'Commit thy way unto the Lord; trust also in Him, and He shall bring it to pass.'"[1]

When she had ceased she became aware that tonight she could not pray. She was alone. And she wondered not a little at this novel consciousness of solitude. For she remembered that it was for the last time.

All at once came a spasm of keen pain — tomorrow it would be all gone …. mother …. father …. the gables …. the chestnuts …. the clematis climbing the porch …. the yellow-legged writing-table in the study, and its litter of old circulars, ends of string, sealing-wax and disused pens …. all would be gone. She would be in a strange room, in a strange house, which she did not know.

And he would be with her.

Often, during the past fortnight, she had tried to realize that the end of the old life was coming; but she had never known, as she knew tonight, that it meant separation from all that had seemed before an inseparable part of her existence. Every day they would sit down to breakfast, to luncheon, to dinner, without her; they would live on, and she would not be there.

---

[1]   Psalms 37. 5.

And, as she knelt, just for a moment, a rebellious longing rushed through her — a passionate yearning to say no — to remain, to be good and gentle and loving to them always, always.

"My queen, my divinity, there will be nothing in my life that is not yours; there will be nothing in your life that is not mine. Henceforth we shall live, each for the other, till death do us part, and the most glorious happiness that God has given will be ours."

Those were his words. She remembered them, every one. Her eyes glistened; for the words sent her blood tingling.

"You are the whole world to me; there is only you, darling. I cannot live without you. I love you, I love you, I love you!"

…. It was where the path in the wood ends — leaves above, leaves around, nothing but leaves; not green, but black and white. Hillier's face, clear cut in the white moonlight, his hands clasping her hands, his cheek pressing her cheek.[2]

And it all seemed to her very wonderful and very grand.

She undressed rapidly, as she was accustomed to do; blew out the candle, and got into bed.

The window was wide open, and the muslin curtains swaying in the breeze bulged towards her, weirdly. She could see the orchard trees bathed in blackness, and above a square of sky, blue-grey, quivering with stifled light, flecked with a disorder of stars that seemed ready to rain upon the earth. After a while, little by little, she distinguished the forms of the trees. Slowly, monstrous, and sleek, the yellow moon was rising.

She was no longer thinking of herself: she had forgotten that tomorrow was her wedding day: for a moment, quite impersonally, she watched the moonlight stealing through the trees.

When recollection returned, it was wrapped, as it were, in a veil of unreality. She had been insisting to herself that it was for her a great moment. Yet it had seemed, and tonight it seemed more so than ever, that, somehow, she was powerless to be present at this turning-point in her life; that as a spectator, on some great height, she was looking down on all that was happening to her. And the distance made things blurred….

It was quite dark when she awoke. She supposed it was about two o'clock. Over there, in the inn opposite, Hillier — was he thinking of her, or was he asleep? No, she was sure that he was awake; eager, excited, impatient, as she was, waiting for the great, unknown happiness. The unknown happiness, of the existence of which, during the past few days, she found herself growing conscious — the unknown, which was to be mysterious and wonderful. Her breath came quickly, in the stillness of the dark she could hear it distinctly….

---

[2]   Hillier is 'Ray' in the *New Review* version of this story. See 'A Commonplace Chapter', *New Review*, 10.57 (February 1894), 242–54.

Tomorrow night he would be with her; she would sink to sleep, her head on his shoulder, his arm protecting her, and, when morning came, he would cover her face with kisses, and he would tell her how he loved her....

She imagined the first breakfast in the cottage which Hillier's uncle had lent him (away in Surrey; it was a grey-coloured county in the school-room map). There was a bow window, and the sunshine streamed in, onto the white cloth. She sat at the bottom of the table; she poured out his coffee, and she asked him how he liked it. Then they went out together through the glass doors — for there were glass doors in the bow window — and they walked round the garden, and she picked some flowers — dog-roses they were — and pinned them in his button-hole, and by-and-bye they went out into the pine-woods, where there was no sound, and where they were alone, quite alone.

*   *   *   *   *

He would be very good to her — she knew that — kind and unselfish, and loving. And she would be unselfish too; she would follow him in everything; he was so clever; he meant some day to become a great writer, of whose name all the world knew.[3]

How different he was from the rest of men! She recalled two others of her acquaintance, and the consciousness of her pride filled her with joy.

Was God away in heaven, looking down on her, she wondered? And she fell to remembering how, as a child, she used to lie staring straight up at the sky, trying to catch a glimpse of God in His glory, seated, surrounded by a shining multitude of angels, somewhere amid the huge billows of white clouds.

Other fragments of her childhood memories came to her too, and some of them she turned over in her mind again and again, beginning each time at the same point, and ending each time where she had ended before....

The sound of the hall clock striking in the hall woke her. How loud it seemed! She felt wide-awake and curiously calm....

II

He was, he told himself, supremely happy. Several times before he had set up a woman's figure on a pedestal, and, for a while, had deluded himself into worshipping her. And when it had passed, he had, to his own satisfaction, succeeded in bedecking the memory of each incident with an appropriate, sentimental halo. He had had too, of course, erotic adventures, purely physical; for he had lived, during his early years, in the unwholesome atmosphere of an expensive public school, and a precocious familiarity with the obscene had

---

[3]   In the original *New Review* version, 'Ray' 'meant to rise to the top of his profession, to be a great lawyer, perhaps a judge, someday'. 'A Commonplace Chapter', *New Review*, p. 244.

left upon his imagination a secret taint, which at moments had asserted itself irresistibly. Growing into manhood he had sinned conventionally with the rest; but for such conduct he frequently professed a sentimental disgust, which, in his case, was more sincere than hypocritical. Yet, in a sense, he was proud of himself; of his ability; of his personal charm; of his physical comeliness; he looked back with pride on many events of his life; on his struggle with poverty; on his conquests of women. The waiting for achievement in his work had never caused him to experience doubt or discouragement; and, when other men paraded these before him, he looked down on them with genuine contempt. His conceit had been sufficiently robust to carry him through that time of struggle; he believed that he had always known that he would not fail. He felt that he was self-satisfied, by reason of a definite gauging of his own powers. Indeed, there was but little perspective in his view of his life, so much of the foreground did his own figure fill.

*   *   *   *   *

During the past two years an unformulated discontent had been growing within him. More and more seldom did his thoughts revert to his past sentimental experiences. Their attractiveness seemed to have faded, like the colour of a much-fingered embroidery. He found that he no longer viewed his management of his own life with the same satisfaction, but rather with a sort of smouldering irritation. Something was wanting; something was unachieved. The restlessness which this sense of void produced, resolved itself, last year, into a concentrated impatience for escape — immediate escape — from the groove in which his life was running. So he travelled alone to Switzerland, and there, during long evenings in drowsy Alpine villages, he started to dream of marriage — an ideal marriage — a simultaneous satisfaction of intellectual, emotional, and physical desires.

And, six months later, in that picturesque Sussex village, he had stumbled across the realization of his dreams.

The whole business was of a piece, he thought; picturesque, yet in no way cheap.

And yet this moment of his marriage had stirred his inmost fibres with an impetuous yearning for regeneration. The manifestation of his love for her had been full of a refinement of fine impulse, of a tense and cultured aspiration. She, Ella, warm and simple-hearted, sweet- and gentle-minded, during the fervour of their engagement trusted in him as a man above all other men; and his very self-absorption made each fresh sign of this trust of hers an acute suffering to him, till, racked by remorse, he longed weakly to besmirch himself altogether in her eyes.

And this same morbid consciousness of the ignoble within him, the cultivation of which brought him a certain relief, since it seemed a final remnant of distinction with which he could bedeck the cloddish brutality of his past conduct, had spurred him to a strenuous devotion to her. He had effaced himself utterly: absorbed himself in her; grown aglow with an ecstasy of passionate, reverential fervour.

For her personality appeared to him abundant in possibilities; and it was — though he never acknowledged it to himself — on these possibilities, rather than on the obvious facts of her nature, that his imagination dwelt. That she might represent to him something entirely different from what he imagined her to represent, now, in this moment of extreme emotional exaltation, would have appeared to him quite preposterous.

Thus he adored her extravagantly, in unconscious insincerity; caressing admiringly the extravagance of his adoration; or telling himself that he loved her with all the forces of his manhood; because she was his, because he had found her, because he knew the great love she was giving him in return.

And he took to describing the relations of sex as a great sacrament.

Physically, at the first glance, he was unlike other men, though it was his habit sedulously to avoid obvious eccentricity of appearance. He was clean-shaven; dark, silky hair; clever, close-set eyes; a thin mouth, drawn a trifle as if by thought at the corners; a clean-cut, intellectual, slightly hatchet-shaped profile; and in his bearing, the unconscious, distinguished ease of fine-breeding. The average man of his age disliked him, generally with impatience; women, on the other hand, were interested in his air of modern picturesqueness. And some, divining beneath his boyish manner a discreet, an intuitive experience of women, and relying on his mobile, emotional nature — that had been said of him, and he knew it — were led to treat him almost as if he were of their own sex.

III

"God is good, Nellie! What a brick He's been!"

"Hush! you mustn't talk like that."

She smiled in quick response to the sudden sound of his voice, and her face flushed a little eagerly. It was a face unattractive according to cheap, conventional standards of prettiness, an unobtrusive face — simple, brown hair, insignificant eyes, and pale lips — a face wearing an unconscious girlishness, and yet a delicate suggestion of maturity. "My wife is so deliciously English," Hillier often said of her afterwards.

"Why not? Before I never thought much about Him. He was like the king of some far-off country, about whom, now and then, one mechanically reads paragraphs in the papers. But now He seems quite near, quite familiar — just like an old pal."

"Hillier, don't! It's blasphemy."

"But it's true. I understand Him quite well now. I suppose it's because I'm happy — so infinitely, splendidly, gloriously happy."

"Are you?"

"Yes; and it's you — all you. You in that adorable blue dress, with that ivory skin, that warm, sparkling hair."

"Stop! you dear — "

"And it's everything else as well. The whole world is changed. The sun is stretching out his big, warm hands to me. Look! the trees are like demure school-girls in new, green frocks, and the cool immensity of that sky. Nell, I understand what it all means."

"Tell me."

"It means that you are adorable — more adorable than any woman who has been, or is, or will be; that I am happier than any man has ever been before on this earth; that the sun knows it, the little green trees know it."

"How wonderfully you talk, Hillier!"

"Darling, come near to me. Give me your hand — a warm, pulsing morsel of your dear self."

"Someone might see. Look! there are people in the road."

"Ha! Dolts, in black coats and ugly, stiff hats."[4]

"They're going to church."

He snorted contempt. Then, presently:

"How everything in the air says that it's Sunday — that all the world is at rest. It's sacrilege to work on such a gorgeous day."

"But lots of people have to."

"Yes, I suppose they do," he answered carelessly.

* * * * *

"Some day when I've become a great writer," and he smiled at his own affectation of conceit, "I'll write a book on the mystery of happiness; where all shall be happiness, profound happiness, like mine, from the first page to the last. There is a man who says that anyone can be happy, if he only will take enough trouble about it."

"Well?"

"That's rot!"

* * * * *

"There are only five days more, and then you will have to go back to work. You will be away all day, and I shall only have you in the evenings, when you're tired out."

---

4   Dolt: a term of contempt for a person supposedly slow-witted or stupid.

"Work! Turn myself once more into a publisher's drudge! I want to live. How can a man work when he's living, when he's feeling things, as I am now? What do they all come to — success, and the petty ambitions to which one sacrifices one's life? Bah! it's a wretched, treadmill sort of existence."

"But you were quite content doing it once?"

"Only a sort of thin, relative contentedness. Because one didn't know any better. Not this sort of ultimate happiness." And he reflected on the felicity of the new-found expression.

A little later she began:

"Hillier, go on telling me what you think about the world and things. It's all so strange — the way you talk of it all, I mean — and I want to understand what is it in me that makes you so happy? Tell me, that's what I want to understand."

"It's just yourself — your hair, your eyes, your mouth, your arms, your hands, your feet. It's your sweetness, your gentleness, your ignorance, your purity."

* * * * *

"Tell me," he said suddenly, "who made love to you before I did?"

"No one — except the little doctor, and he didn't really."

"What! that freckled little chap I saw at the school-treat? I should think not."

"But he was very nice and kind. He used to walk miles and miles to get me flowers. And, Hillier, I sometimes used to like him a great deal."

"Shut up. It's too monstrous. But you don't mean it. Why, you and I were made for each other: as you said the other day, you were just waiting for me all those years down in that quiet, old-fashioned vicarage."

"But, Hillier, why should you mind about the doctor? You've had flirtations too."

"How do you know?"

"I guessed it. How many?"

"I don't know. I've never counted."

"But how many? Three?"

"Oh! yes; more than that."

"Six?"

"Yes."

"More than six?"

"Perhaps."

"Twelve?"

"Yes; about a dozen, I suppose."

"Hillier, is that true?"

He nodded.

"And didn't you care for any of them?"

"No, not really."

"And they ——"

"Well?"

"Didn't they care?"

"Yes; I suppose some did. At least, they pretended to."

"Oh! Hillier, don't talk like that. It's not you; it's like someone else. It's horrible. And did you tell them that you loved them?"

"Yes, sometimes."

A pause. There was trouble on her face: on his, nettled impatience.

"Hillier, did you only flirt with them?"

"What do you mean?"

"Was there nothing — nothing more between you?"

"Come, Ella," he answered with a forced laugh, "you're cross-examining me like a regular lawyer."

"No, I must know — I ought to know!"

"We'll talk about it some other time — not now."

"No — now!"

"Well, if you must know, there was."

"With all of them?"

"With most of them."

*   *   *   *   *

"Well, what are you thinking about?" he began again, with obvious uneasiness.

"Why didn't you tell me before?"

"How could I? Besides, what does it matter now?"

"If I had been like that, what would you have said when I told you?"

"I shouldn't have cared a jot. Do you suppose I only love you for your virtues. I love you for yourself. I want you just as you are."

"But if I'd been different?"

"But you aren't. So there's an end of it."

"But, Hillier, just now you were angry when I told you of the doctor."

"No, I wasn't. Only he's such a puny creature."

"And *they* — were they all so beautiful?"

"Yes, every one," he replied, with brutal pride.

"Much more than me? …. I suppose you said to them all the fine phrases you have been saying to me …. No wonder they come so easily." But she had not the strength to sustain the hard note of sarcasm. She turned her back on him quickly and stared across the lawn. And he, impulsively reminding himself of her purity, of the fineness of his former attitude towards her, upbraided himself helplessly, and, putting his arm round her, soothed her with an outpouring of intense tenderness.

IV

She was awake. The fresh sunshine filled the room. Some birds were twittering as they sported in the creeper outside; inside, the sound of his breathing rose and fell in heavy regularity.

.... Six weeks this morning! But it was like years and years: at least the memories of the old life were faint and blurred; far, far back in the past; to recall them was almost an effort.

She shifted her position in the bed. The hair was dishevelled; the long, colourless cheeks lay inert; the mouth was half open. His handsomeness was gone; at least so she fancied; and the empty expression on his face coarsened it, brutalized it. He looked as she had never seen him look before. She shrank from him, she knew not why. She was his now! How strange that was! for all at once it seemed to her that she knew nothing of him, and the revelation of this ignorance scared her. He was twenty-eight years old. He had been a man for eight years. Eight years! Twice four years! She tried to realize the stretch of time that four years meant. And she knew nothing — nothing, but what he had told her yesterday. She tried to think — what did she know? He had lived in London many years .... he had been very poor once .... then things had changed .... and now he worked for a great publishing firm .... his name appeared sometimes in the London papers .... and he had numbers of friends, celebrated people.

She found herself resenting her ignorance of these eight years. Why had he married her? How came it that she, a simple clergyman's daughter, should mean to him all those wonderful things?

At the corner of High Field Lane she had seen him for the first time. He was sketching, with his back turned towards her. She stopped to look at his picture, and he turned round with a stare so rude, it had seemed, that she hurried away. How odd those beginnings appeared now!

In those days, his tall, thin figure, his clear-sounding voice, each detail of his person, dominated the rest of the world, and his words fascinated her.

Was it changed now? No, it was the same — only, there was yesterday afternoon. But she did not think of that now: she was just yearning for home. The oppressiveness of her sense of isolation increased. Even *he* was asleep, dreaming, perhaps, his thoughts away from her, in places, with people, that she did not know. For the second time since the marriage the tears welled up. She strove to convince herself that it was but childish folly, but she could not keep them back. Then she let them come. To cry was a sweet relief.

A little while and it passed, leaving her numb. And she fell to considering drowsily the long years ahead — twenty, thirty — which must be passed by his side. She wondered how it would be when he was an old man and she an old woman. At least she would know him better then. Perhaps he would love her as he did now; perhaps they would be like old Doctor Manners and his wife, white-haired, wrinkled, yet caressing as young lovers. But she did not think it would be so — something indefinable, instinctive, told her that it would not be.

And then her thoughts went back to home. They would be less poor now, and that cheered her. Times had grown bad of late. The tenant had left the glebe farm,[5] and no other could be found. She knew well to what straits the slender income had been put.

Often she had longed to go out as a governess, and in all probability she would have gone had she but known how to set about it. But she had no qualifications: she could not paint, or play the piano, and she knew no French. This helplessness of hers galled her; there were times when she had grudged the very food she ate. So, when he had appeared, to single her out, to tell her that he loved her, to ask her to be his wife, she had not hesitated. To consult her own feelings, searchingly, never occurred to her. Afterwards she had given herself no sort of merit for this: for when he was with her she was quite happy; and when he was not there too. Only there had been moments when she dreaded the step — when she shrank from the irrevocable, the unknown.

One day he went to London and brought back with him three black leather cases full of jewels. A ring, a brooch, and a bracelet. And, somehow, these jewels made her even less at her ease with him than ever. She couldn't help wondering what they must have cost, and it seemed to her wrong to spend so much on things about which she did not care. She felt, too, with a sort of shame, that she could not help showing him that she did not thank him for them genuinely. But, she noticed, he did not care; he was so pleased with them himself.

When the wedding-day had come, she had not realized it at all; it had all been queer and unreal, like a dream. The service so solemn and beautiful she had thought it, when she read it over to herself; but, in the church, she never listened. Her eyes were fixed on the sapphires in the bracelet he had given her; she was wondering how much they had cost.

This house, too, to which he had brought her, the unfamiliar furniture, and the strange faces of the servants, had only added to her sense of isolation. Yet, after all, it was better now.

*   *   *   *   *

He had slipped his arms round her. He had seen that her cheeks were wet with tears.

"Nell!"

At the sound of his voice, clear and strong, she impulsively nestled her head on his shoulder.

"Come, little one, what is it? Out with the secret grief."

---

[5]   A glebe farm is granted to a clergyman as part of his benefice.

"I was thinking of home. You are so good to me, Hillier. You won't mind, will you?" And the yearning to pour out what was in her heart gave her courage. "I've never been away from them before — and — and it seems so strange."

She paused: he was stroking her wrist; the soothing was delicious.

"They are so poor. Father hasn't had any rent from the glebe farm for two years …. And you've made me so rich …. It doesn't seem fair."

"Darling one, what isn't fair is that I haven't a thousand times more to give you."

"But what have I done that I should have so much?"

"Nothing of course, except existed."

She smiled absently.

"Hillier, I do wish I could do something to help them."

"Send then a hundred pounds," he answered.

"A hundred pounds! You will give me a hundred pounds to send to them?"

She covered his face with kisses; his eyes, his cheeks, his mouth.

He submitted with an affectation of resistance.

"I wonder if there is another man on earth like you, Hillier," she murmured.

V

The hundred pounds were duly dispatched — ten clean, crackling bank-notes in a registered envelope. And, when it was all finished, they went out into the garden, hand in hand.

He could ill afford the money; but that fact spurred him the more to send it; and in an hour or two his interest in the matter had faded: he referred to it but once with a carelessness that was not assumed. But on her, the incident made an impression of no slight depth: late at night, and early in the morning, the remembrance of it was with her: such generosity seemed wonderful. Traces of its influence were discernible in each small phase of her attitude towards him: she reproached herself for not having done justice in her own mind to his generosity before: yet she set to work eagerly to discover ways of pleasing him: she reproduced a little of his extravagance of language, and stimulated with rare tact his exuberant expression of opinion, even when the topic was unfamiliar and uncongenial to her.

From her upbringing — from the methodical monotony of her home life — she had learned the habit of mental precision. She had begun, by a sort of classification of his sayings, to endeavour to arrive at the nature of his thoughts, to discover what was his faith in religion, in Christ, and she waited always for the day when he should talk to her on these matters.

The passionateness of his love communicated itself irresistibly to her. This had troubled her, she did not know whether it was right or wrong. She had sought vainly, in the teaching of her life, for guidance. But such was the ignorance in which her girlhood had been spent that she found nothing.

Now, however, all these misgivings were merged in her aspiration to be worthy of him, to please him absolutely.

And thus his satisfaction in her, and in himself for having found her, grew in completeness, as the days of the honeymoon drew to their close.

VI

She sat in the garden alone. The hum of insects, and a faint scent of sweet hay was in the air; the trees, robed in the sombre green of midsummer, stood solid and still; masses of cloud, ponderous and white, crowded the sky.

She saw all these things, and yet she was unconscious of them. Her eyes were restless with excitement.

Yes, she was beginning to see clearer now, or rather to realize her immediate surroundings.

London! — the broad, white streets, the never-ceasing flow of cabs and carriages, the shining shop-windows, and the black crowd on the pavement — tomorrow she would be there; she was impatient for it to come.

She would become a Londoner; soon she would be quite at home in the great city. Hillier would take her to the theatre; to the opera; she would be mistress of his house, and sit at the bottom of the table when they had dinner-parties: and when she had grown quite familiar with it all, father and mother should come; she saw herself walking through the streets with them, naming to them all the famous people as they rolled by in their carriages. And she felt very, very happy.

VII

They were quite strange, these first impressions of London: at least, so they seemed, when she recalled them afterwards; as if, in those days, the forms of the buildings had been altogether altered.

Disappointment — disappointment which, for a while, she had refused to recognize — disappointment which, later, she had struggled to suppress — that was what she had first felt.

The hansom,[6] which brought them from the station, rattled past the long line of porticoes, stretching away and away, in spacious monotony, down the Cromwell Road:[7] then halted. And the house — which was to be theirs — looked lonely, cheerless, dreary, with its expanse of grey-black wall. The sense

[6] See note 7 on p. 84.
[7] The Cromwell Road, west London, starts as West Cromwell Road in Kensington then runs eastwards to Exhibition Road.

of separation from every surrounding of her country home, each hallowed by its particular associations — the green garden-seats under the trees, the shrubbery-walks, the flowers, the bright colours — came back to her.

Radiant and eager, he led her through all the house, from the basement to the servants' bedrooms under the roof. At the beginning, she made some effort to echo his laughter, to emulate his buoyancy; but, before they had come to the end, she was following him wearily, sick at heart, longing for it to be over, that she might be alone with her own thoughts.

It was only when they were having tea, by themselves in the drawing-room, that he perceived her dejection. And he questioned her so gently, that, in one generous impulse, she gave him all that was in her heart, pouring out her disappointment and her distress, reproaching herself the while for her weakness and for her ingratitude. He seated himself by her side on the sofa, and soothed her, till he had changed her sadness to hesitating happiness, and from hesitating happiness to the rest of pure delight.

In a corner of the bare, half-furnished drawing-room, while, outside, the rattle of wheels rose, shook the windows, and died away in the distance, he talked, narrating his love for her, till all the vista of the future became tinged with gold.

After dinner, while he smoked, she sat on a cushion at his feet, resting her head between his knees.

And when at last they went upstairs, she remembered nothing but his goodness, and the abandonment to the intoxication of his love.

VIII

There were three days before he must go back to his work — three days more to be passed together; and then, morning after morning, he would have to set off to his work; and all day, till the late afternoon, she would be alone.

They had talked together of this daily separation, many times — he resenting it unreasonably, she bravely concealing her dread — a double dread of solitude, and of those friends of his with whom she must become acquainted. For she divined that there would be no affinity between them and her.

But they were busy days; for the furniture that the house possessed was quite scanty, and they had but a single, temporary servant.

So full of their joy as to be oblivious of all that was not directly concerned in it, they wandered through many spacious shops, hesitating at the entrance to consult a voluminous list which she had conscientiously compiled; then, after starting in the wake of some stately shopman, halting continually, calling the one to the other, purchasing capriciously. Just at first his joyous recklessness roused her scruples: soon, she became entirely infected with his exuberance.

In the evenings, they were eager to have done with their dinner, that they might the sooner attack the pile of packages encumbering the hall, and spread their contents on the dining-room table, critically, as if for exhibition.

And, besides, there were servants to be engaged. Hillier was charmed by her timid avowal of inexperience, and good-humouredly took the matter into his own hands, inserting advertisements in the newspapers. So on the morning of their last day they breakfasted earlier than usual: then, as soon as the cloth was cleared, seated themselves, in judgment as it were, at one end of the long table.

And the invasion began. In rapid succession they appeared; portly women in smart bonnets; chubby country-girls; maids with prim, genteel voices; bouncing, garrulous creatures of all shapes and sizes.

Hillier attacked each one with the same determination, questioning and cross-questioning with a confident fluency that filled her with amazement and admiration. So, by luncheon-time, their household was completed.

And all the while, to know that the separation was at hand, lent to the close companionship of these first days in London — the last of the honeymoon, she named them to herself — a subtle excitement and a precious charm.

IX

"How far is it?"

"About three miles. You'd only better come as far as the Circus."[8]

"Oh! let me come all the way, please."

"There, poor little girl, of course you shall, if you want to."

The morning sunlight was gladdening the city, gilding the roof-tops, driving the dirt from the houses, lending to the pavement a dazzling whiteness, paving the roadway with burnished nuggets, glinting on the panels of carriages, and on the flanks of horses.

"Look, Hillier! what a beautiful morning!"

Something of the glad spirit entered into her, as, by his side, she walked past the great yellow museum, all agleam in the insolence of its ugliness. To glance down at her bright-blue dress, which she was wearing for the first time, gave her a sense of elation, of kinship with the day's mood.

Hillier was jubilant; talking, jesting, laughing loudly; so that, as they passed, people turned to look at them. And when he noticed this, he jested the louder.

They turned into the Park, and away across the green towards Rotten Row.[9]

---

[8] The Circus: here, Piccadilly Circus in central London.

[9] Rotten Row (originally *Route de Roi*) is a wide avenue flanked by trees extending along the southern boundary of Hyde Park. 'In the morning, between 11 and 1' it is 'crowded with ladies and gentleman on horseback, representatives of "the upper ten."' Charles Eyre Pascoe, *London Of To-Day: An Illustrated Handbook From 1891*, 7th edn (London: Simpkin, Marshall, Hamilton, Kent, & Co., 1891), p. 89.

In the distance the trees, all veiled in blue haze, were merging themselves, indistinct and indefinite, in the glowing sky. Hillier exclaimed how that exquisite atmospheric effect was to be seen but there, and in Corot's best work.[10] She wondered who Corot was; she fancied his name must be spelt Coreau.

There they sauntered a little, watching the riders as they cantered past. Once an acquaintance of Hillier's raised his hat. She divined, quickly, that the obvious curiosity with which the man eyed her was distasteful to him; for he started to narrate, in a forced, jocular manner, his peculiarities. She felt that the edge of her happiness was dulling; as if something, coming between them, had alienated his sympathy from her.

When they reached Piccadilly, she was thinking of the return home; the way seemed long, and she would be alone: she was recapitulating all the occupations with which she had told herself last night she would fill the day till his return.

Moreover, she was acutely conscious that, for the moment, she had no place in his thoughts. She heard him explaining a quarrel between a famous author and the firm of publishers who employed him as reader, and she knew that he had never noticed that she was not listening. Then he spoke of the future, of the people who would call on her, who would ask them to dinner, and whom they would have to entertain in return. To hear all these names, with which she was quite unfamiliar, made her heart sink lower and lower.

At the crossing they paused, for several omnibuses blocked the road: from behind, from each side, the people crowded to the pavement-edge, waiting to cross.

And still he went on talking.

The soreness of her wounded pride grew intolerable.

"I shall go back now," she said: but she was keenly hoping that he would ask her to come on.

"Poor little Nell! you're tired. I'll put you into a hansom."

"I'd rather walk," she answered curtly.

He looked at her doubtfully, then —

"No, you can't," he remonstrated.

"I'd rather — at least the bit across the Park."

"Goodbye," he said. Next, with a glimmer of how things were, he added, "The little wife must take great care of herself. I shall dash home in the swiftest hansom in the Strand."

The omnibuses had moved on; the roadway was clear; the people, pressing forward, swallowed him up.

---

[10]   Corot: Jean-Baptist Camille Corot (1796–1875). French painter of portraits and landscapes, he was influential on the later impressionist painters. Hillier Haselton's enthusiasm for Corot reflects the high estimation of his work shown by Pater and, before him, Gautier and Baudelaire.

She noticed that he had not touched her hand, or raised his hat to her. Back, against the tide of men and women flowing towards the City, she turned; dreary-hearted, isolated, in the midst of this crowd that pushed past her, in whose life she had no part. Everyone seemed to be watching her, staring at her, hardly, hostilely. She felt more and more awkward, and different from the rest.

X

During the late afternoon he returned, bringing her some bunches of violets. She found herself almost shy of him: she told him so, and they laughed together.

In the evening a band struck up near the house, so they carried chairs and rugs onto the balcony and sat there, talking a little, while the music played. He was pleased that she was thus tender, subdued in manner towards him. Her companionship cost him no effort, and he reminded himself how, in marrying her, he had done well.

Later, in the silence of the night, she listened to the passionate expression of his love, and the memory of the walk, of the parting, of the dreary loneliness in which the day had been spent, faded till it had grown vague and insignificant. Only the next morning she did not offer to accompany him: he did not suggest it: he just kissed her in the hall, his hat on his head, his stick in his hand, and went.

She was not sorry that it was thus.

XI

So the days went by.

She went to work seriously, methodically, to accustom herself to the new routine, resolute to learn, to make herself at ease in her new life. She was uneasy on account of her ignorance of the ways of people in London; yet she shrank from communicating her uneasiness to him — partly from a desire to conceal her shortcomings, and partly, perhaps, because she feared lest, in betraying them, she would be risking something — of the precise nature of which she had no idea.

And she was busy making progress. From conversations listened to in the drawing-rooms she visited, she acquired a glib familiarity with the jargon of her new surroundings; she learnt to manipulate easily, without effort, just those turns of phrase calculated to sustain amiable conversation.

Besides, from books, from review articles, from his talk, she was getting a queer, jumbled knowledge of modern thought — of Ibsen, of the labour question, of impressionism, of the works of George Meredith, of the emancipation of women.[11] It was the pressure of a constant consciousness of her husband's superiority that impelled her to struggle with all these things. "Hillier wants me to be clever," she had said to herself. But, as yet, her labour bore no fruit; only the sense of her own ignorance and of her own stupidity came of it. Now and then, with a glimmering perception of the wickedness of the world, she revolted against what she read: but she was generally too preoccupied with the thoughts that were at work in the background of her own mind to grasp intelligently the author's meaning.

XII

The innumerable small signs of her love for him, of her submission to him in all things, afforded his vanity a continual regalement such as it had never known before: beside no other woman had he experienced that sense of complete mastery. He attributed his contentment to the depth of his love. At the same time, the period of dissatisfaction with the various sentimental experiences, which other women had bequeathed to him, closed. He had already almost persuaded himself that they were a not inappropriate prelude to the adoration which his wife laid at his feet.

Thus, the best that was in him was brought to the surface.

He had visioned himself as treating her with forbearance, indulgence, sweetness, after having displayed an intelligent unworldliness in marrying her. During the honeymoon, and the first days in London, he had achieved this attitude quite satisfactorily, and since he had found that achievement easy, he glided into a complacent security with regard to the future.

After the strangeness of the first days had worn off, he had been busy with dreams of his own possibilities as her husband. Her entire lack of all that small knowledge, of which, in London, she would stand in such need, did not daunt him; it excited him, while her responsiveness, her eagerness to accept him as a teacher, swelled his self-confidence.

And her continual recognition of his kindness towards her, and her avowals of her faith in him, led him insensibly to shirk the knowledge that, after all, he was not what she believed him to be.

XIII

A sullen buzz of voices, a dazzle of light, a crowded confusion of men and women, huddled together.

[11] These topics of current interest would each merit inclusion in *The Albermarle: A Monthly Review*, the journal Crackanthorpe co-edited in 1892.

They passed the doorway, but they could get no further: the room was quite full.

The faces she saw were quite strange: a grey-haired woman in a low-cut dress lifted some glasses with a long handle to her eyes and stared. Some man nodded to Hillier: the rest did not move.

So they stood there, hemmed in on all sides, looking round them. She wanted to ask Hillier who the people were. But she dared not, they were all so near.

Disjointed words, fragments of phrases reached her ears. After a while, quite close, a woman's voice was saying —

"A simple, country girl. Before she met him her mind must have been a blank. I guess it's pretty well scored with his scribblings though by this time. She takes him, I hear, with prodigious solemnity — and herself too, for that matter."

"Yes, it's a great pity. Somebody should have done something. But no one knew of it till it was done. He's made a huge fool of himself." The voice was a man's.

The woman's voice answered something which she could not hear.

She looked, and saw them standing quite close, with their backs turned towards her.

"He's very devoted to her?" the woman's voice began again.

The man said something in a lower tone and the woman laughed.

"What girl wouldn't under the circumstances?" he added.

"She's sweetly pretty, people say."

"Bah! the world's stuffed full of pretty women."

Hillier's hand gripped her arm.

"Come, let's get on," she heard him saying.

The roughness of his tone startled her. She saw the tight look on his face. What was the matter?

He pressed forward, and, as there was not space for her to follow, he dragged at her arm. But there were no gaps in the human wall in front. The floor was blocked.

Next, a young man shook hands with Hillier, who introduced him to her. He made some remark about the great crowd.

The voices began again; the woman was speaking.

"If it's as you say, she'll be a great drag on him."

"He's not the sort of man to enjoy recognizing his own mistakes — especially one of that kind."

"Perhaps he will never recognize it."

"Life is long," answered the man's voice.

She noticed that the young man who had been introduced to her was talking to someone else. The voices were indistinct now. Next she caught the words: —

"And, you know, he might have married Mrs. Hendrick."

Mrs. Hendrick! Mrs. Hendrick was a friend of Hillier's. In a flash it came to her that it was of her — and of Hillier — that they were talking. For a moment the meaning of their words vanished, while resentment, hot and reckless, rose. She wanted to walk straight up to them — there before everybody — to tell them that they were mean, cowardly, hateful. Then the words returned, bringing dull pain. She longed to be alone with him, she was hungering for his comfort.

"Let's get out of this," he blurted.

He had heard it all, too.

He pushed his way towards the door; she following, dazed. She seemed to hear the voices still talking, indistinctly, behind her.

When they reached the landing, and were free of the crowd, her dress caught behind her. But he strode on, holding her arm so tightly that she could not stop, and the stuff tore loudly.

* * * * *

He had not spoken since they left the house. In the obscurity of the cab she could not see his face, and, till she had read its expression, she shrank from speaking. Several times, as they shot past a lamp-post, she threw a furtive glance at him. But his hat was tilted over his eyes, and the light was gone, before she could distinguish anything. She rubbed the moisture from off a corner of the window-pane, and peered out. Everything was dark and deserted; only the gas-lamps seemed awake. And the cab shot by them — one after another — rapidly.

* * * * *

He half wanted to speak to her, for he was aware that his silence was cruel; that he was playing an entirely ugly part. And the consciousness of how much a word of comfort would mean to her, of his own impotence to speak it, and the suspicion that she was crying, increased his exasperation considerably, tempting him to address her brutally.

He blamed her; yet he knew he had no right to do so: he disliked her; yet he knew that he was causing her to suffer.

They reached home in silence.

In the hall, a small impulse of remorse prompted him to lift off her cloak for her; but, as he came forward, she stepped past him with an assumption of haughtiness, so that he could not touch her. Immediately the full flame of his anger flared forth: he tasted an exasperated joy in that she had at last afforded him a pretext for losing his self-control.

He stepped into the study, and slammed the door behind him with all his force.

*   *   *   *   *

In her room, she sat down mechanically, without taking off her cloak. Her expression was blank: she could not cry.

Then she struggled to comfort herself. After all, perhaps it didn't matter what people said of her. It would be just the same tomorrow.

She whispered to herself some old words of his: — "You are the whole world to me: I cannot live without you, I love you, I love you, I love you." Three times he had said it; she shivered: for, somehow, they brought her no warmth.

How long would he be down there?

*   *   *   *   *

Oh! why had it ever been?

*   *   *   *   *

And, all at once, her whole being rose in fierce rebellion against her married life; she recalled, with added bitterness, her first revolt against the revelation which marriage had brought.

She felt that she hated the whole world, that there was no sweet savour left in life. Human nature, men and women, seemed hideous, degraded. And she hated herself because she had become like the rest.

She recalled the calm days of her girlhood with exceeding bitterness. She could never be like that again.

Then she felt that she could not bear to speak to him again tonight. When he came up she pretended to be asleep. He made no attempt to wake her; and, before long, he was heavily sleeping by her side.

XIV

The next morning, as they were preparing to get up: —

"I wish you'd put on that blue dress you used to wear when we were engaged," he said.

She had already learned the intonations of his voice, and, as he spoke, she recoiled a little.

"That old thing. I couldn't."

"I don't see why not. You used to look fifty times better in that than in all these new gaudy arrangements."

The harshness of his tone hurt her the more because it had come suddenly, at the very beginning of the day.

"Oh, Hillier! you never said you didn't like my new dresses," she faltered.

"I only say the other one suits you, and they don't."

She remembered the money they had cost, and how she had resolved to make each last as long as possible to compensate for the extravagance of buying them.

"What's wrong with them?"

"I don't know," he answered pettishly.

"But tell me what you don't like about them, and I will try to get them altered."

"That's no good; get a fresh lot. A different shape, more flowing lines, not tight and stiff." He did not look up: he was rummaging among some proofs on the bed.

"But it's so expensive," she pleaded.

"I tell you they don't suit you. How can you wear things that don't suit you?"

"I think you're horrid," she broke out, as he went into his dressing-room.

When she came downstairs, he was sitting reading the proofs which were littered on the floor around his chair. He took no notice of her as she entered.

"I believe it's all because of what those people said last night." Before the words were all uttered she was vaguely astonished at herself, and afraid of him.

"Don't go on nagging like that, you little fool! Do you hear?" he retorted loudly.

She turned to the breakfast-table. She glanced back at him; he did not look as if he were sorry that he had so spoken. Her resentment swelled tumultuously: she was shaking all over. If she had been a dog he could not have spoken more brutally; and he had said it just as if he were accustomed to speak to her so. Then the scene, that Sunday morning, in the garden, during the honeymoon, came back to her. Those words, that tone, he had thrown them at some one of the other women, and they had returned for her to hear, like an echo from the past. All through breakfast she continued to nurse this idea till she could not trust herself to speak to him, so bitterly did she feel.

He went on reading his proofs while he ate, and when he had done, gathered them together ostentatiously, saying that he was pressed for time.

A few minutes later the hall-door slammed.

A wild impulse prompted her to write to her mother; to tell her about last night and about this morning, that he no longer cared for her, that she wanted to come home, back to the old life, never to leave them again.

But as she dipped the pen in the ink the reaction came. Such a letter would seem silly, excited, absurd. She left the writing-table and started to busy herself with other things.

XV

Meanwhile he was walking towards Hyde Park Corner, irritated against the people who obstructed his path.

An obstreperous November wind, gusty and biting, was rushing about the streets: several ragged, dark clouds were careering across a leaden slab of sky. It was the beginning of winter, and he cursed the vile climate of London as only fit for cattle and dogs.

A press of work owing to the approach of Christmas had obliged him to cut short his morning's walk: and this, for want of a better pretext, increased his annoyance.

As he passed the French Embassy, a hansom drove by, carrying a woman wearing a white veil, who stared round at him through the side glass. Before he could raise his hat in recognition she was gone. It was Mrs. Hendrick.

The words "and he might have married Mrs. Hendrick" threw a whole new light upon her, revealing of a sudden the reason of many things in the past. How blind he must have been never to have perceived it before! Of course it was him that she wanted. How she had done her best to tell him this, and how obstinately he had shut his eyes! If he had only known, all sorts of curious things might have happened.

Probably she was quite forty; for she had wrinkles under her eyes and round her mouth, and her skin, white as it was, was altogether opaque. Yes, certainly she looked best in evening dress; or, at twilight, in a pallid-gold tea-gown which matched her hair.[12] And she had seven thousand a year.

He recalled his meeting with that ruffian Hendrick, her husband, a fortnight after she had divorced him — jovial and superb in spite of his grey hairs — banking in the baccarat-rooms at Aix-les-Bains.[13] He had chatted with the fellow afterwards on the balcony of the *Cercle*.[14] Hendrick had talked the case over shamelessly.

He remembered certain things which the man had hinted to him concerning her — things which no one but Hendrick could have known; and he wondered more than ever at himself how it was he had never noticed.

Mrs. Hendrick had never been to see Ella. The juxtaposition of the two women in his mind produced an only half-stifled movement of repentance, and of shame at his own behaviour this morning. Yet, he argued, there was nothing against Mrs. Hendrick; few women could have gone through such a case so satisfactorily.

*   *   *   *   *

[12]   A tea-gown is a long, loose fitting dress generally made of fine fabric and trimmed with lace, worn at afternoon tea.
[13]   Aix-les-Bains, with its thermal baths, was a fashionable town in the department of Savoie, south-east France.
[14]   The *Cercle*: the Casino Grand-Cercle was established in Aix in 1850 and was instrumental in attracting European high society to the Savoie area. Crackanthorpe's familiarity with casino culture is evident from his story 'When Greek Meets Greek', in *Wreckage*, pp. 165–214.

By-and-bye,[15] in the afternoon, he received a commission to write for an important review, a survey of the year's literature.

This unexpected stroke of good fortune, and the thought that he might have married Mrs. Hendrick, lent an elasticity to his gait as he walked home.

XVI

"Oh! I'm so glad!" she exclaimed, when he had finished telling her of his success. "And, Hillier, Mrs. Hendrick has been here."

"She ought to have come before." There was an insincere note of grievance in his tone. "Well, how did she seem?"

"I don't know .... she was very nice, and stayed a long time. She said she had seen you from a hansom this morning, and that reminded her of her negligence. She asked me to go to see her on Tuesday .... It's so difficult, Hillier .... She's much older than I expected. I thought she must be quite a young woman."

"Why?"

"Because I heard that man say the other evening that — that you might have married her .... And it seemed so — absurd." She brought out the words bravely, though a little tremulously.

He said nothing; so she went on more hurriedly:

"It isn't true, Hillier, is it? — tell me — that she was one of those .... you know, that afternoon in the garden...."

"No, of course not."

"Will you promise me, Hillier?"

"You don't believe me, then?" he exclaimed, almost angrily.

"Yes, dear — only I wanted to be sure."

"Well, then, I swear it. Now are you satisfied?"

"But she was a great friend of yours."

"I knew her a good deal. She was married to a brute of a man who used to treat her like a dog."

And he told her something of the rest.

"But her husband — where's her husband now?"

"I don't know; in Paris, probably."

"Didn't he care, then?"

"Not a rap."

"How horrible! How long had they been married?"

"Fifteen years. Why on earth she put up with him so long, I can't imagine. It was only when he took to bringing his — mistresses — to the house that she divorced him."

---

[15] Crackanthorpe's idiosyncratic, and consistently deployed, spelling of this phrase is maintained.

"Poor woman! How she must have suffered!"

There was a pause. Then she added —

"Hillier, I'm so glad she came. I want her to like me — to be friends with me — because I think she likes you very much."

"What makes you think that?"

"I don't know — but I'm sure she does."

And he did not mention the article to her.

XVII

There lurked, beneath the sweetness of Mrs. Hendrick's smile, and the gentleness of her voice, and the fragility of her whole appearance, an air of bitterness, restrained and refined. After the exposure of her husband's cruelty, a section of Society had considered itself justified in proclaiming an emphatic sympathy with her wrongs; women discussed her with long-drawn exclamations; men lowered their voices when they spoke to her; people, whose faces were unfamiliar, gushed with affectionate sympathy; some boldly indiscreet; others affecting tact; and those who had known her longer vindicated effusively their right to correct the general curiosity concerning her. Her worn beauty was in harmony with her new position; and those who were busy with her, hailed this harmony with satisfaction, affording, as it did, a fresh subject for comment. And lastly, the large fortune which she inherited just five weeks after she had regained her freedom, made her acquaintances more anxious than ever to assist her in the arrangement of her existence.

But by none of these things was she deceived, for just then she was disinterested enough in the course of her own existence to perceive that it all was entirely natural. And so, her attitude towards the world remained inert, apathetic, full of tired reserve. She repulsed people wearily, though politely; she was aware that she had no appetite for the cheap consolations they had to offer her. To abandon herself to her lassitude, to rest, to sleep, to forget, to put time between the present and the past — these were her longings.

By-and-bye there came with her wealth a clearer realization of her freedom, which made her wearily wonder why she had submitted so long, why she had thus wasted the best years of her life.

At these moments she marvelled bitterly at him who had been her husband: at his jovial insensibility, at the satisfaction, facile and complete, which his simple sensuality afforded him. She hated him; for she knew that he did not care. Thus, indifferent to the present, hopeless with regard to the future, she saw everything as dreary, colourless. It was as if the corner she had just turned had brought her face to face with a dead wall.

Occasionally some sharp phrase of the simple-minded old relative, who had come to live with her, made her conscious of her listlessness; and then, she rated herself morbid, or hard, selfish, incapable of emotion, and mused how it would have been if she had had a child.

Yet she continued to fulfil the engagements which Society made for her, because the effort of escaping from them seemed beyond her strength.

And all this was two years ago.

It was down in Norfolk, at a country-house, where they were fellow-guests, that her acquaintanceship with Hillier Haselton had developed into intimacy.

He, the morning of his arrival, had related to her — with a careless audacity that she set down as rare tact — how he had met Henry Hendrick on the Continent, a fortnight before. This placed him, in her eyes, in a slightly privileged position, which he was not slow to assume. So, somehow she drifted into talking to him about herself; on the terrace after breakfast, smoking a cigarette, he would saunter with her, up and down; he would fetch a basket-chair, and sit by her on the lawn, while the rest played tennis; he would row her on the lake in the late afternoon.

It only lasted a week, but they were much alone together, and their conversation glided insensibly into a tone of intimate seriousness. She hinted to him, at certain moments of eager expansion, of things concerning herself which, when she recalled them afterwards, scared her; yet the next day she would begin again to tell him more. She could not help herself.

Before he left, she had told him of her gratitude; though, indeed, she could not say what it was that he had done for her; only that she understood how un-glad her heart had been before, and that the common things of life looked less cheerless. Perhaps it was a little the consciousness of her wealth, and the new power it brought to her; for she had confided to him, timidly, her secret wish to employ a large — a very large — portion of it towards helping the outcast children of the great cities, and he had taken up this desire of hers, encouraged it, expanded it, given it, as it seemed to her, practical shape. And on this section of human suffering he spoke simply, with no affectation of false sentiment; so that to discuss it with him was in no wise difficult, as was the case with other people.

He seemed to her strong, fearless, a man of fine fibre.

*　*　*　*　*

A month passed, and then they were both back in London. He came one afternoon when she had other visitors: he only stayed a short while, but she learned that he had not forgotten the "scheme," as he called it, that he had been busying himself with its realization. And that, amid the stress of his own work, he should have found time to help her, touched her exceedingly, and intensified her admiration.

She saw him again, not unfrequently, for they had many friends in common; yet they never again got beyond the superficial small-talk of mere acquaintances. She shrank, somehow, from any attempt to renew their intimacy.

Once more he inquired concerning the "scheme"; but on learning that it was proceeding satisfactorily, he passed to another topic. He seemed unwilling that they should talk again as they had talked, in the summer, down in Norfolk.

So they drifted apart: she attributed it to his busy life which left him so little leisure; and she retained in her mind a clear image of him, as he had first appeared to her — strong, fearless, a man of fine fibre.

*   *   *   *   *

And now, he was married — a penniless clergyman's daughter — a love-marriage, accomplished quietly, secretly almost, in defiance of every worldly interest.

She thought it very characteristic of him.

All her interest in him revived. Yes, she might make friends with his wife, help her in little ways; and thus, indirectly, she would be of use to him. This idea grew rapidly in her mind: she was very eager to be friends with his wife.

XVIII

Ella by this time possessed a large number of acquaintances, but she sought out the society of no one of them, content that they should remain on the fringe, as it were, of her life. Her natural reserve exempted her from the temptation to entrust to others a selection of her inmost feelings; and she had no skill in superficial companionship. Thus she made no friends.

It was commonly reported that she "had not much in her"; or by others more shallow in thought and acrid of speech, that she was "quite stupid." Many tongues were busy with explanations of Hillier Haselton's marriage with the commonplace daughter of a country parson, remarking how frequently brilliant men tied themselves to dull women.

And, since the other evening, she had been growing more and more acutely sensible to all this; the smart that had been inflicted had endowed her, for the moment, with bitter perspicacity; she was convincing herself that everyone whom she met regarded her in the same light.

More than ever she sent her heart out towards her husband; starting afresh to urge herself to admire him extravagantly, stifling her sense of feverish insecurity, or attributing it to physical causes.

She was disturbed, puzzled too, by Mrs. Hendrick. She was not jealous; that would have been ridiculous; she did not dislike her, that would have been treacherous. Hillier liked talking to Mrs. Hendrick; when she came to dinner, and when they went to the big house in Grosvenor Place, he was in high spirits, always. And, of late, except on these occasions, he had been moody, dispirited; the edge of his buoyancy was blunted; he was overworking himself.

No, she was not jealous; for Mrs. Hendrick liked talking to her, too, and was constantly proposing that they should drive together in the afternoon — to a private view, or to an afternoon party. No, she did not dislike Mrs. Hendrick; for Mrs. Hendrick was kind, gentle, sweet.

XIX

The greater part of the afternoon he had been in his office, glancing through a manuscript.

Suddenly, while he was crossing the room to consult a volume on the shelves, the impulse to go and see Mrs. Hendrick laid hold upon him. It brought at once a feeling of excited unrest. He felt sick of work and cooped up in the room, which seemed dingy and full of dust. The desire to get out, to some immediate change, some outside excitement, became imperious.

What a long while it was since he had seen her alone! Not since that time two years ago. Certain incidents came back to him again. How was it he had been so indifferent then? He tried to flatter himself by the recollection of this indifference of his; but the effort was unsuccessful.

At that moment he entirely accepted the fact that he was tired of his wife. And, since he attributed this to some vague superiority in himself, it was without a pang that he shattered the whole accumulated fabric of his former conceptions of the possibilities of his marriage. Not that it once seemed that he had committed a piece of folly; for he was ready to blame her that she did not satisfy him. Yes, she did not satisfy him; and he clutched at this explanation as a justification for his recent vague dreamings concerning other women. It was no particular woman that he was picturing to himself, but certain types of women which were wholly different from Ella. The actual possibility of unfaithfulness to her he had never faced; though, perhaps, he had been very near indeed to doing so — certainly much nearer than he himself imagined. But then he had always taken for granted that he was not a brute. He had only been married a few months, and he knew of no one — except notorious scoundrels — who had done that thing after a few months.

So he went out, and drove to Grosvenor Place.

XX

She was at home. The servant showed him into the drawing-room — a charming room arranged in sound taste, he had always thought it. Today the furniture was all clothed in shiny, stiff chintzes, which lent a cold, uncomfortable look. He paced up and down restlessly, anxiously curious concerning what was about to happen. In half-an-hour it would be over, he told himself. What would be his position then? Yet he had no fixed idea as to what he was going to do. He lifted a red book from off the writing-table, opened it, and began to read the names absently — Williamson, Williamson, Williamson, Willie, Willington, Wilkie. He shut the book and replaced it. What was he going to do?

On the mantelpiece he caught sight of Ella's photograph[16] — an old likeness taken before their marriage. The lips were parted in a faint smile, and the rose-tinted background lent delicacy and sweetness to the face. It was very like her. He realized rapidly that his passion had certainly dwindled; that the sight of the photograph caused him no vibration of emotion.

*   *   *   *   *

The door opened, Mrs. Hendrick came forward, her hand outstretched frankly, cordially.

He met her, still holding the photograph in his left hand.

She noticed it, and smiled, then began —

"I'm so glad we've made such friends, Mr. Haselton. I can't tell you how much I like her. You must be very, very happy."

"Yes," he answered instantly. "I am completely happy."

"That's right, for you deserve it."

"Why?" he asked, assuming a blank expression.

"Because — well, you know, I've always thought of you as one of those people who have a right to the best things of life. When I first heard that you were married, before I knew your wife, I was sure you had done the best thing."

"But why?" he repeated mechanically.

"Oh, because I was sure you *would* do the right thing."

He perceived that she was quite genuine in speaking to him thus, and he was not a little disappointed; her seriousness exasperated him; she suddenly became to him wholly uninteresting; he wanted her no longer.

They talked on about his wife; by-and-bye, to change the topic, and to cover his indifference to her, he asked concerning her Home, and she recounted at considerable length how it was thriving, and of the peace of mind that the work had brought her.

When she seemed to have finished he rose, saying that he must be getting home. Laughingly she begged him to replace the photograph, which,

---

[16]   It appears improbable, but the presence of Ella's photograph in Mrs. Hendrick's house might be explained by the fact that Mrs. Hendrick had previously paid a visit to Ella. Even if there is no mention in the text, on that occasion Ella might have given her the photograph, which is now on her mantelpiece.

unconsciously, he had been holding in his left hand all the while. He did so with a well-simulated smile, and offered her a cheque in aid of the Home; but she shook her head, still laughing, telling him to buy his wife a present with it instead.

And she bid him goodbye just as she had met him, frankly, cordially.

In Bond Street he stopped to look at some diamonds flashing in a jeweller's window; two pretty women were giggling together by his side, and he wondered vaguely what he would do if anything were to happen to his wife.

A Commonplace Chapter — II

I

This was four years later.

*   *   *   *   *

She sat in a corner of a large London drawing-room, and the two men stood before her — Hillier Haselton, her husband, and George Swann, her husband's cousin; and, beyond them, the mellow light of shaded candles, vague groupings of black coats, white shirt-fronts, and gay-tinted dresses; and the noisy hum of conversation.

The subject that the two men were discussing — and more especially Swann's blunt earnestness — stirred her, though throughout it she had been unpleasantly conscious of a smallness, almost a pettiness, in Hillier's aspect.

"Well, but why not, my dear Swann? Why not be unjust? man's been unjust to woman for so many years."

Hillier let his voice fall listlessly, as if to rebuke the other's vehemence; and, to hint that he was tired of the topic, looked round at his wife, noting at the same time that Swann was observing how he held her gaze in his meaningly. And the unexpectedness of his own attitude charmed him — his hot defence of an absurd theory, obviously evoked by a lover-like desire to please her. Others, whose admiration he could trust, would, he surmised, have reckoned it a pretty pose. And she, perceiving that Swann seemed to take her husband's sincerity for granted, felt a sting of quick regret that she had ever come to understand him, and that she could not still view him as they all viewed him.

Hillier moved away across the room, and Swann drew a stool beside her chair, and asking her for news of Claude, her little boy, talked to her of other things — quite simply, for they were grown like old friends. He looked at her steadily, stroking his rough, fair beard, as if he were anxious to convey to her something which he could not put into words. She divined: and, a little startled, tried to thank him with her eyes; but, embarrassed by the clumsiness of his own attempt at sympathetic perception, he evidently noticed nothing. And this obtuseness of his disappointed her, since it somehow seemed to confirm her isolation.

She glanced round the room. Hillier stood on the hearthrug, his elbow on the mantelpiece, busily talking with slight, deferential gestures to the great English actress in whose honour the dinner had been given. The light fell on his smooth, glistening hair, on his quick, sensitive face; for the moment, forcing herself to realize him as he appeared to the rest, she felt a thrill of jaded pride in him, in his cleverness, in his reputation, in his social success.

Swann, observing the direction of her gaze, said almost apologetically —
"You must be very proud of him."

She nodded, smiling a faint, assumed smile; then added, adopting his tone —
"His success has made him so happy."

"And you too?" he queried.

"Of course," she answered quickly.

He stayed silent, while she continued to watch her husband absently.

II

Success, an atmosphere of flattery, suited Hillier Haselton, and stimulating his weaknesses, continually encouraged him to display the handsomer portion of his nature. For though he was yet young — and looked still younger — there was always apparent, beneath his frank, boyish relish of praise, a semblance of serious modesty, a strain of genuine reserve. And society — the smart, literary society that had taken him up — found this combination charming. So success had made life pleasant for him in many ways, and he rated its value accordingly; he was too able a man to find pleasure in the facile forms of conceit, or to accept, with more than a certain cynical complacency, the world's generous judgment on his work. Indeed, the whole chorus of admiration did but strengthen his contempt for contemporary literary judgments — a contempt which, lending the dignity of deliberate purpose to his indulgence of his own weakness for adulation — procured him a refined, a private, and an altogether agreeable self-satisfaction. When people set him down as vastly clever, he was pleased; he was unreasonably annoyed when they spoke of him as a great genius.

Life, he would repeat, was of larger moment than literature; and, despite all the freshness of his success, his interest in himself, in the play of his own personality, remained keener, and, in its essence, of more lasting a nature than his ambition for genuine achievement. The world — people with whom he was brought into relation — stimulated him so far as he could assimilate them to his conception of his own attitude; most forms of art too, in great measure — and music altogether — attracted him in the proportion that they played upon his intimate emotions. Similarly his friendships; and for this reason he preferred the companionship of women. But since his egoism was uncommonly dexterous, he seemed endowed with a rare gift of artistic perception, of psychological insight, of personal charm.

It had always been his nature to live almost exclusively in the present; his recollection of past impressions was grown scanty from habitual disuse. His sordid actions in the past he forgot with an ever-increasing facility; his moments of generosity or self-sacrifice he remembered carelessly, and enjoyed a secret pride in their concealment; and the conscious embellishment of subjective experience for the purpose of "copy," he had instinctively disdained.

Since his boyhood, religion had been distasteful to him, though, at rare moments, it had stirred his sensibilities strangely. Now, occasionally, the thought of the nullity of life, of its great, unsatisfying quality, of the horrid squalor of death, would descend upon him with its crushing, paralyzing weight; and he would lament, with bitter, futile regret, his lack of a secure standpoint, and the continual limitations of his self-absorption; but even that, perhaps, was a mere literary melancholy, assimilated from certain passages by Pierre Loti.[17]

But, now, he had published a stout volume of critical essays, and an important volume of poetry, and society had clamorously ratified his own conception of himself. Certainly, now, in the eyes of the world, it was agreed beyond dispute that she, his wife, was of quite the lesser importance. "She was nice and quiet," which meant that she seemed mildly insignificant; "she had a sense of humour," which meant that an odd note of half-stifled cynicism sometimes escaped her. He was evidently very devoted to her, and on that account women trusted him — all the more because her personality possessed no obvious glamour. Perhaps, now and then, his attentions to her in public seemed a little ostentatious; but then, in these modern, uncourtly days, that in itself was distinctive. In private too, especially at the moments when he found life stimulating, he was still tactful and expansive with sympathetic impulse; from habit; from pride in his comprehension of women; from dislike to cheap hypocrisy. How could he have divined that bitter, suppressed seriousness, with which she had taken her disillusionment; when not once in three months did he consider her apart from the play of his own personality; otherwise than in the light of her initial attitude towards him?

And her disillusionment, how had it come? Certainly, not with a rush of sudden, overwhelming revelation: certainly, it was in no wise inspired by the

---

[17]   Pierre Loti: pseudonym for Louis Marie-Julien Viaud (1850–1923), a naval officer and novelist. His works were impressionistic in character, often located in exotic settings.

tragedy of Nora Helmer.[18] It had been a gradual growth, to whose obscure and trivial beginnings she had not had the learning to ascribe their true significance. To sound the current of life was not her way. She was naive by nature; and the ignorance of her girlhood had been due, rather to a natural inobservance, than to carefully-managed surroundings. And yet, she had come to disbelieve in Hillier; to discredit his clever attractiveness: she had become acutely sensitive to his instability, and, with a secret, instinctive obstinacy, to mistrust the world's praise of his work. Perhaps had he made less effort in the beginning to achieve a brilliancy of attitude in her eyes; had he schooled her to expect from him a lesser loftiness of aspiration, things might have been very different; or at least, there might have resulted from the process of her disillusionment a lesser bitterness of conviction. But she had taken her marriage with so keen an earnestness of ideal, had noted every turn in his personality with so intense an expectation. Perhaps, too, had he detected the first totterings of her ideal conception of him; had he aided her, as it were, to descend his figure from that pedestal, where he himself had originally planted it, together they might have set it uninjured on a lower and less exposed plane. But he had never heeded her subtle indications of its insecurity: alone, she had watched its peril, awaiting with a frightened fascination the day when it should roll headlong in the dust. And, at intervals, she would vaguely marvel, when she observed others, whose superior perspicacity she assumed, display no perception of his insincerity. Then the oppressive sense that she — she, his wife, the mother of his child — was the only one who saw him clearly, and the unsurmountable shrinking from the relief of sharing this sense with anyone, made her sourly sensitive to the pettiness, the meanness, the hidden, tragic element in life.

A gulf had grown between them — that was how she described it to herself. Outwardly their relations remained the same; but, frequently, in his continuance of his former attitude, she detected traces of deliberate effort; frequently, when off his guard, he would abandon all pretension to it, and openly betray how little she had come to mean to him. There were, of course, moments also, when, at the echo of his tenderness, she would feverishly compel herself to believe in its genuineness; but a minute later, he would have forgotten his exaltation, and, almost with irritation, would deliberately ignore the tense yearning that was glowing within her.

[18]   Nora Helmer is the female protagonist of Henrik Ibsen's play *A Doll's House* (1879). The role was performed to great acclaim by Janet Achurch at London's Gaiety Theatre in June 1889. The production was attended by many of the leading writers of the day, including Crackanthorpe's friend Ernest Dowson, who thought it 'the very finest play that has been seen for years' (Dowson to Victor Plarr [*c.* 19 June 1889], *The Letters of Ernest Dowson*, ed. by Desmond Flower and Henry Maas (London: Cassell, 1967), p. 85). Nora's decision to leave her marriage and her children at the end of the four-act play, which culminates in her dramatic action of slamming the door on her household, caused a sensation, dividing opinion between shocked upholders of marriage as a sacred institution and progressives and feminists who loudly applauded her act of defiance against the hold of patriarchy.

And so, the coming of his success — a brilliant blossoming into celebrity — had stirred her but fitfully. Critics wrote of the fine sincerity of his poetry; while she clung obstinately to her superstition that fine poetry must be the outcome of a great nobility of character. And, sometimes, she hated all this success of his, because it seemed to emphasize the gulf between them, and, in some inexplicable way, to lessen her value in his eyes; then again, from an impulse of sheer unselfishness, she would succeed in almost welcoming it, because, after all, he was her husband.

But of all this he noted nothing: only now and then he would remind himself vaguely that she had no literary leanings.

The little Claude was three years old. Before his birth, Hillier had dilated much on the mysterious beauty of childhood, had vied with her own awed expectation of the wonderful, coming joy. During her confinement, which had been a severe one, for three nights in succession he had sat, haggard with sleepless anxiety, on a stiff-backed dining-room chair, till all danger was passed. But afterwards, the baby had disappointed him sorely; and later, she thought he came near actively disliking it. Still, reminding herself of the winsomeness of other children at the first awakening of intelligence, she waited with patient hopefulness, fondly fancying a beautiful boy-child; wide, baby eyes; a delicious prattle. Claude, however, attained no prettiness, as he grew: from an unattractive baby he became an unattractive child, with lanky, carroty hair; a squat nose; an ugly, formless mouth. And in addition, he was fretful, mischievous, self-willed. Hillier at this time paid him but a perfunctory attention; avoided discussing him; and, when that was not possible, adopted a subtle, aggrieved tone that cut her to the quick. For she adored the child; adored him because he was hers; adored him for his very defects; adored him because of her own suppressed sadness; adored him for the prospect of the future — his education, his development, his gradual growth into manhood.

From the house in Cromwell Road the Haseltons had moved to a flat near Victoria Station:[19] their means were moderate; but now, through the death of a relative, Hillier was no longer dependent upon literature for a living.

III

George Swann was her husband's cousin; and besides, he had stood godfather to the little Claude. He was the elder by eight years; but Hillier always treated him as if their ages were reversed, and before Ella, used to nickname him the "Anglo-Saxon," because of his loose, physical largeness, his flaxen hair and beard, his strong simplicity of nature. And Swann, with a reticent good humour, acquiesced in Hillier's tone towards him; out of vague regard for his cousin's ability; out of respect for him as Ella's husband.

[19]   Victoria Station: in Victoria Street, near Buckingham Palace and Westminster.

Swann and Ella were near friends. Since their first meeting, the combination of his blunt self-possession, and his uncouth timidity with women, had attracted her. Divining his simplicity, she had felt at once at her ease with him, and, treating him with open, cousinly friendliness, had encouraged him to come often to the house.

A while later, a trivial incident confirmed her regard for him. They had been one evening to the theatre together — she and Hillier and Swann — and afterwards, since it was raining, she and Hillier waited under the doorway, while he sallied out into the Strand to find them a cab. Pushing his way along the crowded street, his eyes scanning the traffic for an empty hansom, he accidentally collided with a woman of the pavement, jostling her off the kerb into the mud of the gutter.[20] Ella watched him stop, gaze ruefully at the woman's splashed skirt, take off his hat and apologize with profuse, impulsive regret. The woman continued her walk, and presently passed the theatre door. She looked middle-aged: her face was hard and animal-like.

One Sunday afternoon — it was summer-time — as she was crossing the Park to pay a call in Gloucester Square, she came across him sauntering alone in Kensington Gardens. She stopped and spoke to him: he seemed much startled to meet her. Three-quarters of an hour later, when she returned, he was sitting on a public bench beside her path; and immediately, from his manner, she half guessed that he had been waiting for her. It was a fortnight after Claude's christening: he started to speak to her of the child, and so, talking together gravely, they turned onto the turf, mounted the slope, and sat down on two chairs beneath the trees.

Touched by his waiting for her, she was anxious to make friends with him; because he was the baby's godfather; because he seemed alone in the world; because she trusted in his goodness. So she led him, directly and indirectly, to talk of himself. At first, in moody embarrassment, he prodded the turf with his stick; and presently responded, unwillingly breaking down his troubled reserve, and alluding to his loneliness confidingly, as if sure of her sympathy.

Unconsciously he made her feel privileged to thus obtain an insight into the inner workings of his heart, and gave her a womanly, sentimental interest in him.

Comely cloud-billows were overhead, and there was not a breath of breeze.

They paused in their talk, and he spoke to her of Kensington Gardens, lovingly, as of a spot which had signified much to him in the past — Kensington Gardens, massively decorous; ceremoniously quiet; pompous, courtly as a king's leisure-park; the slow, opulent contours of portly foliage, sober-green, immobile and indolent; spacious groupings of tree-trunks; a low ceiling of leaves; broad shadows mottling the grass. The Long Water, smooth and dark

---

[20]   A woman of the pavement: a euphemism for a prostitute.

as a mirror; lining its banks, the rhododendrons swelling with colour, cream, purple, and carmine.[21] The peacock's insolent scream; a silently skimming pigeon; the joyous twitterings of birds; the patient bleating of sheep....[22]

At last she rose to go. He accompanied her as far as the Albert Memorial,[23] and when he had left her, she realized, with a thrill of contentment, that he and she had become friends.

IV

That had been the beginning of George Swann's great love for her. His was a slowly moving nature: it was gradually therefore that he came to value, as a matter of almost sacred concern, the sense of her friendship; reverencing her with the single-hearted, unquestioning reverence of a man unfamiliar with women; regarding altogether gravely her relations with him — their talks on serious subjects, the little letters she wrote to him, the books that he had given her — Swinburne's *Century of Roundels*;[24] a tiny edition of Shelley, bound in white parchment; Mrs. Meynell's *Rhythm of Life*.[25] He took to studying her intellectual tastes, the topics that were congenial to her, her opinions on men and women, with a quiet, plodding earnestness; almost as if it were his duty. Thus he learned her love of simple country things; gained a conception of her girlhood's home; of her father and mother, staid country folk. He did not know how to him alone she could talk of these things; or of the warm, deep-seated gratitude she bore him in consequence; but he reverted constantly to the topic, because, under its influence, she always brightened, and it seemed to ratify the bond of sympathy between them.

How much, as the months went by, she came to mean to him, he had not in the least realized: he had never thought of her as playing a part in his own life; only as a beautiful-natured woman, to whom he owed everything, because, by some strange chance, she had made him her friend.

Not even in his moments of idle, vagrant reverie, did he think to ask more

[21]   The Long Water is an artificial lake in Kensington Gardens, created in 1730. The name refers to the long and narrow half of the Serpentine lake.
[22]   In tone and style this descriptive passage is characteristic of the virtuoso performances of the prose poem form which make up Crackanthorpe's *Vignettes* (1896).
[23]   The Albert Memorial is a monument, designed by Sir George Gilbert Scott, to Queen Victoria's husband, Prince Albert of Saxe-Coburg and Gotha, who died in 1861. It was erected in Kensington Gardens in 1872. Victoria outlived Albert by a further forty years.
[24]   *A Century of Roundels* (London: Chatto and Windus, 1883) was dedicated by Swinburne (1837–1909) to Christina Rossetti (1830–1894), who was herself an exponent of the form. A roundel is a variation of the French *rondeau*.
[25]   Alice Meynell (1847–1922) was a poet, writer, later suffragist and literary hostess of Catholic sympathies; she was friends with Johnson and Beardsley. *The Rhythm of Life and Other Essays* was published by Elkin Matthews and John Lane in 1893.

of her than this; to intrude himself further into her life; to offer her more than exactly that which she was expecting of him, naturally never occurred to him. Yet, in a queer, uncomfortable way, he was jealous of other men's familiarity with her — vaguely jealous lest they should supplant him, mistrustful of his own modesty. And there was no service which, if she had asked it of him, he would not have accomplished for her sake; for he had no ties.

But towards Hillier, since he belonged to her, Swann's heart warmed affectionately: she had loved and married him; had made him master of her life. So he instinctively extended to his cousin a portion of the unspoken devotion inspired by Ella. Such was the extent of his reverence for her, and his diffidence regarding himself, that he took for granted that Hillier was an ideal husband, tender, impelled by her to no ordinary daily devotion: for, that it should be otherwise, would have seemed to him a monstrous improbability. Yet latterly, since the coming of Hillier's success, certain incidents had disconcerted him, filled him with ill-defined uneasiness.

From the first, he had been one of Hillier's warmest admirers; praising, whenever an opportunity offered, out of sheer loyalty to Ella, and pride in his cousin, the fineness of form that his poetry revealed. To her, when they were alone, he had talked in the same enthusiastic strain: the first time she had seemed listless and tired, and afterwards he had blamed himself for his want of tact; on another occasion, he had brought her a laudatory article, and she had turned the conversation brusquely into another channel. And, since his love for her — of which as yet he was himself unconscious — caused him to brood over means of pleasing her (he lived alone in the Temple),[26] this indication that he had jarred her sensibilities was not lost upon him.

Hillier's attitude towards the little Claude, and the pain that it was causing her, would in all probability have escaped him, had she not alluded to it once openly, frankly assuming that he had perceived it. It was not indeed that she was in any way tempted to indulge in the transitional treachery of discussing Hillier with him; but that, distressed, yearning for counsel, she was prompted almost irresistibly to turn to Swann, who had stood godfather to the child, who was ready to join her in forming anxious speculations concerning the future.

For of course he had extended his devotion to the child also, who, at Hillier's

---

[26] 'You know the Temple is supposed to be used only by lawyers, but [...] other people do sometimes live here', wrote Arthur Symons, who called it 'an oasis in the heart of London — quietest spot in all the great city, yet with the roar of the Strand only just out of hearing' (Symons to Katherine Willard, 5 February 1891, *Arthur Symons: Selected Letters, 1880–1935*, ed. by Karl Beckson and John M. Munro (Basingstoke: Macmillan, 1989), p. 70). The Temple was home to other figures associated with the Decadent movement, including George Moore, John Gray, Havelock Ellis, and Alexander Teixera de Mattos, and it was to Fountain Court in the Temple that Symons invited Verlaine during his November 1893 visit to England.

suggestion, was taught to call him Uncle George. Naturally his heart went out to children: the little Claude, since the first awakening of his intelligence, had exhibited a freakish, childish liking for him; and, in his presence, always assumed something of the winsomeness of other children.

The child's preference for Swann, his shy mistrust of his father, were sometimes awkwardly apparent; but Hillier, so it seemed to Ella, so far from resenting, readily accepted his cousin's predominance. "Children always instinctively know a good man," he would say, laughing; and Ella would wince inwardly, discerning, beneath his air of complacent humility, how far apart from her he had come to stand.

Thus, insensibly, Swann had become necessary to her, almost the pivot, as it were, of her life: to muse concerning the nature of his feeling towards her; to probe its sentimental aspects, to accept his friendship otherwise than with unconscious ease, that was not her way.

But Hillier noted critically how things were drifting, and even lent encouragement to their progress in a way that was entirely unostentatious; since so cynical an attitude seemed in some measure to justify his own conduct.

V

For he was unfaithful to his wife. It was inevitable that the temptation, in the guise of a craving for change, should come — not from the outside, but from within himself. And he had had no habit of stable purpose with which to withstand it. Not altogether was it a vagrant, generalized lusting after women other than his wife; not a mere harking back to the cruder experiences of his bachelorhood; though, at first, it had seemed so to manifest itself. Rather was it the result of a moody restlessness, of a dissatisfaction (with her, consciously, no; for the more that he sinned against her, the more lovable, precious her figure appeared to him) kindled by continual contact with her natural goodness. It was as if, in his effort to match his personality with hers, he had put too severe a strain upon the better part of him.

He himself had never analyzed the matter more exhaustively than this. The treacherous longing had gripped him at certain moments, holding him helpless as in a vice. He had conceived no reckless passion for another woman: such an eventuality, he dimly surmised, was well-nigh improbable. In his case brain domineered over heart: to meet the first outbursting of his adoration for his wife, he had drained every resource of his sentimentality.

Was it then an idle craving for adventure, a school-boy curiosity clamouring for fresh insight into the heart of women? Mere experience was unnecessary for the attainment of comprehension: "to have lived" did not imply "to have understood": the most pregnant adventures, as he knew, were those which entailed no actual unfaithfulness.

And for these — subtle, psychological intimacies — ample occasion offered. Yet the twist in his nature led him to profess to treat them heedlessly; and, in reality, to prosecute them with no genuine strenuousness. They would have been obvious lapses; Ella would have been pained, pitied perhaps; from that his vanity and his sham chivalry alike shrank.

His unfaithfulness to her, then, had been prompted by no evident motive. Superficially considered, it seemed altogether gratuitous, meaningless. The world — that is, people who knew him and her — would probably have discredited the story, had it come to be bruited.[27] And this fact he had not omitted to consider.

She, the other woman, was of little importance. She belonged to the higher walks of the demi-monde:[28] she was young; beautiful too, in a manner; light-hearted; altogether complaisant. She was not the first; there had been others before her; but these were of no account whatsoever: they had but represented the bald fact of his unfaithfulness. But *she* attracted him: he returned to her again and again; though afterwards, at any rate in the beginning, he was wont to spare himself little in the matter of self-reproach, and even to make some show of resisting the temptation. The discretion of her cynical camaraderie, however, was to be trusted; and that was sufficient to undermine all virtuous resolution. She had the knack, too, of cheering him when depressed, and, curiously enough, of momentarily reinstating him in his own conceit, though, later, on his return to Ella, he would suffer most of the pangs of remorse.

There was something mannish about her — not about her physiognomy, but about her mind — derived, no doubt, from the scantiness of her intercourse with women. Her cynicism was both human and humorous: she was a person of little education, and betrayed none of the conventionality of her class: hence her point of view often struck him as oddly direct and unexpected. He used to talk to her about himself, candidly discussing all manner of random and intimate matters before her, without shyness on his part, without surprise on hers — almost at times as if she were not present — and with an assumption of facile banter, to listen to which tickled his vanity. Only to Ella did he never allude; and in this, of course, she tacitly acquiesced. She possessed a certain quality of sympathetic tact; always attentive to his talk, never critical of it; mindful of all that he had previously recounted. He could always resume his attitude at the very point where he had abandoned it. Between them there was never any aping of sentimentality.

---

[27] Bruited means rumoured.
[28] The demi-monde (literally 'half-world') is a group of people of dubious respectability or morality.

That she comprehended him — with so fatuous a delusion he never coquetted: nor that she interested him as a curious type. She saw no subtle significance in his talk: she understood nothing of its complex promptings: she was ordinary, uneducated, and yet stimulating — that was the contrast which attracted him towards her. Concerning the course of her own existence he did not trouble himself; he accepted her as he found her; deriving a sense of security from the fact that towards him her manner varied but little from visit to visit. But, as these accumulated, becoming more and more regular, and his faith in her discretion blunted the edge of his remorse, he came to notice how she braced[29] him, reconciled him to his treachery; (which, he argued, in any case was inevitable) lent to it a spice almost of pleasantness. Neither had he misgivings of the future, of how it would end. One day she would pass out of his life as easily as she had come into it. His relations with her were odd, though not in the obvious way. About the whole thing he was insensibly coming to feel composed.

And its smoothness, its lack of a disquieting aspect, impelled him to persevere towards Ella in cheerfulness, courteous kindness, and a show of continuous affection; and to repent altogether of those lapses into roughness which had marred the first months of their marriage.

VI

The hansoms whirled their yellow, gleaming eyes down West:[30] hot, flapping gusts went and returned aimlessly; and the mirthless twitterings of the women fell abruptly on the sluggishly shuffling crowd.[31] All the sin of the city seemed crushed to listlessness; vacantly wistful, the figures waited by the street corners.[32]

Then the storm burst. Slow, ponderous drops; a clap of the thunder's wrath; a crinkled rim of light, unveiling a slab of sky, throbbing, sullen and violet; small, giggling screams of alarm, and a stampede of bunchy silhouettes. The thunder clapped again, impatient and imperious; and the rain responded, zealously hissing. Bright stains of liquid gold straggled across the roadway; a sound of splashing accompanied the thud of hoofs, the rumble of wheels, the clanking of chains, and the ceaseless rattle of the drops on the hurried procession of umbrellas.

---

[29] Braced means strengthened.
[30] Down West: here either in, or in the direction of, the west side of London.
[31] This opening passage, ending in 'hurried procession of umbrellas', is imported, very slightly modified, from Crackanthorpe's 'Melodramatic Storm' (*The Speaker*, 8 December 1894, p. 636). Compare Richard Le Gallienne's 'A Ballad of London': 'the hansoms hover, | With jewelled eyes to catch the lover' (lines 9–10), *Second Book of the Rhymers' Club* (London: Elkin Matthews and John Lane, 1894), p. 20.
[32] The 'figures [waiting] by the street corners' are prostitutes.

Swann, from the corner of a crowded omnibus, peered absently through the doorway, while the conductor, leaning into the street, touted mechanically for passengers.

The vehicle stopped. A woman, bare-headed and cloaked, escorted by the umbrella of a restaurant official, hurried to the shelter of a cab, across the wet pavement. A man broke the stream of the hastening crowd; halted beside the wheel to stare. The woman laughed in recognition, noisily. The man stepped rapidly onto the foot-board, and an instant stood there, directing the driver across the roof. The light from a lamp-post caught his face: it was Hillier. The next moment he was seated beside the woman, who was still laughing (Swann could see the gleaming whiteness of her teeth): the driver had loosened the window strap, the glass had slid down, shutting them in. The omnibus jolted forward, and the cab followed in its wake, impatiently, for the street was blocked with traffic.

Immediately, with a fierce vividness, Ella's image sprang up before Swann's eyes — her face with all its pure, natural, simple sweetness. And there — not ten yards distant, behind the obscurity of that blurred glass, Hillier was sitting with another woman — a woman concerning whose status he could not doubt.

He clenched his gloved fists. The wild impulse spurted forth, the impulse to drag the cur from the cab, to bespatter him, to throw him into the mud, to handle him brutally, as he deserved. It was as though Hillier had struck him a cowardly blow in the face.

Then the hansom started to creep past the omnibus. Swann sprang into the roadway. A moment later he was inside another cab, whirling in pursuit down Piccadilly hill.

The horse's hoofs splashed with a rhythmical, accelerated precision: he noticed dully how the crupper-strap[33] flapped from side to side, across the animal's back. Ahead, up the incline, pairs of tiny specks, red and green, were flitting.

"It's the cab with the lady what come out of the restaurant, ain't it, sir?"

"Yes," Swann called back through the trap.

The reins tightened; the horse quickened his trot.

Hyde Park Corner stood empty and resplendent with a. glitter of glamorous gold. The cab turned the corner of Hamilton Place, and the driver lashed the horse into a canter up Park Lane.

"That's 'im — jest in front ——"

"All right. Follow," Swann heard himself answering. And, amid his pain, he was conscious that the man's jaunty tone seemed to indicate that this sort of job was not unfamiliar.

---

[33] The crupper-strap runs from the back of the saddle or harness along the top of the horse's rump, then underneath the tail, in order to keep the saddle from sliding too far forward, or to keep the harness in place.

He struggled to tame the savageness of his indignation; to think out the situation; to realize things coolly, that he might do what was best for her. But the leaping recollection of all her trustfulness, her goodness, filled him with a burning, maddening compassion .... He could see nothing but the great wrong done to her....

Where were they going — the green lights of that cab in front — that woman and Hillier? ... Where would it end, this horrible pursuit — this whirling current which was sweeping him forward? ... It was like a nightmare....

He must stop them — prevent this thing .... but, evidently, this was not the first time .... Hillier and this woman knew one another. He had stopped on catching sight of her, and she had recognized him .... The thing might have been going on for weeks — for months ....

.... Yet he must stop them — not here, in the crowded street (they were in the Edgware Road), but later, when they had reached their destination — where there were no passers — where it could be done without scandal....

.... Yes, he must send Hillier back to her .... And she believed in him — trusted him .... She must know nothing — at all costs, he must spare her the hideous knowledge — the pain of it .... And yet — and yet? ... Hillier — the blackguard — she would have to go on living with him, trusting him, confiding in him, loving him....

And for relief he returned wearily to his indignation.

How was it possible for any man — married to her — to be so vile, so false? ... The consummate hypocrisy of it all....

Swann remembered moments when Hillier's manner towards her had appeared redolent of deference, of suppressed affection. And he — a man of refinement — not a mere coarse-fibred, sensual brute — he who wrote poetry — Swann recalled a couplet full of fine aspiration — that he should have done this loathsome thing — done it callously, openly — anyone might have seen it — deceived her for some common, vulgar, public creature....

Suddenly the cab halted abruptly.

"They're pulled up, across the street there," the driver whispered hoarsely, confidentially; and for his tone Swann could have struck him.

It was an ill-lit street, silent and empty. The houses were low, semi-detached, and separated from the pavement by railing and small gardens.

The woman had got out of the cab and was pushing open the swing-gate. Hillier stood on the foot-board, paying the cabman. Swann, on the opposite side of the street, hesitated. Hillier stepped onto the pavement, and ran lightly up the door-step after the woman. She unlocked the door: it closed behind them. And the hansom which had brought them turned, and trotted away down the street.

Swann stood a moment before the house, irresolute; then re-crossed the street slowly. And a hansom bearing a second couple, drew up at the house next door.

VII

"You can go to bed, Hodgson. I will turn off the light."[34]

The man retired silently. It was a stage-phrase that rose unconsciously to her lips, a stage-situation with which she was momentarily toying.

Alone, she perceived its absurd unreality. Nothing, of course, would happen tonight — though so many days and nights she had been waiting. The details of life were clumsy, cumbersome; the simplification of the stage, of novels, of dozing dreams, seemed, by contrast, bitterly impossible.

She took up the book again, and read on, losing herself for a while in the passion of its pages — a passion that was all glamorous, sentimental felicity, at once vague and penetrating. But, as she paused to reach a paper-knife, she remembered the irrevocable, prosaic groove of existence, and that slow drifting to a dreary commonplace — a commonplace that was *hers* — brought back all her aching listlessness.[35] She let the book slip to the carpet.

Love, she repeated to herself, a silken web, opal-tinted, veiling all life; love, bringing fragrance and radiance; love, with the moonlight streaming across the meadows; love, amid summer-leafed woods, a-sparkle in the morning sun; a simple clasping of hands; a happiness, child-like and thoughtless, secure and intimate....

And she — she had nothing — only the helpless child; her soul was brave and dismantled and dismal; and once again started the gnawing of humiliation — inferior even to the common people, who could be loved and forget, in the midst of promiscuous squalor. Without love, there seemed no reason for life.

Away her thoughts sailed to the tale of the fairy-prince, stepping to shore in his silver armour, come to deliver and to love. She would have been his in all humility, waited on him in fearful submission; she would have asked for nought but his love.

Years ago, once or twice, men had appeared to her like that. And Hillier, before they were married, when they were first engaged. A strange girl she must have been in those days! And now, — now they were like any husband and any wife.

"It happened by chance," the old tale began. Chance! Yes, it was chance that governed all life; mocking, ironical chance, daintily sportive chance, hobbled to the clumsy mechanism of daily existence.

Twelve o'clock struck. Ten minutes more perhaps, and Hillier would be home. She could hear his tread; she could see him enter, take off his coat and gloves gracefully, then lift her face lightly in his two hands, and kiss her on the

---

[34] This is the opening of a passage, ending 'in dumb docility, upstairs to bed', imported from Crackanthorpe's 'Femme incomprise', *The Speaker*, 8 December 1894, p. 636.
[35] Paper-knife: in the nineteenth century books were still sold with unopened pages, and so readers had to use a paper-knife to cut along the (edges of the) leaves.

forehead. He would ask for an account of her day's doings; but he would never heed her manner of answering, for he would have begun to talk of himself. And altogether complacently would he take up the well-worn threads of their common life.

And she would go on waiting, and trifling with hopelessness, for in real life such things were impossible. Men were dull and incomplete, and could not understand a woman's heart....

And so she would wait, till he came in, and when he had played his part, just as she had imagined he would play it, she would follow him, in dumb docility, upstairs to bed....

* * * * *

It was past one o'clock when he appeared. She had fallen asleep in the big arm-chair: her book lay in a heap on the carpet beside her. He crossed the room, but she did not awake.

One hand hung over the arm of the chair, limp and white and fragile; her head, bent over her breast, was coyly resting in the curve of her elbow; her hair was a little dishevelled; her breathing was soft and regular, like a child's.

He sat down noiselessly, awed by this vision of her. The cat, which had lain stretched on the hearthrug, sprang into his lap, purring and caressing. He thought it strange that animals had no sense of human sinfulness, and recalled the devotion of the dog of a prostitute, whom he had known years and years ago....

He watched her, and her unconsciousness loosed within him the sickening pangs of remorse....

He mused vaguely on suicide as the only fitting termination .... And he descended to cheap anathemas upon life....[36]

* * * * *

By-and-bye she awoke, opening her eyes slowly, wonderingly. He was kneeling before her, kissing her hand with reverential precaution.

She saw tears in his eyes: she was still scarcely awake: she made no effort to comprehend; only was impulsively grateful, and slipping her arms behind his head, drew him towards her and kissed him on the eyes. He submitted, and a tear moistened her lips.

Then they went upstairs.

And she, passionately clutching at every memory of their love, feverishly cheated herself into bitter self-upbraiding, into attributing to him a nobility of nature that set him above all other men. And he, at each renewed outburst of

[36] Anathemas are strong denunciations, or curses.

her wild straining towards her ideal, suffered as if she had cut his bare flesh with a whip.

It was his insistent attitude of resentful humility that finally wearied her of the fit of false exaltation. When she sank to sleep, the old ache was at her heart.

VIII

Swann strode into the room. Hillier looked up at him from his writing-table in unfeigned surprise; greeted him cordially, with a couple of trite, cheery remarks concerning the weather, then waited abruptly for an explanation of this morning visit; for Swann's trouble was written on his face.

"You look worried. Is there anything wrong?" Hillier asked presently.

"Yes."

"Well, can I do anything? If I can be of any service to you, old fellow, you know I — "

"I discovered last night what a damned blackguard you are." He spoke savagely, as if his bluntness exulted him: his tone quivered with suppressed passion.

Hillier, with a quick movement of his head, flinched as if he had been struck in the face. And the lines about his mouth were set rigidly.

There was a long, tense silence. Hillier was drawing circles on a corner of the blotting-pad; Swann was standing over him, glaring at him with a fierce, hateful curiosity. Hillier became conscious of the other's expression, and his fist clenched obviously.

"I saw you get into a cab with that woman," Swann went on. "I was in an omnibus going home. I followed you — drove after you. I wanted to stop you — to stop it — I was too late."

"Ah!" An exasperated, sneering note underlined the exclamation. Hillier drove the pen-point into the table. The nib curled and snapped.

The blood rushed to Swann's forehead. In a flash he caught a glimpse of the thought that had crossed Hillier's mind. It was like a personal indignity; he struggled desperately to control himself.

Hillier looked straight into his cousin's distorted face. At the sight the tightness about his own mouth slackened. His composure returned.

"I'm sorry. Forgive me," he said simply.

"How can you be such a brute?" Swann burst out unheeding. "Don't you care? Is it nothing to you to wreck your wife's whole happiness — to spoil her life, to break her heart, to deceive her in the foulest way, to lie to her? Haven't you any conscience, any chivalry?"

The manly anguish in his voice was not lost upon Hillier. He thought he realized clearly how it was for Ella, and not for him, that Swann was so concerned. Once more he took stock of his cousin's agitation, and a quick glitter came into his eyes. He felt as if a mysterious force had been suddenly given to him. Still he said nothing.

"How could you, Hillier? How came you to do it?"

"Sit down." He spoke coldly, clearly, as if he were playing a part which he knew well.

Swann obeyed mechanically.

"It's perfectly natural that you should speak to me like that. You take the view of the world. The view of the world I accept absolutely. Certainly I am utterly unworthy of Ella" (he mentioned her name with a curious intonation of assertive pride). "How I have sunk to this thing — the whole story of how I have come to risk my whole happiness for the sake of another woman, who is nothing — absolutely nothing — to me, to whom I am nothing, I won't attempt to explain. Did I attempt to do so, I see little probability of your understanding it, and little to be gained even if you did so. I choose to let it remain for you a piece of incomprehensible infamy; I have no wish to alter your view of me."

"You don't care .... you've no remorse .... you're callous and cynical .... Good God! it's awful."

"Yes, Swann, I care," Hillier resumed, lowering his voice, and speaking with a slow distinctness, as if he were putting an excessive restraint upon his emotions. "I care more than ever you or anyone will ever know."

"It's horrible .... I don't know what to think .... Don't you see the awfulness of your wife's position? ... Don't you realize the hideousness of what you've done?"

"My dear Swann, nobody is more alive to the consequences of what I've done than I am. I have behaved infamously — I don't need to be told that by you. And whatever comes to me out of this thing" (he spoke with a grave, resigned sadness) "I shall bear it."

"Good God! Can you think of nothing but yourself? Can't you see that you've been a miserable, selfish beast — that what happens to you matters nothing? Can't you see that the only thing that matters is your wife? You're a miserable, skulking cur .... She trusted you — she believed in you, and you've done her an almost irreparable wrong."

Hillier stood suddenly erect.

"What I have done, Swann, is more than a wrong. It is a crime. Within an hour of your leaving this room, I shall have told Ella everything. That is the only thing left for me to do, and I shall not shirk it. I shall take the full responsibility. You did right to come to me as you did. You are right to consider me a miserable, skulking cur" (he brought the words out with an emphasized bravery). "Now you can do no more. The remainder of the matter rests between me and my wife — "

He paused.

"And to think that you — " Swann began passionately.

"There is no object to be gained by our discussing the matter further," Hillier interrupted a little loudly, but with a concentrated calm. "There is no need for you to remain here longer." He put his thumb to the electric-bell.

"The maid will be here in a moment to show you out," he added.

Swann waited, blinking with hesitation. His personality seemed to be slipping from him.

"You are going to tell her?" he repeated slowly.

The door opened: he hurried out of the room.

The outer door slammed: Hillier's face turned a sickly white; his eyes dilated, and he laughed excitedly — a low, short, hysterical laugh. He looked at the clock: the whole scene had lasted but ten minutes. He pulled a chair to the fire, and sat staring at the flames moodily .... The tension of the dramatic situation snapped. Before his new prospect, once again he thought weakly of suicide....

IX

He had told her — not, of course, the whole story — from that his sensitivity had shrunk. Still he had besmirched himself bravely; he had gone through with the interview not without dignity. Beforehand he had nerved himself for a terrible ordeal; yet, somehow, as he reviewed it, now that it was all over, the scene seemed to have fallen flat. The tragedy of her grief, of his own passionate repentance, which he had been expecting, had proved unaccountably tame. She had cried, and at the sight of those tears of hers he had suffered intensely; but she had displayed no suppressed, womanish jealousy; had not, in her despair, appeared to regard his confession as an overwhelming shattering of her faith in him, and so provoked him to reveal the depth of his anguish. He had implored her forgiveness; he had vowed he would efface the memory of his treachery; she had acquiesced dreamily, with apparent heroism. There had been no mention of a separation.

And now the whole thing was ended: tonight he and she were dining out.

He was vaguely uncomfortable; yet his heart was full of a sincere repentance, because of the loosening of the strain of his anxiety; because of the smarting sense of humiliation, when he recollected Swann's words; because he had caused her to suffer in a queer, inarticulate way, which he did not altogether understand, of which he was vaguely afraid....

X

When at last he had left her alone, it was with a curious calmness that she started to reflect upon it all. She supposed it was very strange that his confession had not wholly prostrated her; and glancing furtively backwards, catching a glimpse of her old girlish self, wondered listlessly how it was that, insensibly, all these months, she had grown so hardened....

*   *   *   *   *

By-and-bye, the recent revelation of his unfaithfulness seemed to recede slowly into the misty past, and, fading, losing its sharpness of outline, its distinctness of detail, to resemble an irreparable fact to which familiarity had inured her.

And all the uneasiness of her mistrustfulness, the pain of her fluctuating doubtings ceased; her comprehension of him was all at once clarified, rendered vivid and indisputable; and she was conscious of a certain sense of relief. She was eased of those feverish, spasmodic gaspings of her half-starved love; at first the dullness of sentimental atrophy seemed the more endurable. She jibed at her own natural artlessness; and insisted to herself that she wanted no fool's paradise, that she was even glad to see him as he really was, to terminate, once for all, this futile folly of love; that, after all, his unfaithfulness was no unusual and terrible tragedy, but merely a commonplace chapter in the lives of smiling, chattering women, whom she met at dinners, evening parties, and balls....

*   *   *   *   *

There were some who simpered to her over Hillier as a model of modern husbands; and she must go on listening and smiling....

... And the long years ahead would unroll themselves — a slow tale of decorous lovelessness ...

He would be always the same — that was the hardest to face. His nature could never alter, grow into something different .... never, never change .... always, always the same ....

Oh! it made her dread it all — the restless round of social enjoyments; the greedy exposure of the petty weaknesses of common acquaintance; the ill-natured atmosphere that she felt emanating from people herded together .... All the details of her London life looked unreal, mean, pitiful....

And she longed after the old days of her girlhood, of the smooth, staid country life; she longed after the simple, restful companionship of her old father and mother; after the accumulation of little incidents that she had loved long ago .... She longed too — and the straining at heart-strings grew tenser — she longed after her own lost maidenhood; she longed to be ignorant and careless; to see life once again as a simple, easy matter; to know nothing of evil; to understand nothing of men; to trust — to trust unquestioningly .... All that was gone; she herself was all changed; those days could never come again....

And she cried to herself a little, from weakness of spirit, softly....

* * * * *

Then, gradually, out of the weary turmoil of her bitterness, there came to her a warm impulse of vague sympathy for the countless, unknown tragedies at work around her: she thought of the sufferings of outcast women — of loveless lives, full of mirthless laughter; she thought of the long loneliness of childless women....

She clutched for consolation at the unhappiness of others; but she only discovered the greater ugliness of the world. And she returned to a tired contemplation of her own prospect....

* * * * *

He had broken his vows to her — not only the solemn vow he had taken in the church (she recalled how his voice had trembled with emotion, as he had repeated the words) — but all that passionate series of vows he had made to her during the spring-time of their love....

... Yes, that seemed the worst part of it — that, and not the making love to another woman .... What was she like? ... What was it in her that had attracted him? ... Oh! but what did that matter? ... — only why were men's natures so different from women's? ...

... Now, she must go on — go on alone. Since her marriage she had lost the habit of daily converse with Christ; here in London, somehow, He had seemed so distant, so difficult of approach....

... She must just go on .... She had the little Claude ... It was to help her that God had given her Claude .... Oh! she would pray to God to make him good — to give him a straight, strong, upright, honest nature. And herself, every day, she would watch over his growth, guide him, teach him ... Yes, he *must* grow up good .... into boyhood .... different from other boys .... into manhood, simple, honourable manhood .... She would be everything to him: he and she would come to comprehend each other, to read into each other's hearts .... Perhaps, between them, would spring up perfect love and trust....

XI

Swann had written to her: —

"You are in trouble: let me come." Gradually, between the lines of the note, she understood it all — she read how his love for her had leapt up, now that he knew that she was unhappy; how he wanted to be near her, to comfort her, and perhaps .... perhaps....

She was filled with great sorrow for him — and warm gratitude, too, for his simple, single-hearted love — but sorrow, that she could give him nothing in return, and because it seemed that, somehow, he and she were about to bid one another goodbye: she thought she dimly foresaw how their friendship was doomed to dwindle....

So she let him come.

*   *   *   *   *

... And all this she fancied she read again in the long, grave glance of his greeting, and the firm clasp of his big hand.

When he spoke, his deep, steady voice dominated her: she knew at once that he would do what was right.

"Ella, my poor Ella, how brave you are!" She looked up at him, smiling tremulously, through her quick-starting tears .... The next moment it was as if the words had escaped him — almost as if he regretted them.

He sat down opposite her, and, lightening his voice, asked — just as he always did — for news of the little Claude.

And so their talk ran on.

After awhile, she came to realize that he meant to say no more; the strength of his great reserve became apparent, and a sense of peace stole over her. He talked on, and to the restful sound of his clear, strong voice, she abandoned herself dreamily .... This he had judged the better course .... that he should have adopted any other now seemed inconceivable. Beside him she felt weak and helpless: she remembered the loneliness of his life: he seemed to her altogether noble; and she was vaguely remorseful that she had not perceived from the first that it was from him that her help would come....

She divined, too, the fineness of his sacrifice — that manly, human struggle with himself, through which he had passed to attain it — how he had longed for the right to make her his .... and how he had renounced. The sureness of his victory, and the hidden depths of his nature which it revealed, awed her .... now he would never swerve from what he knew to be right .... And on, through those years to come, she could trust him, always, always....

... At last he bid her goodbye: even at the last his tone remained unchanged.

It was close upon seven o'clock. She went upstairs to dress for dinner, and kneeling beside the bed, prayed to God with an outburst of passionate, pulsing joy....

Ten minutes later Hillier came in from his dressing-room. He clasped his hands round her bare neck, kissing her hair again and again.

"I have been punished, Nellie," he began in a broken whisper. "Good God! it is hard to bear .... Help me, Nellie .... help me to bear it."

She unclasped his fingers, and started to stroke them; a little mechanically, as if it were her duty to ease him of his pain....

Battledore and Shuttlecock

I

"You may smoke, you know, Ron, if you like. I'm afraid I haven't any cigarettes, though."

"All right. I've got some here."

He dipped a spill into the grate, and stretching himself on the hearthrug in front of her, steadied the flame. Helen fell to musing on the gracefulness of the attitude he unconsciously adopted, the natural nobility that, despite their boyish indecision, his features suggested.

"Make haste, or you'll burn your fingers," she exclaimed.

He puffed vigorously, for the paper was almost consumed; then gazed up at her in frank scrutiny.

"Well, what are you thinking about me?" She smiled; her voice was soft and leisurely.

Blinking with surprise, he dropped his cigarette into the fender, and sat up, clasping his hands round his knees.

"How on earth did you know that?"

"It wasn't so very difficult to guess. Now tell me; I'm very curious to know."

"I was thinking how glad I am I've come to live here," he said simply.

"You dear boy!" She was flushing with quick pleasure.

"You see, Helen," he continued seriously, "I should have been beastly dull all alone, and you have to know a man awfully well before you can go into rooms with him. I found that out at Oxford. I used to wonder a great deal what it would be like, my living with you. I think you're changed tremendously."

"Changed — how?"

"I don't know exactly, it's so difficult to explain. But in the old days — that time you came down to Battlebury — you seemed just the same as all other girls. You're absolutely different now. I think it is," he stumbled over his thoughts, "that you're more like a man than anyone I've known. I mean I felt at home with you at once, just as if we were old friends. Most women are so silly to talk to."

"What a queer boy you are!" she laughed.

"I'm not queer a bit," he retorted, picking up the cigarette. "I'm only just a rather dense, ordinary sort of chap."

"So you're really glad you've come?"

"Rather. But I don't mind telling you now that I didn't care much for the idea, when you first wrote about it from India. I wanted to be independent. I was sick of being looked after."

"What made you change your mind?"

"Oh, several things. That second letter you wrote me. I thought you'd be lonely perhaps, now — now that ——" He sent her a quick, shy glance.

"Dear!" Her hand stretched out towards his. "You're right. I did feel utterly lonely; as if the world had suddenly grown empty all around me. And Hal, just before he died — almost the last words" — (her voice was quavering) "said, 'When you get back look after Ronald.' We often talked about you, and he used to wait for your letters so eagerly. He was so fond of you."

Ronald stared stiffly into the fire, struggling with his emotion.

Presently he perceived her eyes glistening.

"Oh! I'm so awfully sorry — I didn't mean to make you cry. What a stupid ass I am!"

"No, dear, it's not your fault. It's nothing. You couldn't help it. Go on talking. It's better to talk about these things."

"I wish I remembered Hal better," he began gravely, after a pause. "You see it's nine years since he went away. I was a lower-boy at Eton then. He and I never saw very much of each other; he was so much older. I used to think about him a good deal though, after mother died. I suppose it was having to be alone with father. That was a beastly time. I used to mark off the days till I went back to Eton on a calendar."

"Why, didn't you get on with your father?"

"Get on with him — no, I never did. I dare say you'll think I oughtn't to talk like this, but I can't help it. Directly I get into the same room with him I feel uncomfortable."

"Oh, Ronald, what a pity!"

"I dare say it's all my fault; but it's just as if I had to bottle myself up, and pretend to see everything just as he does. He makes me feel ever so far beneath him. It was always the same."

"But hadn't you any friends down there?"

"No; no one much. Sometimes some of my Eton friends came to stay; but he always used to treat me before them as if I was a little school-boy — and them too sometimes. I hated it awfully, and of course I never could do anything. You can't imagine how keen fellows at school are about their people."

"And after — when you went to Oxford?"

"Oh! then I used to stay about with people as much as I could. One summer I went on a walking tour round the west coast of Scotland, with a sort of tutor. We had a ripping time. Of course one had an enormous number of friends up at Oxford. That's the worst of Oxford, one knows such a crowd of men. But they're all so much alike, Oxford men, I think. They all say the same things."

*　*　*　*　*

She rose presently from her chair, to look at the clock.

"Why, it's eleven already. What time would you like to breakfast tomorrow?"

"Well, I've got to be at the crammer's at half-past nine."[1]

"Shall I order it for half-past eight then?"

"That'll do splendidly."

"Goodnight, Ronald."

"Goodnight," he answered a little awkwardly, jumping to his feet.

Her hand lingered affectionately in his.

"Put out the lamp when you go up," she added, at the door.

II

When Helen awoke next morning, her first thought was of Ronald. Like a ray of glad sunshine, it came to her. She looked forward eagerly to the companionship of this first breakfast with him, impatient to begin the routine of the life together. So she hurried over her dressing that she might get downstairs quickly, to greet him.

She was tall and loosely-knit; flaxen hair, a swinging gait, and a large simplicity of gesture that seemed inappropriately clothed in widow's weeds. Her features, though faulty and individually insignificant, achieved, in their combination, an immediate charm, by means of the rare spontaneity, fearlessness almost, of regard.

Her marriage with Ronald's elder brother had been an unison almost without flaw. In the gentleness of his unsoiled instincts, backed by sheer robustness, she had definitely realized her ideal of the lovable in man. Alone with him in a beautiful and remote station,[2] where the sequence of dreamy, uneventful days cheated the flight of time, she had drifted, unchecked, into an entire merging of herself in the play of his personality. For she had no child.

Later, when they removed to Calcutta, amid the novelty of strange faces, social tasks, and the annual summer separation, their intimacy was securely sealed, beyond danger of damage.

It was in the spring of the third year there that he died, at the end of five days' fever.

During the night after the funeral, she attempted to take poison; the thought that she was left behind maddened her. There followed a long period of nervous prostration and emotional numbness, while time built for her a barrier between the present and the past.

When she was herself again, she was conscious of but one desire — to avoid

---

[1]   The crammer offered tutoring specifically for the passing of examinations.

[2]   The remote station was the place of residence for British district or garrison officers in imperial India.

the faces who had known him, to be alone with her sorrow. By-and-bye, vague, filtering hopes of relief by the side of his young brother Ronald roused her. She started for England. Sometimes, during the voyage, sitting on deck, watching the lazy rhythm of blue billows, she dimly foresaw how, if the boy failed her, life would be altogether dismal and bare. Then the intolerable ache of yearning would start again, the sickening remembrance that Hal was gone, gone for always, that it was over, that it could never be again. It was but listlessly that she clutched at belief in a meeting after death; she could not escape from the near presence of the irrevocable.

But when Ronald arrived from Oxford, to live with her in her new London house, while he worked for his army examination, her torpor lifted, like a murky fog-curtain, and she beheld the world a-glitter once more. A haze settled down over the memories of the past, blurring their edge, and the traces of her sorrow faded, leaving her bright with vitality.

While she was coiling her hair, she saw him again, as a lanky, unattractive boy, who was stubbornly rude to her because she was engaged to his elder brother. Once Hal had boxed his ears, and sent him in to her to apologize. He stood sheepishly in the doorway, his face aflame, throwing his excuse at her defiantly. And before she could attempt to soothe him, he was gone in ruffled dignity.

How like he had grown to Hal — a certain poise of the head, certain tones of his voice! At first she had recoiled from this resemblance; but now, she was happy in brooding on it. For it removed the strained sense of strangeness, and swathed in a soft tint of melancholy the prospect of her affection for him.

III

Ronald adapted himself to his new surroundings with the quick pliability of youth still innocent of habit; traversing in the transition from boisterous irresponsibility to the restraint of routine no intermediary period of restlessness. The repetition of the daily morning walk to his crammer's; of the return across the Park, all wrapped in the drab haze of lingering day; of the uneventful evenings, when, lulled to drowsy contentment by the day's work, he talked idly to Helen — he accepted its whole quiet monotony with easy cheerfulness.

And he grew to enjoy the hours spent with her. Little by little she encouraged him to assume with her small airs of authority, almost of proprietorship; to insist on her wearing furs when the wind was bitter, or thick boots when the streets were wet. Thus she made him conscious of his male superiority, impregnating with a subtle charm the novelty of his independence. He thought now of his father's attitude towards him with aggressive disgust. Feminine companionship was new to him, and close familiarity with her provoked in him a vague, questioning interest in womankind. His consciousness of sex slept less soundly.

Meanwhile, stimulated by pride in his own conscientiousness, he accomplished his daily tasks thoroughly; looking forward to his profession eagerly, stirred when a regiment passed him in the park, discussing with Helen historical campaigns. Several of the faces at the crammer's were familiar to him; but he purposely restricted all intercourse to conventional greetings; flat comments on the weather or the work; curt, mutual recollections of Oxford men. All proposals for evening amusements he declined, unwilling for change.

IV

One evening, when they had finished dinner, Helen retired to her room. Ronald sat for a while in the drawing-room fidgeting with his notebooks. He was sick of work, sick of the sight of the shiny covers. The sense of cramping confinement chafed him, his legs tingled with pent-up energy, he was eager for activity. He left the house. Tightening his sinews, stiffening his shoulder, ready from sheer excess of vigour to buffet the passers, he strode along.

* * * * *

Immediately he entered the theatre, the sudden sight of the scene stopped him, revealed, as it were, through a great gap. The stage blazed white; masses of recumbent girls, bathed in soft tints, swayed to dreamy cadence of muffled violins, before the quivering, gold-flecked minarets of an Eastern palace. He leaned against the side of the lounge to gaze down across the black belt of heads. The sight bewildered him. By-and-bye he became conscious of a hum of voices and a continual movement behind him. He turned to look.

Men, for the most part in evening dress, were passing in procession to and fro, some women amongst them, smiling as they twittered mirthlessly; now and then he caught glimpses of others seated before little round tables; vacant, impassive, like wax-work figures, he thought. He felt ill-at-ease, almost wished he had not come in. A vision of Helen, pale with headache, flitted before his mind's eye, succeeded by a glimmering perception of the sense of things. He started in chase of this fleeting perception, only to entangle himself amidst the incoherence of novel sensation. Then his face grew hot, the gaze of one of the seated figures was upon him; he turned hastily back to the stage.

He was throbbing with trepidating curiosity, buffeted by irresolution. The music clashed triumphantly, and the dancers massed together, formed a solid, whirling wheel of glittering humanity. Exhilaration and a quiet, tense composure took possession of him. As he faced round again his foot encountered an obstacle.

"I beg your pardon." The exclamation came mechanically.

"It didn't hurt a bit."

Amusement was dancing in her big, baby eyes, and friendliness on her open lips. The strains of the band, the restless flow around him, everything vanished; he was only aware of her face sparkling upon him.

The ceasing of her voice nipped the spell, and he dropped back to consciousness of the external. He comprehended in a flash that he was talking to a girl in the lounge of a music-hall. And the image of Helen flitted past, almost unobserved.

Beside the girl he felt himself clumsy and clownish; he recollected his muddy boots.

"Have you been here before?" she was asking him. He was busy noting her large-brimmed, black velvet hat; the soft duskiness of her skin, which a feather boa caressed; her white, tight-fitting gloves, and the gold bangles on her wrists.

"No, I've only just come," he answered.

Her face still sparkled.

"Have you been here long?" he stammered.

She had not heard him; she was smiling across at someone in the crowd. He imagined that she was slipping from him, and roused himself rudely from his contemplation.

"Aren't there any seats?" His eyes pretended to search the balcony ostentatiously; but in reality everything appeared blurred.

"Let's go and see," she suggested, bringing her glance back to him.

They moved to the gangway, and he sat down beside her in the back row. Her tiny, shell-like ear held his gaze, while he beat his brain for some remark which would cause her to think well of him.

"Did you see the performing birds?" she said. "I love birds. I've got one at home. He sings beautifully."

"No, I didn't see them. Were they good?"

"There are two pigeons, who draw a carriage with some dressed-up sparrows in it, right round the stage."

"By Jove! I wish I'd seen that."

"They've been going on a long while. Haven't you been here before?"

"No."

"Do you generally go to the Alhambra?"[3]

---

[3] The Alhambra was a famous music-hall in Leicester Square, London, built in the Moorish style with two minarets. First opened in 1854, it was rebuilt following a fire in 1882, becoming a leading venue for variety and, particularly, ballet. Its spectacle offered Arthur Symons, in a vibrant display of connoisseurship, 'the one escape into fairy-land which is permitted by that tyranny of the real' ('At the Alhambra: Impressions and Sensations', *The Savoy*, 5 (September 1896), 75–83 (p. 83); repr. in *Arthur Symons: Spiritual Adventures*, ed. by Nicholas Freeman (Cambridge: MHRA, 2017), pp. 89–98). Controversially, its Promenade

"No, I've not been there either yet. I've only been in town a short while, you see. And I'm working very hard."

"You're in business?"

"No, I'm going in for an exam — for the army."

"Is it very difficult?"

"Yes. You see one has to know such a lot of different things."

"You're awfully young," she said presently.

He reddened, apprehensive of her disapprobation.

"Yes, awfully young," she concluded decisively.

She seemed to be thinking to herself. The music had softened again. She was beautiful, he thought, and abandoned himself to the glow of pride at being with her.

"What's your name?" she asked.

"Ronald Thornycroft. And — will you tell me yours?"

"Midge."

"Midge — what?"

"Midge — that's all — nothing else." Her face was sparkling upon him, as when she had first spoken to him. "Do you know any of the girls here?" she began.

"No — do you?"

"Do you live by yourself?"

"Yes, mostly; my father lives in the country and my mother is dead."

"I'm so sorry," she exclaimed. Her tone troubled him instantly; her face, he saw, had grown quite grave.

"It's a long time ago," he explained. Their eyes met, and she smiled at him again.

"Do you know, I'm going home next month — down to the country. I love the country."

"So do I," he answered.

"And the sea-side? Do you care for the sea-side?"

"I don't know. I haven't been there much."

"I was down there in the summer. I'm awfully fond of the roar of the waves and the wind, when the sea gets black and angry, and seems to show its teeth."

The music crashed before stopping; the curtain slid down.

"Shall we go back? The ballet's over. Lend me your programme."

He waited while she wrote with a tiny silver pencil-case. As they regained the lounge, she thrust the programme into his hand, saying:

"There's my address."

He took it and moved forward to a clear space. When he turned to look for her she was gone.

areas offered the opportunity for men to pick up prostitutes, the sight that greets the initially 'bewildered' Ronald in this story.

V

Midge was feeding her canary, humming a waltz-tune to herself the while: lazily lingering over the thrill that filtered through her, as she reminded herself how, since last night, she had fallen in love....

"Don't," she exclaimed, with an affectation of pettishness, roused from her dream-land by the nip of the bird's beak. "What a bother you are, master impatience!" She scattered some hemp seeds over the floor of the cage: the plump little mass of yellow fluff hopped down, vigorously dipping his head.

.... He'd got such a nice face.... If she could just be friends with him .... keep him to herself .... out of the way of harm.... He looked so young .... she could become such friends with a boy like that .... real friends .... different, separate from the others.... He had made her feel so queer, uncomfortable, unhappy almost, last night; she couldn't help running away from him.... he might so easily have spoilt it all for her.... And she had lain awake in the dark, such a long while, dreaming about him.... Yes, she was quite in love with him....

She moved to the window. The hoar-frost had come, decking the trees in the square; and the sky was white with the glare of the winter sun. How pretty everything looked in the clear morning light! A man with a barrow-full of cabbages was moving slowly down the street, leading his donkey, all brown and furry, chanting as he went. She tried to catch the meaning of his cry.... A congregation of fat sparrows were taking their dust-bath and combing their wings in the road-way. One little fellow had lost his tail: he was so comical when he tried to fly.

She crumbled a biscuit on to the window-sill, and hid behind the curtain, peeping and waiting. But they refused to come; they sat in a row on the railings, jerking their heads from side to side, as if by clockwork. She began to hum the waltz-tune over again.... Yes, something about that boy's face was sweet and gentle.... She'd never known anyone quite like him.... She felt certain they would get along together.... How that tune kept running in her head!...

She seated herself before the piano, and started to strum it.

*   *   *   *   *

Of a sudden, in the full, languorous swing of a phrase, the piano-lid crashed, rattling the whole room. She had caught his reflection in the mirror.

"My goodness!" she gasped, half swinging round on the stool. "How you did startle me!"

"I'm very sorry.... I didn't mean to." He stood blinking at her white cheeks.

"There, it's all right now.... It made me feel quite bad.... I never expected you'd come — so soon, I mean.... I was just thinking about you."

There was a red hat-mark across his forehead; otherwise he was just the same as last night; his open stare was unchanged.

"Had breakfast?"

"Yes — at half-past eight."

"Oh! I forgot — you've got a holiday today?"

"It's Sunday."

"So it is!" she cried, her face rippling. "Fancy my not knowing that. How dreadful!" Then, ruefully examining her skirt — "And I'm not fit to be seen."

"But you are, really — you're lovely," he blurted out hastily, combating in all seriousness her depreciation of herself. "I think you're even prettier than last night."

She uttered a quick, nervous laugh.

Her unloosened hair was romping in rich folds over her shoulders; a white flannel dressing-gown clung to her bust, while within the hollow of her falling sleeves he perceived her white arms. She reminded him of some school-picture of a Greek priestess. And his eyes went on devouring her.

"Please sit down. You look so uncomfortable.... I say, are you always solemn like this? You don't know how glum you look. No wonder you startled me."

He coloured, and sat down opposite her stiffly.

"There, don't be vexed; I didn't mean to laugh at you, Ronald. You see I've remembered your name."

His eyes were travelling round the room; he was unaware how she was watching him.

"Is that your canary?" he said at last.

"Come and look at him; he's such a darling."

"Does he do any tricks?" he asked, as they stood together by the cage.

"No — only bites — awfully hard sometimes."

She chirped to the bird, pursing her lips. He felt his heart thump; his teeth began to chatter.

"How cold you are! Go and warm yourself at the fire.... I say, I've got an idea. Do you know a game called Badminton?"

"No; what is it?"

"Oh! it's splendid fun. It's like lawn-tennis, only you play with battledores and shuttlecocks....[4] Here, just move these chairs out of the way.... Now the table.... Mind! you'll spill the flowers.... Wait, I'll help you.... Now for the string. There it is on the piano.... Catch hold of the end — see, it wants knotting.... This nail 'll do.... Tie the other end onto the curtain hook — no, you silly boy, over there, opposite.... Now that anti-macassar[5].... Give us your handkerchief. Spread them out over the string.... That's beautiful.... Now for the battledores. They're on the top of the cupboard.... Get on the table.... Take

---

[4]   A battledore is a racket.

[5]   Anti-macassar: a cloth put over the backs and arms of a chair or armchair, mainly as a protection against Macassar hair oil.

care — you'll fall…. Put your hand on my shoulder…. All right, it doesn't hurt. Lean on me…. Now then, you go the other side…. I'll begin. Ready! Play!"

Pang! pang! pang! pang! … the shuttlecock flew from one to the other. At last it struck the string, hesitated, and toppled over.

"Good stroke!" he cried enthusiastically.

"What's that? Fifteen? How do you count?"

"That's nothing."

"No, no; of course it must count."

"Don't contradict. Play!"

The shuttlecock whizzed to and fro. Both were warming to the game. They were evenly matched, though she played with easy skill, and he with laborious clumsiness. Their countenances grew graver and graver, only intent on the flight of the feathers. For several minutes no comment passed between them, only, at the end of each bout, Ronald mechanically registered the score.

"Take that!" he called suddenly, loosing his energy awkwardly in a slash. But the shuttlecock shot under the string, and tumbled at her feet.

"Hurrah! Game to me!" And she clapped her battledore gleefully.

"Your service," he replied grimly. And, with a renewed volley of battledore blows, the battle raged again.

…. Deuce! … Vantage in! … Midge held the game, playing securely, while Ronald contorted his body to ungainly angles. He seemed on the point of missing every time.

All at once her battledore caught a picture-edge and the shuttlecock alighted on the floor.

"Damn that thing!" she broke out, vindictively staring in its face.

"Come," remonstrated Ronald from across the barrier. "You've another chance yet."

"Play!" she called excitedly. But she failed to reach the return volley. The game was his.

*   *   *   *   *

"Ugh! I *am* hot." She flung herself into an armchair. "Have a cigarette? There's some in that case on the mantelpiece."

He saw two letters, G. S., stamped on the leather inside. Why were they there? he wondered rapidly.

"Well, and me? Aren't you going to offer me one?"

"I beg your pardon."

"Perhaps you think it wrong to smoke?" she queried, roguishly turning her eyes up to him, the cigarette between her lips.

"No, I don't — not at all."

"Then give me a light."

*   *   *   *   *

"I say, you were awfully shy at first, weren't you?" She was pensively flicking the ash with her little finger.

"Yes," he acknowledged, colouring. "But I'm not a bit now," he added, smiling at her frankly.

"No, I see that," she retorted.

"Why did you disappear like that last night? Were you offended with me?"

She sat without answering, perplexedly watching the ascending streak of smoke. Presently she looked up, her expression clear.

"I'll tell you straight out all about it. The minute you spoke to me I liked your face awfully. You somehow seemed to me quite different from all the rest.... You looked so young and shy and bewildered. And then, I was afraid you'd say something — you wouldn't understand how it was I liked you. It was just an idea of mine.... When I got home I thought how jolly it would be if I were to be friends with you — proper friends, I mean. I wouldn't mind if I didn't see you very often; if only I just knew it was like that. I wouldn't bother you; I can look after myself all right." She stopped in anxious expectancy.

He felt himself suddenly overflowing with devotion to her; he longed desperately to be able to afford her some striking proof of his gratitude. And the novel sense of important responsibility towards her swelled his exultation.

"I will be your friend always," he answered simply.

"Perhaps I seem to you ridiculous, talking like this when I have only seen you once before. But I'm like that. I always do things just as they come. It's my way — I can't help it. If I could, perhaps things would have been quite different. Now you know exactly what I am, don't you?"

He flushed crimson: his whole being rose in revolt against the brutal thought she forced upon him. His troubled glance appealed to her, but she did not seem to notice. The moment of silence that followed quickened the whirl of his perplexity.

"Yes," he blurted out, with a supreme effort. "But that doesn't matter.... It doesn't make any difference.... It isn't your fault, I mean.... You aren't any the worse.... I respect you just the same...." Hot shame hustled the words helter-skelter to his lips.

"You're a dear good boy to say that. But you're wrong. I don't mind telling you that. I've got no one to blame but myself.... Promise me you'll come and see me again.... Promise."

"I promise," he said solemnly, "to do whatever you ask me."

As he ceased speaking, she laughed a little excitedly. Then jumping up, with a sudden lightness of tone:

"My goodness! I *am* hungry. Aren't you?"

"Yes, I am, rather."

"Well now, tell me, what would you like for lunch?" He hesitated.

"I'm most awfully sorry — the fact is, I ought to go home. My sister-in-law asked a friend of mine to lunch. But I'll come back as soon as I can."

"No, you mustn't do that."

"I'll stay then. After all, it doesn't matter."

She shook her head.

He felt pride in obeying.

"May I come to see you tomorrow? — in the morning?"

"No; you must go to your work."

"But I must see you," he objected impetuously.

"Well, if you *must* then," she answered, laughing; "would you like to take me out to dinner?"

"Most awfully. Tomorrow?"

"Yes; come to fetch me at half-past seven. Now goodbye, or you'll be late for your friend."

He took her outstretched hand. She looked for a moment straight into his eyes, and then he moved away.

"Goodbye, till tomorrow — at half-past seven," he forced himself to say.

"Goodbye," she repeated quietly.

VI

Faster and faster he walked, struggling to cheat the longing to return to her. The keen air flicked his cheeks, and the crisp, whitened turf of the Park crackled under his tread. Behind the frail tracery of the twigs, peeping between the gaunt arms of the black-skinned trees, dancing over the ripples that shimmered silver across the lake, he beheld her sparkling smile....

.... He was her friend.... her friend.... The word coursed exultantly through him, echoing and re-echoing. The scene lived again; he saw her rippling rivulets of hair; he felt the quick play of her gaze; he heard the ring of her laughter; her voice spoke to him: he replied to her; once more, in a corner of that disordered room, their bond was sealed....

She stood, a white and dazzling figure, blocking the centre of his imagination; exquisite, wonderful, yet having accorded him the intoxicating privilege of familiarity.

He pictured himself by her side, intimate, confidential, grateful, reckless in devotion; or strong, protective, necessary; or again, before the world, masking the bond in proud unobtrusiveness, and so always, on, on, into the misty future....

Only he and she remained in the world — alone, and together the rest faded to thin silhouettes. Helen slipped to the fringe of his life. The luncheon towards which he was walking became unreal, like a stage-scene, in which a part had been set for him. The time till tomorrow evening was as a stretch of colourless waste.

Then, under his care, how beautiful she would look! ... Her tiny, white-gloved hands, and the gold bangles encircling her wrists! And all during dinner, while, with the waiters moving behind, they discussed trivial topics, he would know that she had secretly chosen him — set him apart. His blood quickened with excited anticipation....

Ignorance simplified his whole prospect: blind jealousy of the male, unpricked by the goad of sexual vision, drowsed on; the welling-up of unsullied chivalry held him to the exact letter of her appeal. Eagerly he exchanged the crude name she had driven him to give her for another of gentler import, and that he accepted readily, slurring its significance. His faith in his own exaltation was spontaneous, unquestioning.

And he seemed to see the past months mapped out behind him, hollow, empty of purpose, filled by a senseless accumulation of poor trivialities. Across the newly-kindled glow, he caught flittings of vague possibilities, hints of a life permeated by sound, exhilarating goodness. He remembered, with a twinge of repentant shame, certain tacit acquiescences in obscene college conversations: henceforward he felt himself ennobled, lifted above the common ruck....

Stout, over-clothed ladies, coming from church, passed him; men in smooth-fitting, tight-buttoned coats, carrying along with them a torpid, Sunday air; children trotting gravely, as if oppressed by stiff garments; the streets bare; the houses asleep; the shops barred up and lifeless: from sheer frolic of heart he fell to noting the quaint physiognomy of the London Sabbath.

VII

She was in black; a sleeveless dress, just betraying her breasts, banded at the waist with vivid crimson. Her smooth hair hung low over her nape, as was the fashion, in a dark, heavy coil; and the simplicity of her bare arms and neck was unspoiled by ornament.

And he — she was proud of him in evening attire, straight and lithe and correctly spotless; his hair brushed in a clean sweep back from his forehead, and drifting, above the ears, into crisp curls.

He took command of her at once; authoritatively deciding the place of the dinner, insisting that she was well wrapped at the throat. And to his deferential protection she abandoned herself with delight.

They sped lightly away, the bell on the horse's neck tinkling shrilly, past dark houses and blazing shops.

"It's freezing, I believe," he remarked. "Glass down," he shouted up through the trap.

The window descended slowly: she nestled almost imperceptibly against his shoulder; he was adorable, she told herself.

At the restaurant, she found a room reserved, and a dinner ordered. And, as he relieved her of her cloak and lace wrapper, she became conscious that he had none of that indefinable air of obtrusive proprietorship, adopted on like occasions by other men. For a while she made pretence of chatting carelessly; but his attitude towards her, continuing gravely, a little elaborately, respectful, swelled her gratitude, choked her spirits, and swathed her happiness in sentimental melancholy.

A dreamy mood crept over her irresistibly, evoking blurred glimpses of past scenes: she forgot him, feeling herself curiously alone and isolated. No bitterness flavoured her musings; only fleeting, half-formulated wonderings; no rankling remembrance of male cruelty; no savagely revolting realization of the part she played. She had found men pleasant, affectionate, generous.

So she recalled each one, without rancour; and of one she thought almost tenderly, for he was now dead. Yet when, awakening, she looked across at Ronald, her eyes grew hot, and her sight misty. She felt the rising of a passionate longing to cry — from no grief, for no reason. Clenching her lips she fought with the hungering for tears, struggling to hear his words, to see her plate clearly.

He had noticed her untouched food, her inconsequent replies, the tight lines of her mouth; and the end of the dinner seemed to him interminable.

"What is it, Midge? Are you feeling bad?" he asked quickly, as the door closed behind the obsequious waiter.

"No, of course not. It's nothing."

But the next moment she was sobbing with her head on the table....

.... She felt the firm clasp of his hands round her head, trying to raise it; and between the throbs of her weeping she heard him saying —

".... Don't.... don't cry.... What is it? .... Can't I do anything? ..."

But she let the tears flow on unchecked: they brought her warm relief.... Presently his hands were on her head again: she submitted. And when he had gently lifted the face, a smile was gleaming through her tears, like the sparkle of sunshine across a fleeting shower.

"Aren't I a silly?"

"But what were you crying for?"

"I don't know. It came quite suddenly." She laid her hand on his. "You're a good, kind boy. I'm not often like that."

He remembered quickly how Helen had once spoken to him in that tone; and he felt a great compassion for the frailty of women welling up within him.

"Sit down now and finish your coffee," she continued.

He obeyed.

"I don't remember ever having cried all about nothing before."

She took a banana, and began to peel it slowly; and he carried his chair round the table and sat down by her side, slipping her bare arm under his own.

"Dear Midge! It's all right now, isn't it?"

She nodded, munching the fruit, and turned to him with a smile of affectionate happiness.

"Come, have the other half." And she held the end for him to bite.

"We'll often have dinner here, I vote. It's a jolly little place," he said, caressing her hand.

"Isn't it rather ruinous?"

He named the price. "But you don't know, I've three hundred a year of my own."

"What a fortune! All your very own, do you mean?"

"Yes; my mother left it to me. I came into it when I was twenty-one."

"You're not twenty-one. Don't talk such absurd nonsense."

"Yes, I am — twenty-two. And you, how old are you?"

"Guess."

"Twenty?"

"No — more."

"Twenty-one?"

"More."

"Twenty-two?"

She assented.

"Fancy our being the same age. When's your birthday?"

"The fourteenth of March."

"And mine's on the tenth."

"By Jove! You're just four days older then."

"Split another banana with me."

"No, I couldn't really."

"Do as you're told. Obey your elders, sir."

"Very good, madam," he retorted in mock meekness.

*   *   *   *   *

"What would you like to do now?" he began.

"Nothing. Let's just stay here and talk."

"You wouldn't like to go to the Gaiety?[6] I've taken a box."

---

[6]   The Gaiety Theatre in the Strand, London, opened in 1868. In the 1890s it became well-known for musical comedy through productions such as the highly successful *The Shop Girl* (1894), which launched the era of the 'Gaiety "Girls"' and 'became a shop window for the peerage marriage market, and world famous for its stage door "Johnnies."' (Raymond Mander and Joe Mitchenson, *The Lost Theatres of London* (London: Rupert Hart Davis, 1968), p. 107.) The theatre survived until 1903 when it reopened as The New Gaiety Theatre, on the corner of Aldwych and the Strand.

"How extravagant!"

"You've forgotten the fortune. Why, except tonight, I don't believe I've spent two pounds during the last three weeks. I'm positively saving."

"How shocking! But about that box — it's awfully wasteful. I suppose we ought to go for a little."

"No, not if you'd rather not. Remember, it'll cost a shilling to get there."

"If it comes to that, I don't mind standing the cab." And they laughed together.

*   *   *   *   *

"I say, Ronald, I want to ask you something. Promise to answer truthfully.... Well, have you ever been in love?"

"No."

"Never at all?"

"Never at all."

"Haven't you ever kissed anyone?"

He shook his head.

"But you must have."

"No, I swear I haven't."

"I wish I was like that," she remarked in a more sober tone.

"Have you? — been in love, I mean.... often?" he asked, fingering her hand nervously to hide his embarrassment.

She nodded with gravity. "Yes, lots of times. But never seriously," she continued reflectively. "Just sort of short likings. Men are always awfully good to me."

He saw her lips part in a faint smile, and winced, his pity stung to incoherent sputterings by a sudden recollection of the brutal name men gave to her calling. Unconsciously he let her hand drop.... What had gone before? .... what was her tale?... Those others — who were good to her — what were they like? He drove in wild parade a flock of male faces.... They had all known her before he had.... They knew her now — she and they had common memories.... They had made love to her — kissed — yes, of course, kissed her — those soft, cool arms.... He was the last — he was behind them all.... But no, protested his vanity, he was different — she had said so.... it must be that he was different.... Feverishly he climbed to the pinnacle of his former exaltation, giddily forcing himself to vision her by his side, her white-gloved hands clasping his shoulders, while he shielded her from the yelping pack of other men.... Then he dropped back into the turmoil of perplexity....

He waited in suspense for her to tell him more, yet he shrank from questioning her. When, however, she spoke again, he at once perceived that the drift of her thoughts had altogether changed. And he could not but acquiesce.

"Tell me what you do every day. You go to your tutor's in the morning?"

He described the place to her. She asked him about his evenings.

"I sit and talk to my sister-in-law, when I've no work."

She plied him with an abundance of questions concerning Helen, listening to his replies attentively, encouraging him to hear himself talk. Thus the edge of his curiosity concerning her was, for the moment, dulled.

He again mentioned the empty box at the theatre. She declined, and declared with abrupt decision that she must start for home. He remonstrated, but she retorted firmly, and quickly grew impatient at his persistence, forbidding him to escort her. He continued to repeat his remonstrance; her tone became brusquely imperious. They descended to the street in silence. She entered a hansom[7] and said something to him, which he failed to hear, as the horse swung round. A flock of cabs, whirling down Oxford Street, engulfed her.

Hardly realizing that she was gone, he was left standing on the pavement. The first thing that he remembered was that he had never kissed her...

VIII

Ronald sat amidst the closely packed figures that blackened an omnibus roof, his thoughts spinning aimlessly, like the fitful columns of dust lifted at street corners by a gusty breeze.

* * * * *

The conductor demanding his fare, rousing him from his musings, snapped the train of his thought. Fumbling in his pocket for the coppers, all at once he remembered her....

"She'll git no verdict."

"Not she. Why, 'ee's bin bled for years."

"Well, serve 'im right. 'Ees a bad 'un any'ow. The aristocracy's all rotten nowadays. I say it's because they ain't got to earn their own bread. Them young toffs wouldn't be so free with their cash if they 'ad to sweat for it."

"An' quite right of the women to bleed 'em. Let 'em get all they can, I say. They're druv to it, poor things. Why, I tell you they're worth a damned side more, most of 'em, than them as calls 'emselves gentlemen jest because they wears top 'ats. I'm a regular Socialist, I am. Every man earn his own bread, I say."

Ronald listened with vague curiosity, while before the vision of tangled brown locks, and the soft white dress clinging at the bust, and trimmed with gold braid round the sleeves, the resolve all slipped from his mind.

---

[7] See note 7 on p. 84.

.... They were right, those men, in their rough fashion, he thought. They looked labourers of some kind, with battered hats and rugged, unfinished sort of faces.... It was women like Midge they meant, women trodden down, women driven to it.... He likened her to a beautiful flower cast to the routlings[8] of swine.... And the stirrings of pity sent proud exhilaration bubbling up boisterously within him: his own attitude towards her stood out in clear, luminous contrast....

.... The frost still held.... A team of heavy horses, straining at a waggon-load of casks, staggered by, banging their hoofs on the pavement, while the driver, all muffled in sacks, high up on his perch, cracked his whip with sharp reports over their backs.... A greyish haze daintily blurred the clustering swarm of vehicles, creeping like flies up the hill towards the narrow end of the straight, broad street; and the sun, topping a bank of creamy clouds, set bright specks twinkling on the harness of cabs, and the window-panes ablaze with gold....

.... The omnibus, turning the corner, rumbled down Regent Street. Each jolt carried him further from Thurgate Road.[9] But he did not descend, judging it was yet too early, dallying with his impatience by means of a series of hurried calculations of time, watching the clocks, and, as the face of each one varied, computing afresh how long it would take him to reach her from the different points on the route. When the omnibus halted at the Circus he got down, intending to saunter back the way he had come: soon, however, he was unconsciously walking as fast as his legs could carry him....

An old woman, whom he had seen on his first visit, was kneeling on the doorstep, some rags and a zinc bucket beside her. The door stood ajar.

"She's away," she called, as he came up.

"Away — out of London, do you mean?"

"Yes, I believe so." And she started to scrub noisily.

"Where's she gone?" he asked blankly.

The grating sound ceased.

"Dunno, I'm sure. Wait a minute. I'll ask Mrs. Wraggleston. She'll know."

She disappeared down the passage, and presently returned, followed by a younger woman, whom he guessed to be the landlady.

"Miss Bashford's gone to the country, sir," she began civilly.

"Where?" he asked again.

"I'm sure I can't tell you, sir, for certain — Brighton, I expect."[10]

---

8 Routlings: derived from 'rootlings', an effective neologism for snuffling around (i.e. by pigs' snouts) for food.
9 Thurgate Road is invented.
10 Brighton was (and still is) a 'fashionable watering-place' (*Gazetteer of The British Isles Statistical and Topographical*, ed. by John Bartholomew (Edinburgh: Adam and Charles Black, 1887), p. 101) on the Sussex coast, some 50 miles from London and so relatively accessible by train for Midge to ply her trade.

"You don't know her address?"

"No, sir, I don't."

"Or when she'll be back?"

"It's sure to be in a day or two."

"Thanks." He moved to go.

"Do you wish to leave any message?"

"No; good-morning," he heard himself answering.

A little way down the street he turned to glance at the house. The two women still stood on the doorstep, looking after him, and talking to one another.

*   *   *   *   *

He returned disconsolately to the crammer's, and for two hours scribbled mechanically in his notebooks. As the minutes slipped by, his longing to see her, to be with her, strengthened in aching intensity.... Everything seemed cheerless, dreary.... Why had she gone? ... When would she be back? ... in a day or two.... tomorrow? ... or the next day? ... He might catch a train down to Brighton.... but her address? ... Still he might meet her in some street, on the Parade.... What was the reason for her going? ... Was she alone? ... Who was she with?

The classroom was darkening. Someone lit the gas. Outside he saw snowflakes in the air. At two o'clock he went out to lunch with the others, Harbord, Willson, and Dawkins. They talked of a new burlesque, and retailed some of the jokes. He sat staring gloomily into the street.

It had stopped snowing, but the fog had descended. The gas-lamps were burning, dismally speckling the monotony of the mud-coloured atmosphere, like sickly remains of an unfinished orgy. Some lighted windows opposite cast squares of murky red; a sense of silence and of desolation prevailed, as if some curse had fallen upon the town.

"What's the matter, Thornycroft? In the blues, eh?"

"Given you the chuck, has she? Cheer up, old chap. There are as good fish in the sea as ever came out of it."

The allusion rudely roused him: he blurted out an oath concerning the weather to cover his confusion.

*   *   *   *   *

And the hours of the afternoon loomed ahead of him, long and yellow....

IX

It was a Saturday. In the class-room the hours dragged by sluggishly; he tingled with impatience, and his eyes travelled constantly to the clock. At last it was over. The men rose, clattering their notebooks. Harbord and Willson were planning to spend the afternoon at some music-hall. Ronald shook them off curtly, hailed a cab, and started for Thurgate Road.

The horse lolloped in a senseless sort of canter, rattling the trace-chains and the glass overhead. The streets were crowded; at every instant, it seemed, omnibuses blocked the way. Near the top of Regent Street a policeman stopped the traffic while a string of stout ladies crossed the road. He sat drumming his fingers on the door, convincing himself that she was back, and feverishly anticipating the first moment of meeting. In Portland Place he shouted to the driver; and a heavy lashing roused the horse into a caricature of a gallop.

From the doorstep he vacantly observed some ragged children dancing to the tune of a piano-organ before a public-house at the corner. Then the door opened.

"She's jest come back," said the old woman.

He pushed past her, and stepping over a bundle of rugs, brown-paper parcels, and portmanteaus strewn across the passage, ran up, taking two stairs at a time.

The room was unchanged. There she was kneeling on the hearthrug, holding an open newspaper against the grate, in a brown dress, a dark hat and veil; wearing a stiff collar like a man's with a red sailor's knot beneath. She half turned her head.

"Hulloa! it's you. How did you know I was back? I was just wondering when I should see you."

He came close to her, a glow of warm happiness rising within him. The red tie made her cheeks look quite rosy.

"Let me help," he said, kneeling beside her.

"Thanks. Hold that corner tight or it'll catch fire."

Presently he said simply —

"It is jolly to see you again."

She smiled at him, her face lit up with pleasure.

"I've been awfully lonely without you."

"What nonsense you talk, you silly boy!"

"But I have, really. I came up here every day to try to find out when you'd be back."

"I don't believe you did," she exclaimed quickly.

"Yes, I promise you."

She was leaning on her elbow, one arm still keeping the newspaper in its place. Her disengaged hand slowly found its way across the hearthrug to his. At the soft, gloved pressure, his gaze turned slowly to hers.

"Dear little Midge ——"

But springing up of a sudden, and dragging back the paper, she cut him short.

"I thought it was alight. There, that'll burn, I think…. Now, sit down and talk to me."

She sank into an arm-chair; he remained kneeling on the hearthrug.

"Tell me," he said, "about Brighton. Why did you go?"

"But I want to hear all about you first. What have you been doing?"

"Nothing.... Going to my work just as usual...."

"Tell me, why did you go to Brighton?" he asked suddenly.

"I love the sea. It was beautiful weather — quite warm and sunny. I suppose it was like that in town. We sat on the Parade ——"

"You and someone else?"

"You don't know him," she said shortly.

"Do you like him very much?" he asked.

She nodded.

"What a curious boy you are! What funny questions you do ask! ... I say, take me out to lunch, will you?"

"Of course. Where shall we go?"

She named a restaurant in Great Portland Street. Then —

"Wait a minute while I get an umbrella."

They walked together through the streets, dry and clean with the frost. Men stared at her as she passed, and when he noticed this he felt very proud.

Once during luncheon he reverted hesitatingly to Brighton.

"Don't keep on bothering about that," she retorted, almost crossly.

*   *   *   *   *

Afterwards they went back to Thurgate Road. She wanted, she said, to show him her two new dresses.

Sitting on the floor, she opened the big cardboard boxes, unfolded the tissue-paper with which they seemed filled, and spread the silks on the sofa.

"This, you see," she began, fingering a soft mass of pale pink, "is an evening one. Princess with a Watteau back.[11] Do you like that?" She stopped, rippling with laughter.

"Don't look so horribly puzzled! ... You poor boy, you don't understand a bit, now do you?"

"No, I don't much," he admitted ruefully. "But explain."

She declined, still shaking with mirth.

"But you think them nice all the same?"

---

[11]   A Princess with a Watteau back is a tea gown with a square neckline in printed silk, satin, and lace. The back of the dress is caught in pleats falling unbelted to the floor, as represented in the paintings of French rococo painter Jean-Antoine Watteau (1684–1721). Watteau was back in vogue at this period via Gautier, Baudelaire, Beardsley, and Pater, whose portrait of Watteau, 'A Prince of Court Painters' (conducted through the 'Old French journal' of Marie-Marguerite Pater, the sister of Watteau's pupil, Jean-Baptiste Pater) appeared in *Macmillan's Magazine*, 52, October 1885, pp. 401–14, and subsequently in his *Imaginary Portraits* (1887).

"Lovely."

Then she ran out, and returned with a box of chocolate creams. He took one, and they stood close together with the box between them.

"Midge," he began, "will you tell me a little about yourself?"

"About myself…. There's nothing to tell."

"Why did you go down to Brighton with that man?"

"What a bother you are!"

"But why did you go?" he reiterated obstinately.

"I suppose I can go where I like, can't I? I needn't ask your leave first. Since you're dead keen on knowing — well, I went because I was hard up. — There!"

She caught a little at her breath, and her face was flaming.

"Now are you satisfied?" she concluded bitterly.

"But why didn't you tell me? … I would have given you as much money as you wanted."

He spoke very quietly.

"I don't want your money…. I wouldn't take it."

Her voice trembled; he thought she was going to cry. Looking down, however, her eyes fell on the chocolate-box, and she laughed again through her tears. Then her face clouded again; she recoiled quickly, as he tried to put his arm round her.

"But, Midge…. dear Midge — "

"Don't," she muttered, as if in sudden pain. "Don't spoil things. How stupid you are! Can't you understand a bit?"

Behind the houses opposite the sun was sinking sullenly, against a cold, opaque-grey sky, spattered with black fragments of cloud. It seemed as if the twilight had come all at once.

"Come, Ron," she said gently, "don't let's squabble. Come and sit by the fire. I want to tell you some things."

He sat astride of the arm of her chair, his hand caressing her hair. After waiting a moment for her to speak, he said:

"Midge, I didn't know, I didn't understand till just now. I've never cared for anyone before. I've hardly stopped thinking about you since the first time I saw you." The words came out clumsily; the last phrase, as soon as he had spoken it, he remembered having read in some novel.

She took his hand in hers silently.

"Midge, will you let me love you? I love you better than everything else in the world. Somehow I've got to understand things a lot better just lately. It's no good my going into the army. We'll get married and go away to the colonies."

She lifted his hand to her lips. The next moment his arms were around her; he was passionately kissing her neck.

"Say you love me back a little," he whispered.

"Yes, dear, dear boy. I've never been so happy before."

"And we'll belong to each other for always?"

With a quick excited laugh she answered:

"I'm married, you know."

"Married!"

"I ran away from him," she continued. "He was a brute. He beat me."

"What's his name?"

"Keith. He's an actor."

"But can't you get a divorce?"

"He could. But he's gone to America. That's why I ran away from him. I was afraid to go with him."

"How long ago was it?"

"Nearly a year. I was only married to him six weeks. A friend of his — Ethel Stainer, a sort of actress — helped me to get away. He suspected it, I've always thought. He wouldn't let me out of his sight. It was the evening before the ship sailed that I escaped."

"Won't he come back?"

"I don't know."

"Haven't you heard anything of him?"

"No, nothing. Ethel Stainer said she would try to find out about him for me, but I didn't want her to. You mustn't be jealous of the others. They've been downright good friends to me."

So they sat on in the growing darkness, and she told him the whole story of her life. And it seemed to him horribly, infinitely pathetic, so that when she had finished he felt that he was bound to her irrevocably, whatever might happen.

"Well, that's about the lot," she exclaimed after a pause, with an abrupt hardening of tone. "What do you think of me?"

"I love you just the same, more than ever. Poor Midge, I am so sorry. But I'll make you happier in the future."

"But I'm not down on my luck at all. He made me feel very miserable — lots of things which you wouldn't understand. But I've been quite happy since."

"Midge."

"Don't call me that name. Everyone calls me that. My proper name is Nita. Now promise you'll give up all those mad ideas. I'm all right; don't you get excited about me. Promise me you'll go on working very hard. The army's your profession. How funny it seems to me talking to you like this."

"But ——"

"Now, no buts. Remember you're only a boy: I'm a full-grown woman."

"Won't you let me speak?"

"I'll not let you say anything — at least not now. Goodbye." There was a note of command in her voice; he felt he must obey.

"Mayn't I see you tomorrow?"

"Yes, dear," she answered gently. "Come in the afternoon. I'll buy a cake and get them to make some tea. That'll be great fun, won't it? And now, I'm going to send you home. Your people'll be wondering what's become of you."

With a new joy in doing exactly as she bid him he took her hand — then went.

X

Beneath a clear sun the frost had melted; and of a sudden, as it were, the days grew glittering and altogether warm. It was with a subtle, indefinable gladness that Midge anticipated the coming of spring, and there were moments when, at the sight of the light glancing prettily in the street, she would smile faintly to herself, for no reason, from sheer sunniness of heart.

She saw scarcely anyone but Ronald now; and every day he appeared at odd, unexpected moments. She liked that it should be so, for then each day the thrill of expectancy was renewed. She took to dressing early in the hope that he would look in for ten minutes in the morning on his way to work; she waited for him at tea-time, or later, in case he should come to take her out to dinner. She found a childish delight in awaiting him; living entirely in the present, she thoughtlessly accepted the chastity of their relations as irrevocable. Thus her sentiment for him floated on from day to day in heedless security, and sometimes she mused indolently concerning the past, wondering whether certain memories had not after all been left her by dreams.

One afternoon they went together by train into the country. They wandered from the station into a beech-wood near the line, and sat down on the clean slab left by a freshly-felled tree. After the roar of London — the thronged streets, the rush of cabs, the rattle of vans and omnibuses — the stillness of the beech-wood pervaded her intimately. She forgot Ronald, who lay smoking a cigarette beside her; she felt she would be content to remain there for hours and hours, doing nothing, thinking of nothing, remembering nothing. The sparkling floor, all speckled by the sunlight, was thickly carpeted with brown leaves, one of which, every now and again, would rise to flutter uneasily at her feet. Here and there a bush, decked in infant greenery, shamed the rest, still shivering in the dead garb of winter. Huge trees lifted like pillars their smooth, green trunks; and beyond, through a crowd of straight, slim stems, she could discern the steely gleam of a river, banding the meadows.

Ronald's smoke blew in her face: she shifted her position.

The swelling undulations of the earth, coated in a great patchwork of grey and brown and rank green, carried a crest of ruddy wood, broken at last by a bunch of fruit trees, powdered from head to foot with snow-white blossom.

Faint cries — whether of birds or of men she could not tell — wandered up from the distance.

* * * * *

And when they were back in London, a dull sadness crept over her — a dissatisfaction, a dislike of the sight of streets, and a vague longing for home....

XI

A treacherous, unmanageable wind, screaming as it rushed past, filled the night. The rain fled before it, helter-skelter; and ragged glimmers of gold danced across the wet pavement. The vague mass of a group of people darkened the steps before the entrance-hall of the Star and Garter; by the road-edge a double phaeton,[12] the horses plunging between the bars of light from the carriage lamps.

A crash! then a shout.

"Woa! yer damned fool — stand steady, will yer. Here, a light — he's caught the splinter-bar."[13]

A lantern moved out of the crowd, illuminating the horses' flanks.

"Steady, boy, steady. He's just nicked hi'self. The bar's right enough." And the man tested it vigorously.

"Tell the gentleman to 'urry up," called the ostler. "The 'orses is jest pullin' my arms off."

At that moment the doorway swung open and Ronald appeared. The hard, white electric light struck his face, as he leisurely buttoned his gloves, his hat aslant on his head.

"It's raining, isn't it?" said Midge, coming up behind him.

"Yes, beastly night."

"Mr. Thornycroft, sir," cried a waiter, running up the steps towards them, and speaking excitedly. "Be advised, sir. Don't try to take them horses back to London night. It ain't safe: it ain't indeed, sir."

Ronald threw a quick glance at the people on the steps.

"Here, get me a cigar — a large Habana," he answered, raising his voice.[14]

"Can't you persuade him, miss? The ostler says he knows you can't get home tonight. They ain't fit to be in harness, them animals."

[12]   A phaeton is a light, four-wheeled, open carriage drawn by two horses. In classical myth Phaeton, the son of Helios (the Sun), drove his father's chariot, nearly setting the Earth on fire by driving too close to it, until he was transfixed by a thunderbolt from Zeus; an appropriate choice of vehicle, given the context.
[13]   The splinter-bar is a cross-bar in the front of a carriage to which the traces of the horses are attached.
[14]   The Habana or Havana cigar was an expensive cigar imported from Cuba that became the luxury smoke of choice in the nineteenth century.

A boy in buttons brought some cigars on a plate.

"Have a hansom, Midge?" said Ronald, laconically, as he chose one.

"Come, be quick," she retorted sharply.

They descended the steps, and the people moved aside to let them pass.

"They'll smash up before they're through the town," said a voice.

"It's madness — and the girl too."

"She's no business to go. Can't some one stop her?"

Ronald had swung himself onto the box.

Midge turned to the crowd.

"Well, won't any of you help me up?"

Half-a-dozen figures started forward; in an instant she was strapping the apron[15] round her.

"Why doesn't some one stop them?" repeated a voice.

"There's a spare seat behind, if the gentleman's in a hurry to be home," Midge called back.

"Let 'em go," shouted Ronald.

The off horse plunged again, struggling to rear. Ronald let the reins drop loose, and cut him heavily with the whip. The animal banged against the collar, and the pair broke into a gallop down the hill.

Ronald rammed the brake home, and they steadied a bit when they reached the bottom.

"You're quite sober?" asked Midge, as they clattered through the town.

"It'll be all right when we get outside."

"I say, chuck away that cigar."

"Catch hold of it, will you?"

He lowered his head, and she took it from between his teeth. It hit the road with a shower of sparks.

"Mind the 'bus. It's going to start — I heard the bell. Keep outside, for God's sake!"

He twisted the rein round his wrist by the buckle, and with a steady wrench from the shoulder hauled the horses onto their haunches. Her grip was on his arm — so tight that he almost cried out.

Then they swung round the corner.

Midge clutched her hat: the wind caught them. "This is lovely," she broke out.

Ronald did not answer. The near horse was trying to stop, frightened at something black by the roadside. With a rush he sprang past it, banging his belly against the pole,[16] and away they whirled down the colonnade of lamp posts.

---

[15]   The apron was used to protect clothing from being soiled by the reins or dirt thrown up by the horses' feet.

[16]   The pole is usually a wood member that runs between a pair of horses, from the front axle of a carriage to the head of the horses; it serves as a lever to steer and stop the vehicle.

"I think this is splendid — dashing through the night, with the wind and the rain. I shouldn't mind a scrap if we were to smash up. I'd rather like to be killed with you, Ron," she laughed nervously.

"The fool's been and put them on the cheek."[17]

Still galloping, they shot past a jogging pony-cart.

"You do drive splendidly," she exclaimed presently.

They were on Barnes Common.

As they neared the railway-bridge, he slackened the reins, and the phaeton rocked more heavily, as they mounted the hill at top speed.

"The bay's getting done."

Down past the silent rows of square villas, they rattled over the river into London, the horses shaking the whole bridge with their stamping. The streets swarmed with a crowd of umbrellas, which overflowed on either side into the roadway.

"Lucky it's Sunday. Bother these 'busses."

"Ronald."

"Well?"

"Does anyone — does your sister-in-law know — suspect — me?"

"That I took you out to dinner? No."

"I don't mean that, but — oh! mind that child."

He shouted, and the child scuttled back.

"That we love each other, I mean?"

"I don't see what it's got to do with anyone."

"Ron — "

"Yes."

"What do you think they'll do when they find out? They must find out soon — your relations, I mean."

"You *are* a funny child, Midge. What on earth are you driving at?"

"Because I'd hate for them to know about me and to come between us, that's all."

He noticed the hardness of her tone, and, embarrassed, flicked the whip to and fro.

* * * * *

"This will do. Stop, please. I'll take a hansom from here."

Mechanically he pulled the horses to a standstill. Almost before he had turned to give her his hand, she was in the roadway.

"Goodbye, Ron," and she stepped into a passing hansom.

Absently, for a while, he followed the red specks of the cab-lamps.

[17] On the cheek refers to the side pieces of the horse's bit; the horse is on the snaffle and not the curb, so less easily controlled.

Piccadilly looked dark and dreary; across St. James's Park, he could see the pattern of some lighted windows high up against the sky. How tall those houses were, he thought, as he turned down a side street towards the stables. A sudden jolt brought him to his senses: he had driven over the kerb.

XII

The next night saw the end of it — an end, sudden and unexpected as the beginning had been. He had not seen her all day, and in the evening he had been dining out. It was dark in the hall, when he let himself in: the servants had gone to bed. He lit a candle, the match striking noisily in the stillness of the house. An envelope, addressed to him, lay on the table, and he went into the dining-room to read it.

"DEAR RONALD,

"I *did* enjoy it so yesterday. It was jolly, the dark night, and the galloping horses, and the rain blowing in one's face. After I got home I stayed a long while thinking about it all, and sort of mooning about you and everything. And I don't know why, but I began to feel quite old and sensible, and all my silly feather-brainedness went away. It was awfully strange and queer, Ronald, and I don't believe you'll understand a bit. It came to me quite suddenly that it could never go on like that. It couldn't really. It was too nice and jolly. Something would have happened. I feel quite sure of it. So, as I said, quite suddenly I made up my mind to go back home. I'd been meaning to do so for a long while. Do you remember I told you I was going that first time you spoke to me? I can't explain why I made up my mind suddenly like that — and perhaps you'll think me quite heartless. I should be very sorry for you to think of me like that. But I can't help it if you do, because I am quite certain I'm doing what's best. As I have said, I've been intending to go for a long while, and if I hadn't met you I should have gone before this. No one down there knows anything about what I've been doing in London, and father's getting very old, and he's all alone now. I shall live with him, and become very good and steady.

"Now I want you, dear Ronald — you've been very, very good to me — I want you to promise me one thing. *Never, never to try to find out where I've gone, and never to come down after me.* You will promise me this, won't you, Ronald, for the sake of all the jolly times we've had together? Yes, I know you will, and I shall trust you.

"So now I shall say goodbye, and wish you all good luck. You've been a dear, dear, good, true friend to me, and I shall never, never forget you. Goodbye, once again.

"NITA."

The fire was dead; only cold cinders lay in the grate. But he did not notice the chilliness of the room, but for a long while remained there, staring stupidly at the letter, as he was, in his hat, overcoat, and gloves. The door stood ajar, and the almond-shaped flame of the candle, orange-coloured at the tip, flickered fitfully in the draught.... A clock sounded a single timid note. He started, crumpled the letter in his pocket, and went briskly upstairs, as if he had come to some satisfactory decision.

A streak of light lay under Helen's door: as he crossed the landing, it opened.

"Come in a moment, Ron," said her voice. "I haven't seen you since the morning. Did you have a pleasant evening?

He had never before seen the inside of her room. The dainty refinement of each intimate detail struck him. How orderly everything was! The glistening, silver-backed brushes, ranged on the toilet-table; the white-panelled wardrobes, their edges picked out in gold; the bright-blue bed-curtains; the warm, terra-cotta walls. A fire was cosily blazing, throwing a vague dance of shadows across the ceiling. And she looked white and fragile, in a loose dress that seemed all lace. Irresistibly, he compared her in his mind to Midge. How curiously different they were! ...

"What's the matter?" she asked in a startled voice.

"Nothing's the matter," he answered shortly.

"But there is.... I can see it in your face. I can see you've got something on your mind."

No, I'm all right. Don't you worry about me."

"What is it?" she persisted. "Is it the examination? Don't you think you'll get through?"

He made an impatient sign of dissent.

"Ron, don't shut yourself up from me. Tell me your difficulties.... Let me help you.... I'm sure I could, whatever they are.... Much more than you think."

The strained note of her pleading startled him. How excited she was all of a sudden! She stood waiting for him to speak. He wished she would sit down, and not gaze at him like that. He felt goaded to say something.

"I think I shall give up the idea of the army," he muttered half to himself.

"Give it up! ... Give it up! ... Why?" she asked in blank astonishment.

"The army's rot nowadays. I can't get into a really good regiment as it is, and I should be only cooped up in some poky country town."

"But you used to be so enthusiastic about it all."

"No, I only fancied I was... I shall go out to the colonies — to New Zealand, or somewhere...."

"Ronald!"

There was a silence. The gasp of her exclamation seemed to linger in the air.

"Since when have you had these ideas?"

"Just lately."

"And you really mean them?"

"Yes."

There was another pause. He got up and stood by the mantelpiece, fidgeting with some china ornaments, apprehensively tempted to tell her.... He must tell somebody.... And led by her question, and his reply to it, to believe in the firmness of his decision to sacrifice his career in order to marry her, he was nervously proud of its importance.

"But I don't understand.... What has made you change like this?"

He continued to fidget with the ornaments.

"There must be some reason.... Why won't you trust me? Don't keep me in the dark like this.... It isn't right of you.... It's unkind.... Don't you trust me?" she repeated, catching a glimpse of his irresolution. "Tell me what's made you change?"

"Nothing.... Nothing's made me change."

Her features stiffened slowly, and he felt angrily uncomfortable because he could not help paining her. He turned a little vase round and round in the palm of his hand. The silence was becoming intolerable.

At last he spoke, ostentatiously replacing the vase, and forcing himself to simulate indifference.

"By Jove! it's half-past twelve. I must be going to bed. Goodnight.... Goodnight, Helen."

"Goodnight," she answered mechanically.

He had reached the door, but there the impulse to speak gently to her fought for release.

"Helen — " he began.

"Goodnight," she repeated dully as before.

She sat listening to his footsteps ascending the stairs. His door closed, and she heard his tread overhead. After a while, all sound ceased....

XIII

Twelve years later, on his return from India, he met Midge again.

It was a frosty October evening in a stable-yard at Huntingdon.[18] He was on his way to a country house in the neighbourhood, and had come to hire a horse and trap. Her husband kept the yard, and she was the mother of three chubby-cheeked girls. It was late: the men had all gone to bed, so she held the lantern, while her husband harnessed the mare.

She knew him at once; but because of her husband, refrained from betraying it. And he just glanced carelessly at her and never recognized her.

Then he climbed up beside her husband, and the trap rattled out of the yard.

---

[18]   Huntingdon is a market town in Cambridgeshire, seventy miles due north of London.

In Cumberland

A phantom regiment of giant mist-pillars swept silently across the valley; beaded drops loaded each tuft of coarse, dull-tinted grass; the peat-hags gaped like black, dripping flesh-wounds in the earth's side; the distance suggested rectangular fields and wooded slopes — vague, grey, phantasmagoric;[1] and down over everything floated the damp of fine rain.

Alec's heavy tread crunched the turfed bridle-path rhythmically, and from the stiff rim of his clerical hat the water dribbled onto his shoulders.

It was a rugged, irregular, almost uncouth face, and now the features were vacantly huddled in a set expression, obviously habitual. The cheeks were hunched up, almost concealing the small eyes; a wet wisp of hair straggled over the puckered forehead, and the ragged, fair moustache was spangled by the rain.

At his approach the sheep scampered up the fell-side; then, stood staring through the mist in anxious stupidity. And Alec, shaking the water from his hat, strode forward with an almost imperceptible gleam on his face. It was so that he liked the valley — all colourless and blurred, with the sky close overhead, like a low, leaden ceiling.

By-and-bye, a cluster of cottages loomed ahead — a choppy pool of black slate roofs, wanly a-glimmer in the wet. As he entered the village, a group of hard-featured men threw him a curt chorus of greetings, to which he raised his stick in response, mechanically.

He mounted the hill. Three furnace chimneys craned their thin necks to grime the sky with a dribbling, smoky breath; high on a bank of coal-dust, blurred silhouettes of trucks stood waiting in forlorn strings; women, limp, with unkempt hair, and loose, bedraggled skirts, stood round the doorways in gossiping groups.

"Which is Mrs. Matheson's?" he stopped to ask.

"There — oop there, Mr. Burkett — by yon ash — where them childer's standin'," they answered, all speaking together, eagerly. "Look ye! that be Mrs. Matheson herself."

Alec went up to the woman. His face clouded a little, and the puffs from his pipe came briskly in rapid succession.

"Mrs. Matheson, I've only just heard — Tell me, how did it happen?" he asked gently.

She was a stout, red-faced woman, and her eyes were all bloodshot with much crying. She wiped them hastily with the corner of her apron before answering.

---

[1]   A phantasmagoria was an optical entertainment using magic lanterns to display images. It had come to mean having dream-like visions, hence phantasmagoric suggests a mixture of real and imagined images.

"It was there, Mr. Burkett, by them rails. He was jest playin' aboot in t' road wi' Arnison's childer. At half-past one, t' grandmoother stepped across to fetch me a jug o' fresh water an' she see'd him settin' in door there. Then — mabbee twenty minutes later — t' rain coome on an' I thought to go to fetch him in. But I couldna see na sign of him anywhere. We looked oop and doon, and thought, mabbee, he'd toddled roond to t' back. An' then, all at once, Dan Arnison called to us that he was leein' in t' water, doon in beck-pool. An' Dan ran straight doon, an' carried him oop to me; but 'twas na use. He was quite cold and drownded. An' I went ——" But the sobs, rising thickly, swallowed the rest.

Alec put his hand on her shoulder soothingly.

"Ay, I know'd ye'd be grieved, Mr. Burkett. He was the bonniest boy in all t' parish."

She lifted the apron to her eyes again, while he crossed to the railings. The wood of the posts was splintered and worm-eaten, and the lower rail was broken away. Below, the rock shelved down some fifteen feet to the beck-pool, black and oily-looking.

"It's a very dangerous place," he said, half to himself.

"Ay, Mr. Burkett, you're right," interrupted a bent and wizened old woman, tottering forward.

"This be grandmoother, Mr. Burkett," Mrs. Matheson explained. "'Twas grandmoother that see'd him last ——"

"Ay, Mr. Burkett," the old woman began in a high, tremulous treble. "When I went fer to fill t' jug fer Maggie he was a-settin' on t' steps there playin' with t' kitten, an' he called after me, 'Nanny!' quite happy-like; but I took na notice, but jest went on fer t' water. I shawed Mr. Allison the broken rail last month, when he was gittin' t' rents, and I told him he ought to put it into repair, with all them wee childer playin' all daytime on t' road. Didn't I, Maggie?" Mrs. Matheson assented incoherently. "An' he was very civil-like, was Mr. Allison, and he said he'd hev' it seen to. It's alus that way, Mr. Burkett," the old woman concluded, shaking her head wisely. "Folks wait till some accident occurs, and then they think to bestir themselves."

Alec turned to the mother, and touched her thick, nerveless hand.

"There, there, Mrs. Matheson, don't take on so," he said.

At his touch her sobbing suddenly ceased, and she let her apron fall.

"Will ye na coome inside, Mr. Burkett?" she asked.

And they all three went in together.

The little room had been scrubbed and tidied, and a number of chairs, ranged round the table, blocked the floor.

"We've bin busy all marnin', gittin' things a bit smartened oop for t' inquest. T' coroner's cooming at twelve," the grandmother explained.

"Will ye coome oop-stairs, Mr. Burkett — jest — jest to tak' a look at him?"

Mrs. Matheson asked in a subdued voice.

Alec followed her, squeezing his burly frame up the narrow, creaking staircase.

The child lay on the clean, white bed. A look of still serenity slept on his pallid face. His tawny curls were smoothed back, and some snowdrops were scattered over the coverlet. All was quite simple.

Mrs. Matheson stood in the doorway, struggling noisily with her sobs.

"It is God's will," Alec said quietly.

"He was turned four last week," she blurted out. "Ye'll excuse me, Mr. Burkett, but I'm that overdone that I jest canna help myself," and she sank into a chair.

He knelt by the dead child's side and prayed, while the slow rise and fall of the mother's sobs filled the room. When he rose his eyes were all moist.

"God will help you, if you ask Him. His ways are secret. We cannot understand His purpose. But have faith in Him. He has done it for the best," he said.

"Ay, I know, I know, Mr. Burkett. But ye see he was the youngest, and that bonny ——"

"Let me try to comfort you," he said.

* * * * *

When they came downstairs again, her face was calmer and her voice steadier. The coroner, a dapper man with a bright-red tie, was taking off his gloves and mackintosh; the room was fast filling with silent figures, and the old grandmother was hobbling to and fro with noisy, excited importance.

"Will ye na stay for t' inquest?"

Alec shook his head. "No, I can't stop now. I have a School-board meeting to go to. But I will come up this afternoon."

"Thank'ee, Mr. Burkett, God bless thee," said Mrs. Matheson.

He shook hands with the coroner, who was grumbling concerning the weather; then strode out back down the valley.

Though long since he had grown familiar with the aspects of suffering, that scene in the cottage, by reason of its very simplicity, had affected him strangely. His heart was full of slow sorrow for the woman's trouble, and the image of the child, lying beautiful in its death-sleep, passed and re-passed in his mind.

By-and-bye, the moaning of the wind, the whirling of lost leaves, the inky shingle-beds that stained the fell-sides, inclined his thoughts to a listless brooding.

Life seemed dull, inevitable, draped in sombre, drifting shadows, like the valley-head. Yet in all good he saw the hand of God, a mysterious, invisible force, ever imperiously at work beneath the ravages of suffering and of sin.

It was close upon six o'clock when he reached home. He was drenched to the skin, and as he sat before the fire, dense clouds of steam rose from his mud-stained boots and trousers.

"Now, Mr. Burkett, jest ye gang and tak' off them things, while I make yer tea. Ye'll catch yer death one of these days — I know ye will. I sometimes think ye haven't more sense than a boy, traipsin' about all t' day in t' wet, and niver takin' yer meals proper-like."

A faint smile flickered across his face. He was used to his landlady's scoldings.

"A child was drowned yesterday in the beck up at Beda Cottages. I had to go back there this afternoon to arrange about the funeral," he mumbled, half apologetically.

Mrs. Parkin snorted defiantly, bustling round the table as she spread the cloth. Presently she broke out again:

"An' noo, ye set there lookin' as white as a bogle.[2] Why don't ye go an' git them wet clothes off? Ye're fair wringin'."

He obeyed; though the effort to rise was great. He felt curiously cold: his teeth were clacking, and the warmth from the flames seemed delicious.

In his bedroom a dizziness caught him, and it was a moment before he could recognize the familiar objects. And he realized that he was ill, and looked at himself in the glass with a dull, scared expression. He struggled through his dressing, however, and went back to his tea. But, though he had eaten nothing since the morning, he had no appetite; so, from sheer force of habit, he lit a pipe, wheeling his chair close to the fire.

And, as the heat penetrated him, his thoughts spun aimlessly round the day's events, till these gradually drifted into the background of his mind, as it were, and he and they seemed to have become altogether detached. His forehead was burning, and a drowsy, delicious sense of physical weakness was stealing over his limbs. He was going to be ill, he remembered; and it was with vague relief that he looked forward to the prospect of long days of monotonous inactivity, long days of repose from the daily routine of fatigue. The details of each day's work, the accomplishment of which, before, had appeared so indispensable, now, he felt in his lassitude, had faded to insignificance. Mrs. Parkin was right: he had been overdoing himself; and with a clear conscience he would take a forced holiday in bed. Things in the parish would get along without him till the end of the week. There was only the drowned child's funeral, and, if he could not go, Milner, the neighbouring vicar, would take it for him. His pipe slipped from his hand to the hearthrug noiselessly, and his head sank forward....

He was dreaming of the old churchyard. The trees were rocking their slim, bare arms; drip, drip, drip, the drops pattered onto the tombstones, tight-huddled in the white, wet light of the moon; the breath of the old churchyard tasted warm and moist, like the reek of horses after a long journey.

---

[2]　　Bogle is an archaic form of 'bogey', an evil or mischievous spirit.

The child's funeral was finished. Mrs. Matheson had cried noisily into her apron; the mourners were all gone now; and alone, he sat down on the fresh-dug grave. By the moonlight he tried to decipher the names carved on the slabs; but most of the letters had faded away, and moss-cushions had hidden the rest. Then he found it — "George Matheson, aged four years and five days," and underneath were carved Mrs. Matheson's words: "He was the bonniest boy in all the parish." He sat on, with the dread of death upon him, the thought of that black senselessness ahead, possessing him, so sudden, so near, so intimate, that it seemed entirely strange to have lived on, forgetful of it. By-and-bye, he saw her coming towards him — Ethel, like a figure from a picture, wearing a white dress that trailed behind her, a red rose pinned at the waist, and the old smile on her lips. And she came beside him, and told him how her husband had gone away for ever, and he understood at once that he and she were betrothed again, as it had been five years ago. He tried to answer her, but somehow the words would not come; and, as he was striving to frame them, there came a great crash. A bough clattered down on the tombstones; and with a start he awoke.

A half-burned coal was smoking in the fender. He felt as if he had been sleeping for many hours.

He fell to stupidly watching the red-heat, as it pulsed through the caves of coal, to imagining himself climbing their ashen mountain-ridges, across dark defiles, up the face of treacherous precipices....

Hundreds of times, here, in this room, in this chair, before this fire, he had sat smoking, picturing the old scenes to himself, musing of Ethel Fulton (Ethel Winn she had been then; but, after her marriage, he had forced himself to think of her as bearing her husband's name — that was a mortification from which he had derived a sort of bitter satisfaction). But now, with the long accumulation of his solitude — five years he had been vicar of Scarsdale — he had grown so unconscious of self, so indifferent to the course of his own existence, that every process of his mind had, from sheer lack of external stimulation, stagnated, till, little by little, the growth of mechanical habit had come to mould its shape and determine its limitations. And hence, not for a moment had he ever realized the grip that this habit of sentimental reminiscence had taken on him, nor the grotesque extent of its futile repetition. Such was the fervour of his attitude towards his single chapter of romance.

Five years ago, she and he had promised their lives to one another. And the future had beckoned them onward, gaily, belittling every obstacle in its suffusion of glad, alluring colour. He was poor: he had but his curate's stipend, and she was used to a regular routine of ease. But he would have tended her wants, waiting on her, watching over her, indefatigably; chastening all the best that was in him, that he might lay it at her feet. And together, hand in hand, they would have laboured in God's service. At least so it seemed to him now.

Then had come an enforced separation; and later, after a prolonged, unaccountable delay, a letter from her explaining, in trite, discursive phrases, how it could never be — it was a mistake — she had not known her own mind — now she could see things clearer — she hoped he would forgive and forget her.

A wild determination to go at once to her, to plead with her, gripped him; but for three days he was helpless, bound fast by parish duties. And when at last he found himself free, he had already begun to perceive the hopelessness of such an errand, and, with crushed and dogged despair, to accept his fate as irrevocable.

In his boyhood — at the local grammar-school, where his ugliness had made him the butt of his class — and later, at an insignificant Oxford college, where, to spare his father, whose glebe was at the time untenanted, he had set himself grimly to live on an impossibly slender allowance — at every turn of his life, he had found himself at a disadvantage with his fellows. Thus he had suffered much, dumbly — meekly many would have said — without a sign of resentment, or desire for retaliation. But all the while, in his tenacious, long-suffering way, he was stubbornly inuring himself to an acceptance of his own disqualifications. And so, once rudely awakened from his dream of love, he wondered with heavy curiosity at his faith in its glamorous reality, and, remembering the tenour[3] of his life, suffered bitterly like a man befooled by[4] his own conceit.

Some months after the shattering of his romance, the rumour reached him that James Fulton, a prosperous solicitor in the town, was courting her. The thing was impossible, a piece of idle gossip, he reasoned with himself. Before long, however, he heard it again, in a manner that left no outlet for doubt.

It seemed utterly strange, unaccountable, that she, whose eager echoing of all his own spiritual fervour and enthusiasm for the work of the Church still rang in his ears, should have chosen a man, whose sole talk had seemed to be of dogs and of horses, of guns and of game; a man thick-minded, unthinking, self-complacent; a man whom he himself had carelessly despised as devoid of any spark of spirituality.

And, at this moment, when the first smartings of bitter bewilderment were upon him, the little living of Scarsdale fell vacant, and his rector, perhaps not unmindful of his trouble, suggested that he should apply for it.

The valley was desolate and full of sombre beauty; the parish, sparsely-peopled but extensive; the life there would be monotonous, almost grim, with long hours of lonely brooding. The living was offered to him. He accepted it excitedly.

And there, busied with his new responsibilities, throwing himself into the work with a suppressed, ascetic ardour, news of the outside world reached him vaguely, as if from afar.

---

[3]   Tenour is an archaic form of 'tenor', meaning direction or prevailing course.
[4]   Befooled by: fooled by.

He read of her wedding in the local newspaper: later, a few trite details of her surroundings; and then, nothing more.

But her figure remained still resplendent in his memory, and, as time slipped by, grew into a sort of gleaming shrine, incarnating for him all the beauty of womanhood. And gradually, this incarnation grew detached, as it were, from her real personality, so that, when twice a year he went back to spend Sunday with his old rector, to preach a sermon in the parish church, he felt no shrinking dread lest he should meet her. He had long ceased to bear any resentment against her, or to doubt that she had done what was right. The part that had been his in the little drama seemed altogether of lesser importance.

* * * * *

All night he lay feverishly tossing, turning his pillow aglow with heat, from side to side; anxiously reiterating whole incoherent conversations and jumbled incidents.

At intervals, he was dimly conscious of the hiss of wind-swept leaves outside, and of rain-gusts rattling the window-panes; and later, of the sickly light of early morning streaking the ceiling with curious patterns. By-and-bye, he dropped into a fitful sleep, and forgot the stifling heat of his bed.

Then the room had grown half full of daylight, and Mrs. Parkin was there, fidgeting with the curtains. She said something which he did not hear, and he mumbled that he had slept badly, and that his head was aching.

Some time later — how long he did not know — she appeared again, and a man, whom he presently understood to be a doctor, and who put a thermometer, the touch of which was deliciously cool, under his armpit, and sat down at the table to write. Mrs. Parkin and he talked in whispers at the foot of the bed: they went away; Mrs. Parkin brought him a cup of beef-tea and some toast; and then he remembered only the blurred memories of queer, unfinished dreams.

Consciousness seemed to return to him all of a sudden; and, when it was come, he understood dimly that, somehow, the fatigue of long pain was over, and he tasted the peaceful calm of utter lassitude.

He lay quite still, his gaze following Mrs. Parkin, as she moved to and fro across the room, till it fell on a basket-full of grapes that stood by the bedside. They were unfamiliar, inexplicable; they puzzled him; and for awhile he feebly turned the matter over in his mind. Presently she glanced at him, and he lifted his hand towards the basket.

"Would ye fancy a morsel o' fruit noo? 'Twas Mrs. Fulton that sent 'em," she said.

She held the basket towards him, and he lifted a bunch from it. They were purple grapes, large and luscious-looking. Ethel had sent them. How strange that was! For an instant he doubted if he were awake, and clutched the pillow to make sure that it was real.

"Mrs. Fulton sent them?" he repeated.

"Ay, her coachman came yesterday in t' forenoon[5] to inquire how ye were farin', and left that fruit for ye. Ay, Mr. Burkett, but ye've had a mighty quantity o' callers. Most all t' parish has been askin' for news o' ye. An' that poor woman from t' factory cottages has been doon forenoon and night."

"How long have I been in bed?" he asked after a pause.

"Five days and five nights. Ye've bin nigh at death's door, ravin' and moanin' like a madman. But, noo, I mustna keep ye chatterin'. Ye should jest keep yeself quiet till t' doctor coomes. He'll be mighty surprised to find ye so much improved, and in possession of yer faculties."

And she left him alone.

He lay staring at the grapes, while excitement quickened every pulse. Ethel had sent them — they were from Ethel — Ethel had sent them — through his brain, to and fro, boisterously, the thought danced. And then, he started to review the past, dispassionately, critically, as if it were another man's; and soon, every detail, as he lingered on it, seemed to disentangle itself, till it all achieved a curious simplification. The five years at Scarsdale became all blurred: they resembled an eventless waste-level, through which he had been mechanically trudging. But the other day, it seemed, he was with her — he and she betrothed to one another. A dozen scenes passed before his eyes: with a flush of hot, intolerable shame, he saw himself, clumsy, uncouth, devoid of personal charm, viewing her bluntly, selfishly through the cumbrous medium of his own personality. And her attitude was clear too; the glamour, woven of habitual, sentimental reminiscence, faded, as it were, from her figure, and she appeared to him simply and beautifully human; living, vibrating, frail. *Now* he knew the meaning of that last letter of hers — the promptings of each phrase; the outpourings of his ideals, enthusiasms, aspirations — callow, blatant, crude, he named them bitterly — had scared her: she had felt herself unequal to the strain of the life he had offered her: in her lovable, womanish frailty, she had grown to dread it; and he realized all that she had suffered before she had brought herself to end it — the long struggles with doubt and suspense. The veil that had clogged his view was lifted: he knew her now: he could read the writing on her soul: he was securely equipped for loving her; and now, she had passed out of his life, beyond recall. In his blindness he had not recognized her, and had driven her away.

How came it that today, for the first time, all these things were made clear?

The clock struck; and while he was listening to its fading note, the door-handle clicked briskly, and the doctor walked in. He talked cheerily of the crops damaged by the storm, and the sound of his voice seemed to vibrate harshly through the room.

[5]   See note 11 on p. 136.

"There's a heavy shower coming up," he remarked. "By the way, you're quite alone here, Mr. Burkett, I believe. Have you no relatives whom you would like to send for?"

"No — no one," Alec answered. "Mrs. Parkin will look after me."

"Yes — but you see," and he came and sat down by the bedside, "I don't say there's any immediate danger; but you've had a very near touch of it. Now isn't there any old friend? — you ought not to be alone like this." He spoke the last words with emphasis.

Alec shook his head. His gaze had fallen on the basket of grapes again: he was incoherently musing of Ethel.

"Mind, I don't say there's any immediate danger," he heard the man repeating; "but I must tell you that you're not altogether out of the wood yet."

He paused.

"You ought to be prepared for the worst, Mr. Burkett."

The last phrase lingered in Alec's mind; and slowly its meaning dawned upon him.

"You mean I might die at any moment?" he asked.

"No, no — I don't say that," the other answered evasively. "But you see the fever has left you very weak; and of course in such cases one can never be quite sure ——"

The rest did not reach Alec's ears; he was only vaguely aware of the murmur of the man's voice.

Presently he perceived that he had risen.

"I will come back in the afternoon," he was saying.

"I'll tell Mrs. — Mrs. Parker to bring you in some breakfast."

After the doctor had gone he dozed a little....

Then remembered the man's words — "No immediate danger, but you must be prepared for the worst." The sense of it all flashed upon him: he understood what the man had meant: that was the way doctors always told such things, he guessed. So the end was near ... He wondered, a little curiously, if it would come before tonight, or tomorrow ... It was near, quite near, he repeated to himself; and gradually, a peacefulness permeated his whole being, and he was vaguely glad to be alone....

A little while, and he would be near God. He felt himself detached from the world, and at peace with all men.

His life, as he regarded it trailing behind him, across the stretch of past years, seemed inadequate, useless, pitiable almost; of his own personality, as he now realized it, he was ashamed — petty mortifications, groping efforts, a grotesque capacity for futile, melancholy brooding — he rejoiced that he was to have done with it. The end was near, quite near, he repeated once again.

Then, afterwards, would come rest — the infinite rest of the Saviour's tenderness, and the strange, wonderful expectation of the mysterious life to come ... A glimpse of his own serenity, of his own fearlessness, came to him; and he was moved by a quick flush of gratitude towards God. He thought of the terror of the atheist's death — the world, a clod of dead matter blindly careering through space; humanity, a casual, senseless growth, like the pullulating insects on a rottening tree....

A little while, only a little while, and he would be near God. And, softly, under his breath, he implored pardon for the countless shortcomings of his service....

The German clock on the mantelpiece ticked with methodical fussiness: the flames in the grate flickered lower and lower; and one by one dropped, leaving dull-red cinders. Through the window, under the half-drawn blind, was the sky, cold with the hard, white glare of the winter sun, flashing above the bare, bony mountain-backs; and he called to mind spots in the little, desolate parish, which, with a grim, clinging love, he had come to regard as his own for always. Who would come after him, live in this house of his, officiate in the square, grey-walled church, move and work in God's service among the people? ...

And, while he lay drowsily musing on the unfinished dream, a muffled murmur of women's voices reached his ears. By an intuition, akin perhaps to animal instinct, he knew all at once that it was she, talking with Mrs. Parkin down in the room below. Prompted by a rush of imperious impulse he raised himself on his elbow to listen.

There was a rustling of skirts in the passage and the sound of the voices grew clearer.

"Good day, ma'am, and thank ye very kindly, I'm sure," Mrs. Parkin was saying.

No reply came, though he was straining every nerve to catch it ... At last, subdued, but altogether distinct, *her* voice ——

"You're sure there's nothing else I can send?"

The door of his room was ajar. He dug his nails into the panel-edge, and tried to swing it open. But he could scarcely move it, and in a moment she would be gone.

Suddenly he heard his own voice — loud and queer it sounded:

"Ethel — Ethel!"

Hurried steps mounted the stairs, and Mrs. Parkin's white cap and spectacled face appeared.

"What be t' matter, Mr. Burkett?" she asked breathlessly.

"Stop her — tell her."

"Dearie, dearie me, he's off wanderin' agin."

"No, no; I'm all right — tell — ask Mrs. Fulton if she would come up to see me?"

"There, there, Mr. Burkett, don't ye excite yeself. Ye're not fit to see anyone, ye know that. Lie ye doon agin, or ye'll be catchin' yer death o'cauld."

"Ask her to come, please — just for a minute."

"For Heaven's sake lie doon. Ye'll be workin' yeself into a fever next. There, there, I'll ask her for ye, though I've na notion what t' doctor 'ud say."

She drew down the blind and retired, closing the door quietly behind her.

The next thing he saw was Ethel standing by his bedside.

He lay watching her without speaking. She wore a red dress trimmed with fur; a gold bracelet was round her gloved wrist, and a veil half hid her features.

Presently he perceived that she was very white, that her mouth was twitching, and that her eyes were full of tears.

"Alec — I'm so sorry you're so ill ... Are you in pain?

He shook his head absently. Her veil and the fur on her cloak looked odd, he thought, in the half-light of the room.

"You will be better soon: the worst is over."

"No," he answered, with a dreary smile. "I am going to die."

She burst into sobs.

"No, no, Alec ... You must not think that."

He stretched his arm over the coverlet towards her, and felt the soft pressure of her gloved hand.

"Forgive me, Ethel, I'm sorry. I didn't mean to pain you. But it is so; the doctor told me this morning."

She sat down by the bedside, still crying, pressing her handkerchief to her eyes.

"Ethel, how strange it seems. Do you know I haven't seen you since I left Cockermouth?"[6] The words came deliberately, for his mind had grown quite calm. "How the time has flown!"

Her grasp on his hand tightened, but she made no answer.

"It was very kind of you to come all this way, Ethel, to see me. Will you stay a little and let me talk to you? It's more than five years since we talked together, you know," and he smiled faintly. "Don't cry so, Ethel dear. I did not mean to make you cry. There's no cause to cry, dear; you've made me so happy."

"My poor, poor Alec," she sobbed.

"You'd almost forgotten the old days, perhaps," he continued dreamily, talking half to himself; "for it's a long while ago now. But to me it seems as if it had all just happened. You see I've been vegetating rather, here in this lonely, little place ... Don't go on crying, Ethel dear ... let me tell you about things a little. There's no harm in it now, because you know I'm ——"

"Oh! don't — don't say that. You'll get better. I know you will."

"No, Ethel, I shan't. Something within me tells me that my course is done.

---

[6]   Cockermouth: old market town in Cumberland, now Cumbria, north-west England.

Besides, I don't want to get better. I'm so happy ... Stay a little with me, Ethel ... I wanted to explain ... I was stupid, selfish, in the old days ——"

"It was I — I who ——" she protested through her tears.

"No, you were quite right to write me that letter. I've thought that almost from the first ... I'm sure of it," he added, as if convincing himself definitely. "It could never be ... it was my fault ... I was stupid and boorish and wrapped up in myself. I did not try to understand your nature ... I didn't understand anything about women ... I never had a sister ... I took for granted that you were always thinking and feeling just as I was. I never tried to understand you, Ethel ... I was not fit to be entrusted with you."

"Alec, Alec, it is not true. You were too good, too noble-hearted. I felt you were far above me. Beside you I felt I was silly and frivolous. Your standards about everything seemed so high ——"

But he interrupted, unheeding her:

"You don't know, Ethel, how happy you've made me ... I have thought of you every day. In the evenings, I used to sit alone, remembering you and all the happy days we had together, and the remembrance of them has been a great joy to me. I used to go over them all, again and again. The day that we all went to Morecambe, and that walk along the sea-shore, when the tide caught us, and I carried you across the water ...[7] the time that we went to those ruins, and you wore the primroses I picked for you. And I used to read over all your letters, and remember all the things you used to say. Downstairs, under the writing-table, there is a black, tin cash-box — the key is on my bunch — Mrs. Parkin will give it you. It's where I've kept everything that has reminded me of you, all this time. Will you take it back with you? ... You don't know how you've helped me all these years — I wanted to tell you that ... When I was in difficulties, I used to wonder how you would have liked me to act ... When I was lonely and low-spirited, I used to tell myself that you were happy." He paused for breath, and his voice died slowly in the stillness of the room. "You were quite right," he murmured almost inaudibly, "I see it all, quite clearly now."

She was bending over him, and was framing his face in her two hands.

"Say I was wrong," she pleaded passionately. "Say I was wicked, wrong. I loved you, Alec ... I was promised to you. I should have been so happy with you, dear ... Alec, my Alec, do not die ... God will not let you die ... He cannot be so cruel ... Come back, Alec .... I love you ... Do you hear, my Alec? I love you .... Ethel loves you ... Before God I love you ... I was promised to you ... I broke my word ... I loved you all the time, but I did not know it ... Forgive me,

---

[7]   This refers to the dangers of crossing Morecambe Bay (which stretches from the south-west coast of Cumbria to Fleetwood, Lancashire) on foot at low tide, which before the railway was built in the 1850s was a matter of economic necessity. It remains a notoriously hazardous activity, due to fast moving tides and quicksands: twenty-three Chinese cockle-pickers were cut off by the tides and died in 2004.

my Alec ... forgive me ... I shall love you always."

He passed his fingers over her forehead tentatively, as if he were in darkness.

"Ethel, every day, every hour, all these years, you have been with me. And now I am going away. Kiss me — just once — just once. There can be no wrong in it now."

She tore her veil from her face: their lips met, and her head rested a moment, sobbing, on his shoulder.

"Hush! don't cry, Ethel dear, don't cry. You have made me so glad ... And you will remember to take the box ... And you will think of me sometimes ... And I shall pray God to make you happy, and I shall wait for you, Ethel, and be with you in thought, and if you have trouble, you will know that I shall be sorrowing with you. Isn't it so, dear? ... Now, goodbye, dear one — goodbye. May God watch over you."

She had moved away. She came back again, however, and kissed his forehead reverently. But he was not aware of her return, for his mind had begun to wander.

She brushed past Mrs. Parkin in the passage, bidding her an incoherent goodbye: she was instinctively impatient to escape to the protection of familiar surroundings. Inside the house, she felt helpless, dizzy; the melodrama of the whole scene had stunned her senses, and pity for him was rushing through her in waves of pulsing emotion.

As she passed the various landmarks, which she had noted on her outward journey — a group of Scotch firs, a roofless cattle-shed, a pile of felled trees — each seemed to wear an altered aspect. With what a strange suddenness it had all happened! Yesterday the groom had brought back word that he was in delirium, and had told her of the loneliness of the house. It had seemed so sad. His lying ill, all alone: the thought had preyed on her conscience, till she had started to drive out there to inquire if there was anything she could do to help him. Now, every corner round which the cart swung, lengthened the stretch of road that separated her from that tragic scene in his room ... Perhaps it was not right for her to drive home and leave him? But she couldn't bear to stay; it was all so dreadful. Besides, she assured herself, she could do no good. There was the doctor, and that old woman who nursed him — they would see to everything ... Poor, poor Alec — alone in that grey-walled cottage, pitched at the far end of this long, bleak valley — the half-darkened room — his wasted, feverish face — and his *knowing* that he could not live — it all came back to her vividly, and she shivered as if with cold. Death seemed hideous, awful, almost wicked in the cruelty of its ruthlessness. And the homeward drive loomed ahead, interminably — for two hours she would have to wait with the dreadful, flaring remembrance of it all — two hours — for the horse was tired, and it was thirteen miles, a man by the roadside had told her....

He was noble-hearted, saint-like ... Her pity for him welled up once more, and she convinced herself that she could have loved him, worshipped him, been worthy of him as a husband — and now he lay dying. He had revealed his whole nature to her, it seemed. No one had ever understood, as she did now, what a fine character he was in reality. Her cheeks grew hot with indignation and shame, as she remembered how she had heard people laugh at him behind his back, refer to him mockingly as the "love-sick curate." And all this while — for five whole years — he had gone on caring for her — thinking of her each day, reading her letters, recalling the things she used to say — yes, those were his very words. Before, she had never suspected that it was in his nature to take it so horribly tragically; yet, somehow, directly he had fixed his eyes on her in that excited way, she had half guessed it....

The horse's trot slackened to a walk, and the wheels crunched over a bed of newly strewn stones ... She was considering how much of what had happened she could relate to Jim. Oh! the awfulness of his *knowing beforehand* like that! She had kissed him: she had told him that she cared for him: she hadn't been able to help doing that. There was no harm in it; she had made him happier — he had said so himself ... But Jim wouldn't understand: he would be angry with her for having gone, perhaps. He wouldn't see that she couldn't have done anything else. No, she couldn't bear to tell him: besides, it seemed somehow like treachery to Alec ... Oh! it must be awful to *know beforehand* like that! ... The doctor should never have told him. It was horrible, cruel ... In the past how she had been to blame — she saw that now: thoughtless, selfish, altogether beneath him.

It was like a chapter in a novel. His loving her silently all these years, and telling her about it on his deathbed. At the thought of it she thrilled with subtle pride; it illuminated the whole ordinariness of her life. The next moment the train of her own thoughts shamed her. Poor, poor Alec ... And to reinforce her pity, she recalled the tragic setting of the scene.

That woman — his landlady — could she have heard anything? she wondered with a twinge of dread. No, the door was shut, and his voice had been very low.

The horse turned onto the main road, and pricking his ears, quickened his pace.

She would remember him always. Every day, she would think of him, as he had asked her to do — she would never forget to do that. And, if she were in trouble, or difficulty, she would turn her thoughts towards him, just as he had told her he used to do. She would try to become better — more religious — for his sake. She would read her Bible each morning, as she knew had been his habit. These little things were all she could do now. Her attitude in the future she would make worthy of his in the past ... He would become the secret guiding-star of her life; *it* would be her hidden chapter of romance....

The box — that box which he had asked her to take. She had promised, and she had forgotten it. How could she get it? It was too late to turn back now. Jim would be waiting for her. She would only just be in time for dinner as it was ... How could she get it? If she wrote to his landlady, and asked her to send it — it was under the writing-table in the sitting-room he had said ... She *must* get it, somehow....

It was dark before she reached home. Jim was angry with her for being late, and for having driven all the way without a servant. She paid no heed to his upbraiding; but told him shortly that Alec was still in great danger. He muttered some perfunctory expression of regret, and went off to the stables to order a bran-mash for the horse. His insensibility to the importance of the tragedy she had been witnessing, exasperated her: she felt bitterly mortified that he could not divine all that she had been suffering.

*   *   *   *   *

The last of the winter months went, and life in the valley swept its sluggish course onwards. The bleak, spring winds rollicked, hooting from hill to hill. The cattle waited for evening, huddled under the walls of untrimmed stone; and before the fireside, in every farmhouse, new-born lambs lay helplessly bleating. On Sundays the men would loaf in churlish groups about the church door, jerk curt greetings at one another, and ask for news of Parson Burkett. It was a curate from Cockermouth who took the services in his stead — one of the new-fangled sort; a young gentleman from London way, who mouthed his words like a girl, carried company manners, and had a sight of strange clerical practices.

Alec was slowly recovering. The fever had altogether left him: a straw-coloured beard now covered his chin, and his cheeks were grown hollow and peaky-looking. But by the hay-harvest, the doctor reckoned, he would be as strong as ever again — so it was commonly reported.

Mrs. Parkin declared that the illness had done him a world o' good. "It's rested his mind like, and kept him from frettin'. He was alus ower given to studyin' on his own thoughts, till he got dazed like and took na notice o' things. An' noo," she would conclude, "ye should jest see him, smilin' as free as a child."

So day after day floated vaguely by, and to Alec the calm of their unbroken regularity was delicious. He was content to lie still for hours, thinking of nothing, remembering nothing, tasting the torpor of dreamy contemplation; watching through the window the slow drifting of the shadows; listening to the cackling of geese, and the plaintive bleating of sheep....

By-and-bye, with returning strength, his senses quickened, and grew sensitive to every passing impression. To eat with elaborate deliberation his invalid meals; to watch the myriad specks of gold dancing across a bar of sunlight — these were sources of keen, exciting delight. But in the foreground of his mind, transfiguring with its glamour every trivial thought, flashed the memory of Ethel's visit. He lived through the whole scene again and again, picturing her veiled figure as it had stood by the bedside, wrapped in the red, fur cloak; and her protesting words, her passionate tears, seemed to form a mystic, indissoluble bond between them, that brightened all the future with rainbow colours.

God had given him back to her. Whether circumstances brought them together frequently, or whether they were forced to live their lives almost wholly apart, would, he told himself, matter but little. Their spiritual communion would remain unbroken. Indeed, the prospect of such separations, proving, as it did to him, the sureness of the bond between them, almost elated him. There would be unquestioning trust between them, and, though the world had separated them, the best that was in him belonged to her. When at length they met, there would be no need for insistence on common points of feeling, for repeated handling of past threads, as was customary with ordinary friendships. Since each could read the other's heart, that sure intuition born of chastened, spiritual love would be theirs. If trouble came to her, he would be there to sacrifice all at a moment's bidding, after the fashion of the knights of old. Because she knew him, she would have faith in him. To do her service would be his greatest joy.

At first the immobile, isolated hours of his convalescence made all these things appear simple and inevitable, like the events of a great dream. As time went on, however, he grew to chafe against his long confinement, to weary of his weakness, and of the familiar sight of every object in the room; and in the mornings, when Mrs. Parkin brought him his breakfast, he found himself longing for a letter from her — some brief word of joy that he was recovering. He yearned for some material object, the touch of which would recall her to him, as if a particle of her personality had impregnated the atoms.

Sometimes, he would force himself into believing that she would appear again, drive out to learn the progress of his recovery ... After luncheon she would leave home ... about half-past one, probably ... soon after three, he would see her ... Now, she was nearing the cross-roads ... now climbing the hill past Longrigg's farm ... she would have to walk the horse there ... now, crossing the old bridge. He would lie watching the clock; and when the suspense grew intolerable, to cheat it, he would bury his head in the pillow to count up to a thousand, before glancing at the hands again. So would slip by the hour of her arrival; still, he would struggle to delude himself with all manner of excuses for her — she had been delayed — she had missed the turning, and had been compelled to retrace her steps. And, when at length the twilight had come, he would start to assure himself that it was to be tomorrow, and sink into a fitful dozing, recounting waking dreams of her, subtly intoxicating.

*   *   *   *   *

In April came a foretaste of summer, and, for an hour or two every day, he was able to hobble downstairs. He perceived the box at once, lying in its accustomed place, and concluded that on learning that he was out of danger, she had sent it back to him. The sight of it cheered him with indefinable hope: it seemed to signify a fresh token of her faith in him: it had travelled with her back to Cockermouth on that wonderful day which had brought them together; and now, in his eyes, it was invested with a new preciousness. He unlocked it, and, somehow, to discover that its contents had not been disturbed, was a keen disappointment. He longed for proof that she had been curious to look into it, that she had thus been able to realize how he had prized every tiny object that had been consecrated for him by her. Then it flashed across him that she herself might have brought the box back, and fearing to disturb him, had gone home again without asking to see him. All that evening he brooded over this supposition; yet shrank from putting any question to Mrs. Parkin. But the following morning, a sudden impulse overcame his repugnance; and the next moment he had learned the truth. Untouched, unmoved, the box had remained all the while — she had never taken it — she had forgotten it. And depression swept through him; for it seemed that his ideal had tottered.

His prolonged isolation and his physical lassitude had quickened his emotions to an abnormal sensibility, and had led him to a constant fingering, as it were, of his successive sentimental phases. And these, since they constituted his sole diversion, he had unconsciously come to regard as of supreme importance. The cumbersome, complex details of life in the outside world had assumed the simplification of an indistinct background: in his vision of her figure he had perceived no perspective.

But now the grain of doubt was sown: it germinated insidiously; and soon, the whole complexion of his attitude towards her was transformed. All at once he saw a whole network of unforeseen obstacles, besetting each detail of the prospect he had been planning. Swarming uncertainty fastened on him at every turn; till at last, goaded to desperation, he stripped the gilding from the accumulated fabric of his idealized future.

And then his passion for her flamed up — ardent, unreasoning, human. After all, he loved as other men loved — that was the truth; the rest was mere calfish meandering. Stubbornly he vindicated to himself his right to love her.... He was a man — a creature of flesh and blood, and every fibre within him was crying out for her — for the sight of her face; the sound of her voice; the clasp of her hand. Body and soul he loved her; body and soul he yearned for her .... She had come back to him, she was his again — with passionate tears she had told him that she loved him. To fight for her, he was ready to abandon all else. At the world's laws he gibed bitterly; before God they were man and wife.

The knowledge that it lay in his power to make her his for life, to bind her to him irrevocably, brought him intoxicating relief. Henceforward he would live on, but for that end. Existence without her would be dreary, unbearable. He would resign his living and leave the Church. Together they would go away, abroad; he would find some work to do in the great cities of Australia…. She was another man's wife — but the sin would be *his* — his, not hers — God would so judge it; and for her sake he would suffer the punishment. Besides, he told himself exultantly, the sin, was it not already committed? "Whosoever looketh on a woman to lust after her, hath committed adultery with her already in his heart."[8]

He would go to her, say to her simply that he was come for her. It should be done openly, honestly in the full light of day. New strength and deep-rooted confidence glowed within him. The wretched vacillation of his former self was put away like an old garment. Once more he sent her words of love sounding in his ears — the words that had made them man and wife before God. And on, the train of his thoughts whirled; visions of a hundred scenes flitted before his eyes — he and she together as man and wife, in a new home across the seas, where the past was all forgotten, and the present was redolent of the sure joy of perfect love.

* * * * *

He was growing steadily stronger. Pacing the floor of his room, or the gravel-path before the house, when the sun was shining, each day he would methodically measure the progress of his strength. He hinted of a long sea voyage to the doctor: the man declared that it would be madness to start before ten days had elapsed. Ten days — the stretch of time seemed absurd, intolerable. But a quantity of small matters relating to the parish remained to be set in order: he had determined to leave no confusion behind him. So he mapped out a daily task for himself: thus he could already begin to work for her: thus each day's accomplishment would bring him doubly nearer to her. The curate, who had been taking his duty, came once or twice at his request to help him; for he was jealously nursing his small stock of strength. He broke the news of his approaching departure to Mrs. Parkin, and asked her to accept the greater portion of his furniture, as an inadequate token of his gratitude towards her for all she had done for him. The good creature wept copiously, pestered him with questions concerning his destination, and begged him to give her news of him in the future. Next he sent for a dealer from Cockermouth to buy the remainder, and disputed with him the price of each object tenaciously.

One afternoon his former rector appeared, and with tremulous cordiality

---

[8]   Matthew 5. 28.

wished him God-speed, assuming that the sea voyage was the result of doctor's advice. And it was when the old man was gone, and he was alone again, that, for the first time, with a spasm of pain, he caught a glimpse of the deception he was practising. But some irresistible force within him urged him forward — he was powerless — to look back was impossible now — there was more yet to be done — he must go on — there was no time to stop to think. So to deaden the rising conscience-pangs he fiercely reminded himself that now, but five days more separated her from him. He sat down to write to his bishop and resign his living, struggling with ambiguous, formal phrases, impetuously attributing to his physical weakness his inability to frame them.

The letter at length finished, instinctively dreading fresh gnawings of uneasiness, he forced himself feverishly into thinking of plans for the future, busying his mind with time-tables, searching for particulars of steamers, turning over the leaves of his bank-book. All the money which his father had left to him had remained untouched: for three years they could live comfortably on the capital; meanwhile he would have found some work.

At last, when, with the growing twilight, the hills outside were hurriedly darkening, he sank back wearily in his chair. And all at once he perceived with dismay that nothing remained for him to do, nothing with which he could occupy his mind. For the moment he was alone with himself, and looking backwards, realization of the eager facility with which he had successively severed each link, and the rapidity with which he had set himself drifting towards a future, impenetrable with mysterious uncertainty, stole over him. He had done it all, he told himself, deliberately, unaided; bewildered, he tried to bring himself face to face with his former self, to survey himself as he had been before the fever — that afternoon when he had gone up to Beda Cottages — plodding indifferently through life in the joyless, walled-in valley, which, he now understood, had in a measure reflected the spirit of his own listless broodings. Scared remorse seized him. The prospect of departure, now that it was close at hand, frightened him; left him aching as with the burden of dead weight, so that, for a while, he remained inert, dully acquiescing in his accumulating disquietude.

Then, in desperation, he invoked her figure, imagining a dozen incoherent versions of the coming scene — the tense words of greeting, his passionate pleading, her impulsive yielding, and the acknowledgment of her trust in him....

By-and-bye, Mrs. Parkin brought him his dinner. He chatted to her with apparent unconcern, jested regarding his appetite; for a curious calm, the lucidity evoked by suppressed elation, pervaded him.

But through the night he tossed restlessly, waking in the darkness to find himself throbbing with triumphant exhilaration; each time striking matches to examine the face of his watch, and beginning afresh to calculate the hours

that separated him from the moment that was to bind them together — the
irrevocable starting towards the future years.

*   *   *   *   *

She stood in the bow-window of her drawing-room, arranging some cut
flowers in slender pink and blue vases, striped with enamel of imitation gold.
Behind her, the room, uncomfortably ornamental, repeated the three notes of
colour — gilt paper shavings filling the grate; gilt-legged chairs and tables; stiff,
shiny, pink chintzes encasing the furniture; on the wall a blue-patterned paper,
all speckled with stars of gold.

Outside, the little lawn, bathed in the fresh morning sunlight, glowed a
luscious green, and the trim flower-beds swelled with heightened colours. A
white fox-terrier came waddling along the garden path: she lifted the animal
inside the window, stroking his sleek sides with an effusive demonstration
of affection. Would Jim remember to be home in good time? she was idly
wondering; she had forgotten to remind him before he went to his office, that
tonight she was to sing at a local concert.

Suddenly, she caught sight of a man's figure crossing the lawn. For an instant
she thought it was an old clerk, whom Jim sometimes employed to carry
messages. Then she saw that it was Alec — coming straight towards her. Her
first impulse was to escape from him; but noticing that his gaze was fixed on
the ground, she retreated behind an angle of the window, and stood watching
him … Poor Alec! He was going away on a sea voyage for his health, so Jim had
heard it said in the town; and she formed a hasty resolve to be very kind to the
poor fellow. Yet her vanity felt a prick of pique, as she noticed that his gait was
grown more gaunt, more ungainly than ever; and she resented that his haggard
face, his stubbly beard, which, when he lay ill, had signified tense tragedy,
should now seem simply uncouth. Still, she awaited his appearance excitedly;
anticipating a renewed proof of his touching, dog-like devotion to her, and with
a fresh thrill of unconscious gratitude to him for having supplied that scene to
which she could look back with secret, sentimental pride.

The maid let him into the room. As he advanced towards her, she saw
him brush his forehead with his hand impatiently, as if to rid his brain of an
importunate thought. He took her outstretched hand: the forced cheeriness of
her phrase of greeting died away, as she felt his gaze searching her face.

"Let us sit down," he said abruptly.

"I'm all right again, now," he began with a brisk, level laugh; and it occurred
to her that perhaps the illness had affected his mind.

"I'm so glad of that," she stammered in reply; "so very glad … And you're
going away, aren't you, for a long sea voyage? That will do you ever so much
good ——"

But before she had finished speaking, he was kneeling on the carpet before her, pouring out incoherent phrases. Bewildered, she gazed at him, only noticing the clumsy breadth of his shoulders.

"Listen to me, Ethel, listen," he was saying. "Everything is ready — I've given it all up — my living — the Church. I can't bear it any longer — life without you, I mean ... You are everything to me — I only want you — I care for nothing else now. I am going away to Australia. You will come with me, Ethel — you said you loved me ... We love one another — come with me — let us start life afresh. I can't go on living without you ... I thought it would be easy for you to come; I see now that perhaps it's difficult. You have your home: I see that ... But have trust in me — I will make it up to you. Together we will start afresh — make a new home — a new life. I will give you every moment; I will be your slave ... Listen to me, Ethel; let us go away. Everything is ready — I've got money — I've arranged everything. We can go up to London tomorrow. The steamer starts on Thursday."

The sound of his voice ceased. She was staring at the door, filled with dread lest it should open, and the maid should see him kneeling on the carpet.

"Don't," she exclaimed, grasping his coat. "Get up, quick."

He rose, awkwardly she thought, and stood before her.

"We were so happy together once, dear — do you remember — in the first days, when you promised yourself to me? And now I know that in your heart you still care for me. You said so. Say you will come — say you will trust me — you will start tomorrow. If you can't come so soon I will wait, wait till you can come," he added, and she felt the trembling touch of his hands on hers, and his breath beating on her face.

"Don't, please," and she pushed back his hands. "Someone might see."

"What does it matter, my darling? We are going to belong to one another for always. I am going to wait for you, darling — to be your slave — to give up every moment of my life to you ... It's the thought of you that's made me live, dear ... You brought me back to life, that day you came ... I've thought of nothing but you since. I've been arranging it all ——"

"It's impossible," she interrupted.

"No, dear, it's not impossible," he pleaded.

"You've resigned your living — left the Church?" she asked incredulously.

"Yes, everything," he answered proudly.

"And all because you cared so for me?"

"I can't begin to live again without you. I would suffer eternal punishment gladly to win you ... You will trust yourself to me, darling; say you will trust me."

"Of course, Alec, I trust you. But you've no right to ——"

"Oh! because you're married, and it's a sin, and I'm a clergyman. But I'm a man first. And for you I've given it all up — everything. You don't understand my love for you."

"Yes, yes, I do," she answered quickly, alarmed by the earnestness of his passion, yet remembering vaguely that she had read of such things in books.

"You will come tomorrow, darling — you will have trust in me?"

"You are mad, Alec. You don't know what you are saying. It would be absurd."

"It's because you don't understand how I love you, that you say that," he broke out fiercely. "You can't understand — you can't understand."

"Yes, I can," she protested, instinctively eager to vie with his display of emotion.

"Then say you will come — promise it, promise it," he cried; and his features were all distorted by suspense.

But at this climax of his insistence, she lost consciousness of her own attitude. She seemed suddenly to see all that clumsiness which had made her refuse him before.

"It's altogether ridiculous," she answered shortly. He recoiled from her: he seemed to stiffen a little all over; and she felt rising impatience at his grotesque denseness in persisting.

"You say it's altogether ridiculous?" he repeated after her slowly.

"Yes, of course it's ridiculous," she repeated with uneasy emphasis. "I'm very sorry you should mind — feel it so — but it isn't my fault."

"Why did you say then that before God you loved me, when you came that day?" he burst out with concentrated bitterness.

"Because I thought you were dying." The bald statement of the truth sprang to her lips — a spontaneous, irresistible betrayal.

"I see — I see," he muttered. His hands clenched till the knuckles showed white.

"I'm very sorry," she added lamely. Her tone was gentler, for his dumb suffering moved her sensibilities. In her agitation, the crudity of her avowal had slipped her notice.

"That's no use," he answered wearily.

"Alec, don't be angry with me. Can't we be friends? Don't you see yourself now that it was mad, absurd?" she argued, eager to reinstate herself in his eyes. Then, as he made no answer, "Let us be friends, Alec, and you will go back to Scarsdale, when you are well and strong. You will give up nothing for my sake. I should not wish that, you know, Alec."

"Yes," he assented mechanically, "I shall go back."

"I shall always think of this morning," she continued, growing sentimentally remorseful as the sensation of rising relief pervaded her. "And you will soon forget all about it," she added, with a cheeriness of tone that rang false; and paused, awaiting his answer.

"And I shall forget all about it," he repeated after her.

To mask her disappointment, she assumed a silly, nervous gaiety.

"And I shall keep it quite secret that you were so naughty as to ask me to run away with you. I sha'n't even tell Jim."

He nodded stupidly.

With a thin, empty smile on her face, she was debating how best to part with him, when, of a sudden, he rose, and, without a word, walked out of the room.

He strode away across the lawn, and, as she watched his retreating figure, she felt for him a shallow compassion, not unmingled with contempt.

Modern Melodrama

The pink shade of a single lamp supplied an air of subdued mystery; the fire burned red and still; in place of door and windows hung curtains, obscure, formless; the furniture, dainty, but sparse, stood detached and incoördinate like the furniture of a stage-scene; the atmosphere was heavy with heat, and a scent of stale tobacco; some cut flowers, half-withered, tissue-paper still wrapping their stalks, lay on a gilt, cane-bottomed chair.

"Will you give me a sheet of paper, please?"

He had crossed the room, to seat himself before the principal table. He wore a fur-lined overcoat, and he was tall, and broad, and bald; a sleek face, made grave by gold-rimmed spectacles.

The other man was in evening dress; his back leaning against the mantelpiece, his hands in his pockets: he was moodily scraping the hearthrug with his toe. Clean-shaved; stolid and coarsely regular features; black, shiny hair, flattened onto his head; undersized eyes, moist and glistening; the tint of his face uniform, the tint of discoloured ivory; he looked a man who ate well and lived hard.

"Certainly, sir, certainly," and he started to hurry about the room.

"Daisy," he exclaimed roughly, a moment later, "where the deuce do you keep the notepaper?"

"I don't know if there is any, but the girl always has some." She spoke in a slow tone — insolent and fatigued.

A couple of bed-pillows were supporting her head, and a scarlet plush cloak, trimmed with white down, was covering her feet, as she lay curled on the sofa. The fire-light glinted on the metallic gold of her hair, which clashed with the black of her eyebrows; and the full, blue eyes, wide-set, contradicted the hard line of her vivid-red lips. She drummed her fingers on the sofa-edge, nervously.

"Never mind," said the bald man shortly, producing a notebook from his breast-pocket, and tearing a leaf from it.

He wrote, and the other two stayed silent; the man returned to the hearthrug, lifting his coat-tails under his arms; the girl went on drumming the sofa-edge.

"There," sliding back his chair, and looking from the one to the other, evidently uncertain which of the two he should address. "Here is the prescription. Get it made up tonight, a table-spoonful at a time, in a wine-glassful of water at lunch-time, at dinner-time and before going to bed. Go on with the port wine twice a day, and" (to the girl deliberately and distinctly) "you *must* keep quite quiet; avoid all sort of excitement — that is extremely important. Of course you must on no account go out at night. Go to bed early, take regular meals, and keep always warm."

"I say," broke in the girl, "tell us, it isn't bad — dangerous, I mean?"

"Dangerous! — no, not if you do what I tell you."

He glanced at his watch, and rose, buttoning his coat.

"Good evening," he said gravely.

At first she paid no heed; she was vacantly staring before her: then, suddenly conscious that he was waiting, she looked up at him.

"Goodnight, doctor."

She held out her hand, and he took it.

"I'll get all right, won't I?" she asked, still looking up at him.

"All right — of course you will — of course. But remember you must do what I tell you."

The other man handed him his hat and umbrella, opened the door for him, and it closed behind them.

＊　＊　＊　＊　＊

The girl remained quiet, sharply blinking her eyes, her whole expression eager, intense.

A murmur of voices, a muffled tread of footsteps descending the stairs — the gentle shutting of a door — stillness.

She raised herself on her elbow, listening; the cloak slipped noiselessly to the floor. Quickly her arm shot out to the bell-rope: she pulled it violently; waited, expectant; and pulled again.

A slatternly figure appeared — a woman of middle age — her arms, bared to the elbows, smeared with dirt; a grimy apron over her knees.

"What's up? — I was smashin' coal," she explained.

"Come here," hoarsely whispered the girl — "here — no — nearer — quite close. Where's he gone?"

"Gone? 'oo?"

"That man that was here."

"I s'ppose 'ee's in the downstairs room. I ain't 'eard the front door slam."

"And Dick, where's he?"

"They're both in there together, I s'ppose."

"I want you to go down — quietly — without making a noise — listen at the door — come up, and tell me what they're saying."

"What? Down there?" Jerking her thumb over her shoulder.

"Yes, of course — at once," answered the girl, impatiently.

"And if they catches me — a nice fool I looks. No, I'm jest blowed if I do!" she concluded. "Whatever's up?"

"You must," the girl broke out excitedly. "I tell you, you must."

"Must — must — an' if I do, what am I goin' to get out of it?" She paused, reflecting; then added: "Look 'ere — I tell yer what — I'll do it for half a quid,[1]

---

[1]   Half a quid: slang for half a pound, i.e. ten shillings. A domestic servant in the 1890s would have earned no more than twenty pounds a year, that is, just over seven shillings a week.

there!"

"Yes — yes — all right — only make haste."

"An' 'ow d' I know as I'll git it?" she objected doggedly. "It's a jolly risk, yer know."

The girl sprang up, flushed and feverish.

"Quick — or he'll be gone. I don't know where it is — but you shall have it — I promise — quick — please go — quick."

The other hesitated, her lips pressed together; turned, and went out.

And the girl, catching at her breath, clutched a chair.

*   *   *   *   *

A flame flickered up in the fire, buzzing spasmodically. A creak outside. She had come up. But the curtains did not move. Why didn't she come in? She was going past. The girl hastened across the room, the intensity of the impulse lending her strength.

"Come — come in," she gasped. "Quick — I'm slipping."

She struck at the wall; but with the flat of her hand, for there was no grip. The woman bursting in, caught her, and led her back to the sofa.

"There, there, dearie," tucking the cloak round her feet. "Lift up the piller, my 'ands are that mucky. Will yer 'ave anythin'?"

She shook her head. "It's gone," she muttered. "Now — tell me."

"Tell yer? — tell yer what? Why — why — there ain't jest nothin' to tell yer."

"What were they saying? Quick."

"I didn't 'ear nothin'. They was talkin' about some ballet-woman."

The girl began to cry, feeble, helplessly, like a child in pain.

"You might tell me, Liz. You might tell me. I've been a good sort to you."

"That yer 'ave. I knows yer 'ave, dearie. There, there, don't yer take on like that. Yer'll only make yerself bad again."

"Tell me — tell me," she wailed. "I've been a good sort to you, Liz."

"Well, they wasn't talkin' of no ballet-woman — that's straight," the woman blurted out savagely.

"What did he say? — tell me." Her voice was weaker now.

"I can't tell yer — don't yer ask me — for God's sake, don't yer ask me!"

With a low crooning the girl cried again.

"Oh! for God's sake, don't yer take on like that! — it's awful — I can't stand it. There, dearie, stop that cryin' an' I'll tell yer — I will indeed. It was jest this way — I slips my shoes off, an' I goes down as careful — jest as careful as a cat — an' when I gets to the door I crouches myself down, listenin' as 'ard as ever I could. The first thing as I 'ears was Mr. Dick speakin' thick-like — like as if 'ee'd bin drinkin' — an' t'other chap 'ee says somethin' about lungs, using some long word — I missed that — there was a van or somethin' rackettin' on the road. Then 'ee says 'gallopin', gallopin',' jest like as if 'ee was talkin' of a 'orse. An' Mr. Dick, 'ee says, 'ain't there no chance — no'ow?' and 'ee give a sort of a grunt. I was awful sorry for 'im, that I was, 'ee must 'ave been crool bad, 'ee's mostly so quiet-like, ain't 'ee? An', in a minute, 'ee sort o' groans out somethin', an' t'other chap 'ee answer 'im quite cool-like, that 'ee don't properly know: but, anyways, it 'ud be over afore the end of February. There, I've done it. Oh! dearie, it's awful, awful, that's jest what it is. An' I 'ad no intention to tell yer — not a blessed word — that I didn't — may God strike me blind if I did! Some'ow it all come out, seein' yer chokin' that 'ard an' feelin' at the wall there. Yer 'ad no right to ask me to do it — 'ow was I to know 'ee was a doctor?"

She put the two corners of her apron to her eyes, gurgling loudly.

"Look 'ere, don't yer b'lieve a word of it — I don't — I tell yer they're a 'umbuggin' lot,[2] them doctors, all together. I know it. Yer take my word for that — yer'll git all right again. Yer'll be as well as I am, afore yer've done — Oh, Lord! — it's jest awful — I feel that upset — I'd like to cut my tongue out, for 'avin' told yer — but I jest couldn't 'elp myself." She was retreating towards the door, wiping her eyes, and snorting out loud sobs — "An' don't yer offer me that half-quid — I couldn't take it of yer — that I couldn't."

* * * * *

She shivered, sat up, and dragged the cloak tight round her shoulders. In her desire to get warm she forgot what had happened. She extended the palms of her hands towards the grate: the heat was delicious. A smoking lump of coal clattered onto the fender: she lifted the tongs, but the sickening remembrance arrested her. The things in the room were receding, dancing round: the fire was growing taller and taller. The woollen scarf chafed her skin: she wrenched it off. Then hope, keen and bitter, shot up, hurting her. "How could he know? Of course he couldn't know. She'd been a lot better this last fortnight — the other doctor said so — she didn't believe it — she didn't care —— Anyway, it would be over before the end of February!"

Suddenly the crooning wail started again; next, spasms of weeping, harsh and gasping.

By-and-bye she understood that she was crying noisily, and that she was alone in the room: like a light in a wind, the sobbing fit ceased.

"Let me live — let me live — I'll be straight — I'll go to church — I'll do anything! Take it away — it hurts — I can't bear it!"

Once more the sound of her own voice in the empty room calmed her. But the tension of emotion slackened, only to tighten again: immediately she was jeering at herself. What was she wasting her breath for? What had Jesus ever done for her? She'd had her fling, and it was no thanks to Him.

"'Dy-sy — Dy-sy ——'"

From the street below, boisterous and loud, the refrain came up. And, as the footsteps tramped away, the words reached her once more, indistinct in the distance:

---

2   'Umbugging lot: i.e. a 'humbugging', tricking or deceiving, lot.

"'I'm jest cry-zy, all for the love o' you.'"[3]

She felt frightened. It was like a thing in a play. It was as if someone was there, in the room — hiding — watching her.

Then a coughing fit started, racking her. In the middle, she struggled to cry for help; she thought she was going to suffocate.

Afterwards she sank back, limp, tired, and sleepy.

The end of February — she was going to die — it was important, exciting — what would it be like? Everybody else died. Midge had died in the summer — but that was worry and going the pace. And they said that Annie Evans was going off too. Damn it! she wasn't going to be chicken-hearted. She'd face it. She had had a jolly time. She'd be game till the end. Hell-fire — that was all stuff and nonsense — she knew that. It would be just nothing — like a sleep. Not even painful: she'd be just shut down in a coffin, and she wouldn't know that they were doing it. Ah! but they might do it before she was quite dead! It had happened sometimes. And she wouldn't be able to get out. The lid would be nailed, and there would be earth on the top. And if she called no one would hear.

Ugh! what a fit of the blues she wasgetting! It was beastly, being alone. Why the devil didn't Dick come back?

That noise! What was that?

Bah! only someone in the street. What a fool she was!

She winced again as the fierce feeling of revolt swept through her, the wild longing to fight. It was damned rough — four months! A year, six months even, was a long time. The pain grew acute, different from anything she had felt before.

"Good Lord! what am I maundering on about? Four months — I'll go out with a fizzle like a firework. Why the devil doesn't Dick come? — or Liz — or somebody? What do they leave me alone like this for?"

She dragged at the bell-rope.

*   *   *   *   *

He came in, white and blear-eyed.

"Whatever have you been doing all this time?" she began angrily.

"I've been chatting with the doctor." He was pretending to read a newspaper; there was something funny about his voice.

"It's ripping. He says you'll soon be fit again, as long as you don't get colds,

---

[3]   From the chorus of the popular music-hall song 'Daisy Bell (A Bicycle Built For Two)'. Written by the songwriter 'Harry Dacre' (the pen-name of Frank Dean (1857–1922)) in 1892, and so very much of the moment for Crackanthorpe's readers; it was partly inspired by the bicycling craze of the period and possibly the figure of Daisy Greville, Countess of Warwick, one of the Prince of Wales' mistresses.

or that sort of thing. Yes, he says you'll soon be fit again" — a quick, crackling noise — he had gripped the newspaper in his fist.

She looked at him, surprised, in spite of herself. She would never have thought he'd have done it like that. He was a good sort, after all. But — she didn't know why — she broke out furiously:

"You infernal liar! — I know. I shall be done for by the end of February — ha! ha!"

Seizing a vase of flowers, she flung it into the grate. The crash and the shrivelling of the leaves in the flames brought her an instant's relief. Then she said quietly:

"There — I've made an idiot of myself; but" (weakly) "I didn't know — I didn't know — I thought it was different."

He hesitated, embarrassed by his own emotion. Presently he went up to her and put his hands round her cheeks.

"No," she said, "that's no good, I don't want that. Get me something to drink. I feel bad."

He hurried to the cupboard and fumbled with the cork of a champagne bottle. It flew out with a bang. She started violently.

"You clumsy fool!" she exclaimed.

She drank off the wine at a gulp.

"Daisy," he began.

She was staring stonily at the empty glass.

"Daisy," he repeated.

She tapped her toe against the fender-rail.

At this sign, he went on —

"How did you know?"

"I sent Liz to listen," she answered mechanically.

He looked about him, helpless.

"I think I'll smoke," he said feebly.

She made no answer.

"Here, put the glass down," she said.

He obeyed.

He lit a cigarette over the lamp, sat down opposite her, puffing dense clouds of smoke.

And, for a long while, neither spoke.

"Is that doctor a good man?"

"I don't know. People say so," he answered.

Lisa-La-Folle

Up on the top of the hill she lived alone, in the shed with the peaked roof. No one could tell you how old she was; and only old Cauhapé knew how long she had been there.[1] Old Cauhapé's legs were paralyzed, and when the sun shone, he used to sit, wrapped in sacking, before the *débit de tabac*[2] which his little great-niece kept for him. And if you could but get him to talk, he would narrate to you, in his stumbling, jerky fashion, how many, many years ago, when Lisa-la-folle was black-haired, and handsome, and devilish proud, the soldiers had come one day to gallop about the valley, and how another day they were all gone back to Paris, they and the officers, in their great plumed hats, and red cloaks reaching below the heels, and Lisa-la-folle with them.

It was a glamorous, sinful life she had led there, with carriages and horses and servants, and a gorgeous mansion, where the nobles played with dice, and sang ribald songs all the night long, till the candles sputtered low in their sockets — at least, so old Cauhapé had heard tell. And many a shameful deed was done in that gorgeous mansion of hers — deeds over which old Cauhapé wagged his head solemnly.

Then, one sweltering Sunday afternoon, she had come back. Everywhere the land was cracking with thirst; for there had fallen no rain through the summer, old Cauhapé remembered.

All the village was going in to vespers[3] as she tottered past the church door, white-haired, bare-footed, and ragged, grimed with much travelling, chattering and laughing to herself the while about things which had no sense. And some of the lads had jeered at her, and one or two had thrown stones, and the young women had run screaming into the church. But she took no notice of anyone: just went by, chattering and laughing to herself. (All the way from Paris she had come so; nearly a thousand kilometres Monsieur le curé had reckoned it.)[4]

That evening the rain had come — a noisy, battering rain, and Monsieur le curé had found her in the lane behind his house, sitting drenched to the skin, still laughing to herself at her own thoughts. And Monsieur le curé had taken her inside, and given her food and wine, and had talked to her softly in good French — she had forgotten the language of the *pays*[5] — and by-and-bye she grew to be quiet and reasonable, and used to work for Monsieur le curé, hoeing and digging in his garden. And when Monsieur le curé died, out of charity, they

---

[1]   Old Cauhapé is a recurring figure in *A Set of Village Tales*, appearing in four of the six tales.
[2]   *Débit de tabac*: tobacconist.
[3]   Vespers is the Christian late afternoon or evening service, or 'evensong'.
[4]   Monsieur le curé: the parish priest.
[5]   *Pays*: country or native land.

set her to mend the roads; for she was strong and a brave worker, and cared nothing for wind or rain. Four kilometres of the road to Hagetmau[6] they allotted her, between the crucifix and the thirteenth milestone; and for thirty-eight years she had tended those four kilometres of road, in rain, sunshine, and storm, and had never missed a day. And she had gone to live, up on the hill, in the shed with the peaked roof; and in the evenings the Annous, who were neighbours, could see her digging her bit of garden, and hanging her rags to dry before the door.

But she was still mad, old Cauhapé asserted; for she had never again remembered the language of the *pays*; but always spoke French — the strange French of the people of Paris, with words that even Monsieur le curé did not know; and sometimes, still, as you passed along the road, you might hear her laughing and chattering to herself, just as she had done that Sunday afternoon, when she had first come back to the village.

All the same she was a brave worker, and never did harm to anyone, and so now no one paid much heed to her. Only she was getting broken at last, and the inspector had grumbled, saying that her time was almost done.

II

Every morning at half-past seven, and every evening at half-past six, Lisa-la-folle, carrying her big blue umbrella and bundle of provisions, used to pass my gate. For a whole fortnight after my talk with old Cauhapé, I never missed wishing her good morning and goodnight. At first she would pretend not to hear me; by-and-bye she took to sending me a quick, suspicious glance, like the start of a frightened animal; last of all, she gave me a mumbling answer.

A little while later, as I rode by her at work, I stopped to speak to her. She stepped forward, laid her hand on the mare's bridle, and motioned me to dismount. I did as she bid me, and we sat down side by side on a grass-grown mud-heap.

"You are a stranger: you are not of the country," she said. "You are young, and you have a beautiful wife. Stay a moment, and I will tell you something, something that I have never told to any of them," and she pointed up the road towards the village. "You shall hear it, and then you can tell it to the people of the land from which you come.

"You do not know the great sun. No, how can you? You are young, and I am old. I have lived with him; I have waited on him many a long, long year. I know him; I know the great sun; I have talked with him: when he is glad and rollicking; when he is sulky and shuts his face; when he is angry and rages over

---

[6]   Hagetmau is a commune in the Landes department in Nouvelle-Aquitaine, south-west France.

the heavens; when he is sorrowful and drips blood-red tears onto the earth. Yes, I have talked with him; in the old time, before the great sun's life was all changed; in the old time, when he and the moon were happy all the day's length, wandering about the cloud-mountains; and at night-fall they slept side by side beneath the shadow of the earth. The moon loved him with a clinging love — a love surpassing the deepest love of woman — a love that you cannot understand, and she was ever joyous and rosy, and they were never apart, neither day nor night. Then, one hot summer evening, the spirit of wantonness clipped the moon, and she slipped from the great sun as he slept, and did him a foul wrong. And in the morning he awoke, full of red wrath to find the moon gone from his side, and that day he put her away from him, for ever and ever.

"And now, while the great sun sleeps, down there, beneath the shadow of the earth, the moon walks the heavens alone, wan and thin and wasted, and when he returns with the day, she flees to hide her white face for shame."

Etienne Mattou

I

It was the fair at Amou.[1] On the ox-market, under the plane-trees, a sea of blue bérets; an incoherent waving of ox-goads;[2] hundreds of sleek, fawn-coloured backs and curved, bristling horns.

Etienne Mattou had been found murdered.

A boy from Baigts had just brought the news,[3] as I drove into the town, and the murmur of it had started to run like wild-fire through the throng. For in those parts they all knew Etienne Mattou; and so everyone could feel an eager, personal interest in the crime.

The boy had soon related all he knew. The express from Toulouse[4] pulled up, close to the level crossing which his mother kept. The *chef-de-train*[5] and three other officials between them carried the body into his mother's house and laid it on the kitchen table. And the blood trickled all down their trousers, and reddened the cloth which they spread over the face. The *chef-de-train* went back to the train and walked along the foot-board, asking at every window for a doctor, till at last a stout gentleman in a tall hat clambered down from a first-class carriage.

Then the gendarmes came, and the engine-driver, who related how he had seen something lying across the rails, but had not been able to stop the train in time. The stout gentleman explained that Etienne Mattou had been dead for some time before the wheels had crushed his head, and showed some wounds on his chest, which, he said, had been done with a knife. After which they all went away together, and the train from Toulouse steamed off again. And the gendarmes found from some papers in the dead man's pockets, and from the marking on his clothes, that he was Etienne Mattou, and the *maréchal des logis*[6] said it was quite clear that he had been murdered in the night, and that the assassin had placed the body across the rails, that people might think it was the train that had done it.

"And Jeanne? She's in the market. I saw her just now, bargaining for some chickens. Someone must tell her."

---

[1]   Amou is a commune in the Landes department in the Nouvelle-Aquitaine region, south-west France.
[2]   Ox-goads: wooden tools, fitted with an iron spike, used to spur oxen as they pull a plough or cart.
[3]   Baigts is a commune in the Landes department in Nouvelle-Aquitaine.
[4]   The express from Toulouse: the express train from Toulouse, now the capital of the Occitanie region, south-west France.
[5]   *Chef-de-train*: conductor or head guard.
[6]   *Maréchal des logis*: sergeant.

But as the old man spoke, she came in sight, walking alone in the middle of the road, with a straggling, gaping crowd behind her. Up there in the fruit-market, she had heard the news, and she had come straight away like that, looking neither to the right nor to the left, with a wild, scared gaze in her dry eyes. She had taken it so strangely that the women were afraid of her, and no one had dared to speak to her.

"Someone must see to her," the old man muttered.

I went up to her, and said, pointing to the dog-cart[7] —

"I will drive you, Jeanne. The mare is fresh."

"Thank you," she answered in a hard voice, keeping her gaze fixed on the ground before her.

We got into the cart together, and the peasants all crowded round to see us start, and the old man swore at the boys and drove them away.

"Will you go home, or to Baigts?" I asked when we had crossed the river.

"Home, if you please. Shall I have to recognize the body?"

"Yes," I answered.

I busied myself with driving the mare as fast as she would go. The road was crowded with flocks of sheep, droves of young horses, ox-carts filled with calves and pigs and poultry, peasant men and peasant women, all on their way to the fair. They stood aside as we rattled past, and several bid me good morning. But none of them had as yet heard the news. A chilly breeze blew in our faces, and the day was draped with heavy folds of lowering clouds. Jeanne never spoke a word; she sat quite still, her hands folded loosely on her lap. Was it the stoniness of compressed anguish, or the stolidity of indifference?

I recalled Etienne's polled, conical-shaped skull, his furtive, sunken eyes, his thin, hooked nose, his egg-coloured moustache and imperial;[8] and now the engine-wheels had smashed it all hideously, and before that, in the dark of the night — I remembered how the lashing of the wind against the window-pane had awoken me — someone had set upon him savagely, and stabbed him again and again.... And Jeanne was beside me, dry-eyed and motionless.... There was something brutal about the silence of this drive. For the mere sake of speaking, I struggled to find some ordinary phrase of consolation, some good word for the dead man. But I could not; for Jeanne was aware that I had had cause to hate him, as much as anyone in the country. So nothing passed between us; there was only the monotonous clatter of the mare's swinging trot.

A fierce haggler, a man of many wiles, a man of stubborn greed, a man without pity, a bully, an evil-natured cheat — Etienne Mattou had been all that. Ostensibly, he had carried on an extensive trade in ham-curing, buying the pigs

---

7　　See note 3 on p. 81.
8　　An imperial is a small pointed beard below the lower lip.

from the peasants, and sending the meat to Bayonne and to Bordeaux;[9] but he had a multitude of other occupations — he was a money-lender, a horse-dealer, a wine-merchant, a road-contractor, and a speculator in land. And many a tale of his ruthlessness in each of these capacities was told about the country.[10]

Jeanne was yet young, and I had often wondered what her life must have been, in that dank, dilapidated château of theirs. People said that she had grown evil-hearted too, and that it was she who had turned the cask-binder out into the road, because he had become slow and infirm.

The rain came before we reached the house — a listless, silently flowing rain. The sky descended like a low ceiling; the breath of the breeze dropped, and a heavy odour of sodden soil came from the land.

"You'll get wet," I said to Jeanne.

She gave me no answer.

… And all the past month Etienne had been busier than ever — he had sold everything — his lands, his ham-trade, his horses; he had dismissed his men. The lease of the château was almost at an end. Etienne was going to retire. In another fortnight he would have been gone — back to the Tarn-et-Garonne,[11] his own country — gone with all his ill-gotten riches.

That the vengeance of some poor devil whom he had outwitted — it must have been that, I thought — should have fallen upon him at that moment, seemed like an awful judgment of God.

We turned within the old stone gateway, all yellow with moss. Inside, as we drove noiselessly over the grass-grown drive, under the thick-leafed trees, the air tasted hot and rank. The house, every shutter closed and the stucco peeling from the walls, stood desolate, rotting, dead-looking.

Jeanne got down, mounted the flight of green, cracked steps, pulled a key from her pocket, and pushed open the great, creaking door. Then, suddenly remembering me, she turned and nodded curtly.

"Thank you!"

"No one has come," I said. And, as she did not speak, I asked: "What are you going to do?"

"I shall wait." She still stood half inside the house.

"Can I do anything?"

"No, nothing," she interrupted. She went inside, and the door closed behind her with a heavy noise.

---

9   Bayonne and Bordeaux: two cities in south-west France of commercial and industrial importance during the nineteenth century, suggesting something of the extent of Etienne Mattou's business activities.

10   Etienne Mattou, 'the money-lender', makes a brief appearance in Crackanthorpe's 'The White Maize', in *Sentimental Studies & A Set of Village Tales*.

11   Tarn-et-Garonne is a department in the Occitanie region, south-west France, through which run the rivers Tarn and Garonne.

II

Since our strange drive together that drizzling April morning, I have never seen Jeanne again. And to this day the gendarmes have not discovered Etienne Mattou's murderer. Old Cauhapé, I remember, for a whole week, grew quite garrulous over the mysterious crime, propounded half-a-dozen theories concerning it, and came to the brutal conclusion that, after all, the rascal only got what he deserved. Jeanne lived on in the dilapidated château, she and an old serving-woman. She was richer than ever now; for Etienne's life had been insured for eighty thousand francs. And people began to speak of her more kindly, and reminded one another that her parents had forced her into marrying Etienne, because he was a man of great fortune.

III

Truth is stranger than fiction; and so it proved in the matter of Etienne Mattou.

One night towards the end of the year, I was at Havre,[12] awaiting the Southampton steamer. When I entered the Café du Port, a flaccid-faced man stood on the platform, chanting a comic song.

> "Brunes et blondes, brunes et blondes,
> Les p'tites cocottes, les p'tites cocottes,"[13]

went the refrain.

"Une cannette de Strasbourg!"[14] called a voice — a rasping, deep-toned voice — a voice that I knew. Those furtive, sunken eyes, that thin, hooked nose — where had I seen them before? The man sat alone, smoking a cigarette, moodily contemplating his glass.

In a flash it came upon me. It was Etienne Mattou. He wore a beard, and a workman's blouse. But it was him — that trick of blinking his eyes, of pressing the ball of his thumb under his nose, as he meditated.

The resemblance was extraordinary, yet the thing was impossible; Etienne had been dead nearly a year.

Fascinated, I watched the man. Presently he began to drum his finger on the marble table. "Les pioupious d'Auvergne,"[15] — I had heard Etienne drum that tune in Eudore's house, the day after the sale.

With an irresistible impulse, I rose and sat down opposite him. His drumming ceased at once, and he fixed his gaze on me, violently blinking his

---

[12]   Havre, i.e. Le Havre, a major city and port in Normandy.
[13]   Brunes et blondes […] les p'tites cocottes: Brunettes and blondes […] the little sweeties.
[14]   Une canette de Strasbourg: a can of Strasbourg beer. Now capital of the French Grand Est region, Strasbourg was annexed by Germany following the Franco-Prussian war of 1870–1871, permanently reverting to France in 1945.
[15]   Les pioupious d'Auvergne: slang for infantrymen of the Auvergne.

small, sunken eyes. I sat there, as if hypnotized, unable to take my eyes off him. The singer came and jingled his plate-full of coppers between us. I let him pass. I felt that to move would break the spell. Then a reckless longing to make the man speak, to hear that rasping, deep-pitched voice, seized me —

"Vous êtes ici depuis longtemps, monsieur?"[16] I began.

"Mais foutez-moi la paix. Je ne vous connais pas."[17]

It was the voice — Etienne's voice. And all at once my courage came back.

"Pardon," I said, "mais vous me connaissez parfaitement. Vous vous appelez Etienne Mattou."[18]

Yes, it was he. Under the eyes he had turned all white.

"Voulez-vous me laissez tranquille?"[19]

"I want to know why you are not dead?" My heart was thumping with excitement; I never heeded the grotesqueness of the question.

"You are mad, I think."

"What are you doing here?"

He struck a match, and, as he steadied the flame, while the sulphur sputtered, his hand shook, rattling the stud of his shirt-cuff.

"I work here. I am a porter on the quay."

"But you are Etienne Mattou. I know you perfectly well now."

He dropped the lighted match on the table, and, leaning across, said in a low voice —

"Come outside."

We went into the street.

"And Jeanne? Where is Jeanne?" he asked:

"Jeanne believes you are dead — murdered by the railway."

"Is she still there — in the country?"

"Yes; and you ——?"

"And I ——?"

"They suppose it was your body that was found by the railway. How was that?"

"I can't tell," he replied sullenly. Then added — "Are you staying long here?"

"No, I go tonight, at half-past eleven — to England, by the steamer."

We were walking along the quay: a few passers were hurrying by, and the water was licking the harbour-wall.

"You are starting without fail tonight then?"

"Yes, without fail."

[16] "Vous êtes ici depuis longtemps, monsieur?": have you been here, long, sir?
[17] "Mais foutez-moi la paix. Je ne vous connais pas.": but leave me in peace. I don't know you.
[18] "Mais vous me connaissez parfaitement. Vous vous appelez Etienne Mattou.": but you know me, very well. You're called Etienne Mattou.
[19] "Voulez-vous me laissez tranquille?": will you please leave me alone?

"You must tell no one that you have seen me."

"Why?"

"Because I am going back there tomorrow — to see after Jeanne — to give her a little surprise."

The light from a café illuminated his face. We had stopped, and he held out two fingers of his right hand.

"Goodnight."

I watched him walk rapidly away. Then I went on board.

Later in the night, as we were ploughing across the Channel, I remembered the look on his face as he had bid me goodbye, and I understood how it had all happened. Etienne had met some beggar in the dark, had changed clothes with him, killed him, and placed the body across the rails, so that it might never be recognized. Afterwards he had escaped to Havre, and had been waiting there for Jeanne to join him with the insurance-money. But Jeanne had never come.

IV

I do not think he ever returned to give Jeanne that little surprise. At least, no one out there ever saw him. Jeanne still lives in the country. She has made over all her money to the convent of the Sacré-cœur at Navarreux,[20] and now she is a cloistered nun, and will never come out till the end of her days.

[20] Navarreux is a commune in the department of Pyrénées-Atlantiques, west and south-west France.

From
Last Studies (1897)

Anthony Garstin's Courtship

I

A stampede of huddled sheep, wildly scampering over the slaty shingle, emerged from the leaden mist that muffled the fell-top, and a shrill shepherd's whistle broke the damp stillness of the air. And presently a man's figure appeared, following the sheep down the hillside. He halted a moment to whistle curtly to his two dogs, who, laying back their ears, chased the sheep at top-speed beyond the brow; then, his hands deep in his pockets, he strode vigorously forward. A streak of white smoke from a toiling train was creeping silently across the distance: the great, grey, desolate undulations of treeless country showed no other sign of life.

The sheep hurried in single file along a tiny track worn threadbare amid the brown, lumpy grass: and, as the man came round the mountain's shoulder, a narrow valley opened out beneath him — a scanty patchwork of green fields, and, here and there, a whitewashed farm, flanked by a dark cluster of sheltering trees.

The man walked with a loose, swinging gait. His figure was spare and angular: he wore a battered, black felt hat and clumsy, iron-bound boots: his clothes were dingy from long exposure to the weather. He had close-set, insignificant eyes, much wrinkled, and stubbly eyebrows streaked with grey. His mouth was close-shaven, and drawn by his abstraction into hard and taciturn lines; beneath his chin bristled an unkempt fringe of sandy-coloured hair.

When he reached the foot of the fell, the twilight was already blurring the distance. The sheep scurried, with a noisy rustling, across a flat, swampy stretch, over-grown with rushes, while the dogs headed them towards a gap in a low, ragged wall built of loosely-heaped boulders. The man swung the gate to after them, and waited, whistling peremptorily, recalling the dogs. A moment later, the animals re-appeared, cringing as they crawled through the bars of the gate. He kicked out at them contemptuously, and mounting a stone stile a few yards further up the road, dropped into a narrow lane.

Presently, as he passed a row of lighted windows, he heard a voice call to him. He stopped, and perceived a crooked, white-bearded figure, wearing clerical clothes, standing in the garden gateway.

"Good evening, Anthony. A raw evening this."

"Ay, Mr. Blencarn, it's a bit frittish,"[1] he answered. "I've jest bin gittin' a few lambs off t' fell. I hope ye're keepin' fairly, an' Miss Rosa too." He spoke briefly, with a loud, spontaneous cordiality.

---

[1]   Frittish means cold.

"Thank ye, Anthony, thank ye. Rosa's down at the church, playing over the hymns for tomorrow. How's Mrs. Garstin?"

"Nicely, thank ye, Mr. Blencarn. She's wonderful active, is mother."

"Well, goodnight to ye, Anthony," said the old man, clicking the gate.

"Goodnight, Mr. Blencarn," he called back.

A few minutes later the twinkling lights of the village came in sight, and from within the sombre form of the square-towered church, looming by the roadside, the slow, solemn strains of the organ floated out on the evening air. Anthony lightened his tread: then paused, listening; but, presently, becoming aware that a man stood, listening also, on the bridge some few yards distant, he moved forward again. Slackening his pace, as he approached, he eyed the figure keenly; but the man paid no heed to him, remaining, with his back turned, gazing over the parapet into the dark, gurgling stream.

Anthony trudged along the empty village street, past the gleaming squares of ruddy gold, starting on either side out of the darkness. Now and then he looked furtively backwards. The straight open road lay behind him, glimmering wanly: the organ seemed to have ceased: the figure on the bridge had left the parapet, and appeared to be moving away towards the church. Anthony halted, watching it till it had disappeared into the blackness beneath the churchyard trees. Then, after a moment's hesitation, he left the road, and mounted an upland meadow towards his mother's farm.

It was a bare, oblong house. In front, a whitewashed porch, and a narrow garden-plot, enclosed by a low iron railing, were dimly discernible: behind, the steep fell-side loomed like a monstrous, mysterious curtain hung across the night. He passed round the back into the twilight of a wide yard, cobbled and partially grass-grown, vaguely flanked by the shadowy outlines of long, low farm-buildings. All was wrapped in darkness: somewhere overhead a bat fluttered, darting its puny scream.

Inside, a blazing peat-fire scattered capering shadows across the smooth, stone floor, flickered among the dim rows of hams suspended from the ceiling and on the panelled cupboards of dark, glistening oak. A servant-girl, spreading the cloth for supper, clattered her clogs in and out of the kitchen: old Mrs. Garstin was stooping before the hearth, tremulously turning some girdle-cakes[2] that lay roasting in the embers.

At the sound of Anthony's heavy tread in the passage, she rose, glancing sharply at the clock above the chimney-piece. She was a heavy-built woman, upright, stalwart almost, despite her years. Her face was gaunt and sallow; deep wrinkles accentuated the hardness of her features. She wore a black widow's cap above her iron-grey hair, gold-rimmed spectacles, and a soiled, chequered apron.

[2] Girdle-cakes: a dialect version of 'griddle-cakes', cooked on a metal plate over an open fire.

"Ye're varra late, Tony," she remarked querulously.

He unloosened his woollen neckerchief, and when he had hung it methodically with his hat behind the door, answered:

"'Twas terrible thick on t' fell-top, an' them two bitches be that senseless."

She caught his sleeve, and, through her spectacles, suspiciously scrutinized his face.

"Ye did na meet wi' Rosa Blencarn?"

"Nay, she was in church, hymn-playin', wi' Luke Stock hangin' roond door," he retorted bitterly, rebuffing her with rough impatience.

She moved away, nodding sententiously to herself. They began supper: neither spoke: Anthony sat slowly stirring his tea, and staring moodily into the flames: the bacon on his plate lay untouched. From time to time his mother, laying down her knife and fork, looked across at him in unconcealed asperity, pursing her wide, ungainly mouth. At last, abruptly setting down her cup, she broke out:

"I wonder ye hav'na mare pride, Tony. For hoo lang are ye goin' t' continue settin' mopin' and broodin' like a seck sheep? Ye'll jest mak yessell ill, an' then I reckon what ye'll prove satisfied. Ay, but I wonder ye hav'na more pride."

But he made no answer, remaining unmoved, as if he had not heard.

Presently, half to himself, without raising his eyes, he murmured:

"Luke be goin' South, Monday."

"Well, ye canna tak' oop wi' his leavin's anyways. It hasna coom t' that, has it? Ye doan't intend settin' all t' parish a laughin' at ye a second occasion?"

He flushed dully, and bending over his plate, mechanically began his supper.

"Wa dang it," he broke out a minute later, "d'ye think I heed the cacklin' o' fifty parishes? Na, not I," and, with a short, grim laugh, he brought his fist down heavily on the oak table.

"Ye're daft, Tony," the old woman blurted.

"Daft or na daft, I tell ye this, mother, that I be forty-six year o' age this back-end,[3] and there be some things I will na listen to. Rosa Blencarn's bonny enough for me."

"Ay, bonny enough — I've na patience wi' ye. Bonny enough — tricked oot in her furbelows,[4] gallivantin' wi' every royster[5] fra Pe'rith.[6] Bonny enough — that be all ye think on. She's bin a proper parson's niece — the giddy, feckless creature, an she'd mak' ye a proper sort o' wife, Tony Garstin, ye great, fond booby."

She pushed back her chair, and, hurriedly clattering the crockery, began to clear away the supper.

---

3   This back-end: this autumn.
4   Furbelows: a pleated or gathered piece of material.
5   Royster: variant spelling (obsolete) of roister: here someone who enjoys boisterous fun.
6   Pe'rith: Penrith. See note 19 on p. 280.

"T' hoose be mine, t' Lord be praised," she continued in a loud, hard voice, "an' as long as he spare me, Tony, I'll na see Rosa Blencarn set foot inside it."

Anthony scowled, without replying, and drew his chair to the hearth. His mother bustled about the room behind him. After a while she asked:

"Did ye pen t' lambs in t' back field?"

"Na, they're in Hullam bottom," he answered curtly.

The door closed behind her, and by and by he could hear her moving overhead. Meditatively blinking, he filled his pipe clumsily, and pulling a crumpled newspaper from his pocket, sat on over the smouldering fire, reading and stolidly puffing.

II

The music rolled through the dark, empty church. The last, leaden flicker of daylight glimmered in through the pointed windows, and beyond the level rows of dusky pews, tenanted only by a litter of prayer-books, two guttering candles revealed the organ pipes, and the young girl's swaying figure.

She played vigorously. Once or twice the tune stumbled, and she recovered it impatiently, bending over the keyboard, showily flourishing her wrists as she touched the stops. She was bare-headed (her hat and cloak lay beside her on a stool). She had fair, fluffy hair, cut short behind her neck; large, round eyes, heightened by a fringe of dark lashes; rough, ruddy cheeks, and a rosy, full-lipped, unstable mouth. She was dressed quite simply, in a black, close-fitting bodice, a little frayed at the sleeves. Her hands and neck were coarsely fashioned: her comeliness was brawny, literal, unfinished, as it were.

When at last the ponderous chords of the Amen faded slowly into the twilight, flushed, breathing a little quickly, she paused, listening to the stillness of the church. Presently a small boy emerged from behind the organ.

"Good-evenin', Miss Rosa," he called, trotting briskly away down the aisle.

"Goodnight, Robert," she answered, absently.

After a while, with an impatient gesture, as if to shake some importunate thought from her mind, she rose abruptly, pinned on her hat, threw her cloak round her shoulders, blew out the candles, and groped her way through the church, towards the half-open door. As she hurried along the narrow pathway that led across the churchyard, of a sudden, a figure started out of the blackness.

"Who's that?" she cried, in a loud, frightened voice.

A man's uneasy laugh answered her.

"It's only me, Rosa. I didna think t' scare ye. I've bin waitin' for ye, this hoor past."

She made no reply, but quickened her pace. He strode on beside her.

"I'm off, Monday, ye know," he continued. And, as she said nothing,

"Will ye na stop jest a minnit? I'd like t' speak a few words wi' ye before I go, an tomorrow I hev t' git over t' Scarsdale betimes," he persisted.[7]

"I don't want t' speak wi' ye: I don't want ever to see ye agin. I jest hate the sight o' ye." She spoke with a vehement, concentrated hoarseness.

"Nay, but ye must listen to me. I will na be put off wi' fratchin[8] speeches."

And gripping her arm, he forced her to stop.

"Loose me, ye great beast," she broke out.

"I'll na hould ye, if ye'll jest stand quiet-like. I meant t' speak fair t' ye, Rosa."

They stood at a bend in the road, face to face, quite close together. Behind his burly form stretched the dimness of a grey, ghostly field.

"What is't ye hev to say to me? Hev done wi' it quick," she said sullenly.

"It be jest this, Rosa," he began with dogged gravity. "I want t' tell ye that ef any trouble comes t' ye after I'm gone — ye know t' what I refer — I want t' tell ye that I'm prepared t' act square by ye. I've written out on an envelope my address in London. Luke Stock, care o' Purcell & Co., Smithfield Market, London."[9]

"Ye're a bad, sinful man. I jest hate t' sight o' ye. I wish ye were dead."

"Ay, but I reckon what ye'd ha best thought o' that before. Ye've changed yer whistle considerably since Tuesday. Nay, hould on," he added, as she struggled to push past him. "Here's t' envelope."

She snatched the paper, and tore it passionately, scattering the fragments onto the road. When she had finished, he burst out angrily:

"Ye cussed, unreasonable fool."

"Let me pass, ef ye've nought mare t' say," she cried.

"Nay, I'll na part wi' ye this fashion. Ye can speak soft enough when ye choose." And seizing her shoulders, he forced her backwards against the wall.

"Ye do look fine, an' na mistake, when ye're jest ablaze wi' ragin'," he laughed bluntly, lowering his face to hers.

"Loose me, loose me, ye great coward," she gasped, striving to free her arms.

Holding her fast, he expostulated:

"Coom, Rosa, can we na part friends?"

"Part friends, indeed," she retorted bitterly. "Friends wi' the likes o' you. What d'ye tak me for? Let me git home, I tell ye. An' please God I'll never set eyes on ye again. I hate t' sight o' ye."

"Be off wi' ye, then," he answered, pushing her roughly back into the road. "Be off wi' ye, ye silly. Ye canna say I hav na spak fair t' ye, an', by goom, ye'll na see me shally-wallyin[10] this fashion agin. Be off wi' ye: ye can jest shift for

---

[7] Scarsdale is invented.

[8] Fratchin means quarrelling.

[9] Smithfield Market: 'Smithfield Market, Newgate Street, City, is the great meat-market of London.' (Baedeker, London and Its Environs, p. 26).

[10] Shally-wallyin: acting in a silly or stupid manner.

yerself, since ye canna keep a civil tongue in yer head."

The girl, catching at her breath, stood as if dazed, watching his retreating figure; then starting forward at a run, disappeared up the hill, into the darkness.

III

Old Mr. Blencarn concluded his husky sermon. The scanty congregation, who had been sitting, stolidly immobile in their stiff, Sunday clothes, shuffled to their feet, and the pewful of school children, in clamorous chorus, intoned the final hymn. Anthony stood near the organ, absently contemplating, while the rude melody resounded through the church, Rosa's deft manipulation of the key-board. The rugged lines of his face were relaxed to a vacant, thoughtful limpness, that aged his expression not a little: now and then, as if for reference, he glanced questioningly at the girl's profile.

A few minutes later the service was over, and the congregation sauntered out down the aisle. A gawky group of men remained loitering by the church door: one of them called to Anthony; but, nodding curtly, he passed on, and strode away down the road, across the grey upland meadows, towards home. As soon as he had breasted the hill, however, and was no longer visible from below, he turned abruptly to the left, along a small, swampy hollow, till he had reached the lane that led down from the fellside.

He clambered over a rugged, moss-grown wall, and stood, gazing expectantly down the dark, disused roadway; then, after a moment's hesitation, perceiving nobody, seated himself beneath the wall, on a projecting slab of stone.

Overhead hung a sombre, drifting sky. A gusty wind rollicked down from the fell — huge masses of chilly grey, stripped of the last night's mist. A few dead leaves fluttered over the stones, and from off the fellside there floated the plaintive, quavering rumour[11] of many bleating sheep.

Before long, he caught sight of two figures coming towards him, slowly climbing the hill. He sat awaiting their approach, fidgeting with his sandy beard, and abstractedly grinding the ground beneath his heel. At the brow they halted: plunging his hands deep into his pockets, he strolled sheepishly towards them.

"Ah! good day t' ye, Anthony," called the old man, in a shrill, breathless voice. "'Tis a long hill, an' my legs are not what they were. Time was when I'd think nought o' a whole day's tramp on t' fells. Ay, I'm gittin' feeble, Anthony, that's what 'tis. And if Rosa here wasn't the great, strong lass she is, I don't know how her old uncle 'd manage;" and he turned to the girl with a proud, tremulous smile.

---

[11] Rumour: here deployed by Crackanthorpe in the traditional sense of a soft, low, indistinct sound, approximating to a murmur.

"Will ye tak my arm a bit, Mr. Blencarn? Miss Rosa'll be tired, likely," Anthony asked.

"Nay, Mr. Garstin, but I can manage nicely," the girl interrupted sharply.

Anthony looked up at her as she spoke. She wore a straw hat, trimmed with crimson velvet, and a black, fur-edged cape, that seemed to set off mightily the fine whiteness of her neck. Her large, dark eyes were fixed upon him. He shifted his feet uneasily, and dropped his glance.

She linked her uncle's arm in hers, and the three moved slowly forward. Old Mr. Blencarn walked with difficulty, pausing at intervals for breath. Anthony, his eyes bent on the ground, sauntered beside him, clumsily kicking at the cobbles that lay in his path.

When they reached the vicarage gate, the old man asked him to come inside.

"Not jest now, thank ye, Mr. Blencarn. I've that lot o' lambs t' see to before dinner. It's a grand marnin', this," he added, inconsequently.

"Uncle's bought a nice lot o' Leghorns,[12] Tuesday," Rosa remarked. Anthony met her gaze; there was a grave, subdued expression on her face this morning, that made her look more of a woman, less of a girl.

"Ay, do ye show him the birds, Rosa. I'd be glad to have his opinion on 'em."

The old man turned to hobble into the house, and Rosa, as she supported his arm, called back over her shoulder:

"I'll not be a minute, Mr. Garstin."

Anthony strolled round to the yard behind the house, and waited, watching a flock of glossy-white poultry that strutted, perkily pecking, over the grass-grown cobbles.

"Ay, Miss Rosa, they're a bonny lot," he remarked, as the girl joined him.

"Are they not?" she rejoined, scattering a handful of corn before her.

The birds scuttled across the yard with greedy, outstretched necks. The two stood, side by side, gazing at them.

"What did he give for 'em?" Anthony asked.

"Fifty-five shillings."

"Ay," he assented, nodding absently.

"Was Dr. Sanderson na seein' o' yer father yesterday?" he asked, after a moment.

"He came in t' forenoon.[13] He said he was jest na worse."

"Ye knaw, Miss Rosa, as I'm still thinkin' on ye," he began abruptly, without looking up.

"I reckon it ain't much use," she answered shortly, scattering another handful of corn towards the birds. "I reckon I'll never marry. I'm jest weary o' bein' courted ——"

---

[12] Leghorns are a type of chicken.
[13] See note 11 on p. 136.

"I would na weary ye wi' courtin'," he interrupted.

She laughed noisily.

"Ye are a queer customer, an' na mistake."

"I'm a match for Luke Stock anyway," he continued fiercely. "Ye think nought o' taking oop wi' him — about as ranty, wild a young feller as ever stepped."[14]

The girl reddened, and bit her lip.

"I don't know what you mean, Mr. Garstin. It seems to me ye're mighty hasty in jumpin' t' conclusions."

"Mabbe I kin see a thing or two," he retorted doggedly.

"Luke Stock's gone to London, anyway."

"Ay, an' a powerful good job too, in t' opinion o' some folks."

"Ye're jest jealous," she exclaimed, with a forced titter. "Ye're jest jealous o' Luke Stock."

"Nay, but ye need na fill yer head wi' that nonsense. I'm too deep set on ye t' feel jealousy," he answered, gravely.

The smile faded from her face, as she murmured:

"I canna mak ye out, Mr. Garstin."

"Nay, that ye canna. An' I suppose it's natural, considerin' ye're little more than a child, an' I'm a'most old enough to be yer father," he retorted, with blunt bitterness.

"But ye know yer mother's took that dislike t' me. She'd never abide the sight o' me at Hootsey."[15]

He remained silent a moment, moodily reflecting.

"She'd jest ha' t' git ower it. I see nought in that objection," he declared.

"Nay, Mr. Garstin, it canna be. Indeed it canna be at all. Ye'd best jest put it right from yer mind, once and for all."

"I'd jest best put it off my mind, had I? Ye talk like a child!" he burst out scornfully. "I intend ye t' coom t' love me, an' I will na tak ye till ye do. I'll jest go on waitin' for ye, an', mark my words, my day 'ull coom at last."

He spoke loudly, in a slow, stubborn voice, and stepped suddenly towards her. With a faint, frightened cry she shrank back into the doorway of the hen-house.

"Ye talk like a prophet. Ye sort o' skeer me."

He laughed grimly, and paused, reflectively scanning her face. He seemed about to continue in the same strain; but, instead, turned abruptly on his heel, and strode away through the garden gate.

IV

For three hundred years there had been a Garstin at Hootsey: generation

[14] Ranty means wild or boisterous.
[15] Hootsey is invented.

after generation had tramped the grey stretch of upland, in the spring-time scattering their flocks over the fell-sides, and, at the "back-end," on dark, winter afternoons, driving them home again, down the broad bridle-path that led over the "raise."[16] They had been a race of few words, "keeping themselves to themselves," as the phrase goes; beholden to no man, filled with a dogged, churlish pride — an upright, old-fashioned race, stubborn, long-lived, rude in speech, slow of resolve.

Anthony had never seen his father, who had died one night, upon the fell-top, he and his shepherd, engulfed in the great snowstorm of 1849. Folks had said that he was the only Garstin who had failed to make old man's bones.

After his death, Jake Atkinson, from Ribblehead in Yorkshire, had come to live at Hootsey. Jake was a fine farmer, a canny bargainer, and very handy among the sheep, till he took to drink, and roystering every week with the town wenches up at Carlisle.[17] He was a corpulent, deep-voiced, free-handed fellow: when his time came, though he died very hardly,[18] he remained festive and convivial to the last. And for years afterwards, in the valley, his memory lingered: men spoke of him regretfully, recalling his quips, his feats of strength, and his choice breed of Herdwicke rams. But he left behind him a host of debts up at Carlisle, in Penrith,[19] and in almost every market town — debts that he had long ago pretended to have paid with money that belonged to his sister. The widow Garstin sold the twelve Herdwicke rams, and nine acres of land: within six weeks she had cleared off every penny, and for thirteen months, on Sundays, wore her mourning with a mute, forbidding grimness: the bitter thought that, unbeknown to her, Jake had acted dishonestly in money matters, and that he had ended his days in riotous sin, soured her pride, imbued her with a rancorous hostility against all the world. For she was a very proud woman, independent, holding her head high, so folks said, like a Garstin bred and born; and Anthony, although some reckoned him quiet and of little account, came to take after her as he grew into manhood.

She took into her own hands the management of the Hootsey farm, and set the boy to work for her along with the two farm servants. It was twenty-five years now since his uncle Jake's death: there were grey hairs in his sandy beard; but he still worked for his mother, as he had done when a growing lad.

And now that times were grown to be bad (of late years the price of stock had

---

[16]   A raise is a rising stretch of ground.
[17]   Carlisle was the 'co[unty] town of Cumberland, on river Eden, 60 miles W. of Newcastle'. (Bartholomew (ed.), *Gazetteer of The British Isles*, p. 134).
[18]   Hardly means harshly or painfully.
[19]   Penrith, a market town in Cumberland south-east of Carlisle which in the late 1880s had a population of just over 9000 and a railway station, and boasted four newspapers. It was the nearest town to Newbiggin Hall, the Cumberland family home of the Crackanthorpes (*Gazetteer of The British Isles*, p. 135).

been steadily falling; and the hay harvests had drifted from bad to worse)[20] the widow Garstin no longer kept any labouring men; but lived, she and her son, year in and year out, in a close parsimonious way.

That had been Anthony Garstin's life — a dull, eventless sort of business, the sluggish incrustation of monotonous years. And until Rosa Blencarn had come to keep house for her uncle, he had never thought twice on a woman's face.

The Garstins had always been good church-goers, and Anthony, for years, had acted as churchwarden. It was one summer evening, up at the vicarage, whilst he was checking the offertory account, that he first set eyes upon her. She was fresh back from school at Leeds:[21] she was dressed in a white dress: she looked, he thought, like a London lady.

She stood by the window, tall and straight and queenly, dreamily gazing out into the summer twilight, whilst he and her uncle sat over their business. When he rose to go, she glanced at him with quick curiosity; he hurried away, muttering a sheepish goodnight.

The next time that he saw her was in church on Sunday. He watched her shyly, with a hesitating, reverential discretion: her beauty seemed to him wonderful, distant, enigmatic. In the afternoon, young Mrs. Forsyth, from Longscale, dropped in for a cup of tea with his mother, and the two set off gossiping of Rosa Blencarn, speaking of her freely, in tones of acrimonious contempt. For a long while he sat silent, puffing at his pipe; but at last, when his mother concluded with, "She looks t' me fair stuck-oop, full o' toonish[22] airs an' graces," despite himself, he burst out: "Ye're jest wastin' yer breath wi' that cackle. I reckon Miss Blencarn's o' a different clay to us folks." Young Mrs. Forsyth tittered immoderately, and the next week it was rumoured about the valley that "Tony Garstin was gone luny[23] over t' parson's niece."

But of all this he knew nothing — keeping to himself, as was his wont, and being, besides, very busy with the hay harvest — until one day, at dinner-time, Henry Sisson asked if he'd started his courting; Jacob Sowerby cried that Tony'd been too slow in getting to work, for that the girl had been seen spooning in Crosby Shaws[24] with Curbison the auctioneer, and the others (there were half-a-dozen of them lounging round the hay-waggon) burst into a boisterous

[20] A reflection of the impact of the agricultural depression in Britain from the mid-1870s to the mid-1890s, partly attributable to the increase in cheap imports of grain from abroad.
[21] Leeds: a major city in the West Riding of Yorkshire, north-east of Manchester, south-west of York.
[22] Toonish: i.e. townish: 'a townish girl as she's become by now. I never cared much about her', is the verdict of Widow Edlin on Sue Bridehead in Thomas Hardy's *Jude the Obscure* (1895), II, ch. vi.
[23] Luny: i.e. loony; mad, as in 'lunatic'.
[24] Spooning is being amorous or behaving amorously; see also 'spoony', note 22 on p. 303. Crosby Shaws: possibly the woods in Crosby, a hamlet in east Cumberland, north-east of Carlisle.

guffaw. Anthony flushed dully, looking hesitatingly from the one to the other; then slowly put down his beer-can, and of a sudden, seizing Jacob by the neck, swung him heavily on the grass. He fell against the waggon-wheel, and when he rose the blood was streaming from an ugly cut in his forehead. And henceforward Tony Garstin's courtship was the common jest of all the parish.

As yet, however, he had scarcely spoken to her, though twice he had passed her in the lane that led up to the vicarage. She had given him a frank, friendly smile; but he had not found the resolution to do more than lift his hat. He and Henry Sisson stacked the hay in the yard behind the house; there was no further mention made of Rosa Blencarn; but all day long Anthony, as he knelt thatching the rick, brooded over the strange sweetness of her face, and on the fell-top, while he tramped after the ewes over the dry, crackling heather, and as he jogged along the narrow, rickety road, driving his cartload of lambs into the auction mart.

Thus, as the weeks slipped by, he was content with blunt, wistful ruminations upon her indistinct image. Jacob Sowerby's accusation, and several kindred innuendoes let fall by his mother, left him coolly incredulous; the girl still seemed to him altogether distant; but from the first sight of her face he had evolved a stolid, unfaltering conception of her difference from the ruck of her sex.

But one evening, as he passed the vicarage on his way down from the fells, she called to him, and with a childish, confiding[25] familiarity asked for advice concerning the feeding of the poultry. In his eagerness to answer her as best he could, he forgot his customary embarrassment, and grew, for the moment, almost voluble, and quite at his ease in her presence. Directly her flow of questions ceased, however, the returning perception of her rosy, hesitating smile, and of her large, deep eyes looking straight into his face, perturbed him strangely, and, reddening, he remembered the quarrel in the hay-field and the tale of Crosby Shaws.

After this, the poultry became a link between them — a link which he regarded in all seriousness, blindly unconscious that there was aught else to bring them together, only feeling himself in awe of her, because of her schooling, her townish manners, her ladylike mode of dress. And soon, he came to take a sturdy, secret pride in her friendly familiarity towards him. Several times a week he would meet her in the lane, and they would loiter a moment together; she would admire his dogs, though he assured her earnestly that they were but sorry curs; and once, laughing at his staidness, she nicknamed him "Mr. Churchwarden."

That the girl was not liked in the valley he suspected, curtly attributing her unpopularity to the women's senseless jealousy. Of gossip concerning her he

[25] See note 3 on p. 147.

heard no further hint; but instinctively, and partly from that rugged, natural reserve of his, shrank from mentioning her name, even incidentally, to his mother.

Now, on Sunday evenings, he often strolled up to the vicarage, each time quitting his mother with the same awkward affectation of casualness; and, on his return, becoming vaguely conscious of how she refrained from any comment on his absence, and appeared oddly oblivious of the existence of parson Blencarn's niece.

She had always been a sour-tongued woman; but, as the days shortened with the approach of the long winter months, she seemed to him to grow more fretful than ever; at times it was almost as if she bore him some smouldering, sullen resentment. He was of stubborn fibre, however, toughened by long habit of a bleak, unruly climate; he revolved the matter in his mind deliberately, and when, at last, after much plodding thought, it dawned upon him that she resented his acquaintance with Rosa Blencarn, he accepted the solution with an unflinching phlegm, and merely shifted his attitude towards the girl, calculating each day the likelihood of his meeting her, and making, in her presence, persistent efforts to break down, once for all, the barrier of his own timidity. He was a man not to be clumsily driven, still less, so he prided himself, a man to be craftily led.

It was close upon Christmas time before the crisis came. His mother was just home from Penrith market. The spring-cart stood in the yard, the old grey horse was steaming heavily in the still, frosty air.

"I reckon ye've come fast. T' ould horse is over hot," he remarked bluntly, as he went to the animal's head.

She clambered down hastily, and, coming to his side, began breathlessly:

"Ye ought t' hev coom t' market, Tony. There's bin pretty goin's on in Pe'rith today. I was helpin' Anna Forsyth t' choose six yards o' sheetin' in Dockroy,[26] when we sees Rosa Blencarn coom oot o' t' 'Bell and Bullock' in company wi' Curbison and young Joe Smethwick. Smethwick was fair reelin' drunk, and Curbison and t' girl were a-houldin' onto him, to keep him fra fallin'; and then, after a bit, he puts his arm round the girl t' stiddy hisself, and that fashion they goes off, right oop t' public street ——"

He continued to unload the packages, and to carry them mechanically one by one into the house. Each time, when he re-appeared, she was standing by the steaming horse, busy with her tale.

"An' on t' road hame we passed t' three on' em in Curbison's trap, with Smethwick leein' in t' bottom, singin' maudlin' songs. They were passin' Dunscale village,[27] an' t' folks coom runnin' oot o' houses t' see 'em go past ——"

---

[26] Dockroy, a misspelling of Dockray, a 'hamlet with hotel, 8 miles E. of Keswick, W. Cumberland' (*Gazetteer of The British Isles*, p. 228).

[27] Dunscale is invented.

He led the cart away towards the stable, leaving her to cry the remainder after him across the yard.

Half-an-hour later he came in for his dinner. During the meal not a word passed between them, and directly he had finished he strode out of the house. About nine o'clock he returned, lit his pipe, and sat down to smoke it over the kitchen fire.

"Where've ye bin, Tony?" she asked.

"Oop t' vicarage, courtin'," he retorted defiantly, with his pipe in his mouth.

This was ten months ago; ever since he had been doggedly waiting. That evening he had set his mind on the girl, he intended to have her; and while his mother gibed, as she did now upon every opportunity, his patience remained grimly unflagging. She would remind him that the farm belonged to her, that he would have to wait till her death before he could bring the hussy to Hootsey: he would retort that as soon as the girl would have him, he intended taking a smallholding over at Scarsdale. Then she would give way, and for a while piteously upbraid him with her old age, and with the memory of all the years she and he had spent together, and he would comfort her with a display of brusque, evasive remorse.

But, nonetheless, on the morrow, his thoughts would return to dwell on the haunting vision of the girl's face, while his own rude, credulous chivalry, kindled by the recollection of her beauty, stifled his misgivings concerning her conduct.

Meanwhile she dallied with him, and amused herself with the younger men. Her old uncle fell ill in the spring, and could scarcely leave the house. She declared that she found life in the valley intolerably dull, that she hated the quiet of the place, that she longed for Leeds, and the exciting bustle of the streets; and in the evenings she wrote long letters to the girl-friends she had left behind there, describing with petulant vivacity her tribe of rustic admirers. At the harvest-time she went back on a fortnight's visit to friends; the evening before her departure she promised Anthony to give him her answer on her return. But, instead, she avoided him, pretended to have promised in jest, and took up with Luke Stock, a cattle-dealer from Wigton.[28]

V

It was three weeks since he had fetched his flock down from the fell.

After dinner he and his mother sat together in the parlour: they had done so every Sunday afternoon, year in and year out, as far back as he could remember.

A row of mahogany chairs, with shiny, horse-hair seats, were ranged round the room. A great collection of agricultural prize-tickets were pinned over the

[28] Wigton is a market town in Cumberland (now Cumbria), twelve miles south-west of Carlisle.

wall; and, on a heavy, highly-polished sideboard stood several silver cups. A heap of gilt-edged shavings filled the unused grate: there were gaudily-tinted roses along the mantelpiece, and, on a small table by the window, beneath a glass-case, a gilt basket filled with imitation flowers. Every object was disposed with a scrupulous precision: the carpet and the red-patterned cloth on the centre table were much faded. The room was spotlessly clean, and wore, in the chilly winter sunlight, a rigid, comfortless air.

Neither spoke, or appeared conscious of the other's presence. Old Mrs. Garstin, wrapped in a woollen shawl, sat knitting: Anthony dozed fitfully on a stiff-backed chair.

Of a sudden, in the distance, a bell started tolling. Anthony rubbed his eyes drowsily, and taking from the table his Sunday hat, strolled out across the dusky fields. Presently, reaching a rude wooden seat, built beside the bridle-path, he sat down and relit his pipe. The air was very still; below him a white filmy mist hung across the valley: the fell sides, vaguely grouped, resembled hulking masses of sombre shadow; and, as he looked back, three squares of glimmering gold revealed the lighted windows of the square-towered church.

He sat smoking; pondering, with placid and reverential contemplation, on the Mighty Maker of the world — a world majestically and inevitably ordered; a world where, he argued, each object — each fissure in the fells, the winding course of each tumbling stream — possesses its mysterious purport, its inevitable signification....

At the end of the field two rams were fighting; retreating, then running together, and, leaping from the ground, butting head to head and horn to horn. Anthony watched them absently, pursuing his rude meditations.

... And the succession of bad seasons, the slow ruination of the farmers throughout the country, were but punishment meted out for the accumulated wickedness of the world. In the olden time God rained plagues upon the land: now-a-days, in His wrath, He spoiled the produce of the earth, which, with His own hands, He had fashioned and bestowed upon men.[29]

He rose and continued his walk along the bridle-path. A multitude of rabbits scuttled up the hill at his approach; and a great cloud of plovers, rising from the rushes, circled overhead, filling the air with a profusion of their querulous cries. All at once he heard a rattling of stones, and perceived a number of small pieces of shingle bounding in front of him down the grassy slope.

A woman's figure was moving among the rocks above him. The next moment, by the trimming of crimson velvet on her hat, he had recognized her. He mounted the slope with springing strides, wondering the while how it was she came to be there, that she was not in church playing the organ at afternoon service.

[29] 'In the olden time [...] He had fashioned and bestowed upon men' (Exodus 9. 14–25).

Before she was aware of his approach, he was beside her.

"I thought ye'd be in church ——" he began.

She started: then, gradually regaining her composure, answered, weakly smiling:

"Mr. Jenkinson, the new school-master, wanted to try the organ."

He came towards her impulsively: she saw the odd flickers in his eyes as she stepped back in dismay.

"Nay, but I will na harm ye," he said. "Only I reckon what 'tis a special turn o' Providence, meetin' wi' ye oop here. I reckon what ye'll hev t' give me a square answer noo. Ye canna dilly-dally everlastingly."

He spoke almost brutally; and she stood, white and gasping, staring at him with large, frightened eyes. The sheep-walk was but a tiny threadlike track: the slope of the shingle on either side was very steep: below them lay the valley; distant, lifeless, all blurred by the evening dusk. She looked about her helplessly for a means of escape.

"Miss Rosa," he continued, in a husky voice, "can ye na coom t' think on me? Think ye, I've bin waitin' nigh upon two year for ye. I've watched ye tak oop, first wi' this young fellar, and then wi' that, till soomtimes my heart's fit t' burst. Many a day, oop on t' fell-top, t' thought o' ye's nigh driven me daft, and I've left my shepherdin' jest t' set on a cairn in t' mist, picturin' an' broodin' on yer face. Many an evenin' I've started oop t' vicarage, wi' t' resolution t' speak right oot t' ye; but when it coomed t' point, a sort o' timidity seemed t' hould me back, I was that feared t' displease ye. I knaw I'm na scholar, an' mabbe ye think I'm rough-mannered. I knaw I've spoken sharply to ye once or twice lately. But it's jest because I'm that mad wi' love for ye: I jest canna help myself soomtimes ——"

He waited, peering into her face. She could see the beads of sweat above his bristling eyebrows: the damp had settled on his sandy beard: his horny fingers were twitching at the buttons of his black Sunday coat.

She struggled to summon a smile; but her underlip quivered, and her large dark eyes filled slowly with tears.

And he went on:

"Ye've coom t' mean jest everything to me. Ef ye will na hev me, I care for nought else. I canna speak t' ye in phrases: I'm jest a plain, unscholarly man: I canna wheedle ye, wi' cunnin' after t' fashion o' toon folks. But I can love ye wi' all my might, an' watch over ye, and work for ye better than any one o' em ——"

She was crying to herself, silently, while he spoke. He noticed nothing, however: the twilight hid her face from him.

"There's nought against me," he persisted. "I'm as good a man as anyone on 'em. Ay, as good a man as anyone on 'em," he repeated defiantly, raising his voice.

"It's impossible, Mr. Garstin, it's impossible. Ye've been very kind to me ——"

she added, in a choking voice.

"Wa dang it, I didna mean t' mak ye cry, lass," he exclaimed, with a softening of his tone. "There's nought for ye t' cry ower."

She sank onto the stones, passionately sobbing in hysterical and defenceless despair. Anthony stood a moment, gazing at her in clumsy perplexity: then, coming close to her, put his hand on her shoulder, and said gently:

"Coom, lass, what's trouble? Ye can trust me."

She shook her head faintly.

"Ay, but ye can though," he asserted, firmly. "Come, what is 't?"

Heedless of him, she continued to rock herself to and fro, crooning in her distress:

"Oh! I wish I were dead! ... I wish I could die!"

— "Wish ye could die?" he repeated. "Why, whatever can't be that's troublin' ye like this? There, there, lassie, give ower: it 'ull all coom right, whatever it be ——"

"No, no," she wailed. "I wish I could die! ... I wish I could die!"

Lights were twinkling in the village below; and across the valley darkness was draping the hills. The girl lifted her face from her hands, and looked up at him with a scared, bewildered expression.

"I must go home: I must be getting home," she muttered.

"Nay, but there's sommut mighty amiss wi' ye."

"No, it's nothing ... I don't know — I'm not well ... I mean it's nothing ... it'll pass over ... you mustn't think anything of it."

"Nay, but I canna stand by an see ye in sich trouble."

"It's nothing, Mr. Garstin, indeed it's nothing," she repeated.

"Ay, but I canna credit that," he objected stubbornly.

She sent him a shifting, hunted glance.

"Let me get home ... you must let me get home."

She made a tremulous, pitiful attempt at firmness. Eyeing her keenly, he barred her path: she flushed scarlet, and looked hastily away across the valley.

"If ye'll tell me yer distress, mabbe I can help ye."

"No, no, it's nothing ... it's nothing."

"If ye'll tell me yer distress, mabbe I can help ye," he repeated, with a solemn, deliberate sternness. She shivered, and looked away again, vaguely, across the valley.

"You can do nothing: there's nought to be done," she murmured drearily.

"There's a man in this business," he declared.

"Let me go! Let me go!" she pleaded desperately.

"Who is't that's bin puttin' ye into this distress?" His voice sounded loud and harsh.

"No one, no one. I canna tell ye, Mr. Garstin.... It's no one," she protested weakly. The white, twisted look on his face frightened her.

"My God!" he burst out, gripping her wrist, "an' a proper soft fool ye've made o' me. Who is't, I tell ye? Who's t' man?"

"Ye're hurtin' me. Let me go. I canna tell ye."

"And ye're fond o' him?"

"No, no. He's a wicked, sinful man. I pray God I may never set eyes on him again. I told him so."

"But ef he's got ye into trouble, he'll hev t' marry ye," he persisted with a brutal bitterness.

"I will not. I hate him!" she cried fiercely.

"But is he *willin'* t' marry ye?"

"I don't know … I don't care … he said so before he went away … But I'd kill myself sooner than live with him."

He let her hands fall and stepped back from her. She could only see his figure, like a sombre cloud, standing before her. The whole fell-side seemed still and dark and lonely. Presently she heard his voice again:

"I reckon what there's one road oot o' yer distress."

She shook her head drearily. "There's none. I'm a lost woman."

"An' ef ye took me instead?" he said eagerly.

"I — I don't understand ——"

"Ef ye married me instead of Luke Stock?"

"But that's impossible — the — the ——"

"Ay, t' child. I know. But I'll tak t' child as mine."

She remained silent. After a moment he heard her voice answer in a queer, distant tone:

"You mean that — that ye're ready to marry me, and adopt the child?"

"I do," he answered doggedly.

"But people — your mother ——?"

"Folks 'ull jest know nought about it. It's none o' their business. T' child 'ull pass as mine. Ye'll accept that?"

"Yes," she answered, in a low, rapid voice.

"Ye'll consent t' hev me, ef I git ye oot o' yer trouble?"

"Yes," she repeated, in the same tone.

She heard him draw a long breath.

"I said 't was a turn o' Providence, meetin' wi' ye oop here," he exclaimed, with half-suppressed exultation.

Her teeth began to chatter a little: she felt that he was peering at her, curiously, through the darkness.

"An' noo," he continued briskly, "ye'd best be gettin' home. Give me ye're hand, an' I'll stiddy ye ower t' stones."

He helped her down the bank of shingle, exclaiming: "By goom, ye're stony cauld." Once or twice she slipped: he supported her, roughly gripping her knuckles. The stones rolled down the steps, noisily, disappearing into the night.

Presently they struck the turf bridle-path, and, as they descended silently towards the lights of the village, he said gravely:

"I always reckoned what my day 'ud coom."

She made no reply; and he added grimly:

"There'll be terrible work wi' mother over this."

He accompanied her down the narrow lane that led past her uncle's house. When the lighted windows came in sight he halted.

"Goodnight, lassie," he said kindly. "Do ye give ower distressin' yeself."

"Goodnight, Mr. Garstin," she answered, in the same low, rapid voice in which she had given him her answer up on the fell.

"We're man an' wife plighted now, are we not?" he blurted timidly.

She held her face to his, and he kissed her on the cheek, clumsily.

VI

The next morning the frost had set in. The sky was still clear and glittering: the whitened fields sparkled in the chilly sunlight: here and there, on high, distant peaks, gleamed dainty caps of snow. All the week Anthony was to be busy at the fell-foot, wall-building against the coming of the winter storms: the work was heavy, for he was single-handed, and the stone had to be fetched from off the fell-side. Two or three times a day he led his rickety, lumbering cart along the lane that passed the vicarage gate, pausing on each journey to glance furtively up at the windows. But he saw no sign of Rosa Blencarn; and, indeed, he felt no longing to see her: he was grimly exultant over the remembrance of his wooing of her, and over the knowledge that she was his. There glowed within him a stolid pride in himself: he thought of the others who had courted her, and the means by which he had won her seemed to him a fine stroke of cleverness.

And so he refrained from any mention of the matter; relishing, as he worked, all alone, the days through, the consciousness of his secret triumph, and anticipating, with inward chucklings, the discomforted cackle of his mother's female friends. He foresaw, without misgiving, her bitter opposition: he felt himself strong; and his heart warmed towards the girl. And when, at intervals, the brusque realization that, after all, he was to possess her swept over him, he gripped the stones, and swung them almost fiercely into their places.

All around him the white, empty fields seemed slumbering breathlessly. The stillness stiffened the leafless trees. The frosty air flicked his blood: singing vigorously to himself he worked with a stubborn, unflagging resolution, methodically postponing, till the length of the wall should be completed, the announcement of his betrothal.

After his reticent, solitary fashion, he was very happy, reviewing his future prospects, with a plain and steady assurance, and, as the week-end approached, coming to ignore the irregularity of the whole business: almost to assume, in the exaltation of his pride, that he had won her honestly; and to discard, stolidly, all thought of Luke Stock, of his relations with her, of the coming child that was to pass for his own.

And there were moments too, when, as he sauntered homewards through the dusk at the end of his day's work, his heart grew full to overflowing of a rugged, superstitious gratitude towards God in Heaven who had granted his desires.

About three o'clock on the Saturday afternoon he finished the length of wall. He went home, washed, shaved, put on his Sunday coat; and, avoiding the kitchen, where his mother sat knitting by the fireside, strode up to the vicarage.

It was Rosa who opened the door to him. On recognizing him she started, and he followed her into the dining-room. He seated himself, and began, brusquely:

"I've coom, Miss Rosa, t' speak t' Mr. Blencarn."

Then added, eyeing her closely:

"Ye're lookin' sick, lass."

Her faint smile accentuated the worn, white look on her face.

"I reckon ye've been frettin' yeself," he continued gently, "leein' awake o' nights, hev'n't yee, noo?"

She smiled vaguely.

"Well, but ye see I've coom t' settle t' whole business for ye. Ye thought mabbe that I was na a man o' my word."

"No, no, not that," she protested, "but — but ——"

"But what then?"

"Ye must not do it, Mr. Garstin ... I must just bear my own trouble the best I can ——" she broke out.

"D'ye fancy I'm takin' ye oot of charity? Ye little reckon the sort o' stuff my love for ye's made of. Nay, Miss Rosa, but ye canna draw back noo."

"But ye cannot do it, Mr. Garstin. Ye know your mother will na have me at Hootsey.... I could na live there with your mother.... I'd sooner bear my trouble alone, as best I can.... She's that stern is Mrs. Garstin. I couldn't look her in the face.... I can go away somewhere.... I could keep it all from uncle."

Her colour came and went: she stood before him, looking away from him, dully, out of the window.

"I intend ye t' coom t' Hootsey. I'm na lad: I reckon I can choose my own wife. Mother'll hev ye at t' farm, right enough: ye need na distress yeself on that point ——"

"Nay, Mr. Garstin, but indeed she will not, never.... I know she will not.... She always set herself against me, right from the first."

"Ay, but that was different. T' case is all changed noo," he objected doggedly.

"She'll support the sight of me all the less," the girl faltered.

"Mother'll hev ye at Hootsey — receive ye willin' of her own free wish — of her own free wish, d'ye hear? I'll answer for that."

He struck the table with his fist heavily. His tone of determination awed her: she glanced at him hurriedly, struggling with her irresolution.

"I knaw hoo t' manage mother. An' now," he concluded, changing his tone, "is yer uncle about t' place?"

"He's up the paddock, I think," she answered.

"Well, I'll jest step oop and hev a word wi' him."

"Ye're.... ye will na tell him."

"Tut, tut, na harrowin' tales, ye need na fear, lass. I reckon ef I can tackle mother, I can accommodate myself t' parson Blencarn."

He rose, and coming close to her, scanned her face.

"Ye must git t' roses back t' yer cheeks," he exclaimed, with a short laugh, "I canna be takin' a ghost t' church."

She smiled tremulously, and he continued, laying one hand affectionately on her shoulder:

"Nay, but I was but jestin'. Roses or na roses, ye'll be t' bonniest bride in all Coomberland. I'll meet ye in Hullam lane, after church time, tomorrow," he added, moving towards the door.

After he had gone, she hurried to the backdoor furtively. His retreating figure was already mounting the grey upland field. Presently, beyond him, she perceived her uncle, emerging through the paddock gate. She ran across the poultry yard, and mounting a tub, stood watching the two figures as they moved towards one another along the brow, Anthony vigorously trudging, with his hands thrust deep in his pockets; her uncle, his wideawake[30] tilted over his nose, hobbling, and leaning stiffly on his pair of sticks. They met; she saw Anthony take her uncle's arm: the two, turning together, strolled away towards the fell.

She went back into the house. Anthony's dog came towards her, slinking along the passage. She caught the animal's head in her hands, and bent over it caressingly, in an impulsive outburst of almost hysterical affection.

VII

The two men returned towards the vicarage. At the paddock gate they halted, and the old man concluded:

"I could not have wished a better man for her, Anthony. Mabbe the Lord'll not be minded to spare me much longer. After I'm gone Rosa'll hev all I possess.

[30] A wideawake is a soft, wide-brimmed felt hat.

She was my poor brother Isaac's only child. After her mother was taken, he, poor fellow, went altogether to the bad, and until she came here she mostly lived among strangers. It's been a wretched sort of childhood for her — a wretched sort of childhood. Ye'll take care of her, Anthony, will ye not? ... Nay, but I could not hev wished for a better man for her, and there's my hand on 't."

"Thank ee, Mr. Blencarn, thank ee," Anthony answered huskily, gripping the old man's hand.

And he started off down the lane homewards.

His heart was full of a strange, rugged exaltation. He felt with a swelling pride that God had entrusted to him this great charge — to tend her; to make up to her, tenfold, for all that loving care, which, in her childhood, she had never known. And together with a stubborn confidence in himself, there welled up within him a great pity for her — a tender pity, that, chastening with his passion, made her seem to him, as he brooded over that lonely childhood of hers, the more distinctly beautiful, the more profoundly precious. He pictured to himself, tremulously, almost incredulously, their married life — in the winter, his return home at nightfall to find her awaiting him with a glad, trustful smile; their evenings, passed together, sitting in silent happiness over the smouldering logs; or, in summer-time, the mid-day rest in the hay-fields when, wearing perhaps a large-brimmed hat fastened with a red ribbon, beneath her chin, he would catch sight of her, carrying his dinner, coming across the upland.

She had not been brought up to be a farmer's wife: she was but a child still, as the old parson had said. She should not have to work as other men's wives worked: she should dress like a lady, and on Sundays, in church, wear fine bonnets, and remain, as she had always been, the belle of all the parish.

And, meanwhile, he would farm as he had never farmed before, watching his opportunities, driving cunning bargains, spending nothing on himself, hoarding every penny that she might have what she wanted.... And, as he strode through the village, he seemed to foresee a general brightening of prospects, a sobering of the fever of speculation in sheep, a cessation of the insensate glutting, year after year, of the great winter marts throughout the North, a slackening of the foreign competition followed by a steady revival of the price of fatted stocks — a period of prosperity in store for the farmer at last.... And the future years appeared to open out before him, spread like a distant, glittering plain, across which, he and she, hand in hand, were called to travel together....

And then, suddenly, as his iron-bound boots clattered over the cobbled yard, he remembered, with brutal determination, his mother, and the stormy struggle that awaited him.

He waited till supper was over, till his mother had moved from the table to her place by the chimney corner. For several minutes he remained debating with himself the best method of breaking the news to her. Of a sudden he glanced up at her: her knitting had slipped onto her lap: she was sitting, bunched of a heap in her chair, nodding with sleep. By the flickering light of the wood fire, she looked worn and broken: he felt a twinge of clumsy compunction. And then he remembered the piteous, hunted look in the girl's eyes, and the old man's words when they had parted at the paddock gate, and he blurted out:

"I doot but what I'll hev t' marry Rosa Blencarn after all."

She started, and blinking her eyes, said:

"I was jest takin' a wink o' sleep. What was 't ye were saying, Tony?"

He hesitated a moment, puckering his forehead into coarse rugged lines, and fidgeting noisily with his tea-cup. Presently he repeated:

"I doot but what I'll hev t' marry Rosa Blencarn after all."

She rose stiffly, and stepping down from the hearth, came towards him.

"Mabbe I did na hear ye aright, Tony." She spoke hurriedly, and though she was quite close to him, steadying herself with one hand clutching the back of his chair, her voice sounded weak, distant almost.

"Look oop at me. Look oop into my face," she commanded fiercely.

He obeyed sullenly.

"Noo oot wi 't. What's yer meanin', Tony?"

"I mean what I say," he retorted doggedly, averting his gaze.

"What d'ye mean by sayin' that ye've *got* t' marry her?"

"I tell yer I mean what I say," he repeated dully.

"Ye mean ye've bin an' put t' girl in trouble?"

He said nothing; but sat staring stupidly at the floor.

"Look oop at me, and answer," she commanded, gripping his shoulder and shaking him.

He raised his face slowly, and met her glance.

"Ay, that's aboot it," he answered.

"This'll na be truth. It'll be jest a piece o' wanton trickery!" she cried.

"Nay, but 't is truth," he answered deliberately.

"Ye will na swear t' it?" she persisted.

"I see na necessity for swearin'."

"Then ye canna swear t' it," she burst out triumphantly.

He paused an instant; then said quietly:

"Ay, but I'll swear t' it easy enough. Fetch t' Book."

She lifted the heavy, tattered Bible from the chimney-piece, and placed it before him on the table. He laid his lumpish fist on it.

"Say," she continued with a tense tremulousness, "say, I swear t' ye, mother, that 't is t' truth, t' whole truth, and noat but t' truth, s'help me God."

"I swear t' ye, mother, it's truth, t' whole truth, and nothin' but t' truth, s'help me God," he repeated after her.

"Kiss t' Book," she ordered.

He lifted the Bible to his lips. As he replaced it on the table, he burst out into a short laugh:

"Be ye satisfied noo?"

She went back to the chimney corner without a word. The logs on the hearth hissed and crackled. Outside, amid the blackness the wind was rising, hooting through the firs, and past the windows.

After a long while he roused himself, and drawing his pipe from his pocket almost steadily, proceeded leisurely to pare in the palm of his hand a lump of black tobacco.

"We'll be asked in church Sunday," he remarked bluntly.

She made no answer.

He looked across at her.

Her mouth was drawn tight at the corners: her face wore a queer, rigid aspect. She looked, he thought, like a figure of stone.

"Ye're not feeling poorly, are ye, mother?" he asked.

She shook her head grimly: then, hobbling out into the room, began to speak in a shrill, tuneless voice.

"Ye talked at one time o' takin' a farm over Scarsdale way. But ye'd best stop here. I'll no hinder ye. Ye can have t' large bedroom in t' front, and I'll move ower to what used to be my brother Jake's room. Ye knaw I've never had no opinion of t' girl, but I'll do what's right by her, ef I break my sperrit in t' doin' on't. I'll mak' t' girl welcome here: I'll stand by her proper-like: mebbe I'll finish by findin' soom good in her. But from this day forward, Tony, ye're na son o' mine. Ye've dishonoured yeself: ye've laid a trap for me — ay, laid a trap, that's t' word. Ye've brought shame and bitterness on yer ould mother in her ould age. Ye've made me despise t' varra seet o' ye. Ye can stop on here, but ye shall niver touch a penny of my money; every shillin' of 't shall go t' yer child, or to your child's children. Ay," she went on, raising her voice, "ay, ye've got yer way at last, and mebbe ye reckon ye've chosen a mighty smart way. But time 'ull coom when ye'll regret this day, when ye eat oot yer repentance in doost an' ashes. Ay, Lord 'ull punish ye, Tony, chastise ye properly. Ye'll learn that marriage begun in sin can end in nought but sin. Ay," she concluded, as she reached the door, raising her skinny hand prophetically, "ay, after I'm deed and gone, ye mind ye o' t' words o' t' apostle — 'For them that hev sinned without t' law, shall also perish without t' law.'"[31]

And she slammed the door behind her.

---

[31] 'For as many as have sinned without law shall also perish without law' (Romans 2. 12). The story draws on the Bible, mainly the Old Testament, in the representation of a cruel and vengeful God.

Trevor Perkins
A Platonic Episode

Trevor Perkins, when he had hung up his hat, sat down, adjusted his spectacles, and ran his fingers through his lanky hair. The long, low room presented an ill-scoured and impoverished aspect. It was almost deserted: a woman in a gaudy bonnet, poring over a half-penny newspaper, sat absently munching thick slices of bread-and-butter; at the far end two elderly gentlemen in shabby tall hats clicked their dominoes over the marble-topped table. The atmosphere was heavy with the scent of stale food, and the waitresses — three anæmic young women, wearing white caps and black, close-fitting dresses — stood stationed in weary, listless attitudes. From outside, through the half-opened door, drifted the rumble of the Strand and the shuffle of hurrying feet; and behind the blurred glass of the shop-window flitted the ceaseless passage of dim silhouettes.

"Good afternoon, Mr. Perkins. You're quite a stranger," the waitress began, standing before him and leaning in a vaguely coquettish attitude, her knuckles on the greasy, marble-topped table.

"Yes, I've been troubled all the spring with a disagreeable cough," the young man answered.

His voice was precise and without tone. His head was wide and overgrown; he sat in a limp, ungraceful attitude; his shoulders were narrow and sloping; his whole frame meagre, almost puny. He fingered his scraggy, immature moustache, and his face, behind the gold-rimmed spectacles, wore the pale placidity of a thoughtful mind.

"Most likely it'll be on account of this funny, changeable weather we've been having. It's more seasonable today though, isn't it? You're not looking very flash," she added. "Tea and tea-cake, I suppose?"

"Yes, if you please, and I think I could fancy an egg."

"I'll pick you out a nice one," said the girl as she turned away.

For a moment he let his eyes follow her retreating figure, then once more ran his fingers slowly through his lanky hair.

Presently, drawing a book from his pocket, he opened it before him and began to read.

"When a man does some violence to his own nature in adhering to the parent bulk; when its character and aspirations are not repeated in him; when his duty to himself runs counter to his outward obligations; when the component parts of the State, its institutions, must have mainstays passed round them to hold them together; when the family is no longer the State in miniature, and woman demurs to what is expected of her; when the populace breaks over its natural barriers; when the faculty of building ceases; when the Ideal and the Practical seem mutually antagonistic, and the youth must crush his genius into cleverness if he will catch on as a citizen — then of that State it may be said that its day, as a State, is over; that nature is no longer in it; and that endless disintegration is its portion ——"[1]

The girl, clattering her tray onto the table, interrupted him; he looked up at her with an impatient gesture; then, while she arranged the tea-things before him, turned again to his book. When he ceased reading, she had moved away.

The words, "When a man does some violence to his own nature in adhering to the parent bulk ... when his duty to himself runs counter to his outward obligations," sang in his ears as he stirred his tea. And, pondering on the significance of his past life, he seemed to realize the profundity of the phrase.

Yes, the curse of decadence lay over the land. The ancient idols had been cast down in the market-place. A new generation had arisen; a generation old before its time — "Venue trop tard dans un siècle trop vieux," as the French poet had sung;[2] a generation doomed to the irreparable loss of the happy illusions of youth; a generation incapable of faith, groaning beneath an accumulation of precocious experience, eternally haunted by the hideous habit of introspection.

Yes, and in his own case how true it all was! As he finished his egg all his boyhood came back to him: the lengthy, dreary Sunday morning hours spent beside his father and mother in that bare Baptist chapel off the Pentonville Road;[3] the attitude of bawling familiarity, half cringing, half patronizing,

---

[1] 'When a man [...] disintegration is its portion': transcribed, verbatim, from 'Vox Clamantis', in *Two Essays on The Remnant*, 2nd edn (Dublin: Whaley, 1895), pp. 16–17, a compact volume Trevor could have drawn easily 'from his pocket' (*Last Studies*, p. 73). The author is the Irish writer, librarian and editor 'John Eglinton' (William Kirkpatrick Magee, 1868–1961). Yeats described Eglington's *The Remnant* as 'a passionate and lofty appeal to the "idealists" to come out of the modern world as the children of Egypt came out of Egypt' (quoted in W. B. Yeats, *Memoirs*, ed. by Denis Donoghue (Basingstoke: Macmillan, 1972; 1988), p. 149 n. 1). Remnants were 'aristocrats whether of blood, or intellect or by ordeal', suggests Ian Fletcher, whose 'real power is to come' (*W. B. Yeats and his Contemporaries* (Brighton: Harvester Press, 1987), p. 117). Eglinton also appears in the 'Scylla and Charybdis' episode of James Joyce's *Ulysses* (1922) as the National Library of Ireland librarian that he was in real life.
[2] From 'Rolla' by the French Romantic poet Alfred de Musset (1810–1857) in *Poésies Complètes De Alfred Musset* (Paris: Charpentier, 1844), pp. 295–331. The fuller quotation is: 'Je ne crois pas, ô Christ! à ta parole sainte; | Je suis venu trop tard dans un monde trop vieux; | D'un siècle sans espoir naît un siècle sans crainte; | Les comètes du notre ont dépeuplé les cieux' (lines 54–57): 'I do not believe, oh Christ, in your holy word: | I was born too late into a world too old. | From a century without hope is born a century without fear. | Our own comets have depopulated the heavens'.
[3] Pentonville Road: a road opened in London in 1756 for transporting livestock on its way to Smithfield. Since then it developed as a residential area full of shops and lodging houses,

adopted by the minister towards the Deity; his own first boyish, timorous doubtings, resolving themselves later into long, secret searchings of heart; then the stern resolve to learn, to judge things for himself; the nights spent in sifting the truth, absorbed in Voltaire, Rousseau, and Herbert Spencer;[4] and finally, that eventful morning of his great revolt — his dramatic refusal to accompany his father to chapel, his defiant proclamation of his intellectual emancipation.... He recalled all the details of the crisis with a mild and complacent pride.

And yet — and yet, he mused bitterly, of what avail had these things proved? To the sensitive the fruit of the tree of knowledge tasted bitter as Dead Sea fruit[5] — that was the inexorable law. He finished his tea thoughtfully, and reminded himself how he had elected to live his own life — apart, shrinking instinctively from the heedless and facile animality of his fellow-salesmen, acquiescing in their disdain of him, effacing himself during shop-hours, and allowing those of coarser fibre to oust him from promotion, to push their way past him, up into the superior departments. Upon none of these things, he told himself, had he set his heart: he had preferred to stand aside calmly while the others jostled past him in their senseless race for worldly success, jealously preserving his pride in himself, and in the evenings, in the cheerless solitude of his bedroom, awakening to a pent-up consciousness of the play of his own personality.

Thus he had passed through many phases. Thus, in his way, he had become a dilettante, cultivating with no slight care that "state of mind at once very intelligent and very voluptuous which inclines us towards diverse forms of life, and leads us to lend ourselves to each one of these in turn, without giving ourselves up to any one of them."[6]

He had studied Shakespeare diligently, and to elevate his conception of life, had committed to memory the more philosophical passages. He had read *Wilhelm Meister* from beginning to end; he worshipped Goethe vaguely as the highest human type.[7] Ruskin had been to him a revelation from which

with a very poor and dense population.

[4] 'Voltaire, Rousseau, and Herbert Spencer': François-Marie Arouet Voltaire (1694–1778), Jean-Jacques Rousseau (1712–1778), and Herbert Spencer (1820–1903), highly influential anti-clerical or materialist thinkers, spanning the Enlightenment and the mid-late Victorian age.

[5] Dead Sea fruit: something that appears full of promise but offers only disappointment.

[6] The source of this quotation is Paul Bourget's essay on Ernest Renan (Section II: 'Du Dilettantisme') in his *Essais de Psychologie Contemporaine*, 3rd edn (Paris: Alphonse Lemerre, 1885): 'une disposition de l'esprit, très intelligente à la fois et très voluptueuse, qui nous incline tour à tour ver les formes diverses de la vie et nous conduit à nous prêter à toutes ces formes sans nous donner à aucune' (p. 59).

[7] *Wilhelm Meister's Apprenticeship* (*Wilhelm Meisters Lehrjahre*) (1795–1796), the founding text of the *Bildungsroman*, by Johann Wolfgang von Goethe (1749–1832), poet, critic, statesman, generally regarded as the most significant figure in German literary history. His other classic work is the highly influential, early Romantic *Die Leiden des jungen Werthers* (*The Sorrows of Young Werther*) (1774).

he had never altogether recovered, though latterly the theory of "Art for Art's sake" had, upon consideration, seemed to him curiously alluring.[8] He judged Carlyle to be a man of genius,[9] and Byron to be a great poet,[10] and he was wont to pride himself upon the modernity of his contempt for the vulgar works of Charles Dickens.[11] He possessed two volumes of the suppressed English translation of M. Zola's works:[12] he believed Paris to be an immoral city. He considered himself to be a passionate lover of books, like Charles Lamb[13] or the late Lord Macaulay;[14] he read with avidity the strenuous productions of certain contemporary novelists and the literary page of the *Daily Chronicle*.[15] He kept

[8] John Ruskin (1819–1900), the leading art critic of the Victorian period, had reacted violently against the American impressionist painter James Whistler (1834–1903) and his painting 'Nocturne in Black and Gold: The Falling Rocket' (shown in the Grosvenor Gallery, London, in 1877), accusing him of 'flinging a pot of paint in the public's face'. Whistler sued Ruskin for libel; a famous court case at the Old Bailey resulted, splitting the art world, and Whistler was awarded a farthing in damages. Whistler's innovative, impressionist painting challenged Ruskin's belief that art should have some moral or didactic purpose.

[9] Thomas Carlyle (1795–1881), Scottish historian and essayist, whose major works include *The French Revolution* (1837) and *On Heroes, Hero-Worship, and the Heroic in History* (1841). Trevor is here more in tune with the wider reading public than with contemporary critical opinion: 'Crowds of Carlyle devotees', wrote J. M. Barrie, 'came to inspect the birthplace in Ecclefechan'; his home in Cheyne Walk, Chelsea was 'bought by public subscription in 1895' (Philip Waller, *Writers, Readers and Reputations: Literary Life in Britain 1870–1918* (Oxford: Oxford University Press, 2006), pp. 379, 379 n. 77). But the critic George Saintsbury observed in 1893 that 'ardent admiration' for Carlyle indicated 'a man's having reached the fogey, and of his approaching the fossil stage of intellectual existence'. Quoted in Peter Keating, *The Haunted Study: A Social History of the English Novel 1875–1914* (London: Secker and Warburg, 1989), p. 146.

[10] George Gordon Byron, sixth Baron Byron (1788–1824), Romantic poet and satirist whose poetry and personality captured the imagination of Europe but whose scandalous reputation lowered him in the eyes of Victorian critics; he was the subject of an influential article, destructive of his reputation (*Fraser's Magazine*, 2.1 (March 1830), 129–43). Trevor's view of Byron is thus notably modern and not at all Victorian.

[11] The vulgar works of Charles Dickens: Trevor's assessment chimes with the decline, during the decades following his death in 1870, of Dickens's reputation as a novelist among literary critics, if not the wider reading public. 'If literary fame could be safely measured by popularity with the half-educated', Leslie Stephen wrote, sniffily, in his *DNB* entry of 1888, 'Dickens must claim the highest position among English novelists' (*Charles Dickens: The Critical Heritage*, ed. by Philip Collins (London: Routledge, 1970), p. 17).

[12] These could be any two from *La Terre*, *Nana*, or *Pot-Bouille*, novels singled out in the controversial prosecution of the publisher Henry Vizetelly for 'obscene libel' in 1888.

[13] Charles Lamb (1775–1834), English poet, essayist, and critic, best known for his *Essays of Elia* (1823–1833) and, with his sister Mary, *Tales from Shakespeare* (1807), a re-telling of the plays for children. The Lambs' *Poetry for Children* had been re-issued in 1892.

[14] Thomas Babington Macaulay (1800–1859), English Whig politician, essayist, poet, and historian, best known for his *History of England* (1849–1861), which secured his status as one of the originators of the Whig interpretation of history.

[15] Arguably a mark of Trevor's good judgement, since the *Daily Chronicle*, under its literary editor, H. W. Massingham (succeeded by Henry Norman in 1895), was earning plaudits for the best literary coverage by any national daily paper of the 1890s. That 'wonderful

a psychological diary — an elaborate record of his thoughts and sensations — and once upon a time he had written an essay upon "Life's Ultimate Aim," which had been accepted, but never published, by a weekly journal of advanced thought.

He was alone in the world. He had discovered that for his parents he had no genuine affection, and this discovery he was wont to deplore, upbraiding himself weakly that he could not overlook the crude bigotry of their point of view. He had no real friends: he had found no one to whom he could unbosom his intimate thoughts. So, though outwardly he appeared to mix with the world, to assume an indifferent acquiescence in its ways, inwardly he lived the life of a recluse, communing in solitude with himself alone. Instinctively he shrank from the coarse contact of men — from their blatant glorification of their animal instincts, — and there were moments when his soul yearned vaguely for the subtle companionship of a woman's delicate mind.

Not that, in his time, he had not experienced the whole gamut of love. Five years ago, on the very threshold of life, he had given his heart to a woman, and during three weeks he had lived, as it seemed to him now, through all the wonderful and tormenting ecstasy of love. He had made himself her slave: he had worshipped the ground on which she trod; and then, one day she had ignobly betrayed him. He had traversed all the heights and depths of human passion, and he had suffered as only the sensitive know how to suffer. For five years had this dearly bought knowledge of the perfidy of woman and the haunting consciousness of his own disillusionment restrained him from further amorous experience. All the confident spontaneity of his youth was turned to bitterness and gall: he had grown cynical and pessimistic, he looked upon his faith in human nature as irrevocably shattered.

But latterly, an indefinable disquietude, a strange and morbid dissatisfaction, seemed to have taken possession of his being, and finally, one evening, after reading an English translation of one of M. Bourget's novels[16] he had felt

literary page', wrote Massingham's obituarist, H. N. Brailsford, in 1924, was 'a vehicle for every group of thinkers and artists which was struggling to escape from the prison house of Victorian convention [...] I should doubt if any force approached [the *Chronicle*] as a formative influence for those who were in their twenties towards the end of the last century' (H. N. Brailsford, 'A Great Journalist: Mr. Massingham's Work', *The New Leader* (5 September 1924), p. 10, cols 1–3 (cols 1–2)). See Alfred F. Havighurst, *Radical Journalist: H. W. Massingham (1860–1924)* (Cambridge: Cambridge University Press, 1974), p. 60. This verdict on the influence of the *Daily Chronicle* might also apply to Crackanthorpe, three years Brailsford's senior.

[16] Possibly *Un Crime d'Amour* (1886), translated as *A Love Crime*. Henry Vizetelly's translation of the novel helped to bring about the charge of 'obscene libel' for which he was fined and later imprisoned for three months in 1889. Paul Bourget (1854–1933) was a well-regarded novelist, a friend of Henry James's, and the part subject of Crackanthorpe's own posthumously published essay 'Notes for a Paper on Barrès and Bourget', *To-Morrow*, 3 (1897), 83–92. *To-Morrow* was edited by J. T. Grein, the innovative theatre manager, well known to the Crackanthorpes.

this wistful conviction steal over him — that where his fellow-men failed to comprehend his secluded attitude, a woman might succeed; and that a woman might appreciate him for that very sensitivity of his which was so apt to excite the coarser sex to active hostility; and that perhaps, after all, Life was more important than Literature, and that an assiduous cultivation of self, by means of a cunning management of experience, represented the last word of a *fin-de-siècle* philosophy.

The two elderly gentlemen adjusted their shabby tall hats and prepared to relinquish their dominoes. The woman in the gaudy bonnet was gone. Trevor Perkins roused himself from his reverie, and, glancing round the room, caught the eye of the waitress. She smiled responsively and came towards him.

Her name was Emily Hammond, and she lived with her married sister, whose husband kept a tobacconist's shop off the Euston Road. She had confided to him that she was not happy at home, and from time to time (he had frequented the shop for more than a year) he had talked to her of his loneliness, hinted at the great grief of his early boyhood, and explained something of the bitterness of his disillusionment. She had not altogether comprehended his meaning, but she would listen to him with a sympathetic attention that seemed to him, when he reflected on it, almost pathetic; and he found that their talks together stimulated him to a keener realization of himself.

So, one Easter Monday afternoon, he had taken her to Olympia,[17] and afterwards, at tea on the Rialto (the entertainment consisted of a representation of Venice in London),[18] he had talked to her of the Renaissance — of that wonderful revival of learning in Italy after the darkness of the Middle Ages[19] — and when he had finished she had told him shyly how his cleverness

---

[17]   The Olympia, Hammersmith Road, west London, opened in 1884 as the National Agricultural Hall, then changed to Olympia in 1886 'when it staged its first circus, the Paris Hippodrome, which included 400 animals, a chariot race and a stag hunt'; thereafter it staged 'spectacular shows which combined education with entertainment' (*The London Encyclopaedia*, ed. by Ben Weinreb and others, 3rd edn (London: Macmillan, 2008), p. 603). In the twentieth century, in enlarged premises, it was notable for hosting the *Daily Mail Ideal Home Exhibition* and *Cruft's Dog Show*.

[18]   Trevor and Emily's refreshments were probably taken courtesy of Joseph 'Joe' Lyons (the founder of 'Lyons Corner Houses'), who had won the concession for supplying food and drink for Olympia's 'Venice in London' spectacle which ran for thirteen months from 26 December 1891. The recreation of Venice (for up to 8000 spectators) 'featured streets of ancient houses [...] canals, a hundred Venetian Gondoliers and thirty imported gondalas [...] the twice-daily show ending in a ballet of a thousand dancers' (John Glanfield, *Earls Court and Olympia: From Buffalo Bill to The 'Brits'* (Stroud: Sutton Publishing, 2003), pp. 35–36).

[19]   The re-discovery of the art and culture of the Renaissance in the late nineteenth century articulated a reaction in the arts to Victorian medievalism, led by Walter Pater's seminal *Studies in the History of the Renaissance* (1873), in which he located and upheld 'the care for physical beauty, the worship of the body, the breaking down of those limits which the religious system of the middle age imposed on the heart and the imagination' ('Preface' to *Studies in the History of the Renaissance*, ed. by Beaumont, p. 5).

intimidated her. Then, in a moment of weakness he had fondly dreamed that her simple, unaffected companionship might have proved a solace to him, and that together they might have achieved that most perfect of human relationships — real friendship between man and woman. But before long he had discovered that she was in the habit of frequenting the minor music-halls with a cousin of hers, a gaudy youth from the City;[20] and remembering his own sensitivity, he had cynically set to work to shatter this, perhaps the last of his illusions. With that quick pride that was characteristic of him he had let his intimacy with her brusquely lapse. Yet even so he did not escape certain pangs of remorse: he was afraid that she would not have appreciated his motives, and that she might have misconstrued his behaviour. Their first meeting just now had perhaps been somewhat strained: as she came up to the table he felt prompted to reassure her, to convey to her that he bore her no ill-will.

"Well, Miss Hammond, and what have you been doing with yourself?" he began, with a forced jauntiness.

"Oh, nothing wonderful! Just jogging along — same song, same tune."

"Do you know, I've been intending to come round to look you up for ever so long?"

He looked up at her quickly: he fancied he detected a note of resentment in her voice, and he added hastily

"I suppose you thought I'd forgotten all about you?"

"Perhaps I didn't think anything at all about it."

He smiled indulgently.

"Come, don't be angry," he continued.

"Angry! I'm sure I don't know what you mean."

"But you're offended with me, I can see."

"What a funny man you are, to be sure, Mr. Perkins!" she retorted.

He felt reassured: they were friends again once more. "Don't go," he went on insinuatingly; "I want to ask you something."

She paused, leaning her wrists on the table: her lips were expectantly parted.

"Will you come out with me on Sunday evening?" he asked, lowering his voice.

He expected a coquettish refusal. But she answered simply —

"Certainly, Mr. Perkins."

"Shall we meet, then, at Hyde Park Corner at half-past eight?"

"I shall be very pleased," she answered in the same tone.

"And you don't think too badly of me?"

"But really, Mr. Perkins, I don't think badly of you at all. I'm sure I don't know where you get these funny ideas from."

"I want you to think well of me," he murmured.

---

[20] See note 2 on p. 147.

She glanced nervously over her shoulder. Behind her an elderly gentleman was impatiently rapping his plate. She moved away, smiling in mock ruefulness.

He lingered for some minutes, affectionately watching her as she flitted to and fro about the room. Once or twice she smiled back at him sympathetically. And when at length he rose to go, her eyes sparkled upon him with simple, unfeigned pleasure.

He mounted an omnibus, and as the vehicle rumbled on towards Charing Cross, he felt his heart respond in vague exhilaration to all the murky, golden splendour of the glamorous London night.

II

They met, greeted each other simply, and turned silently into the Park. Overhead a dark, romantic sky quivered with a myriad glittering stars — an infinity of distant worlds, dimly winking through measureless miles of space.

"What a nice warm evening! It's quite summery," she murmured.

He made no answer, but pressing her arm, drew it gently beneath his own.

They crossed the road, and as they turned down the long avenue, beneath the spreading branches of the great elms, the moon appeared, a monstrous disc of glistening silver, slowly climbing the sky, to preside, as it were, over all the Park. A subdued rumour[21] of decorous footfalls waited on the still night air; down the stately avenue and beneath the ancient trees the vague silhouettes of countless couples were flitting through the pale moonlight.

"Dear Miss Hammond!" he whispered, bending his face to hers.

"Oh, Mr. Perkins, don't be unkind!" she answered, gently rebuffing him.

"Unkind? But how am I unkind?"

"Don't be unkind," she repeated vaguely.

Disconcerted, he looked away from her, and they resumed their walk.

He gazed up at the stars, and tried to lose himself in the wondrous immensity of the firmament, to comprehend the infinite insignificance of human life. And, as his eyes travelled over the great glittering assemblage, he recalled, with a dreamy wonder, the vast range of human aspiration, the persistent progress of scientific achievement, the unflagging effort of each successive generation. And presently an overwhelming sense of the grotesque futility of it all oppressed him. He thought of himself — of his lonely life, of his unsatisfied melancholy, of the bitterness of his experience, of that welling spring of happiness which had been irreparably poisoned. He looked at the girl by his side: their eyes met: her lips parted in a faint, tremulous smile. Ah! *she* was happy: *she* could not understand this haunting sense of the pitiful hollowness of things!

How fresh and sweet and simple she looked in the pale moonlight! Could he not, during one short, mad hour, escape from himself?

[21] See note 11 on p. 277.

"Are you not getting tired, Miss Hammond?" he asked gently.

"Well, I do think we might rest a bit," she answered.

They walked on, looking about them, for most of the benches seemed already occupied. At last they discovered one that was half empty. A couple — the man was a soldier — was in possession of the one corner; Trevor and Emily sat down on the other.

All the Park seemed alive with lovers, sauntering in silent embrace beneath the gleaming, full-faced moon. The heavy breath of human love seemed to float through the warm, still, night air; and now and then from out the distant darkness there sounded a woman's strident laugh.

"Emily!" he murmured, drawing her towards him.

"Mr. Perkins!" she whispered softly in reply.

"Look up at the stars," he continued.

"Yes, isn't it a fine night?"

"How wonderful to think that they are all different worlds, millions and millions of miles away!"

"Do you think they can see us?" she asked.

"I dare say. Who knows?" he answered dreamily.

"What a spoony[22] lot they must think us!"

He joined in her laugh uneasily. Her remark jarred vaguely upon his sensitivity. And parenthetically he deplored his own fastidious and exacting taste.

They relapsed into silence, while she nestled towards him shyly. He kissed her on the forehead; she made no resistance, but began —

"You know Lottie Blandford, that tall scarecrow of a girl — you know, what serves in the front at our place. She's awfully jealous of me and you. When you were talking to me the other day in the shop, didn't you notice how she kept edging and trying to catch what you were saying? She's a real mean, spiteful thing — that's what she is. And the other evening I could stand her nasty prying ways no longer, and I says to her straight out ..."

He let her prattle on, while his thoughts drifted towards profounder things.... She looked up to him: she believed in him; she cared for him after her guileless, untutored fashion. By a dozen touchingly feminine movements she had betrayed herself.... Was there, then, no response that he could make? Must he let her suffer — suffer as he had suffered? ... Could he not rather watch over and preserve intact those bright, girlish illusions of hers concerning him? ... Could he not be kind — yes, infinitely kind: her simple little heart would, he divined, demand but little else.... Could he not sacrifice himself, mask all the bitterness of his cynicism — the tragic aridity of his heart? Would not that, after all, prove a finely modern part?

[22] Spoony means sentimentally amorous.

"Emily," he murmured, drawing her face to his, "dear little Emily."

She laughed — a low, rippling laugh.

"Oh, Mr. Perkins, what a way you have, to be sure!"

"You're no longer cross with me? You don't think badly of me?"

"I sha'n't tell you what I think of you. It might make you think too much of yourself," she answered coquettishly.

"You don't know how lonely, how isolated my life is, Emily."

"Well, I have noticed you seem sort of sad-like and dreadful down on your luck. I don't see why you should be, though. You've a nice position."

"I can't explain to you now, Emily. Some day, perhaps, you'll understand."

"I believe it's reading too many books. I knew a girl who went just the same way. I never could see the sense of all this book-reading myself."

He laughed gently, assuring himself that such artlessness was quaintly charming.

"Never mind, Emily; you must be patient and bear with me. You will, won't you, Emily, darling?"

She paused, then asked gravely —

"What's up now?"

"If only I had a real friend," he went on dreamily; "an honest, loyal little friend — a friend like you, Emily — a friend who would be patient and bear with me."

"You talk that vague-like, Mr. Perkins, I don't know exactly what to say. I'm sure we're chummy enough."

"Call me Trevor," he whispered.

"I'm a funny sort of a girl," she continued, "but I do like to know where I am with folks. I've kept company before, you know, and I like folks to mean what they say."

"And you don't believe in me — in my sincerity?" he asked bitterly.

"Oh, you're too deep for me, Mr. Perkins," she answered shortly.

"You're not going to quarrel with me, Emily?" he expostulated.

"Oh, Lord! I'm sure I can't see anything to quarrel about. You do jump at things so, Mr. Perkins."

"Then you don't think badly of me after all?"

"You are a rum sort and no mistake," she concluded.

He looked down at her. The moonlight was playing on her face: her skin, he thought, looked white as driven snow, and, all at once, he felt his whole being throb with a mad, passionate yearning. The whole world, so he fancied, swam before his eyes: he took her into his arms, and he kissed her with a fierce and feverish desperation. Yet, even in this wild moment of ecstasy, he retained a vivid consciousness of the relativeness of things, and more than ever he realized the profundity of his disillusionment.

"Oh! Trevor dear," she expostulated softly, "I am so happy!"

"Are you, darling?" he answered, with a vague uneasiness.

Then, bending over her, he kissed her again.

"You are a spoony man," she exclaimed with a brusque laugh.

Yet, after all, he debated with himself, why should he tell her that he had no heart to give her? Why should he spoil this short moment of her delight? Why should he not play his part to the end with a desperate and cynical recklessness? … And yet — and yet, as the thought formulated itself he felt his better self rise in revolt. She trusted him … she loved him, perhaps…. And once more the temptation returned.

This time he faced it without flinching. He felt her warm, soft hand steal its way into his, and, with a supreme effort, he determined to be true to his better self.

He became conscious of the return of his self-possession. And all at once he felt strangely cool — master of himself: he realized that he had definitely reconquered his personality.

He seemed to see the vast obscurity of the Park, peopled with a multitude of wandering lovers, and there welled up in his heart that great compassion for the helplessness of humanity of which he had read in books. He understood all the pitifulness of human love, its crude, primitive basis, the curiously blinding glamour of its endless elaboration.

Her head rested on his shoulder, and her hat, pushed all awry, shaded her face from the white light of the moon. Her eyes were closed, her lips listlessly parted, and her plump, girlish frame throbbed in silence with all the tremulous rhythm of her hurried breath. He watched her, and there stole over him a certain subtle pride in his own power of tranquil self-detachment. And because of this self-satisfaction of his he pitied her vaguely, for the helplessness of her emotion and for the unconsciousness of his own attitude towards her. And, letting his thoughts drift onwards, he brooded aimlessly on the whole fragility of woman.

Yet, a moment later, he heard himself saying to her, with supreme inconsequence —

"Dearest Emily, you do care for me a little?"

She nodded mutely — gave him a long, slow look; then closed her eyes again wearily.

"My own dear little Emily," he went on, tenderly.

"Dear Mr. Perkins, you don't mean that?" she murmured.

"Of course I do. You are the whole world to me," he protested hastily.

For a long while they remained locked in silent embrace. By and by the soldier and the woman at the other end of the bench, rising to go, roused them.

"We must be thinking of moving," he said abruptly.

"Oh, no! Not yet. It's so jolly here!" she answered.

He acquiesced with a strange, sudden impatience, and started to wonder, after his old cynical fashion, how it would all end for him....

The faint notes of a distant clock tower floated through the still, warm air....

"I really must be getting home," he began five minutes later.

"Oh, dear, must you really?" she asked reproachfully. "What a fidget you are! Why, it's only ten o'clock."

He put his arm around her, she laid her head on his shoulder, and together they moved away slowly down the stately moonlit avenue.

The Turn of the Wheel

I

The city was disgorging.

All along the Strand, down the great, ebbing tide, the omnibuses, a congested press of gaudy craft, drifting westwards, jostling and jamming their tall, loaded decks, with a clanking of chains, a rumble of lumbering wheels, a thudding of quick-loosed brakes, a humming of hammering hoofs....

The empty hansoms[1] crept silently past: the street-hawkers[2] — a lengthy row of dingy figures — lined the pavement edge: troops of frenzied newsboys darted yelling through the traffic; and, here and there, a sullen-faced woman struggled to stem the tide of men.

Somewhere, behind Pall Mall,[3] unheeded the sun had set: the sky was powdered with dull-crimson dust: one by one the shops gleamed out, blazing their windows of burnished glass: the twilight throbbed with a ceaseless shuffle of hurrying feet; and over all things hovered the spirit of London's grim unrest....[4]

So Eardley Lingard mused; leaning his elbows over the cab-doors, relishing complacently the nimbleness of his fancy, savouring every fragile modulation of the dusky pageantry, sedulously enhancing, with the nicety of a virtuoso, the keenness of his exhilaration.

And presently, he anticipated Hilda's joyful reception of the news, and his own pleasure in confiding it to *her*, the first of all. He visioned her quick flush of pride in him: his thoughts lingered almost boastfully on the distinction of her beauty, on her intellectual promise. And he reminded himself how she was *his* daughter, and in no way her mother's....

Then, his thoughts deflected at random towards the future satisfactions of his new position, its easy, congenial routine, the agreeable leisure it would afford him.... And a sudden pride in himself, in the intensity of his personality, sparkled within him — pride in his tireless, intellectual vitality, which had set him privileged above the crowd; respect, too, for the whole course of his double career, commercial and political, rich in accumulated achievement.

His exhilaration quickened: he felt himself buoyant with elasticity, eager for

---

[1]   See note 7 on p. 84.

[2]   Street-hawkers are street-sellers.

[3]   Pall Mall: 'one of the most famous thoroughfares of London, deriving its present prestige from its club-houses' (Pascoe, *London Of To-Day*, p. 318). Eardley is looking westwards on his cab journey from the Strand, through St. James's, en route to his home in Pimlico (see note 5, below).

[4]   'The city was disgorging [...] the spirit of London's grim unrest': a verbatim importation of Crackanthorpe's 'In The Strand'; see pp. 382–83.

new interests, new possibilities, a new lease of life.

Presently, in St. James's Park, he passed Greaves Chamney, walking homewards. The young man waved his hand with an effusive gesture; Eardley, smiling back benignly, bethought himself to ascertain how things were between him and Hilda. Chamney had a future before him: his face wore the smooth stamp of success. And his admiration for Hilda was undisguised. But she — she, on this point, was still enigmatical, as yet she had given no sign.

* * * * *

When at last he had reached Belgrave Street,[5] and stood beneath the portico fitting the latch-key into the door, he revealed himself a little man, almost insignificant — a white, emphatic forehead; vaguely sunken eyes, alight with a vagrant, incisive flicker; drawn cheeks; a wiry, meagre mouth, well-worn, and hinting at a tale of long effort.

II

It had been his wife's day at home; and all the afternoon, throughout the long succession of callers, filling and refilling the room — the women, over-clothed and glib; the men, correctly affable — the rumour of his appointment had hovered irresolute. She had listened complaisantly to the string of hinted congratulations, weakly, tremulously smiling; but Hilda had met them coldly, with a persistent attitude of tense unconcern, and occasionally, it had seemed, with some show of compressed resentment.

About half-past six the mother and daughter were left alone.

Bessie Lingard remained, staring listlessly before her, her face inertly immobile with fatigue; her gown of dull-green velvet falling to the carpet in clumsy folds; her hair tightly parted and braided behind her head in rigid coils, and one hand hanging limp beside her, the fingers loaded with rings, whose stones sparkled in the firelight…. An indefinite face; just now, despite the mellow lamp-light, appearing jaded by the afternoon's effort, absorbed by a hebetude of over-ripe middle-age, a lax and puffy lethargy.

* * * * *

A footman brought in an evening paper. She unfolded it nervously.

"They say in an article here that Mr. Bulkeley ought to be appointed."

Hilda made no answer, but looked suddenly away from her mother.

"Mr. Bulkeley's worked hard for the party. Perhaps after all he's better claims."

---

[5] Belgrave Street is listed in Baedeker's *London* (1889) in well-to-do Pimlico, now part of Lower Belgrave Street, west of Victoria Station.

Hilda opened a book at random with a quick, exasperated movement.

"You know I'm going to Tukenton tomorrow, Hilda," Mrs. Lingard began after a pause.

"Are you?" her voice was deliberately hard: she did not look up from her book.

"The new conservatory was finished yesterday. I shall be all alone till the end of the week when Lady Whyte comes. I wish you'd come, Hilda. A little country air would do you good. You've no engagements except the Assheton's ball. You could ride Carlo, and have the Machens and Mr. Walsh over for some tennis." She spoke hurriedly, in an eager tone of forced indifference.

"Of course I can't, mother. How absurd you are! You know Mrs. Mathurin has promised to take me." Her head remained buried in her book.

Of a sudden she sprang up.

"There's the hall door. That'll be father."

And she left the room brusquely.

*   *   *   *   *

The sound of voices came up from the hall: Eardley's cheery, spontaneous; Hilda's subdued, earnestly confidential. Then the abrupt closing of a door. They had gone together into the library.

She guessed that it was true. And now, down there, in the library, he was telling it to Hilda....

The sting of thwarted curiosity prompted within her — not of a sudden, but insensibly — a dull resentment, a sense of her own isolation, a vague knowledge that Hilda had altogether supplanted her, driven her into the background, transformed her into a person of no consequence.

But from the discomfort of this assertion of herself she quietly shrank, relapsed into her former passivity, her incurious acceptance of the plain facts of her life, till, presently, that he should have come to tell her the news first, would have seemed irregular, almost perplexing.

The twenty-five years of her married life, whenever she inadvertently surveyed them, seemed to her so entirely usual, and the conclusion that they had achieved so entirely inevitable, that the musing on them brought no keenness of regret, no sentiment of insufficiency. In her own eyes she appeared precisely fitted for the part she had come to play.

Only occasionally did she shrink from the crudity of Hilda's indifference. To the rest she had become numbed — a middle-aged woman, her sentimentality, long untouched, grown musty; prosaicly contented, anticipating little, sluggishly living from day to day.

*   *   *   *   *

She sat on, waiting for Eardley. And her thoughts drifted to Tukenton (where she had lived during the greater part of the year) to certain trivial changes to be made in the garden.

* * * * *

By and by they came in together. Hilda's flushed cheeks betrayed that he had been appointed.

He came forward and took both her hands in his, gravely, affectionately. Hilda, she saw, paused behind him embarrassed.

"I've been telling Hilda the good news. You're glad, too, aren't you, Bessie?"

"Of course I am glad, Eardley, very, very glad. Everyone was saying this afternoon that it ought to be you. But somehow I never believed it could be true."

He let her hands fall, smiling to himself at his own thoughts.

And she caught a quick glimpse of all that this meant to him, of how, for years, his tireless ambition had been straining towards this final achievement; and there came to her out of the past, quite slowly, quite faintly, like the hesitation of a distant rumour,[6] the memory of an evening, years and years ago, when Hilda was a toddling child, when they were poor, and lived in lodgings. He had spoken to her of this jestingly, trying the title on her name. She remembered her word to him just now with a strange impotent yearning to say more, to let him see that she understood, a little.

But Hilda and he were talking together without her.

"What time does it begin?" he was asking.

"It's a splendid position for you, Eardley," she remarked.

He looked across at her, a momentary, scrutinizing glance; but Hilda interrupted —

"It's not till nine, dad."

"Very well, child, order the carriage."

They were accustomed to settle things without her, but she asked shrinkingly —

"You're going out?"

"Yes," he answered lightly, "Hilda is taking me to the play.... By the way, Bessie, are you going to Tukenton tomorrow?"

"Yes, dear. I wrote to Hedges this morning to tell him to meet the 4.45."

He nodded unconcernedly, and went upstairs to dress.

* * * * *

"I knew all along that dad would be appointed. He was the only man

---

6   See note 11 on p. 277.

possible," Hilda remarked triumphantly.

"How did you know?"

"Oh! just instinctively. I was quite certain of it from the first."

"But you never said so."

"No, I never said so."

"I'm afraid Mrs. Bulkeley will be very disappointed."

Hilda tossed her head contemptuously.

"Mr. Bulkeley's simply an ingenious machine. He's no real intellect. Look at all dad's done — the way he's made his career from the first — never asked anything of anyone."

"Yes, dear, I know," the mother assented vaguely.

For a moment Hilda stood considering her abstractedly, toying with some train of thought.

"Dad says that it's not to be mentioned to anyone yet."

"Very well, dear," the other answered meekly. Then added — "It's twenty past seven, Hilda. You'd better go to dress."

The girl went, sauntering deliberately, slightly conscious of her self-possession, rustling with a certain artificial grace her fashionable, elaborately-fitting silk dress.

III

Hilda was three-and-twenty — possessing that cold regularity of feature, which, according to society's facile and conventional standards, passes for beauty; that intelligent superciliousness of demeanour that passes for obvious superiority.

Women acknowledged her handsomeness freely, praising the delicacy of her complexion, the symmetry of her carriage; but her mother perceived that, nevertheless, most men she failed to move. Old Lady Whyte — after her trenchant fashion — declared that the girl obtruded her intellectual superiority without tact; and, moreover, that her persistent insensibility of expression dispelled all feminine charm. And in this summary of the matter her mother had acquiesced limply, with a vague sentiment of helpless, maternal disappointment.

As a child she had promised altogether differently.

For a while, it was as if her physical growth were clumsily draining at her vitality; she was always pale, and often ailing. Later, it was as if her personality were convulsively struggling to assert itself: she became tormented by a morbid scrupulousness, by strange fits of persistent, childish, introspection. And, especially, her attitude towards her mother grew freakish; now petulantly, and at times passionately, insurgent, now marked by outbursts of an overwrought, conscientious docility. She developed, too, a fondness for solitude, wandering alone for hours in the garden at Tukenton, chatting to the flowers, telling herself stories concerning the lives of the insects, the birds, the trees. From companionship with children of her own age she would rebelliously escape.

It was to counteract this phase that she was sent to school.

She came home more reticent in manner, more observant of herself, full of a bookish caprice, an exasperated craving for knowledge, and professing a dogmatic scorn for the amusements of her age. She spent her leisure poring over histories; filling notebooks in her attempts to master subjects, working for her school examinations with a zealous and febrile restlessness. Her devotion to her father expanded suddenly into an intense veneration for his ability; she would listen to him earnestly, question him eagerly, absorbing his words. And he took an open pride in her acuteness of apprehension, in teaching her, in furthering her intellectual development. During the holidays they became close companions. She came to understand him, and he to confide in her. With her mother her manner was inattentive.

So, till she was eighteen, till she "came out," as the phrase goes, till she took her place in the world.

Then, with a rapid transition, she appeared to throw off the last remnants of childishness, and definitely to assume consciousness of her *rôle*.

Now, she dressed elaborately, with a considerable affectation of smartness; cultivated an artificiality of manner, a tone of fashionable frivolity, contrasted with a deliberate, cynical attitude of worldliness, and a habit of shrewd, thoughtful conversation, both suggestive of a mind self-reliant to no common degree.

Her devotion to her father remained undiminished, rather, beneath a more conventional surface, did it take deeper root; and while, as time went on, her mother — seeing her only as she appeared in public — comprehended her less and less; he, on the other hand, was easily able to maintain his old intimacy with her, to keep in touch with the progress of her capricious development.

He saw that she was reasonable rather than sentimental: from her demeanour towards men he surmised that she was endowed with a touch of the virginal temperament; in no way eager for marriage, fastidiously expecting of it a lasting companionship and an intellectual union. He saw, too, that while she appeared content to let the trivialities of society absorb her time, the intimate portions of her mind remained unfrequented: throughout her subserviency to fashion she retained, half-unconsciously, a secret, intellectual liberty.

He understood how she was frankly eager for life, for a masculine comprehension of the activities of the world; and, in the keen vitality of her intellect, he recognized, with supreme satisfaction, an echoing of his own personality. The disproportion between her perspicacity and her experience, and continued proofs of the unexpected extent of her bookish knowledge, delighted him; but, after all, and perhaps quite illogically, he took the greater pride in her personal beauty, and in her skill in bedecking it. For in the confection of her clothes her mother had no voice.

IV

It was in commerce that Eardley Lingard had made his fortune; in the House of Commons his reputation. Twenty-seven years ago, at Oxford, he had taken a very brilliant degree. It was supposed that he would read for the bar, for which Jowett[7] had more than once laid emphasis on his special aptitude. But to the surprise of his friends he had forfeited his fellowship in order to marry — over-hastily, and quite foolishly, it was thought, a pretty-faced, penniless girl. She was the daughter of an Oxford doctor; he had gone to bid her and her father goodbye; the girl had burst into a flood of tears. And then, in an impulse of cerebral chivalry (his intercourse with women had been of the slightest) he had engaged himself to her. A month later, during the vacation, they were married unostentatiously at Oxford, and, in lodgings in London, began life together. And he was forced to accept a subordinate situation in the shipping firm of Aitken and Aitken.

His hours at the office were long; and he made no effort to mitigate their exactions; concentrated every energy of his intellect on the business; mastered its details with an astonishing rapidity, left upon everything he touched the impress of his acumen.

It was only at the end of his hard day's work that he and his wife met; their relations quickly drifted into daily superficiality.

She was untutored in perception, ingenuously unreceptive, without subtlety of penetration, acquiescing credulously in his superiority. For a long while she remained unconscious of her own inadequacy; she was incapable of appreciating — except through incidents explicitly significant of his neglect (which came later) — the entire lack of mental kinship between them.

*   *   *   *   *

So the years slipped by, and her position with regard to him grew to seem altogether natural. Moreover, after Hilda's birth, the care of the child filled her days and her mind. She would have it brought down to the drawing-room, and

---

7   Benjamin Jowett (1817–1893), fellow of Balliol College, Oxford (1838), Regius Professor of Greek at Oxford (1855), longstanding Platonist and Master of Balliol College from 1870. Associated with the Broad Church movement, his essay 'On the Interpretation of Scripture' in the liberal-minded *Essays and Reviews* (1860) sought to relax the boundaries between Anglicanism and Dissent. 'Generations of Balliol men', wrote his obituarist in *The Athenaeum*, 'felt the charm of his presence, and tested the value of his constant friendship and kindness.' *The Athenaeum*, 3441 (7 October 1893), 491–92 (p. 492).

her friends, when they called, would find her romping on the floor, her hair all dishevelled. Eardley thought her foolish, and told her so; at that time the child interested him little; he had wanted, she knew, a boy, though she had no conception of the bitterness of his disappointment.

Then, little by little, so insensibly that she was scarcely aware of its progress, came the change. With the capricious awakening of the child's intelligence, Eardley began to take notice of her, and, occasionally, in the evenings, to read aloud to her, or to tell her fairy tales. His ascendency over her started to declare itself: towards her mother the child grew less and less responsive, so that before she had perceived how things were drifting, she had already learned to tolerate her isolation.

Meanwhile, old Rupert Aitken, the head of the firm, had detected young Lingard's ability, and had come to repose in him no ordinary confidence. The firm had been in great difficulties: Eardley had somehow retrieved the situation, and shortly afterwards was made a partner — she knew no more than this, for he never talked to her of his work. Hilda was about ten years old when Mr. Aitken died: by his will the chief control of the business was left to Eardley. Almost immediately its scope expanded: from a humdrum, old-fashioned concern, it blossomed into a thriving, modern enterprise.

And, all at once, they were rich. They moved to a house in Belgrave Street: he bought Tukenton Court; and at a bye-election was returned, unopposed, for the county.

Politically, his success was as speedy as it had been commercially. She knew that he had served on committee after committee, on each of which his vitality, his clearness of perception, his power of concentration had accentuated the value of his personality. He was cited in the Press as a coming man.[8]

And now her isolation, from him and from Hilda, grew greater than ever. Each year she became less familiar with him; living mostly at Tukenton, with old Lady Whyte, an invalid aunt of his, for company; busying herself with the garden, with tending her pets, with visiting the village poor.

Hilda remained on in Belgrave Street, keeping house for her father; and three or four times a year they both came to stay at Tukenton, bringing with them a party of guests. Of late, however, his visits had been rare and hurried, and he had appeared strangely white and worn of expression. She had been secretly apprehensive at the double strain of his work — in the City every day,[9] and in the House till late at night,[10] — to which he relentlessly submitted himself. People warned her that he was over-working; she replied mechanically that she

[8]   A coming man: a journalistic appellation of the 1890s for a young, rising figure in public life.
[9]   See note 2 on p. 147.
[10]   The House: a metonym for the House of Commons, prior to Eardley's elevation to the House of Lords as a newly-appointed peer.

would interfere, but, of course, there was nothing that she could do.

But, henceforward, things would be different. He was to be made a peer; he had said, too, that he contemplated retiring from active participation in the business. Yet so firm was her habit of her life grown, that it was only with an apathetic content that she looked forward to the future....

V

On the Tuesday she went down to Tukenton — alone with her maid. Hilda remained with her father in London: there was no further proposal that she should leave him.

The mother and daughter were not to meet again for a month; but their parting was perfunctory — a stereotyped effusion of household affection. Hilda had an appointment with her dressmaker, which prevented her from going to the station.

The Assheton's ball was on Friday; and Hilda, after her mother had gone, wrote, at her father's suggestion, to ask Mrs. Mathurin to dinner. It was Mrs. Mathurin, who, though no relation, only an old friend, frequently chaperoned her; and on several previous occasions, it had seemed pleasant that she should come to dine in Belgrave Street beforehand.

Hilda was still upstairs dressing, and Eardley alone in the drawing-room, glancing through an uncut novel, when she was announced.

He noticed at once that she was in black — a massive dress of black satin — that she wore in her hair a large diamond star; and he remembered how he had once said to her that these suited her admirably. As he crossed the room to meet her, he thought she looked more resplendent than ever, in all the richness of her exuberant maturity. He grasped her hand, thanking her for the warm letter of congratulation she had written him.

She read his undisguised admiration: her face flushed beneath her heavy, dark hair: he had not looked at her so for many months.

"I feel so proud of you, Eardley," she said, seating herself on the sofa. "You're going to retire from business, too?"

He nodded, standing on the hearthrug smiling, with his hands behind his coat-tails. Beside her his smallness of stature seemed accentuated.

"I'm immensely glad. You were over-working yourself terribly. Now you'll have lots of leisure," she added.

He nodded again, looking at her curiously, half-closing his eyes, quickly, with a trick that was habitual to him.

He was wondering how marvellously she had managed to preserve her youth, computing that at least she must be five-and-forty. At moments she possessed the stately luxuriance of a portrait by Rubens[11] with a suggestion of latent passion in the full-veined, almost muscular firmness of her throat. The heaviness of her chin, though it lent, in certain light, a coarseness to her face, in others betokened an almost animal-like tenacity of purpose, a stubborn consciousness of desire. She was large-limbed and massive and dark; and while she sat fanning herself with a slow deliberation, breathing a little heavily, the opulent folds of her dress half-filled the sofa around her.

"How is dear Hilda?" she asked.

"She'll be down presently."

"And Bessie, when did she go?"

"On Tuesday."

"Dear Bessie, how strange of her to go away, just now of all times." She spoke in a tone of smooth patronage.

He shrugged his shoulders imperceptibly.

A sound of rustling came from the stairs: it was Hilda.

"When will you come to tea, Eardley?" she asked hurriedly.

"Not this week. I shall be in the City till late every day."

"Monday?"

The door opened. He nodded.

She rose to greet Hilda, kissing her effusively.

"It was sweet of you to come."

"You're looking perfectly lovely, dear."

Dinner was announced. Eardley gave Mrs. Mathurin his arm.

＊　＊　＊　＊　＊

During dinner the conversation flagged repeatedly. Mrs. Mathurin talked persistently of literature, addressing herself to Eardley, a little loudly, in complacent condemnation of the feebleness of contemporary productions. Hilda tried ineffectually to turn the topic, perceiving that her father was inattentive and tired; but Mrs. Mathurin passed glibly to French poetry, ruthlessly mangling the titles of books.

Afterwards, in the drawing-room, Hilda, with intuitive tact, sat down before the piano. She played a series of Strauss waltzes — facile, sensuous airs, which she knew always pleased her father, and whenever for a moment she paused, Mrs. Mathurin begged her to continue, and when she had finished, praised her playing with an excessive effusion, exclaiming how she adored the old simple tunes.

Then, while Mrs. Mathurin lingered with her father, she went upstairs to put on her cloak. As she came back into the drawing- room, their conversation

---

[11]   Peter Paul Rubens (1577–1640), Flemish artist, regarded as the greatest exponent of Baroque painting.

ceased: she thought it was of her that they had been talking.

In the brougham,[12] Mrs. Mathurin complimented her on the scheme of her dress, and offered her a seat in her box at the Opera, suggesting that she should persuade her father to escort her, and adding, in a tone of assumed carelessness, that Greaves Chamney would be there. Hilda reddened in the obscurity of the carriage, and hastily protested some vague previous engagement. Mrs. Mathurin was pressing her, when the carriage stopped.

VI

The ball-room was ablaze with light: the floor shook with a prismatic whirling of high-keyed tints — pale blue, and green, and rose — of bare arms and shoulders, gleaming white against the men's black coats.

Hilda at once perceived Greaves Chamney standing in the doorway. He came towards her: she took his arm. They danced a turn or two, jostling through the throng.

"What a crush!" he remarked, "let's go and find a seat."

He pushed his way through the onlookers, she clinging to his arm, and up the stairs. They turned the landing, and sat down alone and out of sight. From below, through the buzz of conversation, and the loud iteration of the butler's voice announcing the guests, drifted the muffled strains of the string band.

"You came with Mrs. Mathurin, I suppose?" he asked.

"Yes, she dined with us first."

"Your mother's gone to Tukenton, then?"

"Yes," she answered, unconscious of the train of his thoughts.

"How's your father?"

"He's dreadfully overworked. He needs a long rest."

"Yes, but he'll want some absorbing occupation: he's been accustomed to it all his life."

The music ceased: the buzz of voices swelled, and the couples came crowding up the staircase. He rose to let them pass, standing against the wall.

She was thinking that he was handsome beyond a doubt — with his keen, decisive profile; graceful, too, in his well-built clothes. There was something elusive, impenetrable, about his faultlessly smoothed hair; the firm lines of his smile. She wondered if she really knew him....

Yet it was for that very impenetrableness of his that she admired him: it was that which had first made her curious concerning him, conscious of his ability: she had judged it a sign of strength. He was looking down at her fixedly: she

[12] Brougham: a closed, four-wheeled carriage with the driver's seat outside, more expensive than the more common two-wheeled hansom cab; named after the Whig jurist and statesman Lord Henry Brougham (1778–1868).

guessed that he had resolved to propose to her tonight; and she meditated without agitation on the manner he was likely to adopt.

He had seated himself again beside her: but the music started almost immediately.

"You'll give me another dance?" he asked, fingering her programme.

She handed him the pencil. He bracketed two numbers, writing his initials opposite them deliberately. Then, after an instant, included a third, without comment. And they went back into the ball-room.

As she stood with another partner, exchanging commonplaces concerning the details of the dance, she noticed him on a sofa in a corner beside Mrs. Mathurin; talking to her at his ease, with his head thrown back. Mrs. Mathurin was gazing in her direction, thoughtfully. It was of her that they were speaking, she suspected, and she turned away hastily.

She liked Greaves Chamney: he interested her: he was brilliant: he would succeed at the Bar, her father had said so often: he was standing for Parliament at the next election. She had been ready to accept him, almost from the first: she had contentedly, without perturbation, let things drift towards this proposal: she had grown to imagine herself his wife with familiarity — the details of their companionship, the groove of their common life. But, as the moment drew near, at the vision of him talking to Mrs. Mathurin, at his ease, with his head thrown back, there crept over her a curious, wayward repulsion: she felt doubtful, apprehensive, afraid, scared lest, after all, he had imposed himself upon her. She shrank from the prospect of coming to a decision, longing to take counsel of someone — her father, but he wanted her to marry Greaves Chamney; she had suspected that long ago....

Then Stephen Walsh's figure entered her mind — his slow, open face, his dog-like look following her....

And she knew instinctively that *he* loved her in a different way....

Mechanically, she went through the routine of the succeeding dances. At last his turn came. He was moving towards her, smiling his smooth smile. She felt herself smiling too: she took his arm, half admiring his self-possession, and half resenting it. As they crossed the room she rapidly imagined herself married to the other — a prosperous country life; eventless wealth; isolation from the pulse of London; the round of county society; their evenings together; his commonplace comments on the contents of the day's paper, on the incidents of his day's sport.

*　*　*　*　*

And, somehow, she was still curious concerning the manner he would adopt. "It's cooler in the conservatory: this place is like an oven."

His suggestion nettled her. That he should choose the conservatory seemed almost a personal slight: the twilight of the place, its unexpected seats beneath the dim shadows of the palms, appeared stupidly sentimental. She glanced at him critically, asking herself a little bitterly if he would begin by begging permission to call her by her Christian name. They sat down; and she waited for him to speak.

"I want you, Hilda, to be my wife." He uttered the words quietly, in his usual, even voice; but, through the obscurity, she was conscious that his gaze was concentrated upon her.

"My practice is fast growing. Next year I shall be in Parliament. I know you like me as a friend: we have seen a great deal of each other: we have already much in common. For three years I have been working for you, almost ever since I have known you ——"

He paused, and since she did not speak ——

"Perhaps you would rather not give me a reply now. You would rather wait?"

She was busy framing her answer, when he continued

"Yes, I think you would rather wait ——"

She felt the touch of his hand on hers: she resisted feebly. He was leaning forward gazing into her face. She laughed weakly: she thought he smiled in response: she knew that he was waiting for her to speak.

"We will wait," she heard herself saying, "and see. You are right.... I would rather wait.... I do not know ——"

He clasped her hand gratefully: she surmised that the tension of his emotion had snapped; that, for the moment, he was content with her answer.

From the ball-room floated the languorous phrase of a waltz-tune. Her blood tingled; and a contradictory consciousness that he had attained this understanding with her with entire ease, and that, had he insisted, he could have achieved more, galled her not a little. All at once she found herself full of an intense longing to end the situation, to escape from the obscurity of the conservatory, from him.

"Would you tell me what the time is?" There was a note of strained ceremony in her voice.

He looked at his watch and answered —

"Twenty past one."

"Twenty past one! Oh! I must go at once. I'd no idea it was so late. I promised Mrs. Mathurin to come at one."

His gesture of expostulation was almost imperceptible. Then he had offered her his arm, and was leading her across the room.

"I'm so sorry to have kept you. But I'm quite ready to come now," she exclaimed.

Mrs. Mathurin looked from one to the other meaningly, and rose, smiling.

Greaves Chamney escorted them to the carriage.

On the way home, no reference to him passed; and Hilda sat, for the most part, silent. But when they parted, Mrs. Mathurin bid her goodnight with an affectation of discretion, and emphasized affection.

And Hilda drove onto Belgrave Street, alone, ill-at-ease, dissatisfied with herself.

VII

The following afternoon she received a letter from him, in which he assumed an indefinite understanding between them, and insisted on his love for her in lengthy, symmetrical, slightly elaborate phrases. The letter, which she read carefully, left her unmoved, as his proposal had done. And she vaguely took for granted that in the course of time she would marry him, rating herself grown cold of temperament, unattracted by men, deliberately deciding that she was insensible to the ordinary agitations of love.

Not that she had never experienced the sentimental imaginings of girlhood. There had been a period when she was continually fancying herself enthralled, now by one man, now by another. But these phases of exaltation had all proved quite transient: the ardour of each secret attachment had in turn gently faded. One after another she recalled them all; and because it was now more than eighteen months since the extinction of the most recent of them, she judged them mere school-girl vapourings, which, coming into womanhood, she had outgrown. And in explanation of her apathetic attitude toward Greaves Chamney, and of her matter-of-fact acceptance of him, she referred, with hasty confidence, to her own experience of society, which, she argued, had given her glimpses enough of the practical success of make-shift marriage bargains. Besides, life with him promised to be full of interest; his companionship was stimulating; and there would be the progress of his success, the glamour of which she would enhance and share.

And to the event of the ceremony, too, she looked forward. It was pleasant to plan its details — a fashionable wedding, at St. Peter's, Eaton Square;[13] seven bridesmaids; a full choral service; and a crowded reception afterwards.

A honeymoon on the Riviera; and then the life in London resumed. But on a larger, freer scale — mistress of her own house entertaining her own guests, collecting about her a brilliant circle of distinguished men.

In the course of her social engagements she met Greaves Chamney frequently. He would discuss political and other gossip with her, maintaining a certain serious deference of tone, and permitting himself no more familiarity than the ease of well-tried friendship. When they were alone, he occasionally called her by her Christian name; but he refrained, with a rare tact she thought, from any semblance of a caress.

[13]   Eaton Square is in Chelsea, London.

And the faultless discretion of his attitude reconciled her to him more and more, though she still shrank from mentioning, even to her father, the tacit understanding between them.

VIII

The butler announced him — "Lord Lingard of Tukenton."

Across the familiar, ornate drawing-room, she smiled at him with an obvious, suppressed eagerness. Cynically, he guessed that the new-sounding title had moved her.

"How sweet of you to come, Eardley. I've said 'not at home to anyone;' so we can have a real, long chat. You'll have some tea?"

He pictured to himself how she had been sitting there, all the afternoon, pretending to read, waiting for him; and uneasily he saw what was coming.

"Thanks; no sugar."

"It's ages since I've seen anything of you. You've been so dreadfully busy."

And the conversation dragged on with a clumsy pleasantness, in a vein of uncomfortable pretence. He was apprehensive of a pause.

At last it came.

*   *   *   *   *

"I've been so unhappy all these months, Eardley," she began.

He bent towards her, simulating a surprised concern.

"I felt so that you and I were somehow drifting apart."

He dissented soothingly.

"My life is so lonely ——"

He rapidly recalled her social activity, her routine of busy pleasure. The role of Ariadne,[14] he thought, was singularly unbecoming to her.

"Society is so hollow ——"

He assented suavely, smiling imperceptibly. The false note she had adopted was irksome to him. And for the rest he waited with some impatience.

"Life is so difficult…. If only I knew how to please you?"

"But, my dear Bertha ——" he expostulated.

"You've never understood how I worship you — your wonderful personality. Sometimes I am terribly afraid about the future — I am afraid I am growing old. All these months I have been waiting for you to come back to me."

The disparity between her phrase and her air of prosperous maturity

---

[14] Ariadne was the daughter of the Cretan king Minos in Greek mythology. According to legend, she gave the Athenian hero Theseus a ball of thread to help him escape the Labyrinth after killing the Minotaur. The reference here draws on the fact that she was abandoned by Theseus in the myth. But in that her name means 'holy or chaste woman' it might also be the spur to Eardley's sardonic view of Bertha's affecting the role of social wallflower.

impressed him, in his irritation, as melodrama grown grotesque. He noticed her want of tact, and how blindly she was effacing that odd, florid charm of hers, which in the past had attracted him towards her. And, at the prospect of her insistence, he let her continue.

And the suavity of his manner intensified.

*   *   *   *   *

Suddenly, she understood how it was.

"You have no heart, Eardley," she broke out, bitterly. "If I only knew how to please you.... I would do anything...."

Her cry of humiliation touched him.

"I am so sorry, Bertha. Cannot we still be friends — old, dear friends?"

The words sounded like a stereotyped formula. He regretted them immediately, but she did not seem to have heard them.

Mechanically he took up a book, and began to turn over its pages; then, lest the action should appear to her brutally callous, replaced it hastily.

She was gazing at him fixedly. Her expression had grown listless and heavy: her face seemed to have aged strangely.

"My poor Bertha ——" he began.

At the sound of his voice — his tone was very tender — the drawn lines about her mouth slackened. He saw that she still hoped. Out of pity for her, he had not the courage to undeceive her. He took her hand.

"I did not mean to pain you.... I did not know how it was.... I have been very overwrought.... I am not quite myself."

Impulsively she lifted his hand to her lips.

He flushed almost angrily: the situation was intolerable.

"Hilda tells me we are to come to the Opera with you on the 13th."

"You will come? ... How good you are to me, Eardley."

A few minutes later he took leave of her, pressing her hand warmly.

In the street, as he walked home, he realized that her personality was growing definitely distasteful to him.

*   *   *   *   *

And she sat on in her ornate drawing-room, goading herself with hope into an uneasy belief that, after all, he would come back to her.

IX

It was a summer afternoon. The butler had wheeled Lady Whyte's invalid chair on to the gravel before the porch, and, since luncheon, she and Lady Bessie Lingard had been sitting there.

The Dutch flower-beds, glowing in the sunlight, heaped lumpy patches of live colour about the velvety lawn: the persistent whirring of a mowing-machine filled the stillness of the air; and, beyond the garden, through a gap in the bank of rhododendrons, one caught a glimpse of the country-side — the well-upholstered undulations of the English midlands.[15]

Lady Whyte, wrapped in her shawls, sat alertly surveying the landscape; her face retaining, despite the tufts of white hair protruding beneath her cap, a wizened precision of glance, a firm consciousness of expression. Presently, briskly adjusting her spectacles, she recommenced the clicking of her knitting-needles.

"When does Hilda arrive, Bessie?"

"She will be here almost directly."

"How long did you say she is coming for?"

"I don't know — only till Monday, I expect."

She nodded sententiously, pursing her lips.

"I shall talk to her," she exclaimed tartly.

Bessie Lingard started. The *Queen*[16] that lay on her lap slipped onto the gravel.

"I shall talk to her, I say — The way that girl behaves, Bessie, is perfectly odious."

"But, Caroline, it isn't right that you should."

"I know it's not my business, but I shall do it, I say. The way she neglects you!"

"Please, Caroline, promise me you won't —— It would altogether upset me.... I don't know what I should do.... It will all come right someday.... I feel it will," she added, half to herself.

"I think matters are growing worse and worse. She goes everywhere with that Mrs. Mathurin. It's abominable of Eardley."

The scattered sheets of the newspaper flapped in the breeze. Bessie stooped mechanically to collect them.

"You know you can do no good. It's cruel of you, Caroline, to persist in talking like this."

"I tell you, I think Eardley's going to the House of Lords, and especially his retiring from business, the worst possible thing." And she set her knitting-needles clicking with renewed vigour.

"And I suppose that woman is everlastingly at Belgrave Street? ——"

There was no answer: she turned her head sharply, scrutinizing the suffering on the other's face.

"There, there, Bessie.... I'm a cantankerous old woman.... But this whole

[15] Compare 'The English Midlands, sluggishly effluent, a massy profusion of well-upholstered undulations' in Crackanthorpe's 'Rêverie April 15', p. 383.

[16] *The Queen* was a lavishly illustrated weekly society publication, founded in 1861, which had achieved impressive circulation figures by the 1890s. It appeared in later twentieth-century incarnations as *Harper's & Queen*, then *Harper's Bazaar*.

business makes my blood boil for you — to see you going on submitting year after year like this. Sometimes I feel as if I must speak out ——" And, as the other winced audibly, she added: "No, not to Eardley, I don't mean that. But to Hilda."

"It will all come right someday," Bessie repeated feebly.

Lady Whyte began a fresh inspection of the landscape, while the mother's eyes, listless with dull pain, mechanically followed the movements of the two gardeners, crossing and re-crossing the far end of the lawn.

Five minutes later, the sound of approaching wheels drowned the whirring of the mowing-machine: the landau[17] swung round the sweep, and Hilda, wearing a mannish travelling dress, stepped out, her lips parted in a small artificial smile.

X

In her room on the dressing-table she found a bowlful of roses. She guessed that it was her mother, and not the maid, who had arranged them. She sat down before the glass, burying her face in the flowers. A wave of weakness seemed to sweep over her: of a sudden, she felt strangely heavy-headed. Hot tears started to her eyes — why she could not tell: she only knew that to cry was a vague relief....

And then it passed. She brushed away the traces hurriedly, settled her hat on her head, and went downstairs. In the hall a thrill of glad expectation reminded her that tomorrow morning she would have a letter from her father.

A saddled horse was being led away down the drive, and a man's figure was seated by the tea-table with her mother and Lady Whyte. She guessed at once that it was Stephen Walsh.

She greeted him with a well-simulated air of casual friendliness: he responded with the masculine stiffness that was habitual to him.

The conversation flickered: he, trying clumsy civilities; her mother, listless and silent; Lady Whyte allusively hostile. The old lady's sarcastic inferences stung Hilda to resentment: once or twice she replied almost rudely: Lady Whyte merely lifted her eyebrows in nettled contempt. Stephen Walsh awkwardly handled his tea-cup; and Hilda turned defiantly to chat airily to her mother.

Lady Whyte declared abruptly that the air was growing chilly. The butler appeared, and as the man wheeled her back into the house, the others walked beside her chair. Hilda lingered by the porch, fingering the jasmine creeper.

A minute later Stephen Walsh joined her.

"It's 'Bijou' you're riding?" she remarked.

"Yes, he's improved wonderfully since you last saw him. I've had him out at grass. Have you been riding at all in London?"

---

[17]   A landau is a type of a horse-drawn, four-wheeled, enclosed carriage.

"No, only once or twice. What have you been doing with yourself?" She stood still by the porch, in a graceful attitude, toying with the creeper.

"Oh, nothing much — haymaking," he answered, laughing. "I promised your mother I'd see Bloxam about some rose-cuttings. Will you come as far as the greenhouse?"

She assented, and they strolled together across the lawn.

"We might have a gallop tomorrow on the old race-course."

"No, I don't think so.... I'll see."

"You'll stay for the bazaar at Courtlands, I suppose?"

"No, I'm going back on Monday."

The gardener met them by the coach-house. While Stephen Walsh talked to him, she went into the stables. When he joined her there, she was in the loose-box, feeding her pony from her hand.

They moved across to 'Bijou,' who stood, still saddled, hitched to the pillar-reins.

"Take care," he called, "he's as tricky as ever."

"He's still dangerous to ride?"

"No, we've got used to one another now." She admired him for thus taking his own courage for granted.

Then they visited the three carriage-horses in turn. The coachman came in, and talked a moment to Stephen with deferential familiarity.

They walked home through the kitchen-garden.

His companionship — the harmoniousness of his contented interest in the natural incidents of his existence — was very restful to her. She forgot how he was in love with her, how he was waiting to plead with her again. Realizing his slow, masculine simplicity, in an impulse of intimate friendliness, that was almost sisterly, her heart warmed towards him. She was grateful to him, too, because his open, English face made her instinctively conscious of the sure stability of his attitude towards her.

He stooped to pick some strawberries, piling them in the palm of his hand; and they sat down on a garden-seat.

The blackbirds cluttered, chasing one another through the currant-bushes. He went to gather her some more fruit: while he was away, she remembered Greaves Chamney, and wondered a little maliciously, if he could be jealous.... He was returning towards her.... She noted his straight, athletic figure.... In his simple way, she mused, he would be very faithful to her....

Presently he took her hand, and the firmness of his grasp thrilled her. And then, suddenly, without a word, his arms were about her: she felt the rough touch of his moustache: the blood rose fast to her cheeks: she perceived that his face was all distraught with emotion.

"Hilda, ... my darling Hilda," he stammered.

She found herself smiling easily at his confusion.

"Tell me there is some chance for me?"

"Do you really care so much?"

"You know how I love you with all my might. I would slave every hour to make you happy.... I'm not clever, I know that: I'm countrified, and can't talk about books and things.... But I'd give up everything.... We'd live in London, if you liked ——"

He stopped short. She was shaking her head slowly; but there were tears in her eyes.

"Then there is someone else?"

She nodded gravely.

A minute later she glanced at him. He looked so dazed, that her heart grew full of impulsive pity for him. She rose; and they turned in silence, back towards the house.

Before the door he bid her goodbye hastily. When he was gone, she thought she comprehended, with a vague bitterness, how good a husband he would have made her.... And with doses of self-pity she assuaged her irresolution.

XI

... The proposal, but for his kissing her passionately, would, she mused, have been quite commonplace....

She dropped to sleep, dreaming blurred dreams of him. Then, all at once, found herself awake, thinking with a strange, searching lucidity....

... She seemed to see herself clearly — not clever, only intelligent; selfish, lacking in sympathy, absorbed by the insignificant mechanism of her own experience, groping at random amid a world which she did not understand, and believing the while in the superiority of her own penetration.... And against the intellectual limitation of her girlhood she rebelled, jealous of men, feverishly longing to probe the real meanings of things....

By and by she fell to brooding on her father, on that worn expression of his; and a tremulous, emotional remorse welled up within her. The fineness of his nature, appearing, as it did to her, so aloof from the pettiness of the world, filled her with a fearful pity for him — an indefinable dread lest some harm should happen to him. A score of intimate tokens of his love for her flitted through her mind: she felt hotly ashamed that she had not requited him more worthily.

She thought of him as a young man, unsparing of his strength, fighting his way upwards, carving his career, by dint of sheer superiority of fibre: she imagined long years of unflinching, self-denying ambition. She remembered his words to her, when he had first told her the news of his peerage: "I'm glad, child, to think that it makes you so happy." And now that his work was accomplished, she was anxiously impatient for his life to be full of sunshine; planning how she would try to merge her own pleasures in the effort to please him, to prove herself continually thoughtful for him, to make the days of his leisure altogether pleasant. And when, some day, she was married, he and she should be together as much as ever.

When she got back to Belgrave Street (and, parenthetically, she resolved to go on Sunday night) she would tell him about Greaves: that, she knew, would make him glad. He was fond of Greaves: he believed in his coming success; and now that she thought of them together, she saw how much they were alike....

Stephen Walsh — poor fellow! He was very miserable now, she supposed: he was the sort of man to take it badly — not to show it, but to nurse it in his heart, for years, stubbornly....

And, perhaps, after all, life with him would have been pleasant.

... How strange, when one reflected upon it, was his kissing her like that — he, so ill-at-ease, so *gauche*[18] with women.... To love like that — to be carried right out of oneself ... she tried to realize it ... it was very strange ... and yet, and yet, to possess that power over a man, to be able to command him by a word, a look, and the while to retain complete control over oneself ... yes, she would be kind to him ... she would ride with him tomorrow ... she would send him a note by the groom — a casually-worded note which would show him she still wished to be friends with him as before....

And Greaves — she could not imagine him kissing her so.... Oh! but after all, what was the use of thinking over the big things of life? ... And, turning on her pillow, she sank again to sleep.

XII

She was talking volubly, indiscriminately, of the jealousies with which she had to contend at the theatre, of the obstinacy of the author, of the small-mindedness of the manager; feverishly pacing the tiny boudoir,[19] her sallow cheeks delicately flushed, her dark eyes dilated till they seemed to fill all her face. Eardley sat on a sofa, his legs crossed, alternately surveying her and puffing reflectively at his cigarette. The movements of her slim, supple figure — they were suave as a cat's — seemed, as she crossed and re-crossed in front of him, to attain a definite symbolization of that tense and neurotic restlessness, dubbed modern — an hysterical caging of spasmodic and inadequate emotion. And the softly lit room, through the blue haze of smoke, completed his impression — the Japanese prints hanging against a Morris wall-paper; exotic, Eastern objects piled beside large sheaves of theatrical photographs; severely mediæval

---

[18] *Gauche*: awkward.
[19] A boudoir is a woman's bedroom or private sitting room.

furniture, backed by hangings of Liberty silk.[20]

"You're a wonderful creature ——" he interrupted deliberately.

She halted abruptly before him, irresolute, impulsively weighing his words.

"Do you really think that, after all, I shall make a great actress?"

"Perhaps … perhaps … I dare say … that's not what I meant."

She sank into an armchair; he let his gaze wander slowly once again round the boudoir till at length it rested on her figure.

"Talk to me," she began eagerly, "about myself. Tell me why I'm wonderful."

"No — you wouldn't understand."

"Why are you so exasperating?"

"Go on telling me about your childhood, out there in Melbourne."

"Oh! I can't. The other things have driven it all out of my head. Besides, it's so long ago. It's all dull and stupid, and I've forgotten it…. Do you know what some people would say if they knew you were here at this time of night?" she added mischievously.

"They would repeat, very properly, what I remarked just now."

"I often wonder," she began after a pause, during which he was occupied in lighting another cigarette, — "I often wonder if you are in love with me, or if ——"

"So do I, Nina, often."

"You'd have no business to ——"

"Nor you to receive me, alone, at a quarter to twelve."

"I should like to feel certain of you."

"Yes, that's natural."

"Do you know, I'm a little afraid of you sometimes."

"Ah!"

"Not exactly afraid of you, but afraid of your coolness. And yet I sometimes feel half sorry for you."

"Yes, I understand that."

"You always say you understand. It makes it very hard to talk to you."

"Why, shouldn't it make it easier?"

"No, it doesn't; you seem to judge me so hardly."

"And just now?"

"Yes, occasionally you pay me mysterious compliments. But I never know what you mean. I should like enormously to know whether ——"

"Well?"

"Well whether, for instance, you consider me respectable."

"I've never considered the matter."

"But if your wife knew that you came here as you do."

---

[20]   The fashionably advanced aesthetic of Nina Whittingham's taste in interior decoration is clear enough.

"My wife and I have been married twenty-five years."

"You think it's bad form of me to mention your wife?"

"I think it characteristic of you."

"Then you think me bad form?"

"I told you just now what I thought of you."

"And you really think it?"

"There was no need for me to say it otherwise. You did not expect it."

"I adore frankness."

"Of course."

"But everyone doesn't."

"Yes, whenever it's agreeable."

"Charlie Strudwicke dined here this evening," she broke off.

He made no answer; he was relighting his cigarette.

"He made me a passionate proposal."

"Really. He's a very foolish young man."

"Foolish because he adores me, and decent enough to ask me to marry him," she retorted hotly.

"On the contrary, that's the most creditable thing I've heard of him."

"He's a dear, good boy."

"Let me congratulate you."

"But I refused him."

"On having refused him."

She bit her lip; then resumed.

"Is Miss Lingard returned to town?"

"Yes, she came this evening."

"I've been wanting to ask you a favour — to do me a little kindness. Only — only I'm afraid you might refuse...."

"Then wouldn't it be better not to ask it?"

"You can guess what it is?"

He nodded gravely.

"And you won't?"

"Not at present."

"Some day?"

"Perhaps."

She rose, and walked impatiently across the room.

"If you were anyone else, I should hate you."

"I am sorry," he said, rising. "Think a little, and you will understand why, and then you will be less angry with me. Goodnight."

"You must go?" she asked, in a voice of forced carelessness.

"It is past twelve."

"Goodnight," she answered, turning up the lamp, and standing with her back towards him.

Slipping his crush-hat under his arm, he went. She caught his reflection in a mirror as he opened the door; his face wore a pleasant, impassive expression.

XIII

He walked home through St. James's Park.

A sullen glow throbbed overhead! golden will o' wisps threaded the shadowy groupings of gaunt-limbed trees, and the dull, distant rumour of feverish London waited on the still, night air. The lights of Hyde Park Corner, blazing like some monster, gilded constellation, shamed the dingy stars; and across the East flared a sky-sign — a gaudy, crimson arabesque....[21]

And all the air hung draped in the mysterious, sumptuous splendour of a murky London night....[22]

As he walked, his thoughts strayed back complacently to the scene in Nina Whittingham's boudoir: he surveyed himself playing upon her personality, as upon some delicate, responsive instrument, and, convincing himself of his ascendency over her, reviewed each detail of her penetrating charm ... At fifty, he told himself with elation, he was ready to begin life again, to wander afresh about the wide garden of emotional experience, and, remembering his youth — a barren period of unflagging toil — he looked back on it with a contemptuous, and almost rancorous, regret.

In no way timorous of experience, and without misgiving concerning the sureness of his discrimination, he dwelt, with a quickening, courageous exhilaration, upon the consciousness of his magnetic ascendency over women, and jading[23] the satisfactions of his ambition, till he had come to regard them as a senseless accumulation of deceptive effort, hailed exultantly the freedom of his leisure.

His thoughts reverted to Nina Whittingham: he foresaw each successive stage of his domination over her — a whole vague, subtle *liaison*, discreet, infinitely stimulating....

And he felt boyishly expectant of the future; confidently awaiting a prescriptive enjoyment of women. He thought of Bessie, with a compassionate affection that was mildly soothing, resolving to write to her that evening and

---

[21] An ornate, elaborate pattern derived from Islamic art. This was an attractive figure for Decadent writers and artists, given their receptivity to the blending of the arts, including ballet, music, and painting, but was also applied by the artist Aubrey Beardsley to the spectacle of advertising in the metropolis: 'against a leaden sky', he wrote, 'skysigns will trace their formal arabesque. Beauty has laid siege to the City' (quoted in John Stokes, *Oscar Wilde: Myths, Miracles, and Imitations* (Cambridge: Cambridge University Press, 1996), p. 122).

[22] 'He walked home [...] murky London night', draws, virtually verbatim, on Crackanthorpe's 'In St. James's Park, January 15', p. 382.

[23] Jading means becoming dull or worn-out from overwork or overuse.

to run down to Tukenton before long — there were addresses of congratulation from his constituents, and a presentation of some kind from the county; of Bertha Mathurin, too, of those drawn lines about her mouth that destroyed her attractiveness, with a certain compunction, reminding himself she still was stubbornly hoping....

Tomorrow, for the first time, he was to speak in the Lords: sardonically, he bethought himself of the dreary lack of humour of English politics ... of the age grown strangely picturesque; of the rich, enfeebled by monstrous ease; of the shivering poor, clamouring nightly for justice; of a helpless democracy, vast revolt of the ill-informed; of priests, striving to be rational; of sentimental moralists protecting iniquity; of middle-class princes; of sybaritic[24] saints; of complacent and pompous politicians; of doctors, hurrying the degeneration of the race; of artists, discarding possibilities for limitations; of press-men, befooling[25] a pretentious public; of critics, refining upon the 'busman's methods: of inhabitants of Camberwell chattering of culture;[26] of ladies of the pavement,[27] aping the conventionality of nonconformist circles....

And, leaving the Park, he mused almost sentimentally on the great, dreamy town; on her myriad, fleeting moods; on the charm of her portentous provinciality;[28] and realizing the vitality of his imagination, reconsidered Nina Whittingham and her attitude towards him....

XIV

She told her father of her engagement. They were to be married, it was settled, in the autumn: every morning came letters and notes of congratulation. She let herself drift with the current of events, busying her mind with a hurried accumulation of trifles, shrinking instinctively from a probing of her emotions.

She wrote to her mother; and received in reply an agitated letter, full of anxious, maternal doubtings, and of tremulous wishes, and concluding with a suggestion that she and Greaves should come down to Tukenton from a Saturday till Monday.

[24] Sybaritic: loving or involving expensive or luxurious things.
[25] Befooling: i.e. fooling.
[26] Camberwell is a district of south London which, as an expanding suburb in the 1890s, saw an exponential growth in housing which catered for the expanding lower-middle class. The latter's pretensions to high culture and enjoyment of popular culture are memorably captured in George Gissing's novel *In the Year of Jubilee* (1894), mainly set in Camberwell. For Gissing, like Crackanthorpe, hearing 'inhabitants of Camberwell chattering of culture' would produce an effect of vulgarity and embarrassment.
[27] See note 20 on p. 187.
[28] The passage 'of the age grown strangely picturesque [...] portentous provinciality', draws heavily on Crackanthorpe's 'Rêverie, December 25' in *Vignettes*. 'Portentous' here means pretentious.

The letter left upon her an uncomfortable, disturbing impression, reviving, as it did, an echo of her original misgivings, so that she resented unreasonably its tactless tone, and blamed her mother for not viewing the matter with that sincere, unquestioning satisfaction which her father had displayed.

Greaves Chamney came constantly to dine in Belgrave Street: they had not a few little genial dinners, all three together, during which she noted the dilatation[29] of her father's liking for the young man.

With Greaves, whenever he and she were alone, it was of the practical details of the future that they talked — of houses, of furniture, of servants; but occasionally lapsing into either a flippant sentimentalism, or a forced sententious attitude towards one another. He petted her with *verve*, with discernment; made her momentarily forget that feeling of uneasiness, which was to return directly she had parted with him.

Mechanically, she grew accustomed to his mood; but familiarity with his several aspects brought her no sense of unconstraint. Rather, on the contrary, did it rigidly confine her within the strict limits of her *rôle* as his *fiancée*. Their engagement, in its intimacy, was altogether unromantic; for which, somehow, she felt she was responsible. To be altogether at her ease with him was more than she could compass: there lurked always, in the background of her mind, the shadowy sentiment that he had imposed himself upon her.... So, in the superficial companionship of her girl friends, she took refuge.

Since the night of the Asshetons' ball Mrs. Mathurin had not been once to Belgrave Street. Hilda guessed it was because, almost at the last moment, her father had remembered an important previous engagement which he had overlooked, and was unable to go to the Opera as he had promised. Once, a fortnight later, she passed her in the Park, looking, so she thought, tired and worn; and she heard that in August she was going to Aix.

Her mother's letters contained casual references to Stephen Walsh; evidently, the outward routine of his life was in no way disordered: he was busy as before with the horses and his gardening ... and yet, and yet, she wondered, she wondered....

Her father at this time was in splendid spirits: he appeared to be growing visibly younger day by day. The season was flaunting its crowded, glittering close: he and Hilda were to be seen almost everywhere together — in the Row[30] in the morning (he had taken to riding again); under the Achilles statue[31]

---

[29] Dilatation: here, expansion.
[30] Rotten Row, Hyde Park, London: see note 9 on p. 167.
[31] The Achilles statue in Park Lane, London, north of Hyde Park Corner, was cast in bronze from captured French guns and 'erected in 1822 with money subscribed by English ladies, in honour of Arthur, Duke of Wellington, and his brave companions in arms' (Baedeker, *London and Its Environs*, p. 260). It overlooks Apsley House, the Wellington family town residence.

in the late afternoon; at dinners, receptions, balls. Her beauty, discarding its former insensibility, seemed to have blossomed into an exuberant expression of radiant happiness. And the women who knew her, sentimentally ascribed the change to her engagement to Greaves Chamney.

XV

"My daughter: Mrs. Whittingham."

It was in the hall of the New Gallery:[32] they had just passed the turnstile: she was going out.

She was veiled, and in black. She gave an impression of discreet and exquisite sobriety, of a daintily intentional unobtrusiveness. Suavely smiling, she held out her hand.

"I've been wanting to know you so much." She spoke with a naive, girlish candour. Admiration of her suppleness made him forget her adroitness in forcing his hand.

Hilda smiled vaguely. And she continued:

"You do not know, perhaps, how kind your father has been to me?"

He blinked his eyes with that quick, almost imperceptible movement of his: he comprehended the bent of her impulse now, and met Hilda's glance of surprise with a faint, well-simulated gesture of protestation.

"Yes," she continued, still fluently smiling, and looking from one to the other, "I dare say he has never even spoken to you of me. He does good by stealth; that is his way."

And full of impulsive, expectant gratitude, her eyes rested upon Eardley.

"I should be so pleased, Miss Lingard," she went on, turning again to Hilda, "if you would come to see me. Indeed your father has half promised he would bring you to tea on Saturday. May I count on you?"

"I am afraid I am going into the country on Saturday," Hilda answered, embarrassed.

"Ah! I am sorry. Well, perhaps some other day he will bring you. Goodbye.... Goodbye, Lord Lingard. I am pertinacious, you see. I intend you to keep your promise."

And still girlishly smiling, she turned back into the Gallery, fading away amid the crowd.

* * * * *

---

[32] The New Gallery, Regent Street, London, was founded in 1888, becoming an important exhibiting venue for Pre-Raphaelite artists and those of the Aesthetic and Arts and Crafts movements. Its first exhibition in 1888, directed by Walter Crane, showcased the industrial and applied arts. It held a major Burne-Jones retrospective in 1892–1893 and continued as a gallery until 1910, when it was turned into a restaurant and, in 1913, a cinema.

"How different she looks off the stage," Hilda remarked absently, as they moved round before the pictures. "You never told me that you knew her?"

He did not seem to hear: instinctively she postponed the topic.

*　*　*　*　*

An hour later, she reverted to it. Her father had gone off to keep some engagement; and Greaves, who had met them in the Gallery, was seated beside her.

They were talking fitfully, leisurely watching the crowd as it shifted before them.

"We met Mrs. Whittingham just now."

"Yes, I passed her as I came in."

"How pretty she is off the stage — so quiet and young-looking. Dad introduced me to her. I expected she'd be quite different. Have you seen her in the new piece?"

"No, not yet."

"Dad's going to take me to see her. She's very interesting, I should imagine."

"Yes, to men: not to women."

"What do you mean?" she asked, looking up quickly.

"There are some women who are more attractive to men than to women, just as there are some men, whom men like, and women don't care for."

"Yes," she answered thoughtfully, "I see what you mean."

And they talked of other things.

XVI

And Bessie, down at Tukenton, full of timorous apprehensions, brooded over Hilda's approaching marriage, till at last, little by little, there crept over her a bitter consciousness of the helplessness of her own isolation, till her life seemed to have grown altogether empty and tasteless.

Not that she bore any resentment against Eardley: long ago had she learned to acquiesce in his attitude towards her. Only, feeling herself grown old, and surveying the past, trailing behind her in all its irrevocable inadequacy, she deplored the exceeding pity of it.

Ah! how different it might have been. Ah! why was it that it had not been different? She thought of Hilda as a little child, dimpling her baby cheeks as she smiled, prattling confidentially as they played together. She recalled how eagerly she had planned the childish frocks; how she had nursed her, watching by her bedside night after night. And now, and now, it was all forgotten; it was as if it had never been. And the instinct of her maternity clamoured within her — after all, was not Hilda her child — of her own flesh and blood — had she not a right to her love, to demand it, to claim it?

Yet now, now it was all forgotten: it was as if it had never been.

* * * * *

If anything were to happen to her, perhaps Hilda would see it all then, perhaps then she would be sorry, would come back to her ... perhaps? ... perhaps? ...

But in the autumn, after the wedding, she was going away — away to her own life in London.... She foresaw how henceforward they would drift altogether apart.

And Greaves Chamney, would he be good to her? Or, after a year or two, would it be as it had been with her and Eardley?...

She comprehended now how it was, as the years slipped by, that she had come to mean nothing to Hilda; how she had done wrong to isolate herself down here at Tukenton; not to have had the courage to face the life in London....

... And yet the humiliation of it all — how could she have endured that? — living on in Belgrave Street, in that house which she had come to hate — there between Eardley and Bertha Mathurin?

And now, she suspected, there were others too.... An actress' name had been hinted to her....

After all, this marriage must be the best thing — and then, perhaps, someday, Hilda would come to see things differently, to realize how harshly she had judged her mother, to understand her silent suffering all these years.

* * * * *

Yes, some day, it must all come right.

XVII

All the week she had been looking forward to taking Greaves down to Tukenton. Her father, these last days, had been but seldom at home; and she was fast wearying of London crowds. She pictured herself strolling over the park with him, while he chatted to her wittily of their London acquaintances.

But, on the Saturday, almost as soon as they had arrived, Lady Whyte's blunt hostility towards him, and, more especially, her mother's obviously anxious curiosity concerning him, falsified all her expectations.

And he seemed ill-at-ease, almost *gauche*; and, on his behalf, she resented hotly the atmosphere that showed him at a disadvantage. She had been expecting that, by his cleverness, he would impose himself upon them: her mother's apprehensive observance of his manner wounded her pride.

Thus irksomely, but without incident, the two days passed.

* * * * *

On the Sunday evening, after dinner (Greaves had gone off to the smoking-room) Hilda and her mother sat alone in the library. For a while they chatted of trivialities. Then, abruptly, her mother began — "I want you to tell me about your engagement, Hilda. You've never talked to me of it. What are your plans?"

"I don't know that there's anything to tell. We're going to Paris for our honeymoon, and of course we shall live in London. I want to be as close to dad as possible."

"And you're very happy, darling? You're very fond of him?"

"Oh! I like him well enough or I shouldn't have accepted him. And dad's very pleased."

"But you yourself, Hilda. I want to know."

"Oh! that's all right. We shall jog along together all right, like everyone else, I suppose."

"Hilda, I can't bear to hear you talk like that."

"Like what?"

"As if you didn't care — as if affection counted for nothing."

"How absurd you are, mother."

"You don't know what a loveless marriage means."

Hilda looked up, surprised at her mother's suddenly strained voice.

Then, after a moment, she answered, laughing hardly —

"Oh! it works now-a-days as well as anything else. Paul and Virginie's[33] all very well on a desert island, or in the remoter Midlands."

"But he — he, at least, is in love with you?"

"Yes, I suppose he is — he thinks so anyway. Men can believe anything of themselves."

"Hilda, you don't know how you're making me suffer."

"I'm sorry, mother; but I can't help it; it isn't my fault. It's better to be frank."

"Oh! but you don't know — you don't understand."

"I know the folly of working oneself up to a pitch of ridiculous illusions, and I know dozens of instances of common-sense marriages turning out admirably."

"Hilda, I implore you — break this thing off — before it is too late. You don't know what you're doing. Listen to me. I am your mother, after all."

"How absurd you are, mother. You see you don't understand me a bit. I realize exactly what I'm doing. I'm not a child. You don't suppose I've resolved upon this without due consideration.... Come, mother, don't give way like this.... There's no cause to make yourself unhappy.... Remember, 'nothing venture, nothing win.' Besides, we shall get on splendidly. In many ways we're simply admirably suited."

The door opened, and Lady Whyte appeared, wheeled in by the butler. Lady Lingard brushed her eyes with her handkerchief, and left the room hurriedly.

---

[33] Paul and Virginie are the devoted young lovers of Bernadin de Saint Pierre's classic novel *Paul et Virginie* (1787), set on the island of Mauritius.

"What's the matter with your mother?" Lady Whyte asked sharply.

"She's been working herself into a state about my engagement. It's too absurd," Hilda retorted aggressively. "If only people would leave one alone," she added.

"You don't care for this man, that's evident. You're only in a childish hurry to get married."

"That's all you know about it," Hilda retorted angrily.

"Don't be rude and lose your temper, but sit down and listen to me. Your conduct towards your poor mother is perfectly heartless. It would be quite abominable, if you weren't very young and very ignorant. I tell you, Hilda, you're behaving in a perfectly heartless way."

"And how, pray? I suppose because I wish to marry to please myself. Both you and mother have conceived a ridiculous and unreasonable dislike to Greaves. I really can't hold myself responsible for that."

"You're your father's child all over — a complacent egotist ——"

"How dare you talk like that — how dare you say a word against dad?"

"Because it's high time you were brought to your senses, and that your eyes were opened, before you rush into this marriage. Sit down," the old lady called, "don't keep walking up and down the room like that. Sit down and, for once, listen to me."

Hilda obeyed sullenly.

"Your father's not fit to black Bessie's boots ——"

"Really!" Hilda interrupted with a concentrated sneer.

"Has no reason ever occurred to you why your mother should live down here by herself ——"

"London doesn't agree with mother — she doesn't care for society — she's essentially a country person. Besides ——"

"Your mother lives down here because long ago your father's conduct made it impossible for her to live in London. For years he's been deceiving her ——"

"How dare you talk like this, Aunt Caroline? ——" Her voice rang through the room: she stood erect before the old woman's chair, her eyes flashing, her lips quite bloodless, her hands convulsively clenched.

"Yes, how dare I?" Lady Whyte retorted. "Because for years I've watched this abomination going on. I've seen your mother suffering and submitting in silent misery, till all her life and gladness has gone from her. Because I've seen you, who ought to have helped her, and been her great consolation, avoiding her, neglecting her, sneering at her. And I've seen Mrs. Mathurin, that brazen-faced woman, coming to the house, and your poor mother having to sit smiling between your father and her."

Hilda gripped her by the arm.

"It's a lie, it's a lie, an abominable lie."

And, breaking into a peal of hysterical laughter, slammed the door behind her.

XVIII

She turned the key in her bedroom door, threw open the window, and gazed a moment out into the night; then, suddenly turning, flung herself upon the bed. She did these things deliberately, almost ostentatiously, as if someone were watching her. As yet, she was only conscious of an obscure sense that the scene, downstairs in the library, resembled some hideous climax in a play.

For a long while she lay quite still, her eyes wide open. Aunt Caroline had been foully slandering her father, trying to poison her mind against him — the phrase rang feverishly through her brain, and its melodramatic quality thrilled her with a strange excitement.

Outside, in the blackness, the trees were rustling: beneath her window some of the maids were loudly laughing together.

And hurriedly, her heart filled full of a warm pity for her father — for his white, worn face.... She longed to go to him, to comfort him, ... she longed to avenge him by some striking deed.

She closed her eyes, as if in sudden pain ... She must think the whole thing out, clearly, calmly — what was best for her to do.... If only she were a man, and Aunt Caroline were a man.... Dad — if only she could go back to him tonight....

It was a lie, a lie, she told herself passionately ... a lie, he was the very soul of honour ... something must be done ... Why had she done nothing, said nothing? ... Why was she so alone?

She sprang up.

Greaves — she would go down to him in the smoking-room....

No, but she couldn't — she couldn't speak to him of it.... Oh! but it was a lie ... it must be a lie ... dad, poor dad — how it would make him suffer if he knew.... Greaves would tell her at once that it was a lie ... he would know what was best to be done.

Impulsively she fumbled with the lock and hurried downstairs.

*   *   *   *   *

He was lying in a big arm-chair, smoking a cigar, reading a French novel.

At the sight of her face he started, exclaiming —

"What's the matter, Hilda?"

"I want to talk to you — to consult you. Something very terrible has just happened." As she spoke, she became aware of her own concentrated calm, and of a half-formulated desire to act admirably.

And she began to walk up and down the room.

"It's difficult to know how to tell you.... After dinner, Aunt Caroline and I were together in the library, and she began to say the most abominable things against dad — that the reason why mother always lives down here is because of Mrs. Mathurin — that — that dad's been behaving wickedly for years — that now — he's in love with some actress — Mrs. Whittingham, whom, you know, dad has helped, and been kind to ——"

"Good God! She's been saying all that to you.... Is that all? Did she say anything else?"

"I wouldn't listen. I went upstairs to my room."

"Where was your mother?"

"She'd gone away.... I don't know ... I don't understand.... Aunt Caroline was furious with me."

"But, explain, why was she furious?"

"She said I've been neglecting mother — I don't know — perhaps she was right.... She said that now I was going to be married, it was time my eyes were opened — those were her words."

He threw his cigar across the room into the grate, and waited hesitatingly.

"You don't doubt him too?" she broke out. "You don't believe these abominable things? Do say something — speak. Say you don't believe them."

"No, no, how can you think such a thing," he answered hurriedly.

He came close to her and put his hand on her shoulder.

"Hilda, I will see what's to be done. You must leave this matter in my hands absolutely. You must trust me. There's been some dreadful misunderstanding."

She was gazing at him doubtfully: gradually, his smooth, authoritative tone convinced her.

"What are you going to do?" she asked weakly.

"I shall see Lady Whyte."

"Tonight?"

"Yes, tonight."

"What will you say?"

"I shall find out her motive for saying those things. I shall clear it all up absolutely."

"Father must never know ——"

"No, no, of course not," he answered hastily.

"Greaves, will you swear to me that it's not true — I'm only a girl: I don't understand things. But you know dad — you're a man of the world — you know that it's impossible — impossible that he could have behaved wickedly. Give me your word of honour, Greaves, and then I will obey you absolutely."

"There, Hilda, it isn't true — of course it isn't true."

"You give me your word of honour."

"I give you my word of honour," he repeated steadily. "And now you must go straight up to bed. You're worn out with excitement."

"Very well," she answered submissively. "Goodnight. You don't know how you've comforted me. I trust you absolutely. And in the morning you'll tell me everything?"

"Yes, in the morning."

She put her arms round his neck, and kissed him on the forehead, reverently.

*   *   *   *   *

When she was gone, he lit a fresh cigar, and mused with a cheap, contemptuous cynicism on the blundering irony of life.

XIX

They were nearing London. Through the fog the wilderness of black slate roofs glimmered wanly: in the distance, like a monstrous, phantasmagoric[34] fortress, some gasworks loomed. The train stopped, and Greaves, peering out, caught a glimpse below the viaduct of a double row of low-walled, brown brick houses — jaded creepers pushing their grimy greenery around the windows; slatternly women lounging in the doorways, troops of squalid children sprawling over the pavement. And for a moment he mused curiously on the degraded simplification of the lives of these creatures.[35]

He turned to Hilda. She had opened her eyes vaguely, but meeting his glance, closed them again. They were alone in the carriage — she pretending to sleep; he, opposite watching her, busy conjecturing why, with a certain ostentation, she had throughout the journey avoided all reference to the episode of last night. After she had left him over a second cigar, he had decided that obviously his course was to stand by and watch the situation (which, despite its somewhat grotesque elements, struck him as quaintly pathetic) work itself out.

At the station, telling the footman to bring on her luggage, she hurried to the carriage, and drove away, bidding him a mechanical goodbye. He remained standing on the platform, gazing at the retreating brougham, and her expression, as he recalled it, seemed all at once to betoken the important impatience of some irksome resolve.

An accumulation of work absorbed him till the following afternoon, when, full of an ironical and expectant curiosity, he called at Belgrave Street.

From the butler he learned the news that Lord Lingard was seriously ill, that Lady Lingard had been telegraphed for, and was expected every moment.

[34]   See note 1 on p. 233.
[35]   This paragraph draws on Crackanthorpe's 'Pleasant Court' in *Vignettes*. However, the phrase 'the degraded simplification of the lives of these creatures' is an importation with a degenerationist slant which conveys something of Chamney's disdain for the poor.

He went into the library, and presently Hilda appeared. Her face was pale and worn, and the tired, tense look in her eyes accentuated, so he thought, her resemblance to her father.

He hastened towards her, making an ineffectual gesture to take both her hands in his. She repulsed him quite definitely.

"What is it?" he asked.

"Pneumonia, brought on by travelling back to London with a bad cold." Her voice startled him. It was strangely deliberate and almost hard.

"He had gone out of town?"

"Yes. It appears that he went down to Maidenhead on Saturday to Mrs. Whittingham's, and came back yesterday with the fever on him."

"Mrs. Whittingham's?" he murmured.

Their eyes met. In the steadiness of her gaze he read the riddle of her stony composure.

"How is he now?" he asked mechanically.

"He's dozing. In the night he was very delirious."

"You look worn-out. Have you got a nurse?"

"Yes."

"Is there anything I can do?"

"Mother will be here presently," she answered curtly.

"There's no danger?"

"Not immediately.... I think he will die."

"Good God!"

At that moment Mrs. Mathurin's voice sounded in the hall outside, excitedly questioning the butler, then asking to see Miss Lingard.

Greaves, recovering himself, started towards the door to intercept her. But he was too late. She had pushed past him into the room.

"Hilda, tell me about this dreadful news.... What is the matter with him? ... It can't be really pneumonia.... How did it happen? ... He's not in danger?"

She spoke incoherently, in a rapid, husky whisper.

Hilda paused before answering, and her features stiffened.

"No, not at present."

"Who's attending him? What do the doctors say? Have you got proper nurses?"

"Everything is being done that can be done. I am expecting mother every minute." She spoke with icy fluency; then turning stiffly, left the room.

It was almost a minute before Mrs. Mathurin realized what had happened. Her eyes dilated: she caught at her breath, looking round the room with a helpless, frightened expression. Clutching at the table, she sank into a chair.

Greaves, who had been standing in the window, came towards her.

"Your arm ... to my carriage, ..." she gasped.

He led her to the brougham, and when she was inside, called to the coachman "Home."

And, as he walked away up the street, the Lingard carriage rolled past him. Through the closed window he caught a glimpse of Lady Lingard's indefinite profile.

XX

During his delirium he had been very violent, calling at intervals fiercely upon Bertha, and pleading with some other unknown woman. But the fever left him at last; and now, quite lucidly, he was slowly dying, lying exhausted day after day, staring vacantly at the wall before him. His face was grown wizened like a very old man's: a ragged white beard disfigured his chin.

For nine days Bessie had scarcely left him. So habituated had she become to the subdued routine of the sick-room, that sometimes she wondered dully whether, in reality, she had not been living there during many months. And while the day-nurse watched by his bedside, she would take her place before the window, to gaze out at the houses opposite, to wait, strangely benumbed, for the end....

The long afternoon faded into the dreary, evening twilight: she lost all consciousness of the present, and across the misty wilderness of the past her thoughts wandered stumbling. For hours, dazed as in a dream, she sat reviewing the past, till it was as if he were already gone, as if her life with him were already ended — a blurred, tangled tale, of which the last page was turned.

By and by, one by one, sprang up vivid memories of her childhood, of her girlhood, of her father, of her mother, of the little yellow house in the High Street at Oxford, of a hundred incidents that had long lain forgotten. And then of a sudden there crept over her, like a brutal interruption, the deadening sense that her father and mother were gone years and years ago, that the little yellow house was pulled down, that never, never could the old days come again; and bitterly, silently, she cried to herself....

And with a desperate, piteous persistence, she reverted to the memories of her youth.

* * * * *

She turned, and at the sight of his tired, aged face, she remembered all the tireless activity of his life, and sat stupidly watching him, sullenly incredulous of the great change that had come over him.

She moved to the bedside and took the nurse's place. He was sleeping with one hand stretched across the coverlet towards her. He opened his eyes, and lay for a while looking at her feebly. The nurse had left the room; he and she were alone. There was no sound but the hurried ticking of the clock, and the faint distant rumour of the traffic. A great yearning for a reconciliation welled up within her, a yearning to tell him how she forgave him; to tell him how she had guessed how things were all these years; how she had come to understand that she was not good enough for him; how now that during those mad nights of his delirium she had learned the truth from his own lips, she found no blame for him in her heart....

But he had closed his eyes again wearily.

She fell to thinking vaguely of the after-world. There, she imagined, the past would be made altogether clear; there each would know the secrets of the other's heart. Then she would tell him of her forgiveness: then he would see how all these years she had come to understand.

And bending over the bed as he slept, she whispered to God to help him in hasty incoherent phrases.

* * * * *

Later, after the visit of the two doctors, from the nurse's manner she guessed that he would not survive the night; and the sense of her own helplessness, face to face with the inexorableness of death, terrified her. She longed passionately for him to live, rebelling desperately against the horrible extinction of his being; wildly, abjectly praying to God to spare him.

If only he would live.... Feverishly, piteously she pictured the details of a peaceful future — down at Tukenton; he convalescent, she tending him with eager, unremitting care.

After midnight he fell asleep, and at the nurse's suggestion, she lay down to rest on the sofa by the window. An hour later the nurse woke her gently, and all at once she knew that the end was come. He had died quite peacefully in his sleep.

She went up to the bed. He lay there, quite still, and so unchanged that the first sight of him caused her no shock. Then gradually she understood that it was not he, but his dead body that was stretched between the sheets, and she broke into a faint, frightened fit of sobbing.

* * * * *

The door opened, and Hilda came in. She stood by the bedside, rigid, her face set. Then turned, and went without a word.

But Bessie was conscious of nothing, but of the whole irrevocable story of their common life trailing interminably across her mind — her own inadequacy, and his superiority to her — and as she sobbed, her heart was aching with an immense, a passionate pity for him.

XXI

The day after the funeral Hilda went down to Tukenton with her maid. She told no one beforehand of her departure; only left a scribbled note for her mother.

Every detail of the house in Belgrave Street, reminding her, as it did, of her father, had become hateful to her; and, above all, her mother's presence — the constant sight of her patient expression of dumb suffering — was intolerable.

She longed imperiously to escape, to be alone with her own crowding thoughts.

*   *   *   *   *

And, down at Tukenton, all day long she nursed the bitterness of her anguish....

Since his death, she had never cried; she felt no grief; she was only embittered against the humiliation of the smirched memory he had left behind him.

Occasionally, this consciousness of her own hardness startled her: she made spasmodic and insincere efforts to soften towards him, while the keen remembrance of his words during that first night of his delirium stung her incessantly to a fresh sense of her humiliation.

And realizing the overwhelming cruelty of her own deception, in self-pity she was moved almost to tears — how she had worshipped him, reverenced him, jealously excluded others from any share in her affection. Looking backwards, she saw him once more, as she had always seen him, a being set above the rest of the world, sacred, wonderful, almost mysterious, so that, often, in the presence of strangers, she had felt consciously proud of her familiarity with him....

... Oh! why had she learned to believe in these things — in honour that was a society fashion, in fidelity that meant ceremonious deceit? ... Bitterly she recalled how, in her shallow folly, she had proclaimed that marriage was a mere arrangement; how, in her pretentious ignorance, she had scoffed at her mother's old-fashioned ideas; how she had once complacently pitied a girl-acquaintance, whose father had disgraced himself, and been forced to escape abroad. And, remorselessly, she railed at herself, at the miserable mockery of her former pride....

For her father she had found no indulgence; for her mother she felt no sympathy — only a vague artificial pity. Little by little she came to comprehend that her mother's inadequacy had been the cause of his treachery; that, inferior to him intellectually, she had proved no help-mate to him in the time of his struggle for success; that she had made no effort; that, weakly, she had abandoned him, to live alone, and apart from him, and that, later, she had known; and *she had acquiesced....*

Her past, too, had been ignominious; she, too, had been content to live a lie.

* * * * *

Thus, blindly, in her pain, she probed the hollowness of her former unquestioning faith, till she had gauged the whole gaping extent of its mockery. Then, shivering, she seemed to see the whole world tainted — men and women evil-hearted, inwardly contemptuous of honour, glibly smiling, preserving a smooth, decorous demeanour. And at intervals, the rhythmically recurring consciousness that he, her own father, who had been everything to her, all her life, had lived ignobly with the rest; that his memory would remain irretrievably soiled, stunned her into a dull, a leaden despair.

* * * * *

One evening, her thoughts reverted constantly to Greaves Chamney; she realized that, somehow, his figure had become altogether repulsive; that she mistrusted him definitely. She sat down to write to him, and found a momentary, hurried relief in a deliberate rupture of their engagement.

And, by and by, there arose within her a weary yearning after goodness; a burning remorse for the empty, useless egoism of her former self; and an impulsive impatience to devote herself in some striking way to the service of others — to become a hospital nurse; to work among the poor; to relieve suffering; to do good, to be surrounded by gratitude and love.

XXII

The house in Belgrave Street was to be sold; in the future they were to be considerably poorer. Bessie came down to Tukenton, and resumed listlessly the tranquil routine of her old life. She appeared aged, and not a little enfeebled: her daily stock of strength seemed altogether scanty.

Old Lady Whyte was away at Bath: the mother and daughter were alone. But they lived apart, meeting only at meal-times, when Hilda's greeting would express a certain perfunctory and shallow solicitude.

Yet, sometimes, during the restless broodings of sleepless nights, forcing herself to contemplate the long years of her mother's suffering, and the bitter part that her own harsh attitude had contributed, with a sudden, spasm of compassionate contrition, she seemed to perceive herself grown heartless; caring for no one; incapable of affection — a personification of withered egoism. And, touched by the consciousness of her own misery, she sobbed to herself, and resolved that, in the morning, she would start to comfort her mother with uncommon tact.

Nevertheless, she continued, day after day, to shrink from the effort of a movement of tenderness, till, little by little, their estrangement stiffened, attained the rigidity of an unbroken habit. It was as if an intangible and unsurmountable barrier had grown up between them.

And now, an aching longing for her dead father crept over her — a gnawing grief; an incessant, hopeless despair, when she remembered his dead, still face; when she remembered that he was gone for ever — that never, never would she see him again.... And sullenly, to herself, she would insist that she could never forget that her mother had been to blame; that his dishonour had, in great measure, been her mother's fault. A stubborn, half-stifled rancour smouldered within her; and the mere approach of her mother's figure recalling in a rush the ugly, crowding memories became hateful. She took to devising hasty excuses for reducing their meetings; to avoiding her almost deliberately.

* * * * *

So time flitted past. By and by it was as if her mother had come to acquiesce in the bare formality of their daily intercourse, for she, too, seemed to shrink from any attempt at intimacy, living on, day after day, vacantly brooding, talking but seldom, dully contented with the regular round of her small, monotonous occupations.

One evening Hilda, with some embarrassment, abruptly announced that she had broken off her engagement. A long, uncomfortable pause followed; then her mother replied coldly — "I am very glad, Hilda, you know I never liked him."

And henceforward, somehow, the girl felt happier. Her prickings of conscience grew rarer, and finally the thought of her mother ceased to cause her uneasiness. Her own attitude no longer seemed to need justification; and she became reconciled to the constant sight of the enigmatic figure....

XXIII

Twice she caught a glimpse of Stephen Walsh, riding in the distance. One morning, at the corner of the village, she met him face to face, and he turned and walked back with her to the gates.

He asked her for news of her mother, referring gently to her grief, betraying, beneath a distant discretion, his profound personal admiration for her father. And comprehending quickly that it had been impossible for his frank, upright nature to view him otherwise, all at once her eyes filled full of tears, and she looked up at him in impulsive gratitude....

... Thenceforward, little by little, they came to resume a semblance of their old friendship. He used to join her when she rode with her groom, and together they used to wander through the lanes. They talked often of her father: she encouraged him to remind her that he had suspected nothing; the continual pretence that she, too, sorrowed reverently, soothed her.

And, instinctively, she took refuge, as it were, in the loyal simplicity of his nature: she let him lead their conversations, assenting to his opinions almost timidly. At first this was merely the mechanical subservience of exceeding fatigue; but insensibly, as she listened while he related his reminiscences of the hunting-field, or explained his practical projects for the improvement of his property, or his plans for the bettering of the labourer's lot, a great, confiding[36] respect for him penetrated her. She imagined how, at every turn in his life, it had been easier for him to do right than to do wrong: dimly she divined his unfamiliarity with evil; that the simple virtues — truth and loyalty, patience, chivalry and courage — were his, as naturally as his physical strength. In his presence she never perceived how strangely her former assertiveness had faded: his naïve enjoyment of his occupations, his placid love of his life, dominated her.

Thus, the reaction that was at work within her, caused her to brood dreamily on his personality, while her gratitude towards him led her to shrink instinctively from a fresh recognition of those defects of his, which before she had definitely recognized, and to drift, in unconscious insincerity, into a forced admiration of those qualities, which seemed to her but just lately revealed. When she recalled her former attitude towards him — her shallow, thoughtless contempt — she felt ashamed.

Passively, she let him absorb her; and because at this crisis in her life she found his companionship restful, she deluded herself into the belief that she would always need him, as she needed him now; into a random assumption of the permanence of her own constraint.

That he would never change, she foresaw; and that, if she married him, he would love her submissively, unquestioningly, with the unswerving fidelity of a faithful mastiff. She would be able to trust him implicitly; and without further probing of her feelings towards him, weakly she urged herself into imagining how life with him would be altogether secure, peaceful; into visioning long years of suave and sunny repose....

And her memories of the time of her engagement to the other, grew all blurred, shadowy, unreal. His figure faded from her mind, she forgot him easily, as one forgets a chance acquaintance.

XXIV

Slowly the prospect of his great happiness dawned upon him.

During that long series of dreary days, through which he had lived mechanically — resolutely, by means of a hundred improvised occupations, endeavouring to oust her image from his mind — not once had he accused her of insincerity, of trifling thoughtlessly with his love. For the fact that she could

---

[36]   See note 3 on p. 147.

not care for him, he had blamed only himself — his own dulness, his own clumsiness, his own obvious inferiority. He bore his heart-burnings with an uncomplaining, dogged stolidity; still stubbornly hoping, after his unreasoning instinctive fashion.

But when, for the first time, he met her again, the warm thrill of gladness at being once more beside her, caused him instantaneously to forget the sullen jealousy, the compressed anguish of spirit, with which these last weeks he had been battling: in his impulsive eagerness to be of use to her in her grief, in his sorrow at her sorrow, the whole bitter memory of the scene of his rejection faded from his mind. Pale, grave, changed in manner — grown older he tentatively judged — more beautiful, certainly, than she had ever appeared before, far away, enshrined, as it were, in the mystery of suffering, to long for her then, to start to rebuild his shattered hopes of winning her, would have seemed a sacrilege. Away from her, he thought of little else: her image was ever present: he brooded over her passionate love for her father, and her broken spirit seemed to him infinitely piteous. Thus timorous of his own awkwardness, he approached her with exceeding reverence, puzzling how best to cheer her, wondering laboriously how best he could help her to forget....

One afternoon they sauntered home, side by side, in silence, along the white high road.

He had almost forgotten her, musing to himself on each familiar landmark, dreamily listening to the distant, floating hum of the reaping machines, or to the soft rustle of the beech trees, all spangled with silver in the summer sunlight, or watching the lazy rippling of the swelling, golden fields.

At the gates they stopped, and suddenly realizing his taciturnity, he said ruefully —

"I'm so sorry; I'm afraid I've been more stupid than usual this afternoon."

She took his hand to wish him goodbye, and answered gravely —

"No, you are not stupid; you are kind: I shall never be able to thank you."

And spurring her horse, she trotted up the avenue, towards the house.

He rode slowly home, moved by a profound protecting pity for her, for the solitude of her mourning, which now he comprehended more vividly than he had done before.

Throughout the evening, flushed with simple happy pride, he repeated to himself those parting words of hers — "I shall never be able to thank you." More than ever was he conscious of his own inferiority: the very fact that he had been able to comfort her a little seemed to accentuate the contrast between them, while the delicious sense that she had confided herself to him, allowed him, as it were, to protect her, and the thought that now, at this very moment perhaps, she was thinking of him with gratitude, set all his old love aflame.

All the next day the rain fell in torrents: to ride with her was impossible, and to call, without an adequate excuse, would, he feared, have seemed an intrusion. So he killed the long hours of the afternoon tramping across the slushy fields, methodically recapitulating fragments of their conversations, recalling chance changes of her tone, of her expression, argumentatively reconstructing a fresh fabric of hope.

On the morrow, he waited for her at the gates as usual; and when she appeared talked to her in a strained fashion, of the weather, of the damage done to the harvest by the rain. Her manner had relapsed into her former indifference, so that he almost felt a doubt whether that moment of their last parting had not after all been but a mad fabrication of his fancy. Then at the sight of her pale still face, he stifled his disappointment resolutely, impulsively respectful of her grief.

The days went by; and he continued to hope patiently. And, little by little, the daily renewal of her familiarity, and the persistent recollection of that one phrase of hers, "I shall never be able to thank you," bred at last within him a deep-rooted confidence, an indefinite yet secure trust in her, and lent to these first weeks of autumn the glow of a mysterious joy. Every night he imagined the coming of some signal opportunity of revealing to her his devotion: often in his dreams, he visioned himself gladly giving up his life for her sake. And, looking forward into the future, to the unending happiness of having her by his side, he spent hours in devising golden projects for her delight.

XXV

He helped her to dismount. The groom held the horses, and they entered the church. It was an ancient, picturesque building, with a square, ivy-clad tower. As they had ridden through the village, she had observed that the door was ajar, and had suggested that they should go inside.

"How new and uninteresting!" she exclaimed. "It's been all restored and quite spoilt." They stood together beside one of the stuccoed pillars. With his hat in his hand he scrutinized the ceiling vaguely: then his gaze reverted to her. Presently she became aware that his eyes were fixed upon her, and turning towards him, laughed a little nervously.

"I wonder if one can get onto the top of the tower," she asked.

He found a side-door at the end of the aisle; and they mounted a worn, winding stone staircase. The roof of the tower had been newly overlaid with zinc: they crossed it, and leaned together over the parapet.

A tribe of sparrows, undisturbed by their presence, were boisterously twittering in the ivy: beneath, on the ridge of a thatched cottage a cat sat crouched in ambush: a four-wheeled waggon, laden with corn, was toiling up the hill; the cracking of the carter's whip was carried past them on the breeze; and beyond, the plain lay spread — a wide, undulating patchwork of gold and green, peopled here and there by huddled groups of white-faced hamlets. The sky was cloudless — an empty vault of vast pale blue.

He pointed out to her in the distance the red chimneys of Tukenton, and further, away to the left, Courtlands, where he lived, half-hidden in the trees.

After a while he ceased speaking. She stayed dreamily surveying the country side, mapped out before her, marvelling how intimately it all seemed to have grown associated with him, forming, as it were, the natural background of his figure. Absently she fancied that, in time, she would come to love it, too, in all its detail, as he loved it, with a tranquil, deep-rooted affection.

"It is very beautiful," she murmured, half to herself.

And, prompted by a sudden impulse, she lifted her hand and laid it across his.

"You will be very good to me," she said gently.

He did not move, though she looked up expectantly into his face; only his grasp tightened slowly upon hers.

"You do care for me, after all ——?" he whispered.

For several minutes he remained silent, holding her hand in his, awkwardly caressing the fingers. She watched a horde of rooks, journeying homewards across the valley, cawing one to another, high in the sky, and she told herself, slowly, gravely, how she had given herself to him irrevocably.

And concerning the future, as she gazed out across the landscape, bathed in the full glare of the autumn sun, she wondered, doubtingly, hastily stifling a spasm of hesitating apprehension.

Then brusquely reminding herself of his natural goodness, of the sure faithfulness of his love, she repeated —

"How beautiful it is! I shall be so happy."

"No, no," he answered quickly. "We will travel: we will live in London: I have thought it all out."

"You are wonderful," she said simply.

He laughed, a quick, happy laugh, and looked into her eyes. His lips moved impulsively as if he were about to speak.

And they remained still standing together, leaning over the parapet, hand in hand; she watching curiously the odd, flickering smile that transfigured his face. Vague visions of new countries flitted before her — of snow, peaked mountains, of deep-blue lakes, of ruined Italian cities — filling her with a feverish impatience to have done with the past, to begin the future.... And once more reminding herself, almost triumphantly, of his natural goodness, of the sure faithfulness of his love, she foresaw herself maintaining with ease her present attitude towards him, continuing always contented by his side.

And her confidence in his stability led her to realize in a flash, that he would prove in no way exacting, and that she would be able, without difficulty, to conceal from him that she did not care for him, as he cared for her, while she fondly fancied that, in time, perhaps, she would change; that under the influence of his companionship she would grow to resemble him....

He came nearer to her, as if to kiss her: she drew back hastily, exclaiming —

"We must go down. The horses will be getting chilled, and Hedges will be wondering what has happened."

PART II:
UNCOLLECTED FICTION

He Wins Who Loses

I

Deeper and deeper grew the twilight: longer and blacker grew the shadows. The slim figure of a woman sat in an arm-chair drawn close in to the fire with her feet resting on the fender bar. Rebellious masses of dark brown hair straggled onto her forehead, and her round, grey eyes had a dreamy, far-away look in them. Though she was as slight and supple as a young girl, there were lines across her forehead, little premature wrinkles under the eyes, and a seriousness about the mouth that gave her a quaint, aged look.

Mrs. Hayward had been married only three years, though she was turned five and thirty. Her husband, John Hayward of Coatbridge Hall, Esquire, was a Justice of the Peace and a Deputy Lieutenant for the County of Suffolk.

For the last three days he had been up in London on business. He was coming back this evening by the six o'clock train.

As Mrs. Hayward sat watching the flickering tongues of yellow flame, her thoughts strolled back to her unmarried life in London — to the little flat off the Edgware Road, where for so many years she kept house for her father, at that time editor of a third-rate weekly paper.[1] Hers had been a hard life, and as she recalled the struggles in those old days to make both ends meet, a smile passed across her face — it was all so different now.

She thought of John — as she had seen him for the first time — his burly figure absurdly out of place amid a jabbering roomful of her father's friends, struggling journalists, politicians, artists. And though her father was very polite — almost obsequious to Mr. Hayward, out of deference to his estate in Suffolk, worth five thousand a year, John was so obviously ill at ease that she felt sorry for him, and wondered what in the world had brought him there. She found him a seat by her side, and did her best to talk to him. But he was not communicative; all he did was to stare in a bewildered sort of way at her and at the people. So after a while she gave it up.

The next Sunday he appeared again, and every following Sunday for a month, till it seemed quite natural to see him there. He always stood in the doorway, never speaking to anyone; but when she had done pouring out the tea, he would elbow his way across to her and sit down by her side.

Then he came one afternoon in the week, and, when she had given him a

---

[1]   Edgware Road in London runs north-west from Marble Arch to the suburb of Edgware. By the late nineteenth century parts of it had become notably cosmopolitan and relatively inexpensive.

cup of tea, he asked her quietly to be his wife. She had half expected it, and had resolved to say Yes — chiefly for her father's sake, to whom this rich marriage meant much. And she too was happy, for in spite of his awkwardness and his taciturnity, there was a singleness of heart about him that made her esteem him. He did not seem to have many ideas, he did not look at things as she did, and he was thirteen years older than herself. But she was past thirty, and had long dispensed with the romantic notions of girlhood.

So they were married — a quiet wedding in a big, bare church near the Charing Cross Road. When the ceremony was over, they had come straight down to Coatbridge Hall, and here they had been ever since, with the exception of a month spent in London every spring.

At first how she had looked forward to the going back to London! For weeks beforehand a childish yearning for the bustle of the cabs and omnibuses had haunted her. And then, she could not help being proud of her new position, and there were so many of her father's struggling friends to whom she wanted to be kind.

But somehow it was all a bitter disappointment. Nothing turned out as she had dreamed. John hated going away anywhere; above all he hated London. He was miserable and grumpy the whole time, so that it was quite a relief to her when they were sitting together in the train, once more whirling back to Coatbridge. He disliked her old friends too, and could not help showing it; he was vaguely jealous of them, because they talked to her of things he did not understand; he was nettled that these young men, who were always out at elbows, should know more than he did. Their impecuniosity, too, he looked upon with vague suspicion, and somehow felt that to have so much knowledge and so little ready cash was not respectable. All this produced a constraint between him and his wife, which became more painful and took longer to wear off with each succeeding spring; so this May Mrs. Hayward had come back resolved to give up the London visit next year.

Since then day had followed day, week had followed week, in almost unbroken monotony. More and more solitary her life became. When John was out, which was almost always the case, she would sit for hours, in summer in the garden, in winter by fireside, reading and dreaming, dreaming and reading. There were a certain number of neighbours, but no one that she really cared to see. She felt that she had nothing in common with them. It was as if they did not speak the same language; they did not understand any of the things that she liked; and though, when they called, she always did her best to be agreeable to them, they instinctively felt that she was making an effort; and their visits grew less and less frequent by degrees. John had reproached her, especially of late, with her apathy, and had even insisted on her seeing a doctor from Ipswich. After this she had tried to interest herself in a local election, in which he was taking a prominent part, and, in a half-hearted sort of way, she had succeeded.

Yet this state of continued compression did not make her unhappy. At first, indeed, her isolation in this rambling Georgian house had oppressed her, and the craving for expansion had been hard to stifle. But she had gradually become used to it. Only now and then a strange melancholy would come over her, a yearning for something, vague, indefinable....

On, on her thoughts wandered, till the sound of wheels crunching on the gravel sweep outside roused her reverie.

A minute later she heard John's deep voice in the hall, giving some orders about his luggage, and asking the servant where she was. In he came, with his heavy tread, looking bigger than ever in a fur coat that reached to his heels. He kissed her on the forehead, and, taking off his coat, threw himself into an arm-chair.

"By George, it *was* a cold journey from the station," he exclaimed. "It must be freezing hard — my feet are like stones," he added, as he turned the soles of his boots to the fire.

"You'll have some tea, John, won't you? You must want it after your journey."

When he had drunk it, he got up and stood on the hearthrug with his back to the fire. He was a heavy and rather clumsily made man, with a ruddy face and a bushy, black beard.

"What a relief it is to get back!" he exclaimed, looking complacently round the room. "I can't imagine how anyone can live in such a hole as London. I believe I should have been ill with the fogs if I'd stopped there another day. Well, I did all my business. Went to Keith & Proctor's, saw Blenkinsop about the mortgages. Last night I dined with Chalmers at the House, and stopped for a part of the debate on the Agricultural Holdings Bill. By George, you never heard such nonsense as one of those Radical chaps was talking. There ought to be a public subscription to ship fellows like that off to the colonies. Well, Kate, is there any news?"

"No, nothing," she answered, "I'm so glad you've come back. The place seemed quite deserted without you."

"Oh, by the by," he broke in, "I thought old Bess was getting a bit groggy, so I bought you a new pony. I happened to look in at Tattersall's[2] on Thursday, and I saw just the very thing I wanted for you. A little black beast, a trifle under fourteen hands, showy, but quiet as a sheep. There was a cart and harness going at the same time, so I bought the lot."

"John, it *was* nice of you."

"Oh, another thing! Who do you think I came across? Why, Lord Flamborough, who used to be a great chum of mine at Eton. I hadn't seen him for twenty years. We sat chatting together over old times at the club, till

[2] Tattersall's was (and still is) the leading auctioneer of race horses.

past one, just like a couple of schoolboys. I've asked him down for the covert shooting next week.[3] Of course, I told him I couldn't offer him anything very grand, but he said he hated great slaughters. When I knew him at Eton, he never expected to come into the title. Now you know, he's married and one of the richest peers in the Kingdom. He's a sort of literary, artist chap, too, so you and he will get on famously together, I expect."

"Is Lady Flamborough coming too?" asked Mrs. Hayward.

"His wife? Oh! no. You see I just asked him for the shooting. He's coming on Wednesday, and he will have to get back on the Saturday afternoon. By George! There's the dressing bell. I'm as hungry as a hunter."

II

Again and again during the next three days, Mrs. Hayward found her thoughts reverting to the subject of Lord Flamborough's visit. She tried to recall everything that she had heard about him in London … A rich eccentric nobleman … an artist of no ordinary ability … supposed to have made an unhappy marriage … these few facts came back to her as fragments of conversation heard in her father's house. More than this she did not know, but it was sufficient groundwork for her imagination to work upon, and during the twilight hours she would conjure up all sorts of fanciful portraits of the expected guest.

She was nervous too, for, though a certain number of visitors came to Coatbridge in the course of the year, she had never received so great a personage as Lord Flamborough. In the little world in which she had been brought up, the ways of Society had been as a closed book. She was vaguely ashamed of her fears, yet she could not resist mentioning them to John. He was annoyed, and answered her shortly that of course she was not to put herself out in any way, and that what was good enough for him was good enough for Flamborough. Still she noticed that his consultations with the head-keeper were longer and more frequent than was usual even at this time of the year, and that he was taking special trouble with the shooting arrangements.

When Wednesday evening came, Mrs. Hayward was sitting, as was her wont, over the library fire. John had driven into Coatbridge to meet Lord Flamborough.

At the sound of wheels outside she jumped up. Her heart was throbbing violently, she was trembling from head to foot. Desperately she struggled to compose herself, feeling that her agitation was perfectly ridiculous.

In came John, followed by a short, thick-set man, with a heavy stoop in his shoulders. He was slightly bald, with a high, conical-shaped forehead; his

---

[3]   Covert shooting: shooting game in a sheltered thicket or woodland.

complexion was pallid, and his brown beard was stubbly and badly trimmed. It would not have been a striking face but for the large, prominent, grey eyes, with finely chiselled lids.

"I hope you had a pleasant journey," murmured Mrs. Hayward as she shook hands. She was going to say something more, but her voice sounded strange, and startled her. He was watching her closely, and it made her more and more nervous.

"Yes, thank you," he answered. "It's a very easy journey from town by that train, as I daresay you know."

Then a long pause, during which Mrs. Hayward suffered acutely. She felt that she must say something. Fifty different remarks passed through her mind but she rejected them all as soon as they occurred to her. She knew Lord Flamborough's eyes were fixed curiously upon her. The blood mounted to her cheeks, a hot feeling came over her.

Suddenly John called out from the hall:

"I say, Flamborough, there's only half an hour before dinner, come and let me show you your room."

John had invited a few of the neighbours and their wives to meet Lord Flamborough at dinner. Mrs. Hayward had timidly remonstrated, with an instinctive feeling that they were not the sort of people whom he would care to meet. But John had insisted, declaring that it was the proper thing.

Half an hour later when she came down to the drawing room she found everyone already assembled.

"Years ago, Mrs. Hayward," said Lord Flamborough, as they led the way to the dining room, "I met your father. It was just after I had come down from Oxford, full of all sorts of crude notions about art, literature, and life generally. He gave me I remember, some very sound advice, which I have never forgotten. He was a man of singularly sound judgment, far too able for the position he occupied," he added thoughtfully, half to himself.

Mrs. Hayward looked up at him and said simply,

"Thank you, Lord Flamborough."

He seemed surprised, and glanced quickly at her; then nodded almost imperceptibly, as if to say: "I understand."

From this moment all constraint between them vanished. He gave her news of some of her father's old friends, telling her little anecdotes of one or two of them, which brought the old days vividly back to her. He asked gently about her father, regretting that their lives had drifted so far apart. So they talked on, discovering at each fresh turn in the conversation that they had something more in common.

For Mrs. Hayward the dinner table and the people sitting round it had disappeared. She only knew that she was talking as she had not talked for years, with a sense of exquisite exhilaration in throwing off the state of compression in which she had been living.

It was not till after dinner, when he was sitting by her side in the drawing room, that the absolute frankness with which she was exposing the whole of her inner life to a man whom she had seen for the first time only an hour or two ago, flashed upon her. She had been led on by his extraordinary quickness of comprehension. Almost before she spoke, he seemed to understand the meaning.

She flushed, rose, and crossing the room, began an animated conversation with the fat wife of the county member.

During the rest of the evening they did not exchange another word, but as she bade him goodnight there was a humbled look in her eyes, as if asking pardon for her abruptness.

III

Everyone had gone to bed but John and Lord Flamborough, who sat together in the smoking room over their whisky and cigars. Outside the wind moaned fitfully and drove the rain pelting against the window.

"What a night!" John murmured sleepily. He was tired out, for all day they had been shooting in a bitter east wind.

Presently his cigar rolled on the floor, his head sank on his chest; he was asleep.

Lord Flamborough relit his cigar and went on thinking. He must leave tomorrow morning by the first train. From this fact there was no escape, and the thought of it made his heart ache with a vague unhappiness which he had not felt since he was a child.

So rapidly had his three days at Coatbridge Hall passed that even now he could scarcely realize what had happened. All he knew was that he felt a yearning, an unspeakable yearning, to be with Mrs. Hayward, to talk to her and to hear her voice. It was not love — at least, not love as men generally understand it — for in it there was not even the shadow of a desire. He felt no jealousy of John. "Why should I?" he said to himself, "What have he and she in common?"

There had been but little joy in his life, so little that he had at last grown sceptical of happiness. As a young man his delicate, almost morbid, sensibility had been combined with a passionate devotion to great ideals, to great ambitions. But the world had not handled him gently, and had lost no time in rudely awaking him from his dreams. Shock followed shock in quick succession and these first disenchantments, this first failing of illusions, caused him intense suffering — suffering such as a man of exquisite sensibility alone could know. He winced and writhed till he could bear it no longer; at last, in fierce defiance, he rebelled. He abandoned everything, and plunged into a whirl of dissipation. And, except for hideous moments when the old suffering came back, cruelly, pitilessly, he succeeded in forgetting his pain. After each fresh crisis, he would rush on faster and faster, that there might be no time left for self-analysis.

And so, till he was seven and twenty. Then one morning the news came that his cousin, the young Lord Flamborough, was dead. On that day his whole position changed, and with this change came a sudden weariness of his past mode of life. This weariness, sudden as it was, was, nevertheless, quite complete — so complete that there were moments when he wondered if the past were his or another man's.

From a boy he had possessed considerable artistic gifts and it was to Art that he eagerly turned to fill for him his now empty life. Resolutely he set to, and for years he worked hard, very hard, and made no little progress. His pictures bore the mark of his great natural facility. "Very clever" was what people said of them. But, beyond this, nothing. How could there be? For his interest in life had vanished, the light which had gone out could not be rekindled.

Thus he dragged on year after year, gradually gaining in skill and reputation, yet living listlessly, wearily, taking each day, as it came, never looking forward, scarcely ever looking backward. The doctors told him that he was working too hard, that his constitution was below par; he must go, they said, to Egypt. But he never left England, the energy was wanting.

About three months after this he married, in the same half-absent, half-mechanical way in which he did everything now. He did it because his friends were always urging it upon him, for there was no heir to the title.

When Society heard of the engagement, it said that the match was more Miss Haviland's making than Lord Flamborough's. And for once Society was right. She was a girl of whose life ambition was the mainspring, and, having set herself the task of becoming the Countess of Flamborough, she found it a great deal easier than she had expected. Lord Flamborough she regarded as a quiet, inoffensive creature, whom she would be able to manage and mould without difficulty. She did not care for him, not one bit — she made that quite clear to herself before the marriage. But then, was she capable of caring for anyone? Yet in spite of it all they got on fairly well together; at least, they never quarrelled, that was not Flamborough's way. But in course of time they saw less and less of one another, not out of dislike for each other's society, but because they were simply indifferent to it. And they were childless.

Tonight it was as if he had been suddenly roused from a stupor, as if a flood of light had burst in upon his life. He saw clearly around him at last, and understood whither he had been drifting during the past ten years. Somehow

Mrs. Hayward was the cause of this awakening. He was sure of it, though exactly how it was he did not know. Only it was so.

And back came the heartache with the thought of his departure tomorrow, and the unspeakable yearning to be with her, to talk to her, and to hear her voice.

Ting! ting! ting! — and, as the clock on the mantelpiece began to strike slowly, John woke up with a start. They wished each other goodnight and went off to bed.

IV

My dear Mrs. Hayward,

       I am sincerely sorry that before I left Coatbridge this morning I had not an opportunity of adequately thanking you and John for all your kindness to me during my visit. It was a matter of very deep regret to me that I was not able to stay till Monday as you so kindly asked me to do. But there was an old promise to preside at an annual dinner of artists, and I had not the courage to leave them in the lurch at the last moment.

I cannot tell you what a pleasure it has been to meet you, or the difference it has made in my life. Now that we shall not meet again for some time, I feel all the more strongly that your friendship is of the greatest possible moment to me. It is because I do so much want to keep in touch with you that I beg you to write to me and to let me write to you. I feel that you are absolutely the only person to whom I can say certain things. What things, I can't explain. Do you understand? Anyway, won't you take it on trust?

Though all this is at present quite vague in my own mind, one thing at least I know, that you will not misunderstand me when I ask you to be my friend.

John spoke of running up with you to London for a fortnight at Christmas. If you do, of course you must make my house your headquarters. I am writing to him about it by this post. Hoping for a letter before long,

Very sincerely yours,

Flamborough

Dear Lord Flamborough,

       I have delayed answering your letter till now. It has been so difficult, and writing has not made it easier. How can I answer it? I have asked myself this a hundred times, and always fruitlessly, for in each answer that I fancied myself writing, a something untrue would slip in. All was fair enough whilst actually unwritten, but when it lay there in front of me, the ugliness of it, and the impossibility of sending any reply which should not be as absolutely true as I could make it, overwhelmed me.

Last of all, it has come to me that I will be faithful to myself and to you. I will write what I should certainly say were you here. Would to God you were! I am a timid woman, I dread letters — but I trust you implicitly, though for that I can give no reason to myself, or to you.

How shall I begin? Best perhaps, because it makes things clearest, by telling you that when your letter came, I knew its contents before I opened it. Nothing in it caused me one moment's surprise. Only joy — yes, joy; I will say it once, only once, for it is true, and it will not be said again.

Do you know, does anyone, save my own happy self, know what it means, after years of darkness, and of living in a dim-lit cave, to come abroad and feel the living sunshine all about one, the current of life flowing from the sky to the softly waving tree-tops, across the dancing flowers, and thence to one's own happy heart? An evening sunshine too, that brings peace and blessing, not the restlessness of the morning, nor the fever of mid-day, but the peace and rest of evening at last — at last! (I feel very old, I *am* old, though only thirty-five.) This your visit — you — have brought to me. A new heaven and a new earth are mine. Is all this the mere romancing of a sentimental woman? I don't know — I only know that it is true.

And because it is true I will not take what you offer me — your friendship. It is the very thing I would soonest have on earth — but I will not. Life is very difficult — I mean it is very difficult to do what we know to be right, to keep ideals steadily in front of us. It would be harder than ever to me, so I would rather not see you or write to you again. I won't ask you to forget me — I don't want you to forget me — I want to be remembered, as I shall remember, one chamber in my heart is yours, where no other has the right to enter.

Written words are so treacherous, convey meanings never intended by the writer. Please understand me. *You* will not read anything in it that is not there — others might. Will you destroy it? I should feel safer if you did, and happier if you did not. Do with it as you will.

Goodbye,

Kate Hayward.

My dear Mrs. Hayward,

Forgive me for writing once more. It is the last time — I understand, but it is very, very hard. Goodbye. I am leaving England tonight.

Always yours,

F.

V

More than a year had passed... It was summer-time, and the fresh, morning sunlight was streaming in through the open bow-window of the dining-room. John and Mrs. Hayward were breakfasting. John, the same red-faced, burly figure, Mrs. Hayward a trifle paler and thinner.

"It's queer," suddenly remarked John, as he turned over the *Times*, "how we've lost sight of Flamborough. I've never seen him once since he came back to England. He wrote me such a civil letter too, after he came to shoot that time, and asked us up to stay with him at his house in town."

"I suppose he's been so busy with his painting," answered Mrs. Hayward listlessly.

"Yes, that's what made me think of him. There's an account of one of his pictures in the paper this morning. He seems to have made quite a hit."

Mrs. Hayward looked up quickly —

"What do they say? Read it to me," she said, in a low hurried voice.

"'Dawn', by the Earl of Flamborough. A dark, windswept plain, faintly lit upon the horizon by the first streaks of the rising sun; in the foreground a figure of a man, travel-stained, and bent with fatigue, trudging along towards the light.

Lord Flamborough's work is always full of clever painting, but hitherto even the best of it — as the 'River Scene' exhibited in last year's Academy, for instance — contained little more than great manual dexterity.[4] It was only the work of a very brilliant amateur. But here we have something quite different. The workmanship is still as sound as ever, and, though owing to the size of the canvas, the composition at first sight appears somewhat bald, the picture possesses a grandeur and depth of feeling such as can only emanate from a great artist. Both the landscape and the figure are treated with intense realism, yet with such breadth of handling that they have almost a symbolical meaning. We have no hesitation in bestowing this — the highest praise — on Lord Flamborough's picture, for it is certainly one of the finest that British Art has produced within the last few years."

"How curious," added John, "that a chap in Flamborough's position, a rich peer, with a big place in Yorkshire, should be an artist. I never could quite get to the bottom of him. Could you, Kate?"

"Perhaps," she answered dreamily.

He looked at her impatiently for an instant, then, with a shrug of his shoulders, got up.

"Well, I must be off," he said. "Those beasts I bought at the Ipswich sale arrived last night, and I haven't had a look at them yet."

---

[4] Academy: Flamborough's painting was probably exhibited at the annual Summer Exhibition of the Royal Academy of Arts, established in 1768 and situated, from 1868, at Burlington House, Piccadilly, central London.

A Latter-Day Highwayman
(An Adventure in Miniature)[1]

At the foot of the pass I found an inn. An old man clattered across the cobbled yard, bringing a bucketful of hot meal and water. He was dumb and deaf as a turnpike post; but, touching my arm, he jerked his thumb towards the north and wagged sententiously his timeworn head. The touch of coming snow was in the raw, morning air; a few thin flakes fell stealthily, floating onto the faded grass of the empty village street; ahead, like a monstrous, bulging wall, loomed the fell, all bleak and bare and vaguely white with the last night's sleet, and, wrapping the summit, there hung a lowering glimmer of ugly yellow.

Once more the old man wagged his head, standing beneath the old-fashioned gateway, tremulously fumbling as he rebuckled my bridle. I bid him a Merry New Year; he gave me a sharp, mechanical nod, and I started to climb the fell. The road mounted slowly between high, ragged banks of drifted snow, and at each turn of the pass I caught a glimpse of the Eden Valley[2] spread out beneath me — a spacious, undulating patchwork of dun-colored fields — and beyond, of the lake district hills, vaguely huddled on the horizon like a great herd of sleeping cattle. And, as the valley below me grew little by little distant and altogether blurred, the snow ceased falling; a strange, white twilight crept across the road, and I could discern the black-faced sheep leaping like lambs as they scurried down the fell-side. The mare, pricking her ears, swayed her head from side to side, uneasily; there was a breathless silence in the air, and about the spot a sense of inevitable immutability, of extravagant solitude. I watched the grey wisps of tattered cloud trailing across the desolate snowfields, and I thought, with a certain pride in my undertaking, of the thirty-five miles of moorland that were still to be traversed before nightfall.

The mare started, swerving across the slippery road, and I caught sight of his figure, seated on a fallen sign-post. He came towards me rapidly; and the sudden

---

[1]   Text: *The Star*, 1 February 1896, p. 2, cols 1–2. 'A Latter-Day Highwayman (An Adventure in Miniature)' is the only extant story of Crackanthorpe's published in newspaper form only, and is republished in this edition for the first time. 'The Star began publishing original short stories on a daily basis with the appearance of a tale by Hubert Crackanthorpe on February 1, 1896. From hereon short stories became an established feature of the paper' (*Index to the Fiction Published by The Star*, < http://thestarfictionindex.atwebpages.com/authorsc.htm> [accessed 19 July 2020]). Above the text there is an illustration of the protagonist confronting the 'highwayman', whose appearance owes much to contemporary imagery of the type of the primitive or degenerate — a representation not substantiated in Crackanthorpe's story.
[2]   The Eden Valley, through which runs the river Eden, is west of the Pennines, east of the Lake District.

sight of him chilled all my complacency. A pair of boots were slung over his shoulder; in one hand he carried a bundle wrapped in an ancient handkerchief. He uncovered his head; his hair was close-cropped; and his clothes, I noticed, looked curiously new. A black, stubbly beard covered his chin; his eyes were wizened; his whole face looked dingy and battered; he seemed starved, and weak, and wretched. He spoke huskily, with a Lancashire accent; said he was tramping to Sunderland, and that he hadn't tasted food for twenty-four hours. I gave him half a crown; he took the coin without a word. A few minutes later, at a fresh bend of the road, I perceived his bedraggled, snow-spattered figure, toiling behind me up the pass.

The blizzard broke as I crossed the summit. Just for an instant the great expanse of treeless tableland unfolded itself; and then all was lost in the sudden obscurity of the storm. The mare, laying back her ears like a dog, winced as the wind caught us, and the cold, wet rush of the snow beat in our faces; and, lifting her head, whinnied in a querulous distress. I fancy that no creature — not even the farmyard fowl — can display upon an emergency a greater capacity for folly than the domestic horse. The descent was steep; the road slippery as greasy asphalte. I dismounted to trudge disconsolately beside her, and in her alarm she persisted in nestling affectionately against me, continually starting and sliding the while, jostling me off the road, till I floundered knee-deep among the snowdrifts. She behaved, as horses will sometimes, like a foolish, frightened child.

We were both whitened like sepulchres[3] before we found shelter in a disused cattle-shed. I set to work to burst open the door, while, daintily sniffing the rotten woodwork, she lent me some show of assistance. Inside it was a long narrow building. At one end the roof had fallen in, and the snowflakes, drifting through onto the floor, lent it a fantastic, almost a theatrical, aspect. I unsaddled the mare, and she strolled off to rub her nose in the fast-accumulating snow — the silly thing, as if she hadn't enough of it outside. I piled some peat-sods and some remains of heather bedding onto the rude stone hearth. I wasted half a box of matches in futile efforts to kindle a fire, but the stuff was damp, and the chimney, such as it was, not unnaturally declined to draw; I only succeeded in half-filling the shed with smoke. So I lit a pipe, and sat down to wait, and to rub my smarting eyes — to fancy I was Stanley, or Nansen, or Lieut. Peary.[4]

---

[3]   Sepulchres are burial vaults, tombs, or graves.
[4]   Sir Henry Morton Stanley (1841–1904), British-American explorer of central Africa, famous for his rescue of the Scottish missionary and explorer David Livingston and for his discoveries in and development of the Congo region. He was knighted in 1899. Fridtjof Nansen (1861–1930), Norwegian explorer and scientist, later diplomat and humanitarian, who made the first crossing of the Greenland interior in 1888 and reached a record northern latitude during his expeditions of 1893–1896. 'The issues [of *The Daily Chronicle*] for 2, 3, and 4 November 1896 were increased from ten to twelve pages to carry [...] Nansen's account,

And then, all at once, my little friend appeared in the doorway. He was covered with snow from head to foot; through the blue haze of smoke he resembled a decadent Father Christmas. He stood peering first at me, then at the mare, then at the walls and the roof of the shed.

"It's not much of a place," I explained, greeting him with some assumption of hospitality. "But you'll find nothing better this side of Leadgate."[5]

He said nothing, but uncovering his close-cropped poll, with his thumb ruefully scraped the snow from the brim of his hat. Next he came and sat down beside me.

"Have a smoke?" I asked cheerily.

He took a wisp of tobacco from my pouch, and, rolling it in the palm of his hand, inserted it in his cheek.

"It's bad travelling," I continued. "I had to walk all the way down from the top. The mare could scarcely stand."

*   *   *   *   *

"You'll not get beyond Alston[6] today," I began again after a pause. "This looks precious like a snow-up."

He nodded vaguely, but vouchsafed no answer. I concluded that he was busy with his quid.[7]

"They don't talk much where you come from?" I inquired flippantly.

That roused him. He looked up and blurted,

"What be that t'you?"

"Nothing," I answered soothingly, "you needn't be afraid. I've no prejudices."

But he had returned to his contemplation of the smouldering peat.

Suddenly I felt his hand on my shoulder.

"He'v ye got any more o'them 'alf-croons[8] about ye?"

At the moment I judged this to be his particular mode of pleasantry (you'll think I might have known better, but I didn't), and I replied, "No — none to spare."

And then I caught the little man's eyes. I sprang up, gripping my hunting-crop, and retreated towards the end of the shed.

He came on, muttering odd, uncomplimentary comments concerning my

with drawings, of his recent polar exhibition' (Havighurst, *Radical Journalist: H. W. Massingham*, p. 60). Robert Edwin Peary (1856–1920), US naval officer and Arctic explorer, usually credited with leading the first expedition to reach the North Pole in 1909. His many expeditions to Greenland from 1886 made him a household name.

5   Leadgate, 'a hamlet [...] 2 miles S. of Alston' (*Gazetteer of the British Isles*, p. 474).

6   Alston, a 'market town, E. Cumberland' (*Gazetteer of the British Isles*, p. 14).

7   Quid: here a lump of tobacco.

8   'Alf-croons: i.e. half-crowns: with eight to the old pound, a half-crown was an eighth of a labourer's weekly wage at this period (35s, or about £90 a year).

appearance, till I had got what I wanted — my back against the wall. He halted; and we stood face to face, surveying one another.

"Ye're got a thing or two t'larn yit, my young chicken," he remarked.

I did not dissent; he spoke with an air of conviction. I watched him out of the tail of my eye, and fingered the leaded butt of my crop meaningly, after the fashion of a stage hero. Yet I felt very depressed, I remember. I kept wondering what on earth I should do if when the struggle came I were to break his head. And this apprehension I communicated to him partially.

He seemed to grow reflective again; at least, he gave no sign of beginning his business. His hangdog attitude was, I thought, singularly lacking in dignity. I felt inclined to reason with him, to discuss his proceeding from the point of view of common expediency. But I rejected the impulse; it was for him to speak.

Still he appeared perplexed; it was the hunting-crop that was puzzling him.

"Now then, my young gentleman, ye've jest got t'shell oot, ye knaw." The phrase had a conventional, insincere ring. He shivered a little with the cold; he seemed half-hearted, with, after all, but little stomach for his trade.

"You'll have to fight for it, my good man," I explained, once more calling his attention to the butt of my crop.

He turned away in undisguised disgust, and resumed his seat before the hearth.

I sat down, too, at a respectful distance. The shed was bitterly cold. I had taken infinite pains to set those peat-sods smouldering; it was unfair that he should monopolise the unearned increment of their scanty warmth. But I submitted meekly to my isolation; the poor little chap looked so cold, so starved, it would be barbarous to oust him, I explained to myself speciously. And, moreover, to seat myself beside him, amicably, might provoke a breach of the peace.

The place was still very dark. Outside the snowstorm continued to rage. I had half a mind to face it — to push on as best I could; but I realised that the mare was unsaddled, that the bank down to the road was very abrupt, and by this time probably several inches deep in snow, and that, under the circumstances, it might be difficult, should he abandon his contemplative attitude, to make my exit with decorum. So, par bravade,[9] I relit my pipe.

And all at once he came on again — almost heroic in his assumption of desperate determination.

"Na mare o'yer nonsense," he began.

It would have been quite futile, I realised, to explain to him my entire seriousness of attitude; but none the less his insinuation appeared peculiarly inappropriate, since at that moment I was minded to take him very seriously indeed. The amateurish dilatoriness of his procedure was altogether exasperating.

---

[9] Par bravade: out of bravado.

"Noo thin, what hev ye got about ye? Hand it ower, sharp," he concluded, with some incoherent reference to my internal organs.

He stretched his arm towards me. I rapped him over the knuckles. He withdrew his hand and put it quickly to his mouth.

The gesture was so pitiable, he seemed so hopelessly inadequate for the role he had assumed, that, irresistibly, I felt that, if it came to a struggle between us, I should end by weakly abandoning to him a handsome percentage of my purse. Concerning his miserable, starveling existence I grew almost sentimental. There would have been something ignoble in cracking his skull.

"Look here," I said, "you'd better give over. You're not fit to fight."

I believe he perceived the soundness of the remark: anyway he remained still sucking his knuckle.

"Let's compromise the matter," I continued. "I'm going on now. I'll leave you a packet of sandwiches and a flask of brandy. That's *my* fire, but I give you leave to sit by it after I'm gone. And I'll not split on you when I get down to Alston."

I handed him the flask and the sandwiches, and he retired stolidly to his former position.

He sipped the brandy — not greedily, but tentatively, with something of the deliberation of a connoisseur; though, judged by the aspect of the inn that had provided it, it must have been poor enough liquor. Now and then, furtively, he glanced towards me over his shoulder. After a while he finished the flask bravely, and setting it carefully onto the ground beside him exclaimed confidentially —

"Ye be a green 'un an' na mistake. But ye doan't git ower me, mister, doan't ye go flatterin' yeself. I reckon I'll hev a look at them 'alf-croons afore I've doon."

He looked brighter certainly, less like a hunted, outcast animal.

The air was growing lighter; the blizzard was spent. To reach the door I had to pass by him. As I approached he struggled to his legs and met me with a desperate, drunken rush. I stepped aside; he steadied himself solemnly. But as he came on a second time — not too cautiously — he tripped over a peat-sod, and fell ingloriously to the ground. I went to the doorway and looked out. The wind had dropped, and through the fading snow the sun was glittering on the opposite hills. When I turned, I found him crawling on his hands and knees across the floor, dragging my saddle towards the fire. Then, resolutely, he laid his head upon it, and, with a luxurious sigh, extended his meagre frame.

When I pulled his pillow from under him, he was scarcely courteous. His head met the ground, however, with no slight violence. The mare, as I buckled her girths, stretched her neck towards him, suspiciously sniffing.[10] He waved her aside with an airy sweep of his hand.

Before leaving him, I drew his attention to the packet of sandwiches, that

[10]   Girths: belts or bands of leather tightened around the body of the horse in order to secure the saddle on its back.

lay untouched beside him. And, as I led the mare over the threshold, he raised himself laboriously onto his elbow, and tersely ejaculating his contempt, threw the packet after me. The paper burst, and the things fell scattered in a shower about the floor.

On the whole, as you will agree, the incident was but a paltry one. And yet, as I recall it this evening beside my cosy study fire, it has, too, its pathetic aspect. Ah! how differently they managed matters in the days of "Galloping Dick."[11] Was my little friend's air of sorry burlesque significant of the age, do you think? He may be the last of the gentlemen of the road. Anyway, I wish I had asked him his name.

[11]   This could be a reference either to Dick Ryder, seventeenth-century English highwayman, featured in a collection of short stories by H. B. Marriott Watson, *Galloping Dick: Being Chapters from the Life and Fortune of Richard Ryder* (1896), or to Dick Turpin, the subject of *The Genuine History of the Life of Richard Turpin: An Account of a Highwayman* (1739) by Richard Bayes, who also featured in Harrison Ainsworth's novel *Rookwood* (1834).

A Fellside Tragedy

Hard by the tiny church of Mardale, at the head of Haweswater Lake,[1] stood a house — not a grey Westmorland farm-house, flanked by long, low-roofed, rough-walled buildings, but a smart little villa, with a red-tiled gabled roof, white stucco walls, a freshly-painted green veranda, and a microscopic lawn in front, dotted with queer-shaped beds of bright flowers.

Everything was so strikingly spruce that to the stray tourist at the "Dun Bull" inn it seemed as if the house had been bodily transported from the suburbs of some city, and set down in this lonely Westmorland valley. The walls were of such a dazzling whiteness that in summer, when the sun shone upon them, they could be seen by the people in the trains over the side of Shap Fells, as a glistening white speck under the dark mountain side.

A little, old, widow lady lived there. Years ago, her father had rented the Scartop farm on the other side of the lake, but she had married a commercial traveller and had gone away South. Thirty years later, she had come back to Mardale — to end her days in the peaceful spot, where she had spent her childhood.

The sun had just topped the hills and was beginning to clear away the blue mists that hung round the shores of the lake. It was early yet, and the village still slept. Not a sound save the crowing of a cock at intervals, in a neighbouring farmyard …

Suddenly, from the little white house, a girl stepped into the road. At first glance, there seemed nothing remarkable about her — just a common farm-girl, with a coarse, thick-set figure, but as she moved into the sunlight you might have seen that her face shewed traces of great mental suffering. Her eyes were bloodshot, the lids red and swollen and there was a hard, set look about the mouth.

She glanced up and down the road — not leisurely as if on the lookout for a passer-by with whom to gossip, but rapidly, almost stealthily. Having made sure that no one was in sight, she ran across the road to the church opposite and tried the door. It was locked. After a moment's irresolution, she crossed the churchyard and began to hurry up the mountain side.

Jenny King was a true Westmorland lass, born and bred on the fellsides, who had never travelled farther from her native village than to Penrith[2] on market-days — except last Whit Monday, when she had gone on an excursion trip to Keswick, with "Long Joe" — "Long Joe" was her lover, a fine, strapping young

---

[1] The village of Mardale Green, Westmorland (now Cumbria), is no longer in existence after it was flooded by the Manchester Water Authority in the 1930s to make way for the Haweswater Reservoir.
[2] See note 19 on p. 280.

fellow, who shepherded for the new tenant of the Scartop farm.[3]

After Michaelmas[4] he was to have a rise; and then they were to be married in the tiny church at the head of the lake. But on Saturday a tragedy had roused the sleepy little village to a state of intense excitement — a tragedy which had wrecked all Jenny's hopes. Joe had been helping the Scartop men to "lead" the hay,[5] and had had words with one of them in the big thirty-acre field. Joe's temper was a quick one; words soon changed to blows, and at last in a fit of fury he picked up a pitch-fork and ran his companion through the stomach.

A day and a half of hiding in the forest followed, till he had got enough money to fly the country. It was Jenny who had given him this money. She had taken it from the well in her mistress's writing-table. The theft had cost her no moral struggle, for she had done it almost mechanically, in blind, dog-like fidelity to Joe, without once giving a thought to the consequences, only filled with the idea that he wanted the money and that she must get it for him.

But as soon as he was gone, hastening on his way to Liverpool,[6] a reaction came upon her. It was terrible. First, the grief of her mistress at the disappearance of her savings cut her to the heart, as recollections of the old lady's thousand and one little acts of kindness crowded in upon her memory; then terror — vague, sickening, physical terror — of the police, of the handcuffs, of the prison.

Towards evening, mistrustful looks, whisperings, and at last a general shunning of her presence, told her that she was suspected. Oh! the horror of the night that followed! For hours she had lain awake, motionless, staring fixedly at the wall by her bedside.

She had once seen in a shop-window at Penrith a coloured picture of a female convict crouching in a cell with her face buried in her hands. All through the night that picture haunted her; its crude, glaring colours had appeared not once, but a hundred times, till it covered the walls of her room. Wherever she turned her eyes she was confronted with it; there was no escape. And gradually, as the night wore on, the seated figure grew more and more like herself, till she could see on its forehead the bruise which she had got when she fell down the dairy steps last week.

At last she fell asleep, but still the figure pursued her. The nightmare came, and she was shivering, chained to the bare stone floor of the prison-cell, doomed for ever and ever....

---

[3]   Keswick: a market town in the Lake District on the shores of Derwentwater. It was originally in the county of Cumberland, but in Cumbria since 1974.

[4]   Michaelmas is the Christian feast of Michael and All Angels, observed on 29 September; St Michael is protector against the dark of the night and is the archangel who leads the fight against Satan.

[5]   To 'lead' the hay is to bring home the hay by cart.

[6]   Liverpool was a major port of departure for emigrants from Britain and mainland Europe to the USA, Canada, and Australia.

The girl could bear it no longer. Tomorrow they would come and take her, and she would become like the figure in the picture. She must fly — where? She never once gave a thought to that. Only to escape to the fells away from the horrible convict woman.

… On, on, she climbed, now across stretches of grey shingle, which she sent clattering down the mountain side, now up to her knees in the bracken, now picking her way over a crowd of boulders huddled together in savage disorder.

… On, on, she climbed, while her heart throbbed excitedly, and great beads of sweat started from her forehead. At last she reached the top and threw herself gasping on the grass. There was a buzzing in her ears and a heavy thud, thud, thud against her temples. Yet this sense of physical exhaustion was a relief, after the terrible mental strain of the last three days.

Then by degrees it passed. From where she lay, she could just see the thatched roof of her father's cottage. There was the road along which, as a little girl, she had trudged to school, day after day, summer and winter; next her mind wandered to Joe — to Joe before the murder — she thought of the first time that he had kissed her, one blustering winter afternoon, when she had gone to fetch the milk from the Scartop farm; of the trip to Keswick and of the silver brooch that he had bought her there.

These recollections were not painful to Jenny. She was reviewing them calmly, as if they were incidents in another's life, when with a sharp spasm of pain, came back the thought of her mistress's grief. Oh! she was sorry, bitterly sorry for her — yet there was no hot self-upbraiding. It was the inevitable. She had done the only thing possible — Joe *had* to be saved.

Was he already at Liverpool, she wondered? How long would he be on the sea? Perhaps he would go on a ship like the one in the picture hanging in the waiting-room at Penrith Station. In the picture the deck was black with passengers. Perhaps Joe was one of them. Gradually her thoughts began to wander, and then — and then she was asleep.…

When she woke the sun was high in the sky. It was a minute or two before she realized how she came to be lying there on the wet grass — she shivered.

Look! some people were crossing the road, and coming toward the mountain. Perhaps it was a search party. She must be gone — further away, where they could not find her. She dare not get up lest her figure should be seen by those below, standing out against the sky-line; so she crawled away from the mountain edge; then got up and ran.

The range of mountains was so broad at this point that the summit formed a sort of tableland, several miles in width. It was a barren expanse, not a tree, not a shrub, only bushy tufts of coarse grass growing right down to the edges of the pools of brackish water; and here and there, like great flesh-wounds in the earth's surface, gaping peat-bogs, with black slimy dripping sides. It was a dreary spot, even on this gorgeous summer day.

Jenny hurried on, driving before her a little flock of black-legged mountain sheep, till she had crossed the range. The great lake of Ullswater lay at her feet, glistening like a sheet of molten silver;[7] beyond, the bare, round backs of the lake district mountains rose, one behind the other, till they melted away to a purple haze on the horizon. She stood for a moment, gazing stupidly at the glorious scene; then she slipped down into a peat-bog.

When she came to herself the white, weird light of the moon was shining and a few fleecy clouds were chasing one another lazily across the sky. From far away below came the bleating of sheep; then all was still...

Hark! What was that? A piercing whistle burst through the silence of the night. Another, then another, followed by a cry which made Jenny's blood run cold. It was her own name ringing through the night.

With the instinct of a hunted animal she held her breath, put her fingers between her teeth to keep them from chattering, and flattened herself against the soft, clammy peat. Nearer, nearer they came. Jenny! Jenny! and the cry was re-echoed by the mountains opposite till it seemed to her fevered imagination as if the evil spirits of the hills were tossing her name backwards and forwards to each other in diabolical mockery. The shouts grew fainter and fainter; at length all was still again.

But now came strange, bitter regrets that they had not found her. How horrible the stillness was! She tried to call after them, but the sound of her own voice terrified her so that she gave it up in despair. The pains, too, which she had forgotten in the moment of mortal anxiety, came back.

What was that white thing gleaming on the stones over there? Only the skeleton of a sheep, probably starved to death in winter. Jenny shuddered, and her teeth began to chatter again furiously. Oh, anything but that! The life of a convict woman, rather than such a death. She must go back and give herself up. Surely someone would have pity on her. She burst into a fit of hysterical crying. Then she struggled forward. Her strength was now almost spent. She was shivering all over, yet her head seemed on fire, and hunger — a devouring, overwhelming hunger began to gnaw her.

Still she crawled on desperately; now falling into a peat-bog, now stumbling over a heap of shingle. Thus down the mountain side, while her knees knocked together at every step.

When she reached Farmer Langley's stead she had not the courage to knock for admittance; so she threw herself on a half-finished hay-rick and, covering herself over with hay, slept....

---

7   Ullswater: the second largest lake in the Lake District, very familiar to Crackanthorpe from boyhood (see DC, p. 23). 'Ullswater' is the title of one of Crackanthorpe's 'vignettes', published in *The Speaker*, 8 December 1894, p. 636, but not included in *Vignettes* (1896).

Two hours later, when the sun ushered in another gorgeous June morning, Farmer Langley's men came and finished the rick....

As the days went by a strange, horrible odour came from the rick-yard. They pulled down the rick and found poor Jenny's body. The forks of the men had pierced her through and through. Was it these wounds that had killed her, or had she passed away before the rising of the sun?

Who shall tell?[8]

---

[8]   This shocking ending was evidently too strong for *The Star*, where it was sanitised to 'They pulled down the rick and found poor Jenny's body' (*The Star*, 14 February 1901, p. 4, col. 1). *The Northern Counties Magazine*, publishing the story in the same month, was clearly less squeamish.

PART III:
FROM *VIGNETTES* (1896)

Ascension Day at Arles[1]

The population pours out from mass, flooding every crooked street — rubicund peasants in starched Sunday blouses; olive-skinned, Greek-featured *Arlésiennes* in quaint, lace head-dresses; strutting *petits messieurs en chapeau rond*[2] and tight-fitting *complets;*[3] shouting shoals of boys; zouaves,[4] indolent and superb, in flowing red knickerbockers, white spats, and jauntily-poised fez.

A bleating of lambs, plaintive, incessant and dirge-like, fills the *Place du Forum;*[5] heaped over the gravel they lie, their legs tied under their bellies, and their skinny necks helplessly outstretched: and beyond, the great, green umbrellas of a regiment of wrinkled beldams[6] — fruit-sellers encamped in rows before their baskets..... A strange complication of odours — of cheese, of fish and of flowers — floats in the air: at every alley-corner some auctioneer stands posted — shouting, perspiring vendors of knives, pocket-books, glass-cutters, chromo-lithographs, cement, songs, *sabots.*[7] An old top-hatted Jew nasally vaunts a wine-testing fluid, and tells horrible and interminable tales of vintages manufactured from decayed dates, from vinegar and sugar, or from plaster-of-Paris; a travelling pedicure operates on the box-seat of a gorgeously-painted van, to the accompaniment of a big drum and clashing cymbals; the

---

[1]   On Ascension Day the Solemnity of the Ascension of the Lord commemorates the bodily ascension of Jesus into heaven, traditionally celebrated in the Christian liturgical calendar on a Thursday, the fortieth day of Easter.

[2]   Strutting *petits messieurs en chapeau rond*: strutting young men with their round hats.

[3]   *Complets*: suits.

[4]   Light infantry troops in the French army wearing a costume copied from that of Kabyles in North Africa, adopted after the French conquest of Algiers. The figure of Vincent Van Gogh's 'Le Zouave' (June 1888), painted during his period in Arles (1888–1889), sports a 'jauntily-posed fez' of Crackanthorpe's description.

[5]   Formerly the Forum, the Place du Forum provides the location for Van Gogh's painting 'Le Café de nuit' (1888). Van Gogh enjoyed a highly productive fifteen months in Arles but at the same time experienced a deterioration in his mental condition: 'it was in Arles that he severed his ear in December 1888, and he left [the following May] after the townspeople had petitioned the authorities for his confinement' (*Arthur Symons: Spiritual Adventures*, ed. by Freeman, p. 99). Built into the fabric of the celebrated Nord Pinus hotel on the Place is a Roman pillar, one of many visible Roman 'ruins' which struck a melancholy chord with Arthur Symons, who visited Arles on several occasions, and wrote about it in 1891, 1898, and 1899 (gathered together in *Wanderings* (London and Toronto: J. M. Dent, 1931), pp. 16–30): 'Everything [...] seems to grow out of death, and to be returning thither', he declared in 'Arles' (1898), repr. in *Arthur Symons: Spiritual Adventures*, p. 101. Crackanthorpe could have read Symons's '1891' piece, 'A Night in Arles', in *The Senate*, 2.19 (November 1895), 420–23 (re-edited for *Wanderings*, pp. 16–22). In contrast with Symons's self-conscious accounts of the city, Crackanthorpe's picture, whilst impersonally Flaubertian, conveys an unmistakeable *jouissance*.

[6]   Beldams: an archaic term for old women, with negative connotations (as in 'hag').

[7]   *Sabots*: wooden shoes or clogs.

inevitable strong man defiantly challenges the crowd to split a flag-stone across his bare, hirsute chest; and a blind-folded fortune-telling wench chaunts[8] with mechanical shamelessness the young men's amorous indiscretions.

Outside the town, the boulevard is gay with the glitter of pedlars' wares, and flapping, gaudy stuffs, red, green and yellow and blue; travelling showmen are bustling with final preparations, hammering together their skeleton booths, or gaunt rolls of battered canvas; the steam-orchestra of a *Grand Musée fin de siècle*[9] bellows from its rows of brass-mouthed trumpets a deafening, wheezy tune; and everywhere, beneath the tunnel of pale green plane-trees, a thick, drifting tide of men and women.

In the Basque Country May 23

All day an intense impression of lusty sunlight, of quivering golden-green .... a long, white road that dazzles, between its rustling dark-green walls; blue brawling rivers; swelling upland meadows, flower-thronged, luscious with tall, cool grass; the shepherd's thin-toned pipe; the ragged flocks, blocking the road, cropping at the hedge-rows as they hurry on towards the mountains; the slow, straining teams of jangling mules — wine-carriers coming from Spain; through dank, cobbled village streets, where the pigs pant their bellies in the roadway, and the sandal-makers flatten the hemp before their doors; and then, out again into the lusty sunlight, along the straight, powdery road that dazzles ahead interminably towards a mysterious, hazy horizon, where the land melts into the sky....

And, at last, the cool evening scents; soft shadows stealing beneath the still, silent oaks; and, all at once, a sight of the great snow-mountains, vague, phantasmagoric,[10] like a mirage in the sky; and of the hills, all indigo, rippling towards a pale sunset of liquid gold.

In the Landes May May 27

Since sunrise I had been travelling — along the straight-stretching roads, white with summer sand, interminably striped by the shadows of the poplars; across the great, parched plain, where, all the day's length, the heat dances over

---

8   Chaunts: Crackanthorpe here uses a Pre-Raphaelite archaism, deliberately intended to link 'present songs to those of the past' (Linda Dowling, *Language and Decadence in the Victorian Fin de Siècle* (Princeton: Princeton University Press, 1986), p. 194).
9   *Grand Musée fin de siècle*: a fair-ground steam-organ fit for a museum and probably renamed to fit the times — here the century-end.
10 See note 1 on p. 233.

the waste land, and the cattle bells float their far-away tinkling; through the desolate villages, empty but for the beldames, hunched in the doorways, pulling the flax with horny, tremulous fingers;[11] and on towards the desolate silence of the flowerless pine-forests....

And there the night fell. The sun went down unseen; a dim flickering ruddled[12] the host of tree trunks; and the darkness started to drift through the forest. The road grew narrow as a footpath, and the mare slackening her pace, uneasily strained her white neck ahead.

Out of the darkness a figure sprang beside me. A shout rang out — words of an uncouth *patois* that I did not understand. And the mare, terrified, galloped forward, snorting, and swerving from side to side....

And a strange, superstitious fear crept over me — a dreamy dread of the future; a helpless presentiment of evil days to come; a sense, too, of the ruthless nullity of life, of the futile deception of effort, of bitter revolt against the extinction of death, a yearning after faith in a vague survival beyond....

And the words of the old proverb returned to me mockingly: —
"The eye is not satisfied with seeing
nor the ear with hearing."[13]

On Chelsea Embankment June 26

I have sat there, and seen the winter days finish their short-spanned lives, and all the globes of light, crimson, emerald, and pallid yellow, start, one by one, out of the russet fog that creeps up the river.[14]

But I like the place best on these hot summer nights, when the sky hangs thick with stifled colour, and the stars shine small and shyly. For then the pulse of the city is hushed, and the scales of the water flicker golden and oily under the watching regiment of lamps. The bridge clasps its gaunt arms tight from bank to bank, and the shuffle of a retreating figure sounds loud and alone in the quiet....

There, if you wait long enough, you may hear the long wail of the siren, that seems to tell of the anguish of London, till a train hurries to throttle its dying note, roaring and rushing, thundering and blazing through the night, tossing its white crest of smoke, charging across the bridge, into the dark country beyond....

---

[11] Beldames: see note 6 p. 376.
[12] Ruddle means to make red.
[13] Ecclesiastes 1. 8.
[14] 'Nocturne: Grey and Silver — Chelsea Embankment, Winter', by James McNeill Whistler (1834–1903), offers a deliberate, aesthetic point of reference. Painted in 1871, it was the first of Whistler's impressionist *Nocturnes*.

Our Lady of the Lane Sept. 17

Whenever the London sun touches the small, dusky shops with a jumble of begrimed colour — the old gold and scarlet of hanging meat; the metallic green of mature cabbages; the wavering russet of piled potatoes; the sharp white of fly-bills, pasted all awry — then the moment to see her is come. You will find her, bareheaded and touzled; her dingy, peaked shawl hanging down her back, and in front the bellying expanse of her soiled apron; blocking the pavement; established by her own corner of the Lane, all littered with the cries of children, and the fitful throbbing of the asphalte beneath the hollow hammering of hoofs.

She carries always a baby by her breast; her bare forearms are as bulky as any man's; in her eyes is a froward[15] scowl; and, when she laughs, it is with a harsh, strident gaiety. But she never fails to wear her squalid portliness with a robust and defiant dignity, that makes her figure definitely symbolic of Cockney maternity.

Paris in October October 4

Paris in October — all white and a-glitter under a cold, sparkling sky, and the trees of the boulevards trembling their frail, russet leaves; garish, petulant Paris; complacently content with her sauntering crowds, her monotonous arrangements in pink and white and blue;[16] ever busied with her own publicity, her tiresome, obvious vice, and her parochial modernity coquetting with cosmopolitanism....

La Côte D'or from the Train October 6

Strips of ruddy earth: poplars flecked with gold, and vineyards with autumn red; the dark, sleek Saône;[17] and beyond, the pale green plain, spacious and smooth, stretching away and away towards the blue haze that wraps the Côte d'Or, hesitating and soft as the lines of a woman's body.

[15] Froward is an archaic term meaning perverse or contrary.
[16] This is probably a reference to Whistler's practice of entitling his portraits in particular as colour arrangements; see especially the famous portrait of the artist's mother 'Arrangements in Grey and Black, no. 1'. Whistler is of course connected with Paris, and so Crackanthorpe is asking us to view the city through the lens of this artist, and of impressionist art, more generally.
[17] The river Saône, rising in the Vosges department, is navigable from Corre in the department of Haute-Saône at the confluence of the Coney, and then flows south to Lyon where it meets the river Rhône.

The sun sets, trailing a wash of pale, watery gold; torn, inky clouds spatter the sky; sombre shadows fill the acacia-groves; and on, on, pounds the train, untiring, rhythmically throbbing.

Lausanne October 7

"Tout paysage est un état d'âme."[18]

Often must Amiel,[19] who lived his life on the shores of this great lake, have brooded over her moods. Deep-blue, she lies plunged in silent meditation; wrapped in the opal-tinted mists of evening, she dreams the vague, glad dreams of fancy; now she smiles, she laughs even, as little ripples, all gilded by the sun-rays, trip across her surface; she has her grey days of gloom, and her dark days of despair: she has also her *jours de fête*,[20] and her *jours de grande toilette*,[21] under a sky heavy-loaded with blue: often, in the moonlight, she lies white, tranquil, statuesque, like a beautiful, sleeping woman: at times her humour is bewilderingly capricious; the fleeting, furious rages of a spoilt child sweep across her; or, ink-coloured, she sulks during long hours, sullenly wrathful.

In the Campo Santo at Perugia November 1

The young moon hangs amid a steely sky; the land, empty and darkening, rolls like a billowing sea towards the Western orange glow; and high behind us the tall hill lifts Perugia's ragged silhouette.

Down the steep road they came — grave *bourgeois*; bands of brown-faced youths, chewing thin cigars; aged peasant-women, with faded, wrinkled eyes; chattering country-girls, gaudy handkerchiefs around their hair; toddling children; uncouth men from the mountains, sullenly wrapped in fur-trimmed cloaks, while, posted in rows on either side, the crippled beggars offer their dusty hats, and whine for charity in the Virgin's name.

Before the red gate of the Campo Santo[22] the crowd surges; within, every

---

[18] *"Tout paysage est un état d'âme."*: 'Every landscape is, as it were, a state of the soul, and whoever penetrates into both is astonished to find how much likeness there is in each detail' (Henri-Frédéric Amiel, *Amiel's Journal: The Journal Intime of Henri-Frédéric Amiel*, trans. by Mrs. Humphry Ward, 2nd edn (London: Macmillan and Co., 1889), p. 30 (entry for 31 October 1852)).

[19] Henri-Frédéric Amiel (1821–1881), Swiss moral philosopher, poet, and critic. David Crackanthorpe notes that '[t]he two volumes of Amiel's *Journal intime* carry more numerous and more emphatic markings than any of Hubert's other books' (DC, p. 44).

[20] *Jours de fête*: holidays or feast-days.

[21] *Jours de grande toilette*: dressing-up days.

[22] Campo Santo: 'holy field', i.e. burial-place, cemetery. Perugia: the capital city of Umbria, central Italy.

alley is black with the press of people. It is the day of the dead. To visit the dead all the town is come.

... The pale specks of a myriad, tiny lamps; the glow of garlands against the crowding slabs of snow-white marble, that mark the children's graves; the glitter of every small, spruce mortuary chapel; and the glad scent of freshly-scattered flowers....

Death loses its squalor; and becomes something demure, sociable, almost gay....

Sunrise

To ride alone beneath the stars, through the long indefinite hours of the night; to climb the slumbering mountain-hulks; to hear the dull roar of the river, toiling unwearied through the darkness below; to break, with a sudden clattering of hoofs, the gloomy stillness of distant village-streets, and on through the twilight that precedes the dawn, to journey, without flagging, high up against the sky, across a desolate, limitless plain.

To scout the future; to unlearn the past; and to brood vaguely, as the night broods....

To elude desire; to disdain the thrill of hate; to forget the long aching of love, and to commune, in tender serenity, with the grave-eyed Spirit of Rest.

And then, while the night slinks away across the hills, to push on towards the sunrise; to watch the marshalling of ruddy heralds across the East, and at last to meet the Great God's dazzling glory, bursting in splendour across the empty land.

In Richmond Park

In the wan, lingering light of the winter afternoon, the park stood all deserted; sluggishly drowsing, so it seemed, with its spacious distances muffled in greyness; colourless, fabulous, blurred. One by one, through the damp, misty air, loomed the tall, stark, lifeless, elms. Overhead there lowered a turbid sky, heavy-charged with an unclean yellow. And, amid the ruddy patches of dank and rottening bracken, the little mare picked her way noiselessly. The rumour[23] of life seemed hushed; there was only the vague, listless rhythm of the creaking saddle....

The daylight faded; a shroud of ghostly mist enveloped the earth, and up from the vaporous distance crept slowly the evening darkness....

---

[23]   See note 11 on p. 277.

New Year's Eve   December 31

It was New Year's Eve. The old, old scene. A London night; a heavy-brown atmosphere splashed with liquid, golden lights; the bustling market-place of sin; a silent crowd of black figures drifting over a wet, flickering pavement.

The slow, grave notes from a church tower took command of the night. The last one faded: the old year had slipped by. And then a woman laughed — a strident, level laugh; and there swept through all the crowd a mad, feverish tremor. The women ran one to the other, kissing, wildly welcoming the New Year in; and the men, shouting thickly, snatched at them as they ran. And the cabmen touted eagerly for fares.

Across the road, by a corner, a street missionary stood on a chair — an undersized, poorly clad man, with a wizened, bearded face.

... "Repent ... repent ... and save your souls tonight from the eternal torments of hell-fire."

The women jostled him, pelted him with foul gibes; and one — a young girl — broke into a peal of hysterical laughter.

And I mused wonderingly on the ugliness of sin.

In St. James's Park   January 15

A sullen glow throbs overhead: golden will-o'-wisps are threading their shadowy groupings of gaunt-limbed trees; and the dull, distant rumour[24] of feverish London waits on the still, night air. The lights of Hyde Park corner blaze like some monster, gilded constellation, shaming the dingy stars; and across the East there flares a sky-sign — a gaudy, crimson arabesque...[25]

And all the air hangs draped in the mysterious, sumptuous splendour of a murky London night....

In the Strand   January 27

The city disgorges.

All along the Strand, down the great, ebbing tide, the omnibuses, a congested press of gaudy craft, drift westwards, jostling and jamming their tall, loaded decks, with a clanking of chains, a rumble of lumbering wheels, a thudding of quick-loosed brakes, a humming of hammering hoofs....

---

[24]   See note 11 on p. 277.
[25]   See note 21 on p. 330.

The empty hansoms[26] slink silently past; the street hawkers[27] — a long row of dingy figures — line the pavement-edge; troops of frenzied newsboys dart yelling through the traffic; and here and there a sullen-faced woman struggles to stem the tide of men.

Somewhere, behind Pall Mall,[28] unheeded the sun has set: the sky is powdered with crimson dust; one by one the shops gleam out, blazing their windows of burnished glass; the twilight throbs with a ceaseless shuffle of hurrying feet; and over all things hovers the spirit of London's grim unrest.

Rêverie April 15

The English Midlands, sluggishly effluent, a massy profusion of well-upholstered undulations; Normandy, coquettish, almost dapper, in its discreet rusticity, its finnikin[29] spruceness, its distinguished reticence of detail; the plains of Lombardy in midsummer, all glutted with luscious vegetation; Switzerland, tricked out in cheap sentimentality, in a catch-penny crudity of tone; Andalucia, savagely harsh, with its bitter, exasperated colouring....

In every country there links a personality, and the contemplation of the memories of the lands where one has lived, of the books one has cherished, of the women one has loved, brings with it a strange sense of the incomprehensible promptings of caprice.

With the fluctuations of mood, Musset seems puerile or passionate; Amiel, lachrymose or exquisitely perceptive; Baudelaire, *macabre* or impassively statuesque; Pater, tortuous or infinitely dexterous; Meredith, irksome or gorgeously prismatic.[30]

There are women whom we worshipped years ago, who would certainly fail

---

[26] See note 7 on p. 84.
[27] See note 2 on p. 307.
[28] See note 3 on p. 307.
[29] Finnikin means over-precise.
[30] Musset: Louis-Charles-Alfred de Musset (1810–1857), French Romantic dramatist and poet who is best known for his plays. Amiel: see notes 18 and 19 on p. 380. Baudelaire: Charles-Pierre Baudelaire (1821–1867), French poet and critic, best known for his collection of poems *Les Fleurs du Mal* (1857), with its pervasive images of beauty subject to decay and disconcerting oscillations between expressions of 'spleen' and melancholy. He was influential on Swinburne, the Decadent writers, Wilde, Symons, and Dowson, and, later, T. S. Eliot. Pater: Walter Pater (1839–1894), critic and essayist, was the single most important influence on the evolution of Aestheticism, and the Decadent movement of the 1890s associated with it. Meredith: George Meredith (1828–1909), poet and novelist, held in high esteem by the Decadents. Despite his substantial and critically important body of fiction, which includes *The Ordeal of Richard Feverel* (1859), *The Egoist* (1879), and *One of Our Conquerors* (1891), it is for his startling fifty-stanza work *Modern Love* (1862), with its agonised account of the failure of a marriage, that he is now most celebrated.

to move us today; books that enthralled us in our childhood, which we hesitate to open again; places we had read of with delight, and for that reason shrink from surveying.

* * * * *

And so tonight, beneath the lime-tree, by the dog-rose hedge, whilst the grasshoppers scrape their ceaseless chorus, and the flies roam like specks of gold, and the fawn-coloured cattle stalk home from the pastures, I wonder dreamily how I have come to love so steadfastly the whole wayward grace of this country-side — the melancholy of its wide plains, burnt to dun colour by the Southern sun; the desolate silence of those dark, endless pine forests that lie beyond; the hesitating contours of wooded slopes; the distant Pyrenees, a long, ragged, snow-capped wall; the dazzling-white roads, stretching between their tall, slim poplars, straight towards the horizon; the tumble-down, white-faced villages, huddled on the hilltops; their battered, sloping roofs, tilted all awry, like loose-fitting, peaked caps of faded-red tiles; the farmyards, strewn with dingy ox-bedding, and littered with a decrepit multitude of objects, which, it seems, can never have been new — broken earthenware pots, rickety, rush-bottomed chairs, stacks of dead branches, still rustling their brown, winter leaves; the slow-paced oxen ploughing the land; the peasants, men, women, and children, swaying in line as they sow the maize, with the poultry pecking behind; the jangling bells of the dilapidated, yellow-wheeled courier; the market-days, the sea of blue *bérets*, the press of blue blouses, the incoherent waving of ox-goads, the bristling of curved horns, the shifting mass of sleek, fawn-coloured backs; the narrow, ramshackle streets of the town; the line of plane-trees on the *place d'armes*,[31] beneath which groups of grave *bourgeois* are for ever pacing; and the Gave,[32] spurting over the rocks, under the old Norman bridge....

* * * * *

The sun slips behind a bank of inky cloud, slowly trailing its pale-green stain, and the old, penetrating charm of this tiny corner of the earth returns, and the old longing to bind myself to it, to have my place in its life, always, through the years to come....

* * * * *

The oxen have gone their way along the road; the lengthy twilight shadows steal across the garden; from the church-spire up on the hill the Angelus[33] rings

[31] *Place d'armes*: parade ground.
[32] The Gave de Pau is a river of south-west France which rises in the Pyrenees mountains, taking its name from the city of Pau through which it flows.
[33] The Angelus is a Catholic devotion commemorating the Incarnation, and the subject of

out; quite near at hand a tree-frog starts piping his shrill, clear note, and the cockchafers their angry whirling; and then, of a sudden, the violet night has fallen, wrapping all earth and sky in her mysterious, impenetrable blackness....

Enfantillage April 23

Have you never longed to wander there, in that wonderful cloudland beyond the sea, where, like droves of monstrous cattle, close-huddled and drowsy, they lie the day through — the comely, milk-white summer clouds, slow and sleek and swelling; the quick-scudding darkling clouds, tattered with travelling across the sky; the mighty thunder-clouds, violet and lowering; the flocks of fluffy-white baby clouds; and all the sun's great gaudy guard, from the daintily gilded sunset spars to the blood-red bands that frequent the South?

Sometimes, at even-fall, when the sea lies calm in her opal tints, you may discern the distant lines of their strange, fantastic home, vague, phantasmagoric,[34] like a mirage beyond the horizon.

Perhaps, after death, we may linger there, and watch them silently sail away towards the lands we have loved long ago! ...[35]

a famous painting by Jean-François Millet (composed 1857–1859) in which two peasants bow their heads in prayer.

[34] See note 1 on p. 233.

[35] '[A]s one reads the closing words of his last book, does it not seem as though, unconsciously, he was already bidding us good-bye?' (Richard Le Gallienne, 'Hubert Crackanthorpe: In Memoriam', in *Sleeping Beauty and Other Prose Fancies* (London: John Lane, 1900), pp. 207–11). 'Enfantillage' had first appeared in the *Saturday Review*, 17 August 1895, p. 202, but Le Gallienne is responding to the fact that Crackanthorpe chose it as the finishing touch of *Vignettes*.

PART IV:
NON-FICTION

Realism in France and in England:
An Interview with M. Emile Zola[1]

"Les parvenus se meublent toujours le salon qu'ils ont ambitionné autrefois dans leurs souhaits de jeunes gens pauvres."[2] I had never completely realised the truth of this remark of Balzac's until I stood the other day in M. Zola's gorgeously furnished study in the Rue de Bruxelles, Paris.

I called to mind the struggles of his early years: how, having failed in the one examination which in France leads to everything, he had started in a wretched situation in the docks, not worth three pounds a month.[3] I thought of the three whole years of hand-to-hand battling with starvation that had followed.... Adrift on the pavement, doing nothing, with no future before him.... Hunger, misery, debts, and constant visits to the pawn-shop. How strange life is!

Yes, Balzac was right, *"l'ameublement trahit l'homme"*.[4] M. Zola began his literary career under the influence of Victor Hugo and the poets of 1830,[5] and it is singular how every object in the workroom of the great realist of today

---

[1]   Text: *The Albermarle: A Monthly Review*, 1.2 (February 1892), p. 39. For the context of this interview see Introduction, Section V.

[2]   *"Les parvenus se meublent toujours le salon qu'ils ont ambitionné autrefois dans leurs souhaits de jeunes gens pauvres."*: 'The new rich always furnish their drawing-rooms as they imagined them long ago, when they were young and poor'. There is no literal rendering of this quotation in Balzac, but Crackanthorpe may be recalling a passage from *La Cousine Bette* (1846): 'a bank-clerk, as he enters his manager's drawing-room, dreams of owning one just like it. If he is successful, it will not be the luxury then in fashion that he will install in his house twenty years later, but the out-of-date luxury that charmed him years ago' (Honoré de Balzac, *Cousin Bette*, trans. by Sylvia Raphael (Oxford: Oxford University Press, 2008), p. 121).

[3]   'In 1859, Zola failed the baccalauréat, a school-leaving examination, success in which would have made it possible to attend university or pursue a profession' (Hubert Crackanthorpe, *Wreckage*, ed. by Malcolm, p. 104).

[4]   *"L'ameublement trahit l'homme"*: 'Furniture betrays the man'. Not a literal rendering, but may draw indirectly on a reference to his *Père Goriot* (1835): 'toute sa personne explique la pension, comme la pension implique sa personne': 'everything about her seems to embody her pension, just as her pension invokes her image' (*Père Goriot*, trans. by Burton Raffel (New York: W. W. Norton, 1998), p. 10). Bourget makes a related point when writing of realist novelists' 'préoccupation de noter avec exactitude le milieu ou se meuvent ses personnages' ('preoccupation with noting with exactness the milieu in which his characters move'), observing that 'La chambre òu vit un homme est la figure extérieure des ses habitudes et de ses gestes' ('the room in which a man lives is the outward face of his habits and his behaviour') (*Nouveaux Essais de Psychologie Contemporaine*, 4th edn (Paris: Alphonse Lemerre, 1886), p. 216). Crackanthorpe was familiar with Bourget's *Essais* (see note 6 on p. 297; note 16 on p. 299).

[5]   Victor-Marie Hugo (1802–1885), poet, novelist, and dramatist; the most eminent of the French Romantic writers.

answers to the romanticist of thirty years ago.... the heavy, Oriental carpet, mediæval tapestries on the walls, stained glass in the windows, old Italian and Dutch furniture scattered here and there, the splendidly carved black oak writing-table, with an enormous high-backed chair — almost a throne — behind.

But, as I gaze curiously around, the entry of the great man himself suddenly interrupts my reflections.

"*Bonjour*," he says, buttoning up his smoking-jacket. "Ugh! how cold it is!" and drawing in a chair, vigorously stirs the wood fire on the hearth.

I at once notice several changes in him since we last met. He is considerably thinner, the pointed beard is more grey, the hair — in the old days always cut short — is now long and brushed back; there is, too, a tired, worn look about the cheeks. Yet, after all, it is still the same short, thick-set figure, the heavy gait, which is characteristic of another famous "*littérateur*" [6] — Mr. Walter Pater — the complexion a strange, dull yellow, the eyes small and keen. The most striking feature in his physiognomy is the neck. Its short and bull-like column gives to the whole face a look of power and solid strength.

"Well", continued M. Zola, "*causons*.[7] What are they saying about me in England? My friends over there tell me that one or two of your leading reviews have been devoting articles to the supposed death of realism in France."

"Yes, and is it not so? Are there not on all sides signs of a reaction?"

"Realism dead!" interrupted M. Zola, fidgetting nervously with a paper-cutter. "But you don't know what you are saying. No more realism! You might as well say that there will be no more sun, no more stars, no more trees. Realism, naturalism, whatever name you give it, is but the result of man's continued search after truth. And that search after truth will exist as long as the human race continues to progress. Now, with regard to the literary situation in France. Our conception of realistic fiction is probably destined to be developed, transformed. It would be absurd were it not so. In nature, everything is by degrees developed, transformed. It is the same in art. It may be that we — Flaubert, Daudet, Goncourt[8] and myself — have been a little sectarian, a little

---

[6] A *littérateur* is a man of letters.

[7] *Causons*: let us talk.

[8] All French writers whose works were well-known to Crackanthorpe. Flaubert: Gustave Flaubert (1821–1880), novelist whose pursuit of artistic 'impersonality' in writing was widely influential on later writers, including Crackanthorpe. Regarded as the prime mover of the realist school of French literature, he is best known for his masterpiece *Madame Bovary* (1857), with its pitiless rendering of bourgeois provincial life. Daudet: Alphonse Daudet (1840–1897), French short story writer, novelist, and dramatist, now remembered chiefly for his *Lettres de mon moulin* (1869), tales of provincial life in the south of France with which he was familiar from long association, an influence on Crackanthorpe's *A Set of Village Tales*. Goncourt: Edmond de Goncourt (1822–1896), novelist and writer, who together with his younger brother Jules (1830–1870) formed a long-standing creative partnership as 'les frères

dogmatic. After all, it was but natural, for as leaders of a movement we were obliged to make our formula as definite and as precise as possible. Yes," he added meditatively, "there will be an expansion of our formula."

"And what shape do you think that this expansion will take?"

"Ah!" he answered, shaking his head, "*Je ne sais pas .. je ne sais pas .. que voulez-vous que je vous dise?*[9] We have perhaps been too absolute, too positive. We have studied the human being a little too much from the point of view of the senses; and there will be, I think, a new movement towards the great Unknown — towards — *mais je ne sais pas .. que voulez-vous que je vous dise?*"

"Do you think then that this reaction is near at hand?"

"First of all," rapidly answered M. Zola, restlessly shifting his position, "You must remember that I am not yet dead, and the present naturalistic formula will find it hard to die without me. But besides, I see no signs of its dying at present. Every great movement in literature is the outcome of a corresponding great social movement. Literature is an expression of the life of the nation, and the best literature of each epoch is that which best expresses the national life of that epoch. Now our age is an age which is thirsting after truth. We see this in many ways; in the progress of Positivism,[10] in the development of democracy, and above all in the enormous strides made by science. Our realistic movement represents all these things; thus we are the outcome of the temper of our age.[11] This temper is so far from decaying that it is being developed further and further. And moreover among our young men there is no one strong enough to become the leader of a new school. I therefore see no reason for expecting an immediate reaction in literature, at least as far as the novel is concerned."

"But what about poetry?"

"Ah! poetry! yes, that is a little different. In 1789 we killed our gods, and set up

---

Goncourt'. In works such as *Germinie Lacerteux* (1864), a novel with a degeneration plot and which furnished Crackanthorpe's *Wreckage* with its epigraph, they helped to establish literary naturalism in Europe and also wrote social history and art criticism. They are best remembered for their voluminous *Journal*, kept up from 1851 until shortly before Edmond's death.

[9] "*Je ne sais pas .. je ne sais pas .. que voulez-vous que je vous dise*": I don't know .. I don't know .. what do you want me to say?

[10] Positivism: a social philosophy associated principally with August Comte (1798–1857), whose *System of Positive Polity* (*Système de politique positive*, 4 vols (1851–54)) was first translated into English by J. H. Bridges in 1875. An influence on George Eliot, Meredith, and Gissing and, above all, on the social philosophers Herbert Spencer and Frederic Harrison (who was president of the English Positivist Committee, 1880–1905), it was crucial in the evolution of social science and in particular the development of sociology as a discipline.

[11] Compare Edmond and Jules Goncourt on the novel: 'the great, serious, impassioned form of literary study and social inquiry [...] through analysis and psychological investigation, it is becoming moral, Contemporary History' ('Preface', *Germinie Lacerteux* (1862; Harmondsworth: Penguin, 1984), p. vi).

in their place Science.[12] From her, during these last hundred years, we have been expecting everything, and though I believe that she has done much to brighten our lives, her progress is but gradual and slow, while man's aspirations advance by leaps and bounds. That the weaker and more impatient spirits should at last revolt against her was inevitable. Hence all this so-called symbolist movement in poetry, these attempts to return to the first beginnings of art, only resulting in vague scribbling, in obscure, stuttering verses. These symbolist poets seem to think that by their senseless reaction they can overthrow the literary formula of their epoch. And when we point out to them the folly of it all, they throw the romanticist movement at our heads. The romanticist movement indeed!" continued M. Zola, getting up and walking excitedly up and down the room, "that was the logical outcome of the Revolution and the wars of the first Empire.[13] The language, worn out by three centuries of classicism, was in need of fresh blood, of enrichment, in fact of a complete renovation. But what need has it today of enrichment, of renovation? And what social movement does this symbolism represent? *C'est de la littérature de brasserie*."[14]

"Now, tell me about the novel in England," he said, evidently desirous of changing the subject. "*Qu'est-ce qu'on y fait?*[15] Unfortunately your literature is a sealed book to me, except through translations, and so few of your new writers have been translated. The fact is that we French are very ignorant, and what is worse, we are very indifferent to what goes on beyond our frontiers. Who are your realists?"

"Well, there is Mr. George Moore."[16]

"Ah! yes, of course, my friend Moore. *Il a beaucoup de talent*. I think very highly of his 'Mummer's Wife': it is full of power.[17] But he is almost alone, is he not? Ah! I thought so. You English are so essentially Protestant. We over here cannot understand your Protestantism, just as you can never understand our Catholicity. All this puritanism of yours is very curious. It would seem as if it were almost an element in your national genius, yet I know no literature

[12] 1789: the year in which the French Revolution began.
[13] The First Empire under Napoleon lasted from 1804 until his defeat in 1815. The Second Empire, under Louis-Napoleon Bonaparte, lasted from 1852 until 1870, ending after France's defeat in the Franco-Prussian war.
[14] "*C'est de la littérature de brasserie*": It's café literature.
[15] "*Qu'est-ce qu'on y fait?*": What can one do about it?
[16] George Moore (1852–1933), leading British naturalist novelist, prolific and energetic Francophile, and critic, whose proselytising of the credo of literary naturalism in the 1880s gave way to a more considered aesthetic position from which to view developments in contemporary writing in Britain and France. His most accomplished novel, *Esther Waters* (1894), is a thoughtfully structured, humane study of the trials endured by a vulnerable working-class woman.
[17] *A Mummer's Wife* (1885) by George Moore, a Zola-esque exposé of the acting profession, first published by Henry Vizetelly. It was translated into French as *La Femme du Cabotin* (Paris: G. Charpentier, 1888).

more healthily brutal and vigorous than that of Shakespeare, Jonson, and their contemporaries.[18] However, you have got under the yoke of the puritans, and as long as you remain so, you will never have a really fine literature outburst. But, from what I hear, there are signs of an approaching reaction. Our work is attracting more attention, is it not? It is more freely discussed than it was. And your stage, too, is getting emancipated. This Independent Theatre is an excellent sign. My little 'Thérèse [sic] Raquin' excited quite a little battle, they tell me. All that is good."[19]

"And Ibsen, too," I put in. "We have had several of Ibsen's plays produced in London this year,[20] and one of them at least was a great success."

M. Zola was turning over the uncut pages of M. Ferdinand Fabre's last novel:[21] he did not seem to hear what I was saying.

"What do you think about Ibsen's work?" I continued.

"Ibsen!" he answered without raising his eyes, "c'est bien obscur."

"But wouldn't you say —— ?"

"C'est bien obscur. Tout cela est bien obscur," he repeated, shrugging his shoulders — "parlons d'autre chose."[22]

It was hopeless, I saw. The great man declined to be drawn.

"Which of our English novelists are most appreciated in France?"

"There is no difficulty in answering that question," he replied, smiling at my sudden change of front; "Dickens and Scott, without a doubt, and for this very obvious reason: the novel in France has always been more or less emancipated, while the works of Dickens and Scott can be put into the hands of anyone, which is more than can be said even for the works of George Sand.[23] Besides,

---

[18]   Zola's point is assimilated by Crackanthorpe into his argument in his 'Reticence in Literature' essay that 'the drama flourished in the robust age of Shakespeare and Ben Jonson' as a sign of how '[e]ach epoch instinctively chooses that literary vehicle which is best adapted for the expression of its particular temper', p. 396.

[19]   Thérèse Raquin, Zola's novel of 1867, featured adultery, murder, and double suicide. In its Preface Zola spelt out his credo for naturalist fiction. This was the second controversial play performed by Grein's newly formed Independent Theatre at the Royalty Theatre in August 1891, the first being the legendary London production of Ibsen's Ghosts (1881) that March. The critical response was predictably negative, typified by the report in The Athenaeum: 'In the process of conversion into a play', it wrote, 'it had ceased to be a psychological study, and developed into a somewhat conventional and grimly repellent melodrama' (The Athenaeum, 3338 (17 October 1891), p. 525).

[20]   In 1891 five of Ibsen's plays were staged in London, including Ghosts, Hedda Gabler, and Rosmersholm.

[21]   This is probably Abbé Roitelet (1890). Ferdinand Fabré (1830–1898) from the early 1860s published novels set in the area of the Cevennes, in the south of France, featuring the lives of the inhabitants of the mountain villages of Herault, particularly its priests, of which L'Abbé Tigrane, candidat a la papaute (1873) was his most celebrated.

[22]   "C'est bien obscur. Tout cela est bien obscur, [...] parlons d'autre chose.": It's most obscure. All that is most obscure [...] let's talk about something else.

[23]   George Sand, pseud. of Amantine-Lucile-Aurore Dudevant (1804–1876), influential

Dickens is a poet, a great poet in many ways. He is less English than most of your writers, and that is why we understand him better. But he ignores all the greater side of man — love, and all the big emotions of life — and above all, woman. He knows nothing at all about women."

"And Scott?"

"Scott!" he answered, with an impatient wave of his hand, "*littérature de pensionnat*.[24] There is another reason for Dickens' success over here," he continued, following up his train of thought. "Our opponents have taken him up to use him as an argument against our conception of realism, and at one time our reviews were flooded with articles on Dickens. Tolstoi has been taken up in the same way, but his success was never real, like that of Dickens."

"And Thackeray?"

"Thackeray! Ah! *je ne sais pas*," with a shrug of the shoulders ... "deeper than Dickens, yes, certainly deeper than Dickens. But it is so difficult to understand it at all. It is so English. For instance, there is George Eliot, who has been lauded up to the skies by Brunetière and the Academic party.[25] *Eh bien! ça n'a pas pris du tout*.[26] She was *très savante, très instruite*,[27] but she had no real knowledge of humanity. She gives me the impression of never having been outside her library door. She seems only to know her humanity through books. 'The Mill on the Floss' — *voyons, ça ne vaut pas grand'chose en somme? hein?*[28] Do you think much of it in England?"

I nodded.

"It is all", he repeated, "so utterly opposed to the genius of the French people."

Then after a pause —

"*Voyons, tous le trois ensemble ne valent pas les grandes machines de Balzac?*"[29]

French novelist whose early romantic works featured the struggles of women against the constraints of marriage.

[24] "*Littérature de pensionnat*": boarding-house literature. Zola is clearly not short of expressions of critical contempt.

[25] From the early 1880s the leading conservative literary critic and editor Ferdinand Brunetière (1849–1906) invoked the example of George Eliot's fiction, contra Zola, to show that realism need not involve the rejection of traditional moral values, as he saw it, and looked to the tradition of English fiction as an 'instrument de prédication, d'étude et d'instruction': 'an instrument of preaching, study and education' (Ferdinand Brunetière, 'Le Naturalisme anglaise: Etude sur George Eliot', in *Le Roman naturaliste* (Paris: Calmann-Lévy, 1897), p. 241).

[26] "*Eh bien! ça n'a pas pris du tout.*": So! It didn't catch on at all.

[27] "*Très savante, très instruite*": very wise, very well-educated.

[28] "'The Mill on the Floss' — *voyons, ça ne vaut pas grand'chose en somme? hein?*": The Mill on the Floss — look here, it's not worth much on the whole? Eh? The Mill on The Floss was George Eliot's second novel, published in 1860. Brunetière's success in raising the prestige of Eliot in France by pitting Eliot against Zola (see note 25, above) helps to explain Zola's dismissive evaluation of it here.

[29] "*Voyons, tous le trois ensemble ne valent pas les grandes machines de Balzac?*": Let's see,

At this moment our conversation was interrupted by the furious entry of a little black spaniel, who flew barking and snapping round my chair.

I rose to go.

"*Il ne faut pas que Bibi vous chasse,*"[30] said M. Zola, holding out his hand. "You have been lucky," he said "to get a drawing from Whistler for your first number, .. a great artist, .. a great artist.[31] Well, goodbye. I am very glad to have seen you. I wish you all success. Send me your review when you get another Whistler. Down, Bibi! down! ... don't be afraid, he won't bite," and as I went down the staircase — "*Il vous faut de la patience en Angleterre .. de la patience. Tout vient à qui sait attendre.*"[32]

all three together don't add up to the great Balzacian constructions, do they?

[30] "*Il ne faut pas que Bibi vous chasse*": Don't let Bibi drive you out.

[31] See Introduction, pp. 1–33.

[32] "*Il vous faut de la patience en Angleterre .. de la patience. Tout vient à qui sait attendre.*": You must have patience in England, patience. Everything comes to those who can wait.

Mr. Vizetelly and Literary Freedom[1]

Sir, —— Mr Frank Harris hits the right nail on the head. What we lack in this matter of literary freedom is an organised opinion of artists and men of letters. We have to fight single-handed, one after the other, for the campaign is only beginning.

Still, there has been a very considerable advance in public opinion since the prosecution of Mr. Vizetelly — even Mr. Robert Buchanan and Mr. Frank Harris would, I suppose, admit that.[2]

Now there is one excellent way in which the extent of this advance could be determined, and, at the same time, a decisive manifestation in favour of the cause of literary freedom achieved — namely, by fighting the same battle over again, but this time with the best weapons procurable.

Let us have a test case. Let all those influential men of letters who expressed or felt indignation at the injustice done to Mr. Vizetelly[3] combine to bring about the publication of an English translation of, say, "Nana" or "Au Bonheur des Dames."[4]

And let it be so managed that the brunt of the prosecution, if there be one, is borne, not by a single unfortunate publisher, but by an organisation which includes every writer of eminence who has the cause of literary freedom at heart. —— Sincerely yours,

Hubert Crackanthorpe.

[1]   Text: *Daily Chronicle*, 9 January 1894, p. 3, col. 7.
[2]   Robert Buchanan (1841–1901): poet, novelist, playwright, and literary controversialist, best-known for his attack on Pre-Raphaelite writers in 'The Fleshly School of Poetry' (*Contemporary Review*, 18 (August–November 1871), later rescinded), was a forceful and sometimes ill-tempered harrier of the new, but achieved some success as a dramatist in the 1890s. His criticism, said Symons, 'was all a kind of fighting journalism [...] Like most fighters, Buchanan fought because he could not think' (Arthur Symons, 'Robert Buchanan', in *Studies in Prose and Verse* (London: Dent, 1904), pp. 121–23 (pp. 121–22)). Frank Harris (1855–1931): novelist, short-story writer, and journalist; his main achievements were his tenure as editor of the *Fortnightly Review*, 1886–1894, and the *Saturday Review*, 1894–1898. Harris later published five series of *Contemporary Portraits* (1915–1927) of over a hundred figures in the arts whom he had encountered. His autobiography, *My Life and Loves* (1922–1927), was laced with candid accounts of his sexual exploits.
[3]   See Introduction, pp. 1–33.
[4]   *Nana* and *Au Bonheur des Dames*: novels by Zola, first published in 1880 and 1883, respectively. In a reply to Crackanthorpe, three days later, George Moore took issue with him: 'Many reasons', he said, 'prevent me from agreeing with Mr. Crackanthorpe's suggestion for the republication of "Nana" and "Au Bonheur des Dames"', although he didn't spell these out. A better candidate, he thought, would be Flaubert's *Madame Bovary*, which 'was included in the list of books which the Vigilance Association determines to proceed against' (George Moore, 'Literary Freedom', Letter to the *Daily Chronicle*, 12 January 1894, p. 3, col. 7).

Reticence in Literature:
Some Roundabout Remarks[1]

During the past fifty years, as everyone knows, the art of fiction has been expanding in a manner exceedingly remarkable, till it has grown to be the predominant branch of imaginative literature. But the other day we were assured that poetry only thrives in limited and exquisite editions; that the drama, here in England at least, has practically ceased to be literature at all. Each epoch instinctively chooses that literary vehicle which is best adapted for the expression of its particular temper: just as the drama flourished in the robust age of Shakespeare and Ben Jonson; just as that outburst of lyrical poetry, at the beginning of the century in France, coincided with a period of extreme emotional exaltation; so the novel, facile and flexible in its conventions, with its endless opportunities for accurate delineation of reality, becomes supreme in a time of democracy and of science — to note but these two salient characteristics.

And, if we pursue this light of thought, we find that, on all sides, the novel is being approached in one especial spirit, that it would seem to be striving, for the moment at any rate, to perfect itself within certain definite limitations. To employ a hackneyed, and often quite unintelligent, catchword — the novel is becoming realistic.

Throughout the history of literature, the jealous worship of beauty — which we term idealism — and the jealous worship of truth — which we term realism — have alternately prevailed. Indeed, it is within the compass of these alternations that lies the whole fundamental diversity of literary temper.

Still, the classification is a clumsy one, for no hard and fast line can be drawn between the one spirit and the other. The so-called idealist must take as his point of departure the facts of Nature; the so-called realist must be sensitive to some one or other of the forms of beauty, if each would achieve the fineness of great art. And the pendulum of production is continually swinging, from degenerate idealism to degenerate realism, from effete vapidity to slavish sordidity.

Either term, then, can only be employed in a purely limited and relative sense. Completely idealistic art — art that has no point of contact with the facts of the universe, as we know them — is, of course, an impossible absurdity; similarly, a complete reproduction of Nature by means of words is an absurd impossibility. Neither emphasization[2] nor abstraction can be dispensed with: the one, eliminating the details of no import; the other, exaggerating those which the artist has selected. And, even were such a thing possible, it would not

---

[1] Text: *The Yellow Book: An Illustrated Quarterly*, 2 (July 1894), pp. 259–69.

[2] Emphasization: a neologism.

be Art. The invention of a highly perfected system of coloured photography, for instance, or a skilful recording by means of the phonograph[3] of scenes in real life, would not subtract one whit from the value of the painter's or the playwright's interpretation. Art is not invested with the futile function of perpetually striving after imitation or reproduction of Nature; she endeavours to produce, through the adaptation of a restricted number of natural facts, an harmonious and satisfactory whole. Indeed, in this very process of adaptation and blending together, lies the main and greater task of the artist. And the novel, the short story, even the impression of a mere incident, convey each of them, the imprint of the temper in which their creator has achieved this process of adaptation and blending together of his material. They are inevitably stamped with the hall-mark of his personality. A work of art can never be more than a corner of Nature, seen through the temperament of a single man. Thus, all literature is, must be, essentially subjective; for style is but the power of individual expression. The disparity which separates literature from the reporter's transcript is ineradicable. There is a quality of ultimate suggestiveness to be achieved; for the business of art is, not to explain or to describe, but to suggest. That attitude of objectivity, or of impersonality towards his subject, consciously or unconsciously, assumed by the artist, and which nowadays provokes so considerable an admiration, can be attained only in a limited degree. Every piece of imaginative work must be a kind of autobiography of its creator — significant, if not of the actual facts of his existence, at least of the inner working of his soul. We are each of us conscious, not of the whole world, but of our own world; not of naked reality, but of that aspect of reality which our peculiar temperament enables us to appropriate. Thus, every narrative of an external circumstance is never anything else than the transcript of the impression produced upon ourselves by that circumstance, and, invariably, a degree of individual interpretation is insinuated into every picture, real or imaginary, however objective it may be. So then, the disparity between the so-called idealist and the so-called realist is a matter, not of æsthetic philosophy, but of individual temperament. Each is at work, according to the especial bent of his genius, within precisely the same limits. Realism, as a creed, is as ridiculous as any other literary creed.

Now, it would have been exceedingly curious if this recent specialisation of the art of fiction, this passion for draining from the life, as it were, born, in due season, of the general spirit of the latter half of the nineteenth century, had not provoked a considerable amount of opposition — opposition of just that kind which every new evolution in art inevitably encounters. Between the vanguard and the main body there is perpetual friction.

But time flits quickly in this hurried age of ours, and the opposition to the

3   Phonograph: a precursor of the gramophone.

renascence of fiction as a conscientious interpretation of life is not what it was; its opponents are not the men they were. It is not so long since a publisher was sent to prison for issuing English translations of celebrated specimens of French realism;[4] yet, only the other day, we vied with each other in doing honour to the chief figure-head of that tendency across the Channel,[5] and there was heard but the belated protest of a few worthy individuals, inadequately equipped with the jaunty courage of ignorance, or the insufferable confidence of second-hand knowledge.

And during the past year things have been moving very rapidly. The position of the literary artist towards Nature, his great inspirer, has become more definite, more secure. A sound, organised opinion of men of letters is being acquired; and in the little bouts with the *bourgeois* — if I may be pardoned the use of that wearisome word — no one has to fight single-handed. Heroism is at a discount; Mrs. Grundy is becoming mythological;[6] a crowd of unsuspected supporters collect from all sides, and the deadly conflict of which we had been warned becomes but an interesting skirmish. Books are published, stories are printed, in old-established reviews, which would never have been tolerated a few years ago. On all sides, deference to the tendency of the time is spreading. The truth must be admitted: the roar of unthinking prejudice is dying away.

All this is exceedingly comforting: and yet, perhaps, it is not a matter for absolute congratulation. For, if the enemy are not dying as gamely as we had expected, if they are, as I am afraid, losing heart, and in danger of sinking into a condition of passive indifference, it should be to us a matter of not inconsiderable apprehension. If this new evolution in the art of fiction — this general return of the literary artist towards Nature, on the brink of which we are today hesitating — is to achieve any definite, ultimate fineness of expression, it will benefit enormously by the continued presence of a healthy, vigorous, if not wholly intelligent, body of opponents. Directly or indirectly, they will knock a lot of nonsense out of us, will these opponents; — why should we be ashamed to admit it? They will enable us to find our level, they will spur us on to bring out the best — and only the best — that is within us.

Take, for instance, the gentleman who objects to realistic fiction on moral grounds. If he does not stand the most conspicuous today, at least he was pre-

---

[4] The imprisonment of the publisher Henry Vizetelly for three months, in May 1889, for publishing translations of novels by Zola, Bourget, and Maupassant. See Introduction, pp. 16–17.

[5] Crackanthorpe is referring to the invitation to Emile Zola to visit London by the Institute of Journalists in September 1893, and the week of celebrations in his honour: See Introduction, p. 24.

[6] Mrs. Grundy: the archetypal puritanical and censorious zealot, frequently called upon by critics of Victorian prudery. She makes her first appearance in Thomas Morton's play *Speed the Plough* (1798).

eminent the day before yesterday. He is a hard case, and it is on his especial behalf that I would appeal. For he has been dislodged from the hill top, he has become a target for all manner of unkind chaff, from the ribald youth of Fleet Street and Chelsea.[7] He has been labelled a Philistine:[8] he has been twitted with his middle-age; he has been reported to have compromised himself with that indecent old person, Mrs. Grundy. It is confidently asserted that he comes from Putney, or from Sheffield, and that, when he is not busy abolishing the art of English literature, he is employed in safeguarding the interests of the grocery or tallow-chandler's trade. Strange and cruel tales of him have been printed in the monthly reviews; how, but for him, certain well-known popular writers would have written masterpieces; how, like the ogre in the fairy tale, he consumes every morning at breakfast a hundred pot-boiled young geniuses. For the most part they have been excellently well told, these tales of this moral ogre of ours; but why start to shatter brutally their dainty charm by a soulless process of investigation? No, let us be shamed rather into a more charitable spirit, into making generous amends, into rehabilitating the greatness of our moral ogre.

He is the backbone of our nation; the guardian of our mediocrity; the very foil[9] of our intelligence. Once, you fancied that you could argue with him, that you could dispute his dictum. Ah! how we cherished that day-dream of our extreme youth. But it was not to be. He is still immense; for he is unassailable; he is flawless, for he is complete within himself; his lucidity is yet unimpaired; his impartiality is yet supreme. Who amongst us could judge with a like impartiality the productions of Scandinavia and Charpentier, Walt Whitman, and the Independent Theatre?[10] Let us remember that he has never professed to understand Art, and the deep debt of gratitude that every artist in

---

[7]   Fleet Street and Chelsea are metonyms for young journalists and bohemians.

[8]   Philistine is a derogatory term for people who are antipathetic to the idea of culture and the life of the mind, brought into prominence by Matthew Arnold in *Culture and Anarchy* (1869). Arnold associated these values primarily with the British middle class.

[9]   Foil, literally a leaf of metal used to accentuate the visual quality of a precious stone, here used to delineate a thing or character that makes another's good or bad characteristics all the more noticeable.

[10]   Crackanthorpe presumably has in mind the dramatists Henrik Ibsen (1828–1906) and August Strindberg (1849–1912) and possibly the short story writer, and fellow *Yellow Book* contributor, George Egerton (1859–1945), who was an important mediator of Scandinavian literature into Britain. Charpentier: Gustave Charpentier (1860–1956), French composer whose most recent composition was his orchestral suite, *Impressions d'Italie*, premiered in 1892. Walt Whitman (1819–1892): American poet, journalist, and essayist; his collection of poems *Leaves of Grass* (1855) was highly influential, notably on the poem *Towards Democracy* (1883, with sections added until 1902) by the socialist writer Edward Carpenter (1844–1929). The Independent Theatre, to which Crackanthorpe and his parents both subscribed, was established in London by J. T. Grein in 1891 with a progressive agenda to meet the needs of students of 'the advancing drama'. Grein's first production, Ibsen's *Ghosts*, exemplified his 'policy' of staging a 'play that has a literary and artistic, rather than commercial value' (Stokes, *Resistible Theatres*, p. 138).

the land should consequently owe to him; let us remember that he is above us, for he belongs to the great middle classes; let us remember that he commands votes, that he is candidate for the County Council; let us remember that he is delightful, because he is intelligible.

Yes, he is intelligible; and of how many of us can that be said? His is no complex programme, no subtly exacting demand. A plain moral lesson is all that he asks, and his voice is as of one crying in the ever fertile wilderness of Smith and of Mudie.[11]

And he is right, after all — if he only knew it. The business of art is to create for us fine interests, to make of our human nature a more complete thing: and thus, all great art is moral in the wider and the truer sense of the word. It is precisely on this point of the meaning of the word "moral" that we and our ogre part company. To him, morality is concerned only with the established relations between the sexes and with fair dealing between man and man: to him the subtle, indirect morality of Art is incomprehensible.

Theoretically, Art is non-moral. She is not interested in any ethical code of any age or any nation, except in so far as the breach or observance of that code may furnish her with material on which to work. But, unfortunately, in this complex world of ours, we cannot satisfactorily pursue one interest — no, not even the interest of Art, at the expense of all others — let us look that fact in the face, doggedly, whatever pangs it may cost us — pleading magnanimously for the survival of our moral ogre, for there will be danger to our cause when his voice is no more heard.

If imitation be the sincerest form of flattery, then our moral ogre must indeed have experienced a proud moment, when a follower came to him from the camp of the lovers of Art, and the artistic objector to realistic fiction started on his timid career. I use the word timid in no disparaging sense, but because our artistic objector, had he ventured a little farther from the vicinity of the coat-tails of his powerful protector, might have secured a more adequate recognition of his performances. For he is by no means devoid of adroitness. He can patter to us glibly of the "gospel of ugliness"; of the "cheerlessness of modern literature"; he can even juggle with that honourable property-piece, the maxim of Art for Art's sake. But there have been moments when even this feat has proved ineffective, and someone has started scoffing at his pretended "delight in pure rhythm or music of the phrase," and flippantly assured him that he is talking nonsense, and that style is a mere matter of psychological suggestion. You fancy our performer nonplussed, or at least boldly bracing

---

[11] W. H. Smith (1792–) and Mudie's (1842–1937) were the leading circulating libraries of the Victorian period, increasingly criticised from the 1880s by Moore, Gissing, Hardy, and others for the morally prescriptive criteria they deployed to dictate the choice of fiction for their subscribers. See Introduction, pp. 1–33.

himself to brazen the matter out. No, he passes dexterously to his curtain effect — a fervid denunciation of express trains, evening newspapers, Parisian novels, or the first number of THE YELLOW BOOK. Verily, he is a versatile person.

Sometimes, to listen to him you would imagine that pessimism and regular meals were incompatible; that the world is only ameliorated by those whom it completely satisfies, that good predominates over evil, that the problem of our destiny had been solved long ago. You begin to doubt whether any good thing can come out of this miserable, inadequate age of ours, unless it be a doctored survival of the vocabulary of a past century. The language of the coster and cadger resound in our midst,[12] and, though Velasquez tried to paint like Whistler, Rudyard Kipling cannot write like Pope.[13] And a weird word has been invented to explain the whole business. Decadence, decadence: you are all decadent nowadays. Ibsen, Degas, and the New English Art Club; Zola, Oscar Wilde, and the Second Mrs. Tanqueray.[14] Mr. Richard Le Gallienne is hoist with

[12]   A coster is a street-vendor; a cadger is a beggar or scrounger.

[13]   Diego Velasquez (1599–1660) was the leading artist in the court of King Philip IV of Spain. The artist Charles Furse, in an essay on impressionism for Crackanthorpe's *The Albermarle*, had invoked Velasquez's 'masterly grip of the essentials' (Charles W. Furse, 'Impressionism: What It Means', *The Albermarle: A Monthly Review*, 2.2 (August 1892), 47–51 (p. 49)). The art critics D. S. MacColl and R. A. M. Stevenson thought that Velasquez anticipated 'the technique developed by French artists of the nineteenth century' (Stokes, *In the Nineties*, p. 47). According to the *Pall Mall Gazette* (17 December 1895), Stevenson's comprehensive study of the painter, *The Art of Velasquez* (1895), could have been entitled 'A Defence of Impressionist Painting as Illustrated by the Works of Velasquez' (quoted in Stokes, *In the Nineties*, pp. 47, 176 n. 44), a comment which helps to make sense of Crackanthorpe's initially puzzling conceit. Rudyard Kipling (1865–1936), novelist, short-story writer, and journalist, was the most widely read poet of the decade. Alexander Pope (1688–1744) was the leading British exponent, in poetry, of eighteenth-century satire.

[14]   Ibsen: Henrik Ibsen (1828–1906), the most critically influential playwright of the late nineteenth century. Denigrated at length by Max Nordau in *Degeneration* (1892, English translation 1895), his plays were applauded by both Hubert and Blanche Crackanthorpe, who wrote that his 'grip on humanity [...] holds his audience as in a vice [...] he has established an electric current between them and himself, for this is life as many of them know it' ('Sex in Modern Literature', *Nineteenth Century*, 37 (April 1895), 607–16 (p. 610)). Degas: Edouard Degas (1834–1917), French Impressionist painter who frequently depicted dancers and was revered by art critic D. S. MacColl. Degas' 'L'Absinthe', exhibited in London in 1893, prompted a brief storm of protest led by J. A. Spender, 'The Philistine', who used the painting to attack critics like MacColl. See Stokes, *In the Nineties*, pp. 35–36. The New English Art Club was founded in 1886 and included amongst its members Sickert and Wilson Steer, painters sympathetic to *plein air* impressionism and influenced by Whistler. Zola: Emile Zola (1840–1902), French novelist of the late nineteenth-century, the leading theorist and practitioner of naturalism through his prose writings and his twenty-novel series *Les Rougon-Macquart*. He was a major influence on Crackanthorpe and on realist writers such as Moore and Arthur Morrison. Wilde: Oscar Wilde (1854–1900), critic, poet, dramatist, and the leading proponent of the Aesthetic movement and 'art for art's sake'. Crackanthorpe namechecks Wilde, who was currently enjoying a *succès d'estime* on the strength of his novel *The Picture of Dorian Gray* (1890, 1891) and his comedy *Lady*

his own petard;[15] even the British playwright has not escaped the taint. Ah, what a hideous spectacle. All whirling along towards one common end. And the elegant voice of the artistic objector floating behind: *"Après vous le dèluge."*[16] A wholesale abusing of the tendencies of the age has ever proved, for the superior mind, an inexhaustible source of relief. Few things breed such inward comfort as the contemplation of one's own pessimism — few things produce such discomfort as the remembrance of our neighbour's optimism.

And yet, pessimists though we may be dubbed, some of us, on this point at least, how can we compete with the hopelessness enjoyed by our artistic objector, when the spectacle of his despondency makes us insufferably replete with hope and confidence, so that while he is loftily bewailing or prettily denouncing the completeness of our degradation, we continue to delight in the evil of our ways? Oh, if we could only be sure that he would persevere in reprimanding this persistent study of the pitiable aspects of life, how our hearts would go out towards him? For the man who said that joy is essentially, regrettably inartistic, admitted in the same breath that misery lends itself to artistic treatment twice as easily as joy, and resumed the whole question in a single phrase. Let our artistic objector but weary the world sufficiently with his despair concerning the permanence of the cheerlessness of modern realism, and some day a man will arise who will give us a study of human happiness, as fine, as vital as anything we owe to Guy de Maupassant[17] or to Ibsen. That man will have accomplished the infinitely difficult, and in admiration and in awe shall we bow down our heads before him.

In one radical respect the art of fiction is not in the same position as the other arts. They — music, poetry, painting, sculpture, and the drama — possess a

Windermere's Fan, which opened in 1892 to great acclaim. With his plays *An Ideal Husband* (1895) and *The Importance of Being Earnest* (1895) still to come, there was every prospect of his scaling further heights. The disaster which would strike Wilde down, nine months later, entailing his arrest for 'gross indecency' and subsequent imprisonment in May 1895, all but destroyed him and turned opinion decisively against Aestheticism and Decadence. *The Second Mrs. Tanqueray* is a problem play in melodramatic mode by Sir Arthur Wing Pinero (1855–1934); it opened in May 1893 at the St James Theatre, London, and was evidently a critical and popular success.

[15] To be 'hoist with your own petard' means to be caught out by your own cleverness; the allusion is to Shakespeare, *Hamlet*, III. 4. 206. Its application to Le Gallienne (1866–1943), poet, critic, and literary 'log-roller', is not entirely clear. Taken up by the *Yellow Book* publisher, John Lane, for whom he became the firm's reader, Le Gallienne's ambivalent relationship to Decadence was either complicated or simply self-serving: he affected a Decadent persona, while writing in an anti-Decadent vein, which left him vulnerable to accusations of inconsistency at best, a lack of self-awareness at worst.

[16] *"Après vous le deluge"*: 'After you comes the flood'. The pronouncement is attributed to Louis XV of France (1710–1774).

[17] Guy de Maupassant (1850–1893), French naturalist writer of short stories and novels, the leading French exponent of the short story of the late nineteenth century and a key influence on Crackanthorpe.

magnificent fabric of accumulated tradition. The great traditions of the art of fiction have yet to be made. Ours is a young art, struggling desperately to reach expression, with no great past to guide it. Thus, it should be a matter for wonder, not that we stumble into certain pitfalls, but that we do not fall headlong into a hundred more.

But, if we have no great past, we have the present and the future — the one abundant in facilities, the other abundant in possibilities. Young men of today have enormous chances: we are working under exceedingly favourable conditions. Possibly we stand on the threshold of a very great period. I know, of course, that the literary artist is shamefully ill-paid, and that the man who merely caters for the public taste, amasses a rapid and respectable fortune. But how is it that such an arrangement seems other than entirely equitable? The essential conditions of the two cases are entirely distinct. The one man is free to give untrammelled expression to his own soul, free to fan to the full the flame that burns in his heart: the other is a seller of wares, a unit in national commerce. To the one is allotted liberty and a living wage; to the other, captivity and a consolation in Consols.[18] Let us whine, then, no more concerning the prejudice and the persecution of the Philistine, when even that misanthrope, Mr. Robert Buchanan, admits that there is no power in England to prevent a man writing exactly as he pleases.[19] Before long the battle for literary freedom will be won. A new public has been created — appreciative, eager and determined; a public which, as Mr. Gosse[20] puts it, in one of those admirable essays of his, "has eaten of the apple of knowledge, and will not be satisfied with mere marionnettes. Whatever comes next," Mr. Gosse continues, "we cannot return, in serious novels, to the inanities and impossibilities of the old well-made plot, to the children changed at nurse, to the madonna-heroine and the god-like hero,

---

[18] Consols are British Government consolidated securities which in theory offered investors dependable rates of interest.

[19] Buchanan had told the readers of the *Daily Chronicle* earlier that year that he had 'advocated again and again the right of perfect freedom of speech in literature', but that did not 'prevent [him] from believing and saying that Zolaism is an ugly, a corrupt, and an evil influence of literature, generally' (Buchanan, Letter to the *Daily Chronicle*, 11 January 1894, p. 3, col. 6). Crackanthorpe was expressing impatience with Buchanan, who had initiated the round of correspondence about Zola, censorship, and taste in the *Daily Chronicle*, which had subsequently drawn in Harris, Crackanthorpe himself, Ernest Vizetelly (Henry Vizetelly's son), and Moore (see Buchanan, Letter to the *Daily Chronicle*, 6 January 1894, p. 3, col. 7; Harris, Letter to the *Daily Chronicle*, 8 January 1894, p. 3, col. 5; Ernest A. Vizetelly, Letter to the *Daily Chronicle*, 9 January 1894, p. 3, col. 7; Crackanthorpe, Letter to the *Daily Chronicle*, 9 January 1894, p. 3, col. 7; Buchanan, Letter to the *Daily Chronicle*, 11 January 1894, p. 3, col. 6; Moore, Letter to the *Daily Chronicle*, 12 January, 1894, p. 3, col. 7; Buchanan, Letter to the *Daily Chronicle*, 15 January 1894, p. 3, col. 6).

[20] Edmund Gosse (1849–1928) was an English poet, critic, literary historian, and translator who helped introduce Ibsen to the British public. A prolific writer, he is mainly remembered for his seminal autobiographical work *Father and Son* (1907).

to the impossible virtues and melodramatic vices. In future, even those who sneer at realism and misrepresent it most wilfully, will be obliged to put their productions more in accordance with veritable experience. There will still be novel-writers who address the gallery, and who will keep up the gaudy old convention, and the clumsy *Family Herald* evolution,[21] but they will no longer be distinguished men of genius. They will no longer sign themselves George Sand or Charles Dickens."[22]

Fiction has taken her place amongst the arts. The theory that writing resembles the blacking of boots, the more boots you black, the better you do it, is busy evaporating. The excessive admiration for the mere idea of a book or a story is dwindling; so is the comparative indifference to slovenly treatment. True is it that the society lady, dazzled by the brilliancy of her own conversation, and the serious-minded spinster, bitten by some sociological theory, still decide in the old jaunty spirit, that fiction is the obvious medium through which to astonish or improve the world. Let us beware of the despotism of the intelligent amateur, and cease our toying with that quaint and winsome bogey of ours, the British Philistine, whilst the intelligent amateur, the deadliest of Art's enemies, is creeping up in our midst.

For the familiarity of the man in the street with the material employed by the artist in fiction, will ever militate against the acquisition of a sound, fine, and genuine standard of workmanship. Unlike the musician, the painter, the sculptor, the architect, the artist in fiction enjoys no monopoly in his medium. The word and the phrase are, of necessity, the common property of everybody; the ordinary use of them demands no special training. Hence the popular mind, while willingly acknowledging that there are technical difficulties to be surmounted in the creation of the sonata, the landscape, the statue, the building, in the case of the short story, or of the longer novel, declines to believe even in their existence, persuaded that in order to produce good fiction, an ingenious idea, or "plot," as it is termed, is the one thing needed. The rest is a mere matter of handwriting.

The truth is, and, despite Mr. Waugh,[23] we are near recognition of it, that nowadays there is but scanty merit in the mere selection of any particular subject, however ingenious or daring it may appear at first sight; that a man is not an artist, simply because he writes about heredity or the *demi-monde*,[24]

---

[21] *The Family Herald: A Domestic Magazine of Useful Information & Amusement*, 'an inexpensive weekly containing fiction, published between 1842 and 1940' (Hubert Crackanthorpe, *Wreckage*, ed. by Malcolm, p. 119).

[22] This passage is reproduced, virtually verbatim, from Gosse's essay 'The Limits of Realism in Fiction' (1890), repr. in *Questions At Issue*, pp. 137–54 (pp. 152–53).

[23] Arthur Waugh (1866–1943), critic and writer, and the author of the essay 'Reticence in Literature' (*Yellow Book*, 1 (April 1894), 201–19), to which Crackanthorpe's is a rejoinder.

[24] See note 28 on p. 191.

that to call a spade a spade requires no extraordinary literary gift, and that the essential is contained in the frank, fearless acceptance by every man of his entire artistic temperament, with its qualities and its flaws.

PART V:
APPENDIX

Crackanthorpe's Writings Selected for this Edition: A Bibliographical Survey

Profiles

From *Wreckage: Seven Studies*, pp. 1–53

Translated as 'Profili' in *Hubert Crackanthorpe: Racconti*, traduzione e introduzione di Emanuela Ettorre (Napoli: Edizioni Scientifiche Italiane, 2015), pp. 33–65

Anthologized in *Writing of the 'Nineties: From Wilde to Beerbohm*, ed. by Derek Stanford (London: J. M. Dent, 1971), pp. 76–98

A Conflict of Egoisms

From *Wreckage: Seven Studies* pp. 55–105

Translated as 'Solitude A Deux' [by Jacqueline Ansaloni], *La Nouvelle Revue Des Deux Mondes* (October 1973), pp. 90–111; 'Un conflitto di egoismi' in *Hubert Crackanthorpe: Racconti*, pp. 67–98

Anthologized in *Selections From British Fiction 1880–1900*, ed. by Ian Fletcher (New York: Signet, 1972), pp. 94–116; *Victorian Love Stories: An Oxford Anthology*, ed. by Kate Flint (Oxford: Oxford University Press, 1996), pp. 277–300

The Struggle for Life

From *Wreckage: Seven Studies*, pp. 107–11

Translated as 'La lotta per la vita' in *Hubert Crackanthorpe: Racconti*, pp. 99–102

Anthologized in *British Poetry and Prose 1870–1905*, ed. by Ian Fletcher (Oxford: Oxford University Press, 1987), pp. 387–89

Dissolving View

From *Wreckage: Seven Studies*, pp. 113–24

First published in *The Albermarle: A Monthly Review*, 2.2 (August 1892), 80–83

Translated as 'Dissolvenze' in *Hubert Crackanthorpe: Racconti*, pp. 103–10

Anthologized in *British Poetry and Prose 1870–1905*, pp. 390–95

A Dead Woman

From *Wreckage: Seven Studies*, pp. 125–63
Translated as 'La Morte' (Nouvelle), *La Nouvelle Revue des Deux Mondes*, pp. 338–55

Embers

From *Wreckage: Seven Studies*, pp. 215–32
Translated as 'Braci' in *Hubert Crackanthorpe: Racconti*, pp. 111–21
Anthologized in *Stories of the 'Nineties: A Biographical Anthology* (London: John Baker, 1968), pp. 242–53

A Commonplace Chapter — I

From *Sentimental Studies & A Set of Village Tales*, pp. 3–108
Sections 1–6 were first published as 'A Commonplace Chapter', *New Review*, 57 (February 1894), 242–54; sections 7–20 were first published as 'A Commonplace Chapter', *New Review*, 58 (March 1894), 365–82, both subsequently revised for publication in *Sentimental Studies & A Set of Village Tales* (1895)

A Commonplace Chapter — II

From *Sentimental Studies & A Set of Village Tales*, pp. 64–108
First published as 'The Haseltons', *Yellow Book: An Illustrated Quarterly*, 5 (April 1895), 132–63, revised for publication in *Sentimental Studies & A Set of Village Tales* (1895)
Anthologized in *'The Yellow Book: An Illustrated Quarterly': An Anthology*, ed. by Fraser Harrison (London: Sidgwick and Jackson, 1974), pp. 139–70; *Hubert Crackanthorpe. Wreckage: Seven Studies*, ed. by David Malcolm (Edinburgh: Edinburgh University Press, 2019), pp. 121–42

In Cumberland

From *Sentimental Studies & A Set of Village Tales*, pp. 170–214
First published as 'A Study in Sentimentality', *Yellow Book: An Illustrated Quarterly*, 3 (October 1894), 175–209

Modern Melodrama

From *Sentimental Studies & A Set of Village Tales*, pp. 215–26
First published in *Yellow Book: An Illustrated Quarterly*, 1 (April 1894), 223–32
Anthologized in *The Decadent Short Story: An Annotated Anthology*, ed. by

Kostas Boyiopoulos and others (Edinburgh: Edinburgh University Press, 2015), pp. 104–11; David Malcolm, *The British and Irish Short Story Handbook* (Oxford: Blackwell, 2012), pp. 191–93

Lisa-la-Folle

From *Sentimental Studies & A Set of Village Tales*, pp. 239–43
Anthologized in *Tales of Mystery and Melodrama*, ed. by Leonard R. N. Ashley (Woodbury, NY: Barron's Educational Series, 1977), pp. 312–14

Etienne Mattou

From *Sentimental Studies & A Set of Village Tales*, pp. 252–63
Translated as 'Etienne Mattou' [by Jacqueline Ansaloni], *La Nouvelle Revue des Deux Mondes* (Août 1975), pp. 380–86

Anthony Garstin's Courtship

From *Last Studies*, pp. 1–67
First published in *The Savoy*, 3 (July 1896), 15–39
Anthologized in *The Savoy: Nineties Experiment*, ed. by Stanley Weintraub (University Park & London: Pennsylvania State University Press, 1966), pp. 101–26; *The English Short Story in Transition 1880–1920*, ed. by Helmut E. Gerber (New York: Pegasus, 1967), pp. 149–76; *Victorian Short Stories 2: The Trials of Love*, ed. by Harold Orel (London: Everyman/Dent, 1990), pp. 34–61; *The Wordsworth Collection of Classic Short Stories*, selected by Rosemary Gray (Ware: Wordsworth Editions, 2007), pp. 297–318

Trevor Perkins: A Platonic Episode

From *Last Studies*, pp. 71–98
First published in *The English Illustrated Magazine*, 156 (September 1896), 473–80
Translated as 'Trevor Perkins (Nouvelle)' [by Jacqueline Ansaloni], *La Nouvelle Revue des Deux Mondes* (Août 1974), 353–62
Anthologized in *The Windmill: Stories, Essays, Poems & Pictures by Authors & Artists whose Works are published at the Sign of the Windmill*, ed. by L. Callender (London: William Heinemann, 1923), pp. 182–92

The Turn of the Wheel

From *Last Studies*, pp. 101–223

It incorporates, with changes, four items from *Vignettes*:
'In the Strand January 27' (pp. 55–56) into *Last Studies* (pp. 101–02)
'In St. James's Park January 15' (p. 55) into *Last Studies* (p. 165)
'Rêverie December 25' (pp. 51–52) into *Last Studies* (pp. 167–68)
'Pleasant Court June 28' (pp. 20–23) into *Last Studies* (p. 192)

He Wins Who Loses

First published in *The Albermarle: A Monthly Review*, 1.3 (March 1892), 104–11
Anthologized in *Path and Pavement: Twenty New Tales of Britain By Eminent Authors*, selected with an Introduction by John Rowland (London: Eric Grant: 1937), pp. 203–21

A Latter-Day Highwayman (An Adventure in Miniature)

First published in *The Star*, 1 February 1896, p. 2, cols 1–2; subsequently in *The Penrith Observer*, 11 February 1896, p. 6, cols 4–5

A Fellside Tragedy

First published in *The Northern Counties Magazine*, February 1901, pp. 287–91; subsequently in *The Star*, 14 February 1901, p. 4, col. 1; 'Three Prose Pieces', *The Double-Dealer: A National Magazine From the South Published at New Orleans*, December 1921, pp. 252–55
Anthologized in *Et Cetera: A Collector's Scrap-Book*, ed. by Vincent Starrett (Chicago: Covici, 1924), pp. 71–79; *Strange Assembly*, ed. by John Gawsworth (London: Unicorn Press, 1932), pp. 129–38

Ascension Day at Arles

From *Vignettes: A Miniature Journal of Whim and Sentiment* (London: John Lane, The Bodley Head, 1896), pp. 6–8
First published in *The Speaker: A Review of Politics, Letters, Science and the Arts*, 11.277 (20 April 1895), 437

In the Basque Country

From *Vignettes: A Miniature Journal of Whim and Sentiment*, pp. 15–16
First published in *Saturday Review of Politics, Literature, Science, and Art*, 79 (22 June 1895), 824

In the Landes

From *Vignettes: A Miniature Journal of Whim and Sentiment*, pp. 16–18
First published in *Saturday Review*, 79 (22 June 1895), 824
Translated as 'Dans les Landes', *Homage à Hubert Crackanthorpe*, Association
   Francis Jammes, Bulletin No. 14 (Decembre 1990), pp. 75–76
Anthologized in 'Vignettes: Pastels in Prose', in *Bruno Chap Books*, ed. by
   Guido Bruno, 1.8 (May 1915), 98–106 (p. 105)

On Chelsea Embankment

From *Vignettes: A Miniature Journal of Whim and Sentiment*, pp. 19–20
First published in *Westminster Gazette*, 12 July 1894, p. 3, col. 1
Anthologized in *Fin de Siècle: A Selection of Late 19th Century Literature and
   Art*, ed. by Nevile Wallis (London: Alan Wingate, 1947), p. 54

Our Lady of the Lane

From *Vignettes: A Miniature Journal of Whim and Sentiment*, pp. 24–25
First published in *The Speaker: A Review of Politics, Letters, Science, and the
   Arts*, 10.258 (8 December 1894), 636

Paris in October

From *Vignettes: A Miniature Journal of Whim and Sentiment*, p. 28
First published in *The Speaker: A Review of Politics, Letters, Science, and the
   Arts*, 10.258 (8 December 1894), 637
Anthologized in *Writing of the 'Nineties*, ed. by Stanford, p. 207

La Côte d'Or from the Train

From *Vignettes: A Miniature Journal of Whim and Sentiment*, p. 29
First published in *The Speaker: A Review of Politics, Letters, Science, and the
   Arts*, 11.277 (20 April 1895), 437

Lausanne

From *Vignettes: A Miniature Journal of Whim and Sentiment*, pp. 29–30
First published in *Westminster Gazette*, 12 July 1894, p. 3, col. 1
Anthologized as 'Tout paysage est un état d'âme' ['Lausanne'] in 'Vignettes:
   Pastels in Prose', *Bruno Chap Books*, ed. by Guido Bruno, 1.8 (May 1915), pp.
   98–106 (pp. 100–01)

In the Campo Santo at Perugia

From *Vignettes: A Miniature Journal of Whim and Sentiment* (London: John Lane, The Bodley Head, 1896), pp. 37–39
First published in *The Speaker: A Review of Politics, Letters, Science, and the Arts*, 11.264 (19 January 1895), 75

Sunrise

From *Vignettes: A Miniature Journal of Whim and Sentiment*, p. 49
First published in *Saturday Review*, 82 (31 October 1896), 465

In Richmond Park

From *Vignettes: A Miniature Journal of Whim and Sentiment*, pp. 52–53
First published in *Saturday Review*, 82 (31 October 1896), 465

New Year's Eve

From *Vignettes: A Miniature Journal of Whim and Sentiment*, pp. 53–54
First published in *Saturday Review*, 80 (17 August 1895), 201
Anthologized as 'It Was New Year's Eve', in 'Vignettes: Pastels in Prose', *Bruno Chap Books*, ed. by Guido Bruno, 1.8 (May 1915), 98–106 (p. 102)

In St. James's Park

From *Vignettes: A Miniature Journal of Whim and Sentiment*, p. 55
Incorporated (with changes) into Crackanthorpe, 'The Turn of the Wheel' (*Last Studies*, p. 165)
Anthologized in *Fin de Siècle: A Selection of Late 19th Century Literature and Art*, ed. by Nevile Wallis (London: Alan Wingate, 1947), p. 54; *Writing of the 'Nineties*, ed. by Stanford, p. 208; *Decadent Verse: An Anthology of Late-Victorian Poetry, 1872–1900*, ed. by Caroline Blyth (London: Anthem Press, 2009), pp. 823–24 (p. 823); *A Midwinter Entertainment: Representing An Exclusive Collected Edition of Curious Pieces Written by Various Authors*, ed. by Mark Beech (London: Egaeus Press, 2016), p. 83

In the Strand

From *Vignettes: A Miniature Journal of Whim and Sentiment*, p. 55
First Published in *Saturday Review*, 80 (17 August 1895), 201–02
Incorporated (with changes) into Crackanthorpe, 'The Turn of the Wheel' (*Last Studies*, pp. 101–02)

Anthologized in *Decadent Verse: An Anthology of Late-Victorian Poetry*, ed. by Blyth, pp. 823–24 (p. 824); *Hubert Crackanthorpe. Wreckage: Seven Studies*, ed. by Malcolm, p. 148

Rêverie

From *Vignettes: A Miniature Journal of Whim and Sentiment*, pp. 57–62
First Published in *Saturday Review*, 79 (22 June 1895), 823–24
Translated as 'Reverie', *Homage à Hubert Crackanthorpe*, Association Francis Jammes, Bulletin No. 14 (Decembre 1990), pp. 76–77

Enfantillage

From *Vignettes: A Miniature Journal of Whim and Sentiment*, pp. 62–63
First Published in *Saturday Review*, 80 (17 August 1895), 202
Translated as 'Enfantillage' in *Homage à Hubert Crackanthorpe*, Association Francis Jammes, Bulletin No. 14 (Decembre 1990), p. 78

Realism in France and England: An Interview with M. Emile Zola

Published in *The Albermarle: A Monthly Review*, 1.2 (February 1892), 39–43
Reprinted in *Hubert Crackanthorpe. Wreckage: Seven Studies*, ed. by Malcolm, pp. 104–10

Mr. Vizetelly and Literary Freedom

Published in *Daily Chronicle*, 9 January 1894, p. 3, col. 7

Reticence in Literature: Some Roundabout Remarks

Published in *Yellow Book: An Illustrated Quarterly*, 2 (July 1894), 259–69
Part-extracted in *The Decadent Short Story: An Annotated Anthology*, ed. by Boyiopoulos and others, pp. 411–12
Reprinted in *Hubert Crackanthorpe. Wreckage: Seven Studies*, ed. by Malcolm, pp. 111–20